I0611844

Marti Keller Mysteries Omnibus #1
Books 1 – 3

By

Artemis Greenleaf

PUBLISHED BY:
Black Mare Books
Houston, Texas
www.blackmarebooks.com

ISBN: 978-1-941502-77-8

Marti Keller Mysteries Omnibus #1
Books 1 - 3
Copyright © 2016 by Artemis Greenleaf

The Hanged Man's Wife

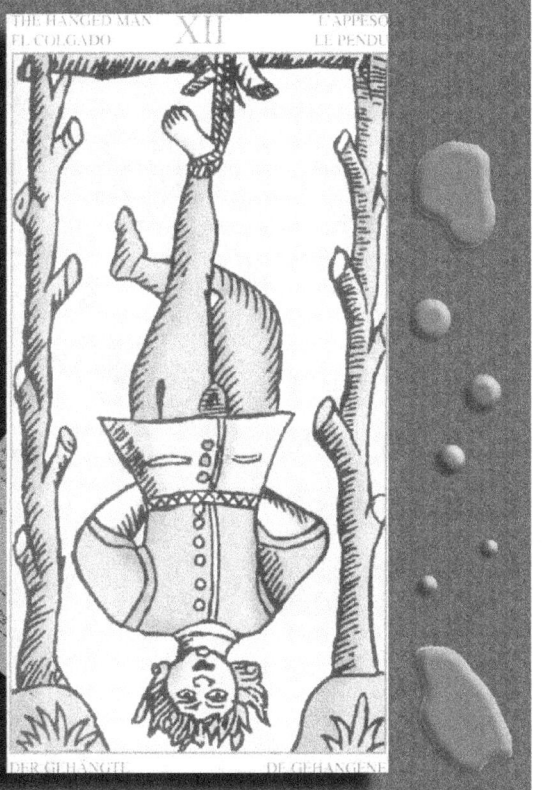

THE HANGED MAN XII L'APPESO
EL COLGADO LE PENDU

DER GEHÄNGTE DE GEHANGENE

Artemis Greenleaf

The Hanged Man's Wife

by

Artemis Greenleaf

Marti Keller Mysteries

Book 1

Acknowledgements

As always, thank you to my wonderful family. This endeavor would not be possible without your love and support. I also appreciate the invaluable editorial and structural help of my critique groups and beta readers. You know who you are, and I couldn't do this without you. Finally, a big shout-out to the Houston Citizen's Police Academy and officers I've had the opportunity and privilege to interact with. Thank you!

Table of Contents

*The universe is full of magical things, patiently waiting
for our wits to grow sharper.*
Eden Phillpotts

Chapter 1
Undiscovered Country

Rural Texas, 12:06 AM

 had just turned out the light and settled back onto the pillow when Amos, my Rottweiler mix, growled. I stroked his back to calm him and felt the hackles standing straight up on his shoulders.

A sharp rap sounded from the wall above the headboard.

Amos shifted and I put my arms around the big dog's neck.

"Who's there?" I asked, knowing I was the only one who was supposed to be in the house. At seventeen, I was old enough to stay home alone while my mother worked the graveyard shift at the truck stop. Dad was a long haul truck driver, and he was gone a lot. Right now, he was on his way back from California, but it would be tomorrow night before he made it home. Too late to help me now.

The silence was thick enough to suffocate me. My heart thudded against my ribs so hard I was afraid it would beat its way out of my chest.

Two sharp knocks cut through the gloom, now coming from the outer wall to my left.

Amos snorted.

I sat up just far enough to peer out the window at the foot of the bed. No one was there.

Maybe it's only an animal in the wall. I didn't believe that for a minute.

Burglars didn't prowl around knocking on the walls, did they?

Four knocks, hard and fast, made me jump. This time, they came from the inner wall on my right, across from the bed.

"Is someone there?" My voice sounded thin and shivery in the dark.

There was no answer. Mom and Dad always told me the noises I heard were just the house settling. I never quite believed them – the sounds were too much like footsteps and whispering. But this knocking. This was different – I'd never heard it before.

"If there's someone there, knock twice for yes and once for no," I called out, pretending to be brave.

Two knocks sounded near the ceiling above my head.

"Are you a man?"

One knock.

"A woman?"

Two knocks.

"Do you live here?"

Two knocks.

That totally freaked me out. I didn't want to know any more about who- or whatever this was. I was done.

Amos sat up and growled. I reached over and snapped on the lamp by my bed. The small pool of light gave me just enough courage to jump out of bed and flip the overhead light switch. Amos remained crouched on the bed, head cocked and staring at the wall. Eventually, I was able to work my way around the house and get all the lights turned on. When I got to the living room, I pulled myself into a ball under the hand-crocheted afghan my grandmother had made and turned on the TV. I watched infomercials until Amos padded into the room and curled up next to me, and I just couldn't stay awake anymore.

Nine Years Later
Mundane Activity Monitoring and Intervention Center (MAMIC)

"I think that's all of them," Quinn said.

"Excellent. You take your team back out to the border and see if you can help shore it up. We'll take care of the refugees," the woman said. She turned and strode down the corridor, her long velvet dress flowing behind her.

"Hey, Aleksei!" Quinn called to a tall Lesovik, who was helping an elderly boggart find a chair. "Have you seen Siobhan recently?"

"Ni. Not since we have arrived here."

Quinn frowned at his blue-skinned friend. "Dame Rowan said to go back out to the breach. Maybe we'll pick Siobhan up on the way."

Aleksei nodded and continued toward a settee with the wispy boggart.

Eoin and Malik, two other members of Quinn's Mundane Intervention Team, stood near the entrance to the great hall. Quinn hurried toward them.

"Have either of you seen Siobhan?"

Eoin blotted some sweat off of his forehead and bare chest. His goat hooves clacked on the floor as he turned to survey the heaving room behind them. "Not since early this morning," he said.

Malik, the djinn, just shook his head as he levitated himself about four feet off the floor in a cross-legged position.

"We're supposed to get back out there, see if we can help," Quinn said. He scanned the great hall one last time. *Might be better if she stays here.*

As soon as Aleksei caught up, they went outside to the emergency portal. Quinn could have left a message with the guard, but decided against it. It was selfish, he knew, but if Siobhan was still here, he wanted her to stay out of harm's way. Things could get ugly in a hurry, where they were going.

They stepped through a full length looking glass in a brass frame and found themselves at the edge of a dark forest. The sky flashed rainbow lightning and dark shapes moved, as if in a fog, just beyond the trees. Fae of all types, along with a few elementals and nature spirits, scurried around like ants after their nest has been poked with a stick.

Demons had definitely been at work here. The realm of Faery overlaps and interpenetrates the Mundane world, and the borders between the two are narrow, but tough. Here, the boundary had been scraped so thin that the shadows of humans were plainly visible. The fae were busy trying to repair it before the demons returned, because the membrane was on the verge of failure. Inexplicably, the demons had left while the locals were being evacuated to the nearby MAMIC.

Demons did not belong in Faery. They didn't belong in the Mundane world, either, but a terrible magickal accident had ripped a hole through space and time and enabled them to escape their world before it tore itself apart. They'd been eradicated from Faery for millennia, but many still prowled the Mundane world, multiplying almost as fast as they were captured. Descendants of those responsible for the accident formed what eventually became MAMIC and trained special teams to hunt those remaining demons. The demons, to be sure, did not appreciate this, and fought back vigorously.

More rainbow lightning flashed. Soon, the shadowy figures disappeared, and there appeared to be a vast meadow just past the trees. The near-breach was sealed. Guards would be posted, to monitor the repair for a few days. If it remained stable, the residents would be allowed to return home. Quinn, Aleksei, Malik and Eoin returned to MAMIC. And they were back before lunch.

Siobhan was still nowhere to be found.

"Malik, do you think you can locate her for me?" Quinn asked.

"As you wish."

The djinn closed his eyes. The smile on his face slid into open-mouthed horror.

"What's wrong? Where is she?" Quinn demanded.

"She is at her cottage in the Mundane world."

"And?"

"Frost Giants have been there."

Fourteen Months Later
Houston, Texas

Ryan was over an hour late coming home.

I glanced up at the clock and then looked out the window, as I'd done for just about every minute since I got back. Ryan was often late from work, but he was usually home by now. It had been chilly and rainy for the third day in a row – not uncommon for a Houston winter – and the wet streets had snarled traffic. I was sure that was all there was to it. Still, congestion was worse than usual today, and the traffic report on the radio said there was police activity on I-10. Usually meant a fatality investigation. What a shame, especially so close to the holidays.

I went into the kitchen and looked in the oven. I'd picked up takeout from Ryan's favorite Thai restaurant on my way home from my shift at the ER, and had put it in there on low to keep it warm. I was a lot of things, but domestic wasn't one of them. I laughed to myself. Jarred pasta sauce and cooked dried spaghetti just didn't rate as special occasion fare. Our third anniversary was only two weeks away, but I couldn't wait that long. Ryan would be so surprised.

I could not stop smiling. I even smiled at the photo of us taken at the zoo that was stuck to the fridge with a tacky tourist magnet from San Francisco. Ryan had a uniquely splendid look. His mother was Vietnamese and his father was Norwegian. His eyes were dark, almost black, and his hair was dark honey blond. He had black belts in both Tae Kwon Do and Hapkido, and had the body to prove it.

A knock at the door interrupted my pouring of the sparkling grape juice.

Who could that be? I really hope it isn't those Jehovah's Witnesses again.

If only it had been Jehovah's Witnesses.

Ryan's shiftmate, Nick, and Frank Helmsly, the Watch Commander, stood on the porch, hats in their hands.

It could only mean one thing, and it was the last thing a policeman's wife ever wanted to see.

All the color drained out of the world and I couldn't seem to get enough air. My hands were shaking so hard I could barely open the door to let them in.

Nick put his arms around me and I sobbed into his chest. I could feel his silent tears on my shoulder. When I was able to get a hold of myself enough to speak, I pulled away from Nick, but didn't let go. It was only then I noticed the splashes of blood on his face. Was it Ryan's? I was afraid to ask.

I closed my eyes in a hopeless attempt to try and contain the waterfall. "Tell me what happened," I whispered.

"Supposed to be a routine traffic stop," Nick answered.

"Don't watch the news tonight, Marti. It's better if you don't," the commander said, patting my shoulder. "We think they were enforcers - they had military grade weapons and body armor. And Russian gang tattoos."

I could feel Nick starting to shake, and I hugged him tighter. "We had no idea what we were getting into," he said. "Ryan pulled them over 'cause they ran a red light. Idiots barely missed getting hit by a bus. Wish they had. Bastards." He paused and took a deep breath, struggling for control. "Their car was stolen, and I rolled up to assist. Before I knew what was happening, there was an AK-102 sticking out of the car window and Ryan was down," said Nick, his voice breaking.

"We got 'em, though, Marti. We got 'em," Helmsly broke in. "There was one holy hell of a chase. I-10 was shut down for four hours because of that and the standoff with the SWAT team. One shooter died at the scene. The other was DOA at Ben Taub. I know that's not much comfort." He shook his head and swallowed hard. "Ryan was a good man and a good officer. We're gonna miss him. The department sends its condolences."

Nick released me and stepped back. "Emily's on her way over. I'll go next door and get your mom."

Ryan and Nick hadn't been just shiftmates . They were also brothers-in-law. I had met Ryan at my sister's wedding. I was Emily's maid of honor and he was Nick's best man.

Commander Helmsly fidgeted on the front porch while Nick went to fetch my mother. I went into the bathroom and tried to vomit, but my stomach was empty. On the way out, I picked up the pregnancy test with its two blue lines and threw it in the trash.

Chapter 2
Information

uinn ran his hand through his thick black hair and sighed with frustration. This mission wasn't going well.

The rumor was that a drug dealer had managed to get his hands on some actual zombie powder. He was planning to use it to enslave dryads and make them hide his product inside trees, where he wouldn't have to worry about it being disturbed, as only the dryads could get it in or out.

Quinn didn't believe that stuff would work on fae, but his team had been sent to investigate, anyway. They'd spent a month hanging out with assorted criminals, junkies, and dealers. They hadn't had any luck, and were about to declare the whole thing a hoax when the first dryad turned up.

She wasn't dead. But she wasn't exactly alive, either. She just shuffled around in a catatonic state, staring blankly ahead of herself, moaning and bumping into objects. Quinn had sent her to Blackthorne in the fae realm to see if she could be helped. Then two more dryads in the same condition appeared, then another. They all died.

Quinn had just run down yet another dead-end lead. He was out of ideas and out of patience. Taking a short-cut, he turned down a grimy alley, and was assaulted by the rusty, salty-sweet odor of blood. Human blood, and lots of it.

A metallic click caught his attention.

A man, wearing nothing but a holey pair of boxers, was advancing down the alley. The handgun he carried was elongated by the silencer attached to the end of the barrel.

"Hey, you! Just let him die, okay?" the gunman said, his voice cracking with hysteria.

Quinn's eyes followed where the gun was pointing. He had to crane his neck to see around a dumpster. A police officer was trying to give first aid to a man who was sprawled on the asphalt in a congealing pool of blood. Quinn could tell by looking at the man's aura that he was a lost cause.

The cop looked up at the gunman. He kept pressure on the injured man's abdomen, trying to cover multiple gunshot wounds. "Easy, now. There's an ambulance on the way. He's going to the hospital. Just put the gun down and back off. Be cool, alright?" His voice was even and calm, but firm.

"I said, let him die! I shot him cuz he's a vampire. Don't help him!" The gunman's hands shook so hard he could barely point his weapon.

Quinn let his serrated teeth show and his eyes go to solid black before he stepped from behind the dumpster. The gunman took one look at him, then screamed and fled, tossing the gun into a pile of trash. Unfortunately for him, he ran smack into the arms of another officer, who was just coming around the corner.

"Vampire! Vampire!" the gunman shrieked, pointing at Quinn. "He's gonna get me!"

"Let me put you in the car, where you'll be nice and safe," the second officer said.

The quivering gunman held out his arms to be cuffed, then scrambled into the back of the police cruiser and cowered on the floor.

"Holy shit! Holy shit!" said Quinn, acting as if he'd just noticed the gunshot victim for the first time. He covered his mouth with his hand before he turned and retched behind the dumpster. No theater there – the taste of human blood made him nauseous – and with that much blood in the open air, the smell was as good as a taste. All he had to do was let his control slip a little.

The approaching ambulance wailed in the near distance like a banshee, foretelling death.

"Wish they were all that easy. Ryan, you okay?" the second officer asked, his eyes on Quinn.

"Yeah. But he's toast," the first officer replied, trying to close the dead man's eyes before he got up. But they stubbornly refused to stay shut, staring blankly at the pale November sky. He glanced at Quinn, who looked perfectly human. "That guy's higher than a kite," he said, nodding toward the police car. He stripped off the blue disposable gloves he'd been wearing and tied them up in a plastic sack. "I'll go bag the shooter's hands and call Homicide."

"So what are you doing hanging out in this alley?" the second officer, whose name tag read N. Benson, asked Quinn pleasantly. But his hand rested on the butt of his gun.

"Me?" Quinn whipped through his mental inventory of cover stories. Seconds ticked by, stinking like fried food and fresh blood. "Just moved here. Looking for a job."

"In an alley?"

Quinn looked at his shoes. "No, man. Had to take a leak."

Benson's lip curled in disgust. "Dude. No. Don't ever let me catch you doing that. You carrying? Got anything sharp in your pockets?"

"No."

"Mind if I check?" Benson asked.

Quinn raised his arms and took a wider stance, and Benson frisked him. Quinn didn't like it, but he knew it looked very suspicious, him showing up in an alley where someone had just been shot, even if someone else was holding the gun. In Benson's place, he would have done the same thing. Best to just go along while he worked out how to turn this obstacle into an opportunity.

Quinn was aware that beat cops know a lot of people in a lot of neighborhoods. They usually have a good idea of who's dealing and who's using, even if they can't prove it. Quinn needed to know what they knew, but he couldn't just come out and ask them. And it was never a good idea to stalk police officers. Maybe, though, they would be interested in some information. And if they thought they were cultivating him, he just might be able to get close enough to find out what he wanted to know and track down the dealer with the zombie powder. But they had to think they had some leverage to use against him. They wouldn't trust someone being helpful for no apparent reason.

By this time, three other patrol cars arrived, EMS had pronounced the victim, and the ambulance had been released in favor of the coroner's van. Yellow police tape blocked off the alley and the Crime Scene Unit was on its way. The first officer, the one who had been attempting first aid, approached Quinn and Benson with a clipboard.

Quinn glanced at the officer's name plate. R. Keller.

"I need to get a statement and some contact information from you, in case the DA wants to call you as a witness. If I could see your ID, please?"

"Sure," Quinn said, reaching for his back pocket. Then he reached for the other pocket. "Shit. It's gone. My wallet's gone!"

Benson rolled his eyes and shook his head.

"When was the last time you had it?" Keller asked.

"I was filling out an application at the dry cleaner a few blocks over. I had it then. Maybe I left it there."

"Maybe. You can go check after I get your statement. What's your name?"

"Marc McLeod. That's Marc with a c, last name m-c-l-e-o-d."

"Address?"

"4003 Allen Parkway. Smitherson House." He'd done a favor once for Tim Arbuckle, the manager of the well-known half-way house, who knew him as Marc McLeod. Quinn knew Arbuckle would vouch for him, if anyone ever called to check on McLeod. The real Marc McLeod was a petty criminal with a heroin habit he couldn't afford. Or he had been, until he tried to rob his dealer and ended up in a Pasadena landfill. He also was not the sort of person anyone would bother to report missing.

Quinn pretended not to notice when the officers exchanged knowing looks. Benson left. Good. He was pretty sure that meant he was going to the patrol car to check out Marc McLeod on the computer. The last time he got his driver license renewed, McLeod had a full beard and the gaunt pallor of a junkie. Quinn could pass for a healthier, clean-shaven version of McLeod, if the officers didn't study the picture too closely. Which is exactly why Quinn sometimes borrowed his identity, although he thought it was a sad commentary on the man's life that he was much more useful dead than he had ever been alive.

Keller's voice derailed Quinn's train of thought. "And a phone number?"

"Don't have one. You can leave a message with the office at Smitherson."

As the officer asked him questions, Quinn tried to locate anything or anyone that could help his cause. The area was filthy and mostly cemented over, and there didn't seem to be any fae or elementals around. Still, he kept calling out for assistance. Other fae could hear him, if they were close enough. But this sound was pitched far above the range of human hearing.

Benson returned and gave Keller the slightest of nods. "What made you decide to shave?" Benson asked casually.

"That was the old me. Trying to get myself straight. Been working out, too." Quinn flexed a bicep. He felt some of the tension drain away. They believed he was McLeod. Now, if he could just find a way to capitalize on this deception.

Keller had almost finished his questions when a ragged and sinister-looking bauchan appeared in a sagging doorway. "What do you want?" it growled at Quinn.

Information, he answered, glad the officers couldn't see or hear it. Something bad must have happed to it to make it so rough. Bauchans are related to leprechauns, and they normally looked more or less like small, cheerful humans.

"About what?" the bauchan grumped.

Who's the dead guy? Why is he here? Quinn suspected he knew the answer to the second question already.

"If I tell you, will you leave me alone?"

Yes.

"They call him Pepé. He sells little crystals and white powder, mostly to humans." The bauchan licked his lips and smirked. "He shouldn't have branched out into new products. Keeps his packages in the AC intake. Now stop bothering me." The bauchan vanished.

"Okay, if you could just sign this," Keller said, holding his clipboard and a ballpoint out to Quinn.

Quinn took it, then frowned. "Couldn't you guys just say you talked to an anonymous bystander or something?"

"You don't want us to use your name?" Benson asked. "Why's that?"

Quinn made a dramatic sigh. "Man, I'm going to catch so much shit if Arbuckle finds out I was down here. I'm serious as a heart attack, sir. I'm clean, I swear. I'll piss in a cup, if you want. But jobs are hard to get right now, 'specially if you've got complications. Rent's due next week and I haven't found nothing. Pepé," Quinn glanced at the corpse, "told me he'd slip me a couple hundred if I ran a package for him."

"What kind of package?" Benson asked.

"Didn't ask." Quinn looked down, scuffing one foot against the other. "But it might be in the AC intake. That's where he used to keep his stash, anyway."

"Nick, why don't you go grab a couple of the guys, take a look. I'll keep Mr. McLeod company," Keller said.

Benson went to talk to some of his colleagues, then they went into Pepé's "office." It didn't take long before they called the crime scene photographer inside.

Benson and Keller had asked Quinn to talk to some Vice Squad officers, but he'd refused, knowing there was a chance that some of them might have encountered the real McLeod. He did say that if he heard anything at the halfway house, he'd pass it along, provided they never used his name on any reports.

After a while, they gave him a cheap, pre-paid cell phone. Five and a half excruciating weeks of giving them information about petty thieves and pimps, and Quinn was no closer to the zombie powder dealer. There was lots of talk from all sorts of folk about the dealer with zombie powder. But no one, fae or human, not even Malik, the djinn, could find a name or point to a location that was of any use. Three more Dryads died. Aleksei and Eoin spent the entire time talking to and watching over dryads. But there was no way to protect them all.

Then, Benson and Keller told him they wanted to set up a meeting between Quinn and an investigator from the DA's office. A man by the name of Ian Chambers. Since Quinn's information on everything else had been spot on, the DA wanted to find out if Quinn knew anything about some home invasion robberies that were about to go to trial.

The day before the meeting, Keller told Quinn he wanted to meet with him privately, after his shift. The spot was off one of the hike-and-bike trails that ran along Buffalo Bayou.

Quinn got there first. The cold drizzle reminded him of home. He was focusing on the smell of rain and the feel of cool water on his face, and allowed himself to be caught off guard when Aleksei stepped from behind an ash tree, appearing human.

"Quinn! You are hard to find this evening."

"Aleksei! Don't sneak up on me like that," he chided, even though he knew it was his own fault for not paying attention. "Is anything wrong?" Aleksei's sudden appearance was not protocol.

"Ni. Nothing wrong. In fact, we have located zombie powder." Aleksei's Ukranian accent was thick and difficult to understand, but Quinn was used to it.

"That's fantastic! How…?"

"You were right. Animal cruelty investigation you said to check."

"Yes!" Quinn hissed as he fist-bumped Aleksei. Sometimes it paid to listen to the officers' radios when he met with them.

"Drug dealer was, how you say? Voodoo queen, from next state over. Used dark magick to hide herself from us, but neighbors did not like for her to be killing chickens in back yard. She is no longer problem."

"Already neutralized? That was quick." Quinn did not envy her fate, especially if the dryads got a chance at her.

"Come. There is much—" Aleksei stopped short when he heard footfalls approaching in the soggy December grass. It had been raining for two days straight, and the park was more puddle than pathway.

"I'm expecting someone. Stay human," Quinn whispered. "Over here," Quinn said to the approaching flashlight. He could easily see Keller holding it, knew he was alone.

"Who's your friend?" the officer asked.

"Him? That's Alek. He's my roomie. Gave me a ride down here."

Aleksei lowered his head slightly. "Is good to meet you. I was just going." He gave Quinn a pointed look. "I see you later at car."

He turned to leave, but the wet Texas gumbo got the better of him. His foot slipped, then stuck in the heavy clay and he lost his balance, tumbled down the bank, and splashed into the bayou.

"He can't swim!" Quinn shouted.

Quinn and Keller scrambled down the bank and found Aleksei holding on to an exposed tree root. The water level was high from all the recent rain, and it was hurrying down towards Galveston Bay as fast as it could. Quinn didn't dare jump in the bayou. Water fae could be extremely territorial, and any that had claimed this area would have known immediately that their space had been violated. Quinn couldn't risk a confrontation and have Keller caught in the middle.

Keller was already holding his baton out to Aleksei. "Grab on. I'll pull you out."

Quinn grabbed Keller's free arm to help anchor him. Aleksei was a lot heavier than he looked.

Aleksei tightened his grip on the root with his left hand and reached for the baton with his right. As soon as Keller started to pull, a floating branch smacked into Aleksei's shoulder and he lost his grip on the baton. He flailed around, but caught the root again before he could be washed downstream.

"Hold on!" yelled Quinn. "We'll try again."

Again, Aleksei reached for the baton. This time, he grabbed on with both hands, and Quinn and Keller hauled him out of the water.

"Diakuiu. I thank you," Aleksei panted, lying on the muddy bank like a beached river dolphin.

"No problem. Just doing my job," Keller replied.

"You okay?" Quinn asked.

"Da."

The three of them struggled back up the slippery bank, using small bushes and tree roots to pull themselves along.

"Do not be long. I've need of dry clothes," Aleksei said to Quinn. "Good night," he nodded to Keller.

"See you in a few," replied Quinn.

"He going to be alright?" asked Keller, eyeing Aleksei's retreating form.

"He'll be fine. You saved my friend's life. I owe you one."

Keller looked around, shining his Maglite into the bushes all around them, as if he was wary that another unexpected guest was going to pop out of the shrubbery. When he seemed to be satisfied that they were alone, he switched off the light.

"You didn't hear this from me. But don't trust Ian Chambers. There's something about that guy...I don't know. I've got to talk to some people about him," Keller said.

Then his cell rang. He'd slid his finger across its face and a thumbnail image of a pretty young woman glowed in the dark. "Hey, Bright Eyes," Keller answered. "Let me call you right back, okay?...Love you, too." Then he hung up and slipped the phone back into his pocket.

"We'll see you tomorrow. Do the street preacher thing. We'll pick you up after lunch. The usual place. I have to go. Watch your back, okay?"

"Thanks for the warning," Quinn replied. "Tomorrow."

But Quinn hadn't seen Keller the next day. Or Ian Chambers.

Benson texted him that the meeting was canceled.

With headlines blaring from every newsstand, it was impossible for Quinn not to realize why. It made him sad – as humans went, Ryan Keller had been a pretty good one. Quinn reminded himself that even the oldest humans were very short-lived, compared to fae. It didn't make him feel any better.

A few days later, Quinn attended the funeral, even admired Keller's pretty widow, whom he recognized from her image on Keller's phone. He wanted to offer his condolences, tell her that her husband had been a good man. But she already knew that, and it was better he stay in the shadows. Besides, he'd gotten what he came for, and it was time for the helpful police informant, Marc McLeod, to skip town. Quinn asked the dryads in Keller's yard to keep an eye on his wife and contact him if she got into any trouble.

Chapter 3
Dinner Theater

Nineteen months later
Memorial Day Weekend, Houston, Texas

assie giggled when her grandmother tickled her chin.

"She is so close to walking now, Mom," I said, shifting the baby on my hip.

"Well, she is her mother's daughter. You walked and talked before you were a year old, Marti," she replied.

"Happy Memorial Day," Nick said as he hugged me.

Emily just waved. Their third child was due a couple of weeks, and even if she weren't holding a huge pan of seven-layer dip, she couldn't get close enough to anyone for a hug. Their twins had already made a break for the ancient swing set.

Mom took the big foil-covered pan from my sister and set it on the picnic table. "Who's your friend, Em?" she asked, looking at the clean-cut, pleasant looking man, about my age, who trailed into the backyard after them.

"Adele, this is Ian Chambers. Ian, this lovely lady is my mother-in-law, Adele Schmidt."

Ian took my mother's hand in his right and clasped her elbow with his left.

"And this is my sister-in-law, Marti Keller." Nick squeezed my arm.

"Hello, Ian. Nice to meet you," I said, barely glancing at the sandy-haired man. I turned and handed Cassie over to my mother. "Nick, I could use your help with the potato salad. If you'll excuse us?"

I hustled Nick into the house. I had to nip this in the bud. Who knows? Ian Chambers might be a great guy and I might even be interested in him, but if I didn't set Nick straight here and now, he'd never stop.

As soon as the door closed I whirled to face my brother-in-law. "I don't need you to fix me up with anybody."

"Come on, Marti. Ian's a nice guy. He saved my life, back in college. He dragged me and three other people out of a burning building. He's a hero."

"I'm sure he is. But I'm not ready. I wasn't ready for the last three guys you tried to set me up with, either."

"Marti, it's been almost two years now. Ryan loved you. He wouldn't want you and Cassie to be all alone."

"We're not all alone. We live next door to my parents. You and Emily are only six doors down."

"That's not what I meant, and you know it. Look at yourself, Marti. You quit your job and hardly see your friends, like a hermit or something. Ryan wouldn't want that for you."

"I don't need you to tell me what Ryan would want. Just back off, Nick. I know you mean well, but it's my life. Got it?" Bottles rattled in the door as I jerked opened the fridge, with more force than I intended.

Nick sighed and shook his head. "Ryan died. You didn't. For Cassie's sake, don't forget that." He started for the back door.

"Where do you think you're going?" I asked him.

He turned around and grunted as I shoved a large, cold bowl of potato salad into his arms. "Don't forget this," I said, with as much smile as I could manage.

After the screen door banged behind him, I went into the bathroom to splash some cold water on my face. I had managed to hold it together while I was talking to Nick, but I was rapidly coming apart now.

"For Cassie's sake…" His words stung. Who the hell did Nick think he was?

Wasn't everything I did (or didn't do) for Cassie's sake? It was for Cassie's sake that I quit my job. She was the only link I had to Ryan, and I couldn't stand the thought of her being in day care, where she would never be as precious to them as she was to me. What if something happened to her? Why didn't I date? It wasn't only because I wasn't really over Ryan. How many times as an ER nurse had I seen children brought in because their mothers' boyfriends hurt them?

Maybe part of the problem was that I never got to say goodbye. Ryan was there…and then he wasn't. There was no closing parenthesis.

I wished for the thousandth time that I hadn't waited the extra day to tell Ryan that we were expecting. I don't suppose it would have made a difference. He'd still most likely be dead. But at least he would have died knowing about our baby. She wouldn't have just been my little secret.

The house that Cassie and I lived in had been a wedding present from Mom and Dad. My car was paid for. I didn't have a lot of expenses, but my savings and the insurance money weren't going to last forever. I needed to come up with a way to get some cash flow before it became a serious problem. I'd have to worry about it later, though. Now, I had to go show my smiling face at the barbeque.

Even after our little talk, Nick still contrived to have Ian sit next to me while we ate. He was actually kind of funny. As an investigator for the district attorney's office, and he'd probably never run out of 'stupid criminal tricks' stories. Kinda reminded me of Ryan like that. Maybe that's why I gave him my email when he asked. I told him I'd only let him have it if he didn't mention it to Nick.

It was four o'clock, and Mom's resin hummingbird garden thermometer read 96°F. Every ice cube in every cooler had melted, in spite of the shady back porch and ceiling fan.

Dad, who was holding my sleeping Cassie, waved at me from across the porch. "Little Sugar, won't you run down to the Stop-n-Go and get some more ice?"

"Sure, Dad." The corner market hadn't been a Stop-n-Go since 1989. The name changed every few years, but to Dad, all convenience stores were Stop-n-Go's.

He was doing well since the accident. In a cosmic spasm of irony, his pickup truck had gotten nailed by an 18-wheeler. He had problems adjusting to the artificial leg and he sometimes had seizures, but all and all, he was doing amazingly well.

Ian was in the bathroom, and I slipped out of the back yard before he came back. I wanted some space. Ian was certainly not hard to look at. And he was smart. And funny. But I needed to step back a little, and use the little grey cells. I stopped by my house on the way and got the little plastic wagon. I didn't want to get in the car to drive three blocks, but I didn't want to carry six bags of ice home in my arms, either.

I found myself humming as I walked along the baking sidewalk. I went out of my way to walk in the shade of the shop awnings to avoid the blistering sun. I squirmed as beads of sweat crawled down into my bra.

I was still trying to decide whether I wanted to hug Nick or slap him for bringing Ian along to the party. Ian was a pretty boy. He didn't have Ryan's body, of course, but he wasn't too shabby. Well, I didn't think he had Ryan's body, but there was only one way to be sure. Marti Renee Keller. Don't even think about going there – you don't know anything about this man. Not entirely true. I knew he worked for the DA, had a cousin who was a circus clown, and had sinfully beautiful blue eyes. Nick thought enough of him to bring him around Dad. He saved Nick's life, back when they were college roommates.

The next thing I knew, I was lying on the sidewalk.

"Oh! I am so sorry!" a plumpish woman leaned over me. "Are you okay, honey?"

"Yeah, I think I'm all right."

Another woman, scrawny with lanky, salt and pepper hair, peeked out from behind a large, battered bookcase that leaned against the brick wall of the storefront. "Did I not just say, 'Lulu, what is that noise?'? But you just kept backing up, knowing you couldn't see around that bookshelf."

"Oh hush, Belinda." The first woman extended her hand to help me up. "I'm Lulu Miranda and this is Belinda Tate. We're opening up a shop here. Trying to get all the counters and whatnot in this week. They won't fit through the back door, so we had to come around to the front. I was going backwards with this shelf and I never even saw you. Sure you're okay?"

I dusted off my butt. "I'm fine. I'm going to go now."

"We'll be open next week, so make sure you come by the shop and choose something for yourself. On me, of course. I didn't catch your name."

"Marti. I'll see you around." I walked away, suddenly aware of how loudly the little wagon rumbled along behind me.

They'd finished this new strip center over six months ago. So far, the only tenant was a nail parlor, although I think that all strip malls are required by law to have nail shops.

Loaded up with ice and headed home, I noticed an enormous sign in Lulu's window:

Coming soon! The Tenth Sphere

– Art * Books * Gifts * New Age –

Featuring original jewelry designs by Belinda's Blessed Beads.

Huh.

But back to Ian. He was good looking, had a stable job with respectable pay, had his own house (in the gentrified Heights, no less), was thirty and had never been married. Why was he still single? Was he really too good to be true, or was I just trying to talk myself out of getting to know him?

I could hear Cassie crying from half a block away. I started to jog, the wagon lurching along behind me, bumping and scraping my heels. She must have woken up from her nap and not seen me. I tried to hurry into the backyard with my payload, but it got stuck in the stepping stones at the gate.

"I've got it. You take care of the baby," Ian said, getting up from his shady camp chair.

"Thanks."

My mother was bouncing Cassie on her knees and singing, but it wasn't helping. I scooped up my little girl, but she was mad at me. Little tears fell on her cheeks and stabbed me right in the heart. I took her inside to see if nursing would calm her down.

On Wednesday, Emily called me. "Hey. Why don't you come over for dinner Friday? Dr. Fredericks scheduled my c-section for Thursday a week, and we wanted to have a last hurrah before the baby comes and we drop off the radar."

Sounded fishy to me. "Who else is going to be there?"

"Oh, Mom, Dad, a friend or two."

"Like maybe Ian Chambers?"

My sister sounded sheepish. "Maybe."

I didn't tell her that Ian had already sent me an email, asking if I'd be at the get-together. I hadn't responded yet. Wasn't like I had any prior commitments. I liked Ian. I liked to look at Ian. But I didn't like to be rushed. It was less complicated to admire him from afar, where the concept couldn't clash with the reality.

"If I come, will you make Nick promise, cross his heart and hope to die, that he will stop trying to fix me up?"

"I promise that I will tell him to promise you."

My sister, the lawyer. "Fine. I'll be there. 7:00?"

"Yep. Bring a pie."

"Got it. Bye."

I replied to Ian's mail, saying I'd be at Emily and Nick's on Friday. I felt a little thrill as I clicked "send." But then I closed the window and saw the wallpaper on my screen, a photo of Ryan and me at Niagara Falls, and I felt horribly guilty, almost like I was having an affair. I decided to take Cassie to the park, where there were no pictures to remind me.

Cassie skipped her Friday morning nap, which meant she had a two and a half hour afternoon nap. While she was sleeping, I tried on every outfit in my closet at least once. I finally decided on a floral print summer dress. It was big enough to cover the scaffolding of the nursing bra and small enough to be cute and maybe just a little flirty. I hung it up on the closet door and put my bum-around-the-house clothes back on.

I did a few quick chores before I sat down to look through a magazine I'd picked up at the bookstore. It promised tip-filled articles on work-at-home jobs for moms.

Appointment setter. No.

Virtual administrative assistant. No.

Computer programmer. No.

Medical billing coder. Maybe.

Tarot card reader. What?

"Learn to read Tarot cards! Be the master of your own destiny with a career that never goes out of style. Set up your own storefront! Entertain at parties! The future is in your hands with this people-pleasing career. For more information, request packet 008799685."

I was going to check in with the interwebs about that, but Cassie started crying. I put her in the high chair with some Cheerios and fruit puffs while I started on the pie. She didn't like to be fed anymore – wanted to do it herself. Which was good, I supposed, but it took her forever to eat. She did okay with finger foods, but she was a menace with the spoon. I put the pie in the oven and wondered if Ian liked coconut cream. It had been Ryan's favorite.

"Da da da!" shouted Cassie as she pounded her tray. I kissed her and gave her a sippy cup with some water in it.

I pointed to myself. "Ma ma. Say Mama, Cassie."

"Da da da!"

"Okay. Be that way." I sighed and forced a smile.

All of the books said that it was developmentally normal for babies to make the "d" sound before the "m" sound. My logical mind accepted this. My emotional mind was another story. Even though I knew it was totally unreasonable, I still felt slighted that she could call for the Dada she'd never meet, but not for the Mama that was there for her 24/7.

I cleaned up the kitchen and pulled the pie out of the oven. I should have made it this morning, so it had time to chill and set up properly. I stuck it in the freezer while I gave Cassie her bath.

When she was all cleaned up and ready, I went back into the kitchen and beat the egg whites. I took the pie out of the freezer. But the pie pan stuck to my damp fingers. I tried to blow hot breath on them, but ended up sticking the tip of my nose in the filling. Well, at least the meringue would hide the hole. It didn't take long to melt the frost. I spread the meringue on top of the custard and popped it in to bake. I checked on it ten minutes later and it looked exactly the same. I hadn't turned on the freaking oven. What is wrong with me?

I knew what was wrong with me, and it was called Ian Chambers. I almost called Emily to say that Cassie was sick and I wouldn't be there, after all. But Mom would be over here in two heartbeats and she'd know I was lying through my teeth. I was too old to sit through that lecture again.

I played finger puppets with Cassie while the meringue browned. Once I took the pie out of the oven, I went to change clothes. I even put on eyeliner. Then I took it back off. I hadn't worn makeup since Ryan died, and if I showed up at the party wearing it, knowing Ian Chambers would be there, Nick would never let me live it down.

Cassie and I were ten minutes late. Part of the meringue had collapsed and I tried to disguise it with toasted coconut. In the end, I gave up and decided to blame it on the pie carrier. Mom grabbed the baby as soon as I walked in, and I put the pie in Emily's fridge. Nick wolf-whistled at me as I came out of the kitchen.

"Don't make me have to smack you," I said.

He chuckled and whispered something in Ian's ear. I didn't want to know what it was.

"Marti! You look great," Ian said, blushing to almost the same color as the hibiscuses on his Hawaiian shirt.

I really didn't want to know what Nick said to him.

"Hey Auntie Marti!" Kyle and Aiden shouted at me as they ran by, squirting each other with water pistols.

"Boys! Not in the house." Nick warned.

They ran out the back door, and Dad limped in, leaving it open.

"Dad!" Emily shouted. "Close the door. You'll let the cat out."

Bojangles was already trotting towards the opening, ready to make his escape.

"TTTSSSSST! TTSSSST!" Ian shouted, waving his arms and lunging towards the cat. Bojangles' hair stood on end as he yowled and took off at top speed towards the back of the house.

On the way, he knocked Cassie over. She had been standing up, holding on to the coffee table. She looked around to make sure everyone was watching before she started to wail.

Ian, who was only a few feet away from her, scooped her up and brought her to me. My knees went a little wobbly when his hand brushed my back after he handed Cassie over. Traitors.

She wasn't hurt, but it had scared the poop out of her. Literally. I felt something wet, warm and squishy on her leg when I shifted her to my hip. There had been a catastrophic breach in the containment field.

"Um, Ian, you might want to go clean up." I was mortified, but it was all I could do to squelch a giggle as I pointed to the streak on his arm. I had a change of baby clothes, but no grown up clothes. "I'll take her back to the house to get cleaned up."

Ian's face froze and he looked at his arm as if it was coated in radioactive waste.

"I'm really sorry about that," I said as I retreated out the door.

Well. That was special. As we hurried home under the street lights, I kissed my baby's head. "So, Cassie-girl, was that an editorial opinion?"

"Da da da!"

When we rejoined the party twenty minutes later, the twins had been sent to the Kids Table, and Dad had already brought in the food he had cooked on the barbeque. My favorite was the grilled peaches. I could be happy eating those and nothing else. The smell of peach, nutmeg, cinnamon and butter made my mouth water as I picked up my dinner plate. They hadn't waited for us. After I buckled Cassie into the high chair, I sat down in the only available seat – next to Ian.

"Sorry about the accident," I said to him.

"Don't worry about it. I know how squirmy babies can be. It's easy to get the diaper on just a little wrong."

I looked at his face. He seemed cheerful enough, even though it almost sounded like a dig. I let it go. I was probably just being hyper-sensitive, given that I managed to go two whole minutes at the get-together before my child besmirched not only me, but him as well. Ryan would have laughed and said, "Poop happens!"

After coffee and a miserable looking (but tasty!) slice of pie, we went into the living room and Nick put the twins to bed. Cassie was wired after her long nap and I knew it was going to be a late night. She was back at the coffee table, holding the edge with both hands. A blue stuffed bunny, Mr. Buns, dangled by the ear from her chubby fingers as she sidled up and down the edge of the table. If it was going to tire her out, I was all for it.

Ian was sitting on the floor near me, and he reached over and scooped Cassie up when she came by. I expected her to start wailing at him for spoiling her fun.

Instead, she giggled and whacked him in the head with the rabbit. "Da da da! Da da da!"

Ian looked surprised.

"Out of the mouths of babes!" Nick said, as he came back into the room at exactly the wrong moment.

I put my head in my hands and shook it. There was no point in trying to explain that she'd been working on that sound for almost two weeks now. Da da this, da da that. When was she ever going to say 'Mama?' "I'll go help Emily in the kitchen."

Mom quickly took my place when I got up.

Pale and sweaty, Emily was trying to arrange leftovers in the fridge.

"Hey Em, anything I can do?"

"No, Marts. I'm just about done. Nick'll get the dishes later."

I sat down, then felt a little guilty. "Why don't you have a seat? You look awful."

"Gee, thanks."

Emily waddled over and pulled out the chair next to me. "So. What do you think of Ian?"

"I'm already pregnant with his child and we're going to elope to Canada."

"You don't have to be sarcastic. I just wanted to know if you liked the guy. Nick thinks you'd make a good pair."

"Sorry. I kinda feel like I'm under a microscope just now. He seems nice enough, easy on the eyes. What do you think of him? He works for the DA – you're bound to have had some lawyerly, public defender contact with him somewhere."

"I mostly know him by reputation, and he works for the other side, remember? They say he's smart, capable, very in control." Emily shrugged. "Sorry, Marts. Wish I had the energy to stay up and chat, but I'm whipped. I'm going to bed. Night." She stood up and ruffled my hair as she walked past.

I made my way back to the living room.

"…and so the guy asks for change, and when the clerk opens the drawer, bad guy pulls out a gun and yells, 'Give me everything in the register!' The clerk hands him all the money in the till and bad guy bolts out the door. There was $5 in the register. And he left the twenty on the counter," Nick said, almost doubling over laughing.

Ian glanced up at me and gave me a quick smile and a wink. I looked down to make sure I hadn't had any wardrobe malfunctions.

"So we had this guy," Ian started, "that went to rob a bank. He had a backpack full of something, and he told the teller it was a bomb. She gave him the money, but he left the backpack, saying he'd detonate it if anybody followed him. So they called out the bomb squad and they found the backpack was filled with books. And his library card."

"No shit!" Nick said.

Mom cleared her throat and he cringed.

"Wait, it gets better," Ian continued. "When the cops asked the teller if the man had any distinguishing characteristics, she said he had horns on his head - some kind of freaky implants - and a tattoo on his forehead, his forehead, that said, 'Born to loose.' He was real hard to pick out of a lineup."

I was afraid Nick was going to wet himself.

"Emily went to bed." I said, plopping down on the couch.

Dad was asleep in the recliner. It was almost like old times, except now it was Ian and Nick talking shop instead of Ryan and Nick.

Cassie had been playing with the twins' blocks, but she left them and crawled towards Ian.

"Hey, baby! Way past your bedtime, isn't it little cutie?" He looked up at me when he said this, then tickled the back of Cassie's neck. She laughed.

"She had a two and a half hour nap this afternoon. But you're right. I should get her home and at least get her jammies on."

"I'll walk you to the house. It's after ten."

I was never bothered about walking alone in this neighborhood at any time day or night. But maybe my safety wasn't what he had in mind.

I really didn't need Ian to walk me six doors down. But I didn't mind it, either.

"In this neighborhood? We'll be fine." I said, protesting more for show than anything else.

"Please allow me to be a gentleman." He flashed perfect, laser-whitened teeth at me.

"If you insist." I scooped up Cassie and the diaper bag and headed towards the door.

"Nice weather we're having," Ian said, looking up at the pale stars sprinkled on the clear charcoal sky.

"Well, at this time of day, yeah."

Ian laughed.

I hummed to Cassie and Ian didn't say anything else until we got to my front porch.

"It was great to see you again tonight. I know it's really short notice, and I understand if you already have other plans, but would you have dinner with me Saturday – tomorrow - night?"

"A dinner date?" Mom could probably watch Cassie. "Yes. I'd like that." Then, I immediately crawfished. "If I can get a babysitter. As you said, it is kind of short notice."

He didn't have to know I'd only leave Cassie with Mom or Emily. And Mom was usually available.

"I'll call you tomorrow afternoon."

"You don't have my number."

"Email it to me."

Duh.

Then he took my non-baby-filled hand and kissed it. "Good night."

Much later on, I fell asleep smiling.

Chapter 4
The Emerald Jar

Bit chilly in here, don't you think?" the man with red hair asked.

"Maybe." Quinn shrugged.

The redhead picked up a log from the stack of wood near the cavernous fireplace and set it in the grate. He smiled at it.

It burst into flames.

"That's better," he said, dusting off his hands and making his way back to the bar.

"If you say so," Quinn said as he set a pint of dark stout in front of the redhead.

He ran his finger along the stein's handle. "I don't trust Malik."

"He's been with my team for ages. I trust him, Kai," Quinn replied.

"Yes, but you introduced him to his wife. He's in your debt, not mine."

Quinn sighed and blotted up a small puddle of beer on the bar. Closing time at the Waterhorse Inn had come and gone, and Kai was the only customer still inside the locked pub. The establishment had belonged to Quinn's family for as long as anyone in Blackthorne could remember, and that gave him a great deal of latitude with the front door key.

Kai took a deep draught of the stout and wiped his mouth with the back of his hand. "Djinn are always wildcards. Never sure what's going to offend them, and nobody carries a grudge like a djinn."

Quinn's smile was half-hearted. "I've heard all that. But Malik has always been solid. He's on my team, and you've got no say about that."

"I'm not asking you to kick him off your team. No," Kai said, crossing his arms. "That would probably be the worst possible thing to do. But this is a joint operation, and I'm just trying to assess liabilities."

"Malik is not a liability."

Kai noted that Quinn's eyes had changed from dark-eyed human to the edge-to-edge black of a kelpie. That often meant he was agitated and having trouble maintaining his current shape. But sometimes he just did it for effect - it totally freaked humans out. This was not one of those times.

Kai raised his glass. "To the unswerving loyalty of true friends." And chugged down the contents.

Quinn snorted and shook his head. His eyes were back to black on white. "Go home."

"See you tomorrow," Kai said as he stood up.

"It is tomorrow. Now get out, Kai."

"That's Mr. Underhill, to you."

Kai clapped Quinn on the shoulder, then turned and sauntered across the room to a floor-to-ceiling picture of a castle. He turned and waved before he stepped into the picture and was gone.

Quinn was tired of holding his human form. He went out to the millpond behind the inn and stripped naked under the platinum sliver of the new moon. As he dove into the water, he let its gelid fingers strip away his human shape. It felt good to be strong, a dreadnought slicing through the water. It wasn't that he felt nothing when he was in his natural kelpie form; but emotions receded into the background and sensations took center stage. The prickle of cold water rushing against his slippery skin. The pressure as he dove to the bottom of the pond. The searing of his lungs, screaming for oxygen, as he forced himself to stay under the surface until the last possible moment. He told himself that it was an exercise to expand his physical abilities. But he knew he was lying.

He wasn't really sure how long Siobhan had been gone. Sometimes it seemed like he'd been missing her for a hundred years, and sometimes it seemed that it was only yesterday that he'd carried her lifeless body, her blood soaking his skin and staining his soul, out of the wreckage of her little cottage. He would never forget that it had happened on a Tuesday, just before lunch. If he took a few moments with a Mundane calendar, he would know it had taken place two years, eight months, and six days ago. But time slipped into irrelevance as he scraped along the muddy pond bottom at top speed.

Quinn stayed out all night. As millponds go, this one was large – it had to be to accommodate generations of Waterhorse Inn kelpies – but it was still only a pond, not a deep loch. He had to be creative to find ways to push himself to exhaustion, and he managed to do so. He'd had a lot of practice. As the eastern sky lightened to grey, he shifted into human form, scooped up his clothes, and went inside.

"Morning, Robbie," Quinn said to the man arranging breakfast plates on the sideboard.

His older brother shook his head. "Put on some breeks, will ya? You'll frighten away the lodgers."

Quinn only smiled and trotted up the stairs. His hair was still damp, but the cool morning breeze had already dried his skin. He dropped his bundle of clothes on the floor and slipped under a heavy featherbed, too tired to dream.

When he woke up, it was well past lunch time. Stomach growling like a Tasmanian devil, he got up and got dressed, brushing one of last night's fish scales out from between his front teeth. Too bad it was only a small pond, with small fish.

The smell of baking bread in the kitchen made Quinn even hungrier. As he raided the pantry for something to eat, his younger brother, Kade, came in. There was one brother younger than him (Graham), and one older than Robbie

(Laurence, but they called him Laurie). Neither of them kept rooms at the Waterhorse.

"So how long are you gone this time?" asked Kade.

"Not sure. A fortnight, probably less, if everything goes well." Quinn knew Kade was just asking because he wanted to make sure the work at the Inn was covered, but having his affairs probed by his younger brother still rankled him.

Kade nodded. "Keep yourself in one piece." He continued through the kitchen and out the back door.

"I always do," Quinn said softly to the closed back door.

Deer season in the Angelina National Forest had been over for months, and this was not a righteous kill. Quinn squatted by the carcass of a white-tailed doe that had been shot and left to rot. It was too late at night for bottle flies, but the scavengers had been busy. Even so, he could see the ragged gunshot holes in the tatters of her stiff hide.

That wasn't the only thing wrong in the forest. It should have smelled like pine trees and earthy leaf litter. But there was an underlying industrial smell, hints of sulfur and plastic that set Quinn's nerves on edge.

"It's gotten really bad here," a quiet voice rasped behind him.

Quinn pivoted around. "Columbia?" he asked, his voice cracking with disbelief.

The dryad should have looked like a pretty young woman. Instead, the tree spirit was gaunt and pale. Oozing sores covered most of her skin, and bald spots glared from her scalp where clumps of her hair had fallen out.

"They poison everything. The trees are dead or dying," she panted.

"Sit down. Rest," Quinn said. "That's why we're here."

Quinn breathed in deeply, trying to quash his anger. He knew if he let it flow, let it control him, he would be blinded by it. But if he could smash it into a smoldering ball of energy deep within himself, he could harness its power later, when he needed it.

Kai's team was drawing off the heavily armed defenders and arranging an encounter between them and the human state police. When Quinn got the signal, his team would sweep in, bind the guards left at the camp and leave them like Christmas presents for the park rangers, who would be on their way. They'd leave the marijuana plants and equipment for the authorities to find. Once the growers were in custody, the forest would have a chance to heal. The pesticides and harsh artificial fertilizer would stop washing into the creek, burning and killing everything they touched.

A tiny ball of light, a flower fae, suddenly glowed by his head, then was gone. It was time.

Quinn whistled like a chuck will's widow three times in quick succession. The first guard never had a chance to grab the Kalashnikov slung over his shoulder as Eoin, the urisk, kicked him in the head with his iron-hard goat hooves. He dropped with a soft grunt and the half-man, half-goat took the guard's weapon, then triple-bound his hands and feet with zip ties.

A second guard had apparently heard something and came to investigate. Quinn slipped up behind him and locked him in a sleeper hold before he could raise an alarm. Eoin again set to work with the zip ties.

"Two down, two to go," Quinn whispered.

He scanned the camp and frowned. He could see as well in the dark as he could in daylight, yet he could detect no movement, no personnel. The growers' camp was too still.

"Something's wrong, Eoin. I can feel it. Not worried about Aleksei and Malik, but Tam's so green."

They crept towards a camo-patterned tent, the kind deer hunters sometimes use. Quinn could see Aleksei standing just behind the tent, although any human who looked at him would see nothing more than a large shrub. A flicker of eye contact, and Aleksei mouthed "Trap!"

But it was too late.

The ground next to Quinn and Eoin erupted and four hulking trolls burst out of the earth. One grabbed Eoin and another snatched Quinn. In human form, Quinn was just over six feet tall, but the troll was easily half again that height. Its hairy arms crushed the air out of his lungs as it picked him up and dragged him out in front of the tent. Eoin fought back, but even his hard hooves were no match for the living stone body of his captor. Quinn fought to breathe, then gagged on the moldy rot of the troll's breath.

"Welcome to the party," said a chunky man, who had been hidden by the tent.

The pupils of his bulging yellow eyes were vertical slits and his reptilian face was a scaly parody of a human's.

What was a demon doing here? No one had mentioned demons were involved. Although, Quinn told himself, one should never be surprised to find demons with their claws in any rotten pie they could find.

The air shimmered behind the demon and Quinn knew that Malik was stalking it.

"Catch!" shouted the demon. It tossed something that glittered green, even in the wan moonlight, in Malik's direction.

When it made contact with the djinn, it started to glow, so brightly that Quinn had to squint and turn his head. Malik seemed to crystalize out of the air, then he crumbled like a sand painting. A colorful stream, grains of Malik, was sucked into the hovering green jar. The demon snatched it out of the air and jammed a stopper into it.

Quinn and Eoin struggled to free themselves, but the trolls just squeezed them tighter, harsh laughter gurgling in their ears.

The demon pulled out a cell phone and sent a short text.

"Special bottle, you see. Carved from a single emerald. Coated in magick. Your djinn friend is mine, all mine. At least, until I sell him for a pile of cash."

The bushes near the demon rustled. No troll was holding Tam, and the young glastyn leaped from the shrubbery, his long horse ears pinned against his black hair and his sharp teeth bared. He scrabbled frantically at the green jar, but the demon coolly caught him by the throat with its free hand. Looking Quinn straight in the eye, it licked its scaly lips and sank its fangs into Tam's throat. He tried to scream, but it came out as a wet, choking gasp.

"No!" Quinn yelled, kicking uselessly at the stony legs of the troll. He heard a bone in his foot snap, but didn't feel it. He shifted into kelpie form, but the other two trolls anticipated this and grabbed his tail and neck. He wasn't any more use to Tam than he had been before. His cousin was going to die and there was nothing he could do to stop it.

Tam shriveled and collapsed in on himself as Quinn, Eoin and Aleksei watched, helpless and horrified. When the demon had finished sucking the last of Tam's life force, it threw his shriveled husk to the ground.

"I'm leaving you alive," the demon said to Quinn, "so that you can crawl back and report to your master that this is what happens to any of you stupid little fae that meddle in Balcones' business." The demon scowled and shook his head. "I can't have a big damn sea monster lying around when he gets here. Shift back to human form."

Quinn shook his head.

Balcones looked at Eoin. "Shift back, or I'm having barbequed goat for breakfast."

Defeated, Quinn shifted.

The demon nodded, and one of the trolls punched Quinn in the face. Everything went dark.

He had no idea how long he had been out, but Quinn awoke to the sound of voices. His head felt like it was in a vise and his broken ribs made breathing painful. He felt soft dirt underneath him and could hear someone nearby, breathing heavily. He hoped it was Eoin.

"And I told you, Chambers. You can have the merchandise as soon as I get a text that the funds have been transferred. Bad things will happen to you if I have to repeat myself."

Chambers. Why did that name sound familiar? There was something he should remember, but it stayed just out of reach, dancing at the dark edges of his memory.

Quinn's eye was swollen nearly shut, but he could open it enough to see the demon, disguised as a human, talking to a sandy-haired man. They were probably twenty yards away, and he doubted the human could see him in the tree-shadowed dark.

Chambers glanced at something in his hand. "My employer is not a patient man," he replied.

"Your employer's gonna have a job opening, if you don't shut up," Balcones snapped.

Chambers shut up.

Quinn let his eye close, and he wasn't aware of anything but the throbbing in his head until an electronic double beep snagged his attention. He opened his painful eye again.

"Money's cleared. Merchandise is yours. Now get back to Houston," the demon said.

He tossed Chambers the emerald bottle.

When Quinn opened his eyes again, his body was well, but his heart was sick. He could tell by the fact that everything was green that he was in a healing room. Quinn sat up and took a deep breath. It felt good to be pain free, at least physically. Then he lay back down and wondered if his mother knew that he'd gotten her cousin's youngest son killed.

"Hey! He's awake."

Quinn turned towards the door to see Kai and Eoin coming to his bedside.

"Weren't sure you were going to make it there, for a bit," Eoin said.

"Well, here I am, all in one piece."

"Kade's downstairs with your mum. He and Robbie have been taking turns sitting with you," Kai said. "She only leaves to eat."

"How long have I been here?"

"Three days," Eoin replied.

"So she knows then. About Tam."

"That was not your fault. Nobody blames you," Kai said, squeezing Quinn's shoulder.

"They should. I knew something was wrong. I should have aborted the mission and sent the team back to the rendezvous point."

"Second guessing yourself doesn't help anything, Quinn," Kai said. He cleared his throat.

"I'll go let your mum know you're awake," Eoin said, taking Kai's hint.

"It's just like before. I couldn't save Siobhan then and I couldn't save Tam now. I'm no good at this. I'll be turning in my resignation as soon as I'm out of here."

"No." Kai's voice was soft, but forceful. "That's just what Balcones wants you to do. If you quit, he wins, and Tam will have died for nothing." Kai shook his head and continued. "Siobhan knew exactly what she was doing. If she hadn't lured the demons away, it would have been a bloodbath. She saved a hundred lives, maybe more. It was her choice to make, not yours."

Quinn turned and faced the wall.

"I didn't even question it when she bought that little house in the Mundane world. She never so much as hinted that she'd volunteered for a suicide mission."

"Because she knew you would have stopped her. Or gone with her." Kai chewed his lip. "I'm sorry about Tam, really, I am. I know he was your cousin. I know you feel responsible. But it isn't your fault. When Tam saw what the situation was, he should have made a tactical retreat and called for reinforcements. That's SOP." Kai paused, his eyes softening and his voice changing from military commander to friend. "Take some time off. Get your head straight. But don't quit."

The door opened and Quinn's mother strode in, followed closely by Kade. She glared at Kai, but did not speak to him.

Kai squeezed Quinn's shoulder. "Think about what I said." Then he turned on his heel and left, avoiding eye contact with Quinn's family.

"How are you feeling?" Quinn's mother asked, laying her hand on his forehead as if he were a feverish child.

"Been better."

"I can see that." She patted his hand. "I hope you've finally come to your senses and you'll give up this ridiculous meddling in the Mundane world. If you really want to save it, you shouldn't be rescuing humans – you should be eating them, and the more the better."

Kade cringed in the background.

"They're not all bad, Mother," Quinn replied.

"Shall I convey that to my cousin Alice? I'm sure that will be very comforting as she's mourning her dead son."

"It was a demon, Mother. A demon killed Tam, not a human. We were ambushed, and Tam failed to follow protocol. He should have gone for help." Quinn struggled to keep his voice even.

"Is that what the red-haired monstrosity told you? His kind is not like us, you know." Her eyes shifted dangerously to all black.

"So, Mumsie," Kade broke in. "Have you managed to contact Graham and Laurie yet?"

"Laurence's wife said he was out teaching the children to catch sturgeon, but she'd pass along the message. I expect he'll be arriving before long."

Quinn suspected that Kade had already contacted Graham. He hoped to see his youngest brother, but knew he would not show himself as long as their mother was around. She and Graham had a bitter falling out over a hundred years ago, and hadn't spoken to each other since. She could not forgive him for getting romantically involved with a human. He could not forgive her for eating his girlfriend.

Quinn leaned dejectedly against the cinderblock wall. He'd slipped out of the Waterhorse Inn during the night, in the middle of his family drama, and come to the Mundane world to find Malik. He'd undoubtedly pay for it when he got back, but now was not the time to think about it. He had worse problems at the moment. There were only about one hundred people with the last name of

Chambers in the Houston white pages. But that didn't include any unlisted numbers or cell phones. How was he going to find Malik before something really bad happened?

A police car drove by. And that's when Quinn remembered. Now he knew where he'd heard the name Chambers.

Quinn pounded his fist into the wall. "Dammit!" All this time, Chambers had been right under his nose. Quinn ran back to the pay phone and looked up 'Chambers' in the tattered white pages that hung from a cable tether underneath the phone. There was neither an 'Ian' nor an 'I' Chambers listed.

At least it wouldn't be too difficult to find out if he was still working for the District Attorney. If not, perhaps he could renew his acquaintance with Officer Benson. He might have some idea where to find Chambers.

The best place to start, he reasoned, was at the DA's office. As soon as he found a way to get downtown.

It took him over an hour to get there on the 53 Briar Forest bus, and he still had to hike eight blocks to the DA's office on Franklin Street. It was nearly 5:00 when he arrived.

"Hey there, miss," he said to the receptionist in his best good-ole-boy American accent. "I'm an old buddy of Ian Chambers' and I was in town for a conference. Thought I'd drop by and say 'hey.' Is he in this afternoon?"

"I'm sorry. Mr. Chambers is out of the office. If you'd care to leave a message?"

"No, thanks. I'll just call him at the house. You have yourself a nice day, now."

Quinn knew that Kai had a team in place for a long-term assignment, and he was certain he could get help from them. They, more than any other fae who still visited the Mundane world, would understand.

One of Kai's team, Lorelei, loaned Quinn her car and gave him a place to crash. That made his life a lot easier. She was away for a few days, but would be back the next evening. He hadn't met her, but Kai had told him where to find the house and car keys inside a faux stone in the backyard.

Quinn arrived at the parking garage around 6:30 AM, then waited until Chambers showed up at ten to eight. He wrote down Chamber's license plate and headed to the tax assessor's office, to get the registration information, which would include Chamber's address. That took two and a half hours, and he had to convince the clerk that he had been sideswiped by that vehicle in a hit and run accident before she would release the information. He stopped for sushi on the way to scope out Chamber's address, a pricey loft in the Heights. The construction was recent, and all of the trees were small. But, three short blocks down, hundred year-old live oaks in front of a gaudily restored Victorian provided excellent shade. And dryads.

Quinn rolled down his window and waited. He was certain that Malik was not at Chambers' home – he'd undoubtedly delivered the emerald jar to his employer the same night Malik was kidnapped. But it could be helpful to see if Chambers had any visitors

It didn't take long before three curious dryads approached him.

"It is strange," said the bravest of the three, "to see one of your kind inside of a human machine."

"Why have you come to this place?" asked another, as she looked at him appraisingly.

"There is a human who lives in the first loft over there. He drives a large gold machine. I need to find out where he goes. He kidnapped my friend."

The dryads twittered among themselves.

"It is the third day of the week," said the last dryad. "He does not come here until late on this night."

"Yes! Sometimes not until the rising of the sun," chimed in the second dryad.

"Thank you," Quinn said, flashing his most charming smile. "I may see you again soon." He put the car in gear and headed back downtown.

There was no way to park close to Chamber's SUV this late in the day, so he parked on the street and fed the meter all afternoon until Chambers left his office around 6:00.

He didn't go very far, taking Quinn to an especially run-down topless bar called Specials. He also noted that it was across the street from a dilapidated motel with a surprising amount of activity, given the state of it. After Chambers disappeared into a back room, Quinn had spread some cash around the bar, but nobody had much to say, other than Chambers came in at least two days a week, and sometimes met up with a couple of cops.

It was 10:30 before Chambers emerged, alone, and went to his car. Quinn followed him back to his luxury loft.

The lights inside Chamber's house went out. Quinn gave up getting any further information and went back to Lorelei's.

He was skinny-dipping in her saltwater pool, wishing it was big enough for him to shift out of human form. Probably just as well, though, in case Lorelei had any nosey night-owl neighbors. When he surfaced underneath the diving board, she was standing at the opposite end of the pool, near the floodlit waterfall.

A sound fell out of his mouth, halfway between a groan and a grunt.

In spite of her name, he had forgotten that she was an actual lorelei. No one, save perhaps those weird sisters themselves, knew what a lorelei really looked like. To any observer, they appeared as the epitome of female beauty, so everyone saw something different.

Quinn saw Siobhan.

He knew it wasn't really her. Couldn't possibly be. His mind knew, but his body reacted anyway. He wanted her. Badly. But, he also knew that, like black widows, the lorelei always devoured their lovers afterwards. Those freshwater mermaids had a little more kink than was good for a body.

Not trusting himself, he stayed as far from her as he could. "Lorelei?"

"Yes. It is I. For you, I have a message. I was told this afternoon that Graham, your brother, requires urgently your presence at your residence."

Great. Just what I need. "Thank you, Lorelei. I'd like to use your portal, if you don't mind?"

"It is no problem."

Quinn had hoped that she'd go in so that he could get out of the pool and get dressed. Looking at her had re-opened old wounds that had been mostly healed, even if the scar tissue was still sore. But she just stood there, torturing him.

"I left your keys on the end table near the front door. Thanks again for letting me borrow your car."

She nodded slightly, then turned and started back towards the house. When she was inside, Quinn pulled himself out of the pool. He hadn't brought a towel out with him, so he just put his clothes on his sopping body. He was loath to interrupt his investigation of Ian Chambers. No telling what his boss had planned for Malik. And he dreaded going home and refereeing a reunion between his mother and youngest brother. But staying here with Lorelei was even worse.

Quinn was usually the peace-maker in the family. But he had been at the Waterhorse for days, and had come no closer to reconciling Graham and their mother. He was ready to abdicate to his older brothers. Nothing ever ruffled Robbie, and Laurie, ever Mother's favorite, had just arrived.

Precious time was slipping away, and Malik was still trapped somewhere in the Mundane world. Taking a break from his family squabbles, Quinn had gone to talk to Malik's wife. She'd cried the whole time, their two children sniffling and clinging to her. The delay was killing him. He had to take action soon.

He was lingering at the edge of the millpond, trying to steal a moment of peace and plan his departure, when he noticed a dryad approaching. She had long, straight hair, and he recognized her instantly - she was from the pine tree in Ryan Keller's yard.

"Daphne?" he asked.

"You said come to you if there was any trouble," the dryad replied.

"What's happened?" He felt his heart beat a little faster.

"Nothing yet. But this man has been coming around late at night, while the house woman is sleeping. He peers in the windows and writes himself notes. He even has asked her to dine with him this night."

"What did she say?"

"She agreed. She does not know he has put under the windows little metal boxes that allow him to listen to what she says. He is dangerous, I fear."

"All the windows?" Quinn asked.

"Just in the back of the house. And one on the side where she parks her transport machine."

Quinn nodded. "Sounds like it's time to repay a debt."

Chapter 5
Cart Before the Horse

om was only too happy to watch Cassie while I had a date with a respectable young man. Ian had called just after lunch to confirm our date. I asked where we were going so I could meet him there. But he said that would ruin the surprise. He would swing by to pick me up at 7:00. I reminded myself that he did work for the DA, so he probably wasn't a serial killer.

"Mom, what am I going to wear?" I complained, looking in my closet. I hadn't gone anywhere I needed nice clothes for a couple of years. The only 'little black dress' I owned, I had worn to Ryan's funeral, and I couldn't bear to look at it. But I couldn't give it away, either.

I had the cash to go buy a brand new dress, but I didn't want to spend it on something so frivolous. I needed to make the money I had last as long as I could. At least until I could get a home business up and running, or Cassie was old enough to go to school and I could go back to work part-time, whichever came first.

"Why don't you ask your sister if she has something you can borrow?" Mom said. She was standing at the baby gate at the doorway to my bedroom, and Cassie was holding on to her leg.

"Because then she'll know I have a date, and I'm not ready to let Nick crow about fixing me up just yet." Especially not after the lecture I gave him at the barbeque.

"Go to the resale shop then. It'll be time for Cassie's nap soon. I'll stay with her."

I put my arms around my mother's neck. "Thanks, Mom."

I tried the two resale shops I usually visit, but didn't find anything I liked. There was a huge Goodwill store on Highway 6. Maybe they'd have something.

The evening wear rack had four items in my size. One was a black crepe pantsuit that was too frumpy for even my mother to wear (and she was the queen of frump). One was a gold-sequined monstrosity that was too low at the top and too high at the bottom. One was a light blue chiffon dress with a beaded bodice that had a very mother-of-the-bride look to it. The last one was a nightmare in pleated fuchsia. I was running out of time, and almost desperate enough to try on the blue chiffon, when an employee came up with a rack of clothes. She pulled out two dresses. One was tangerine, and looked like it would fit a hippopotamus. The other one was a beautiful emerald green with sheer, shimmery organza sleeves. It was perfect – elegant and flattering without being too sexy.

"Excuse me, may I try that one?" I motioned towards the green dress.

"Sure." The employee handed it over and pushed the cart to the next section.

I held my breath and looked at the tag. What were the odds it would be in my size? The tag said it was a size nine. Close enough. I hurried to the dressing room to try it on.

It wasn't a perfect fit. It was too tight across the bust, but the designer probably didn't have nursing moms in mind. It was a little too loose in the waist, but that left extra room for dinner. I paid $15 for the dress and left. There was still a little tag from the dry cleaner on the dress, so I felt okay about wearing it as-is.

I pumped when I got home. Cassie was usually only interested in nursing first thing in the morning or last thing at night. Or if she was upset. Part of me was glad that she was starting to wean herself, and part of me was sad that she was growing up. Either way, I would miss our special bonding time.

Cassie was just starting to stir. Mom went home to check on Dad. He'd gotten more forgetful lately, and she wanted to make sure he'd eaten his lunch. She'd be back around 6:30. That gave me almost three hours with my little sweetie-pie.

When Mom showed up, I was just putting on my earrings.

"You look mah-velous, dahling!"

I laughed. "Thanks. There's fresh milk in the fridge, in the bottle and ready to go. If Cassie gets too fussy or won't go to sleep, call me. I'll come straight home."

"She'll be just fine, Marti. Don't you worry about us." Mom bit her bottom lip. "You do realize you're still wearing your bunny slippers, don't you?"

I hadn't realized.

"Yes, Mom. I know."

Ryan had bought me those slippers as a joke a couple of months before he died. I started wearing them just to tease him. Now, I wore them all the time, and they were getting a bit ragged.

I touched up my eyeliner, then went to the closet and slid on my dress shoes. I never wore heels higher than two inches. At 5'9", I was already tall enough. In fact, that's one reason Emily matched me with Ryan at her wedding. He was 6'3" and the only one of the groomsmen I didn't tower over.

I had to rummage around in the closet to find my evening bag. The doorbell rang while I was still trying to stuff my wallet, cell phone and lipstick into the tiny little purse. I wedged in a fresh pair of nursing pads, just in case.

"Ian, come in," my mother said from the living room. "Marti will be out in just a moment." Eek. Just like in high school.

I gave myself a final once-over in the mirror. It wasn't too late. I could still back out. Maybe take a swig of hydrogen peroxide to make myself vomit and convince them I was sick. I shook my head, took a deep breath, and headed for the living room.

Ian sat on my couch. I would have thought he was making an internal critique of my interior decorating, the way he was scrutinizing the living room, if his right leg hadn't been twitching up and down like a sewing machine. Was he that nervous? It was kind of cute.

"Wow," he said. "You do clean up well."

Not so cute. When had he ever seen me not cleaned up?

"Thanks. You're not so bad yourself." The tan sport coat made him look like a TV detective, but it worked for him. The jacket was almost the same color as his hair, and his blue shirt was only a little darker than his eyes.

I kissed Cassie and my mother before Ian and I went out and climbed into his gold Chevy Suburban.

"So. Where are we going?"

"It's a surprise." Ian grinned at me, but I felt nervous. Why hadn't I insisted that I follow him in my own car?

We made small talk for half an hour or so as we headed east on I-10. I squirmed and shifted in my seat and leaned against the door. My logical brain told me that I wasn't in any danger. People knew I was with him. He worked in the DA's office for goodness' sake. I supposed what was bothering me was lack of control. He was probably just trying to sweep me off my feet, but I felt more trapped than romanced.

As we took the I-45 exit, I said, "You're not taking me to the Rainforest Café in Galveston so you can get me alone in the dark on the Lost River ride, are you?" I was only half joking.

"Nope. Wouldn't dream of it."

A little while later, we took the El Dorado exit and headed east.

"Kemah Boardwalk?"

"Maybe."

Ian paid extra to leave his truck in the parking garage. As soon as I got out of the car, I was caressed by a cool salty breeze. It reminded me of the last time Ryan and I camped at the beach, our standard Thanksgiving getaway. That's how I ended up with my sweet little Cassie.

It was almost 8:00, and the sky over the Kemah Boardwalk was just starting to think about going dark. The lights on the observation tower were on, but looked anemic against the grey blue of the evening sky. To our right, the Boardwalk Bullet roller coaster thundered along wooden tracks. People screamed with fear and delight as they were dropped from a free fall tower. Music from the carousel drifted our way. The kitchens on the restaurant row were in full swing, and I could smell fish, fajitas and pizza – with notes of popcorn and cotton candy. Marquee lights flashed on the Ferris wheel.

Ian took my elbow and guided me towards The Aquarium restaurant. Train tracks ran parallel to the walkway and a little red and black train hooted at us as it passed by. The Boardwalk was heaving with people, mostly families. I swallowed the small, desperate wish that I was here with Ryan and Cassie and smiled at my date.

"You know, the Aquarium downtown would have been a lot closer," I said.

"Yes, but this one has other…features. After you," he said as he opened the door.

The hostess was a youngish bottle blond whom I inexplicably disliked on sight. She addressed Ian with bored eyes and a saccharin smile. "Table for two?"

"I have a reservation. Under Chambers."

She scanned the laminated plastic sheet on the podium and made a mark with a grease pencil. "Of course. Your table will be ready in a few minutes. You can wait in the Dive Lounge, if you'd like." She handed Ian a chunky black alert buzzer.

Ian thanked her, and we made our way to the bar.

I watched the fish swim through the bubble wall while Ian ordered a martini. About the time the server arrived back at the table with the drink, our buzzer went off to let us know our table was ready.

The hostess showed us to a table with an up-front view of the overwhelming aquarium. Actually, it was an up-front view of an ever-changing pack of children with their noses pressed up against the overwhelming aquarium. I wondered if the sharks that cruised the tank had any idea that people were sitting all around them, eating their relatives.

The rail-thin server handed us our menus. Her cheekbones were sharp enough to chop wood, but her low-cut top strained to contain her oversized bosom. At least Ian was a gentleman and didn't blatantly gawk at her. I wondered how many men had bruises on their shins from being kicked under the table by wives or girlfriends when they were in her section.

"I'm Suzette," she said, in a peculiar accent that I was almost certain was fake, "and I'll be taking care of you this evening. May I get you anything to drink?"

Ian debated with Suzette about the wine list. I wasn't much of a drinker, and he could just as easily have ordered Mad Dog for all the difference it would make to me.

"Glass of water for me, please." *And get yourself a sandwich while you're in the kitchen.*

Suzette fetched the wine and my water.

"Would you care for any appetizers?" she chirped.

"Dozen oysters on the half shell," Ian replied. His eyebrow twitched.

I shook my head and Suzette minced back to the kitchen on her stiletto heels.

Ian poured us each a glass of white wine, then raised his glass. "To the Boardwalk."

"To the Boardwalk," I toasted.

The wine was a bit drier than I expected, and it didn't take too many sips for my cheeks to start feeling a little warm. One glass was probably more than I needed for the entire evening. I was very glad I got the glass of water.

Suzette returned with a plate of raw oysters. She set them in the middle of the table, but I could hardly look at them.

"Have you decided what you will be having for your main course tonight?"

"I'll have the mixed grill, and the lady will have the mahi mahi and shrimp."

"Excuse me," I snapped. "The lady will have the Greek salad, thank you."

"Would you like shrimp with the salad? We can do that," Suzette gushed.

"No, thank you. I'm allergic to shellfish."

"So, no shrimp then?"

"Not unless you want to see me go into anaphylactic shock and have to call EMS to the restaurant. Might upset the other diners."

I thought Suzette's eyes would pop out of her head.

"Yes ma'am. One Greek salad and one mixed grill. Excellent choices. Thank you." Suzette's heels clicked briskly on the tile as she left.

"I'm really sorry, Marti. I had no idea," Ian said.

"I believe you were trying to be an old fashioned gentleman. I appreciate that. But don't order food for me again, okay?" I don't appreciate being treated like a child.

"Certainly, if that's how you want it."

He smiled when he said it, but his clipped words were tinged with pique.

The idea drifted into my head that maybe Ian had read an old book on how to romance women, rather than actually knowing how to do it from experience. But that was just silly.

Then he started eating the oysters. I had to excuse myself to the ladies' room while he slurped. I had seen enough septic wounds in the ER that seeing anyone eat something that looked like effluvium made my stomach churn.

I texted my mom to see how Cassie was doing. She'd fallen asleep in the rocking chair with Mom while watching a Baby Einstein video, and was now sleeping like a brick in her crib. I checked my hair and makeup to see if I needed any maintenance. I looked fine. How long would it take him to eat those oysters? I gave him ten minutes before I washed my hands and went back to the table.

When I returned, Ian had not only finished the oysters, but topped off my wine glass, which I ignored. The rest of dinner went unexpectedly well, and I started to relax. He had the rest of the wine while we ate, plus another martini. I was starting to get uneasy about how much he was drinking. When I offered to pay for my meal, he wouldn't hear of it. After he'd paid the check, I enjoyed exploring the Rainforest exhibit with him and seeing the piranhas. They're actually sparkly, and kind of pretty, for vicious little killers.

It had been fun, but I was ready to go. I was tired and starting to fret about Cassie. It was 10:45 and this was the longest I'd ever been away from her. We went outside. When Ian nearly walked into a pole, I tried to decide whether I should drive us back to town or call a taxi.

The earlier crowds had dissipated, and there was hardly anyone around near the restaurant. I started towards the garage.

"What's your hurry?" Ian asked. "You don't want to leave without riding the Ferris wheel, surely?"

"They're just about to shut everything down. I've had a great time, really, Ian, but it's been a long day, and it will take us another forty-five minutes or so for me to drive us home."

"It doesn't have to."

"What? Have you got a teleportation device in your pocket?"

"Better. I've got a beach house on the Island."

Oh, boy. Why didn't I bring my own stupid car? "I'm sure it's very nice and I'd love to see it another time. I'm ready to go home. To my home. Alone. Now."

Ian took a step closer and started to stroke my shoulder. The booze smelled sour on his breath. "Come on, Marti. I-I can treat a lady right." He planted a sloppy kiss underneath my ear.

"Back off, Chambers!" I growled at him and pulled away.

He had a hold on my sleeve and when I jerked my arm backward, the sheer fabric ripped. Ian's mouth worked like a landed fish.

"Is that what you think of me? That I'm some desperate female, who'll just fall into bed with you for no good reason?"

"I…I…I am so sorry," he stammered, organza still clutched in his fingers.

"Let go!"

"Excuse me, Miss. Is there a problem here?"

I turned my head to see a man approaching us. It was hard to tell in the poor light, but he could have been anywhere between twenty and forty. Dark hair brushed his shoulders.

"Is this man troubling you?" He had a slight accent, Scottish, perhaps.

Ian stepped away from me. He looked like a scared kid. A really big scared kid.

"It's okay. Thank you," I said.

The man stayed where he was and watched Ian suspiciously.

"Marti, I don't know what came over me. I can't apologize enough." Ian pulled the car keys out of his pocket. "Let me just take you home."

"I'm not getting in the car with you." I snatched his keys away. "And you don't need to be driving anywhere." Now what was I going to do with his stinkin' keys?

"Ian, you go inside and tell them to call you a taxi."

He stumbled towards the door. I could drive myself home in Ian's car, but then I'd have to park it in front of my house, and wouldn't Nick just love that? But maybe there was a better way.

"You sure you're okay?" the dark-haired man asked.

"I'm fine, thanks. My friend has just had a little too much to drink, that's all. I appreciate your concern."

The man's eyes half-closed and he took a deep breath. "Your arm's bleeding."

I glanced down. There was a smear of blood where Ian had torn my sleeve. He must have caught me with his nails.

"Just a scratch. I'll be fine."

He looked around as if he were counting the stragglers from the earlier crowds. I probably should have been afraid, but I wasn't. When his eyes came back to me, I could see they were very dark, almost black. Like Ryan's. They pulled me in and held me. Run! Run now, before it's too late. Run. Adrenalin, not sure if it was his or mine, made my skin feel alive. If he'd made a move to touch me, I would not have stopped him. And I didn't know why.

I shook myself and looked away. I was not like that. I did not get all hot and bothered by complete strangers.

I knew Ian would be back any second, and I needed to be gone by then. "There is one thing you can do that would really help me out…" I gave him a questioning look.

"Quinn."

"Quinn," I repeated. I took Ian's car key and remote off the ring and tried to stick them in my purse, but they just wouldn't fit. I pretended like I'd planned that all along. "Would you please tell my friend that the parking attendant has his keys when he comes out?"

When Quinn smiled, just for an instant, I could have sworn his teeth were sharp, like the sharks' that we had just eaten dinner with. When I looked again, they were as normal as mine. I knew it was just the dim light, but it was still unsettling, and I felt something that wasn't quite fear.

"Your friend? Friends like that, you probably don't need."

I gave him my best glower. My friends were none of his business. "Thanks for your help," I said crisply.

He only smiled at me, so I turned on my heel and made a show of stalking towards the parking garage. I didn't have the ticket, but I was sure they'd let me out for the max price. I found the car, got inside and adjusted the seat and mirror.

The small white square by the rear view mirror was notably absent. No EZ-Tag? Why would you not have an EZ-Tag, Ian? I didn't have any change or small bills to go through the full service booths, so unless I wanted to stick Ian with a ticket, I'd have to avoid the Tollway. I did consider it, though, after what he'd just put me through.

I counted on Ian being too embarrassed by assaulting me to call the PD and report his car stolen. I would leave his Suburban in the parking lot of the 24-hour Kroger that was about a mile from my house and leave his keys in the gap under the bumper. I'd email him and let him know where it was.

And then what?

After a wrong turn sent me to Dickinson, I bumbled my way back to I-45. I knew how to get home now, so I could chew on what had happened. I liked Ian. Or at least I had, until he started pawing me outside the restaurant. Was this just a one-off, or was this his standard operating procedure? He looked contrite enough, but was that only because Quinn showed up? Ahh, Quinn. I felt an unexpected twinge of sadness that I'd never see him again.

This was all Nick's fault. If he hadn't been so bent on setting me up with somebody. I sighed. No, it was my fault. I accepted the date. I could have said

'No.' I should have. I loved Cassie more than anything in the world, but sometimes, it would be nice to have an adult to talk to besides my mother. It would be nice to feel strong male arms around me. It would be nice to make love. But Ryan was dead and no amount of wishing was going to bring him back. Regardless of what my body might want, my heart was not ready to let him go.

I let the tears roll down my cheeks as I tried to push visions of a wailing Cassie and my frazzled mother out of my head. I found the oldies station and turned up the radio, too loud, and made myself sing along with The Clash.

After I parked Ian's behemoth truck under one of the parking lot lights at the Kroger, I sent him an email from my phone about the location of his vehicle. Ordinarily, a walk in the fresh air would clear my head. But tonight it was so muggy and warm that it just made me cranky.

A Mediterranean gecko scrambled for cover as I came up onto my front porch. Fat June bugs and assorted moths buzzed around the light. I didn't hear a sound coming from the house, so I unlocked the door and crept inside. Dad was asleep in my recliner and Mom was stretched out on the couch. I checked Cassie's room. She was sighing in her sleep, smelling like baby powder and lavender. As softly as I could, I touched her hair and caressed her cheek. "Goodnight, my sweet little thing," I whispered as I left her room.

I did my usual rounds – checked all the doors to make sure they were locked, made sure Alpha and Betty, our pet rats, had food and water. Nick had rescued them from a homicide scene. The dead man had no friends or relatives to take them and the shelter was overflowing, so euthanasia was their best offer. He'd thought Kyle and Aiden would like them, but Emily wouldn't allow them in the house. He knew I never met a stray I didn't rescue, so he brought them to me. As it turned out, the twins weren't as interested as he'd imagined, but I thought the rats were very sweet.

I made one last check on Cassie, standing near her bed and listening to her breathe for a few minutes before I went to bed. How old does your baby have to be before you stop looking in on her each night?

I went to my room and lay on top of the covers. I kept the thermostat on 80 during the summer – cheaper that way – and even with the ceiling fan on high, the heat was oppressive. I tried to figure out what to do about Ian Chambers. I couldn't make up my mind whether he was a habitual jerk or just made a one-time mistake. But it seemed like the more I thought about Ian, the more Quinn's face popped into my head. I finally found a comfortable spot and slowly faded to sleep. I woke up about every two hours, remembering fragments of a dream about riding a horse, and the horse swimming through a wonderful, cool lake.

It was just after lunch on Sunday afternoon. Cassie and I were playing with the shape sorter when the phone rang. I checked Caller ID. It was Ian. Again. I let it go to voice mail. I wasn't ready to talk to him. Not yet. Maybe never.

෬

Cassie had just finished Monday's breakfast. She was covered in oatmeal and had squished her banana chunks together to use as a hair styling product. We were headed towards the bathroom when the doorbell rang.

On the other side of the peephole, stood a young man in a light blue uniform, holding a vase of yellow roses.

"Who is it?" I asked.

"I'm Todd. I've got a delivery from Annabelle's Flowers for a Ms. Marti Keller."

I opened the door.

Todd was holding a vase of flowers, and there were five others lined up on the porch beside him. He handed me the one with the card.

"Six dozen roses? Seriously? Are you sure there's no mistake?"

"No, ma'am. They're all for you."

I signed for them and Todd helped me bring them in the house. They took up nearly all of the breakfast table. I asked Todd if he had a wife or girlfriend who might like to have a dozen yellow roses, but he shook his head.

I looked at the card.

"Dear Marti. I am so, so, so, so, so very sorry. I don't know what came over me. It's just that you are a beautiful, smart, funny lady and I want to get to know you better. I jumped the gun. I shouldn't have tried to rush you. I hope you can find it in your heart to give me another chance."

So. He thought I was beautiful, smart and funny, did he? Maybe that should count for something. Or maybe it was just empty flattery. Was this the same Ian Chambers who pulled Nick and three others out of a burning building? Just who is the real Ian Chambers??

Chapter 6
Listen

an chambers staggered out of the Aquarium restaurant, and Quinn wanted to punch him in the face. He remembered Keller's last words to him, warning that Ian Chambers was not to be trusted. And now, he was courting Keller's widow.

Chambers looked around, confused.

"She's gone," Quinn said, strolling casually over. "Said she was going to leave your keys with the parking attendant."

Chambers swore softly. "And who did you say you were?"

"A friend."

"I don't think I know you." Chambers shook his head, trying to clear the fog.

"I didn't say I was your friend."

Quinn let his eyes go completely black, just for a few seconds. Long enough for Chambers to snort and back up, trip over his own feet, and land hard on his butt.

"I didn't mean anything. I would never have hurt Marti. Please..." he mewled.

"You tied to force yourself on her. You tore her dress."

"It was an accident. I – I—"

Quinn smiled and extended his hand. "Let me help you up."

Chambers' shivering hand was soft and clammy. Quinn pulled him up, then trapped his arm and pulled him in close, so his face was only inches from Chambers'.

"Stay away from Marti. I don't want to hear about you coming around and bothering her. Understand?"

Chambers nodded.

"Go get your keys. I'm sure your taxi will be here any minute," Quinn said.

Chambers wobbled off towards the parking garage, looking over his shoulder. Quinn smiled and waved. He hoped that Chambers was sober enough to remember their conversation, but he wasn't so sure.

A figure moved out of the shadow of the building. "That wasn't the smartest thing you've ever done," Kai said. "Now he knows what you look like, and he's scared of you."

"Maybe. But I got his cell phone."

Kai laughed. "Good luck with that. Doubt he'll have a contact labeled 'Evil Second Boss.' But you ought to get it back to him before he notices it's missing."

Kai did not like to drive. And it was just as well – machines tended to fail under his touch, even when he didn't want them to. As his cover identity was that of a very wealthy philanthropist, he had a driver. His name was Frey, and he'd been burned by dragon fire. He was hard to look at, but he was as loyal as they come. And, he was good with human technology, something Quinn had never really mastered.

"Frey," Quinn said as they got in the car. "That guy I've been following? I got his phone. Not sure if his contact list is going to be much use. Do you have any ideas?"

"What is it that you want to do?" Frey asked, his blind, white eye facing Quinn.

Quinn leaned back in his seat. "I'm looking for the guy he works for, the guy who has Malik. I want to know where Chambers goes and who he talks to."

"Pah. I thought it was going to be something hard. Let me see the phone," Frey answered.

He shook his head. "Not password protected." Then he opened the phone's internet browser and surfed to a website. It took almost two minutes to download an application. "Whose phone number you gonna use to check this?"

"Kai's," Quinn answered.

"That's fine," Kai replied.

Frey typed in some data and turned the phone off. "Next time he makes or receives a call, you'll be able to hear it. If he sends a text or an email, you can read it. He's disabled the GPS on the phone, but the software will turn it on. If he notices, he'll probably turn it back off, though." Frey handed Chambers' phone to Quinn.

"Will he be able to find this program?" Quinn asked.

"Not unless he's really paranoid and runs a virus sweep on his phone with the right software."

"Guess I'd better get it back to him, then."

Quinn gave Frey Chambers' address. They drove past his house, as the taxi had just arrived and Chambers was getting out. They doubled back and Frey parked in the shadows of the old live oaks down the street. They waited until the lights in Chambers windows went dark, then they waited another half hour.

Kai and Quinn got out of the car and walked up to Chamber's front door as if they belonged there. One of Kai's skills was opening locks. He couldn't do anything about barricaded doors, but locks he could pick with a touch, unless they were magickally sealed. Any curious neighbors would think the two men had a key, given how easily the door opened for them. Quinn closed it gently behind them.

Chambers had made it easy for them. He'd left his pants draped over a chair in the kitchen. His keys dangled precariously from one pocket. Quinn slipped the phone into the other front pocket, turning it so that it didn't slide out.

Quinn wrinkled his nose. The place smelled like furniture polish and carpet freshener. He looked around the room. Everything was chrome and granite. Very modern, very sterile. Even the flower arrangement in the middle of the breakfast table was silk.

Kai was already on his way out, and Quinn hurried to catch up. In his haste, he knocked over a lamp that was perched on an end table near the sofa. He lunged for it. He caught it, but made a big thump as he hit the wood floor. He and Kai both froze. Upstairs, Chambers mumbled something. Seconds passed, then minutes. The house remained still and quiet.

Quinn set the lamp back on the table and they made their way out of the house and back into Kai's car.

"That was too close," Kai said.

"Tell me about it," Quinn replied.

Quinn lost track of the number of times he heard Marti's voicemail message, as Chambers called her over and over on Sunday. He liked her voice, he decided. It was clear and firm, but softly blurred at the edges – neither sharp authoritarian nor breathy sex kitten.

Quinn kept in close contact with the dryads in Marti's yard, keeping surveillance on her that way. It felt weird to him, inadvertently spying on her, while spying on Chambers. On the other hand, it did make his life easier. He learned her routine, knew her baby always got up at six thirty and they always went for a morning walk. If he was going to protect her from Chambers, it helped to know her habits.

Chapter 7
Happy Medium

t was just after ten on a Tuesday morning, and the heat was already all but intolerable. Cassie and I were headed home from our morning walk, and she was having a lively conversation with her stuffed rabbit, Mr. Buns. "Marti? Is that you?"

I turned to see Lulu Miranda, the woman who had knocked me over with the bookshelf, carrying a cardboard box through the parking lot of the mostly vacant strip center.

"Hi. We're out for a walk." Admittedly, I was agnostic about this woman's sanity.

"Oh, come on in. Have some cold water and a look around."

A cowbell clattered as Lulu pulled the door open. I looked into the shop. Cassie seemed happy enough. The idea of talking to an adult who wasn't a relative really appealed to me just then.

"Sure, if there's room for the stroller." I always left myself an out.

"Course there is, honey." Lulu smiled as she held the door open for me.

The Tenth Sphere smelled like sandalwood incense and butterscotch. The shop felt different from outside, the same way the weekend feels different from the work week. Very breakable-looking figurines lined the wall nearest the cash register, which was boxed in by jewelry display cases. Another wall had incense sticks, charcoal tablets and reed diffusers. Sturdy wooden shelves were crammed with crystal spheres, salt lamps, pendulums, Tarot cards and loose crystals. There was a vast array of books from astral projection to zoomorphism. Two clothes racks stood against the far wall, displaying robes, cloaks and belly dancing outfits. Belly dancing outfits?

Near the back of the shop, a staircase – closed off with a purple velvet rope – led to the second floor.

"What's up there?" I asked Lulu.

Lulu grinned as she handed me a paper cup with cold water from the cooler by the front door. "Oh, we have some classrooms and private client consultation rooms."

"What do you do in private client consultation rooms?" That sounded like a euphemism for something illegal.

"Well, we do Tarot and astrological readings. Sometimes those get very emotional for the clients, and they prefer to have some privacy."

Seems like lately I could hardly sling a cat without hitting something about Tarot card reading.

"Tarot card readings. You know, I saw something the other day about doing that as a home business."

"Did you really?" Lulu said, looking at me as if she was truly surprised. "Have you ever had your cards read, honey?"

"No. My dad always said that so-called psychic readers were nothing but con artists."

As soon as the words left my mouth, I wished I could take them back. "I mean, not that you, personally, are a con artist. That's just Dad's opinion. About psychics in general, not you." Shut up before you make it any worse.

Lulu sighed. "Well, unfortunately, there are a lot of flim-flammers, and that's a real shame, because it puts a bad light on people who really do have a talent. Tell you what. I owe you one for flattening you the other day. Would you like a reading? On the house, of course. You can judge for yourself."

I looked at Cassie, enthusiastically whacking her bunny against the stroller tray and giggling with delight.

"I don't know. I'll never get the stroller up those stairs and—"

"Don't you worry about that. I'll get Belinda out of the back. She's got four grandbabies, you know." Lulu nodded and leaned towards me, as if she were about to tell me a delicious secret. "Susan Pletcher is going to be coming in on Tuesdays and Thursdays to do readings, starting next week. She is really good. Anyway. Belinda!" Lulu power-walked towards a door marked 'Employees Only.' "Belinda!"

Belinda emerged from the back room with a barcode scanner in her hand and a packing peanut in her hair.

"What is it?" she snapped.

Lulu was unfazed. "B, can you keep an eye on this little lady—," Lulu turned to me, "what's her name, honey?"

"Cassie."

"Miss Cassie while I pop upstairs to give Mama a reading?"

"Course I can. That's the best offer I've had all day." When Belinda smiled, she looked like a fairy godmother.

"I don't know. She can be fussy around people she doesn't know." She takes after her mother.

"Belinda's got a way with babies. If it makes you more comfortable, I'll even leave the curtain open so you can see Miss Cassie during your reading."

I winced as I bit the inside of my cheek a little too hard, chewing on the idea. I wasn't sure I wanted to leave Cassie with a stranger – even if she did have 'a way' with babies. On the other hand, I was extremely curious about Tarot card reading, since it had been coming up over and over. Curiosity killed the cat. Still, it wasn't exactly like I was leaving her – I'd only be half a boutique's length away from her, and I'd be able to see her the whole time. But satisfaction brought it back.

"Alright," I said.

After setting the scanner on the jewelry counter, Belinda moved Cassie's stroller so that she could see both the baby and the front door while she sat in an enormous gnarled chair carved from a cypress tree root.

Cassie grinned at her, with all four and a half teeth, and pounded poor Mr. Buns on the stroller tray. "Da da da!"

She didn't even seem to notice that I was leaving. I looked over my shoulder a couple of times as I followed Lulu upstairs. I alternated between feeling happy that my child was independent and sad that she didn't seem to miss me.

Immediately in front of us, at the top of the stairs, was a conference room with a glass door. To the left of the conference room was a doorway hung with a purple curtain, and to the right was a doorway with a green curtain.

Wooden rings scraped across the metal rod as Lulu whisked the purple curtain out of the way. We entered a room not much bigger than a walk-in closet. A well-used night stand with an artificial African violet and a box of tissues squatted in one corner. We sat down opposite each other on folding chairs at a small round table draped with several layers of fabric.

"How long will this take?" I asked, picking at the cuticle of my thumb. If I sat just a little sideways in my chair, I could look over my shoulder and see Cassie gnawing on Mr. Buns.

"Ten minutes, give or take. Depends on the cards and how many questions you have."

Lulu opened the nightstand drawer and took out a wooden box with leaves and flowers carved on the lid. The over-sized cards she pulled out of it were so worn that they could have been one of the first decks ever made.

"Shuffle the deck until it feels right to you, then cut it with your left hand."

Lulu closed her eyes and took a deep, slow breath.

She sat there like that while I shuffled, then cut the cards. I placed them in front of her. She didn't move. I started to wonder if she'd fallen asleep. Cassie giggled downstairs and I felt a twinge of jealously. Was Belinda more fun than me?

Lulu's eyes popped open, and she leaned forward, startling me enough to gasp.

"Sorry, honey. Now, let's see what we've got here."

Lulu laid out fifteen cards and frowned at them.

She tapped the first card she had turned over. It was a drawing of a man hanging upside down by his right leg in front of a grid. His left leg crossed over at the right knee, making an upside down "4." His arms were stretched wide and nailed to green circles on the grid, and there was a large snake coiled in a pit beneath his head. There was something that looked like a white and green sun at the top of the card, where his right foot was suspended.

"This first card represents you and the kind of problem you are having, or something that is influencing you. When the card's upright like this, he represents redemption, as in undoing damage or getting back something that was lost."

Getting back something that was lost. I would give anything to get Ryan back, but I didn't see how that could be possible.

With her finger still on the card, she continued. "But it may come at a cost. Also, keep in mind that this is usually on a spiritual or emotional level, more than a physical level. You see this thing that looks like a sun at the top, and this dark area with the snake? The Hanged Man represents light descending into dark, or spirit going into matter. If you are feeling lost in the dark, he's here to hand you a flashlight. But you may have to sacrifice your fear to get back home."

I could hear Lulu talking about some of the other cards, but I didn't pay close attention, at least not until the end. I kept thinking about getting back something I'd lost and wishing she was right.

"And here you have the Six of Cups, the Princess of Disks, and the Seven of Wands. A Princess usually represents a young woman. The Seven of Wands, you see here, it's called 'Valor,' represents a struggle, but nothing you can't overcome. The Six of Cups is about happiness and success – that's why it's called 'Pleasure.' What this is saying to me is that you've been having an issue with a young lady, but you'll be happy with the outcome, even though it may be a minor victory. It may come about in as little as 24 hours, but certainly less than two weeks."

Lulu put her hands on the table. "Do you have any questions, honey?"

I wanted to ask her how the Hanged Man could get my lost Ryan back. Instead, I said, "No. No questions. That was very interesting. Thanks."

"My pleasure." Lulu scooped up the cards and put them back in the box with the others. The hint of a smile on her face made me think that she knew something she wasn't telling me.

As we walked toward the stairs, Lulu said, "You know, honey, you ought to come to our mediumship circle on Thursday nights."

"Mediumship circle? What's that about?"

"Well, we do different things each week. Sometimes we reach out to those on the other side—"

"You mean you talk to dead people?"

"That's one way to put it, yes."

Ryan. If I could just talk to him again, even if it was only to say goodbye.

"Does it work? Can you talk to anybody you want?"

"Have you ever been in the bathroom when the phone rang?"

What's that got to do with the other side? "Yeah, sure."

"People on the other side have stuff to do as well, and they can't always drop everything and come running for a little chat. We can usually find someone who wants to talk to us, but it may not be who you're hoping for." Lulu patted me on the shoulder.

I suddenly noticed the absolute silence coming from downstairs.

"Cassie?" I called, peering over the railing as I hurried down the stairs.

My baby was out of her stroller, cruising around the root chair. When she saw me, she let go of the chair and flapped her arms.

"Ma ma! Ma ma!"

"Hey, baby! Did you just say…"

"Mama!"

Cassie suddenly realized she wasn't holding on to anything. She looked from one hand to the other, and squealed with delight. Then she plopped down onto her bottom. I picked her up before she could cry, even though I was almost crying myself. Mama. She'd finally said 'Mama!'

As I hugged my little girl, I realized that it was almost 11:00. If the nap window closed, it would be a wretched afternoon for both of us.

"Thanks, Lulu, for the reading. It was interesting. I appreciate you watching Cassie, Belinda. She seems to really like you. I've got to run – it's time for Cassie's nap, and if I don't get her down..."

Lulu tucked a blue flier into the stroller bag. "Been there, done that. Hope to see you Thursday, honey." She held the door for me as I wrestled the stroller over the threshold.

Cassie was so sleepy by the time we got home she didn't put up much of a fight going down for her nap. I ate my grilled cheese sandwich and looked at Lulu's flier while my baby slept.

Was it really possible to talk to dead people? What if they told you something you didn't want to know? The truth was, especially after my disastrous date with Ian Chambers, I was missing Ryan so badly that I was willing to try anything, even if I was just grasping at straws. My logical mind told me that once your heart stops beating, that's it, there's nothing left. But I didn't really believe that. And the Tarot reading nagged at me. Lulu had predicted a small victory, the attainment of something I'd really wanted, then as soon as I got downstairs, Cassie said, "Mama." I knew it was just a matter of time before she got around to it. But she hadn't seemed to be in any hurry, and Lulu predicted a 'win' within the next 24 hours.

While I was mulling this over, I cleaned Alpha and Betty's cage. When it was ready for them to go back in, I got out some bits of cereal. I decided to let Betty, the friendlier of the two rats, make the decision for me.

"Alright, Miss Betty. You tell me if you think I should go to the mediumship circle on Thursday. If you think I should stay home, take the dark Cheerio first."

Of course, asking a rat to decide whether I should go to a meeting to try and talk to dead people wasn't any less crazy than actually going to the meeting to try and talk to dead people.

I put two Cheerios in my palm. Betty stood up on her back legs and sniffed at the air. Then she bounded over and snatched the pale Cheerio. She crunched it until it was small enough to tuck into her cheek, then grabbed the dark Cheerio in her delicate paws. I scooped her up and put her back into her rat habitat with her buddy.

"Serves me right for asking you."

Betty always preferred the dark Cheerios.

I picked up the phone and called my mother.

"Marti! I was just about to call you."

"What's up?"

"Do you think you'd be able to drop off the twins at robotics camp on Thursday morning? They go from 9:00 to 3:00. I'll pick them up in the afternoon, but I want to be at the hospital when Emily has her c-section."

"Is that this Thursday? I was thinking it was next week. Sure, I can do that. What time is her operation?"

"8:30. Em and Nick finally got around to picking a name. McKenzi Belle. And Marti?" mom asked. "Would you mind hanging around with your dad while I'm at the hospital?"

"What's wrong with Dad?" Worry tugged at my solar plexus.

"Oh, the doctor adjusted his medication last Friday, and he's feeling a little off. I'll have to take him back this Friday if it hasn't straightened itself out."

"Why didn't you tell me?"

"It's just a little tweak, nothing serious. I didn't want—" She stopped herself.

"You didn't want what?"

Mom hesitated. "You've seemed troubled the past couple of days. I didn't want to make it worse. Your dad's situation is under control."

I hadn't told her what happened on Saturday night, but she knew something wasn't right.

"You don't need to protect me. I'm not a child," I huffed at her. "If you must know," I sighed, "Ian wanted me to go home with him, and I said 'No,' and our date ended on a sour note. Nothing more serious than that." I knew if I told her about the kiss and the torn sleeve, she'd tell Nick, and I really didn't want to go there.

"I'm sorry, baby."

"Well, it's not the end of the world."

"So, what is it that you were calling about?"

"Oh. I had wanted to…get together with some friends on Thursday, and I was wondering if you'd watch Cassie. But that doesn't seem like a happenin' thing now."

"Nonsense. You need to get out more. Come on over for dinner and leave Cassie with us. Nick and the boys will be here. It'll be nice."

"Sounds good, Mom. See you Thursday, okay?"

"Bye."

Emily's c-section went about as well as a c-section can go. McKenzi Belle was small, red and wrinkled, with a wild shock of black hair. I took a picture with my cell phone to show Dad. I didn't get to see Emily, but I talked to Nick for a couple of minutes. He was an overly-caffeinated proud papa, and I couldn't stay long – I had to get back to the house to watch over my father.

He was delighted to see the picture of McKenzi. He seemed mostly like his usual self, just a little more tired. We sat in the kitchen, where Cassie was having her pre-nap snack.

"I heard that Ian Chambers fellow has taken quite a shine to you," Dad said, taking a sip of iced tea.

"Has he?" I asked. "And what else has Nick been telling you?"

Dad laughed. "Nick's a big fan of his. Chambers acts nice enough. Can't put my finger on it, but something about that boy bothers me, Little Sugar."

I smiled, wondering if Mom had told him how my date with Ian had turned out. "Well, I'm still not really ready for another guy. Ryan was a pretty tough act to follow."

"Da da da!" Cassie added.

I smiled at her and picked a melted sweet potato puff off her cheek. "She said 'Mama' yesterday."

"That girl'll be talking up a storm in no time. Won't be long before you're telling her to be quiet."

Dad got up and topped off his tea glass before hobbling into the living room. He and Cassie fell asleep watching a Matlock rerun while I tidied up the kitchen.

Nick and the twins showed up just in time for dinner. He kissed me on the cheek. "So, Marti. Ian was asking about you yesterday."

"And what was it he wanted to know?" Probably trying to figure out if I'd told Nick what had happened on Saturday.

"How you're doing. If you're going to be around this weekend, that sort of thing."

"So how's that new baby?" Dad asked.

I nodded my thanks to him and went into the kitchen to help Mom.

After supper, Cassie was so busy playing with Mom and Dad that she didn't even notice I left. And yet, I hadn't even made it to the sidewalk when Nick burst out the front door.

"Where you going?"

"Not that it's any of your business, but I'm going to meet up with some female friends for a little while."

Nick opened his mouth to say something, but I cut him off.

"And stop badgering me about Ian Chambers. See you later."

I started striding towards my house, which was in the same direction as the Tenth Sphere. I heard the screen door bang and checked over my shoulder to be sure Nick had gone inside. There was no sign of him on the porch.

There were already six ladies at the Tenth Sphere when I got there. Another three arrived after me, and Lulu and Belinda made the group an even dozen. I put a ten dollar bill in the jar with the "Love Offering" sign, but I noticed that at least two other ladies put in twenties. I wasn't sure if that made me cheap or thrifty.

We all introduced ourselves. I, apparently, was the only newbie.

"I think that's everybody," Lulu said. Then she locked the front door and we headed up the stairs.

We all sat on the floor in a loose circle. The lights were dim, but at least there were no hokey candelabras. Belinda lit a bundle of sage and started walking around the circle.

"She's smudging the room, to cleanse it of negative energy," Lulu whispered to me.

It was all very relaxing. Until the smoke detector started screeching.

"Hello?" a stern voice boomed like an evil spirit from the intercom in the hallway. "This is PDQ Security. We've received a fire alarm. Is there an emergency here?"

I thought that Marilyn, the lady on my left, was going to jump out of her skin.

Belinda ran out of the room, "No! This is Belinda Tate. It's a false alarm. No emergency." Then she punched in a code on the alarm panel.

"Thank you, ma'am. You have a good night," the voice said, followed by a click.

In the meantime, Lulu had turned the lights up and climbed up on a chair to remove the batteries from the upstairs smoke detector.

"Well," she said. "That was exciting. Sometimes it takes some doing to figure out all the quirks of a new place."

Everyone seemed to have recovered except for Marilyn. She had gotten up and was pacing around the room.

"It's him. It's him. I just know it!" she hissed at Lulu.

"Marilyn, honey, it was nothing more than the smudge stick." She closed her eyes for a moment. "My guides tell me there's no one here that isn't supposed to be. I think I've got some chamomile tea downstairs, if you'd like a cup."

"No, thank you. I'll be alright, I guess."

Marilyn sat back down, but fidgeted with her hair. I noticed a thick scar across the width of her left wrist and felt a chill in my stomach. She must have seen me looking.

"It was a long time ago," she said, wistfully.

She might have said more, but Lulu dimmed the lights. "Let's try this again," she said.

This time when Belinda walked around with the smudge stick, nothing happened.

"Marti, I'm going to start with you, honey, because you've never done this before. First of all, what I want you to do is close your eyes and imagine yourself surrounded by white light. Now, ask your guardian angel to help and protect you. Listen to me! This is important. Never, never, never skip these two steps. There are some bad things out there you do not want to mess with. Got it?"

I nodded.

"Good. Once you've done those two things, start visualizing the person you want to see. Imagine that they're in a familiar place, where you saw them often. See them coming to meet you there. Or, if that doesn't work, think about them being in a crowded room, like at a party. You're standing in the doorway, but you can't go in. They can come over and talk to you, if you can just get them to notice you. Ask your spirit guides to help you get their attention. Keep working on that."

Lulu moved over to Marilyn. She started brushing the air around Marilyn's head and shoulders as if she were clearing away dangling cobwebs. "It's alright, honey. He isn't here."

Marilyn's shoulders dropped, and she swallowed hard. Lulu moved on.

I closed my eyes and pictured Ryan. I could see every detail of his face, every ripple of hard muscle in his body. I tried to imagine him in our living room. No joy. Then I tried a room full of strangers, but I just couldn't see him there, either.

"Girlfriend, he ain't up in there."

I opened my eyes and saw a person standing between Marilyn and myself. I couldn't make up my mind if this individual was a drag queen or just a masculine-looking woman. Either way, she looked like she ought to be singing jazz songs in a seedy nightclub. No one else appeared to notice her.

"Don't you know who I am?" she smiled.

Two rapid, sharp knocks rang out from the wall.

Chapter 8
Severance Package

hen the knocking started, Marilyn screamed and threw herself on the floor. Lulu rushed to her side and pulled her up to a sitting position.

"Shhh. Shhhh. It's okay," she said to Marilyn, as if the woman was a small child afraid of the dark. Lulu's eyes closed and a smile spread across her face. "She says her name's Delilah. She's here with Marti."

"Marti, would you tell Chicken Little there that her stepfather is not coming after her. Not unless she start drinkin' again, anyway," Delilah said.

"Uh, Marilyn, Delilah tells me that your stepfather will only come for you if you start drinking again," I echoed. And this isn't weird. Nope, not at all. Not the least bit weird.

Marilyn started making disturbing little mewing sounds. Belinda helped her to her feet and led her out of the room.

"Her stepfather...did some really bad things to her. He just died on Monday," Lulu said. "Good for you, making such strong contact with your guide on the first try." She went across the circle to talk to a woman in a virulently orange shirt with a matching silk turban and penciled-on eyebrows.

"The first try!" Delilah nearly shouted. "Girl, I been trying to wake you up for years. Thought I did it that one time. Don't you remember? You was all 'Knock twice for yes, once for no' and I was all knock, knock and you got all scared and shit. You ran away."

"That was you?" I surprised myself with how loudly the words fell out of my mouth.

"You don't have to talk out loud, you know. Now, what did I just say? If I'm lyin', I'm dyin'."

Aren't you already dead? That was much less awkward. Nobody gave me strange looks this time.

"Look who knows so much all of a sudden. Maybe I'll just leave you be..."

Don't go! I felt as if I was drowning and a lifeline was slipping through my grasp. Please. I need your help. I really, really want to talk to Ryan.

"And I told you he is not here."

Where is he?

"Girl, I can't tell you that. If he want you to know, he will get in touch."

I groaned with frustration. Why can't you help me? What difference could it possibly make? He's dead! Fear crept over me. A cruel fear that maybe Ryan didn't love me enough to want to get in touch with me. That he even knew about Cassie, but didn't care.

Delilah pursed her lips and shook her head. "Marti, girl, there are some things you just are not meant to know. I can't tell you what Ryan is up to for the same reason I can't tell you tomorrow's Lotto numbers. It's nothin' to do with you. It's just the rules."

Can you at least tell me if he's okay?

"He's happy as a pig in poop. And he's closer than you think." Delilah winked at me.

But I can't talk to him.

"Sorry." Delilah frowned.

Fine, I thought at her, irritated that I wasn't making any headway. I exhaled too loudly, not intending to make such a show of sighing. So you can't tell me any secrets. I get it. But what I don't get is why you've been hanging around all this time. The whole knocking incident was, what, twelve years ago?

Delilah shook her head. But she was smiling, kind of. "Girlfriend, I'm your spirit guide. I been with you your whole life."

Doing what?

Delilah crossed her arms. "What do you think a guide does?"

How do you guide me, if I can't even see you? I shot back.

Delilah's arms uncrossed, and she laughed loudly. At least it was loud to me. "You remember last time at the bookstore, you were all worried and such about money, and you saw that quarter on the floor? When you bent over to pick it up, you saw that magazine about home businesses on the bottom shelf. Who you think put that quarter there?"

I crossed my arms and shifted away from her. I couldn't help feeling a little creeped out, even if she was helping me. Or so she said. Why me? Why you?

With an exaggerated roll of her eyes, she said, "Everybody got spirit guides and guardian angels. Everybody. They don't always listen to 'em, but they got 'em." She gave me a meaningful look. "Angels ain't never had bodies, spirit guides have. We understand stuff about the living they just don't. If we've figured something out, we get matched with somebody that's still working on that same problem, you see?"

So you're telling me that there's like some cosmic dating service to put spirit guides with living people. Seriously?

"Lord have mercy, girl!" Delilah shook her head and looked up at the ceiling in supplication. "It ain't really like that, but if that's how you need to see it, you go ahead."

Don't you get bored, just hanging around, waiting for me to do stuff that needs guidance? I was half genuinely curious, half dismissive. Hedging my bets, I supposed.

"Naw, girl. You ain't the only one I got to attend to. They keep me hoppin'."

Oh. It made sense, in a way. After all, as an ER nurse, no one would expect me to only care for one patient per shift. But it still made me feel a little less special. Do I know any of them? What a dumb thing to say! It made it sound like I was accusing her of having an affair.

Delilah smiled at me and shook her head. "There is something I can tell you, though. You watch out for a black horse, now, you hear?"

And with that cryptic warning, Delilah was gone. I spent the rest of the session trying to get either her or Ryan to come through, with no luck. Lulu turned the lights up, and we filed out of the room and down the stairs for light refreshments.

"I want to talk to you before you go, honey," Lulu said quietly to me as I passed her.

Belinda met us downstairs with an industrial-sized pot of hot tea and a tray of gluten-free cookies, which were surprisingly good. While the rest of the group was jawing about what successes they did or didn't have during the circle, Lulu pulled me through the Employees Only door.

"I know you're itching to get back to Miss Cassie," Lulu said. "But I needed to talk to you. Are you still interested in learning to read Tarot cards for fun and profit?" She raised her perfectly plucked eyebrows and cocked her head to one side.

"Well, I hadn't really thought any more about it."

"You have a gift. The way you just opened up and made contact with Delilah was amazing."

But it didn't get me in touch with Ryan. "Maybe."

"No maybe about it, honey. If you think you might want to develop your gift, why don't you work a party with me on Saturday? That'll give you a chance to see what reading cards," Lulu made air quotes, "'for entertainment purposes only!' looks like. Sometimes just paying attention to someone can make all the difference to that person and you do more good than you realize."

"I don't know. It's kind of short notice, and I have to get a baby sitter…"

"There's a hundred bucks in it for you."

"My mom will probably be available. What time?"

"Be at the shop at seven."

"I'll let you know if there's a problem."

Lulu smiled and handed me a pack of cards. "Have a look at these before Saturday."

I felt guilty asking my mother to babysit yet again. It seemed like lately I was constantly pawning Cassie off on my parents. I felt like a horrible mother and a horrible daughter. But I needed to make some money. This gig didn't pay nearly as well as the ER, but it didn't cost me forty plus hours a week away from my baby. And if the parties or events were a few hours here and a few hours there, mostly at night while Cassie was sleeping, it almost didn't count as being away from her.

Nick had started his paternity leave, and while we visited Emily in the hospital, he took the boys out for breakfast, then to day camp. My sister was doing well. McKenzi was in the room with her when we came in. She looked a whole lot better, hardly wrinkled at all and a nice, healthy pink. What a difference a day makes. They'd be coming home either Monday afternoon or Tuesday morning, depending on when the insurance company booted them out of the hospital.

We stopped for Indian take out on the way home. I had to be really careful what I ordered – Cassie hated it when I ate spicy food. Guess it made my milk taste funny. Dad, on the other hand, was jonesing for a chicken vindaloo.

After lunch, Cassie and I headed back to our house. My phone rang just as we opened the door. Caller ID told me it was Ian Chambers. Again. He'd called me at least twice a day, every day this week. I'd already texted him to stop calling, and blocked his email. I shook my head. I had decided that he was too big a risk to have around my baby. If I never saw him again, it would be too soon.

Once Cassie went down for her nap, I opened up the cards Lulu had given me last night. They were different from the ones she had used to tell my fortune – those had a more or less Art Deco style. These looked medieval. The pictures could have come straight off stained glass windows from a European cathedral. I sat at the table with the instruction booklet, looked at the pictures and wrote down the meaning of each card. Then I tried doing my own reading. I did manage to freak myself out when the first card I turned over was The Hanged Man, just like in Lulu's reading. Otherwise, I was utterly hopeless. Hopefully, Lulu just wanted me to carry stuff for her, and not do any actual fortune telling.

I looked at the instructions again for the meaning of The Hanged Man. Betrayal. Sacrifice. Accusation. What were the other things Lulu had said? Wisdom and seeing things from another perspective. Well, if this card represented Ian Chambers, it was right on the money with the betrayal part. I supposed the six dozen roses he sent were a kind of sacrifice, but I wasn't willing to be bought so easily. But then again, what was he supposed to do to apologize (not that it mattered at this point)? I didn't have an answer for that, so I got up and folded that pesky basket of laundry that had been sitting around since yesterday morning.

I arrived at the Tenth Sphere at 6:55. The door was locked, so I tapped on the glass. I could see Lulu arranging things in the jewelry case that faced away from the door. Something struck me as odd, but it didn't register until she turned around.

Lulu was dressed up like a gypsy fortune teller – corset, chemise, tiered skirt, lacy shawl and coin belt. What have I gotten myself into?

She grinned at me as she jingled towards the door.

"Glad you could make it, honey."

"Nice, um, outfit."

Lulu grinned. "How many other jobs are there where you get to play dress up?"

I shrugged.

"Come on," Lulu said. "Belinda usually works the events with me, but her granddaughter has a dance recital tonight. She said you could borrow her costume. You're both tall and skinny, and the sizing on these things is pretty flexible."

I followed Lulu to the back of the store, where the clothes racks were. There was a pair of saloon doors with a "Fitting Room" sign above them. A garment bag hung on one of the doors. She nodded towards it. "We need to leave in about ten minutes. Everything's already in the car."

"Is a costume really necessary? At least for me? I've never been all that into dress up."

"We are paid entertainers tonight. Chop, chop. Time's a-wastin'."

I sighed. "The $100 is in cash, right?"

Resigned to my fate, I took the garment bag and went into the dressing room. The electric blue of the bodice was not a color I would have chosen for myself. But the Battenberg lace inserts on the sleeves of the chemise were very pretty. Not sure if it was by good luck or good design, but the corset laced in front. I looked in the mirror and shook my head. Halloween came early this year.

The coin belt jangled with every step and jangled my nerves.

"Excellent!" Lulu said before she put a gaudy, bejeweled barrette in my hair.

She looked at me again and chewed her bottom lip. "The tennies don't quite work, though, honey. There should be some shoes in the outer pocket of the garment bag."

I did like Belinda's lace up boots. But we had to stop at the corner market on the way and get some knee-high hose, because they were too tight with socks. Good thing I could tie them loosely.

We headed east, to a ritzy Memorial Area neighborhood. The guard at the gate found Lulu's name on the guest list, but he looked like he was having second thoughts about letting us in. He shook his head as he wrote down Lulu's driver's license number and opened the gate. We wound our way through a maze of McMansions – over-sized houses on under-sized lots – and Lulu finally pulled up in front of a three-story Mediterranean-style house.

It had to have been at least as big as my house, my parents' house, and Emily and Nick's house put together. Twilight was only just starting to settle onto the city, and landscape lighting was beginning to come on. Green floodlights cast eerie palm tree shadows against the beige stucco walls. Taking up most of the postage stamp-sized front yard, a dazzlingly lit, eight foot tall Talavera fountain cascaded into a Talavera-tiled koi pond, dotted with fuchsia water lilies. Ordinarily, I quite like the bright, colorful Mexican tiles, but this was way too much of a good thing.

As I helped Lulu get her gear out of the car, I looked at the surrounding yards: tiny, closely-trimmed patches of St. Augustine grass punctuated with Dr. Seuss-style juniper topiaries near walkways or front doors. No flowers. No unusual shrubs. The yards were all one homogenized strip of what my mother referred to as "blandscaping." I smiled to myself. Bet the neighbors hate that fountain.

The woman who answered the door looked exactly as I would have expected someone who owned an eight foot Talavera fountain to look. She had the "Texas

Blonde" thing going – dark roots and nearly platinum hair – teased into a towering beehive. I wouldn't have thought that a lime green cocktail dress with black polka dots would have been good on anybody, but it worked for her. Green rhinestones sparkled on her zebra-striped manicure as she grabbed Lulu and hugged her.

"I'd like you to meet my associate, Marti Keller," Lulu said when the woman released her. "And Marti, this is our hostess, Mrs. Stella Thorpe."

"Pleased to meet you." I offered her my hand.

Stella pulled me into a rib-cracking hug. I tried not to gasp too loudly for air when she let go.

"Ain't you two just the cutest little things?" She asked in a thick East Texas drawl. "Ya'll come on in now." Stella turned and cupped her hands around her mouth like a megaphone. "Pudge! Come and help the fortune tellers set up, you hear?"

Pudge, followed by the world's ugliest dog, trotted down the stairs. Pudge was small and wiry (except for a pot belly), with greasy, shoulder-length salt-and-pepper hair. Dandruff littered the shoulders of his polyester leisure suit that hadn't been in style since the early seventies. And he had the sniffles.

Except for tufts of long white hair on its head and the end of its tail, the dog was bald with speckled skin and crooked teeth.

Stella kissed Pudge's unshaven cheek and scooped up the dog. "Pudgie, you know Lulu, and this gal here is Marti." Stella batted her false eyelashes at me. "This here's my husband, Geoffrey, but we all call him Pudge." She patted his belly affectionately.

Pudge gave us a glassy-eyed nod. He didn't say a word, but he was very twitchy, and it made me nervous. He wiped his nose on his sleeve, leaving a snail track of bloody snot.

"This little one here," Stella patted the dog in her arms, "is Moo Shu, our Chinese Crested. She's s'posed to look like this, you know."

She must say that a lot.

"This way," Pudge grunted as he picked up the canvas case with Lulu's folding card table and dragged it across the terra cotta tile.

"Bless his heart, I think Pudge has started on his birthday celebration a little early," Stella said, almost apologetically.

We had almost finished setting up when both the caterers and the circus performers arrived. The performers would be out in the backyard (in the heat) putting on their show as best they could in the minute garden. The guests could hang around in the air conditioning, eating canapés, and watch them eating fire and juggling chainsaws and so on.

Once the first few guests trickled in, the floodgates opened, and the house teemed with people. I walked around the crowd periodically, handing out business cards and letting people know where we were. Most of the time, I managed the line – Lulu was doing a brisk trade – and I listened in on the readings as much as I could. I almost felt like I was at Cinderella's ball every time the grandfather clock on the second floor landing tolled out the hour. Customers had thinned to practically none, and Lulu had taken a restroom break. My feet were killing me, and I sat on a folding stool that she had brought. The clock had just finished striking eleven. Even though the party was still going strong, I was ready to turn into a pumpkin.

The front door opened. I'm not sure what made me look up, because people had been coming and going all night.

Two men stepped into the foyer. I couldn't tell if they'd come in together, or just happened to arrive at the same time. The strawberry blond one took Stella's hand and air-kissed her cheek. His dove grey suit looked expensive and Italian. I would not have described him as ugly, but there was something about him that was not quite right.

"Why Tucker Fellowes, you devil!" I heard Stella say. "Your secretary said you weren't coming."

"And miss your party, Stella? I canceled my other plans."

The second man was sharply dressed, but his clothes just didn't look right on him. The brown sport coat he wore was well-made, but didn't fit his muscle-bound frame the way it should have. I wondered if he had borrowed it.

"Mmmm, mmm, mmm. That is one crazy mo-fo, girlfriend. Don't even talk to that man if you don't have to."

I jumped.

Delilah was standing to my left, arms crossed and staring at the latest arrival.

"Jeez, woman! Don't sneak up on me like that," I hissed at her.

The lady in the overstuffed chair near me gave me a strange look before she got up and left.

"You know," Delilah said, "when you talk out loud to folks other people can't see, they kind of think you're crazy."

Better? I thought at her.

"What do you think?" Delilah cocked her head at me. "Lord have mercy! What do we have here?"

I followed her gaze.

A man in a white suit with a black shirt and red tie was in front of the muscle guy who had just come in the door. White Suit was waving his arms, his head cocked oddly to one side, in front of the man's face.

"Look what you've done to me! Look what you've done!" he screamed.

Muscles ignored him. So did all the other guests.

It was only then I noticed that White Suit's hands were missing, and the ends of his pristine, white sleeves were soaked in blood.

Chapter 9
Scavenger Hunt

 he muscle man continued to ignore the man in the white suit. Muscles took a step forward and walked right through him.

"Listen to me!" White Suit's head tilted in a crazy bend as he screamed at Muscles' back.

Muscles kept walking.

Why was everyone ignoring the screaming man in the white suit? This wasn't right, and even the hair on my arms prickled and stood up. Then I realized that they were ignoring him because they couldn't see him.

"This can not be good," I said to Delilah.

"What's that, sugar?" Stella asked me, flute of pink champagne in one hand and a plate of hors d'oeuvres in the other.

I'd been so intent on the guy in the white suit, that I hadn't noticed our hostess passing by. "Oh…I mean, well," I searched the room and my eyes fell on the performers in the backyard. "The flaming chainsaws they're juggling out there. If one goes over the fence and lands in the neighbor's yard, that can not be good."

Stella waved her champagne at me. "Oh, don't be silly. It'd just fall in the Jacuzzi." She walked away, shaking her head.

"I warned you 'bout talking out loud, girlfriend." Delilah said.

Fine. I get it.

White Suit stopped shouting and looked in our direction. Had he heard us? His eyes locked on mine, and he ran over to where we stood, passing through party guests on the way. That was creepy and weird and I started looking for the back door.

"Can you see me?" he shouted.

Yes. And I can hear you too. You don't have to yell.

"Look what he did to me!" White Suit screamed. His head fell backwards at a disturbing angle, and he had to use both arm stumps to drag it back into place.

"Boy, what did girlfriend here just say?" Delilah demanded.

"But he broke my neck, then he cut off my hands so I'd be hard to ID. I didn't even do nuthin', chica."

His head wobbled crazily, and I thought he was going to cry.

"Lots of interesting guests at the party tonight, honey." Lulu had come back from her restroom break and was looking at White Suit with equal amounts of surprise and pity.

White Suit turned to look at her, but his head collapsed onto his chest.

"Come on, Marti. Let me help you fix your make up." Lulu waved at White Suit to follow us.

"Step into my office," Lulu said as she held the door to the biggest bathroom I'd ever seen in somebody's house. It was bigger than my living room. Black polished granite countertops glittered around the double sinks. The toilet was enclosed in its own tiny room and there was a small, red velvet couch against one wall. An enormous vase of birds of paradise, orchids, and protea stood in one corner, and a potted fern stood in another.

"Now what?" White Suit said pitifully.

Lulu ignored him. She squeezed my upper arm. "Marti, you okay with this? I know it can be unsettling at first, when they know you can see them, and they start coming out of the woodwork."

"What are you trying to say?" White Suit glared at her.

Lulu gave him a talk-to-the-hand gesture. Her eyes were soft and kind when she looked at me.

"You are never required to help anybody. But it seems a shame to squander a special gift."

"I'm not sure seeing dead people is a gift. More like a curse." Unless one of those dead people was Ryan.

Lulu smiled. "It can seem that way, sometimes. But you had a career helping living people. Dead people can need help, too – they're just in different circumstances."

Well, that made sense. Nurses helped people in trouble, and ER nurses helped people in bad trouble. Wait a minute…

"Lulu?" I asked, taking a step away from her. "How do you know I used to having a career helping people?"

"When I touch you, honey, I can see an image of you in green scrubs in a very bright room, carrying a tray of medical instruments. You're a nurse, aren't you?"

"Ahem!" The man in the white suit glared at us. "That's all nice and sweet and everything, but what about me? I'm the one in need here."

Lulu looked at him, then back to me. "He came to you, Marti. Must be a reason. I think you should handle it," Lulu said.

"Me?!"

Delilah stood in the corner with the flowers, arms crossed and smirking. I wanted to stomp over and ask her what she thought was so funny. Instead, I turned to Lulu.

"How, exactly, do I handle it? I don't really want to get involved in a murder. It's nothing to do with me."

"How would you like it if somebody killed you and stuffed you in a culvert and nobody would help you?" White Suit asked, his head lying on his shoulder. "I don't want my little boy to grow up not knowing what happened to his papa."

I sighed. I looked for Delilah, but she was gone. Lulu was smiling at me. "Fine," I said. "Where is the culvert? What's your name? Maybe I could tell somebody down at the station."

"What are you going to tell them?" Lulu asked.

"Where he is and who he is, I guess."

"And what are you going to say when they ask how you know this?"

I hadn't thought about that. If I told Nick that a ghost at a party told me where to find this man's body, I'd be in a straightjacket within the hour. Then what would happen to Cassie? What would people think of me if they knew I talked to dead people? The phrase 'Salem Witch Trials' flitted across my brain, and I shuddered.

"I can't get involved," I said.

"People call the cops from pay phones with anonymous tips every day. Don't tell me you ain't heard of Crime Stoppers." White Suit's voice sounded desperate, but I couldn't tell if he was looking down to avoid eye contact, or if he just couldn't help it. I did wonder if his broken neck might have had something to do with an anonymous tip.

"Do they even have pay phones anymore?" I asked, still trying to find an out.

"If you know where to look." White Suit answered.

I didn't have any paper, so I unrolled a few squares of toilet paper. Lulu handed me a pen.

"Where are you located?" I asked White Suit.

"I am right here. My body is in a culvert out in the country somewhere. The main road is 529, but I don't know the street they turned off on. It was gravel, no sign."

"Wow. 529 and BFE. That narrows it down. What's your name?"

White Suit glared at me. "Nelson Ortega. But everybody calls me 'Spam.'"

"Spam?" I wrote down the name and tucked my toilet paper memo into my bra.

"Long story." He frowned and his head lolled forward. "Could I ask you one more favor? Could you get my wallet out of the trash and leave it with my body? I can show you where they threw it."

"You're already pushing your luck, and now you want me to go dumpster diving for you?"

"There's something in it I want my boy to have - a St. Christopher medal I got from my own father. They tossed the wallet on the way here. I've only been dead a couple of hours."

"We can look for it on the way home," Lulu said.

I'd almost forgotten she was standing there. "It'll be dark." I complained.

"I always keep a flashlight in my car. Never know when you're going to need one."

I crossed my arms and stared daggers at Spam. "Okay, but I'm not looking for your body until daylight."

"You know," Lulu said, "the shop doesn't open until noon on Sundays. I could come with you, if want me to."

That would give me a live person to talk to, anyway. "Alright. You want to meet me at your shop around nine?"

"Nine it is," Lulu said.

"And you," I turned to Spam. "I'll help you out, but you need to do something for me."

"Got somebody you want me to go haunt or something?"

He looked awfully eager.

"No. My husband, Ryan, died almost two years ago. I want you to find him and tell him that I really need to see him."

"I'll see what I can do. I got lots of contacts on the other side."

I'm sure you do.

"I heard that."

I looked at Lulu, then back to Spam. "So after we get your wallet, you're not planning to follow me home and watch me get undressed or anything like that are you? Because if I see you hanging around my house, the deal is off. Got it?"

The doorknob rattled.

"Just a minute!" called Lulu. She flushed the toilet and ran the tap for a minute.

We got a strange look from an elderly lady as we came out and she went in. But that wasn't the worst of it.

Not twenty feet away, standing beside the ten-gallon punch bowl was Ian Chambers.

I ducked behind a potted palm tree.

"Lulu!" I whispered.

She looked at me like I'd lost my mind.

"See that guy over there by the punch bowl? In the light pink shirt?"

"What about him?"

"I can't let him see me. I know him. We had a horrid date, and he's been calling me all week. I really, really don't want to talk to him."

"That doesn't seem like enough reason to hide from him," Lulu chided me.

"I stole his car."

"I see."

There was no way to get back to our Tarot table without passing right in front of Ian. Shielded by Lulu, I made my way to the nearest door past the bathroom. I spent the next half-hour in the kitchen, peeking out the door to see if Ian Chambers was gone and trying to stay out of the way of the caterers (although I did end up filling a tray of champagne flutes for them).

"Is he gone?" I asked Lulu when she finally showed back up.

"Went upstairs. It's nearly twelve. We should start packing up."

I followed her, continually glancing over my shoulder at the red marble staircase as we went. The coast remained clear.

"You know that guy?" Spam whispered in my ear. It almost sounded like an accusation.

Had a date with him. Didn't go well.

"No shit," he snorted at me, like I should have known better. If Spam was the career criminal I suspected he was, he wouldn't think much of an investigator from the DA's office.

It didn't take long to fold up all of the table draperies and pack everything away.

"Why don't you start taking stuff out to the car? I'll go find Stella." Lulu handed me her car keys.

After I wrestled the table and tote bags into the trunk of Lulu's car, I caught a blur of motion, just out of the corner of my eye. Something had run around the side of the house.

Holy. Crap. Where were my ghostly friends now, when I needed someone to go investigate something dangerous for me? I checked the glove box for Lulu's flashlight and found it sitting right on top of the Key Map.

A pink Hello Kitty flashlight, Lulu? Maybe if I found a burglar, he'd laugh himself to death. I snapped on the light and the anemic beam barely lit the ground five feet in front of me. I crept around the corner.

"Woof! Woof!"

An unusually large black Labrador retriever sat in front of the six foot brick wall that separated back yard from front. His eyes shone green in the flashlight and his tail thumped on the grass. Something akin to déjà vu washed over me. I shook it off.

The dog barked again. Although he didn't have a collar, he looked well-fed and his coat was shiny. Must belong to somebody. Probably just dug under the fence.

"Nice doggie," I said. I let out the breath I hadn't realized I'd been holding.

I backed away from him slowly, intending to go into the house and let Stella know about the neighbor's dog. That went well until I bumped into something solid.

"Who are you? What are you doing here?" Ian Chambers demanded.

The night was getting more crap-tacular by the second.

I turned around, keeping the flashlight down so he couldn't see my face, and I tried to deepen my voice. "No hablo Ingles."

"¿Quién eres, senorita? ¿Qué haces acqui?"

I only know enough Spanish to get myself into trouble, and this wouldn't be the first time. But I was saved from having to bumble through an answer by a low growl.

The black Lab was standing next to me, teeth bared and hackles raised.

"Good dog," Chambers said. I could see his right hand easing towards his left armpit. "I've got something for you right here."

Of course he'd be carrying. As much as I didn't want to talk to him, I couldn't just stand by and let him shoot the poor dog.

"Excuse me? Is there some reason you're harassing my staff?" Lulu was standing in the light of the Talavera fountain, hands on her hips.

Stella stood next to her, swaying a little on her platform shoes.

"Mrs. Thorpe. Sorry, I thought I'd found some criminal activity. I hadn't realized…"

"Apologize to that girl, then shut your trap and get back in the house. Salinger was looking for you," Stella demanded.

"Lo siento, se pierda," Ian said.

"Gracias." That one was easy, anyway.

Stella and Lulu exchanged perplexed looks as Ian scurried into the house.

"Why was he speaking to you in Spanish?" Lulu asked.

"Case of mistaken identity. Anyway," I said, shining the light on my protector, "your neighbor's dog got loose."

"He don't belong to nobody I know. I see the same people walking the same dogs every day, and I ain't never seen that one," said Stella. "Why don't you keep it? If anybody comes looking for it, I'll let you know."

I needed a dog like I needed a hole in my head.

"I don't know, Stella. I've got a baby at home, and I don't know anything about this dog. Besides, he really looks like he belongs to somebody."

Lulu had narrowed her eyes as she looked at the Lab. "He could be dangerous. It's hard to tell with a dog like that."

"Well, I'll wait until morning to call Animal Control. I'm sure it doesn't live around here." Stella hugged Lulu. "The guests got a real kick out of your fortune telling. Good night, ya'll. Drive safe, now."

After the front door closed, I looked at the dog, then at Lulu. "Do you really think she'll have him sent to the pound?" I didn't like his chances, if that happened.

"She's had a lot to drink. She'll probably forget," Lulu looked hard at the dog, "if he isn't where she can see him. Out of sight, out of mind."

"He did come to my rescue with Ian Chambers. Maybe I should put up some posters and feed him for a day or two until someone claims him." I'd already half-talked myself into taking the dog home. The slope was getting more slippery by the second.

"I don't believe anyone's going to claim that dog," Lulu said, moving towards the car.

The Lab headed towards the car with us. Going once!

"Why do you say that?"

The dog barked and wagged his tail when I touched the car door handle. Going twice!

"Because I don't think he belongs to anybody. He looks like a free agent."

The "free agent" scrambled into the car as soon as I opened the door and plopped himself down on the back seat. I guessed he weighed eighty pounds or more, and it wouldn't be easy to get him out of the car if he didn't want to go. Sold! To the lady in blue.

I had to laugh. "That is exactly the sort of thing my dad's old dog, Jingle, would do. It might be good for Dad to have him around, even if it's only for a few days."

I couldn't tell in the dark whether Lulu's face was sad or angry. "Maybe. But there's something not right about that dog. If he turns out to be dangerous, don't say I didn't warn you. And if he gets carsick, you're cleaning it up."

We got buckled in and Lulu started the car.

"Hey!" Spam's voice came from the back seat. "Why do I have to sit back here with the dog dude?"

The Lab yawned, ignoring the ghost.

"Dog breath. Nice. Glad I can't smell no more," Spam added.

"You don't have to sit anywhere. You could just go away," I reminded him.

"You promised," he retorted, sounding wounded.

"Your wallet. Where is it?" Lulu asked.

Spam directed us to a dumpster behind a grocery store on the northwest side of town.

"Don't look at me, he's your case," Lulu said as she pulled up in front of it.

I took a deep breath, trying to load my lungs with fresh air before I got out and faced the garbage. Hoping to be quick, I left the car door open. Spam appeared at my side.

A pile of moldy cabbage drooped over the edge. I wasn't sure if it was a good thing or a bad thing that the dumpster was mostly full. "Hey, Spam! Why don't you look around and make sure it's still there?"

He disappeared into the trash.

"It's here!" he shouted. "Between the furry cheese and the moldy peaches!"

I stacked some milk crates up so I'd have a better reach. I would have held my nose, if I hadn't had to hold the flashlight. The dumpster smelled like something dead with sour milk and rotten bananas on top of it. I couldn't stop myself from gagging.

I saw the wallet and reached for it.

"Wait!" shouted Spam.

"What?" I asked.

"You need something to pick it up with. Otherwise, you'll get fingerprints all over it."

"You've done this kind of thing before, haven't you?"

Spam shrugged.

I went back to Lulu's car and found some paper napkins in my purse. I wrapped two of them around the wallet and pulled it out of the ooze of rotten fruit.

"I don't want that disgusting thing in my car," Lulu said when I sat down. She popped the trunk. "There's some plastic bags in back. Wrap it up in one of those."

"Don't forget. You promised you'd help me." Spam waved a stump at me, probably forgetting he no longer had fingers. It might have been more effective, if his head hadn't flopped forward onto his chest. He faded into the darkness.

"Good night, Spam," I said with a half-hearted wave before I went back to rummaging around in the trunk.

A small, flat stone rolled out from under some boxes that I moved. I recognized the scratchy markings as a rune, but I didn't know any more about it than that. I found a plastic bag and dropped the wallet inside.

I handed the stone to Lulu as I buckled my seatbelt. "Found this in the trunk."

"Oh! I've been looking for those rune stones. Funny you should find that particular one, honey. It's called Eoh. Means 'horse' and it usually represents a trip or a journey."

"Huh. Delilah said something about a horse Thursday night. I don't see myself going on a trip any time soon. And I certainly can't afford a horse." I picked at my fingernails. "I suppose I should think up something to call him," I said.

"Call who?" asked Lulu.

"The dog."

I looked into the backseat. I could only see his front half, but his tail thunked against the card table.

"How about Pluto," Lulu suggested.

"As in Mickey Mouse's dog?"

"No. As in the God of the Underworld. Hades would probably work just as well."

"You really don't like him, do you Lulu?"

"I don't think bringing that dog home with you was the best decision, no. Don't you think that's awfully convenient that he just happened to show up when Ian Chambers did?"

"What? You think Ian and the dog are playing good cop/bad cop with me? For what purpose?" Even though I'd been talking to a dead guy for the past couple of hours, I still had a tough time believing in ghosts. A psychic dog on top of that was just too much.

"I don't know," Lulu sighed.

We didn't talk the rest of the way home. I actually fell asleep for a few minutes. When we got back to the Tenth Sphere, I left the Lab in the car while I changed clothes.

When I came out of the dressing room, Lulu hung a small pewter medallion around my neck. "If you're going to keep that dog, I want you to have this."

"What is it? Luck with pet care?"

"More like protection."

"Fine." I thought she was being a bit over-protective. He was just a dog, for crying out loud.

Then she handed me a white envelope. Inside were ten crisp twenties. "I thought you said $100."

Lulu shrugged. "Stella's a generous tipper. She used to wait tables in some small town diner, then she and Pudge hit the Lotto. $119 million. She never forgot what it's like to be broke, though."

Cassie was delighted to find a dog in the house when she woke up. She squealed and giggled and threw her Cheerios on the floor. The dog gobbled them up.

I felt a little guilty. "When was the last time you ate, huh fella?"

I cleaned Cassie up and we made a quick trip to the grocery store for a bag of dog chow. I bought some canned food for good measure. Scanning the bin of old movies near the checkout gave me an idea for a name.

I set out a big stainless mixing bowl and filled it to the top with kibble. "Bruce! Come and eat your breakfast!"

Toenails clattered on the wood floor, and the dog appeared in the kitchen doorway. He sat down in front of the bowl of food and sniffed it. Then he cocked his head to one side and whined at me.

"It's dog food. You're a dog. Eat it."

Bruce lay down and rested his head on his paws. His eyebrows wrinkled, and he was the saddest looking dog ever. I'd let him out in the backyard to go to the bathroom when I first got up, so I didn't think that was the problem.

"I don't have time for this, Bruce. I have to meet Lulu in ten minutes."

I opened one of the dog food cans and dumped it on top of the dry food. "Yummy, yummy, Bruce! Nom, nom, nom."

He turned his head and looked even sadder. And he sighed. I couldn't believe it. I picked up the bowl and set it on the table, thinking I should get a fork and mix up the wet and dry foods.

Cassie squealed, and I had to snatch the bowl up before she got her hands in the congealed red paté. I picked up a Cheerio off the high chair and put it under Bruce's nose. He ate it.

"Wretched dog," I mumbled under my breath as I poured a bowl of Cheerios for Bruce. He stood up and started wolfing them down.

"I'll deal with you later, Doggy McStrange."

I had my hands full, and I very nearly forgot Spam's wallet.

Cassie and I pulled up to the Tenth Sphere with about thirty seconds to spare. Lulu was waiting in the air conditioning and came out as soon as we stopped.

Before she even made it to the car, Spam appeared in the front seat. "Shotgun!"

I would have insisted he get in the back, but I really didn't want him sitting next to Cassie. I didn't know if she could see him, but I preferred not to take any chances on him scaring her. I hadn't really wanted to bring her, but I had no choice. Mom was helping Emily with the baby and I couldn't exactly tell Nick that I needed him to babysit so I could go plant evidence at a crime scene. Cassie would be sitting in the car with Lulu in the air conditioning, so she wouldn't be exposed to anything dangerous. I doubted that any bad guys would be hanging out, watching Spam's body – they left him on the far side of nowhere so they could forget about him.

"So. Where's the dog?" Lulu asked as she climbed into the back seat.

She smiled at Cassie, and Cassie cooed at her.

"I left him at home. I didn't know how he'd react to being in the car with a baby." I glanced to my right. "Okay, Spam. How far out on 529 are we talking?"

"Past Katy. I know that much."

I started at Highway 6 and took a left on FM 529. Once we passed FM 362, we were surrounded by rice paddies and cattle.

"Are you sure it's this far out?" I grumbled.

"Yeah. I remember there was a big tree by the turn off. Maybe like an oak or something. A bunch of red and white cows were lying down under it. I remember 'cuz I asked the bossman why we was coming all the way out here." After a few seconds pause, Spam asked, "What do you think FM stands for? Far Mother—"

"No," I cut him off. "Farm to Market. Jeez. And watch your language around Cassie."

Spam sulked.

We drove for another ten minutes before I hit the brakes.

"Did they look like that?" I asked, pointing to a group of polled Herefords on the north side of the road.

"Yeah! That could be them."

"I think it's a little farther on," Lulu said from the back.

"What makes you say that?"

She pointed to the northwest. "Them."

A couple of dozen black vultures circled a point about a mile ahead of us, spiraling down to the ground like a tornado in extreme slow motion.

Chapter 10
Space Invaders

lease don't let them buzzards eat me!" begged Spam, head thrown all the way back over his shoulders.

"I'm sorry, but there's not much we can do about that. I'm going out on a limb leaving your wallet here. I don't want to disturb the crime scene any more than what I'm already doing, and I don't want to get involved."

We turned north onto the gravel road that led to the vulture feast. It wasn't long before we came to a bridge over a dry creek. Red-headed turkey buzzards had joined the party of black vultures and hunched along the guard rail on the bridge. Blow flies buzzed fitfully around the culvert.

"You probably don't want to see this," I said to Spam.

He still followed me to the big pipe. The indignant scavengers moved out of my way and glowered at me from a safe distance. I threw the bag containing Spam's wallet near where the stump of an arm stuck out of the culvert. I could hear flapping and hissing coming from inside the pipe. I really didn't want to look in there.

"Yo! Mujer! You can't leave the bag and napkins. Your fingerprints are all over them."

I groaned.

Spam's corpse hadn't taken long to ripen in the June heat. I held my nose against the sickly-sweet stench and closed my eye that was closest to his body. Even so, I caught a glimpse of it. Scavengers had been at work for a while, and the left arm was gone. There wasn't much left of his face, either. It was all I could do not to toss my cookies.

I shook the wallet out of the plastic bag and picked up the napkins I had used to retrieve it from the dumpster.

The rattling bag alarmed the birds in the culvert, and they rushed out, big wings flapping. One of them paused long enough to vomit on my shoes.

"Ugh! Gross!" I yelled at the turkey buzzard, as little chunks of Spam slid off my feet and onto the ground.

It didn't take too many steps before the vulture vomit started to seep through the tongue of my tennies. I took off my shoes and socks and put them in the plastic bag that had held Spam's wallet. I had to pick my way through the grass burrs back to the car, where Lulu was sitting in the air conditioning with Cassie. Spam marched along by my side, muttering about how somebody was going to pay for this.

I opened the back of my car and dropped the plastic bag-o-nastiness in. When I slid behind the wheel, Lulu asked why I was barefoot and slamming doors.

She laughed at me when I told her what had happened.

"It's not funny. I'm going to have to buy new shoes."

"I'm sorry, honey. It's just that you're the only person I've ever known who's had a buzzard puke on them." Lulu clamped her lips together, trying not to smile.

"I bet Spam doesn't think it's amusing."

I looked around for him, but he was nowhere to be seen.

Before I dropped Lulu off at her shop, I stopped by a truck stop, lobbed my ruined footwear into the dumpster and used their pay phone to call Crime Stoppers to report finding Spam's body.

When we got back to the house, I struggled to pull a wiggly Cassie out of her carseat. She kept grabbing the medallion that Lulu had given me, choking me, and out of frustration, I pulled it off and tossed it into the glove box. At least the temperature of the concrete underneath the carport was bearable. The caliche in the driveway, not so much.

"I guess no good deed goes unpunished," I complained to Cassie as I hopped across the sizzling gravel towards the side door.

A horse whinnied nearby.

"I mean, this has nothing to do with us. Seems like Spam's not even grateful for the help."

Cassie squealed with delight and lurched away from me. I had to clutch her shirt to keep her from falling.

The horse whinnied a second time.

There in my backyard, as if it was the most normal thing in the world, was a shiny black horse. I stared stupidly through the chain-link fence.

"What the—"

A loud crash came from inside the house. Burglars?!

Horse or no horse, I ran to Mom and Dad's house and called the police. I also called Emily's number to see if Nick was at home. He wasn't.

I left Cassie in the house with Mom when two patrol cars arrived a few minutes later. Dad came out with me to talk to the police. I recognized one of the officers from parties of Christmases past – his name was Robert. The other was a lady I hadn't seen before.

"Marti, what happened?" Robert asked me.

"I came back from running an errand and—" I glanced into the backyard. There was no sign of the horse. I wondered if I had imagined it, but Cassie had seen it too. "And I heard some noises coming from inside."

"Good thing you called us. Can't be too careful with something like that," he said.

The side door was locked, so I handed him my keys. The other officer went around to the front door.

Gun drawn, Robert knocked on the side door. "Hello? Anybody in there?"

The only reply was a muffled bark.

Bruce.

I'd forgotten about him. I hoped he wasn't hurt.

"Is that dog loose in the house?" Robert asked.

"He was when I left."

Robert entered the house. I wasn't sure if his partner had gone in the front, or was waiting by the door to catch whomever Robert flushed out. Either way, she wouldn't give her position away by using her radio. Minutes crawled by. Dad squeezed my shoulder and hobbled over to my car and sat down in the driver's seat.

"It's going to be okay, Little Sugar." He cocked his head and frowned. "Where are your shoes?"

"My shoes. Yes. Long story short, I stepped in some…fresh asphalt while I was out and ruined them. I threw them out so I wouldn't get it all over the floors in the house. Because that would be a real mess to clean up." I should probably stop over-explaining now.

Finally, Robert came out the side door.

"There's nobody here. We found your dog shut in the baby's room. He doesn't look hurt."

"Dog? You don't have a dog," Dad said.

"I found him last night."

Dad and I followed Robert into the house. The female officer was taking notes. I opened Cassie's bedroom door. Bruce trotted over to me and put his head under the palm of my hand.

"You okay?" I asked him, scratching his ears.

He answered with a big slurp of his tongue on my wrist.

Robert walked me around the house, asking if anything was disturbed or missing. Even though the front door was now standing wide open, none of my valuables (such as they were), including my laptop and the TV, were missing. The living room, on the other hand, was a disaster.

Couch cushions were strewn across the floor. The drawers from my small filing cabinet had been dumped out. My breath caught in my throat when I saw our wedding photo on the tile, glass broken and picture partially pulled out. All the pictures that had been on the wall were face-down on the floor, some of the frames were broken and the canvases torn. My signed copy of The Mists of Avalon lay open and face-down, the front cover partially torn from the binding.

"You have any idea what the burglar might have been looking for?" the officer I didn't know asked me. Her brass name tag read 'A. Perkins.'

"No. I don't have anything. I don't keep cash in the house, and the few pieces of real jewelry I have are still in the box on my dresser."

I was as puzzled as they were.

A. Perkins looked at Bruce. Robert asked, "You sure the dog didn't do any of this? Sometimes they get real upset being left alone."

"You think the dog was so upset he went through my files and took all of my pictures off the walls? Then he opened the front door and shut himself in Cassie's room?"

Robert shrugged. "Things aren't always what they seem."

They asked me to stay out of the house until they finished collecting evidence. They let me take a few things for Cassie, and the Cheerios for Bruce, and said they'd call me when I could come back.

When Dad, Bruce and I arrived next door, Mom hugged me. Dad got out the phonebook (which I didn't realize they still made) and called one of the big alarm companies to set up an appointment for Monday afternoon.

"I'm so glad you and Cassie weren't hurt," Mom said, stroking my arm. "Good thing you heard that noise."

"Yeah." I thought of Delilah's warning – Watch out for the black horse. I'd have to see just what she knew about that. What had happened to it? How was it connected to the burglary? Did she know who was in my house? And then there was the horse rune in Lulu's trunk. Maybe after my parents and Cassie were asleep, I could try to contact her.

"So tell me about the dog, Little Sugar. He kinda looks like old Jingle."

"Found him wandering around last night. He doesn't look like a stray. I thought I'd take him to the vet and see if he had a microchip, and maybe put up some posters for him, see if anybody claims him. If not, I guess I'll keep him."

"It's good to have a dog around," Mom said.

"If he stays with us, I'll have to have him neutered. I'm not crazy about having a male dog running around, peeing on everything."

Bruce grunted and curled up.

"Tends to keep them from getting out and wandering, too," Mom said.

"He's kind of weird, though. Only thing I've found that he eats is Cheerios."

Bruce leapt to his feet and barked.

The front door rattled.

Both of my parents gasped and my heart pounded against my ribs.

Nick burst through the front door, with Kyle and Aiden close behind.

"Marti! What happened? Are you okay? I saw the patrol cars in front of your house…"

"It's alright, Bruce. Nick is a friend." I gave the dog a pat. "You scared the living crap out of us, Nick."

Then I told him what had happened, starting with pulling into the carport, and editing out the part about the horse.

He nodded and chewed on his lower lip. "I'll keep on top of it." He tilted his head. "Where'd the dog come from?"

"Found him."

"Well, you ought to keep him. You need an alarm system, too."

"Dad's already on it."

"I'll just go next door and see how it's going," Nick said.

Aiden and Kyle coaxed Bruce out into the backyard to play with them. He seemed to be very good with kids: running around in circles like a fool and leaping to catch tennis balls that they threw. No telling where they got them. I hoped, for Bruce's sake, that they weren't moldy.

The police finished with their evidence gathering and cleared us to come home before supper. I opted to spend the night at Mom and Dad's. Even with Bruce around, I wasn't comfortable staying in my own house. That made me angry. It wasn't about the things that the burglar didn't even bother taking. It was about the invasion of my space. Whoever broke into my house had no right to do that. It was my house, dammit. And what if that horse hadn't whinnied and I had walked in with Cassie while he was in the middle of trashing my living room? What would have happened then? If I could get my hands on that jerk, I'd like to remove a few of his favorite body parts and see how he felt about that, see if he felt violated the way I did right now.

Cassie was totally unruffled, but I picked at my food. I was still too upset to eat much of anything. Nick and the boys joined us for dinner.

"Have they started running mounted patrols in this area, Nick?" Mom asked.

"You mean on horses? Don't think so. Not unless HCSO is doing something. Why?"

"The sheriff's department? Maybe. I was sure I heard horses whinnying this afternoon. Didn't see any, though."

"Yeah. Thought I heard one, too. Aren't there some ranchettes a mile or so south of here, where people are allowed to have horses? Maybe they were just trail riding," I said, hoping she'd drop it. The less said about the vanishing equine, the better.

"I thought it was just before you got back, Marti. Maybe it was on TV or something."

I shrugged.

Or something. I had almost convinced myself that I'd imagined the horse in my backyard. But Cassie had seen it, too. Were we both hallucinating? If not, where did it go?

I watched as Kyle surreptitiously fed his carrot soufflé to Bruce, who gobbled it up. If Nick noticed, he didn't let on. Bruce, you are the weirdest dog, ever.

Bruce looked up and pricked his floppy Lab ears as high as they would go. That look only lasted a couple of seconds, until Kyle slipped him some more soufflé.

Nick had left with the boys hours ago. Mom, Dad and Cassie were all asleep. It was 1:30 AM and the pull-out sofa bed was not getting any more comfortable. It wasn't the springs that poked me at every turn that were making me cry. Every time I closed my eyes, I imagined the burglar holed up somewhere, laughing at me. I had given up on trying to sleep long ago and sat cross-legged on a cushion on the lumpy sofa bed in Mom and Dad's living room, flipping through the channels. It didn't seem like there was anything on except old movies and infomercials. And really weird cartoons. Cartoons not intended for children.

I blew my nose yet again. I couldn't stop the tears of frustration, of anger, of sadness that slid down my cheeks and splattered on my shirt.

"Girlfriend, you got to get a hold of yourself." Delilah had materialized next to me on the couch.

"Easy for you to say. You haven't just had your house broken into and your things destroyed."

"Could be worse. You could be Spam."

"Is this meant to be a pep talk, Delilah? Because you're actually making it worse."

"You're talking out loud again."

Do you know anything about the black horse that was in my backyard this morning? You did say something about a black horse earlier.

"Yes. Yes, I do know something about it. You know that amulet that Lulu gave you? You might want to put it back on."

And then she was gone.

I punched the throw pillows. Why did she have to be so freakin' obscure about everything? Who did she think she was, Nostradamus?

Bruce hopped up on the couch and put his head in my lap, tail wagging lazily. I was finally able to go to sleep with both the lamp and the TV on, and Bruce snuggled up against me.

I woke up to the sound of Cassie babbling and shaking the side of the crib. I pushed my way out from under Bruce (who had managed to spread out and take up most of the fold-out) and went to my baby. She was standing up, holding onto the railing, and I swear she was trying to sing.

"You know what, baby? We're going back to our house. I'm not letting some big meanie run our lives. It's our house, and we're taking it back."

I wrote a quick note for Mom, and then Cassie, Bruce and I headed next door. The dog took care of his morning business on the way and he ended up eating more of Cassie's breakfast than she did. She was used to the Pick Up Game – she'd throw stuff on the floor and I'd pick it up. Bruce, however, just ate it. At first, I think she was a little mad, but she soon decided it was funnier that way.

I called the vet that Dad used to take Jingle to. They could see Bruce on Tuesday afternoon. I had gotten most of the living room put back in order by the time the alarm guy showed up at 2:30. Dad was watching for him, and he was at my house before the estimator even got out of his truck. Nick came over as well, although he was really antsy, so I guessed he was anxious about leaving Emily at home with the new baby and the boys.

"Mom is there. They'll be fine," I said.

"The kids make a lot of noise. It'll be obvious that people are home. In case—" Nick stopped himself.

"In case what? The burglar comes back to hit more houses in the neighborhood?" I asked.

Nick looked at the ground. "Yeah."

"Not helping, Nick. Not helping."

"Sorry."

Dad took the estimate from the alarm guy back to the house with him. Nick followed.

When Cassie woke up from her afternoon nap, we went to go see Emily and McKenzi. My sister was still sore and was having trouble getting up and down, but she seemed chipper enough.

"Who is Bruce?" she asked me. "The boys keep talking about playing with him."

"I found a dog. I'd bet money he belongs to somebody. I'm having the vet scan for a chip tomorrow, and I'll get some signs up."

"I hope nobody claims him. Kyle and Aiden would love to have a dog, but I just can't manage one right now. They'd have a blast borrowing yours."

I felt like I almost had to keep Bruce, now. And I was okay with that.

Cassie was easy to get to sleep that night. Bruce curled up on my bed, and I talked to him while I was getting undressed for a much-needed shower. I was tired from my late night, and fell asleep easily, in spite of Bruce's snoring.

The next thing I heard was the shower running. I opened one eye. It was just getting light. The alarm clock read 6:12. Ryan's getting up a little late for work this morning. I rolled over to go back to sleep.

Hang on. It couldn't possibly be Ryan in the shower.

But who was it? Bruce was nowhere to be seen.

The water shut off. Whoever was in my bathroom was whistling. The tune seemed vaguely familiar, but I couldn't think of the name of it.

"Bruce!" I whispered. No response.

I was looking for a heavy, blunt object when the bathroom door opened. Wearing nothing but a towel around his hips, water glistening over his well-formed muscles, stood Quinn, the guy who'd saved me from Ian Chambers in Kemah.

Chapter 11
Creature Feature

uinn?" I asked, trying to pick my jaw up off the floor.

He winked at me and disappeared back into the bathroom.

When he'd intervened in the drama with a drunken Ian Chambers at the Kemah Boardwalk, it hadn't really occurred to me to wonder what he looked like naked. Now that I knew, I was mad at myself for strongly approving.

Why was he in my bathroom? And with no clothes on?

I slipped out of bed, fully conscious that I was only wearing one of Ryan's threadbare tee-shirts and purple polka-dot panties.

I pushed open the bathroom door.

"Hello?"

Bruce's tail thumped against the shower curtain. He used his nose to push the shower faucet lever up, and lapped the water from the faucet. The water squealed and groaned in the pipes from the low flow.

I closed my eyes and rubbed them. I shook my head. When I opened my eyes again, wet Bruce was still in the shower, getting himself a drink.

The only rational explanation was that I was losing my mind.

I put Bruce outside to do his doggy business while I got dressed. As I filled the carafe for the coffee maker, I wondered how much a psychiatrist would cost. I knew some worked on a sliding scale. I wasn't sure I trusted myself around my baby now. If I was hallucinating naked men, no telling what else my crazy brain might come up with. What if it made me hallucinate something that caused me to hurt Cassie? Like that lady who heard voices telling her she should drown her five kids in the bathtub. And she believed them.

I did think about trying to contact Delilah and ask her for help. But somehow, asking an invisible dead person about my hallucination seemed weird and wrong.

But what if there wasn't anything wrong with me? Seems like these visions of ghosts started when I met Lulu. What if she was slipping psychoactive drugs to her unsuspecting clients? That might explain a lot of things, although it wouldn't explain the whole Spam adventure. I fully intended to get a sample of the water in the cooler, for a start. My friend Amanda still worked in the hospital lab, and she'd probably be willing to do me a favor and run some tests.

Cassie and I went for our morning walk, as usual. Except this time, we had Bruce with us. Cassie ignored Mr. Buns and laughed at Bruce as he trotted along, tongue flapping and speckling the sidewalk with little drops of drool.

We arrived at the Tenth Sphere a few minutes before opening time. Bruce plopped down in the shade of the awning.

"Oh, come on," I said to him. "I don't want it to look like we're standing around, waiting for them to open. Don't you have some territory to mark?"

Bruce just lay there, panting.

Cassie banged on her stroller tray. "Da ma da ma!"

Metal clacked against metal as Belinda pushed back the security shutters and unlocked the front door.

"Good morning!" she called to us.

"Morning, Belinda. How are you?" I couldn't help feeling a little wary. I hoped it didn't show. She seemed too nice to spike the water cooler, but in the ER, I'd seen way too many awful things that "really nice" people had done.

"Fine, fine. If you're looking for Lulu, she'll be in after lunch."

I shouldn't have made it so obvious that I was peering over her shoulder and into the shop. "No, that's alright. I wanted to thank you for letting me borrow your outfit for the party on Saturday."

Belinda opened the door a little wider. "You're welcome. You ladies can come inside and tell me about it, if you'd like."

"I'm in a bit of a rush, but I would like a drink of water, if you don't mind. Did Lulu tell you about our trip to the country Sunday?" I wrestled the stroller over the threshold. Bruce sat up and whined, but wouldn't come inside. I tugged on the leash, and he fought back. Finally, I gave up and tied the leash to the bar handle of the door.

"She did. I bet it was pretty grisly. Did you see it on the news? They said they found a wallet, but the body was too badly...damaged to make a positive ID." Belinda shuddered.

"Yes," I said, filling a paper cup from the cooler. "It was pretty gross. Lots of buzzards and flies and stuff." I saluted her with the cup. "Thanks for the water – I've got to run."

We were almost back to my house when a passing car startled a group of iridescent black grackles drinking from a sprinkler puddle in the gutter. One bird bounced off the car's windshield and lay flapping in the street. I set the brake on the stroller, double checked for traffic, then ran out into the road and scooped up the bird. His mouth opened and closed pitifully, and his nictitating membrane closed halfway over his eye.

"Cassie, we may have a trip to the wildlife rehabbers," I said as I pulled the stroller brake up with my toe.

It was hard to steer the stroller with one hand and cradle the injured bird against my body with the other.

In the end, it didn't matter. The bird stopped struggling and his head lolled limp between my fingers. I couldn't feel a heartbeat. After Cassie went to sleep, I buried him under the knockout rose near my patio. Bruce lay nearby, head on his paws, and watched.

I called Amanda, and she agreed to meet me at the California Pizza Kitchen in the mall at 12:30. The lunchtime rush had not thinned out quite enough to be what I would consider 'baby friendly.' The frazzled hostess put us in a booth at the far end of the restaurant, near the restrooms. Cassie sat at the end of the table in a high chair and threw crayons at us while we talked. I wrangled them and herded them into the space between Cassie's cup and the container of finger foods I had brought.

"You dropped off the face of the Earth after you had her," Amanda said. She gave Cassie a vaguely resentful look. I tried not to go into Mama Bear mode.

I put some Cheerios on a napkin for Cassie. One by one, she dropped them on the floor. I wondered if she was missing Bruce.

"Things would have been a lot different if Ryan hadn't died." I often felt like I had to defend my decisions around my former work friends. I supposed that's why I tended to avoid them.

"Molly just finished maternity leave," Amanda said. "She found a really nice daycare lady. She could probably put you in touch if you were interested in coming back to work. ER is way under-staffed right now – I'm sure they'd take you back in a heartbeat."

"Thanks. I'll keep that in mind. So, how's Lance?"

Amanda blushed. "Guess you haven't heard the news."

Uh-oh. Had they broken up?

She held out her left hand. A big honkin' rock glittered on her ring finger.

"Congratulations! Have you set a date?"

"Thanksgiving. Everybody's going to be travelling down anyway, so it seemed like a good time."

"Good for you." I envied her then.

I flashed back to when Ryan had proposed to me. It was 6:00 on a Saturday morning, and the ER was slow, often the case in that timeslot. A cop and one of the doctors came rushing down the hall from one of the ambulance bays with a patient on a stretcher. I was in the zone and didn't even notice the officer was Nick. Not until afterwards, anyway, when he took off his fake moustache. Dr. Vo shouted for the crash cart, so I ran to get it. When I got back, my first clue that something was out of the ordinary was a line drawing of a heart taped to the EKG monitor. Shaking his head and trying hard (but not quite succeeding) to look grave, Dr. Vo told me that the man's heart was missing. I stepped in for a closer look. The "patient" sat up, and I was surprised to see it was Ryan – they'd kept his face hidden from me when they brought him in. He said that since I'd stolen his heart, I may as well take the rest of him, too. Then he gave me his grandmother's ring and asked me to marry him. I couldn't have said 'no' if I had wanted to.

Cassie's squeal snapped me back to the present. "Sorry, I've got something in my eye," I said, dabbing at the moisture that suddenly pooled at the corners of my eyelids.

I had hardly regained my composure when Spam appeared on the seat next to Amanda.

I jumped half out of my seat and knocked over my tea.

Luckily, the tea glass was mostly empty and I had enough napkins to mop up the spill. "Sorry about that. My phone is on vibrate, and it went off in my pocket."

Amanda nodded. Everybody's done that at least once. I pulled out my phone and pretended to read a message.

What are you doing here?! I gave Spam a sharp, quick look.

"There's something you need to see. Go to Specials tonight around six."

I don't know what 'Specials' is.

"It's a club, called Specials, downtown, near West Gray."

And what is it I'm supposed to see there?

"You wouldn't believe me if I told you."

And just like that he was gone. Ghosts had the most annoying habit of disappearing so you couldn't argue with them.

I finished my pretend message and put my phone away. Cassie was gumming the crayons that I had thought were out of reach. "Babies, huh?" I said to Amanda as I traded the green Crayola for some sweet potato puffs.

"So what's the story on this water you want tested?" Amanda asked.

"A friend of mine started having some hallucinations after she started at a new job. She's afraid she's going nuts, but I wanted to find out if there was something simple, like contaminated water, before she blew a wad of cash on a shrink," I said.

"I'll run some strips on it," Amanda said. She looked bewildered as she watched Cassie recapture the green crayon and start trying to shove it up her nose.

Nick had told me I could leave Cassie at their house while I took Bruce to the vet and ran an errand. I couldn't bring myself to ask my mom again. I dropped off a mac and cheese casserole at Emily's when I dropped off Cassie. I was pretty sure that if dinner was up to Nick, Kyle and Aiden would have chips and gummy bears.

"Alright, Bruce. It's just you and me," I said when I got back in the car.

"Easy, there, Bruce" said the vet tech as the hydraulic exam table rose. "Eighty six pounds – he's a big guy." He flashed a thermometer into Bruce's ear. "Ninety-eight. Temps a little low, but that may be because of the AC."

Dr. Anderson reached to shake my hand as she entered the exam room. "Ms. Keller, I'm so sorry about your long wait. We tried calling to reschedule, but you'd already left. Did the front desk tell you I had an emergency surgery? It took a while – I ended up having to amputate the poor dog's leg. When it's car vs. dog, the dog never wins." Dr. Anderson shook her head. "So, who do we have here?"

"Well, I found this dog on Saturday night. I thought I'd have him checked to see if he's got a chip and maybe I'd put out some signs to see if anybody's lost him. If nobody claims him, I guess I'll keep him. I've been calling him Bruce."

"Anthony, would you go get the scanner, please?" Dr. Anderson asked.

The tech disappeared into the back of the clinic. The doctor looked in Bruce's ears and at his feet, then pulled his lips back and checked his teeth. She checked again.

"That's odd. He's got some extra teeth. I would expect to find forty-two. He's got fifty. He's got plenty of room for them, don't see any crowding."

Anthony returned with something that looked like a giant magnifying glass with a digital read-out in the handle. The vet took it from him and waved it over Bruce's neck and back.

"No chip."

Spam appeared in the corner, tapping his wrist.

I ignored him.

Dr. Anderson didn't find out anything else odd or unusual about Bruce, and I decided to hold off on the vaccinations and neutering until I found out whether anybody was looking for him. I did buy a tube of topical flea and heartworm medication, though. The receptionist handed me a crunchy doggie bagel from the jar while I was waiting for my receipt. Bruce made short work of it. Guess those extra teeth came in handy.

"You don't have time to take him home," Spam said as we walked out of the clinic. "It's almost 5:30 now."

I knew he was right, but I didn't like it. I stopped on the way and bought a liter bottle of water and a package of disposable bowls.

I had to drive around a little to find a parking spot in the shade. "Sorry, Bruce. This is the best I can do for now. Stay in the car – I'll be out as soon as I can."

After I rolled down all four of the windows and poured Bruce two bowls of water, I followed Spam to the club entrance.

The bouncer gave me a funny look as I went through the door. Once I got inside and had a look around, I understood why.

I was in a titty bar. And an especially seedy one, at that. Spam directed me to a corner table, and I cringed as I sat on a sticky wooden chair. What would Ryan say if he knew I was in a place like this? He'd laugh at me, then hand me a couple of dollar bills, that's what he'd do.

You might have mentioned what kind of place this was, Spam.

"Maybe, chica. But you might not have come."

I snorted. You think? Now that we're here, what am I looking for? I don't want to be in this place a second longer than I have to be.

"You see that door back on the other side of the stage that says 'Employees Only?' Keep your eyes on who goes in and out."

The odors of alcohol, stale sweat and long gone cigarettes assaulted me. I perched on the edge of the chair and crossed my hands in my lap, trying to minimize contact with anything in this place. Whomever I was supposed to see had better make an appearance soon, because I was on the verge of breaking out the disinfectant wipes that I always kept in my purse. That would probably not be inconspicuous.

A woman in a g-string and high heels slapped a napkin down on my table. "Drink?"

Are you kidding?! "No thanks, not right now. I'm...waiting on somebody."

She shrugged and left.

I wanted to tell her that it wasn't what she thought, that I wasn't the sort of person who frequented places like this, but I managed to keep my mouth shut, for a change. I hope Bruce is okay – whatever Spam wants me to see had better happen soon, because I'm not leaving that dog in the car for long.

I couldn't watch the door without also seeing the stage, and I'd bet money that Spam planned it that way. He seemed to be enjoying the show, but I thought most of the girls looked like they would rather have been anywhere but Specials. Their eyes were glazed and they seemed to be half-heartedly following a choreography that they'd gotten bored of long ago.

Except for one dancer. She looked Marilyn Monroe-esque, with platinum blonde hair, bright red lipstick and a beauty mark on her chin. She'd started out with a white halter dress and full length gloves, and was quickly working her way down to much less. I found her routine with the pole disturbing, both for her relentless enthusiasm and sheer vulgarity. Spam wore a wistful smile. I checked the time on my phone. I'd been there five minutes. If nothing had happened in another five, I was leaving.

"Be sure to avoid that one," a male voice whispered in my ear.

I whipped my head around to find Quinn sitting in the shabby chair to my right. I poked him in the arm.

"What was that for?"

"To see if you're a hallucination."

"Well?"

"You feel solid enough. What are you doing here? Are you following me?" Why were you naked in my bathroom, and where did you go, if you were even really there?

"We seem to be looking for the same person." Quinn smiled. "Seriously, though." He cocked his head towards the stage, "Avoid her like the plague."

Like I was interested in doing anything anywhere near her.

"Why you dissing, GiGi, man? She's smokin' hot – look at those chichis grandes!" Spam said. He didn't act the least bit concerned about the new arrival.

"She's a succubus," Quinn said, maddeningly nonchalant.

"She'll suck your what?" Spam asked, with such a salacious smile I wanted to smack him.

"Your soul," Quinn said. "She's a soul eater. Don't you know anything about demons? With a set-up like this, she doesn't have to go looking for victims. They come to her."

I suddenly snapped that Quinn and Spam were having a conversation. "Wait! You can see him?" I said. I was surprised at the relief I felt that lots of people saw ghosts. "I thought Lulu and I were the only ones that could see him." Maybe I'm not losing my mind, after all.

I glanced back up at GiGi and winced. Her performance made me feel like I was being assaulted. "You mean she's working like a demon. Not that she's an actual demon, right?"

"Says the lady who talks to dead people." Quinn smiled as he said it.

Spam glared at him.

"See what she sees," Quinn answered him, commanding.

He brushed his fingertips over my eyes, almost touching me. I pulled away from him, but when I looked back at the stage, I almost cried out. Instead of a modern-day Marilyn Monroe, something scaly and reptilian with bulging yellow eyes gyrated on stage in a white sequined thong. It felt like someone had poured a glass of ice water over my head and down my back. I glanced at Spam. I expected that he would have gone pale, if there had been any blood to drain from his face. I spent a moment or two being amused by his lusting after The Creature from the Black Lagoon.

"Who are you, really? How did you do that? Why are you here?" I pelted Quinn with questions.

"She wears a disguise, I know how to see through it, that's all," Quinn said. "And I told you, my name is Quinn. And it appears we are looking for the same person, you and I."

I clenched my fists in frustration. He had answered my questions, but told me nothing.

"Look! Look! Look!" shouted Spam.

The 'Employees Only' door opened and a muscle-bound man in a polo shirt and acid-washed jeans, whose appearance screamed 'bouncer,' poked his head out and scanned the room.

"That's Jericho," Spam whispered. "If he's here, Salinger's around somewhere too. He is one sneaky bastard."

Jericho waved to someone behind him. Moments later, Ian Chambers slipped cautiously out the door.

And headed straight for our table.

Chapter 12
Secret Chambers

 looked desperately froM Spam to Quinn. I didn't think Ian had spotted me yet, but it was only a matter of seconds until he did.

"I can't let him see me here!" I said through gritted teeth.

I was trapped in the corner, and the only way out led directly into Ian's path. My heart pounded so hard I wondered if he could hear it.

A warm, strong arm slid around my shoulders and my rickety chair tipped back just a little. Quinn's hot mouth covered my own. My lips, no longer under my control, parted for him. I couldn't remember how to breathe, and my skin felt electrified. It made me think of diving into a deep, icy pool on a sweltering day, shocking and overloading my senses, short-circuiting my brain. He smelled of water on parched earth and pine forests. It seemed to me that I could drown in his embrace, and it wouldn't be a bad thing.

I had never thought the word 'swoon' would be applied to me. But that's just about what I did when Quinn pulled away from me and gently lowered the front legs of my chair back to the floor. Good thing the table was there – it kept me from slithering out of the chair and lying like a limpid pool on the floor. I was dizzy and shaking, almost gasping for air. And that was just from a kiss.

"He didn't see you," said Quinn, licking his lips. He brushed my cheek with the backs of his fingers and I shivered.

It took a moment for his words to register and make sense as my mind drifted back down from the stratosphere. A fleeting aftertaste of bagels forced my mind to focus on reality. I shifted in my chair, planning to get up and follow Ian.

"Wait," said Spam. "He's still here, getting a drink at the bar."

I made sure my back stayed to the bar.

"Why are you looking for Ian Chambers?" I asked Quinn.

"You're welcome," he said.

I glanced into his eyes, then down at the table. It was hard to keep control of myself when I looked at his face. My body was desperate for another kiss like that, but my mind wanted to run as far away, as fast as possible. "Thanks. Again. That's twice, now that you've stepped in between me and Chambers."

"At least."

Before I could ask what he meant by that, one of the dancers came to our table. Her eyes looked blankly at Quinn, and I was as invisible to her as Spam was.

"Dance, mister?"

Even in the poor light, I could tell she was not young, but she probably wasn't nearly as old as she looked, either. Her smile was tired and artificial, and crow's feet cracked through thick layers of foundation and powder.

Quinn shook his head. The woman shifted the chain mail bib necklace that hugged her throat and dangled between her pendulous breasts. As she turned to go, something fluttered to the table, falling from the crease of her breast. I covered my mouth to stop myself from saying anything when I realized that it was a small, dried cockroach. Spam snickered, but I felt incredibly sad for her. How does somebody get to a place in her life where this is normal?

Shut up, Spam. It's not funny.

Quinn tilted his head like a dog does when it hears something its human can't.

"Wait, Miss."

She turned back to him, her face an odd mix of hope and disappointment. He scanned the room before pressing something into her hand.

"Have a good one." His tone was solemn.

Whatever it was, she quickly tucked it into her shoe.

"Ay caramba, dude!" Spam said. "A hundred bucks for nothing?"

"You gave her a hundred dollars? That's quite a gift," I added. Why didn't strangers just walk around and hand me hundred-dollar bills, no strings attached?

"Is it? If they don't find it and take it away from her, I'd be surprised if she doesn't buy enough drugs to overdose."

"Then why did you give it to her?" Surprise made my voice break. "If you knew it might be dangerous? Why?"

"Death isn't necessarily the worst thing that can happen to you. Besides," he shrugged, "she might do something else with it. Everything is a choice, isn't it?"

"Hey, chica, you might want to see this. Don't turn around. Look in the mirror."

What mirror, Spam? What am I looking at?

"On the ceiling. Check out Chambers' new friend."

I looked up to see that sections of the low ceiling were mirrored. If I scooted towards Quinn just a little and tilted my head at the right angle, I could see Ian Chambers.

He was talking to Nick.

I had to struggle not to stomp over and ask him what he was doing in a place like this. If Emily knew, she'd be so disappointed. But then, Nick might wonder what I was doing in a place like this. What was I doing here? Spying on Ian Chambers and making out with a total stranger in a scummy titty bar while my sister took care of her newborn, her twins and my child, that's what. What is wrong with me?

The only thing that I was sure of was that I had to get out of this place, and the sooner the better. Preferably without either Nick or Ian seeing me.

Hey, Spam. Where is the back door in this little shop of horrors?

"Kitchen."

The kitchen, of course, was at the end of the bar. Where Nick was chatting with Ian-Stop-Calling-Me Chambers.

What about the bathrooms?

They were just to the other side of the 'Employees Only' door.

"No door. Might be a window in the senoras bano, but I never been in there."

Could you go look?

Spam tried to cock his head at me, but it only sagged onto his shoulder.

Don't look at me like that. You owe me big time, Spam.

Muttering to himself in Spanish, he vanished.

I was very careful not to look into Quinn's eyes. That seemed to be where I got caught, just fell right in, like a mammoth in the La Brea Tar Pits. That, or when he touched me.

I stared at his hands. There was a slight webbing between his fingers. Not like duck feet – just at the base of his fingers, and extending maybe half an inch up. It was barely noticeable, unless I looked carefully.

"So. Quinn, you said we were looking for the same person. Why are you looking for Ian Chambers?"

"You first."

I risked glancing up at his face. He looked amused. I clenched my teeth and forced myself to take a deep breath before I spoke. Okay, Mr. Slippery. I'll bite, if that's what it takes to get you talking.

I twisted a few strands of hair around my finger. "I haven't been looking for him. We had a blind date – that night I saw you in Kemah – and now it seems like everywhere I go, he turns up." And so do you.

"Hmm. It seems you have some very—" he paused, choosing his next word carefully, "interesting friends."

"I'm baaack! Did you miss me, chica?" Spam reappeared across from Quinn.

Jeez! Stop doing that already. What did you find out?

"There's a tiny window just below the ceiling in the ladies' room, but if you go through the 'Employees Only' door, you can go behind the stage and out through the kitchen door." Spam said.

"Sounds like a terrific plan, Spam. I'm sure the bouncer won't mind at all if I go wandering around backstage." I spoke out loud, so Quinn could hear.

"Maybe if we're lucky, he'll put you to work." Spam grinned.

"Spam, I did what you asked me to. I put your wallet with your body and called in a tip to Crime Stoppers. Why are you still hanging around being a jerk? Aren't you supposed to go into the light or something now?"

Spam's grin faded considerably. "Unfinished business, chica. Unfinished business."

"That has nothing to do with me. Honestly, I don't know why I'm wasting any more of my time with you. You showed me that Ian Chambers hangs out in a cesspool. Big. Fat. Hairy. Deal," I grouched at him.

"You said you would help me. You gave your word," Spam said, each syllable an accusation. Infuriatingly, he vanished.

Quinn cleared his throat. "The bouncer won't mind you being backstage if he doesn't see you."

"And I suppose you're going to loan me your invisibility cloak?"

"No. It wouldn't work on you."

I couldn't tell if his half smile was serious or sarcastic.

"But," he continued, "What I am going to do is create a disturbance. Go to the ladies' room, and when you hear the bouncer run out of the 'Employees Only' door, go through it."

I've heard of worse plans.

"Do you want me to swing by the front and pick you up in the car?" I asked.

"I'll be fine. Don't worry about me."

A quick look into the ceiling mirror showed me that Nick was smiling and talking with his hands. Ian was pale and had dark circles under his eyes. He just nodded along as Nick spoke.

"Thanks." I made the mistake of making eye contact with Quinn. I could feel his kiss all over again and goose bumps popped up on my skin.

He closed his eyes – a long blink - and I glanced back towards Nick and Ian. "Well, those two seem busy enough. There's no time like the present." I got up, cringing as the fabric of my long shirt briefly stuck to the chair. I made my way to the bathroom as casually as I could.

The faded cherry veneer on the door was cracked and buckled, and the hinges squeaked like a startled mouse when I pushed the broken handle. I almost gagged. Specials needed a special plumber for their sewer gas problem. I left the door open just a crack, so I could get some fresh air and see when the bouncer, the one Spam had called Jericho, ran by. Within seconds, I heard glass breaking and a man shout. Did he really say, 'Hey, he stole my clothes!'?

The 'Employees Only' door opened and slammed shut. Heavy footsteps thudded on the worn carpeting towards the bar. Through the crack in the door, I could see the back of a large man moving quickly away from me. Keeping my back towards the fracas, I slipped through the other door.

The corridor was dim, and aged yellow linoleum crackled softly under my feet. A door on my left had 'Office' in peeling black letters on the frosted glass window. Another door to my right had an engraved plastic sign that read 'Stage.' I turned the handle and slowly pushed the door open.

The Marilyn Monroe dancer stood just off stage with her arms crossed, watching a woman in pleather writhing around the pole on stage. Maybe it had something to do with being away from Quinn, but she was back to looking human. She gave me a head-to-toe scan that made my skin crawl. It was more predatory than appreciative.

"You the new girl?" she asked.

"Kitchen. I'm helping in the kitchen." I said, backing away from her.

"Come back after your shift, sweet thing. I could make a meal out of you." She blew me a kiss.

Not today, lizard breath. I was not too proud to scurry like a rat behind the dusty curtains into the murky hallway that separated backstage from the kitchen. I could hear a dishwasher running, and something that sounded like deep-fat frying, but I didn't see anyone. I tip-toed to the exit and made a break for my car.

Behind Specials, there were a few employee parking spaces and a dumpster. An eight foot wooden fence blocked me from leaving in the direction of my car.

I had to make my way down the driveway and take the long way back to where I was parked.

Bruce sat behind the steering wheel and whuffed when he saw me.

"Move over, you big lug. You can't drive." I was happy to see that sitting in the car for almost fifteen minutes hadn't harmed him.

Bruce squeezed into the back.

I tossed my purse into the passenger seat, then popped the trunk and raided the emergency baby change kit for a beach towel, which I used to cover the driver's seat. Then I emptied the water bowls onto a thirsty patch of grass. Bruce didn't seem to have drunk any of it, so I wondered why his head was wet. If it was drool, I didn't want to think about how it got between his ears.

I reached between the seats and patted the dog's chest. "You know, Bruce, it's pretty bad when a wet dog smells better than the place you've just been in."

I drove around the front of Specials, just in case, but there was no sign of either Quinn or an altercation. I still felt uneasy as I drove away.

"What do you think, Bruce? Think Quinn's all right? I know he said not to worry about him, but I hate leaving without knowing he's okay."

The crazy dog pushed his head between the two front seats and slobbered all over my neck, trying to lick my face.

"Okay, okay. We're going home."

Specials had a stench that went far deeper than surface grime, and I didn't want it in my house. I stripped naked and threw my clothes and the beach towel in the washer before I left the garage. I didn't like washing such a tiny load, but sometimes the bullet must be bitten. Bruce sat by the door and supervised.

I took a quick shower before he and I went to pick up Cassie. Emily asked me to stay for coffee, and Bruce exercised the boys in the back yard until dark. If Nick had noticed me at Specials earlier, he didn't say anything.

I was wiped out by the time we got home. It was too late, and I was too tired to put my mini-load on the clothesline, so I guiltily plopped it in the dryer. I fell asleep in the rocking chair, nursing Cassie. It wasn't anywhere near the first time I'd done that - I always put her in a sling during bedtime nummies for that very reason. It was close to midnight when I tucked her into her crib. I topped off Alpha and Betty's food and filled their water bottle on the way to my room.

"Come on Bruce." I yawned and patted the bed.

I felt the mattress sag as he jumped on it, but I was out before he finished getting comfortable.

I felt myself drifting up out of sleep. I was hot, sweating from the warm body snuggled up against me. I was lying on my right side and an arm, a male arm, draped across my waist and curled around me. Hot breath on the back of my neck made me quiver.

Relief washed over me like a warm shower. I'd been having this horrible dream where Ryan was dead. And now I was waking up and there he was, right where he belonged. I wanted to dance and shout. I snuggled up tighter against him.

Maybe I should wake him up.

I twisted a little so I could run my hand down his thigh. But something felt off. Some indefinable thing wasn't right. The joy (and lust) I had been feeling only a moment before started to congeal into cold little blobs of anxiety.

The warm body next to me stirred. The arm across my waist shifted, and the hand cupped around my shoulder.

I reached up and ran my fingers over that hand on my shoulder. There was no wedding band. My stomach lurched.

Then a word. A single word from dreaming male lips: "Siobhan"

Siobhan? Who the hell is Siobhan?

I shoved the arm off of me, sat up and snapped on the bedside lamp.

The silver lining was that Ryan wasn't having an affair with some chick named Siobhan.

The towering, five mile high, black-as-sin thunder cloud remained, however. What the freaking bloody hell was Quinn doing in my bed, laying there like a Playgirl centerfold?

Shock and disappointment were a one-two punch that took my breath away. I almost tripped myself up as I scrambled out of bed, taking the sheet with me to cover up my verging-on-transparent threadbare tee shirt.

Quinn squeezed his eyelids together, then rubbed them.

I hit him. On the shoulder, as hard as I could.

"What was that for?" he asked, opening one eye.

"What are you doing in my bed? Naked?"

"Lots of people sleep naked."

"Not in my bed." I shook my head.

Quinn sat up. A languid smile turned up the corners of his lips. "You invited me."

"I most certainly did not."

Quinn breathed in deeply, then he shimmered and flickered. In an instant, Bruce lounged in his place. He thumped his tail on the quilt and gave a low bark. Bruce shimmered and Quinn was back.

"Okay. I know I'm dreaming now. That did not just happen. It's a trick. You only see stuff like that in the movies. People don't just turn into dogs and back again."

"You're right. Humans don't. But I'm not human."

His dark, dark eyes fixed on mine. I felt like a deer in the headlights. I couldn't move, didn't want to move.

"W-What are you, then?" I stammered. Maybe I'm not awake, after all.

I felt his hold on me relax. When he smiled, there was a flash of sharp teeth, just like the very first time I saw him at the Kemah Aquarium. "I'm a kelpie."

I stared at him. Meant nothing to me.

"A water horse?" he tried again.

I shrugged.

"Surely you've heard of the Loch Ness Monster?"

"You're telling me that you are the Loch Ness Monster?" I arched an eyebrow and tilted my head away from him.

"Only once, when I was visiting my cousin, Vanessa. There are a lot of us, actually. Most large bodies of fresh water have lake monsters. Haven't you ever heard of Champ, the Lake Champlain monster? Or Tessie, in Lake Tahoe?"

Quinn stretched and put his hands behind his head. The move highlighted the well-defined muscles in his chest. I swallowed and looked away, remembering his kiss at Specials.

"Why don't you put some clothes on?" I asked. Less distracting that way.

"Why? Is this form not pleasing to you?" His eyes were bright, teasing me.

"I'm not in the habit of entertaining naked sea monsters in my bedroom." I tried on my best schoolmarm voice, but I could feel heat in my cheeks.

"Kelpies live in fresh water, not the ocean. Besides, I don't have any."

Funny, it looks to me like you've got some to spare. "Any what?" I was staring again. I tore my eyes away from his body.

"Clothes."

I sighed. I had never gotten around to donating Ryan's things to the homeless shelter. It didn't seem right, somehow, offering them to a stranger now. A stranger who had turned up in my bed in the altogether. But it seemed even less right to sit and talk to said naked stranger lying in my bed.

I went over to the dresser. I could feel Quinn's eyes on my back. It made my skin tingle, but how much of that was dread and how much was delight was hard to say. I didn't know what to think about Quinn. The whole turning into a dog thing had to be a trick, somehow. My mind flatly refused to accept that it was possible for a man to turn into a dog and back again, even if I did just see it happen.

"Here. Put these on," I said, handing a pair of cargo shorts and a t-shirt to Quinn. He was a little shorter and a little slimmer than Ryan, but the fit would probably be close enough.

"As you like."

I turned my back while he got dressed. Silly, I know. I'd already seen every blessed inch of him. I suppose what I didn't want to see was the way his muscles moved under his skin. Or the way he looked at me with those big, dark eyes that were so much like Ryan's.

"So. Tell me about kelpies," I said to him, my back still turned. I heard fabric slide on his skin and the zip and snap of shorts being fastened.

"We can take several forms. Normal, human, dog, horse."

"Horse! Was that you in my backyard on Sunday afternoon?"

"Yes. I needed to keep you from going inside. You can turn around now."

Seeing Quinn sitting on my bed, wearing Ryan's clothes, was almost as much of a shock as seeing him there naked. My hands flew to my mouth and I staggered back a step. I couldn't help the tears that spilled out of my eyes. The aching disappointment I had felt when I realized that I hadn't dreamed Ryan's death was sharper now.

Quinn came to me then, put his hands on my shoulders and kissed the top of my head, as if I were a child. "What makes you so sad, now?"

I pulled away from him. This was wrong, very wrong. I hardly knew the man. Or monster, if he was what he said he was. And yet, I could think of nothing I wanted more at that moment than to feel his arms around me.

That was when the dam burst and a river of tears flooded down my face, cascading onto my throat and soaking Quinn's shirt. I didn't care that he was hardly more than a stranger, and a very strange one, at that. I sobbed against his chest until I was dry.

"I'm sorry," I finally said. It felt good to be held by a man, and I wasn't quite ready to push him away.

"About what?" Quinn's voice was pure black velvet.

"When I woke up, and you were there, I thought…I thought you were Ryan, my husband, and that I'd only been dreaming that he was dead." I sniffled. "It's nothing against you," even if you are a sea monster, "I just thought I'd woken up from a nightmare and then found I hadn't. And what were you doing in my bed, anyway?"

I pulled away from him then, and he let me go. Part of me wished he hadn't.

"I told you – you invited me."

"No," I said, putting my hands on my hips, "I invited Bruce, the dog."

Quinn laughed. "Can't have one without the other, I'm afraid." Then his face became more serious. "I'm not offended. It is hard to lose a mate."

I suppose he meant that to be comforting, but it felt like he was mashing a bruise. I closed my eyes for a long moment.

A peek at the clock told me it was 4:27 AM. Cassie would be asleep for another couple of hours. Maybe I could get some answers from Quinn this time.

"Who is Siobhan?"

"She was…a colleague." Quinn closed his eyes and bit his bottom lip. "It's hard to explain to you. She was killed."

I wondered if he had ever kissed her the way he'd kissed me, and I was startled by this twinge of jealousy.

"I'm sorry," I said.

"She was—" he stopped himself. "It happens. She knew the risks when she accepted the job." Pain flickered across his eyes, but was quickly gone.

It was enough to stop me from asking any more questions about her, though, even if I was very curious what risks she knew about and how she ended up dead. I'd best change the subject.

"So. How do you know Ian Chambers?" I asked.

"I don't. It's his boss I'm looking for."

I folded my arms across my chest. "The District Attorney?" That wouldn't take much looking.

"His other boss. The one who pays for his beach house and his designer suits."

"Other boss? What are you saying? Are you telling me that you think Ian Chambers is dirty?" Cold fear gripped my innards. Why hadn't it occurred to me to wonder how Chambers had enough money to afford a beach house and a house in The Heights on an investigator's salary?

"I'm saying he plays both sides. He was the one who ransacked your house, by the way."

"What? Why would he do that?"

"I think that your husband might have had something of his, something that made him wonder what Chambers was up to. Once your husband died, Chambers probably thought people were done asking questions about him. But when I showed up, with more questions, he panicked and started trying to find whatever it is. He also bugged your house."

"Bugged my house? How do you know this?"

"Someone saw him. Under the back windows and the side one by the carport. They got blasted by the sprinklers though. Don't work anymore."

"I haven't been running the sprinklers."

Quinn smiled.

"Oh." I found I was gnawing on my thumbnail. "What could he be looking for? And why would Ryan have it? I don't think he even knew the guy."

But then I thought back to last night at Specials. Nick knew Ian Chambers well enough. And Ryan and Nick sometimes had a drink after work. Had Ryan known Chambers? I felt a little betrayed that Nick wouldn't mention this to me, even though there was no real reason why he should. And there was an unpleasant little shock when it occurred to me that Ryan might have gone to Specials with them.

I had to sit down, so I dropped myself on the cedar chest at the end of the bed with a thud.

"This second boss. Tell me about him."

"I'll tell you about him, chica. Calls himself Diablo. He was the one who had me killed!" Spam shouted, almost in my ear.

Startled, I fell off the chest, sprawling on the floor. "You've got to stop doing that!" I snarled at him as I picked myself up.

"What?"

"Just popping up out of nowhere and shouting at me. It's extremely annoying."

I suddenly became very conscious of being wrapped in a thin sheet over a verging-on- transparent threadbare shirt with two strange men in my room. Even though one of them was dead and one only looked like a man. Still felt uncomfortable.

"Spam, what did I tell you about hanging around my house? I'll deal with you later. Just go."

He glowered at me, but disappeared in a puff of wispy vapor.

I checked Cassie's room to make sure the noise hadn't woken her up. She was still blissfully a-snooze. I went back to my bedroom. And Quinn.

"Okay," I said to him as I sat on the bed. "Without waking the baby, tell me why you are looking for Ian Chambers' alleged second boss. Please."

"He took something from me. I need it back," Quinn said.

"What was that?"

"You wouldn't believe me if I told you."

"Try me. I've seen a lot of unbelievable things lately."

"What he stole is a small green bottle." Quinn took a deep breath and closed his eyes. "It's carved from a single chunk of emerald."

He avoided looking at me. There was something he wasn't telling me.

"What's in the bottle?"

"A djinn."

Chapter 13
Gate Crasher

 Djinn? He stole a djinn from you?" I asked. I immediately thought of one of Cassie's favorite picture books, How the Camel Got His Hump. "You mean like a swirling cloud of dust, a genie in a bottle, three wishes and all that?"

"Well, unbound djinn aren't obligated to give anyone any wishes. Some of them do it for their own entertainment, though."

I closed my eyes. I tapped my heels together three times. "There's no place like home. There's no place like home. There's no place like home."

When I opened my eyes, Quinn, in Ryan's clothes, was still sitting next to me on the bed, looking puzzled.

"What are you doing?" he asked.

"I seem to have fallen into the Twilight Zone, where a bunch of made up stuff, like sea monsters, ghosts and genies are real. I was just hoping to get home. It worked for Dorothy, anyway."

I smiled to cover up how scared I was. I had very clear ideas about what was fact and what was fiction, and now someone was changing the rules on me.

Quinn crossed his arms and glared at me before he got up and strode to the other side of the room. When he spoke, his voice was deeper, rougher. "Made-up stuff? I find that very offensive. My kind have been around long before you hairless apes showed up. I'm the one who pointed out Jupiter's moons to Galileo, and I'm not even middle-aged yet. Just because you are ignorant, that's no excuse to go around insulting people, especially people who have been trying to help you."

His eyes flickered, and the near-black iris suddenly bled across his entire eye, swallowing up any traces of white. I was afraid of him then. At that moment, I absolutely believed he could shift into something monstrous. I was scared, and yet...I didn't want him to go. Every logical brain cell in my head screamed at me to tell him to leave and never come back, call 911 if I had to, anything just to get him gone.

Instead, I apologized.

"I'm sorry. I was brought up being told that there was no such thing as ghosts. That sea monsters were just misidentified animals or flotsam. That fairy tales are nothing more than cautionary stories for children. It's really, really hard to accept that you are what you say you are, even if I did actually see you change into a dog. You don't understand how hard this is for me to believe. I didn't mean to offend you." What was I thinking?

Quinn's eyes softened, but his arms stayed crossed. "We get that a lot. That's why most of us don't even bother interacting with humans."

"Okay, let's just rewind and start over. Why don't you tell me more about kelpies? What do they eat? How do they spend their time?"

"Okay, a do-over works for me. Kelpies are solitary fae, and we have to live near water. What we eat depends on what form we've taken. If I'm a horse, I eat grass."

"When you're a dog, you don't eat dog food."

"Have you ever tasted dog food?"

"Point taken. What about when you're in normal kelpie form, whatever that may be?"

Quinn put his hands on top of his thighs, and then found a loose thread on the comforter to pick at. "Whatever that may be?" he quoted me. "Come on. Everyone's seen the infamous Surgeon's Photo of the Loch Ness Monster."

"Wasn't that a hoax?"

"No, not at all. But it was important for people to think it was. Chris Spurling was good enough to confess to making the model and naming the other so-called hoaxers, who had conveniently died. As to what we eat, you know. The normal stuff. Fish. Humans. Livestock."

"Wait! Did you just say 'humans?'"

"Well, not me, really. Humans give me terrible indigestion, so I go out of my way to avoid them. It's been years since the last time. Seriously."

"So what you're saying is that you could turn into a monster at any moment and gobble up my daughter and I?"

"Technically." Quinn's jaw worked from side to side. "But you know how some people can't have dairy products? Same for me with humans."

"Really? The only reason you haven't eaten us is because you're lactose intolerant? I'm not sure how to respond to that."

"No. That's not the only reason. Besides, how many times have I protected you from Ian Chambers already? If I was planning to hurt you, I would have done it ages ago. We could help each other. We're both trying to find the same guy."

"No. You're trying to find him. I'm going to talk to Nick, let him handle it through official channels. I don't need to get involved in taking down Ian Chambers and his alleged second boss."

Quinn laughed quietly. "Do you really think Nick will believe anything bad about Chambers? Your husband was suspicious of him; he must have known something. Otherwise Chambers wouldn't have turned your house over. Aren't you the least bit curious?"

"Not if it puts my daughter at risk." I crossed my arms, now.

"Hate to break it to you, but she's already at risk, and so are you. If Chambers gets desperate enough, he'll use any leverage he can find."

"So you're saying that I have no choice but to trust you?" I resented being pushed into a corner by anybody. "I don't think so. Nick may not want to believe anything bad about Chambers, but he's not unreasonable. And if he doesn't want to listen to me, I'll take it to Captain Helmsley. Somebody, somewhere will listen to me."

"Maybe. If you had proof. But what are you going to tell them? A sea monster told you that Chambers was a bad guy?" The corners of Quinn's mouth curled up into a mocking smirk.

"You said it yourself: Ryan hid something in the house. If I could find it…"

Quinn sat back down on the bed. "But you don't even know what it is."

"Well, maybe Chambers got it. He won't have any reason to come after me, then."

"Are you willing to bet your life on that? Cassie's life?"

"Then tell me what you think Ryan had. Tell me what you know about Chambers' other boss."

"That's the problem. I don't know. Ryan must have had something small – but that could be anything – a piece of jewelry, a photo, a thumb drive." Quinn threw up his hands. "And his master? That's even trickier. I know he's somewhere in the Greater Houston Area, which narrows it down to about five million people. Lots of visitors come and go from Chambers' place. One of them might be the boss man. Or not. I can't just walk up and ask them, now can I? I do know this – Mr. X has his fingers in a lot of pies, but drugs and prostitutes are his main source of income, and he has some very dangerous friends."

"And you know this how?"

"I've seen Boris Cherngelanov going into his house. He's the top dog in the local Russian brotherhood."

"Brotherhood?"

"Mafia."

I got up and stalked to the sliding glass door. I looked for the pot of red zinnias on the bistro table that took up most of the small patio. I could see nothing but reflections of the room and myself in the dark glass, and I watched Quinn watching me. I saw him get up and come stand behind me, too close. He didn't touch me, just looked out the window over my shoulder. My body was aware of him, though. My skin tingled and the little hairs along my arms stood up, alerted by danger and desire. Damned gonads. I dug my fingernails hard into the palm of my hand, trying to draw blood, trying to distract myself. Punishment for wanting him.

"What do you see?" His voice was not much more than a whisper.

"Dark."

Quinn reached past me to the light switch and flicked it off. As he brought his hand back to his body, he brushed his fingertips close to my forehead, just like he did at Specials. "Look again," he said.

Now there were small lights, like fireflies, except they didn't flicker on and off, floating around the zinnias on the table. Two young ladies in gossamer dresses were sitting in the bistro chairs, chatting away. When the light went off, they looked up briefly and smiled, most likely at Quinn, since they probably had no idea I could see them. As I looked beyond the patio, I could see dozens, maybe even hundreds of little lights dancing around the plants all the way to the back of the garden. I felt like I had fallen into a Disneyland version of my own backyard.

"What is this? Why are there people sitting on my patio, and who are they?" I tried to turn towards him, but his cool, strong hands on my shoulders stopped me.

"They're dryads. The one on the left is from the pine tree, the other is from the oak. They like your patio."

"What about the little glowing things buzzing around the flowers?"

"Flower fae. They're a little bit like guardian angels for plants."

"Is this like at Specials, with the succubus? You did something to make me see them?"

"Yes. There's a whole universe of things, Marti, that most humans have no awareness of. I've seen how you treated Bruce, how you treat Alpha and Betty. I watched you try to help the bird that got hit by a car. Your yard is a giant butterfly garden. I thought maybe you were one of those rare few who would be willing to help."

"Help? Help with what?"

"Shifting the balance. There are those - some human, some not – who prefer darkness to light. Right now, they seem to be winning."

I looked at Quinn's reflection in the glass. His face looked serious, earnest, somber. "I think you need a super hero, not a single mom. Sounds too lofty for someone like me."

"It isn't that lofty, not if everybody that can does a little bit." There was a note of something that might have been longing in his voice.

I frowned at the darkness and picked at my thumbnail.

Quinn continued. "The guy that Chambers is working for is very bad, even by human standards. The thought of him with a djinn is unbelievably horrifying."

He took a step back from me.

I immediately felt the empty space where he had been, and I sighed. "You really want your djinn back, don't you?"

"He isn't mine. His name is Malik. He has a family, and he doesn't deserve to be a prisoner. He also doesn't deserve what will happen to him if Chambers' boss finds a sahir willing to work for him."

"A sahir? What is a sahir, and what would one of those do to him?" I kept watching the dancing lights around the flowers. Were those really there all the time?

"A sahir is a sorcerer that specializes in djinn. He knows how to bind one to an object, enslaving the djinn. Can you imagine what would happen if a bad guy, a really bad guy, had unlimited power?"

"I thought you said they didn't have to grant wishes if they didn't want to."

"I said unbound djinn are not obligated to. Bound djinn are a different story. What if the first wish is to be emperor of the world?"

"People wouldn't stand for it. They'd fight back."

"What if they forgot they had ever lived any other way?"

I whirled to face him, fantasy panorama forgotten. "That's impossible! He couldn't do that."

Quinn shimmered and changed into Bruce, who looked utterly ridiculous in Ryan's shorts and tee shirt. He came to me and licked my hand. Suddenly Quinn stood in his place, so close I could feel the heat from his body. "Don't try to tell me about impossible. You don't know the half of it." His voice had a hard edge to it, and what had been so funny a moment before was now deadly serious.

My jaw clenched. There was no need for him to talk down to me. "If this is so apocalypse/Armageddon/ end-of-the-world important, why are you trying to do this on your own?"

"I'm not. But we could use all the help we can get. Besides, we have a fallback position. You don't."

Even in the pre-dawn gloom, I could see his face was drawn, as if he knew more than he was saying, shielding me from the worst of it. I wanted to reach out to him, but I didn't dare.

"I need to think," I said.

Quinn nodded and slipped away from me through the darkness. He closed the bedroom door behind him. A little part of me was mad that he had left so easily, didn't want to stay with me. In my bedroom. That little part was going to get me into trouble, no doubt about it.

I sat on the bed and watched the dancing lights in the backyard. I thought it was rude to stare at the two young ladies sitting at my bistro table, but I let my eyes pass over them from time to time. I wondered if they would talk to me, or just run away if I went outside. Surely, this was just a dream. None of it could possibly be real. And yet…the heat of Quinn's body against my skin hadn't felt at all like imagination. If this was a dream, there was no harm in exploring. If it was real, well, that was a little tougher.

I tried to get my head around Quinn's nightmare scenario. Bad guy with unlimited power. Evil world dictator. And genie power. But it was just too fantastical, too unreal. I couldn't make that leap. In a book or a movie, sure. In the real world? I couldn't believe it. My eyelids started to get heavy, and I was afraid that if I went to sleep, I wouldn't be able to see the dryads and fairies anymore when I woke up. I decided to step outside and see what would happen.

My hand was on the lever lock of the door when the dryads stopped talking and looked sharply at the back of the yard. Something large was moving in the dark. It trotted towards the door. As it moved past flowerbeds, the little dancing lights were extinguished. The dryads fled. The shape seemed doglike, and for a second, I wondered if it was Quinn. As it got closer, it broke into a lope, covering the short distance with long strides. It stopped at the glass and peered up at me.

The thing was huge, and at first I might have thought it was a timber wolf. But there was something about its proportions that was not right – body too long, chest too heavy. The distorted canid rose onto its hind legs and stood like a man. Its huge paws slid on the door like hands, searching for a handle. Heavy claws screeched on the slick surface. Less than six inches away from my face, fierce teeth glinted in the dying moonlight as slavering lips pulled back into a snarl. Hot breath fogged the glass, but I could still see its eyes, glowing like campfire embers.

Run! Get away, now! Flight response had kicked in. Except that my feet weren't listening.

I could have sworn the beast smiled before it took a few steps backward, then threw itself at the door. The frame creaked, and the house shuddered. It backed up and tried again. This time, the first layer of the double glazing cracked. I was too terrified to breathe, let alone move.

I had the distinct impression that this monster wanted to get at me for no reason other than the sheer delight it would feel in watching me die in a horror-fest of blood and gore. And there seemed to be nothing I could do about it. Would it be satisfied with me, and leave Cassie alone? I thought of my baby, asleep in her crib, and rage flowed through me. If I was going down, I was going to take this thing with me. It was not going near Cassie, not while I was still breathing.

I started a mental inventory of possible defensive weapons. Both Ryan's Sig Sauer pistol and his grandfather's silver-inlaid kiem sword were packed safely away in the attic. Didn't matter – I had no time to get to them, and I didn't have any bullets for the gun, anyway.

The weird wolf backed up again, getting ready to make another run at the cracked glass.

The bedroom door opened, and the creature paused. It seemed to be looking over my shoulder.

"Whatever you do, do not turn around," Quinn said, not far behind me.

You can count on that. The air around me suddenly went cold and damp. It felt like I was standing in heavy fog, only everything looked the same. Fear crawled across my skin like a nest of spiders. I didn't have to look at Quinn to know he'd turned into his kelpie form. There wasn't enough money on the planet for me to turn around and see that. But instinct got the better of me, and I turned to look at the grey blur of motion in the mirror. I whipped my head back around, even putting my hand to the side of my face to block my peripheral vision. But not before I caught a glimpse of a long neck and a crocodile-like snout.

The monster outside twisted its head from side to side, then cowered and slunk away.

I swallowed hard, and noticed my breath was coming in fast, shallow bursts. I felt Quinn's hand on my shoulder. At least, I hoped it was a hand.

"Are you okay?"

I turned and melted against him, gasping in deep ragged breaths of air to stop the hyperventilation. He caught me when my knees buckled, and carried me to the bed.

"What was that?" I hated the way my voice quivered and broke.

"Seriously? I thought everybody'd heard of werewolves."

"There's no such thing as werewolves."

"Go outside and tell him that."

I looked at the cracked glass and started shaking. I tried to stand up, but my legs were pure gelatin, and I fell back on the bed.

"Where are you going?" Quinn asked.

"I need to check on Cassie."

"She's fine."

"I need to see her."

Quinn sighed. "Stay here."

He got up, silent as a shadow, and came back a moment later with a sleeping Cassie in his arms. He put her gently on the bed next to me. She groaned and rolled over. Tears of relief rained onto the quilt. I didn't want to cry, but the tears were cleansing, washing away the fear and evil that had shrouded me only a few minutes ago.

I knew if I touched her too much, it would chase the sleep away, but I kissed the top of her head and caressed her cheek anyway. Her nose twitched.

Quinn handed me a tissue. "You don't want to wake her up with Chinese water torture, now do you?"

I snorted, and Cassie opened her eyes. She started to cry, but I scooped her up and took her to the rocking chair. It didn't take long to get her to sleep. I decided there wasn't much point in going back to bed, so I put my baby in her crib and headed toward the kitchen, with Quinn close behind me.

"Coffee?" I asked as I filled the carafe.

"No, thanks."

"How do you like your eggs?" I normally avoided cooking as much as possible, except when I was nervous. It gave me something to do, and everybody has to eat.

"Scrambled," Quinn answered.

I heated olive oil in the skillet while I beat the daylights out of four innocent little eggs and a tablespoon of water.

"Could you find the garlic press for me?" I pointed to one of the drawers under the countertop closest to him.

I peeled two cloves of garlic while Quinn rummaged around in the drawer. He finally chose something and held it out to me.

"That would be a citrus reamer. A garlic press is a squeezy thing with handles and a basket."

"This?"

"Yep."

I deliberately brushed my hand over his when I took the gadget. I studied his face, checking for any reaction. One eyebrow twitched. That was something, anyway.

I added salt, pepper and garlic to the eggs and poured them into the hot pan. My stomach growled as the warm smell of cooking eggs filled the kitchen. I popped a couple of slices of bread in the toaster.

I looked at Quinn. "Why do you suppose that a werewolf was using himself as a battering ram at my side door? Do you think Chambers' boss is into them, too?"

"Don't know. It may not have anything to do with Chambers. Could be someone trying to set me up."

"How so?"

"Kill you and Cassie, make it look like I did it."

"Why?"

"That's a whole 'nother story. Let's just say 'revenge' and leave it at that. There are some individuals who are not above framing me for something I didn't do." Quinn frowned, "I don't think Chambers knows about me, not yet, anyway." Then he shook his head. "Werewolves are demonic, so there could be a demon behind the attack. And demons would definitely do something like that."

Demons. Oh, good. Because I need more problems in my life just now.

I dished out the eggs and got a jar of orange marmalade from the fridge.

"Your friend at the metaphysical shop. Is she any good at warding?" Quinn asked.

"I don't even know what that is."

I spread marmalade on my toast, pretending we weren't having a conversation about werewolves attacking my house.

"Protection spells."

"Spells. Right. I can ask her." Well, we've already got fairies, werewolves and lake monsters. Why not witches, too?

"I know you're getting a burglar alarm installed. That'll help against bad humans, but it isn't much use against demons, though. As soon as it gets light, I need to go out. Not sure when I'll be back, but definitely before dark."

"Is that a good idea? I mean, if this werewolf is looking for you, maybe you shouldn't be here." I shuddered, remembering the fangs on that thing.

Quinn frowned. "It knows I'm here. But it won't take me on without its pack, if it has one. Besides, what if Ian Chambers comes back to finish what he started on Sunday? Do you want to be here by yourself, you and your baby?"

I liked the idea of Quinn/Bruce being around, but I couldn't help but wonder why he did it. There must have been a dozen other ways for him to follow Ian Chambers without involving me.

"What if he found whatever he was looking for?"

"What if he didn't? Besides, I could be wrong. The werewolf may have come for you. Maybe Chambers knows more than I think he does. Wouldn't surprise me if Chambers' boss is the kind who'd make an alliance with demons."

"A pact with the devil?"

"The devil? I don't know what that is, but long story short, demons existed in an ancient, unstable universe that ripped itself apart. Demons are all about chaos and destruction. They shouldn't be here, except some managed to crawl through a hole in time – something I believe you'd call a wormhole."

Sci-fi, too. It just keeps getting better. I picked up a scrambled egg curd and popped it into my mouth. I swallowed it, and wished I wasn't out of orange juice.

"So I'm between a rock and a hard place then. It's dangerous if you stay, dangerous if you don't." If Ryan's parents were still alive, I'd go stay with them for a while in Vermont. I just wished I could take Cassie and get the hell out of Dodge right now.

"Looks that way," Quinn said around a mouthful of toast.

I stabbed viciously at a clot of egg. "I never had these problems until I started dabbling in this stupid card-reading psychic stuff."

"Ian Chambers has been a problem for a while. You just didn't know it."

"Maybe. But I didn't fish a wallet out of a nasty dumpster for him." Or tamper with a crime scene. I really hope you appreciate that, Spam.

Quinn shook his head, a hint of a smile on his mouth.

I stared out the bay window, and noticed that the black silk night had started to fade to grey. Pink and gold smudges peeked through the neighbor's trees, letting me know that the werewolf-banishing sun was on its way. At least that's how I hoped it worked, anyway.

"I guess you'll be going soon," I said.

"Yeah. You could say I have to see a man about a dog."

I groaned.

"Ma da da maaaaa!" Cassie shouted from her crib.

"I'll be right back," I said.

When I returned with Cassie on my hip, she took one look at Quinn and squealed. "Booce!"

Chapter 14
One Small Step

 ow did—?" I shook my head. "That's not possible."

"Babies remember a lot, but they can't talk about it. By the time they can talk about it, they've mostly forgotten," Quinn said. He smiled and waved at Cassie.

"What could babies possibly remember?"

"Where they came from before they came here."

"You mean Heaven?"

"If that's what you want to call it." He got up and surveyed the backyard. "I think it's light enough that you'll be safe, now. I'll be back before dark."

He didn't wait for me to answer before he pushed open the door and was gone. Part of me was glad he was gone, and part of me wanted to run after him. I'd wanted to ask him more questions, but they'd have to wait. Besides, I had a hungry baby to feed. A beautiful baby who meant the world to me.

"Girlfriend, what did I say about putting on that amulet?" Delilah stood in front of me, hands on hips.

"I wondered where you'd gotten to. We've been having some excitement around here."

I was a little cross with her for poofing in with some cryptic message, then poofing out again before I could get any answers.

I purposely walked right through Delilah, heading towards my rocking chair. Felt like stepping in to a walk-in freezer. Cassie's shiver pricked me with guilt.

"That's what I'm talking about, girl," Delilah said, drifting along behind me. "You need to be a little less excited 'bout that shifter."

I sat down, got myself ready, and Cassie latched on hungrily. It felt like she was going to suck my spine out, as well.

"What are you talking about, Delilah?"

Her hands went from her hips to across her chest. "Your new boyfriend, that shapeshifter. Can't nobody trust a shifter. That's why Lulu gave you that amulet, girl. It keeps a shifter from shifting, but you have to wear it. It don't do nobody no good sitting in your glove box."

"I don't need the attitude, thanks. If you and Lulu want me to know something, why don't you just come out and tell me, instead of making me guess at your crazy riddles? And then you act like I'm stupid if I don't know what you're talking about."

Cassie squirmed and complained, but didn't let go. Could she taste my irritation?

I patted her back and took a few deep breaths. The baby settled in and started feeding in earnest. That child must be having another growth spurt.

Then I had an idea. "What about werewolves? Does that charm work against them?"

Delilah's outline shivered. "Werewolves. Girlfriend, they are some bad juju. They ain't natural. But you know, silver the only thing can hurt them."

"A werewolf tried to knock down my door this morning."

"I know that."

"Then you also know that Quinn scared it away."

"Girl, how do you know those two ain't friends?"

"If Quinn wanted to hurt me, he's had lots of opportunities." I surprised myself at how quickly I came to his defense.

Delilah glowered at me while I switched Cassie to the other side. I decided the subject needed changing. "So. Do you know if Lulu is any good at warding?" I asked.

"Pretty good. She kept your boyfriend out of her shop." Smirking was not attractive on Delilah.

"I wish you'd stop referring to him as my boyfriend. It isn't like that. His name is Quinn."

"You mean it isn't like that...yet." One thinly plucked eyebrow arched smugly.

"And what's it to you, anyway? I'm a grown woman. I can do whatever, whomever, I want," I snapped back at her.

Cassie started to cry, but whether it was because I was dry or angry, I couldn't tell. I stormed past Delilah into the kitchen to get yogurt and cereal for my little girl.

Thankfully, the ghost didn't follow me, and I was able to cool down a little. I got Cassie ready to go for our walk. Wouldn't hurt to ask Lulu about the warding. I knew that Amanda wouldn't find anything in the water I had asked her to test, so there wasn't any reason to avoid The Tenth Sphere. Truth was, I kind of missed the shop. Maybe I'd even do the mediumship circle tomorrow night, if Mom was available to stay with Cassie.

The Tenth Sphere was still closed when we walked past it. It seemed weird, not having Bruce, or rather, Quinn, with us. He was, as they say, conspicuous by his absence. I hadn't counted on that.

The humidity made the air tangible and the morning sun bright and thick, crouching on my shoulders like the Old Man of the Sea. By the time we had finished our loop and made it back to the shop, I had made a valiant effort to convince myself that I'd imagined the whole werewolf adventure. The cowbell jangled more loudly than I remembered when I opened the door and pushed the stroller inside.

Lulu popped up from behind the counter. "Marti! Where've you been, honey?" She looked behind me, out the door. Her eyes narrowed a little. "Where's that dog? Did he run away?" She almost looked hopeful.

"Cassie and I have just been hanging, doing lunch. That sort of thing." I thought about the anti-shifter amulet, and wondered if I was taking the right approach. "No, Bruce hasn't run away. So. Tell me what makes you think he's a shapeshifter." I smiled, kept my voice even, non-accusatory.

Lulu smiled back. "He just has that look about him. Guess you could call it his aura. Are you okay? He hasn't tried anything, has he?"

"What do you mean?" I figured playing dumb would get more information than starting out with details.

"I mean fae are dangerous. Humans are easily enthralled by them. They can make anything seem like a really good idea – jumping off a bridge, playing in traffic, having sex with them."

Enthralled...was that what I felt when Quinn looked at me? "I see. And just for argument's sake, what would be so dangerous about having sex with them?"

"No. Please tell me you haven't..."

"Lulu. He's a dog. Not my type."

She frowned slightly. "It isn't uncommon for people to die."

"Die! Seriously? Why?" Reflexively, I glanced at Cassie. She was too busy gnawing on Mr. Buns' ear to get up to anything else. Please, teeth. Hurry up.

"When the faery consort leaves, and they always do, the abandoned human often pines away and dies. They lose all interest in the Mundane world and human lovers."

I couldn't resist. "Once you've had fae, there's no other way?"

"It's not a joke, Marti. That's why I gave you the amulet. If he is what I think he is, and shifts into human form, do not, under any circumstances, let him touch you."

Too late for that. "He saved me from a werewolf last night."

Her eyes narrowed. "Did he tell you it was a werewolf, or did you actually see it?" Lulu wasn't cutting Quinn any slack.

"It was hurling itself against my patio door. It was clearly a werewolf."

Lulu scowled, and it was a minute or so before she answered. "Werewolves and fae are usually chalk and cheese. But stranger alliances have been made."

Because it's perfectly normal to have werewolves in the back yard and lake monsters in the kitchen. "Well, Delilah's not too crazy about him, either."

"Good for her."

The bell on the door clanged, and the UPS man pushed a dolly with two boxes up to the counter. He left them near the cash register.

"Have a good one, Ms. Miranda," the deliveryman nodded at Lulu as he left.

"B! Your shipment is here!"

Belinda fairly burst out of the 'Employees Only' door. She struggled to lift one of the boxes onto the counter, then sliced it open with a pair of scissors. "Oh, they're beautiful!" she cried as she pulled out a paperback book.

Lulu handed one to me. The title, Dragon by Knight, and the author's name, Coda Sterling, graced the cover in light green. A very hot guy, wearing only jeans and holding a large sword, stood in front of a seaside castle. Over his shoulder, a dragon flew underneath the full moon.

The bell jangled again, and a group of women came in. I recognized the one with the turban from the mediumship circle last week. Today, the hat was turquoise. In the daylight, I realized that her eyebrows were drawn on with pencil, not because they were plucked, but because she didn't have any. No eyelashes, either. Chemo. I wondered what kind of cancer she had.

"I saw the UPS truck. Are they here yet?" she asked.

Lulu hugged her. "Ellen! Great to see you, honey. How are you feeling?"

"Today's a good day. I'm so glad I could make it out and get a copy of Belinda's latest, hot off the presses."

Belinda's latest?

"This one's kind of steamy – you may need a cold shower," Belinda joked.

She took a pen from the cup by the cash register and signed the book in her hand – "To Ellen. Fight the good fight! Love, Coda Sterling" She signed books for the other four women, who lined up to pay. Lulu refused to take any money from Ellen.

"I have to run, sweetie. I'm due at Anderson in twenty-five," she said.

Belinda squeezed her hand. "You let us know what the doctor says, you hear?"

Ellen smiled and nodded. With that, the ladies trooped out the door. I hoped if I was older and sick that I'd have friends that took me to the hospital and sat with me. Well, I certainly wouldn't if I kept pushing them away, I scolded myself. I sighed and looked down at Cassie, who was bashing the now soggy Mr. Buns on the stroller tray.

I was curious about Ellen, but I thought it would be too tacky to ask. I guess Lulu could tell, because she said, "Ellen's had a setback. Her breast cancer had been in remission for four years, but then she developed leukemia from the chemo. She just got out of the hospital for chemo on that, and now they may have to remove her spleen."

"AML – Acute Myeloid Leukemia?" I nodded knowingly, although it was something I'd only heard of, not seen – most of the time, they went straight to M.D. Anderson, since it's the cancer research hospital. But I knew the prognosis wasn't usually very good.

The cozy atmosphere in the store had turned grim. I wanted to shake it off as best I could, so I turned to Belinda. "I didn't know you were an author."

She blushed. "Well, it's just something I do on the side, really."

I turned the book I still held in my hand over and scanned the back. It looked like it was a bodice ripper set in medieval times, with knights and dragons and all the trappings. But maybe not.

After a chance encounter with a devastatingly handsome knight, Lisabeth Stuart finds herself at the Dragon's Lair Pleasure Faire resort in Galveston. She's supposed to be reporting back to her investor cousin, but she's hoping to enjoy the merriment and feasting, and especially time with the mysterious and delectable Sir Tristan. Just when Lisabeth starts to think she's found exactly what she wants, old enemies and even older secrets threaten to take everything from her. Will finding true love save her…or kill her?

"I'll buy your book. Looks interesting." I am normally not into romance novels, but I thought it was cool to have a signed copy of a book written by someone I knew.

Belinda signed it – "To Marti – Look for the dragons in the world. Love, Coda Sterling"

While Lulu was ringing me up, she said, "Belinda and I were talking. With all the classes we've got going on, we're up to our eyeballs with paperwork. We were thinking it might be good to get someone in part time, like half a day, two or three days a week. That gives me some space to do all the back-room stuff during the day instead of staying up late to do it. I was wondering if you might be interested? Of course, you can bring your little princess." She smiled at Cassie, who shouted "Ma da da da ma ning!" Ning? That's new.

"Oh," I said. Her offer surprised me a little. "What would I be doing?"

"Mostly running the till. Maybe a little re-stocking, answering the phone. That sort of thing."

"Can I sleep on it?"

"Of course you can. Oh, listen. There's a new product we're trying. Totali-TEA. You want to have a sample and tell us what you think?"

"Sure, why not?" Cassie was back to chewing on Mr. Buns and didn't seem at all bothered about hanging with Lulu and Belinda. Having tea would give me a chance to ask Lulu about warding. I sat down in the cypress root chair while Lulu disappeared into the back.

The bell jangled, and an older couple came in. Belinda showed them some salt lamps.

The Tenth Sphere was busier than I thought it would be on a Wednesday morning. That was good. I was 99% sure I would accept Lulu's job offer, and having worked retail in college, I knew busy was better.

"Here you go, honey." Lulu handed me a cup of hot tea.

"Thanks." The tea smelled wonderful and floral. I guessed it had lavender and jasmine flowers in it. I filled the spoon and blew on it, trying to cool the tea down enough that it wouldn't scald my palate. "So, Lulu. About the werewolf that showed up last night. Would you happen to know anyone who might know how to do some warding to keep it out of my yard?"

"Oh, I could do that for you, no problem. How about this evening, when the shop closes?"

"That would be great. The tea is excellent, by the way." It ought to be for $16.99 a box.

It was almost 3:30 and there was no sign of Quinn. Cassie was having her afternoon nap, and I lazed on the couch with Belinda's book. I could see what she meant about the cold shower. I would never look at Belinda the same way again. The book wasn't actually set in medieval times, but at an adults-only Renaissance-themed resort. With an actual dragon.

I heard scratching at the door. Quinn, in the form of Bruce, sat panting on the back porch. I opened the door for him.

"You could just open the door and come on in."

The dog shimmered and Quinn stood next to me. "What would the neighbors think?" He smiled at me, and I smiled back at him. Enthralled?

"Did you talk to your friend about the warding?" he asked.

"Good afternoon to you, too."

Quinn was unfazed. "I hope that's a yes."

"Lulu's coming this evening after the shop closes."

"Good. We managed to track the werewolf. And you wouldn't believe where he went."

Before I could ask where, Cassie began to wail. After a dry diaper and a snack, she was a much happier camper. We sat in the living room while Cassie cruised around the furniture and cooed at Quinn. Apparently, he wasn't comfortable talking about werewolves in front of a soon-to-be eleven-month old baby.

BamBamBamBamBam! Sombody or something was banging on the back door.

I froze, and I was sure my heart stopped.

"Aunt Marti! Aunt Marti! Can we play with Bruce?"

I think that was the most grateful I've ever been to hear Kyle and Aiden shouting at the tops of their lungs.

Quinn shifted into dog form and beat me to the back door. At four in the afternoon on a summer day in Houston, it wouldn't take long for the heat to suck the life right out of them. Cassie tried to keep up, but she couldn't crawl nearly as fast as they could run.

So she got up and walked.

Not very well or very far, but she had taken her first unassisted steps. This called for a celebration.

"Hey, guys! Do you want popsicles or ice cream sandwiches?" I shouted to the boys.

"Popsicles!"

I got one for each child and an ice cream sandwich for myself. Had to take a picture of Cassie, who got more of the popsicle on her than in her. I felt genuinely happy. Except for Lulu's warning about Quinn, which kept buzzing at the edges of my consciousness like a mosquito at three AM. Every time I get any warm fuzzies towards Quinn, I questioned whether it was real or I was just enthralled by him. True, he had been protecting me, but was it only because he thought he needed me to help find his emerald jar?

According to the old clock/thermometer/hygrometer on the wall, Lulu'd be here in half an hour, give or take.

I picked up a tennis ball that lay near my feet. "Bruce! Here, boy."

He came bounding up to me, and I threw the ball. He caught it on the second bounce and brought it back to me. I scratched his ears and lowered my voice to a whisper. "Lulu's coming soon. I'm going to do something you may not like, but you have to trust me. I'll explain it to you when she's gone. We need to talk, anyway."

I threw the ball again, but he didn't fetch it. Hackles raised, he barked and snarled at the back gate. Nick had started to open it, but reconsidered.

"Easy, there, boy," he said.

That just made Bruce/Quinn snarl louder.

"Bruce! Come!"

He grudgingly came and plopped himself down at my feet with a grunt. His eyes stayed on Nick.

"That's just the kind of dog you need, Marti." Nick did not come into the yard. "Boys! Come wash up for supper!"

"Bye, Aunt Marti! Thanks, Bruce!"

Nick was gone before I even had a chance to tell him Cassie had taken her first steps. I was bursting to tell someone. Maybe I'd get a chance to call Mom before Lulu showed up. I got my car keys and got the anti-shifting amulet from my car. I felt bad putting it on, but I didn't want to risk Quinn taking human form and talking to her while she was here. And I wanted Lulu to feel like her advice had been taken.

Bruce/Quinn's dejected eyes said it all as the three of us went back into the relative cool of the house. I didn't want to hurt him, and I very nearly took the amulet off, even had my hand on it, when Lulu knocked at the door.

"This is what I was talking about earlier. Please trust me." I tried to pat him on the head, but he avoided my touch. What have I done?

Lulu had a fabric shopping bag slung over her shoulder. "Wow. You've really done some updates on this house. It looks so modern on the inside."

The house may be twice my age, but it's paid for. "Well, Ryan did most of the work. He said that it was like a moving meditation, very zen and all that. He was Buddhist."

"Honey, I don't want to be rude, but I've had something come up and I need to do this quickly. Can we start in back?"

"I hope it's nothing too serious." I shifted Cassie to the other hip and led the way to the back yard.

Lulu rolled her eyes and shook her head. "There's a turf war going on between my Home Owners Association incumbent president and the challenger. Lot of BS, if you ask me, but since I'm the secretary, I have to show up at the meetings, even if they only give me three hours' notice."

Bruce/Quinn slunk along behind us. He was going to be mad at me for a while. I hoped he'd get over it.

Lulu went to the northeast corner of the backyard. She pulled out a small yellow cotton bag. Quartz crystals and some dried leaves peeked out of the top of it. She lit some dried sage and placed it in a censer. She muttered something about 'spirits of air,' then pulled out a trowel. She lifted off the layer of sod like a pro, and when she was done burying the bag, I couldn't even tell there had been a hole.

Next we visited the southeast corner, in the front yard, where she buried a red bag; the southwest corner where she buried a blue bag; and the northwest corner, where she buried a green bag. The sage smoke reminded me of stuffing, and I wondered for a second what I was going to do about supper.

"Okay, honey," Lulu said. "That should fix you up. Never can tell about werewolves, though. Some of them are strong enough to punch through the best wardings."

I scooped up Cassie, led Lulu through the gate and out to the sidewalk. Bruce/Quinn stayed panting under the oak tree in the far corner.

"Thank you so much, Lulu. I'll see you tomorrow. Have fun at your meeting."

She snorted. "You take care," she said, tossing her bag into the back seat of her car. I waved as she drove away.

A slamming screen door to my left caught my attention.

Nick ran down the sidewalk towards me.

"Marti!" he bellowed.

I waited the few seconds it took for him to sprint to me. His face was flushed and his chest heaved. I knew it wasn't from running the short distance from his house. Anger flowed off of him in hot, palpable waves. "Nick, what is wrong?"

"I'm being investigated." His voice was hoarse.

"For what?!" Arrows were crooked, compared to Nick.

"Internal Affairs was contacted by the DA's office. They said they had a tip from some gang punk trying to cop a plea that certain officers were looking the other way on some drug dealers for a cut of the profits. I was on the list."

"That's just crazy."

"But listen. They may show up at your house with a search warrant."

"My house?" A tip from the DA's office? Was Ian Chambers now trying to have my house officially searched because he didn't find what he wanted on his own? "Have you talked to Ian? Can he tell you anything?"

"Can't find him. But there's something you need to know. That little POS claimed that Ryan was the original ringleader."

Chapter 15
Stalking Horse

almost dropped cassie. The extra-sticky coating of popsicle juice may have been what saved her. "What did you just say?"

"I said, they think Ryan took the money and organized other cops to leave the pushers alone. This kid couldn't have been more than twelve when Ryan died. Doesn't make any sense. I have no idea where this is coming from." Nick's fists clenched by his sides.

I think I know exactly where this is coming from. "It'll be okay, Nick. You didn't do anything wrong, and neither did Ryan. They won't find any evidence, because there is nothing to find." I used the calmest ER nurse voice I could summon. I had to convince myself as well as him.

"I hope you're right. I have a meeting with the union rep first thing in the morning. I can't just stand around. I have to try and clear my head – just need to move. Later." Nick sprinted off down the sidewalk.

I watched him go, and felt my own anger welling up inside me. Some friend you are, Ian Chambers. Nick's been on the waiting list for the SWAT team for almost three years and this false accusation better not torpedo his chances. But attacking Ryan, who isn't even around to defend himself? That is lower than low, and there is no way in hell I'm going to let you get away with that.

I ran up the steps and slammed the side door behind me. The noise made Cassie cry. I ran the bath and sang absently to her while I tried to figure out what to do. It did give me a chance to cool down a little. I took off the anti-shape-shifting amulet and left it on the dining table. Bruce/Quinn remained outside. Whatever. I could only deal with one crisis at a time.

I almost didn't need my own shower by the time Cassie was done with her bath. After dinner, she was too tired to put up much of a fight, and she went to sleep quickly. I crept out of her room, and found Quinn sitting at the kitchen table, his face grim.

"I'm sorry," I said.

"So am I."

"What is that supposed to mean?" I had a bad feeling about this.

"I never should have involved you. You clearly don't trust me. I thought that you could help, that you wanted to help." His voice was like frozen blades of grass - cold, sharp and brittle.

"Don't blame me for not fully trusting you, when you used some kind of hocus-pocus magic power to make me want you." Had I just said too much?

"I am what I am. I told you up front that I wasn't human, so don't be so surprised if I don't think like one."

I crossed my arms and glared at him. Hard to argue with his logic, but I didn't have to like it.

Quinn got up and walked into the dining room.

Was that it? He was just going to get up and leave? I sat there, stunned.

He returned a few seconds later, carrying the anti-shifting amulet as if it were a piece of rotting garbage. Quietly, he placed it in front of me, then sat back down.

"Do you know what this is?" he asked.

"An anti-shape shifting amulet." Duh.

"But how is it made? Any idea?"

I had a feeling I wouldn't like the answer. "No."

"Shapeshifters, generally, are pretty strong. If you want to control them, you have to get the strongest shapeshifter of them all – a dragon – and bind it to this amulet. It no longer has any free will. Every time the amulet is used to stop a shift, a little more of the dragon's power, a little more of its life, is torn away. It suffers horribly until it dies. And dragons live practically forever."

I felt pretty much the same way that I felt when I heard about LD-50 tests – where testers force-feed beauty products to a group of animals until half of them die – and the bottom dropped out of my anger. "I didn't know." Does Lulu?

"I thought not."

"Can the dragon be released?"

"If you unmake the amulet."

"What, do I have to throw it in a live volcano or something?"

"It's not that bad. Ryan said —"

"You knew Ryan?" Who else was going to turn up that Ryan had known but I had no idea existed?

"Yes. He was a good man, and he helped us out, although I don't think he realized it. He had some questions about Ian Chambers and, unfortunately I didn't have any answers."

Quinn's expression was drawn and wistful, and I waited for the thunk of the other shoe hitting the floor.

"Did he know what you really are?"

Quinn shook his head. "No."

Well, at least I was in on one little secret. Yay, me.

"So, basically, you were investigating Ian Chambers and I stumbled into your way." My rational mind told me that I should have felt relieved that I was only on the periphery of the weirdness, rather than at its center. Even so, I was oddly disappointed that I only had a walk-on role in this drama.

"That isn't true. Ryan was crazy about you. I felt I owed it to him to keep an eye on you after he died."

"You owed him?"

"One of my colleagues fell into Buffalo Bayou. Ryan pulled him out. Saved his life, so I owed Ryan a favor."

So, instead of a guardian angel, I had a guardian lake monster. That's unique. Still, I wasn't entirely sure how to take that. Kind of sweet or kind of creepy – could go either way. But I did see an opportunity.

"If you feel you owe Ryan anything, you can help me now. Somebody in the DA's office, and I think we both know who that is, has made some allegations that Ryan and Nick are dirty, that they took money from drug dealers. I know that isn't true, but I don't know how to prove it. Help me find a way to clear them."

"You know what that means," Quinn said.

"What?"

"That Chambers didn't find what he was looking for. The only way to clear Ryan is to get Chambers and his boss."

"I was afraid you were going to say that. So what do we do?"

"You never asked where the werewolf went," Quinn said.

I rearranged the salt and pepper shakers on the kitchen table. "I'd forgotten about him. Where did he go?" I don't see what that has to do with clearing Ryan and Nick.

"We tracked him to Specials."

"They already have a pet succubus. Why not a werewolf?" I shrugged.

Quinn's lips made a pale imitation of a smile. "I don't think it was a coincidence that you went to Specials in the afternoon and their so-called pet werewolf showed up at your door later that night."

"You know that's right."

I looked up to see Delilah standing by the refrigerator.

"Girlfriend, I have a message for you from Spam, since you don't want him popping up in your house. He told me to tell you that Salinger saw you at Specials. He knows who you are."

"Salinger? Now is he that muscle-bound dude from Stella's party that broke Spam's neck?"

"That's the one," Delilah answered.

I chewed my thumbnail. I only did that when I was scared and pretending I wasn't. "So what's the problem with that? He doesn't know that I know he killed Spam."

"And yet a werewolf came to kill you," Quinn said.

"I don't have time to deal with Spam's stuff right now. I've got to help Nick and clear Ryan's name. That's more important."

Quinn propped both elbows on the table and rested his chin in his hands. "Come Tuesday morning, neither of those things may matter."

"What you talking about, shifter?" Delilah asked, planting her hands on her hips.

"I got word this afternoon that one of the sahirs we've been keeping an eye on is on the move, and in the general direction of Houston. The good news is, he can't take a plane – he's on a terrorist watch list. The bad news is, he doesn't need to. He's working his way around all the wardings and shields between here and there, so the person summoning him must not have a portal. It's taking him some extra time, but he'll be here for the full moon on Monday. That's when they'll do the binding."

"Binding?" Delilah's arms relaxed and slid to her sides.

"They're going to bind a djinn to some kind of object, probably a talisman or a ring, to give the possessor almost unlimited power. And by 'they,' I mean some really bad guys," Quinn answered.

"Oh, that is not good," Delilah answered.

I still couldn't get my head around the evil-world-dictator-for-life scenario. But I really didn't have to. What I could understand was that Chambers and company needed to be stopped, and stopped soon, or else Nick's career and Ryan's reputation were in the toilet. I'd just go with that.

"It's Thursday night," I said. "That gives us Friday, Saturday, Sunday and Monday."

"Until moonrise on Monday," Quinn corrected.

"Fine. Moonrise. What's the plan?"

Quinn looked at Delilah, then back at me. "Marti, I don't think you realize how dangerous these people are. This is not a TV show. They will kill you. Or worse."

Or worse? "I can't sit around at home and hope you get the bad guys. Ryan and Nick deserve better from me." How could I look at my little girl, knowing I didn't do everything I could to clear her daddy's name?

"I'm not asking you to sit around. I also don't think you want Cassie to lose both of her parents. You can do some digging. Find out who owns Specials. Do they own any other businesses? Whose name is on the liquor license? That sort of thing will help, if you want to clear Ryan. Investigators love paper trails."

I was only mad because I didn't want to admit that he was right about Cassie. "I don't really see how Spam's stuff is going to help," I pouted, not willing to concede entirely.

"Ian Chambers didn't just go there for a drink. He came out of the back office, remember? He's connected to Specials. You need to find out how. I'm sure that's why Spam took you there."

"Fine." I still felt like I was being given busy work to keep me out of the way.

Quinn looked at Delilah. "How strong is the warding?"

"Good as it gets, shifter."

"Glad to hear it." He looked back at me. "I have to go. If you haven't heard from me by noon on Sunday, assume the worst and do whatever you have to do to keep yourself alive."

I had to swallow hard before I could speak, the coppery taste of fear flavoring my words. "You have to win." I inwardly cringed. My words came out sounding too much like a plea, like begging.

"I know." He stood up and pushed his chair in, lifting it slightly so the legs didn't scrape on the floor and wake Cassie.

I stood up and walked him to the door, under Delilah's watchful eye. He said nothing else, but he turned and brushed my cheek with the back of his fingers in a way that made my knees weak. I didn't know if that was a promise or a final goodbye. "Keep yourself in one piece," he said.

Then he stepped out of the door and melted into the twilight.

A twisting tidal wave of emotions washed over me. Fear, anger, loss, hope, desire, regret, frustration, hate, pain. I didn't know whether to scream or curl up in a fetal position under the covers. Or both. I covered my face with my hands, took a deep breath, held it as long as I could, then let it out. Dropping my hands back to my sides, I turned to Delilah. "The last thing I can afford to do right now is fall apart like a cheap plastic toy. I'm going to go take a shower. A hot shower makes everything better."

Delilah nodded and faded away.

I stood under the hot water until it started to go cold. My emotions were still vacillating wildly between terror and fury, but at least I'd narrowed the range down to two. I was drying my arms when I noticed the mirror.

It was fogged up from the hot shower. But someone had written two words on it: "Ryans File."

I really hoped that Delilah was the one creeping around in my bathroom while I was in the shower, but I tried not to think about it too much. Maybe this was something I could use. I quickly combed out my hair and put on a nightshirt, all the while thinking about which of Ryan's files this clue could mean. I looked through every file in the two-drawer cabinet. Nothing but mundane stuff – insurance papers, bank statements, tax returns and such. All very familiar, as I'd just re-organized them after Ian Chambers broke into my house and tossed them all over the floor.

It was just after ten when I picked up the phone and called my sister's house. Nick answered after three rings.

"Marti? What's wrong?" Nick's voice was deep and raspy, the way it got when he'd been drinking.

"Nothing's wrong. Nick, how hard would it be for you to get a hold of Ryan's file. The investigation of his death?"

"I can maybe talk to somebody Monday –"

"I can't wait until Monday. I need it tomorrow."

"Why?"

Good question. How can I answer that without sounding like a nutcase? "I just need to see it. Maybe there's something in there that can help get you off the hook."

"Doubt it, but I'll see what I can do after my union guy meeting."

"Thanks. And Nick? Hydrate and go to bed. You don't want to be hung over in the morning. Goodnight." I hung up before he could argue with me.

I hoped that Lulu's warding would work. I didn't need werewolves coming in my backyard at will. What had Delilah said? Only silver can hurt a werewolf. I hoped that there didn't have to be a critical mass, and any amount of silver would work. I pulled down the stairs to the attic and climbed up. The small, naked bulb didn't do much to alleviate the creepy shadows in the corners. I grabbed the box with Ryan's grandfather's sword and scooted back down the rickety steps. I would keep it with me, just in case.

I was able to use the Texas Alcoholic Beverage Commission public inquiry webpage to find out about Specials' liquor license. The listed owner, irony notwithstanding, was Friar Enterprises, LLC. I found an address for them, an executive suite at Greenway Plaza, as it turned out. According to their website, Friar Enterprises owned a wide range of strip clubs, from the dingy to the deluxe. I supposed that wasn't so unusual, but it seemed odd, for a company with that many holdings, to only have one tiny executive suite, rather than actual office space somewhere.

It was a quarter of one, and I'd decided I had done all I could do for the night. I looked in on Cassie, who was sleeping like a rock. It felt odd, walking around my house with a sword, but extraordinary times called for extraordinary measures, or something like that.

Tired as I was, I had a hard time settling down and going to sleep, my brain assaulting me with too many problems and issues: dragons and djinn, liars and louts. I worried about Nick, and Ryan's reputation, and wondered if Quinn would be okay. I had gotten used to Bruce/Quinn sleeping on the bed, and now that I was alone, it was hard to tell if I felt smaller or the bed felt bigger. And who wrote those words on the bathroom mirror? Exhaustion finally won out, and I slept.

Who needs an alarm clock when you have a baby? I could set my watch by Cassie – up at 6:30. Every. Single. Morning.

After the usual preparations, we went to the kitchen for some solid food. Cassie threw her Cheerios off her tray and looked hopefully at the door. Bruce did not come. She sulked.

"Don't worry, sweetie. He'll be back." I hope.

I was restless and didn't really want to be alone. Well, Cassie counted as company, but not company that I could have a rational conversation with. We stopped by the Tenth Sphere on the way back from our morning walk. Besides, I had an ulterior motive. What Quinn had told me about the suffering dragon was jabbing my conscience, and I needed to see how much Lulu knew about it.

Cassie was being especially fussy and insisted on being carried. I walked her around the shop while she gnawed on her fingers as if she hadn't eaten in weeks. Talking to Lulu between customers and a cranky baby wasn't easy, but I managed to snatch an opportunity.

"So, Lulu. That amulet you gave me. Did you make that?"

She set down the packs of Tarot cards she'd been rearranging and looked at me like I was crazy. "Are you kidding, honey? I don't have the time or patience to do those. And I don't know anything about metalwork. No. I get them from a company in Oregon. They're expensive, but they're handmade and they really work."

"So you don't know how they're made?"

"Not really. All I know is it takes three days to make one. Are you thinking of starting an amulet business?"

Maybe the dragon rescuing business.

I shifted Cassie to my other hip. "No. I was just wondering. It's beautiful, and nobody would ever think it was anything other than just a piece of jewelry. Curious about their secret, that's all."

She offered to send me the owner's email address later, and I said that would be fine. I felt relieved that she didn't know about the dragon. I would tell her next week, if the world didn't end, and see if I could get her to help me release the creature.

In the end, Cassie's incoming new teeth were giving her a lot of grief, and she was just too grouchy to continue inflicting her on innocent bystanders.

When we got home, I gave Cassie some baby ibuprofen. Betty and Alpha climbed to the top of their cage, hoping for a treat. I gave them each a yogurt drop and felt a little guilty for ignoring them for the past few days. Even with the ibuprofen, Cassie's gums were bothering her too much to allow her to sleep. I thought distraction might help, so I slipped the rats' tiny harnesses and leashes on, and the four of us girls sat in the shade under the live oak tree in the back yard. The pain reliever finally kicked in, and Cassie tried walking some more. She was getting better at it, but still had a long way to go. The little rats seemed to be enjoying sniffing around in the grass and eating the occasional pill bug. It didn't take very long for the sun's ferocity to drive us back indoors.

We had just started lunch when Nick walked in the back door, without knocking, and plopped a large brown envelope on the kitchen table. Peppery stubble littered his face, and his usual spikey hair lay flat and limp on his head.

"Jeez, Nick. You look like something the cat dragged in."

"Whatever. Here's the file you asked for. Gotta have it back first thing Monday morning."

"Thanks. How did your meeting go?"

Nick flipped one of the breakfast chairs around, and sat straddling it, resting his chin on the back. "I am so screwed. IAD is focused on nailing dirty cops, not clearing innocent ones. Even if they don't come up with a shred of evidence, I'm still tainted."

It hurt me to see Nick in this state. I was sure he'd bounce back, once he had a little time to get over the initial shock. "I'm so sorry this happened to you. But they also went after Ryan, and I'm not going to let either one of you get railroaded."

Nick smiled. "Emily says the same thing."

"Well, there you go. The Schmidt Sisters are on the case. How can you lose?" I paused long enough to give him a reassuring look. "You know, it might do you some good to take the boys to the Museum of Natural Science. Maybe you could catch the IMAX and get your mind off of this for a little bit. And you know Kyle and Aiden never get tired of seeing the enormous hall of dinosaurs."

"Maybe."

Nick looked around the room. "Hey. Where's your dog?"

"Bruce? He's…at the vet, getting a flea bath." I hated lying to Nick, even if it was a teeny white one. But I couldn't exactly tell him the truth, either.

"You need to make sure your back door's locked, especially if you're by yourself." Nick stood up to go.

⁍

Once Cassie was down for her afternoon nap, I hopped back on the internet and started researching Friar Enterprises, LLC. It was privately held, and there wasn't much to find, although I did discover that the executive director was named Cynthia Ashland.

I suppose I had put off looking at Ryan's file for as long as I could. My hands shook as I picked up the unmarked mailing envelope and slid the file out. There were some loose crime scene photographs in the folder that I couldn't bear to look at, so I held them against the front cover to keep them face down when I opened it. The file was not very thick – the case was cut and dried. Traffic stop goes bad. High speed chase and stand-off. SWAT called. Bad guys dead. The end. As much as I thought that the idea of time-travelling Russian literary stars with machine guns would make a great Quentin Tarantino movie, I didn't believe for a second that Anton Chekhov and Fydor Dostoyevsky were the shooters' real names.

I read every piece of paper, save anything that might be trapped between the photos, at least three times. The time of 12:55, when the 'Officer Down' call hit dispatch, stuck in my head. Still, I couldn't find a single thing that would do Ryan or Nick any good. Some tip this turned out to be. I picked up the loose papers and tried to get them back in some semblance of order before I clipped them back in.

A grimy, dog-eared Post-It note fluttered to the floor. I picked it up. In smeared pencil, it read: "EMT: suspect said, 'Hey, fellows!' and then expired."

Well. Interesting bit of trivia, but completely useless. Dying people often say bizarre things.

The question now was whether I'd missed something, or my mirror-writing source was wrong. Just to see if there was some report or scrap of paper I'd missed, I picked up the photos one by one, careful to keep them face-down. I'd seen some very grisly things in the ER, but none of them had involved Ryan. I needed for the pictures of him I kept in my head to stay uncontaminated. It had been necessary for the funeral service to be closed-casket.

I tucked all of the papers and photos back into the folder and slipped it into the large envelope. I texted Nick that I was done with the file, but didn't get a reply.

I had managed to get through the file without blubbering. That was something, anyway. But now, I felt dull and depressed. I made a pitcher of iced-tea and stood in the kitchen, looking out the back door. I hoped the sunlight would burn off the gloom, but it was merely hot, rather than purifying. I knew Cassie would be up any minute, and I hoped I could force myself into a better mood before then. Wondering what Quinn was doing wasn't helpful, and Delilah didn't seem to be around, either.

I went in the living room and turned on the TV.

The phone rang. I could tell by caller ID that it was Amanda. She had called to tell me there was nothing wrong with the water sample I'd given her. And to remind me that the ER was hiring.

I hung up the phone and flipped mindlessly through the channels until I heard Cassie squawking in her crib. After I brought her into the living room, she didn't want to do anything but have me hold her hands so she could walk around the house. We did that until my back cramped up and I could barely stand upright.

I called Emily to see if she needed anything, and Cassie and I ended up going over there. Nick had taken the boys out, and I was able to have a good visit with my sister – just girl talk - even though we avoided the 600 pound gorilla that was the manufactured charges against Nick and Ryan. We stayed for dinner, but I made a point of getting home before dark. I hadn't brought the sword with me – thought I'd avoid the awkward questions and explanations.

At 3:42 AM, I was awakened by someone tapping, actually, it was more like banging, on the sliding glass door in my bedroom. The same glass door that the charging werewolf had cracked. It took a moment for my brain to wake up and my hands to grab the sword. Raising it above my head, I went to the door and turned on the outside light. There was a group of four people standing on the patio. No, make that five. Someone was draped over the shoulder of one of the men. The person's backside was towards me and I could tell it was a man, but I couldn't tell if he was alive or dead.

"Let us in!" demanded a red-haired man.

I waved the sword, just to make sure they saw it. "Who are you?"

The redhead said something to the man who was carrying the body. He turned around and I gasped. Even with the hair matted to it with blood, I recognized the face.

Quinn.

Chapter 16
Bitter Grapes

 uinn hated leaving Marti and Cassie. But he also knew that it was the only way to protect them. And at this point, it went far beyond saving a pretty woman and her baby. For ten thousand years, maybe longer, there were humans who had thought they could control djinn. Even bound djinn were not as helpless as they might seem, and binding them seemed to make the djinn go a bit mad. Between Malik's tricks and Chambers' employer's wishes, there was no telling what would happen. And none of it was likely to be good. Quinn was certain that the boss had paid a lot of money for Malik – the demon who kidnapped him said as much - and he probably wouldn't do that unless he had something really big and really bad planned. Why else would he need the power of a djinn? How did he even know about djinn, anyway? Were demons involved in that, too? If that was true, it added a whole other level of ugly – it could change the situation from potentially catastrophic to potentially apocalyptic. His head throbbed, from the crown all the way down into his shoulders.

Kai's car was waiting around the corner.

"Frey," Quinn said as he climbed in.

"Evening," Frey replied, then drove in silence to Kai's house.

As usual, when Frey drove, all the traffic lights were green. The journey took less than twenty minutes.

When they arrived, Quinn hurried up the stairs to the large bedroom that served as the war room for Kai's team. The walls were brightly painted, but whether it was dark yellow or light orange was hard for Quinn to say. He wasn't sure he liked the color, but he did always feel energized in that room. An oval mahogany table with a highly polished grey and orange granite top stood in the center of the room, surrounded by six matching chairs. Kai's laptop perched on one end of the table, its back to a large flatscreen, which took up most of the wall on one of the room's shorter sides. The longer sides of the room were old school, lined with whiteboards and corkboards.

He forced a grim smile when he saw those already gathered.

Eoin and Aleksei sat at the table opposite each other, eating sandwiches. Kai was on his feet, fidgeting around near the computer. And of course, there was Breena, who'd just met him at the door. Well, there were five of them, and teams were always made up of five. It should be enough. He hoped. They were going to rescue a captured team member. That's all they had to do to make the bad guys' plan fall apart. Just a day's work for a Mundane Intervention Team.

"Food is on the table," Breena said, tucking dark hair behind her ear. She gestured towards a side table spread with fresh fruit, sandwiches, and a selection of fruit juices before she moved to the table and sat down.

Quinn wasn't really hungry, but thought he ought to at least have something for politeness' sake. As he reached for the pitcher of orange juice, he caught Marti's scent on his hand. When this was over, when Malik was recovered, when the bad guys were dealt with, when Marti was safe, then what was he going to do? The obvious answer was to go back to the Waterhorse Inn and serve up pints and sandwiches until another mission called. It would certainly keep Marti safe from his mother. It would be better for Marti and Cassie both, for a lot of reasons, if he just left her alone. But he wasn't sure he could.

"We may as well get started," Kai said. He pushed a button on his smartphone and the flatscreen flared to life. A map of the Port of Houston appeared on it in high definition. As he talked, the map zoomed in on one terminal. "Now, the source who's been tracking the sahir tells me that he's on a Liberian-flagged container ship, the MV Albatross. Best guess is that he's pretending to be one of the crew. When the ship docks at Barbours Cut Terminal, we assume he's going to slip off the boat as its being unloaded. What we don't know is how he's getting to the place they're keeping Malik. And since we don't know where that is, either, we'll have to follow him. Once we have a location, we can start planning. The ship should arrive sometime tomorrow."

Quinn knew they were necessary, but he hated planning sessions. He just wanted to get started, get things done. He shifted in his chair and tried to force himself to pay attention.

Kai clicked the button again. "This is what he looks like." An image of an elderly, leather-faced man appeared on the wall. His eyes were a nearly colorless grey, and they matched his thick, grizzled beard. "He's only human. He can't shift or use glamour. But he is likely to be disguised. And he's also probably the only one that will be sneaking out of the terminal."

"Is he travelling alone?" Eoin asked.

"Excellent question. I don't know," Kai said.

"If he is user of dark magick, is easy to tell," Aleksei added.

"Maybe. If he isn't expecting anyone to be looking for him and he hasn't bothered shielding himself. But one doesn't get to be as old as he is without being paranoid. Not sure we can count on seeing the anti-glow," Kai said.

Quinn knew that all living things have an aura, a field of glowing colors that surround them. Most humans have trained themselves not to notice it, but they can see it, with a little practice. People who do good things glow brightly, while those who do bad are dimmer. He saw it all the time, and had taken it for granted. Still, he hadn't thought about magick. Add magick, and the effects are amplified. Magick itself isn't good or bad, but when it is used for bad things, the aura of the person using it glows dimmer and dimmer, until he finally has a negative aura, as if light is being sucked away – an anti-glow.

"There is one thing to look for – he always wears a ring on the middle finger of his right hand. Has a large peridot stone in the middle and some ancient script on the sides. It's the source of his power – he won't take it off." The picture zoomed in to a cocktail ring-sized green stone on the sahir's hand. "Now what I was thinking," Kai continued, "is that one of us could be inside the terminal, watching the boat, and the rest of us could be keeping an eye on the exit."

"Security's going to be really tight there, could be a problem," Quinn said.

"Maybe not, if that individual was in the water."

Quinn's smile was more grimace than grin. "Because you know how much I love swimming in nasty seaport water."

"I'm sure Malik would do it for you," Kai shot back.

"Of course he would." He was the only one, apparently, who recognized Kai's dig at Malik.

More pictures were displayed and all the organizational details were worked out. Quinn didn't relish simply hiding in the port water, keeping only his eyes and nostrils above the surface, so he'd simply look like flotsam, if anyone spotted him. He hated waiting – he preferred doing.

"Alright," Kai said. "I think we should try and get some rest. It's going to be a long day tomorrow."

There were enough bedrooms in the house for each of the guests to have their own, but Aleksei and Eoin preferred to sleep outside in the back yard. The marble tiles inside were too slippery for Eoin's hooves, and Aleksei needed to get his toes in the soil to recharge.

Upstairs, Quinn lay on a soft bed, staring at the pale blue ceiling. He was too tired to sleep. Or perhaps it wasn't that at all. His arm stretched across the empty expanse of the bed. He'd quickly gotten used to not sleeping alone, even if he had been in dog form. He forced his mind in another direction, focusing on tomorrow's plan. He visualized the mission going smoothly, recovering Malik, introducing Chambers and his boss to the human authorities. His debt to Ryan Keller would be repaid. And then what? He couldn't think about that, not now. He started over with the visualization.

Quinn and company left early in the morning, while it was still dark, and drove about an hour to Seabrook. No one there would pay much attention to a wade fisherman in the surf. Quinn eased himself further into the water, deeper and deeper, until he could slip under the swells and shift. He swam out into Galveston Bay and followed the line of ships until he found the one he was looking for. The Albatross had not been difficult to locate. It was queued up to enter the mouth of the San Jacinto River and move into the Ship Channel. Once he spotted it, it would be nearly impossible to miss. All of the other ships were stacked high with generic yellow, white and grey containers. But the Albatross also had one small, sea-green refrigerated container with grapes painted on it.

He kept himself submerged as much as possible – but he could only hold his breath about two hours, if he was mostly still. He got as close to the ship as he dared, but he made sure he stayed well away from the depth finder, and especially far from the boat's thirty foot propellers.

Watching an anchored ship was excruciatingly boring. The crew was below decks in the shade, rather than soaking up the punishing Texas summer sun. Quinn amused himself by catching redfish for his breakfast. Finally, the tugboat and the channel pilot came out to the Albatross, and the ship began to move towards the terminal. It wasn't moving quickly, but it was moving.

Quinn's relief was short-lived.

He had just gotten a breath when he saw it. It was medium grey, hints of vertical stripes, with a blunt nose and low, wide dorsal fin. Tiger shark.

At fifteen feet, it wasn't much smaller than he was. The shark was probably attracted by the scraps of Quinn's fish, but it wouldn't be opposed to having a meal of kelpie with a redfish garnish. He knew it would approach slowly, trying not to spook him, then when it got close enough, it would attack, its powerful tail giving it a burst of speed that he couldn't match. So the trick was not letting it get close enough.

Quinn dove, swimming away from the shark faster than it was moving, but not at his top speed. He wasn't as fast as the shark, but he was more maneuverable. The shark picked up its pace, easily shadowing him. Quinn skimmed along the bottom, twisting and turning to avoid debris and other hazards. He was making for one of the many abandoned oil platforms, or a shell reef, whichever came first, across the river in Trinity Bay. With any luck, the tiger shark would decide that the schools of fish that swarmed the submerged structures were easier pickings than Quinn.

He ducked behind a pipe stand that looked like over-sized, barnacle-encrusted monkey bars. He stuck his head over the top of it and looked for the shark. It was nowhere to be seen. Perhaps it had given up. Swimming far and quickly had depleted Quinn's air reserves, and he needed to get to the surface. He checked again. No sign of the shark. He started to rise, slowly, carefully. The water wasn't deep, scarcely more than the millpond at the Waterhorse. Quinn tilted his head upward, so he could just break the surface with his nostrils.

The shark hit him from behind, crashing into his side and grabbing one of his flippers in its mouth. The teeth were so sharp he didn't feel them cutting into his skin, and he was momentarily amazed by the dark cloud of his own blood floating around him. The shark shook its head, tearing at the flipper. Quinn's lungs were burning. He had to have air, and soon. Even sooner, he had to get twelve hundred pounds of shark off of him.

Sharks aren't the only ones with mouths full of razor sharp weapons. Quinn sank his own teeth into the flesh just before the fish's stumpy dorsal fin. The shark wasn't used to its prey biting back. Startled, it stopped the attack and reversed course, thrashing and snapping its bristling jaws. Quinn let it go. His straining lungs would force him to gulp in seawater instead of air if he didn't get to the surface soon.

His head shot out of the water, and he gasped for oxygen. A startled fisherman nearly fell out of his bass boat. Quinn gave him a toothy grin. Cursing and fumbling, the man started his outboard motor and sped away.

Quinn had to get out of the water. Between his bleeding flipper and the injured shark nearby, other sharks would be coming to investigate. And this would quickly become a very unhealthy place to be. He swam towards the opposite bank the fisherman had headed to, and he let himself take on human form as he left the water.

The shark had bitten his arm all the way to the bone, and it was bleeding badly. Muscle and skin hung in strips. He sat on the beach and put the ragged flesh back in place as best he could, then he had to apply pressure so the tissue could knit itself together properly. He covered most of the wound with his hand and other arm, and after a minute or two, the bleeding slowed considerably. Kelpies heal very quickly. In two hours' time, there would hardly be a scar. Nevertheless, he was light-headed from blood loss.

But now the mission was compromised. He'd lost track of the Albatross. And he couldn't risk getting back into the water until the shark bite healed, or at the very least, stopped bleeding. And if those problems weren't enough, his clothes were somewhere on the opposite side of the bay, so he couldn't go walking around to get back into the water further away from the shark.

Quinn looked around, trying to get his bearings. He was surrounded by brackish estuary, low, scrubby bushes, and thick marsh grass. He sat partially in the water so it wasn't obvious that he was nude. The last thing he needed was somebody wandering by and calling the police.

A shadow seeped across Quinn's face.

"You're out of your element, kelpie," a hoarse voice croaked.

Quinn turned his head to see an especially ugly ichthyuxoris standing over him. She was mostly human-shaped, with large external gills that started behind where her ear would be if she were human and ended at the base of her throat. They dangled and swayed like fat, spiky earthworms in the breeze. Her face was more frog than human, with bulging tawny eyes and an unpleasantly wide mouth filled with jagged bony plates, like some prehistoric fish. Sunlight glinted off of her green-black scales.

There are virtually no reports of these creatures, partly because they are very rare, and partly because humans who saw them almost never lived to tell anyone about it. In fact, the favorite hobby of ichthyuxori is tipping over small boats and drowning the occupants. Still, Quinn knew the reason the ancient Romans had called them Fish Wives.

Quinn raised his injured arm. "I'll be on my way in a bit, as soon as this heals enough."

"This is my territory. Get out," the ichthyuxoris snarled, pointing a dangerously clawed, webbed hand toward the land.

"I understand that. I'm not planning on staying here, and I'm not hunting. I just need to rest for a little while."

The ichthyuxoris hissed and took another step towards him. "Leave!"

In human form, Quinn didn't stand a chance against her, especially not in his weakened state. In his kelpie form, he was clumsy on land, but still quite dangerous, and he would have the advantage. He couldn't leave via land, and she would fight him if he got in the water. He didn't wish to hurt her, but he had to get back to the other side of the bay, and see if he could still find the Albatross and salvage the mission. Without being torn apart by frenzied sharks.

Blood still oozed from his arm, but it was a lot better than it had been a few minutes ago. He eased himself slightly deeper into the water, as if the swells were carrying him out into the bay.

"Not that way!" the ichthyuxoris growled. "My territory."

Quinn stood up, as if he were going to come on shore. Then he hurled himself backwards into the water, changing into kelpie form as he did so. The water was a little shallow, and he scraped his belly on the rocky bottom, but he shot away from the ichthyuxoris. With a screech, she dove under the waves and followed him. He'd counted on that.

Quinn built up speed, stretching out like a long-necked torpedo. He headed straight towards where he'd left the injured shark.

So far, it was holding its own against some small sharks that had come, hoping for an easy meal. The big tiger's teeth added some of their blood to its own. Larger sharks would not be far away.

As soon as the ichthyuxoris saw the wounded tiger shark, she broke off her pursuit, swam to it, and lovingly stroked its nose. Surveying the small sharks harassing the injured tiger, she opened her mouth wide and emitted an infrasonic growl that nearly knocked Quinn over. Its frequency was too low for humans to hear, but the attacking sharks couldn't get away from her fast enough. Quinn twisted his long neck around as he shook his head to clear the ringing in his ears. The ichthyuxoris was guiding the shark by its dorsal fin, most likely to her lair to treat its injuries. Fish Wife, indeed. Quinn wished there were more of her kind.

The line of ships waiting to enter the channel was easy to find. The Albatross was not. It must already be in the terminal. The channel was relatively narrow and shallow, with lots of traffic. He'd have to maneuver his large body perfectly, if he wanted to avoid being converted into chum by the huge propellers. The problem was, his eyesight was blurry and his head seemed like it was no longer attached to his neck. Quinn's flipper felt like it was on fire. The strain of frantic swimming had been too much for the healing wound. It hadn't held, and now he was pouring blood into the bay again. He wasn't going to do Malik any good if he bled to death, so he reluctantly made his way back to the shore.

He converted to human form as soon as the water got shallow enough. He heaved himself onto the crushed concrete, and lay partially submerged in the shade of a rotting pier. He held pressure on his arm. It took a lot longer for the bleeding to stop this time. The water in the Gulf of Mexico during summer is like bathwater, and the warm gentle waves caressed and relaxed his exhausted body. His mind drifted with the whitecaps, not really awake, but not quite asleep. Something brushed against his thigh.

"Marti?" he mumbled.

But it was only a clump of seaweed.

೪

When Quinn opened his eyes, Breena was pouring something cool down his throat. It tasted green and sweet – like mint and basil and thyme and honey, all mixed together.

He swallowed and coughed.

"Welcome back," she said.

Quinn was lying on the second row of seats in Kai's SUV. His clothes were on, although his shirt was backwards. His arm was bandaged.

"When you didn't check in, we got worried. Frey found you." Breena helped him sit up. "You may still feel dizzy. It'll pass soon. You're going to be fine, although it will probably be tomorrow before you're a hundred percent."

Quinn nodded his thanks to Frey, who was playing a game on his cell phone.

"Then it's a good thing we're just doing recon today," Quinn replied.

Kai, who was sitting in the front passenger seat, put down his binoculars and turned to Quinn. "What happened?"

Quinn told them.

"You saw an ichthyuxoris?" Kai asked. "That's amazing. There are only about three of them in the entire Gulf of Mexico. I think one's near Padre and the other is in the Florida Keys."

"Okay. Good to know. I'd rather have seen the sahir."

"Yeah, well, you have to take whatever wins you can get, sometimes," Kai replied.

The remark irritated Quinn. It wasn't his fault he got attacked by a shark, was it? It might be possible later for him to slip into the water from the other side of Barbours Cut Boulevard and swim into the terminal to watch the water side of the Albatross, but right now, he was too weak and clumsy from the shark attack to be able to pull it off. If the sahir had brought diving gear, and if he waited until well after dark, he just might be able to slip over the side of the ship and make his way out of the terminal underwater, away from the watchful eyes of the Coast Guard and the Port Police. He'd escape while Quinn and his team all sat in the car, wondering what to do. If Quinn had just taken the time to eat breakfast and left the stupid redfish alone, the shark wouldn't have showed up, and he'd be in place, ready to intercept the wretched sahir. He wanted to hit something, but didn't dare, not in the vehicle's close quarters with the others nearby. With any luck, he'd be strong enough to get back in the water in a few hours, and could still redeem himself. If the sahir was not stopped, Malik would be enslaved. And it would be all Quinn's fault.

Quinn sighed and looked out the window. "Is it my imagination, or are we really parked in front of a cemetery in the middle of a cargo terminal?"

Breena snorted softly.

"Morgan's Point Cemetery. It was here long before the terminal. Quite handy for Aleksei to get up in those trees in the corner. He and Eoin can watch the ship, we can watch the exit." Kai handed Quinn a pair of binoculars before he put his own pair back up to his eyes. Quinn glanced to the back row, slightly ashamed he hadn't even noticed that Aleksei and Eoin were missing. He lifted the glasses and focused on the gate.

It was 4:30. The gates would close at 5:00. If anyone was planning on leaving tonight, they'd have to do it soon. Quinn watched the exiting vehicles. Silver pickup. Green pickup. White semi. White semi. Orange semi. Red semi.

"Now that's interesting," Quinn said.

"What's that?" asked Kai.

"That pickup truck with the flatbed trailer. He's taking one half-sized, refrigerated container. I'm sure it was on the Albatross. I haven't seen any other green containers with grapes painted on them."

"Are you thinking what I'm thinking?"

"That the sahir isn't in the crew – he's in the container."

"Bingo."

Frey flashed the SUV's headlights. Eoin and Aleksei were at the doors within a minute.

"Think we've found him," Kai said.

Frey pulled slowly out of the parking lot and turned onto Barbours Cut Boulevard. The pickup was just ahead of them. Aleksei and Eoin ducked below the windows and Quinn lay back down on the seat, bending his knees so Breena would have space to sit. If the pickup driver noticed the SUV, two men and a lady probably wouldn't look suspicious. Five men and a lady might.

They followed the driver until he pulled into a warehouse near the train depot in downtown Houston. Frey passed the driveway and parked around the corner a few blocks over. They could see if anyone entered or left the premises, but they couldn't see anything that was going on in the yard.

Frey scowled at the steering wheel.

"What's wrong?" asked Kai.

"Perhaps it's nothing. It just seems that he went well out of his way to get here. He should have just stayed on 225. There was no reason at all for him to go all the way down to the Beltway and back up on 288."

"Maybe he just took a wrong turn?" Breena asked.

"If so, he's a bloody bad driver," Frey responded.

"The great thing about walking a dog is that you can wander around all kinds of places, and no one thinks twice about it," Kai said.

Eoin chuckled.

"You be gentle with him. His arm's still healing," Breena said sternly. "Maybe I should do it."

"No. They'll notice you. They won't pay any attention to a male. I think Aleksei should go with him," Kai replied.

Quinn shifted into dog form, and Aleksei forced his blue skin into a more human shade. They strolled down the sidewalk, pausing for a sniff here and a dig there. He only limped a little bit – the arm bandage was far too big for a dog leg and had to be removed. The skin had healed, but the muscles were still weak. Aleksei and Quinn verified that there were no back exits to the warehouse yard.

They could even see the nose of the truck sticking out from behind the warehouse. Eight vertical feet of chain link fence, topped with razor wire, encircled the yard. A faded, rust-flecked sign on the front gate read "Beware of Dog." That was all there was to report when they returned to the SUV.

By the time it was dark, the warehouse district was asleep. A few security guards occasionally appeared and disappeared around corners. No one had left the warehouse. The truck was still parked behind the building.

"I don't like this," Breena whispered loudly.

"Did you notice any place that a dog might be able to get into the yard?" Kai asked.

"Where the gates join in the middle is not quite flush. If somebody pushed on the bottom half of one, I could probably squeeze in."

Breena frowned after he and Aleksei as they left the SUV and headed towards the warehouse, knowing Quinn wasn't fully healed.

Aleksei looked around. There was no one is sight. The chain rattled as he pushed against the lower half of the gate. His feet were strong, like the roots of a tree, and the metal was no match for him. The gate started to bend, and Quinn slipped through, wagging his tail.

He snuffled around and trotted towards the truck. The trailer was still attached to it, but the container was gone. Must be inside.

Light poured out of the windows and left square puddles on the ground. Quinn found some five gallon buckets stacked along one wall, and a couple of them were under windows. He cringed as each click of his toenails was amplified by the empty containers. He stood on his hind legs to peer in, but the three men inside didn't seem to notice. One was tall and beefy, probably a body guard. He stood with his arms crossed and feet apart. Next to him was a man with reddish blond hair, who was doing a lot of talking. The other man had a grizzled beard and leathery skin. The sahir. He was holding the emerald jar. A jewelry box, a stick of chalk, a box of charcoal tabs, cone incense and a censer lay haphazardly on the table next to him.

Quinn climbed down from the buckets as quietly as he could, then bounded toward the gate. Aleksei pushed the bottom open for Quinn and he slipped out. He galloped toward Kai's SUV as fast as his three good legs could go. He heard Aleksei pounding along behind. Eoin opened the back door and Quinn leaped in, then shifted to human form.

"They aren't waiting," he panted. "Looks like they're getting ready for the ritual right now."

"Damn," Kai said.

Aleksei clambered into the middle row. "What is plan?" he asked.

"How many?" asked Kai.

"Three," answered Quinn. "That I saw, anyway."

"We are five," Aleksei said.

"We should probably count the sahir as two," Kai said.

"And the body guard," Quinn added.

"They probably aren't expecting any visitors," Eoin said. "We could just barge in. Surprise will be on our side."

"He's right. I doubt we'll be able to sneak in and get the bottle," Breena said. "Not if they're just about to perform the binding ritual."

"Right. Not much of a plan, but we're out of time. Let's go in there and see what happens," Kai said.

They started getting out of the SUV. Breena closed the door on Quinn. "You might want your clothes on first."

When they got to the warehouse gate, the padlock came off in Kai's hand as if it had never been locked. He opened the gate quietly. The other four slipped in, and he pulled the gate shut behind him. The heavy smell of incense leaked from the windows and hung stagnant in the moist air.

The warehouse had a drive-through passage, with garage doors on either end. On the end nearest the gate, a metal door opened into a small office, which opened into the warehouse. The opposite end of the warehouse had another metal door next to the garage door. Quinn and Eoin went to the far door, while Kai, Breena and Aleksei crept in through the office. They burst into the warehouse more or less simultaneously. The strawberry blond sat on a table, his legs dangling. The sahir sat in the middle of a twelve foot chalk circle. The emerald jar was in his lap.

"You're a little too late," said the man on the table. If he was surprised by their appearance, it didn't show.

The sahir chanted, getting gradually louder. Quinn could see the cone of energy, a swirling blue flame, surrounding the chalk circle. They would not be able to get inside it. The only way they could save Malik was to get the sahir to come out and break the circle.

"I thought you said there were three of them," Eoin said softly.

Quinn glanced around. "There were."

A wooden crate near the sahir burst into flames. Then another. Then the wooden table. It was good to have a firestarter on your team.

"Get out! This whole place is going to go up!" shouted the strawberry blond. "We'll do this later!" He got halfway towards the far door, and looked over his shoulder. The sahir had stood up and was pacing the circumference of the circle, chanting, oblivious to the intruders. The man shook his head. "You idiot! Come on," he shouted at the sahir.

Then he stopped, looked at Quinn and smiled. A bad kind of smile.

Quinn started to turn his head and glimpsed a blur of brown fur as the werewolf barreled through the door and sank its teeth into his shoulder. It had been aiming for his jugular, but he'd had a split second to move out of the way. He cried out as his collar bone splintered.

Without even thinking, he shifted into kelpie form. His long neck snaked around the werewolf and grabbed its leg. It yowled and let go of him, scratching and clawing at Quinn's body as he pulled it away from himself. He shook the werewolf like a rag doll and flung it into the flaming blue cone. The impact was enough to knock the sahir out of the circle. As soon as he crossed the chalk line, the blue flames vanished. Aleksei strode forward, snatched the emerald jar from him and pinned his arms. Breena took his ring and handed it to Kai. He set it on the concrete floor and stared at it. The ring started to melt.

"No! Stop! You cannot do this!" screamed the sahir. His face was white with terror.

An amorphous, boiling cloud began to form over the molten gold and the loose gemstone. Lightning flashed around it, and fountains of sparks erupted as the bolts of energy struck the metal framework of the warehouse.

"That would be one really pissed-off djinn. We need to go. Now," said Kai.

The far door banged shut. The strawberry blond man was gone.

Aleksei ran to help Eoin with Quinn, who had reverted to human shape.

"No!" Eoin shouted. "Get back. Did you not see that werewolf?" He hoisted Quinn onto his shoulders, and the five of them fled out the back door.

Frey was waiting for them at the gate. Aleksei opened the SUV's back door and Eoin pushed Quinn inside, then got in with him. Tires squealed as Frey took off, not waiting for Kai's door to close.

"I don't know how, but they knew we were coming," Kai blurted out. "They were expecting us."

"I see. Where to?" Frey asked.

"Can't take him to our place. Too much MAMIC traffic, and this mission was beyond unauthorized. Take him to his girlfriend's house," Kai said.

"She's not my girlfriend," Quinn replied weakly from the back.

Eoin pulled some paper towels off of the big roll in the cargo area and used them to help staunch the bleeding as he held Quinn's shoulder tightly. "What about Malik? Can you free him? We could do with his help."

Kai shook his head. "No. I don't know how far they got with the ritual. He might be compromised. If we let him out, he might kill us all."

Chapter 17
If Wishes Were Horses

 threw down the sword and fumbled with the lock, flipping the lever and jerking the door back along its track.

"No! Don't touch him! He's covered in blood," a dark-haired woman shouted at me as I lunged towards Quinn.

I felt that familiar helpless dread, like my soul was being sucked down a bathtub drain with the dirty water. Not again.

"What happened? Is he...?"

"Dead?" asked the woman. "No. Not yet, and not if I can help it."

She went out to the patio and started talking, apparently, to the zinnias in the pot on the bistro table. The man who had been carrying Quinn laid him down on my bed. That's when I noticed that only the top half of him was a man. The goat-legged bottom half was very disturbing.

I turned on the overhead light. Quinn looked bad. His eyes had rolled back in his head, so mostly white was showing. A huge bite mark marred his left shoulder and part of his neck. Many, less serious, cuts and bruises dotted his body. As I watched, he started to twitch and shiver.

"Hurry!" the redhead called to the woman.

"He's seizing!" I yelled.

The red haired man held onto my arm and prevented me from going to Quinn. "Don't touch him! Are you deaf, woman?"

I could have sworn that I saw a disembodied hand suddenly appear in front of the woman on the patio and pass her a two-handled cup. However she got it, she came in and drizzled some of the cobalt-colored liquid on Quinn's gaping shoulder wound. It hissed and smoked when it touched the bloody areas.

"I need a spoon for the smaller areas – more precision," she said, not looking at me.

Obediently, I trotted into the kitchen and retrieved both a regular spoon and a serving spoon. That wound on his shoulder was big.

When I got back, the redhead, the half-goat and the third man were holding Quinn down on the bed as he thrashed and moaned. His shredded clothes were lying in a pile by the door. The woman was trying to dress his wounds with the blue stuff, but he was doing his best not to let her. I'd seen scary grand mal seizures before, but this was worse. He snarled like a trapped animal and groaned as if he were in unbearable pain. I shut the door behind me, hoping to muffle the noise enough not to wake Cassie. I didn't need to contend with her as well.

"Here!" I said handing the woman the spoons.

"Good. You take the small spoon and put the medicine on any place you can find where the skin is broken. He won't like it. Don't let the liquid get on your skin. And whatever you do, don't touch his blood. Eoin's immune. You're not."

I would ask her what Eoin was immune to later. Now, I had work to do. I took the spoon from her and dipped it into the cup. My ER training made dabbing smelly stuff on a struggling body seem like second nature. While I was searching out punctures, I could feel Goatboy's eyes on me. It seemed that he wasn't just looking at me, but into me; peeling away the layers of myself, until he could see my bare soul. I didn't have time to worry about being uncomfortable.

The third man grumbled. "I don't understand why you wanted to bring him here. We should have just taken him to—"

The red-haired man shushed him and nodded towards me. "Aleksei. You know he can't go there if he's infected."

Infected? There it was again. Infected with what?

I looked at the third man, who was holding one of Quinn's legs. I knew he was there, but he seemed to fade into the background and I had to concentrate to notice him. His face was greyish-blue and elongated, and something about it made me think of gnarled, ancient trees.

The woman had finished with the big wound. To my surprise, it was already starting to close. She helped me medicate the last few scratches on his front and sides.

"Roll him on his side," she ordered the men holding Quinn.

Fortunately, there weren't many wounds on his back – we were almost out of the blue serum.

"Gotta get him out of this blood," the woman said. "It may be live."

Live?

The men lifted Quinn while she stripped off the sheets. There was one small spot where Quinn's blood had soaked through the pad and into the mattress.

"That mattress is going to have to go. Sorry," the redhead said.

They laid Quinn back down, as far away from the spot as possible. He had stopped struggling, and appeared to be asleep. I shook my head in disbelief. The enormous wound on his neck and shoulder was completely closed, covered by new, pink flesh. There was no sign of the other cuts and scratches.

The woman gasped. "Blood!" she shouted to the red-haired man.

A deep red streak stood out in shocking relief against his pale wrist. She grabbed the spoon from me and smeared the residue of the cobalt liquid on the blood. Then she did the same with the other spoon. The blood sizzled and smoked as it evaporated.

"That was close. Please tell me no one else is contaminated."

The four of them checked each other for blood spots, then the woman gave me a careful once-over. Everyone was clean.

I opened the cedar chest at the end of the bed and pulled out a cotton blanket. Careful not to touch him, I draped it over the unconscious Quinn.

The red-haired man took out his mobile phone and started sending a text.

"Okay," I said. "Can someone please tell me what is going on? What happened to Quinn?"

"Werewolf," said the woman. "Big nasty one, too."

I really hoped that it was the same one that had come to my door. I didn't want to think that there was a whole pack of them prowling around. "Did he kill it?" I asked, hopeful.

"Not sure," said the red-haired man. "There was a lot going on when we left."

I looked at Quinn. "Will he be all right?"

The red-haired man looked at the woman, and there seemed to be some unspoken communication between them, but it was nothing I could decipher.

"Maybe," she replied, glancing at me. "Werewolves are kind of like Komodo dragons. Except instead of lethal bacteria, their saliva contains parasites, which can infect the victim and turn him or her into a werewolf, too, if there is a sufficient load. That's why you can't touch his blood – it may be full of them. Eoin's an urisk – think Scottish satyr – and the parasites can't live in his blood. The rest of us are all susceptible, and humans are particularly vulnerable." She shook her head slightly and looked at Quinn. "We killed off as many as we could, but it's up to him, now. If his body can fight off the invaders, he'll be fine."

"And if it doesn't?" I was fairly sure I already knew the answer.

"He'll either die slowly and painfully, or the parasites will take him over and we'll have to kill him," Aleksei said quietly.

That seemed incredibly unfair. "Isn't there some kind of antibiotic or anthelmintic you can give him?"

"A dewormer? I wish there was," said the woman, with a sigh. "Sunlight helps some."

"Got no shortage of that," I replied. "Well, at least we won't in another couple of hours. How did Quinn get attacked by a werewolf?" Guilt was already gnawing at me. Had he taken on that monster to protect me? My eyes lingered on his face, so peaceful now. Please, please, please be okay.

"We were retrieving some stolen property," the redhead said, "and it ambushed us."

Stolen property? Could it be the bottle containing Malik, the djinn? Might be just what the doctor ordered.

"Were you able to get your stuff back?" I asked.

Another long look between him and the woman. "Yes," he said, with no elaboration.

"That's nice," I said. These folks don't give anything away, do they? I continued. "We haven't been introduced. I'm –"

"Marti Keller. We know. I am Mr. Underhill," he replied. One corner of his mouth quivered, as if an automatic smile was suddenly quashed.

Quinn moaned softly and his fingers twitched as if he were dreaming. I watched him carefully.

"You can go to him now, if you want," the woman said. "He's cleaned up, should be safe enough. For now, anyway."

I tried not to be too dismayed as I went and sat on the edge of the bed. I stroked his forearm and the back of his left hand. "Just because I said there was no such thing as werewolves, you didn't have to go and try to prove it. I believe you. You're going to be just fine. All you need is some rest."

I leaned over and kissed his forehead. "I'll see you soon."

I hadn't noticed Eoin and Aleksei leaving, but when I turned around, they were nowhere to be seen.

I got up and made my way to the dark-haired woman. "How long does it take? To know if he's going to become a werewolf?" I whispered.

"If he hasn't turned by Tuesday morning, he isn't going to," she replied.

"Tuesday? Today is Saturday. Where are you going to take him to recover? Can I come visit him?"

"Take him? He's too unstable to be moved."

The last thing in the world I needed was a werewolf incubating in my bedroom. But I couldn't just throw Quinn out and risk his recovery, either. Do I choose Scylla or Charybdis?

"Won't the werewolf come back to finish Quinn off? It knows where I live, and it knows Quinn has been staying here."

"Unlikely," Mr. Underhill answered. "For one thing, it was badly injured – I think Quinn broke one of its legs. For another, if our treatment doesn't work, either Quinn will die or he'll turn. If he turns, he'll seek out the alpha, the one who infected him. No real reason for the werewolf to come back. Besides, you've got a pretty good warding set up."

"Worst-case scenario: what happens? I have to know what to do to protect my child."

"In the worst-case scenario, there's really nothing you can do, other than to not be here. If he starts to turn and takes us out before we can neutralize him, he becomes a full-blown werewolf. If the parasites are able to harness his full kelpie strength, well, I don't fancy anyone's chances against him."

Fantastic. "On a slightly different subject, there was an event, with a sahir, on Monday night that Quinn was concerned about. Is that—"

"That situation is under control," Mr. Underhill said, cutting me off.

I seemed to mostly have traded one crisis for another, except that now I was back to square one on taking down Ian Chambers and his boss. The world might be safe from an evil dictator, but Nick and Quinn (and Ryan's reputation) were still in jeopardy. The more I thought about it, the more I knew what I had to do. I just hoped I hadn't missed my chance.

"I need to go to the restroom. If you'll excuse me?" I went into the bathroom and locked the door behind me, turned on the exhaust fan, then flipped down the lid and sat on the toilet.

"Delilah!" I thought as hard as I could.

"Girlfriend, what have you gotten yourself into now?" She stood directly in front of me, shaking her head.

I need your help. Can you find out which one of them has the bottle with the djinn?

"They can see and hear me, remember? Nothing I can do about that."

Damn.

"Since you wouldn't take my advice about the shifter, I know you ain't gonna take my advice about messin' around with djinn. But I'm gonna tell you anyway. Do not even go there. You think that shifter's friends are slippery. They ain't nothin' compared to a djinn. I know what you're thinking and you need to just forget about it."

But don't you see? It would fix all of the problems in one easy step.

"Baby girl, I got two words for you: unintended consequences. You think you're the first person to fool around with stuff like that? Ain't nobody, in the history of time, ever got what they thought they would."

What do you want me to do? Quinn may turn into a werewolf and be killed by his friends. Nick's career may be finished, and Ryan's reputation could be tarnished forever if I don't do something.

Delilah's eyes softened. "Marti, why do you think this is all on you? Nick's union lawyer will take care of him. When he's cleared, Ryan's cleared. There's not a thing you can do for that shifter. He'll either be okay or he won't. But it's not about you."

I never said it was. I can't just sit around and hope things will work out. I have to do something. It's the way I'm made.

Delilah shook her head. "Girl, I knew you were going to say that. Please let that djinn alone. And when you ride the black horse, don't trust its driver."

And poof! Delilah was gone.

Aaaarrrgh! Ghosts could be so annoying.

I flushed the toilet and washed my hands, just in case they were listening outside in the bedroom. If they had a djinn in a bottle, who was Quinn's friend, why didn't they just ask the djinn to heal him? There was probably some elaborate protocol, red tape and paperwork, I reasoned. At least that's what I hoped it was. But me, I had plausible deniability. I could just plead ignorance.

I brushed my teeth and splashed some water on my face. Man, I look rough. Still another hour before Cassie got up. I may as well have breakfast.

I did a very poor job of stifling a yawn as I went back into the bedroom. Quinn hadn't moved, but the woman was sitting on the cedar chest, and "Mr. Underhill" had his cell phone held up to one ear with his finger stuffed in the opposite one.

"I'm starved," I announced. "You guys want some breakfast?"

The woman hesitated. "Do you have any fresh fruit?"

"Always."

She followed me into the kitchen and rooted through the fruit bowl while I put the coffee on. I had hoped to get a chance to talk to her. But she washed the peach she had chosen, ate it over the sink and was gone before I could think up anything more or less intelligent to say. I am so not a morning person.

What am I going to do? I can't abandon my house to these strangers. I think they're trying to help Quinn, but I can't be certain. Quinn did say that someone might be trying to get revenge against him, so I suppose it's possible that this whole thing is a crazy conspiracy. But if they wanted revenge, it seemed weird they would have bothered patching him up. Besides, Delilah never said anything against them. And Quinn had said 'we' several times. I didn't think he meant the royal we, as in 'We are not amused.' What if Cassie and I left the house and Kyle and Aiden came to play with Bruce, but found a were-kelpie-wolf in his place? How would I explain that to Emily and Nick? 'I'm so sorry that your kids were eaten by a werewolf...' I had to keep Cassie safe. Not like I could leave her at Mom's for three days. I wanted to help Quinn, if I could, but I wasn't sure that any of my nursing skills translated into de-wolfing someone. And what about Nick and Ryan? How was I supposed to work on nailing Ian Chambers with a possibly mortally wounded Quinn lying on my bed and being watched over by people who just might have to kill him? And me, for that matter. All this made my head hurt. Maybe coffee would help.

I had propped my elbows on the table and cradled my chin in my hands, just to rest my eyes for a moment. I didn't realize I had fallen asleep until Cassie's wakeup alarm sounded. The coffee had thickened and scorched while I had been sleeping, filling the kitchen with a bitter reek. I unplugged the machine and went to get my little sweetie.

I stopped by my bedroom on the way, to check on Quinn. I suppose no news was good news.

Once Cassie was dressed and ready to come into the kitchen, I set her in the high chair. She dropped Cheerios on the floor and looked around expectantly. When Bruce didn't come, she cried.

"It's okay, baby," I said, stroking her short, wispy hair. I picked her up and carried her around the house. "Let's go for our walk, okay my dumpling?"

I knew it wasn't required, but I checked in with the dark-haired woman, whom I decided to start calling Morgaine (just not to her face).

"Ba ba ning!" Cassie exclaimed, flapping her hands.

The woman smiled, and Cassie grinned back at her.

"How's he doing?" I asked.

"No change," she replied, shaking her head gently.

"We're going out for our morning walk. Need anything from the corner market?"

Morgaine opened her mouth as if she were going to say something, then shut it again. "No, nothing, thanks. Have fun."

I was hoping the fresh air, make that dense, muggy air, would help me find a new perspective, to look at these multiple problems from a different angle. That, and the Tenth Sphere was on the way. Maybe Lulu would have some insight into demonic parasites.

I could hear the rumble of a big truck outside. Odd. It wasn't garbage day. I looked out the front window and saw a furniture delivery truck parked in front of my house. Two men were lowering the ramp.

"New mattress," Mr. Underhill said. "You didn't really want to keep the blood-soaked, parasite-infected one, did you?"

"Not when you put it that way."

"They'll also take all of the contaminated clothes, sheets and so on and dispose of them properly."

I nodded. I never expected to have a bio-hazard containment team in my house. Even if it had to be done, I didn't want to watch them take away the mattress from the bed I'd shared with Ryan. I grabbed Cassie and we hurried to the Tenth Sphere.

"So, honey," Lulu asked as soon as I walked in the door. "Have you thought any more about coming to work here at the shop?" She was dusting the Tibetan singing bowls.

"Yes. Yes, I'd love to do it. When do you want me to start?"

"How about Monday?" Lulu wiped down the counters with glass cleaner.

"How about Tuesday?" Morgaine said we would know one way or the other by then.

"Deal."

I sighed. The walk hadn't done diddly-squat for my perspective. If anybody could help, it would be Lulu. And I needed every ounce of help I could get. After all, she had accompanied me to tamper with a crime scene. If I couldn't trust her, I couldn't trust anybody. "So. How much do you know about werewolves? Delilah said the only thing that can hurt a werewolf is silver. Is that true? If so, will wearing a silver bracelet help?" I was trying my best to come up with ways to protect Cassie that wouldn't make me look like a tinfoil-hatter to the casual observer.

"They do seem to be allergic to it – blisters them on contact and it'll kill them if it gets in their bloodstream. Not sure how well a bracelet would work, but it couldn't hurt, I suppose. Is that werewolf still giving you trouble?" she asked. "Didn't the warding help?"

"It's not that. I wish that was it. It's Quinn. Well, you know him as Bruce, the dog. He's been attacked by a werewolf."

"Goddess help us!" Lulu exclaimed. "Well, honey, I did tell you not to take that dog home," Lulu said. "But anybody that is fighting werewolves can't be all bad." Then her eyes narrowed. "How do you know that's what happened? And I'm not even going to ask how you know his name is Quinn."

"They told me when they brought him to my house at 3:30 this morning."

"They who?" she shot back.

"A man that calls himself Mr. Underhill, a dark-haired woman, a goat man, and a guy that made me think of trees, if that makes sense."

Lulu dropped the duster. "Does this Mr. Underhill have red hair by any chance?"

I felt my jaw go limp. "How did you know that?"

I shifted Cassie to my other hip. She'd been gnawing on her fingers and drooling like a faucet. My left shoulder was soaking.

"If this Mr. Underhill is who and what I think he is, any anti-werewolf measures he's got are miles better than the best I could come up with. Excuse me, honey."

She left to help a customer choose a Tarot deck and some incense.

"Patchouli," she said when she came back.

I snorted. "Hmph. He going home to fire up a joint?" I snarked.

Lulu gave me such a look that I felt like I should run out to the parking lot to apologize to the man for something he didn't even hear me say.

"Patchouli is good for divination – it boosts clairvoyance. Fertility, too, if you must know."

"That's very nice," I snapped. I was pacing back and forth behind the cypress root chair and bouncing Cassie a little harder than I probably should have. "But I have to know: how could you possibly know Mr. Underhill?"

I puffed out my cheeks and exhaled my frustrations. Didn't help any. I shifted Cassie to my other hip. The air conditioning blowing right on my head and slimy shirt didn't make me feel any more cheerful.

"I don't know him," Lulu replied. "I know of him."

"And?"

Lulu shrugged. "He's fae. He and his group are about as much on our side as their kind are ever likely to be."

"What's that supposed to mean?"

The door jingled and a woman wearing a gauzy, flowing skirt in a floral print strolled in.

"Oh, dear," Lulu muttered just loud enough for me to hear. "Hold that thought, Marti." She cleared her throat and smiled rigidly as she went to greet the customer. "Virginia! What brings you to this side of town?"

"Lu! Love the shop. This is a great location for you."

She ran her fingers over the glass counter as she went by the cash register, passing Lulu and making her way deeper into the shop.

"Yes," Lulu said. "We're liking it a lot. Well, thanks for stopping by."

"Oh, my, my, my. I'm in no rush." She cast her eye around to the shelves nearest her. "I thought I'd have a look at your loose crystals."

Lulu never let the strained smile slip. "Of course you did." She turned to me and mouthed something. It looked like 'Go get Belinda,' so that's what I did.

I found her in the store room, organizing inventory.

"Hey, Belinda? Lulu asked me to come find you. Some woman named Virginia is up front."

Belinda' eyebrows arched into fearsome points and her nostrils flared. I was concerned for her blood pressure, the way her face darkened.

"Yeah, well, I think Cassie and I will be on our way now." I backed away from her. Whatever was going on with this Virginia person looked like way more than I was willing to get involved with right now.

I wished I could have hung around the shop and helped a little bit, but between Virginia (whoever she was) and trying to keep Cassie from making the acquaintance of any number of breakables, I was stretched too thin. It was time for Cassie's nap, anyway. We went back to the house. Wasn't sure how that was going to work when I reported for duty on Tuesday, but I supposed I would find out. If it was just half a day, two or three days a week, my mother might even be able to swing watching her. But how on Earth did Lulu know about Mr. Underhill? Stupid Virginia. She couldn't have waited five minutes to waltz through the door and mess everything up?

I hadn't intended to, but I surprised the alleged Mr. Underhill sitting at the kitchen table with the green bottle-o-djinn in his hands. He quickly stuffed it back into his left pocket. Now at least, I knew where it was. No idea how to get it, but I'd worry about that later.

Cassie struggled against sleep, but lost the battle. She would be giving up her morning nap soon, I guessed. Soon, but not yet.

I got a drink of water and went to my bedroom.

"How's the patient?" I asked Morgaine.

"He's stirring a little. Why don't you try and talk to him?"

She hovered in the doorway when I went to see Quinn. I couldn't tell who she was watching more closely, me or him.

I laid my hand on top if his. "Quinn? How are you feeling?"

His smile was weak and half-hearted. When he opened his eyes, I pulled back and gasped. I hadn't meant to.

Instead of near-black, his eyes were orange, and burned with fever.

"Is that supposed to happen?" I asked, glancing over my shoulder to the woman in the doorway.

"It's not a good sign," she answered. "But he isn't lost yet."

"Marti?" Quinn's voice was quiet, but it was a hoarse growl that turned my insides to ice.

"I'm here." I squeezed his hand harder.

"Sorry. Didn't. Get. Him." He rasped.

"It's okay," I said. "We'll get him later. You need to rest, and get yourself well."

His lips parted, as if he was going to say something else, but I put my finger against them. "You can tell me all about it later." The fact was, his rough new voice frightened me, and I refused to think about what it meant. He was losing the battle and I knew it. I'd seen the signs all too often in the ER.

I had to act now, before it was too late. If I didn't do something, and right now, Quinn was going to die. Or become a werewolf. Not sure which was worse.

"Be back in a minute," I told Morgaine on my way out.

Fortune smiled upon me. Mr. Underhill was headed down the hall towards me. I adjusted my pace so that I would pass him just at the open door of the half-bath.

I pretended to trip on the throw rug and fell into him. Instinctively, he reached up to catch me. I plunged my hand into his left pocket and felt the emerald jar, cold and sharp-edged. He must have felt me pulling it out. He tried to grab me, but I twisted away and ducked into the powder room, slamming the door behind me and slapping the bolt latch closed. The door was an old-fashioned solid wood one, not the flimsy hollow core ones that most people have inside their houses. Still, I knew the latch wouldn't keep him out for long. But hopefully, it would be long enough. I wedged the laundry hamper under the doorknob for good measure.

I hadn't really thought through what I was going to do when I got my hands on the emerald bottle, so I was going to have to wing it.

"I claim this bottle," I said. "And the djinn within," I added for emphasis.

"Open the door, Marti!" Mr. Underhill shouted. "You don't know what you're doing."

"No! I know exactly how to fix everything. Go away!"

My hands were shaking from adrenalin and my heart pounded. I almost dropped the bottle on the tile when I tapped it with my fingernail. I wasn't sure how to get Malik's attention, and that seemed like a good idea.

Out of the corner of my eye, I saw the door's bolt latch sliding open. I grabbed the little knob on top and slammed it closed. I leaned on the hamper and door and didn't dare let go of the latch. Whatever Mr. Underhill was using on the other side to pull the latch back was strong and I struggled to hold it in place. I wasn't sure if the laundry hamper was hurting or helping at this point.

I addressed the bottle. "I have a deal for you. One wish for your freedom."

I twisted the cork top out of the mouth of the jar. I expected smoke to pour out and turn into someone who looked more or less like Mr. Clean.

Nothing seemed to happen. I had to drop the bottle onto the rug and hold the latch with both hands now.

"Don't let him out!" shouted Mr. Underhill. "Open the door!"

"Well? Aren't you going to answer him?" asked a deep voice.

I looked over my shoulder to see a man in a wool sport coat standing between the toilet and the sink. His pale lavender silk tie was impeccably knotted and held in place by a diamond tie-tack. A carefully shaped and closely trimmed beard hugged his chin and jaws. The only thing that prevented him from looking like he'd just stepped out of a Fortune 500 shareholders' meeting was his weirdly green eyes. They were absolutely the wrong shade for eyes – pale and metallic – and it seemed to me that there was a cold fire raging behind them.

Mr. Underhill pounded on the door. "Marti? What have you done?"

My fingers ached from holding the tiny knob on the latch. I knew it was only moments before my grip failed. I leaned against it even harder.

"A trade," I said to the djinn. "One wish for your freedom."

"A single wish? Nothing more than that?" he replied.

"Marti! Stop!" pleaded Mr. Underhill from behind the door.

"I wish I was back to the day before Ryan died."

The room began to spin. I threw out my arms for balance. I felt the powder room door opening and pushing against my body as I faded away.

I heard Mr. Underhill shout, from what sounded like a very great distance away, "Malik! She doesn't know what she's doing. Give her an out!"

"Oh, very well," the djinn grumbled. "You have chosen to change history and create an alternate timeline. I cannot prevent you from forgetting this version of reality, but I can slow it. You have thirty-six hours before your memories of this timeline are completely erased. You can change your mind until then."

And I was utterly alone in the dark.

Chapter 18
Horses for Courses

opened and closed my eyes. Made no difference. The blackness was absolute. Then I started to fall. I flailed my arms and kicked my legs, searching for a non-existent solid something to grab onto. I tried to scream, but nothing would come out of my mouth.

I landed hard on my back and gasped for air. I was cold and felt mildly claustrophobic, almost like I was trapped in goo in a small space.

I smelled something spicy and familiar. My eyes flew open.

I was lying in my own bed. The bathroom door was ajar, and Ryan was just finishing up shaving, wearing nothing but his boxer-briefs, as usual. And what a delicious sight that was. He hummed to himself as he stretched his lips and chin for the razor. I almost laughed out loud. I knew he'd think I was having some kind of episode if I ran in there and hugged him, so I stayed under the covers, basking in my secret good fortune.

It was still dark, and he didn't have to be at work until eight. He usually went to the gym first, unless I could persuade him to skip it. But that wasn't going to happen today. I felt queasy and I was over a week late. I would wait until after Ryan left to take the test, just in case I was wrong. But I knew I wasn't. Still, I'd need something to show Ryan – he'd want proof. I thought of Cassie and smiled.

Everything was put back to where it should have been. Ryan was alive, and I'd tell him about the baby before he left for work. Not sure how I'd stop him from pulling over that car tomorrow, but I'd come up with something – I had to. It was now almost two years before Quinn would encounter the werewolf, and if Ryan didn't die, and Ian Chambers had no reason to come to my house, perhaps Quinn and the werewolf would never even meet, and he'd be safe. Maybe I'd even changed things enough that Malik would never be imprisoned in the emerald jar. I could hope, anyway. I could expose Ian Chambers before he had the opportunity to frame Ryan and Nick, and they'd be safe. But most important, I had Ryan back and Cassie would have a chance to grow up knowing her daddy. It was an all-around win.

Ryan stepped out of the bathroom and pulled a t-shirt and sweats out of the dresser. He was half dressed before he noticed me watching him.

"Hey, Bright Eyes."

"Hey, yourself." That was it. I couldn't lie there and not touch him. I peeled back the warm covers and swung my legs out of bed. And lay back down. There wasn't anything in my stomach, but damned if it wasn't trying to come up anyway.

"You okay?" Ryan asked, concerned.

"Yeah. Just got up too fast, that's all," I fibbed.

Ryan scowled. "I hope you're not getting that flu that's been going around."

"I'm sure it's not the flu. I'm fine. Actually, I think it's something else. Something very, very different." I stood up and took the few steps I needed to join him by the dresser.

He wrapped his arms around me, and started to kiss me. But I wouldn't let him. I hadn't brushed my teeth yet. I nestled my head against his shoulder, savoring the feel of his body, the smell of his aftershave, the beating of his heart. If I got any happier I would explode. Now was my big chance to tell him.

The first heave wasn't too strong, and was easy to stifle. But I knew the next one wouldn't be. I pulled away from Ryan, more slowly than I needed to, but faster than I wanted to.

"Bathroom," I said, smiling at him.

He nodded and went back to getting dressed.

Behind the closed bathroom door, I tried drinking some water. But the sound of the running faucet made me really have to pee. I tore open the pregnancy test I'd stashed under the towels in the étagère above the toilet. I held up the tiny plastic cup. Seriously? But I had to go – it was that or nothing.

Drinking the water had been a bad idea. Now there was something to heave up. I knew I had fifteen weeks of vomiting to look forward to. Or was it twelve? Details were starting to get a little fuzzy already. I supposed that was a good thing.

I completed the test and set it on the floor beside the toilet to let it develop while I brushed my teeth so I could give Ryan a proper send off.

"Ryan?"

No answer. He can't have left already. I haven't told him!

I ran into the kitchen and looked out the back door window. His car was just pulling onto the street. No! I'd never stop him now. I had no choice but to wait until tonight. I could call him, I supposed, but this was the kind of news that ought to be told in person. I sighed and told myself that regardless of what happened tomorrow, he'd still know about the baby.

I went back to the bathroom. The second line had appeared, as I knew it would. I left it on the vanity where Ryan could see it when he came home. Today, I was working the two-to-ten shift, and he'd be home first. The last time, I'd kept it hidden. But now that I had another shot at it, I wasn't going to blow it. I missed holding Cassie, but I knew she was in the safest place she could possibly be. In another eight months or so, both Ryan and I would have the chance to hold her.

I walked around my house, touching the curtains, straightening the picture frames, like I had just moved in. I reveled in my second chance – I was the cat who got the cream. Before I knew it, it was time for lunch.

Lunch…Officer down at 12:55. That was it! I'd get Ryan to have lunch with me tomorrow. That's what would stop him from pulling over that car – he would be safe and sound in a restaurant. I didn't know what Mr. Underhill had been so upset about. This was a piece of cake.

My shift in the ER was busy, as usual. The only thing that stood out was just before I was scheduled to go off duty, a couple brought in a six year-old boy. He was a beautiful child, with enormous hazel-brown eyes and milk chocolate brown hair. And a broken arm. The mother was frantic. I recognized the father. I knew him from somewhere, but I just couldn't place him. 'Spam,' the mother had called him. I couldn't think of a reason why I would know Spam, but I was sure that I did. Something bad had happened to him. He didn't seem to know me, though, and he even got edgy with me at one point. Could Ryan have arrested him? Maybe, but how would I know about it?

"Take a picture chica; it'll last longer," he snapped at me.

"I'm sorry. I was sure I knew you from somewhere. Must be mistaken."

Maybe he was from the other reality, the bad reality that was fading away. It couldn't fade fast enough for me.

Ryan met me at the door when I got home.

"Is that what I think it is in the bathroom?"

I grinned at him.

And then we celebrated. Right there in the middle of the living room floor.

After we migrated into the bed, I snuggled against Ryan, and he draped a territorial leg over mine. He fell asleep almost immediately. It was early December, and the Christmas lights across the street bled in around the edges of the mini-blinds, blinking and flashing. I blamed them for keeping me awake, but, if I were really honest with myself, I'd have to admit that I was afraid if I went to sleep, I'd wake up and Ryan would be dead again.

So, I tried to organize my life. Had I done any shopping? I'd check my closet in the morning. That's where I hid everything. Maybe stepping into my life exactly where I'd left off almost two years ago wasn't quite as easy as I thought, but it sure beat the alternative.

The sound of Ryan's slow, deep breathing was starting to lull me to sleep. My eyelids were now so heavy I couldn't keep them open.

A sharp rap pierced the cozy quiet of the room.

My eyes flew open like cartoon window shades. The noise had come from the wall above the headboard, on Ryan's side.

At first, I couldn't see anything, but as I stared into the darkness, a pale mist seemed to be floating next to the bed. Or it could have been my imagination. Then, I remembered.

"Darla!" I whispered as loudly as I thought I could without waking Ryan.

"Darla? Girlfriend, that is messed up. Delilah. My name is Delilah. And you're talking out loud, again."

"Oh. Right. Why are you here?" I asked. I hadn't learned to see her until after Ryan died.

"I'm always around, Marti-girl. Even if you don't see me. I'm trying to help you. You need to undo this wish."

You are out of your mind. No way in hell I would change this. I've got Ryan back, and there are some other things I'm sure I fixed. I will not un-wish.

I could only see a faint mist, but I imagined that Delilah shook her head, and I could hear the sigh in her words. "Remember that I warned you."

The mist faded away, and I slipped into an uneasy sleep.

Nick and Ryan met me at 12:39 at the IHOP. It was too soon to tell Nick our good news, but he could tell we were hiding something. I have no doubt he guessed at what it was, especially given my sudden and obvious aversion to food. I was equally sure that Nick would wheedle it out of Ryan. That was okay. I'd already told Emily, but sworn her to secrecy.

I didn't pay very much attention to the conversation – my attention was on the green plastic clock on the far wall. 12:50. I squirmed in my seat.

"Do you need to get out so you can go to the ladies room?" Ryan asked.

"No, I'm fine."

12:55 came and went with no fanfare. I knew it was an important milestone. And that it had something to do with Ryan, but I couldn't quite remember what. Only that it was good that it had passed.

Outside of the IHOP, a man stood on the sidewalk in the parking lot. He wore a sandwich board made from two ragged pieces of cardboard. The message scrawled on the front with a ball point pen read, "The end is near! Repent, sinners!" and on the back, it read "World ends December 18! Believe it!" He flapped a handful of photocopied, handwritten fliers at anyone who didn't walk across the parking lot to avoid him.

"Are you saved?" the man shouted at Ryan.

"Sorry, sir. You're going to have to move along. You're trespassing," he replied.

The man handed Ryan a flyer, which he folded and put in his pocket. I guessed he did that just to be polite. That, and there was no trash can around.

"Fine, fine. The truth is too much for these wretched sinners to handle, anyway," the man grumbled as he started to shamble away.

He paused to look at me when he passed by. His eyes were dark, almost black, and they were clear and bright. Not the vacant eyes of the addict or the intense eyes of the psychopath. The dirt on his face looked cosmetic, not the ingrained grime of the long-term homeless. In fact, he smelled more like evergreens and rain than unwashed masses. I was horrified that his scent made my heart skip a beat. I glanced at Ryan and Nick, but their expressions gave nothing away.

The preacher took off his sandwich board and tossed it to the sidewalk.

"Hey! Pick that up. You're littering," Nick called after him.

The man waved one arm, as if he were swatting at Nick, and kept walking.

"That's it. We're going to have to run you in," Ryan said.

"Do what you've got to do," he replied.

Ryan cuffed the preacher and put him in the car while Nick put his makeshift sign and flyers in the trash.

Idiot. It was almost like he wanted to get arrested.

Thoughts of the incongruous street preacher niggled at me as I drove to work. And Delilah's warning from last night didn't help, either. I hadn't even clocked in when Ryan called on my mobile.

"Hey! What's up?" I asked.

"Marti," his voice was soft, and I was suddenly afraid. "Your mom was out shopping with Emily and the boys. Some guys ran a red light and hit her car. Adele and Kyle are okay, just bumps and bruises. Aiden's been Life-Flighted to Hermann hospital."

"Oh, God." How could this happen to a four-year old boy? It wasn't fair. It took me a second to count heads. "Emily. You didn't say anything about her."

"I am so sorry."

"No. My sister is not dead. She wouldn't leave her boys right before Christmas. You're wrong." It couldn't be true if I refused to believe it, right?

Ryan didn't argue with me. "I just dropped Nick off at the hospital. I'm on my way to pick you up. Be there in about twenty. I love you."

My hands shook so hard that it took three tries to get my phone back into my handbag and I could barely see through tear-blurred eyes.

Mom and Dad had taken Kyle out to feed the ducks and get something to eat. Ryan and I sat with Nick, who looked more like a wax figure of Nick than the actual person. I had to look closely to see if he was breathing. I was still waiting for Emily to come around the corner and say, "Ha ha! Fooled you!"

It was almost 5:00 when Aiden came out of surgery. Both his legs were broken, he had a ruptured spleen, and a fractured skull. Even though he had taken off his surgical scrubs, the doctor's scent was a sour cocktail of latex, iodine and sweat, and he looked exhausted.

"Aiden had a subarachnoid hemorrhage. We had to perform a craniotomy, that's cutting a hole in his skull, to relieve the pressure and stop the bleeding. If he makes it through the night, there's a reasonable chance he might pull through. We've put him in a drug-induced coma to help the swelling go down and give the brain a better chance to recover. You need to know that both cognitive and physical disabilities are common with this kind of injury."

As soon as he had said 'subarachnoid hemorrhage,' I knew it was bad. Really bad.

Smart-ass, swaggering Nick stared blankly at the doctor. I'd never seen him like that, and it broke my heart.

"Can we see him?" Ryan asked.

"In about half an hour, you can go to the ICU."

I couldn't look at Nick, and I felt too guilty to cling to Ryan while Nick was sitting there all alone, so I stood up and looked out the small window in the waiting area. Winter dark was already descending, and the city was on the night side of twilight.

Somehow, this was my fault. I wasn't sure how it could be, but I knew it was. Not the first time I'd wished for a CTRL-ALT-DEL in real life. My stomach was a little crampy, but I figured that was because I'd eaten six saltines and half of a pancake all day. I left the waiting area to find a drink of water, but it didn't help much.

Ryan had followed me out into the hall.

"So," I said. "Did they at least get the person who did this?"

"Yes and no. Adele was westbound on Memorial and there was a Metro bus headed east. The southbound SUV hit your mom's car, pushing it across three lanes of traffic. The bus T-boned them immediately after."

"Them?"

"Two men, we think. Car was registered to Friar Enterprises. But it's going to take some time to identify the occupants."

I cringed. Enough details. Back in the waiting area, a woman in scrubs was talking to Nick. I wasn't sure if she was a nurse or a doctor, but she had come to take us to Aiden.

We stumbled like zombies to the ICU. I got a Snickers bar from the vending machine on the way. My hands were starting to shake, and the cramps were getting worse. Even so, I couldn't bring myself to eat the candy bar.

Aiden was dwarfed by the machinery that surrounded him. Tubes stuck out of his head and his throat and his arms. Drain tubes, trach tube, IVs. He was so pale. EKG and EEG readouts scrolled along above his head. The respirator clicked and hissed. I was too numb to cry. This couldn't be happening.

But my day wasn't bad enough.

The cramps I'd been having suddenly got worse. A whole lot worse. It felt like my entire midsection was being crushed in a vise. I hadn't meant to cry out as I doubled over and hit the floor. I must have peed myself, because something hot and wet was running down my leg.

I stayed curled in a fetal position on the floor. I could hear Ryan swearing (he never did that) and rubber-soled shoes scurrying around the room. Then the clatter of a gurney, and hands lifting me up.

I heard someone moaning and groaning as they wheeled me down the corridor. I wondered if it was me. I found the smell of hospital disinfectant oddly comforting.

"Was she pregnant?" a female voice asked.

Was? What do you mean was? Is. Was is past tense. I am pregnant.

"Yes." Ryan's voice was hoarse.

Another wave of mega-cramps hit me. I was sure I heard the word 'miscarriage' floating in the air above my head.

NO. No. No. No. No. I am not losing my baby, too.

Too much. Too much tragedy for one day. I didn't think I could survive it. I tried to say something, but the only thing that came out was a whimper.

"Is there supposed to be that much blood?" Ryan asked. His voice was edged with panic.

I didn't hear what the woman said because someone was whispering in my ear. "Marti? You're almost out of time, girlfriend. If you're gonna un-wish this, you better do it quick."

Un-wish? I could almost remember something about making a wish, but it skirted the edges of my memory.

"You can go back to where you were before you made the wish. Ryan is dead, but your baby, her name is Cassie, is alive, and Emily and Aiden are fine. Or you can stay here."

Cassie? The baby's a girl? I'd always wanted a little girl, but I'm not sure I would have named her Cassie.

If Ryan was alive, I could probably have another baby. Wouldn't be this baby, but lots of women had miscarriages and went on to have healthy babies. Happened every day. The ER docs always said most early miscarriages were due to chromosomal abnormalities.

If my choice was to sacrifice Ryan for an unviable baby, there was no contest.

But it wouldn't bring back Emily. I'd lose my sister, Mom and Dad would lose their daughter, Nick would lose his wife, and Kyle would lose his mommy.

I thought of Aiden, lying in the ICU, so small and so very fragile. A medically-induced coma was a Hail Mary, a last resort. Something they did when there was nothing left to lose. He was only four.

And I did this to them. I knew it in my bones, even if I couldn't figure out how.

Why do I have to choose? Ryan or my baby, my sister, and my nephew. That's so unfair.

"Sorry, girlfriend. I don't make the rules."

My baby, though. Carrie?

"Cassie."

She's healthy? Nothing wrong with her? And Emily and Aiden are fine?

"Yes. She's beautiful. You have to choose now."

Dammit. Dammit. Dammit. I knew, if I were able to ask Ryan to choose, what his choice would be. Why? Why did this life have to be so damned hard?

I opened my eyes and looked up at Ryan. I needed to see his face. I squeezed his hand. My throat was so tight with misery and pain that I could barely get the words out. "I love you," I wheezed.

And then, I un-wished.

I fell up, spinning away into the night sky. The stars glittered coldly, so bright and so close. I felt nothing, no fear, no pain, no joy. I was just...aware. Galaxies spun. Stars died and were born. I watched it all and I didn't know if I was there for a millisecond or a millennium before I started to fall back down.

Faster and faster I went, feeling as if the breath was being pushed out of me, and there was too much pressure to let my lungs expand and take in more. Fear gripped my innards with icy fingers and sharp claws. Just when I thought I must surely implode, everything stopped. I gasped for air and opened my eyes.

Chapter 19
Down to the Sea in Ships

I sprawled in the middle of the powder room floor, the fallen laundry hamper on one of my legs. Mr. Underhill bent over me and snatched the emerald bottle and its stopper out of my hands.

"What did you do?" he asked.

"I didn't do anything. There was nothing in the bottle," I snapped at him. Still, I wondered why my cheeks were wet with tears and my abdomen felt like the Jolly Green Giant had squeezed me nearly in half.

He frowned. "What did you think would be in it?"

I took a deep breath and let it out. No reason to keep it a secret anymore. "Quinn told me that his friend, Malik the djinn, was trapped in a bottle made from an emerald. When you said that you had gotten what you were looking for, I assumed it was Malik. I thought I could save everybody if I wished myself back to the day before Ryan died. He wouldn't get killed, Quinn wouldn't have to fight the werewolf, and Ian Chambers would have no reason to frame Ryan and Nick. But the bottle was empty. Nothing happened." I didn't know whether to be angrier with myself, for believing in some stupid fairy tale genie, or Mr. Underhill, for treating me like a naughty child. Or the fact the whole crazy plan didn't work.

"What is the last thing you remember?"

Oh, for Pete's sake. "You pounding on the door and yelling at me."

What could have possibly happened in the nanosecond between me opening the bottle and him crashing through the door?

I picked myself up off the fuzzy rug and pushed my way past Mr. Underhill, shoulders back and chin up, trying to salvage the remaining shreds of my dignity. All the noise had woken Cassie up, and I had to go to her.

I sat her in her high chair with a sippy cup and veggie puffs while I cut up grapes for her. She didn't throw anything on the floor for Bruce to eat, and that made me a little sad.

Something shiny caught my eye. The anti-shifter amulet was still on the table where Quinn had left it. Once Cassie was done eating and wiped down, I took the amulet into my bedroom and gave it to the dark-haired woman.

"I don't know if this will help. It's an anti-shifting amulet. Quinn says there's a dragon bound to it."

She shrugged. "Maybe. Werewolves are unnatural shifters, so the type of magic in the amulet doesn't sync with theirs. But then again, dragons are powerful healers. Can't hurt to try."

I could tell by her expression that she didn't think it would do much good, but she hung it around Quinn's neck, anyway.

He immediately started groaning and writhing. The strange characters on the amulet glowed pale blue. His eyes darkened from bright orange to amber.

"That's good, right?" I asked.

"Not sure," she replied.

The noises Quinn was making frightened Cassie, so I had to take her out of the room. In fact, the walls were closing in on me and I really needed to get out of the house.

Mr. Underhill sat in the living room, messing with his phone.

Fae, huh? And all this time, I thought fairies were tiny little women in skimpy dresses with sparkly butterfly wings. And just what is it, Mr. Underhill, that you do that makes you so locally well known that even Lulu has heard of you?

"I'm low on diapers, so I'm going to get a few things from the store. Need anything?" I asked him.

He didn't look up. "No, thanks."

The HEB grocery store was about three miles from my house. Kroger was closer, but I had HEB diaper coupons. We were a little over halfway there when the giant primer grey and red Suburban on my left decided to change lanes. Unfortunately, he didn't bother checking to see if the lane was occupied.

There wasn't a lot I could do to avoid him. I laid on the horn and ran up on the curb. He still sideswiped my fender before he took off, tires squealing. His windows were tinted too dark for me to get a look at the driver and I couldn't see his license plate – there was an over-sized spare tire bolted to the back. Cassie and I were shaken up, but unhurt.

As I was getting her out of the car, a metallic blue convertible Ferrari pulled up in front of us and the driver got out, "Hey Miss! You okay? I saw what happened."

"Thanks for stopping," I said. Where did I know this guy from?

"No problem." He handed me a business card. 'Tucker Fellowes, Attorney at Law Board Certified Estate Planning and Probate.' An address and phone numbers followed. "If you need a witness, just give me a call."

"I appreciate that. I was just calling my insurance."

The fender could have been worse, but the front tire on the passenger side was flat, and I was afraid the axle was bent. Great. Just what I needed.

I thought it was a little odd that Tucker Fellowes waited around while I talked to my agent. She was sending a tow truck. I used my phone to take photos of the damage and email them to her, as well as Tucker Fellowes' contact information. Then it suddenly occurred to me where I had seen him.

"You know Stella and Pudge? I'm sure I saw you at their party last Saturday."

A broad grin spread across his face. I wouldn't say he was handsome, but his features were well chiseled, and if anything, he was over-groomed. Clear nail polish on men really didn't work for me, though. "Yes, I was there. Sorry that we didn't meet at the party."

He said this while staring at my chest, and I found that I wasn't particularly sorry we hadn't been introduced.

"Excuse me for a minute, okay?" I said.

I tried to call Nick to see if he could come and get Cassie and me, but I couldn't get a signal. Of all the times for my cell to crap out. It had been working fine a few minutes ago.

Flashing yellow lights at the next traffic signal made me feel better. The wrecker driver would be here in a minute.

"You Marti Keller?" the driver asked when he got out of the tow truck. The name Earl was embroidered on his blue uniform shirt.

"Yes, I am,"

Earl handed me a card from the towing company. "Let's get 'em hooked up here." He spat tobacco juice on the sidewalk and then walked around my car.

Tucker Fellowes even helped Earl get the car lined up to pull it onto the flatbed truck. Once it was secured, I thought Cassie and I would ride to the dealership with him. If my phone didn't work there, at least they'd have a landline I could use.

But there was a problem.

There was enough room in the cab for Cassie or me, but not both.

"Can I just hold the baby in my lap?" I asked the driver.

"No ma'am. Can't do that. Insurance won't let me."

"Can I give you a lift somewhere?" Fellowes asked.

I weighed my options. Walk about two miles with a twenty-three pound baby in a carrier - a squirmy twenty-three pound baby who did not want to be in the carrier – or get into a sports car that cost about three times more than my house with a board certified probate attorney who freely gave his name and contact info to my insurance agent. Fellowes might be a creep, but I didn't think he was dangerous.

"Will the baby carrier fit in the back of your car?" I asked. There was that out again.

"Are you kidding? A baby is about all that will fit in that back seat," Fellowes said with a chuckle.

Even with the top down, it took a lot of contortion and awkwardness, but I got the baby bucket strapped into one of the miniscule back seats. I wasn't convinced that the two seats in the back were intended for anything other than decoration. Or maybe for chauffeuring Pomeranians around.

The front seat, on the other hand, reeked of luxury. Leather seats, satellite navigation, back-up camera. All very high tech and very expensive. If I won the Lotto, I don't think I'd buy a car like this, but I didn't object to going for a ride in it.

My plan was to have Fellowes drop me off at the Tenth Sphere. Close enough to easily walk home, and he wouldn't know exactly where my house was. I gave him directions.

We were on surface streets, but the top was down and the engine was loud. Sometimes it was hard to understand him, and I had to shout to make myself heard.

"What are you doing, chica?"

I could see him hunched in the back seat, next to Cassie. Getting a ride home, Spam. What did you expect me to do, hitchhike? With a baby? Where have you been, anyway?

"How do you know Stella and Pudge?" Fellowes asked.

"Stuff to do, people to see," Spam replied.

Having two completely separate conversations with two different people is a lot harder than it looks. I turned to Fellowes. "I don't exactly know them. I was there working with Lulu, the Tarot card reader."

Glancing up into the rearview mirror, I thought at Spam. What are you doing here?

"I remember there were entertainers there. How long have you been in the business?" Fellowes asked.

"'Bout a week," I answered, trying to look calm, cool and collected.

"Why'd you get in the car with this pendejo? What were you thinking?"

What am I supposed to think, Spam? I was getting more irritated with him by the second. If he wanted to tell me something, why couldn't he just come out and say it?

Fellowes continued through the light.

"Um, you missed the turn. You should have made a left there."

"Oh, did I? Sorry." But he kept driving.

"Told you," Spam chirped.

If you aren't going to help, go get someone who will, like maybe Delilah?

"Okay. This has gone far enough. Just pull over and let us out." I tried to sound calm, but my voice was scratchy and cracked from all the shouting.

"Can't do that, Marti. You decided to stick your nose in my business, so now you're going to get to experience it first-hand," Fellowes said, with a rancid smile.

I did not like the sound of that. "I thought you were a probate attorney. What are you going to do? Force me to read wills?" If I sounded flippant, maybe he wouldn't realize how scared I was.

"You're a funny lady, Marti. My estate planning practice is just the entrée, gets my foot in the door. Helps me find clients for my real business," Fellowes replied.

"And what would that be?" It had only just occurred to me the Ferrari logo was a black horse on a yellow background. "When you ride the black horse, don't trust its driver," Delilah had said. Crap.

"Haven't you guessed by now?" Fellowes asked, his tone implying I was stupid.

No, I haven't guessed what the business is, but I bet I know one of the employees. "Would Ian Chambers know?"

More laughter. "We'll be seeing him later. Why don't you ask him then? But out of the goodness of my heart, I'll give you a hint: Cynthia Ashland, since I know you've been doing some research. You have been to my website, after all."

Cynthia Ashland? The name seemed familiar, but I struggled to recall where I'd seen it. I mentally back tracked through the websites I'd been researching. Which one was Tucker Fellowes'?

"He owns Specials," Spam said.

You could have mentioned that earlier, Spam.

"No, I couldn't have. You have to be here. Sorry."

I looked at the back seat in the rear view mirror. Spam was fading away, and Cassie was getting glassy-eyed. There was no way I could jump out of the car without leaving my little girl behind.

At the next red light, a couple of homeless men were going from car to car with a paper cup.

"Help me!" I shouted at them. "Call the cops!"

Tucker Fellowes laughed. "You do realize you're asking junkies to call the police?"

I casually put my hand in my shorts pocket, where my cell phone was. Surely I'd get a signal by now. That dead spot had to have been a fluke. I ran my fingers over keys, trying to remember where the numbers started and the special characters ended. I hoped I was dialing 911.

Tucker Fellowes just smiled.

Nothing happened, so I tried again. Still nothing. Damn.

Then I suddenly remembered where I'd heard of Cynthia Ashland. She was the executive director of Friar Enterprises, LLC. Which owned Specials and a range of titty bars. Must be a front for Fellowes. That explained why Friar Enterprises only needed an executive suite – it was just a puppet theater. It also wasn't too hard to guess what types of services Friar Enterprises might be providing. So Tucker Fellowes wanted me to experience his business first-hand, and he was a pimp. I shuddered.

When we got to the Beltway, we headed south. I had tried calling 911 twelve times now.

I looked back at Cassie. She was falling asleep. Car rides did that to her. "Where are we going?" I asked.

"Boat ride." Fellowes answered. "And just an FYI – I turned on the cell phone jammer, so you can give up trying to call anyone. Might save yourself a lot of effort and frustration. I let you call the insurance agent and tow truck to get your car off the road so it wouldn't be attracting any unwanted attention. Your mother has already gotten a text saying that you and the baby are visiting a friend in Austin over the weekend. By the time anyone misses you, you'll be long gone."

I swallowed against the metallic taste of adrenalin and tried to force myself to breathe deeply. If I did that, my heart might stop thumping against my ribs like a caged animal. "Gone where?" I tried to sound casual. But my voice split the difference between 'terrified' and 'casual' and came out 'concerned.'

"Probably Asia, but we'll have to bleach your hair – they prefer blondes. Don't look so worried. You're way too old to go to Bangkok. I expect you'll go to a private collection. In fact, I've already contacted several likely interested parties. One of them likes to make snuff films, but I don't think he will be able to afford what I'm asking for you."

Knowing Fellowes was trying to intimidate me, I closed my eyes. I'd only caught a glimpse of Quinn in kelpie form on the night of the werewolf attack, so I substituted a mosasaur. I pictured it snapping up Tucker Fellowes in its huge jaws and swallowing him, screaming for his mama, in one gulp. There. You're not so tough.

Then I had another thought. I was afraid of the answer, but I had to ask. "What about Cassie?"

"The baby? She's not old enough to sell on to Bangkok." He smiled a greasy smile at me, knowing that wasn't at all what I meant. "If you cooperate, I won't hurt her. I could have her left at a hospital or fire station, with her name pinned on her shirt and everything. Your mother would get her back eventually. But only if you do exactly what I tell you."

That didn't make me feel a whole lot better.

I knew it was grasping at straws, but I had nothing else to grasp at. I may not be able to transmit anything from my phone, but I could record. It was a long shot, but I couldn't think of anything else. I fumbled with the buttons.

"So. Just out of curiosity. Why did you have Spam killed, Fellowes?"

"Spam? You run in interesting social circles, Ms. Keller. Yes, I was disappointed that they were able to find and identify him so quickly. But then you wouldn't know anything about that, would you?" He paused for me to answer, but continued when I said nothing. "Spam was a long time employee. He was good at doing odd jobs and procurement. It's a real shame he started to develop a conscience and began questioning some of my business practices. It was only a matter of time before he started running his mouth to the wrong people."

Spam did like to run his mouth. "What kind of procurement?"

"Well, well. Aren't you full of questions?" Fellowes downshifted and took the I-45 exit off the Beltway. "Do you have any idea how expensive law school is? Neither did I, until I enrolled. I cooked meth to pay my way. Spam smurfed for me. Yep. If there was something you needed, Spam could get it."

"I'm sure he could." I shifted in my seat, feeling more sickened by Fellowes by the second.

"Estate planning and probate didn't pay nearly as much as I thought it would, so I had to branch out, add goods and services to my line of offerings."

"You disgust me."

"You'll have plenty of practice being disgusted once I've received payment and shipped you to the buyer."

If I didn't think it would make him crash the car and possibly hurt Cassie, I would have slapped his smarmy face. I pushed the button on the phone again, ending the recording. I didn't want to talk to Fellowes any more. Right now, I was too angry to be scared. But I knew that would change.

When we got to the private marina where Fellowes had his yacht docked, he raised the top and locked me in the car while he took Cassie out of the back seat. Then he opened the door for me. I had no choice but to follow as he carried my sleeping baby along the pier.

"Did you really name your yacht 'Mary Celeste'?"

Fellowes grinned. "I couldn't resist. We'll be here for a few minutes, until the others can join us."

Anybody who would name a boat after an infamous ghost ship really liked to push his luck, was all I could say.

Fellowes found a shady spot under an overhang and set down the carrier. He pulled up a deck chair and sat next to Cassie, blocking my access. I paced back and forth in the glaring sun, looking for a way out. There wasn't a soul on this side of the marina. And what was I going to do if there was? Fellowes had Cassie. No telling what he'd say if the cops showed up – nasty custody battle that I'd lost? I was a stalker? I'd be the one getting arrested, and by the time they figured everything out, he'd be long gone with my baby.

Still, the sun shone and the waves sparkled. White boats bobbed on the swells. In the distance, a rainbow triangle skated over the water, pulling a sailboat along underneath it. The luxuriant frivolity pissed me off.

The ugly primer and red Suburban that had run me into the curb pulled up in the parking lot. Ian Chambers and Salinger-Spam-Killer got out of the truck. They pulled a large duffle bag from the back and Salinger slung it over his shoulder, more or less fireman style. The two men came down the pier and climbed aboard the boat.

I didn't know what had happened to Salinger, but I'd hate to see the other guy. Both of his eyes were blackened, although the bruises were a little blotchy, like they were a day or two old. Two deep, scabby cuts barely missed his left eye and skidded down the side of his neck to his collar bone. He limped badly under the weight of the duffle.

"Ian, can you get her cell phone? It's in her right pocket," Fellowes said.

Chambers complied, refusing to look me in the eye, and handed the phone to Fellowes, who sealed it in a cardboard envelope. "I picked a random storefront in Austin to FedEx this to. You can run it up to the drop box before we leave."

Ian Chambers paused before following Salinger below decks. "I'm sorry it had to come to this, Marti."

"I'll bet you are."

"Let's all go below, shall we?" Fellowes said with a gesture. "After you, mademoiselle."

He had Cassie's baby bucket, so there wasn't much I could do but curse him silently and shuffle down the steep stairs.

Chambers fixed himself a drink at the minibar. Salinger plopped the duffle on the floor, where it toppled over. I was sure I heard a groan. He opened a drawer and worked a fresh roll of duct tape out of a large multi-pack. He pulled some off and came over to me. He taped my hands together behind my back.

"Sit down," he said, nodding toward the built-in bench sofa behind me.

I sat, and he taped my ankles together.

"Really?" I asked. "Where is it you think I'm going to go?"

Salinger responded by slapping a piece of tape across my mouth. Asshole.

Tucker Fellowes had taken Cassie into another cabin.

"Hey, Fellowes," Salinger called.

I suddenly thought of the dog-eared sticky note in Ryan's file. Hey, Fellowes. Hey, fellows! Isn't that what the guy who shot Ryan, Fydor Dostoyevsky, said in the ambulance just before he died? Holy shit. What is going on here?

"What?" Fellowes came back in without Cassie.

Salinger prodded the duffle bag with his foot. "Leave him in or tape him?"

Fellowes looked at me with a wolfish grin. "By all means, tape him. I don't want my property damaged."

Chambers set down his drink and helped Salinger open the duffle bag and shake its contents onto the white Berber carpeting.

Mouth freshly bloodied, and still wearing the anti-shifter amulet, lay Quinn, looking much the worse for wear.

Chapter 20
Pretty Maids All in a Row

"hat have you done to him?" I tried, without much luck, to shout at Salinger. He only smirked at me.

I hopped over to Quinn and flopped down awkwardly beside him. Laying my head on his chest, I could hear his heartbeat, slow but steady, and I felt his breath on my cheek. I wanted to peel back an eyelid and see what color his eyes were, but it was impossible with my hands taped behind me. Had they darkened or turned even more fiery? And what had happened to Mr. Underhill and the dark-haired woman?

I sat up and glared at Salinger. I tried scowling at Salinger, but the duct tape on my mouth was too stiff. Then I looked back at Quinn.

Salinger didn't try to roll Quinn over, just taped his hands in front of him, then his ankles. He didn't bother taping Quinn's mouth – maybe he didn't think it would stick with all the blood.

When he was done, he tossed the duct tape back in the drawer, looked at Chambers and nodded toward the stairs. Chambers picked up his drink, which was sweating almost as profusely as he was, and started for the steps. He paused to give me a sad, lingering look. I imagined hundreds of little knives flying out of my eyes and ripping him to shreds. He sighed and left. Salinger closed the door on his way out and locked it.

I don't know how long our boat ride lasted. It felt like several years, but I was sure that it really wasn't more than a couple of hours. It was long enough for me to make myself sick with worry, at any rate. Was Cassie okay? Where was she? Would I be able to get us out of this mess before I ended up in a brothel? Was Quinn still Quinn? Where the hell was Fellowes taking us, anyway?

If there is a way to get comfortable while bound and gagged with duct tape, I couldn't find it. Eventually, I sat next to Quinn and used his prone body to prop myself up.

Someone cut the engine and the boat stopped moving forward, but it still rocked enough to make me feel a little ill. I could hear men shouting and Cassie crying. I cried along with her. It'll be okay, sweetie. It'll be okay. Mama loves you. I struggled against the duct tape, but nothing I did seemed to help much. My shoulders ached from my arms being pulled behind my back and the stink from the tape on my mouth was giving me a headache.

I wished yet again that Lulu's anti-shifting amulet wasn't hanging around Quinn's neck. It was probably the one time ever that I needed him to turn into a big, nasty monster, and he couldn't do it. But then again, I couldn't be sure what kind of big, nasty monster he would turn into now, so maybe it was just as well.

I didn't know what Fellowes' plan for him was, but I was sure it wouldn't be good. I was reviewing my options (currently, none), when heavy footfalls thudded down the stairs. Then the snick of metal on metal as the lock turned, followed by a squeal of the door being opened. Salinger loomed in the doorway.

"We're here." He went to the mini-bar and opened the cabinet high above it. When he turned to face us, he had a box cutter.

He used it to cut the duct tape from our ankles. He wasn't very careful and he nicked my shin. He wiped the blood off of my leg with his finger, and then licked it. I gagged. He grinned.

Salinger got a chilled bottle of water from the mini-bar and splashed it on Quinn's face. His lids fluttered (but not enough for me to see what was going on with his eyes) and he groaned. "Wake up, you little sneak," Salinger snarled at him, before dragging him roughly to his feet. Semi-conscious, Quinn staggered and stumbled up the metal stairs ahead of me. He went to his knees twice on the way up, and I winced for him both times. That's going to leave a mark.

Out on the deck, I filled my lungs with the fresh, salty air. I quite liked the smell of the sea. Although, the smell of the sea, mingled with duct tape stench, was not so nice. It was late in the afternoon, and the yacht was moored to the barnacle-encrusted leg of an oil platform. A shabby nylon rope ladder dangled down the side, its tattered ends drifting it the water next to the boat. Were they expecting us to climb up that? A diesel engine growled to life somewhere above us. I looked up to see that a crane high above was lowering what looked like a giant metal basket towards us. Quinn collapsed to his knees on the deck, leaning his head against the side railing.

"I'll deal with you later," Salinger growled at him.

Then he stood behind me, hands on my shoulders.

Something bad was about to happen.

Tucker Fellowes picked up Cassie's baby carrier. She started to cry, I was sure she was wet and hungry, and I ached to hold her. Salinger's nails dug into me.

"You know how I said that I could leave her at a hospital or a fire station for your mother? I could...but I won't."

And then he dropped her over the side of the boat.

I jumped after her, but Salinger was expecting that, and grabbed me around the waist. I screamed as well as I could with duct tape over my mouth. I kicked that muscle-bound idiot for all I was worth. I thrashed around and head-butted him. Still, he didn't let go. I am not small, but he was a mountain of meanness and muscle. I didn't think I could save Cassie with my hands taped together, but I'd rather drown with her than stay on the wretched boat. Out of the corner of my eye, I saw Quinn lunge for the gunwale and topple over the railing. His hands were taped together and he was wearing the anti-shifter amulet. What was he thinking? Now, I'd lost both of them.

Salinger jerked up on my wrists until I heard a wet crunch and felt one of my shoulders pop out of joint. The pain was nothing compared to watching Fellowes drop Cassie overboard like she was a piece of trash.

It was too late to do anything now. Despair and hopelessness closed in on me, and I stopped fighting. Salinger dumped me into the middle of the basket and sat down with his feet on me so I couldn't get up. The metal floor was unpleasantly hot and stank of ammonia.

Fellowes looked over the side of the boat where Quinn had thrown himself in. "Well. That saves me a lot of trouble."

He and Chambers stepped onto the basket, and I felt us being lifted up. I couldn't bear to open my eyes and look at the horrible murky water that had swallowed up Cassie and Quinn. If I didn't see it, it wasn't real. Inside, I was dead. Why wouldn't my heart stop beating? How could it work when it had been shattered into a million tiny fragments? I curled more tightly into a fetal position and focused on the throbbing of my dislocated shoulder. Maybe it would distract me from the unbearable pain in my heart.

On the platform, Fellowes and Chambers scrambled out of the personnel basket, which hovered just above the deck. Salinger picked me up and handed me to Chambers. I went completely limp, forcing him to carry me.

"Put her in with the others, for now," Fellowes said.

I was carried and dragged down a couple of flights of metal stairs. A door was unlocked and it scraped across the cement floor when it was opened. Chambers set me down carefully on the floor of a dimly lit room. He peeled off the tape from my mouth, then my hands. It hurt like hell when he moved my dislocated arm, and I let out an involuntary cry.

"I'm so sorry, Marti," he whispered before he left, and the door slammed shut and locked.

In one corner of the room, a girl sat with her knees clasped to her chest, rocking herself. It was hard to tell in the poor lighting, but she looked about fifteen. Her face was bruised and her pants were crusted with something dark. Dried blood? Another girl, more or less the same age, I guessed, cowered against the wall near her. Long brown hair covered her face. Two other girls watched me from the shadows.

There was one other girl. I knew she was dead – a ghost – because I could see through the gaping hole in her chest. Her pale face was spattered with blood, and she used both hands to cup something small against her belly. She said nothing, only glared. I didn't have either the strength or the will to try and contact her.

"Welcome to Hell," said a voice behind me.

No shit. I sat up gingerly and turned to face her, grimacing as my dislocated arm dragged along my thigh. This girl looked closer to twenty than the others, but I didn't think she was there yet. "I need out," I answered. "I'm going to disembowel Tucker Fellowes and hang him with his own intestines." I felt like I was watching a movie of myself. Cue the action hero to swoop in for a daring rescue.

The girl snorted. "You and what army? I'm Rayne, by the way." She indicated the two girls in the shadows. "That's Mercedes and Daniella. The other two are Veronica and Crystal. Don't think we haven't tried to get out of this shithole."

"He threw my baby overboard," I said. Though my logical mind told me there was only one possible outcome, I refused to accept it. It wasn't real, true, or possible. It just couldn't be.

The ghost girl raised her head and took a step closer.

"I'm very sorry about that," Rayne said, glancing at the other girls. "But we're on an abandoned oil platform on the far side of nowhere. Nobody is coming to help us. Nobody is going to make him pay."

Dolphins. Dolphins often help shipwreck survivors and drowning people. Maybe there were dolphins that could save Cassie and Quinn. Please, let there be dolphins.

I said nothing, absently watching the ghost girl. I was sure she knew I could see her, but she made no move to speak to me. She kept looking at whatever it was in her hands.

"Boats," Rayne said, apparently feeling the need to explain. "Easy pick up and drop off. There was even a chopper here two days ago. They took Charlotte." She looked down at the filthy floor.

The rusty door skreeked across the cement floor again. A scrawny man with bad teeth and a stained ribbed tank top appeared in the doorway. He had an electric cattle prod in one hand and a large plastic dog bowl filled with an unidentifiable mass in the other.

"Here, bitches! Supper." He laughed as he roughly dropped the bowl on the floor, and a fair amount of the contents slopped out.

He brandished the cattle prod, causing Veronica and Crystal to shrink against the wall and cry.

"Get out," I snarled. After all, I had nothing left to lose, and there was nothing he could do to me that would be anywhere near as bad as what had already happened.

He took a big step towards me.

I did not back down. All of the impotent rage that I thought had burned itself out on the deck of Fellowes' yacht suddenly crystalized into a cold-blooded need to make somebody pay. And he was available.

He must have read the intention on my face, because he backed away and scuttered out the door like the vermin that he was.

The door slammed and locked.

"You go, girl," said Rayne.

Behind her, the other four girls were using their hands to scoop the mush out of the dog bowl and eat it. Under other circumstances, I probably would have been appalled. But I found it hard to care much at the moment.

"There has to be a way out of here," I said.

"Yeah, sure. Just ask Billy nicely and I'm sure he'll let you out." Rayne's voice dripped sarcasm. "And if you get out, what do you think you're going to do? This platform is sixty miles offshore. At least that's what they told me, anyway."

The door scraped open again. This time, Salinger hulked in the opening. "Keller, Mr. Fellowes wants you to join him for dinner."

"Not hungry."

"Then you can watch him eat."

He grabbed my dislocated arm and dragged me through the door. It brought tears to my eyes, but I refused to cry. Not in front of him.

I tried to visualize dolphins, lifting Cassie and Quinn out of the water on their wide backs, taking them to the safety of a passing boat.

We tramped up two flights of metal stairs and ended up in a cafeteria-style dining area. There were several plastic tables, but only one had a crisp, white tablecloth. And a putrid scumball called Tucker Fellowes.

Salinger pushed me down into a plastic chair. I winced as he patted my shoulder.

"Not again!" Fellowes' voice bristled with irritation. "What have I told you? It costs me money when they're damaged. I have to give a discount. It's coming out of your pay, that's all I can say."

Salinger grunted and lumbered off.

Ignoring the plate of lobster scampi in front of me, I leaned back in my fancy plastic lawn chair as far as I dared. I tried to cross my arms, but quickly decided against it as hot pain stabbed my dislocated shoulder.

"I have great news. I found a buyer for you. He'll be here for a test drive in the morning, and if he likes, he'll take you with him."

I considered eating the lobster tail. If I went into anaphylactic shock and died, it would serve Fellowes right. I'd be with Cassie and Ryan, away from this horrible, horrible place. I smiled a wicked little smile at this idea.

"You'll get your own room, here on the upper deck," Fellowes continued. "After all, my client will expect a play area. You'll get your hair done in a little while - this one likes redheads. And you get a shower. Oh, and I get a fat wad of cash. What's not to like?"

I examined his face, wondering if I could jam the plastic knife by my plate far enough into his eye socket to reach his brain before it broke.

"Oh, come on. The poor are the nation's greatest untapped natural resource. Crystal's mother sold her to me for five rocks of crack. I can get her conditioned, clean her up for almost nothing, then turn around and sell her for maybe ten grand. It's all in the presentation. I get a fantastic return on investment, and she gets a job. How is that bad?"

"Are there many dolphins out here?" I asked.

"Dolphins?" Fellowes looked both puzzled by my question and genuinely surprised that I didn't congratulate him on his jobs creation program.

Death by shellfish was looking more attractive by the second. I closed my eyes. I could just about see Ryan standing there, Cassie in one arm, the other open to welcome me. The joke's on you, Fellowes. I couldn't help laughing.

Page 163

I opened my eyes when I heard Fellowes sigh. He was shaking his head.

"Well, eat up. I don't want you looking drawn and waxy when my client comes to shop. In fact, I think I'll give you a little something to keep you going later. The client is…quite vigorous."

I smiled at Fellowes as I thought of Cassie and speared an especially large hunk of lobster with my fork. It kept sliding off the plastic, so I grabbed the big chunk in one hand and a smaller piece in the other hand. This was going to be so easy. Two bites of lobster, then I'd be free, and there would be nothing Fellowes could do about it.

With the worst timing in the world, Ian Chambers came into the dining room. "Here's the number you wanted. Hey, Marti, I thought you were deathly allergic to shellfish."

Fellowes dived across the table, knocking my chair over and trying to pin my wrists to the floor.

"No! Let go of me!" I screamed at Fellowes, kicking and snapping at him with my teeth. I got close enough to the piece of lobster in my right hand to taste the garlic butter sauce, but Fellowes smashed my wrist against the concrete floor until my hand went numb and he scraped the shellfish out of my cupped palm. I had no strength in my injured arm, and he had both hands free to pry the little bite of lobster, my salvation, out of my other hand. But not before I bit his forearm hard enough to draw blood. He rewarded me with a hard slap across the face.

"Nice try. But I'm not going to let you cheat me out of my hard-earned money. Chambers, take her to the Honeymoon Suite." Fellowes got to his feet and wrapped a paper napkin around his bloody arm, cursing softly.

If I couldn't join Cassie in death, then she must somehow be alive. The dolphins must have come to save her. I was sure of it. Now, I just had to find a way to get to her.

Ian Chambers held my arm and guided me through a labyrinth of low, narrow corridors. He stopped and opened a door painted a cheerless, gaudy red. "After you," he said, gesturing inside.

There was a king-sized bed with a faux fur leopard blanket over zebra print sheets. The ceiling was mirrored and sex toys spilled out of a compartment in the lighted headboard. A fake bearskin rug stretched across the floor at the end of the bed, lying on top of white shag carpeting.

Ian Chambers looked both ways down the hall before he stepped into the room and closed the door behind him.

"I'm going to get the key tonight," he said, slumping down onto the bed.

"Key to what?" I asked. I stayed as near the door as possible. If I could just get out to the water, the dolphins would take me to Cassie. Maybe they'd saved Quinn, too.

"The key that unlocks the cockpit of Fellowes' yacht. Then I'm going to get you, and the girls downstairs, and we're going to leave this hellhole."

"Fellowes will kill you," I said. And if he doesn't, I might.

"Nick'll kill me, when he finds out what I've been doing. Either way, I'm a dead man walking." Ian's lips smiled, but his eyes glistened with pain.

I didn't care. I just wanted out.

"Don't know how I got here, Marti. It was never meant to be like this. I was supposed to be one of the good guys, you know? And have the house with white picket fence and a dog." His voice was soft, and thick with tears I knew he would not cry.

"How did you get mixed up with Fellowes, anyway?" Dumb thing to say. I did not want to be his confessor. I didn't have the strength to forgive him for his sins. I just wanted to find the dolphins, and if I kept him talking, maybe he'd let his guard down, and I could escape.

They call him Flipper, Flipper...

Ian looked at the floor. "You know Fellowes runs crank and hookers between Houston and Tulsa, right? Well, not all of them are female."

I swayed to the music in my head. Faster than lightning...

"You're a male prostitute?!" I asked.

No one you see is smarter than he...

Ian almost laughed as he shook his head. "Not me, but I...receive their services."

That took a minute to sink in, and it interrupted my little song. It was the only dolphin song I knew.

He'd gotten my attention, at least for a minute. "So. Catching a DA investigator doing something illegal was too good to pass up?"

"That, and he covered some gambling debts for me in Vegas."

It was my turn to shake my head. "How did Nick not know about this? About you not liking girls, I mean." And I had thought he was just being a gentleman at the restaurant, when he didn't ogle the waitress with the too-low top.

"Well, you know Nick. He's 110% Alpha male. It would never occur to him that another man wouldn't want the same things he does. And I did everything I could to hide it. If Nick wanted to go jump out of airplanes, I was the first to say, 'Hell, yeah!' He was always fixing me up with girls. I think most of them knew, on some level, anyway, that nothing was ever going to happen between us."

"Okay, so now I have to know. If you don't even like girls, why did you ask me on a date and try to rip my clothes off?" I started humming the theme to Flipper again.

"Yeah. Sorry about that. I had to get drunk to come on to you, and I overdid it. It was never about getting in your pants. It was about getting in your house. I had to figure out where Ryan had hidden it."

Hidden it? I swallowed hard. "What did he have on you?"

Ian closed his eyes and shook his head. "A credit card receipt. Sounds stupid, I know. But Nick and Ryan had picked up one of Fellowes' mules, Richard Murphy, for DWI and possession. He only used Fellowes' street name – he calls himself Diablo - but Murphy did way too much talking for his continued good health. Three hours after he made bail, he was found in a dumpster with his neck broken. I was supposed to be deposing him at the time he was killed. Instead, I was having a beer with Nick and Ryan."

"The guy didn't show. You did something else. That's not a crime." I said, still not understanding why a credit card receipt mattered so much.

"It is when you falsify court documents."

"You just made up his deposition?" I said, too loudly.

"No. Fellowes had it messengered over. And I filed it. With a huge red timestamp on it that declared I had deposed Murphy at the same time I was sitting on a stool at Specials. It was in my valise, which got kicked over, and Ryan helped me pick up the papers that fell out. I knew he saw it. In spite of Nick's cheerleading, he never liked me, never trusted me. It was only a matter of time until he put two and two together, if he hadn't already."

I did not like where this was going, and I felt cold, in spite of the heat. "What did you do?" I couldn't control the quiver in my voice. It reminded me of a dolphin chattering.

"I didn't know at the time that they'd already iced Murphy. I swear, Marti. If I had—" Ian's voice broke and he gasped for air. "I would never have told Fellowes about Ryan. I knew he was a heartless bastard, but I didn't realize he was a cold-blooded killer. That's not exactly true. He keeps his hands clean. He's always got someone else to do his dirty work. That traffic stop, it didn't just go bad. It was an execution. And it's my fault."

I felt like Ian had just thrown me over a cliff. The oxygen-depleted world spun until I could finally stop it. Now I understood why the dying shooter was talking about Fellowes.

In three strides, I was pounding on his chest with my fists, although my injured arm was too weak to do any harm. "You. Worthless. Piece. Of. Shit," I snarled at him.

Chambers managed to grab my wrists and held on to them until I stopped trying to hit him. I wanted to scream with rage. But I pushed it down, holding it in reserve. I knew I'd need it later. I turned my back on Chambers and stalked to the door. Then I leaned my back against it, pressing myself as far away from him as I could get.

"I never intended for Ryan to get killed. I don't know what I thought. Maybe that Fellowes would change his operation, or lay low for a while. This has been eating me alive for almost two years now." His cheeks glistened and he snuffled, a deep, wet, miserable sound that shook his entire body. "I knew when Spam turned up dead that I was probably next. Regardless of what happens out here, I sent a FedEx to the DA. First thing Monday morning, an envelope will arrive containing my resignation and a full confession. I detailed how I set Ryan and Nick up. I named every name I could think of, and I even included my journal in case I left someone out." Ian sighed deeply. "I know it doesn't bring your husband or your baby back. I wish..."

His misery washed over me and broke on the rock that used to be my heart. Inside, I had become a frozen wasteland – harsh, implacable ice. I didn't object to getting the girls out of this place, but I also knew if we left Tucker Fellowes alive on this platform, he'd either escape and go somewhere with no extradition treaty, or some way, somehow, he'd manage to bend the law in his favor and get a slap on the wrist, if that. I could almost see the dolphins swimming away, breaching and chattering in the setting sun. Without Cassie.

A weight, a cold oppressiveness, settled on me like a granite cloak, squeezing out any glints of hope. "There aren't any dolphins around here, are there?"

Chambers frowned. "I have no idea."

I was going to make sure Tucker Fellowes, that despicable excuse for a human being who took my family away from me, was going down, or I would die trying. And I was okay with that.

Chapter 21
Tangled Web

 e can't just sneak out and leave Fellowes here. He'll find some way to escape," I said.

"I can radio the Coast Guard from the boat. He won't get away."

The problem was, I knew Ian Chambers was a double agent. I had no way of knowing if this was some Machiavellian plot to get me to trust him and manipulate me into doing what Fellowes wanted me to, or if he'd really had a change of heart. If he was acting, he was damned good, and really should try out for the Alley Theatre Company. That is, if he survived.

But ultimately, I didn't really have a choice. I could sit here, passively waiting to be raped and living the life of the walking dead, or I could try to save those girls and get them on the boat. And then get Fellowes myself. Trustworthy or not, Chambers was the only chance they had. Besides, I had no chance of taking down Fellowes if I was locked up in this tragic and cheesy porno hell room.

"What's your plan?" I asked.

"Fellowes has to go to sleep at some point. I'll slip in and get the keys to the yacht, then I'll get you and the girls and we'll climb down the rope ladder onto the boat. "

"And what could possibly go wrong?"

"If you have a better idea, let's hear it," he snapped.

I started to cross my arms again, but my shoulder screamed at me. "What about Salinger? And there's at least one other goon. I saw him when I was locked in with the girls." And I'm not leaving Fellowes behind, alive and well on this stinkin' platform.

Chambers scowled. "There are two of them, Billy and Trey. And he's got a cook, Charles."

"I saw what they're feeding those girls. I don't know why you call him a cook."

"He isn't that kind of cook. He's a chemist. Fellowes built a state-of-the-art meth lab on the top deck. He puts out primo stuff."

"Can we torch the lab?" That might be a great diversion.

"Not likely. It's designed to be fire proof."

Chambers looked at his watch. "I've been here too long already. I have to get back before Fellowes misses me."

"Doesn't he trust you?" I toned down the sarcasm, but it still came out too harshly.

"He doesn't trust anybody. That's why he's still alive."

Chambers locked me in the room. I tried pacing, but each step jolted my shoulder. I lay down on the bed, hoping to give it some support. It helped a little, but not much. I needed a sling, or at least a pillowcase and a pair of scissors. I had a pillowcase, anyway.

The bedspread smelled like new carpet that had been sprayed with fabric deodorizer. Sleep wasn't an option, and I knew I should try to come up with a plan. I didn't know very much about the layout of this place and the whole thing was a game of chess. But I was the world's crappiest chess player. I couldn't even beat Kyle, and he was only six.

"Chica?"

I turned my head to see Spam standing near the end of the bed. I didn't want to admit I was glad to see him. "Long time, no see."

"I tried warning you about this pendejo. You should have listened better."

"You said Salinger killed you. How was I supposed to know he worked for Fellowes?"

Spam shrugged. "Guess it doesn't matter. He was going to grab you anyway. You just made it easier for him."

"Did you just pop in to criticize me, or are you planning to do something useful?"

"Don't count on Chambers, chica."

"I knew it! I knew it was some kind of miserable plot." I slapped the bed with my good hand.

"No. Fellowes brought him out here to get rid of him. Chambers is becoming a liability. Just like I was. Fellowes is going to shoot him up with smack and leave him on the beach by his house. It'll look like just another dead dumbass, messin' with stuff he couldn't handle."

"Or suicide, when the DA gets his confession. Does Fellowes know what Chambers sent to the DA?"

Spam's smile was grim. "No. But the DA ain't gonna catch Fellowes. He's got too many escape holes. Something bad's only gonna happen to Fellowes if the Russians find out he's been shorting them. You got no idea what he's capable of."

I looked around the room. "I think I do."

"No, chica. You don't. Fellowes paid some Russian hackers to break into the EZ Tag system. He can track anybody that gets on any tollroad in Texas. That's why Chambers wouldn't put a tag in his car. If it has an EZ tag, Fellowes knows if it's coming his way. He can listen to any cop's cell, not just the scanners. He's also jacked into TranStar and the traffic camera net."

"I thought that was strange that Chambers didn't have an EZ tag. But haven't they turned off the red light cameras?"

"Just because the city ain't using them, doesn't mean Fellowes isn't."

I nodded.

"I gotta tell you something," Spam said. "I was there."

I sat up. "You were where?"

"I was there when they killed your husband."

If Spam had still been alive, I would have strangled him, dislocated shoulder notwithstanding. "You were there? And you've been hanging around, acting like you're here to help and asking me to do stuff for you? You're a bigger tool than Chambers," I spat, out loud for God and everybody to hear.

"It wasn't like that, chica. They didn't know I was there, but I was tailin' them the whole time. They were a present from the Russians, and Fellowes wanted to get rid of them – they were too sloppy, and probably spies. He also wanted to get rid of your husband. He thought he could do both at the same time. After they pulled the trigger, they ran, because that's what Fellowes told them to do. But he double-crossed 'em. He was supposed to have a second vehicle waiting for them in a parking garage, so they could switch cars, but it wasn't there. They couldn't even get in the garage – that's why they headed for the freeway, instead of just hiding inside. Once the cops stopped them, it was my job to make sure they left in body bags. Those pendejos were going to get out of the car and give up. If that happened, Fellowes was gonna kill me. You see how it was? Me or them. I knew he'd look at the message, thinking it was instructions from Fellowes, so I sent the driver a 'shopped picture of his girlfriend bangin' a cop. That's why he started shooting."

"Spam?"

"What?"

"I'm glad you're dead."

"That's cold, chica."

"So are you, you heartless son of a bitch."

Spam faded away. I suppose it was good information, about Chambers. He might want to know that Fellowes was planning to kill him, if it wasn't already too late. There was no clock, here in the Museum of Tacky. It seemed like such a long time between Spam leaving and Chambers showing up, that I had convinced myself that he wasn't coming. I couldn't allow myself to think about Cassie, or I wouldn't be able to function. But it was especially hard not to think about her. It must be way past her bedtime, because my breasts were engorged and sore. It was just one more layer of hurt piled on to this already unbearable day.

I stared at what looked like a small bloodstain on the wall as I scrambled to think of something else. Anything else. My thoughts wandered to Quinn. Was he trying to help my poor, sweet baby? I guess I'd never know. I had gotten used to having him around, and his absence was more painful than I would have expected. I had to force myself to stop thinking about him, too. That left Mr. Underhill and the woman. I don't think they liked me, especially, but they were Quinn's friends. I hoped they were okay. I called for Delilah, but she didn't answer.

I jumped when the lock turned and the door started to open.

"Are you ready to go?" Chambers half-entered the room and whispered.

"Past ready." I said as I slipped out of the Porn Palace. I noticed something shiny on the threshold. It was a key. Chambers must have dropped it, so I picked it up and stuck it in my pocket.

Chambers was already a dozen yards down the dimly lit corridor, so I pushed the door shut and turned the bolt to lock it, then hurried to catch up.

We crept down the hallway, our footsteps echoing on the metal floor. I stayed as close to Chambers as I could. I had no idea where we were or where we were going.

"Did you know Fellowes is planning to kill you?" I whispered to Chambers.

"Not surprising. Did he tell you that?"

"Not directly."

"You overheard it?"

"Something like that." Now, I wished I hadn't said anything.

Footsteps clanged on the metal floor, coming towards us.

Shit. I'd forgotten about my hair appointment.

"They're supposed to dye my hair tonight," I whispered in Chambers' ear.

"Then we'd better get a move on."

"Hey!" a voice shouted. Salinger. He'd seen us and he started running our way, his footsteps thundering on the metal flooring.

"Go that way!" Chambers pointed to a darkened hallway up ahead.

I sprinted for the connecting passage, but Chambers ran back the way we had come. Guess Salinger couldn't follow both of us. I ran a short distance and came to a T-intersection. I hung a right and plastered myself against a wall to listen for a second. The only sounds were my heavy breathing and pounding heart. I'm going to have to start doing more cardio, if I get out of this alive.

This part of the platform didn't appear to be used much – there were no lights and it smelled rusty and dank. Once I had turned the corner, it was almost like being in a cave. I felt my way along the wall and tested the floor with each step. It was slow going, but the only appointment I had was with Fellowes, and it was flexible.

I could hear water dripping, somewhere off to my left, and something scuttled around in the dark. I really hoped it was roaches. They were big and disgusting, especially when they flew straight at your face, but they wouldn't stop me from getting Fellowes.

The wall suddenly disappeared, and I fell through the stairwell opening and tumbled down a few stairs.

I was sitting on the top step, trying to shake it off, when the dead girl I had seen earlier appeared in front of me, two stair steps below.

"This way," she beckoned. Her eyes flashed a metallic green that made my skin crawl.

I need to get to Rayne and the others, I thought at her, not sure where she intended to lead me, and not sure I wanted to go.

"I know."

What did you say your name was?

"Kamli."

She glided down the stairs so fast it was hard for me to keep up with her. She waited for me at the bottom. Kamli was still holding something in her left hand, petting it with two fingers from her right. Only this time, she was clutching it up to her chest, where her heart would have been if there hadn't been a yawning hole there.

"Not his to take," the ghost said, frowning.

What wasn't?

A smile flickered across her face and she hugged whatever she held in her hands closer. "Josh promised he would marry me. Promised. But then he said he didn't want no stupid tramp to be the mama to his babies. Josh sold me to Tucker Fellowes."

She chose a corridor and started floating down it. I followed her.

And Fellowes did this to you?

"Nah. It was that big ole guy that works for him. Too bad he cain't see me, or I woulda got him, just like I got Josh."

Oh?

"I stood at the end of his bed every night. Just stood there and stared at 'im. Didn't take long before he was sittin' in the corner, talkin' to the walls. His mama had to haul him off to the crazy house."

I see.

"Guilt'll do that to a person, eat ya up like a cancer."

That's true. Are we nearly there? It didn't seem to me that we were going the right way. It was too dark.

"Almost."

Kamli led me deeper into the musty labyrinth. I was just about tell her I thought she'd made a wrong turn when she stopped.

"Here. Open this door."

Are you sure? This doesn't look like the same door.

"Open it."

I frowned at the door, but pushed down the handle and went into the room. I couldn't see my hand in front of my face. But I could hear the ocean and feel a little breeze. It seemed to be coming from the floor. I froze, afraid to take another step. I could hear the wush-wush of my pulse pounding in my ears.

Kamli? What's going on?

She giggled behind me. I turned to look at her. She held up the thing she'd been cradling, and it seemed to stretch, nearly doubling in size. I dropped to my knees.

Mr. Buns, Cassie's lovie, dangled from Kamli's fingers. He glowed, the same way she did. Her giggles turned to guffaws.

"How did you get that?" I shrieked at her, struggling for air.

"This old thing?" Kamli asked.

Then she tossed Mr. Buns over my head, towards the corner of the room. I snatched at him as he sailed past, but I missed badly – one arm was useless and the other was exhausted. Instead of landing on the floor, the stuffed rabbit disappeared through it.

"Why did you do that?" I couldn't stop the sobs that powered their way out of my chest, so I sat back on my heels and let them come.

"Revenge," Kamli said sweetly.

Then she started to shimmer and twist in the air. A man stood where the girl had been a moment before. He had a carefully shaped, closely cropped beard. He looked very business-like in his expensive sport coat, a diamond tie-tack holding down his silk tie. Except for his weird, metallic green eyes.

"What happened to –"

"Kamli. Malik. Same difference."

"Malik? I-I tried to release you. You weren't in the bottle," I stammered.

"Of course I was. You just don't remember."

The djinn waved his hand at me, and a flash flood of memories washed over me, nearly drowning me in misery. The pregnancy test. Making love with Ryan. The car accident. Losing my baby. Losing Ryan. Again.

"Stop!" I screamed at him. "Stop this!"

Malik only smiled. "You begged me for a wish. Do you remember?"

"Yes," I whispered.

"And then you spurned my generous gift to you! You unwished it." Malik's eyes blazed.

"I had to. I had Ryan back, but I lost my baby, my sister and my nephew. It just made things worse for everybody." My voice was squeaky and pathetic.

"You can't shift one part of a timeline without affecting the rest of it," Malik said, as if he were scolding a naughty child.

"I didn't know! How was I supposed to know that?"

Malik raised one eyebrow and shrugged.

"I thought I was helping you by letting you out of that bottle. I would have been better off just letting Mr. Underhill keep it," I snapped at him.

Malik's face darkened, and his eyes burned bonfire bright.

My body reacted, leaning away from him. I lost my balance and toppled over to my side. "I am sorry. I am so sorry I offended you. Please. I beg your forgiveness." I had to get out of here, and telling him what he wanted to hear seemed the quickest way to do it.

Malik crossed his arms and the fire in his eyes dimmed a little. "It is only because you freed me that I am giving you a chance."

The djinn raised both his arms, his hands circling as they rose. A dim light appeared on the ceiling. I could see that there was a hole about the size of a large pizza box in the floor behind me, where Mr. Buns had vanished. On the wall in front of me were three doors, frames glowing neon green.

"One door leads to certain death. One door is the exit. The other door…is a surprise. Choose wisely."

"What if I don't choose?" I asked, knowing that wasn't really an option.

Malik cocked an eyebrow. I heard a splash behind me. I spun around to see that another pizza box-sized chunk of floor was gone.

"One will fall every minute that you don't choose."

With a grin, he was gone.

Chapter 22
Eenie Meanie

 looked at the double pizza box-sized hole in the floor. I guestimated that the room was ten pizza boxes wide by twelve pizza boxes long. That gave me about two hours.

I stared at the three glowing doors. Malik was wrong. I didn't have to choose. I could just wait until the floor dropped out from under me, and I joined Cassie in the water. It was tempting.

But that wouldn't get Fellowes. And it wouldn't save the girls. If I ever needed guidance, it was now.

"Delilah! Where are you? I really need your help!" I said to the middle door.

Behind me, another tile dropped.

To my great relief, Delilah appeared next to me, hands on her hips. "Girlfriend –"

A blue light surrounded her and she froze.

"Delilah?!"

She didn't move.

Then I heard Malik's disembodied voice. "Unh-uh-uh. That's cheating."

His laughter faded, but Delilah remained a statue.

Dammit. I looked at the doors again.

Another tile splashed into the sea. There didn't seem to be an entire minute between each splash, but perhaps my perception was distorted.

The doors were identical. There were no visible clues as to what might be behind them. I scrambled to the first one and put my ear against it. I held my breath, listening. Silence. Same with the other two. There was no keyhole to peer through. I even tried sniffing at the border where door met frame. Nothing.

Another tile dropped. The first row was about halfway gone.

I growled with frustration. For lack of a better idea, I started "Eenie, meanie, miney, mo. Catch a tiger by his toe. If he hollers let him go. My mother told me to pick this one." I was pointing to the door on the right.

I took a deep breath. As I pulled the door open with my left hand, I gripped the frame tightly with my right, hoping I could pull myself back if it looked like I was facing certain death.

Instead, I found myself in my own kitchen. I had just come in from the outside door. I smelled tobacco. Not the bitter smell of cigarettes, nor the dusty smell of cigars, but tobacco from a pouch, earthy and sweet.

"Oh, there you are, darling," said Quinn. He sat at the table, hair oiled back, wearing slacks, a button down shirt (with an undershirt), reading a newspaper. And smoking a pipe.

"I just wanted to bring in yesterday's mail," I said, looking at the envelopes in my hands. It was then I noticed that I was wearing a cotton A-line dress and a ruffled apron. I knew the ring on my finger was my wedding ring, but it seemed alien, wrong somehow.

I felt like I had just woken from a dream, but strands of it lingered, dusty, obscure cobwebs in my head that fluttered away every time I tried to grab at them.

"Don't forget to take the cinnamon rolls out of the oven, Dear," Quinn said.

"Oh! I had forgotten about them."

I got an oven mitt and pulled a pan out of the oven. The rolls weren't burned, but they were on the far side of the done spectrum. There was a bowl of frosting sitting on the countertop, and I started spreading the contents on the bread.

Quinn came over and eyed the rolls. "Tsk, tsk. You're completely useless in the kitchen." He smiled as he said this. Then he patted my butt. "It's a good thing I love you for your other, much more accomplished skills."

As he walked away, I wanted to smack him across the face and tell him just where he could shove that steaming hot pan of cinnamon rolls.

Instead, I said. "Yes, Dear, I know. I'm so lucky to have married you."

I didn't have a lot of control over what I did, and even less over what I said. I seemed to be trapped inside the body of a 1950s sitcom wife. This had to be the dream, the nightmare, and the other thing I couldn't quite remember had to be reality. Now, if I could just figure out how to wake up.

Four children, two boys and twin girls bounded into the kitchen. The boys book-ended the girls, and the youngest looked six-ish while the oldest looked twelve-ish. I would guess the girls were eight or nine.

The oldest child looked disapprovingly at the pan, rolls half-smeared with icing.

"Father said you had a snack for us, before he took Harry and me out to ride bikes," he said.

What about the girls? Don't they get to go ride?

"Yes, David. But you know how I am in the kitchen. Why don't you children just wait at the table. I'm sure I'll get this done in a minute."

Where is the stapler, so I can just staple my lips together and not spew this tripe all over the place? I am going to make myself ill. The side door. If I can just get to the side door.

I put a cinnamon roll on each of four plates, along with a knife and fork. I served the boys first, and when the four of them were finished, the girls picked up all of the plates and put them in the sink.

The boys left with their father. By the time they came back an hour later, the girls and I had washed the dishes, dusted the knick-knacks and swept the floors. I did manage to wrest a fragment of control from the automaton who was hosting me.

"Didn't you girls want to go and ride bikes as well?" I finally managed to ask.

The looked at each other, then back at me. "Mother!" said Peony. "We're not boys!"

Then she and Petunia trotted up the stairs to play with their dolls. I sighed and started mopping the floor. Peony and Petunia? Harry and David? Who named these children? I had hoped I could work my way to the side door and escape, but I just wasn't able to force my hands to turn the door knob.

Quinn came downstairs, hair oil-free and still damp from his shower. I didn't think this was the actual Quinn, but a creation that looked like him.

"You know what would be good, Darling?" he asked.

"I'm sure I don't," I said, wanting to gag on those words.

"If we had some fresh-cut flowers for the table when my boss and his wife come over for dinner tonight."

So, I have to cook a fancy dinner for the boss and his wife, after Quinn's been ragging on me about how I can't cook?. Fantastic. "That's a splendid idea." The automaton smiled, and I smiled along with it as I retrieved the hand pruner and my gloves from a drawer and headed towards the side door.

"Where are you going?" Quinn asked. "You know the roses are out front."

The outside smile stayed full. "Of course! What was I thinking? Sometimes, I'm such a dummy." The inside smile faded to black.

The front yard had a bed of rose bushes, alstroemeria, and daisies. The rest of it was a bland stretch of perfectly edged lawn.

I didn't recognize the tune I hummed as I cut enough flowers for a bouquet. I did figure out how to manipulate the body just a little. If I could learn to do it a little, I could learn to do it a lot. Then I could walk out that side door.

I put the flowers in a vase and added water, then went to put them on the kitchen table, out of the way. As I neared the side door, I had an idea. The linoleum was still wet from being mopped. If I put my foot wrong...

It worked.

I slipped and fell hard against the side door, breaking the glass window and crashing through it. I was suddenly back on the oil platform.

The first thing I noticed was that blood was running into my eyes from a cut on my head. The second thing I noticed was that Malik had lied. The tiles had been falling the whole time I was in that existentialist time warp hell, and now there were only four left.

Plop.

Make that three. The door I had just come through had vanished. I opened the next door over. I still had broken pieces of vase in my hand, and I wedged them against the jamb so the door couldn't close all the way.

On the other side of the door, it was pitch-black and smelled musky. Yellow eyes suddenly glowed in the darkness. Very large yellow eyes. I didn't want to see what they were attached to, but it made me think of Where the Wild Things Are. The thing behind the eyes snarled and charged at me. I ran for the door. I was only a couple of steps away, and I could see a faint shaft of light where I'd propped it open. I've never been so grateful for broken glass in my entire life. I hurled myself at the light, scrambling for the doorknob. My leg burned as the creature's claws raked me from knee to ankle.

My momentum nearly carried me over the edge of the tile. I stopped myself by flopping back against the wall, where the door had been, and huddling against it. I tried to catch my breath. There was one door left, and it had to be the exit. Maybe I'd survive Malik's revenge, after all, and have a chance at my own.

As I started to step over to the next tile and open the exit door, the piece I was standing on dropped. I lunged forward, and found myself draped over the last tile. I hadn't fallen into the ocean, but I couldn't open the door, either. And I had less than one minute to fix the problem and save myself.

I eased over on my side and dragged my hips onto the tile. The blood streaming from my leg made the tile and my hands slippery. I reached up and grabbed the door handle.

The tile dropped out from under me.

I caught the threshold of the door with my nails as I fell. I grabbed on tightly, and clung to the metal strip. Even without a dislocated shoulder and exhaustion, I would have had trouble pulling myself up into the hallway. My fingers were cramping, my arms were burning, and my shoulder was screaming.

"Easy there, girlfriend!"

Delilah stood in the doorway.

"How—?"

"Later. Let go!"

"What?"

"There's a cat walk about ten feet below you. Don't miss, girl."

With all the blood I'd been dripping into the ocean, every shark within a twenty mile radius was bound to either be here or on the way. If I missed, the end would probably be quick.

I took a deep breath and let go.

Chapter 23
The Female of the Species

 t takes approximately one second to complete a ten foot drop. Either Delilah was wrong about the distance, or this was the longest second in the history of the universe.

I wished it had been longer.

I moaned when I hit the railing. I felt my ribs cave. Searing pain shot through my chest when I tried to breathe. I didn't want to think about moving.

"Come on, girl. Get up!" Delilah said, suddenly beside me.

Not sure I can. I gasped as I tried to sit up.

Talking only made the pain worse. I could manage it with short, shallow breaths that didn't move my ribs too much. Then it was merely excruciating, instead of unbearable. On the up side, I wasn't noticing my shoulder so much now.

"You went through all this to get Fellowes, and you're just going to lay there and let him get back on his boat?"

I knew she was right. But that didn't make it any easier. The cut on my head had mostly clotted, so I didn't worry much about it. I whimpered as I took off my shirt and used it to bandage my leg. It was still bleeding, and moving would just make it worse.

I cried, big hot tears scorching down my cheeks, as I struggled to my feet. I held onto the railing as a coughing fit shook my body. I tasted blood. Of course. I needed a punctured lung to go with the broken ribs. Why break up such a nicely matched set?

"I know it hurts, Marti. But you got a job to do. You got to let those girls out. That's the only way anything gonna happen to Fellowes today. Come. On."

I struggled to keep up with Delilah. I was dizzy and felt I might vomit at any time. But I would have crawled through broken glass to take Tucker Fellowes down. And I did crawl up three flights of no-slip grip metal stairs, which was pretty much the same thing.

"We're here," Delilah said.

I had to lean against the door frame to catch my breath. I heard a gurgle as the air went in and a rattle as it went out. That was so not good. I also heard crying on the other side of the door, so I knew we were in the right place. I turned the dead bolt and opened it.

"Girls," I whispered as loudly as I could. "It's me, Marti. C'mon, let's get out of here."

They were very cautious in coming to the door. I assumed they were expecting a nasty trick. Or perhaps it was because I looked like a refugee from a slasher film. Either way, I understood, but they were wasting precious time by being so timid.

"Hurry up! We don't have a lot of time." I don't have a lot of time. Rayne shooed them along.

"What happened to you?" Rayne asked.

"Long story. Tell you on the boat. Can you get there?" I had to lean on the door to keep myself upright.

"Sort of. I had to help them unload groceries once."

"Go. Don't wait for me."

Rayne led and I staggered behind. Crystal, the one with the bloody stains on her pants and bruised face, was leaning on Veronica. Then she stumbled and fell to her knees. She was pale and sweaty. Veronica helped her up.

"Sorry. I'm just a little lightheaded," Crystal said.

"It's okay. Do the best you can," I said.

I wondered if she had internal injuries, because she sure looked shocky. And there wasn't a damned thing I could do for her out here. Me either, for that matter. She was going to shut down if she didn't get help soon. That made two of us. But I only had to make it long enough to get Tucker Fellowes. After that, it didn't much matter.

Rayne got us to the upper deck. Progress was slow, but we made it.

Delilah appeared and held up her hands "Stop."

"Wait," I rasped. I leaned against a crate and panted, trying not to cry from the pain.

I really hoped there was nobody on the receiving platform – they would see us, if they took the time to look. There were still traces of the sun on the western horizon, but it was dark. An enormous orange moon was just breaking the eastern horizon. I guessed it was somewhere between 8:30 and 9:00. Artificial daylight blazed on the deck, bleaching colors and darkening shadows.

Voices came from the opposite side of the deck, and we stayed put. Tucker Fellowes opened a door and Salinger dragged something heavy through it. It was Ian Chambers. He was at the very least unconscious, but I was too far away to see anything more.

"Yeah, well Billy and Trey couldn't find their asses with both hands. You go look for that bitch," Fellowes barked. "She's getting to be more trouble than she's worth."

Salinger disappeared into the innards of the rig.

I had hoped that Fellowes would follow him, but he didn't. I don't know what I thought I was going to do. I could barely stand up. Even if I could sneak up on him, and if I had a weapon (two pretty big ifs), I didn't have the strength to use it. My original plan had been to knock him out, tape him up and turn him over to Nick. And tell him that he was the one who killed Ryan and blackmailed Chambers. Unfortunately, I didn't have a Plan B, the one that outlined how to capture Fellowes when I was somewhere between half and three-quarters dead.

My legs were shaking so hard that I had to sit down. I unstuck my raw palms from the crate, leaving bright bloody handprints, and slid to the deck against the crate that had been holding me up. My eyes didn't want to stay open. If I could just have a nap, everything would be clearer. Maybe just rest my eyes for a minute.

A scrabbling sound interrupted my snooze.

"Where is she?" A woman emerged from the dark behind a stack of boxes. I couldn't be sure, but she looked like the stripper Quinn had given $100 to at Specials.

"Waynette. What a nice surprise." Fellowes answered, unperturbed. "Just out of curiosity, how'd you get out here? Happened to be in the neighborhood?"

"Cut the crap. My aunt said you took her. Where is Veronica?"

"I don't know. I don't have her," Fellowes said, taking a step backward.

"Mom!" Veronica shouted as she ran out onto the deck.

"You bastard! You told me if I worked for you, you'd leave her alone," Waynette shrieked at Fellows, her voice rough with fury and loathing.

"And you believed me?" Fellowes was easing his way towards the woman, and she was backing away at the same pace.

She raised both her arms, chest level, hands clasped together. The barrel of a handgun gleamed in the harsh floodlights. Veronica stood frozen on the deck. Both she and her mother were crying.

"I'm warning you! I will shoot," Waynette shouted.

"No, you won't. You're just strung out. You're going to give me the gun, then we'll go up to the lab and Charles will fix you up. Then you'll be back at work tomorrow." Fellowes voice was calm and soothing.

"Not another step!"

Fellowes took another step.

A small black hole suddenly appeared between his eyes, followed immediately by an earsplitting bang. I've never seen anyone look more surprised as he sank to his knees and toppled over, face down. He bet wrong on that one.

I was torn between the intense satisfaction of Fellowes getting what he deserved and the disappointment of it being someone other than me who gave it to him. The acrid smell of spent gunpowder drifted past me, and it made me think of Ryan, on days when he came home from the firing range, that smell clinging to his clothes.

Veronica ran onto the platform. "Mom! Mom!" she yelled as she threw herself at her mother.

Still holding the pistol, Waynette wrapped her arms around her daughter. They held each other and sobbed.

There was no sign of any bad guys, and they had surely heard the gunshot. The rest of the girls ventured out to where Veronica and Waynette were standing, and milled around the two of them.

Then there was a loud clunk, as if a heavy switch had been pulled, and all the lights went out.

I was grateful for the light from the almost-full moon, but it still took some time for my eyes to adjust.

Something snarled and snuffled in the shadows. Two points of red light hovered about three and a half feet off the ground. I recognized those eyes. They belonged to a werewolf, maybe even the same one that had hurled itself against my patio door a few nights ago.

It burst into the open, destroying the distance between it and the girls with frightening speed, fangs glinting in the silvery moonlight.

I saw a muzzle flash and heard another bang. The creature was knocked back a little. A dark stain spread through the pale fur on its chest, but it didn't slow down much. Waynette squeezed the trigger again. Nothing happened. The monster was closing in for the kill. Waynette frantically shook the pistol and pulled the trigger again. There was an explosion from the back of the gun, and Waynette collapsed.

I knew I wasn't going to make it.

I couldn't keep my eyes open any longer. But at least had the satisfaction of knowing Fellowes wasn't going to hurt anyone else. Ever.

I thought of Ryan and Cassie, and let myself relax into the dark.

Chapter 24
Flight

 arti, girl! Get up and come with me. Somebody need to talk to you."

Delilah? What's going on? I – where am I?

"Just come with me, girlfriend."

I couldn't tell if my eyes were open or closed, and I stretched out my arms in front of myself to feel my way. Pudgy fingers closed around my hand.

"Come on, Marti."

Delilah and I shuffled through the dark. I'm glad one of us knew where we were going. I gradually became aware of light. Then Delilah was gone and I was in a strange room where the floor, walls and ceiling were all bright white. It was hard to tell where one left off and the other started.

"Hey, Bright Eyes."

I turned to see Ryan standing behind me. I ran towards him, but I seemed to be on a treadmill. I ran and ran, but he never got any closer. Finally, I stopped.

"Ryan? Why can't I reach you?"

"Because you don't belong here. You have to go back."

"Aren't I dead?"

He smiled and shook his head. "Temporarily. But you can't stay here."

Why was he smiling? "I saw you, and I assumed that you were here to take me to the other side, and you, me and…wait a minute. Where's Cassie? You do know about Cassie, don't you?"

Ryan laughed. "Of course I know about Cassie."

I felt a little disappointed. "She didn't come with you?"

"She's not dead."

"I saw Tucker Fellowes drop her over the side of the boat."

"Maybe, but she's waiting for you back there. But first, you have a visitor."

"Hey, chica."

"Spam."

"You know that unfinished business? It's finished now. Couldn't have done it without you." Spam grew a little more transparent.

On the one hand, I didn't like Spam. He was a self-centered jerk who was responsible for a lot of human misery. On the other hand, he helped stop someone who was responsible for a whole lot more human misery, and who had arranged to have Ryan killed. If he hadn't shown up at the party, Tucker Fellowes would still be trafficking young women, selling drugs, and living well off other people's suffering. Grudgingly, I said, "Thank you, Spam. If it wasn't for you, I would never have known what really happened to Ryan."

Spam grinned. "Yeah, well you know Waynette bought that gun at a pawn shop with the c-note Quinn slipped her at Specials."

"So you want credit for stopping Fellowes as well?"

"Un poquito," he said, measuring a small space between two fingers.

An elderly couple with a small baby in a frilly dress popped up next to Spam.

"Mamá! Papi!" He hugged them both and took the baby from the old woman. "Maria, me buena." They all got brighter and brighter until I couldn't look at them anymore. And then they were gone.

"You have to go now." Ryan said. He still looked highly amused.

"You don't have to look so happy about it," I complained.

"Seems weird, doesn't it? But every time you look into Cassie's eyes, you'll see me there. I'm always with you. Always."

"Not sure if that makes it better or worse. But at least I get the chance to say goodbye this time."

"Not goodbye. Until next time, Bright Eyes. You've got a lot more living left to do. And it shouldn't involve living in a convent." He cocked his head and lifted one eyebrow.

I smiled back at him. "Hint, hint, nudge, nudge?"

"Be happy. I love you."

"I love you, too."

I felt like I was falling, and reached out to try and stop my fall. I was shocked that my hands made contact with something firm and warm.

I opened my eyes. The sun had just cleared the eastern horizon, and Quinn was sitting next to me. My fingers were digging into his thigh.

"Sorry!" I said, quickly releasing him.

"Welcome back."

His eyes were dark, almost black, the way they were supposed to be. I smiled at him, glad to see him looking werewolf free.

"Not that I mind, but you might want this." Quinn handed me a tee-shirt.

It took me a second to remember that I was only wearing shorts and a nursing bra. "Thanks," I said, pulling the shirt over my head.

"Somebody's been looking for you."

A woman I didn't recognize came over, carrying something.

She was holding Cassie.

I leaped to my feet and snatched my baby from her arms. I hugged that child so tightly that she squirmed and fussed. I knew my eyes were streaming, and I must have looked like I'd been through a blender, but I was too happy to care. I held her at arms' length to look at her. She was wearing the same dress, although there was something that might have been banana smeared all over the front of it. And instead of a diaper, she had some shop towels duct taped to her bottom. She grinned at me. "Mama! Mama!"

I looked at Quinn. He shrugged. "The Coast Guard didn't have any diapers. This was the best we could do."

"The Coast Guard? There's a whole lot of this story that you need to fill me in on."

And that is when I realized that my shoulder and ribs didn't hurt and I could breathe without gurgling. I tore the bloody shirt off of my leg. If I looked carefully, I could see four thin white scars.

"Did you do this?"

"Not me. I just know the right people."

I thought of the woman with dark hair, and wondered if he meant her.

Quinn chuckled a little as he stood up. "Now. Where were we? I'll start where we parted company. First of all, do you know how much Styrofoam those baby carriers have in them? They're extremely buoyant. I don't know if you saw Cassie floating around after Fellowes dropped her in the water. Some of my friends looked after her and kept her under the platform so she didn't get sunburned and dehydrated. They gave her something to eat, too. Don't ask me what, because I don't know, but she seems happy enough."

He reached out and tickled the side of Cassie's neck. She squealed with delight and hid her face against my shoulder. Then she looked around, eager for him to do it again. He didn't, but he motioned for us to follow him down the stairs. The woman stayed on the upper deck. We ended up on the level where Fellowes had kept the five girls imprisoned. I felt cold and oppressed just being down here. Residual energy, perhaps.

"Before they snatched me yesterday afternoon, I could feel Salinger coming for me. Maybe because he's the one who infected me, I was hyper-sensitive to him."

"Wait, Salinger was the werewolf?"

"I thought you knew that."

"I only knew that you'd tracked the werewolf to Specials."

Quinn rummaged through some large cabinets and storage lockers as he spoke. "Sorry. Anyway, I knew Salinger was coming, and that he'd kill anyone in the house with me, so I asked them to take me outside, into the sun, and leave me alone. They did, and when Salinger and Chambers came for me, I pretended to be sicker than I really was. They dropped me trying to get me into the back of the SUV – that's how my lip got busted."

"I thought they'd beaten you up."

"No. They thought I was coming over to their side. And they were right. The werewolf parasites were winning. I couldn't fight them much longer. I knew that the best thing I could do was drown," Quinn continued.

"Drown? You don't look dead to me."

"Well, of course not. Water can't kill me. I am water. But what lying on the bottom of the ocean for an hour did do to my human form was to make it inhospitable enough to the parasite to kill it. And as powerful as dragons are, they are not as powerful as an entire ocean. Because I was in the sea, I was able to override the amulet."

"I thought you weren't a sea monster."

Quinn shrugged. "Water is water. A little salt doesn't make all that much difference, although I couldn't live in the ocean full time. It dries out my skin and makes me itchy." He winked at me. "By the way, did you want to keep it?" He pulled the anti-shifting amulet from his pocket.

"No. I want to unmake it."

"That's what I thought."

He found a metal tank and rubbed some dust off the label, then checked the pressure gauge. He attached a hose to it, and rummaged around until he found a welder's helmet in one of the cabinets.

"You might want to step around the corner. This is going to be bright."

I took Cassie a little way down the hall and sang her a song. She looked so much like her daddy that it hurt, sometimes. I though she also might be hungry. I was right. I ran my finger along her jaw as she nursed.

I could see Ryan clearly in my mind, standing in that white, white room, smiling at me and joking around like he always did. I supposed what I had now was closure. I'd gotten to say goodbye, at long last. And got his not-so-subtle hint that I should move on. After all this time, I finally felt at peace, that whatever happened would be okay. I leaned against the wall, and closed my eyes. Behind us, I could hear the hiss of an acetylene torch, and smelled hot metal.

Cassie was finished and burped before Quinn joined us in the corridor. He held a chain with half of a melted pewter circle suspended from it, all that remained of the anti-shifting amulet.

"That should do it," he said.

We went back up the stairs and came out onto the deck, washed in fresh new sunlight. Seagulls were already diving and squawking around the platform. Quinn led me to the edge of the deck. I heard a splash and then saw an enormous creature rising from the water. It made Fellowes' yacht look like a bath toy bobbing next to the platform leg. Above the metallic aquamarine body, bat-like wings unfolded and stretched. It raised its snaky neck up until it was almost level with us. Its emerald green eye was bigger than my head. Then it opened its armored jaws and roared.

It was so loud it shook the platform, and it made Cassie cry. I patted her back and jiggled her gently up and down with my hip.

"That's dragon for 'thank you,'" Quinn said.

Water fell on us like rain as the creature flapped its wings and rose into the air. Cassie stopped crying and stared at the dragon as she flew higher in the sky, her silhouette soaring above the orange morning sun.

"There she goes!" said Quinn, waving.

"Won't people see her?" I asked.

"Not unless she wants them to."

We watched the dragon until she faded into the horizon. After discovering kelpies, dryads and werewolves, a dragon seemed perfectly normal to me, no more unusual than a mocking bird in the backyard. I was glad she was free.

"So…just out of curiosity, why was a dragon living underneath the oil platform? I didn't think they lived in water."

"They don't. Dragons fly, of course, but they also travel through the earth. Being bound to the amulet, she was forced to follow it around. It wasn't her fault there was 1,200' feet of water over the little bit of the Earth's crust she was hiding in. Remember, they're the ultimate shapeshifters. They can take any form you can imagine, and quite a few you can't."

"So, while I had the amulet, there was a dragon hanging out under my house?"

Quinn nodded.

What the HOA didn't know wouldn't hurt them. "Where do you think she's going?" I asked.

"I don't know. Watch the news for earthquakes in the next day or two. That'll probably be it. They move around a lot, trying to get settled in."

"Earthquakes. Right." I nodded. "Now, tell me about the Coast Guard."

Quinn led us over towards the personnel basket that had lifted us from Fellowes' boat yesterday afternoon.

"That was all Delilah. She's a wizard with electricity and radio. She called in an SOS from this location. Coast Guard Search and Rescue arrived just after the shots were fired."

"She could have called someone earlier, like when Salinger ran my car off the road."

"She could have. But then no one would have known to rescue the girls he had locked up out here, and Fellowes and Salinger wouldn't have gotten what was coming to them. And I'd be a werewolf by now."

"Funny how things work out, huh?" I looked at Quinn, very glad that he wasn't a werewolf.

Quinn picked up Cassie's waterlogged car seat and put it in the metal basket, then helped us in. An engine rattled to life, and the basket shuddered and lifted off the deck.

I held tightly to Cassie as the arm swung out over the water and the personnel basket started to descend.

"The Coast Guard found the three bodies - Fellowes, Salinger and Chambers - on the deck. Turns out that Waynette used silver slugs. No idea where she found those. The bullet she put in Salinger got him, eventually, but using those rounds also caused her gun to blow up. The slide hit her in the face and fractured her skull. I don't know if she'll survive. It's hard to tell with these things. They took her, her daughter and one other girl by chopper. The remaining girls, the chemist, and the dead ones, went by boat. I hid you and Cassie while he was working on putting you back together. Didn't think you'd mind."

"He? Anybody I know?"

Quinn looked down to the deck. "Kind of. It was Malik."

Anger surged up from my belly. "That's awfully decent of him, since he's the one who nearly killed me."

"Technically, you were dead. And I can't blame you for being upset with him—"

I threw my free hand in the air. "Upset?" I snapped. "It goes way beyond upset."

"I hear you. I was quite angry with him, too, when he told me what had happened. But keep in mind that he'd just been attacked by a sahir who was trying to make him a slave. His mind was poisoned. He wasn't himself. He hoped healing your body would go some way in making it up to you."

It made sense. But it wasn't so easy to forget what he'd put me through. "I'll keep that in mind."

"He also tweaked the girls' memories. As far as they remember, Waynette rescued them. It's like you were never here."

That would save me a very uncomfortable conversation with Nick.

"Speaking of Waynette," I asked as I shifted Cassie to the other hip. "How did she get here and how did you know to give her the money for the gun?"

"The first part's easy. She packed herself into one of the supply crates Salinger took out to the yacht. The second part is a little more complicated. Let's just call it intuition and leave it at that."

I didn't want to leave it at that, but I suspected Quinn wasn't going to tell me any more about it. He had turned away from me, watching the boat below us. Sweat stuck his loose cotton shirt to his back. The image of him in my bed flickered across my memory and I felt myself smile. Then I looked at Cassie and blushed. Still, I wondered if I'd have a different reaction than hopping out of bed and wrapping up in a sheet, if I ever found myself in a similar situation with him.

Cassie squawked when the basket bumped down on the deck of Fellowes' yacht. We stepped out of it, and it rose off the deck. When the basket was back on the platform, the diesel engine stopped. A dark blur sliced into the water near the boat, as if someone had dived off the deck.

"Don't worry about her. She lives here," Quinn said, then frowned at the locked door.

I took the key out of my pocket and unlocked the cockpit. I suddenly realized that not everyone was accounted for.

"And what about the other two? Fellowes had a couple of guys here on the platform other than the cook."

"They won't be causing you any more trouble. You think they've got any fizzy drinks on this boat? I've got terrible indigestion."

Bonus Material

Last Night at the Roquefort

aul Samson pulled the plug from the bathtub, and listened to all the sweat and grime from his longshoreman's job gurgle down the drain with the bathwater as he dried off. He'd have to hurry if he was going to make it to Club Roquefort on time. He quickly dusted his body with lilac scented powder, then tucked the hot pink box underneath a towel in the linen closet. He had brought his elderly mother to live with him after his sister moved to the west coast, and he would just as soon not have a discussion with her about why a lifelong bachelor would have fancy ladies' powder in his bathroom.

Paul had brought his clothes into the bathroom with him. He pulled a stretch knit panty girdle most of the way up. Then he folded a small towel and tucked it inside, carefully arranging his parts and using the towel to smooth out any bulges. He shaved again, slicked his damp hair back, then dressed in khakis and a pale denim shirt.

In the living room, his mother had fallen asleep on the couch, bible in her lap. He kissed her softly on the top of the head, then pulled an aluminum travel case out of the hall closet and left.

Club Roquefort was far from being the Moulin Rouge, Paul's dream venue. Even in its heyday in the mid-1920s, the Roquefort had been neither grand nor new. Ten years later, was tired and dingy, but it was a fixture. It was the sort of place his mother had told him never, *ever* to go near when his banker father had uprooted the family of five from New Orleans, Louisiana and replanted them in New York City. That had been 1916, and Paul was nearly a grown man then.

The bouncer looked up when Paul came in through the grimy stage entrance, then went back to his newspaper. The dressing room door stuck, as usual, and Paul had to put his shoulder against it to shove it open. He'd been performing here on Friday and Saturday nights for a dozen years, and in all that time, the door had never been fixed. Bursting into the room like Eliot Ness had become a ritual for Paul, almost like a mini rebirth.

He set his burden down on the dressing table and fumbled in his pocket for the key. The Halliburton locking aluminum case – the hot new thing - had been a splurge, but it made Paul feel safer. The Great Depression had caused a social backlash against the mores of the freewheeling 20s that had been slow to dissipate. He feared what might happen if strangers knew what was inside.

He hung up the sequined red gown and set the corset, stockings and makeup box on the table. He'd made the dress himself, spending many a wee hour hand-sewing the sequins while his mother was sleeping. He'd often toyed with the idea of opening a dress shop and designing fabulous custom gowns. After all, if Main Bocher could design Wallis Simpson's wedding dress, and gowns for Mary Pickford, there was no reason Paul couldn't do the same thing. But somehow, there was never enough time, or money, or this, or that, and Paul kept working at the docks.

He sprayed the perfume atomizer around the room, hoping to cover up the eau de mildew of the place while he got ready. It took the better part of an hour to apply the makeup and get the wig just so. Paul slipped on white cotton gloves so that his labor-roughened hands wouldn't damage his stockings. No amount of buffing or lotion ever made the thick callouses truly go away, the price he paid for nine years working at the docks. Before that, he had worked for his father, until that fateful day in 1929 when the bank failed and his proud, but financially ruined, father opted to take a header out of a twenty story window. He'd been thinking of his father a lot, lately. Especially, since he'd been having a recurring dream where his father came home from work, tottering crazily on smashed and broken legs, blood covering one side of his face, and asked to have fried eggs for supper.

Paul sucked in his stomach. The corset had been getting tighter over the last few months. He'd been promoted and was doing less manual labor. It was just as well, because he wasn't as young as he used to be, and as he neared middle age, a certain softness was settling in around his body. It made for nice cleavage, though.

The stage hand knocked on the dressing room door. "You're on in five."

"Zip me up, Irv?"

"Sure thing." Irv stepped in and tugged the long zipper up Paul's back. "You look great," he said.

"Thanks.

Paul strapped on his heels and made his way to the stage wings.

"Please give it up for Nehi, the Indian Princess!" the MC boomed into a bulky silver microphone.

The crowd was not large and the applause was not loud. Nehi, whose wife knew him as Jim, minced off the stage, swinging long black hair.

"And now, what you've all been waiting for! The one and only! The spectacular! The faaaabulous Miiiiss Deeeeeliiiiilaaaah!"

Paul took a deep breath and let *her* out. She strutted out to the MC and took the mic. Miss Delilah owned the stage. She was everything Paul was not – stylish, powerful, and happy. She surveyed the audience. The Roquefort was half full, three-quarters if she counted the patrons who were no longer living. The dead ones came, attracted to drunk people like flies to carrion. They crowded in, hoping to steal energy, memories, life from those who spent their time trying to drown their misery in alcohol. Unfortunately, misery floats.

"How y'all doing tonight?" In spite of living so many years in New York City, Delilah had not only kept her unique New Orleans accent, but embellished it with faux southern-ness. The regulars hooted and cat-called.

The spotlight came on and the footlights went out. Delilah closed her eyes. Tiny rhinestones glittered on her eyelids. The pianist stroked the keys.

Delilah's smoky voice eased into her set, a selection of popular torch songs and a Gershwin medley.

When Delilah finished her act, she got a standing ovation. Delilah always got standing ovations.

She went backstage, then came into the bar from the front. Rudy, the bartender, handed her a glass of tepid water. She perched on a barstool and waited. After the main show was over, and the paying customers had either left or were too drunk to care, the manager let some aspiring performers take the stage – comics, singers, strippers and occasionally, sideshow working acts.

"Great show tonight, Delilah! Good on ya," a young man said as he approached her. He was handsome, blonde, and had been dead for almost a hundred years. She hardly even noticed the gash on his head or the bloodstain on his shirt anymore. He'd fled the Potato Famine, only to die here three months later.

Thanks, Bram, she thought, knowing he could hear her. She'd talked to dead people all of her life, and had been twelve years old before she realized that most people didn't see them.

The majority of the ghosts in the place were ugly, leering, nasty. But Bram had been killed in a textile mill accident nearby. The owner had covered it up. The mill was long gone, but Bram's bones were still buried in the now cement-filled basement.

"Now would you look at that?" he said.

Delilah followed his pointing finger. A strange, misty blob hovered over the head of one of the patrons. A half-empty bottle of whiskey and an empty shot glass sat in front of him. Delilah guessed that he had no clue that a cloud, flickering with what looked like red and orange heat lightning, was slowly lowering itself towards his head. *What is that?*

"Have you never seen them before? Not sure what the educated fellas ud call 'em, but I rekon they're a sort of parasite. It's like a possession – they take over yer mind and make you do all and such as you'd ne'er do on yer own."

Come with me. Delilah got up and went to the man's table. "Mind if I sit down?" she asked, pulling out the chair across from him. Bram floated behind her.

The man looked up slowly, his eyes half closed. "It's a free country."

His breath stank of whiskey and despair.

"I ain't seen you around. First time here?" Delilah asked the man. *What are you? What do you want?* She thought at the cloud. It was almost touching the whiskey drinker now.

"Leave us alone!" the cloud screeched at her, its voice like shattering glass.

Delilah imagined a large bubble, formed from pure white light, enclosing the table, surrounding herself, Bram, and the drunk.

The cloud flashed dark red and screamed, a shrill keening that made Delilah's temples throb. But it left, moving off to hover against the high ceiling in the corner.

"Well, mister, I hope you enjoyed the show." Delilah stood up. The drunk grunted and poured more whiskey.

"Lady D! You bring your gorgeous self over here!" Princess Nehi called from the end of the bar, surrounded by the other performers and a handful of patrons.

"Girl, ain't nobody tell me what to do," Delilah answered with mock indignation. She took her glass of water and joined the group.

It was close to 3:30 AM when Delilah went to the restroom. She would have to revert back to being drab, lonely Paul soon, and she was putting it off as long as possible.

"Psst!" a voice from the shadows called.

"*Who* is that up in there? Are you *really* hissing at me?" Delilah's fists planted themselves on her hips.

The drunk from earlier stepped from the shadowy hallway. "Miss Delilah? Is that your name?" He appeared to have sobered up considerably.

"What do you want?"

The man lunged at her, pushing her against the wall and pinning her there with his forearm across her throat. "Just wanted to show you some appreciation, that's all." He grabbed hard at her crotch.

"What the hell?" he shouted as he stumbled backwards.

He doesn't know. Oh. My. God. He doesn't know. "Sweetheart, this is Club Roquefort. What did you *expect* to find down there?" Delilah smoothed her dress and fixed her wig. Her heart raced and she just wanted to get back to the safety of her friends. But she would be damned if she would let this piece of human garbage intimidate her. She may even have let Paul out to pop him upside the head a few times.

When he looked up at her, Delilah saw red lightning flashing behind his eyes. Somehow, he'd found the baseball bat that the bouncer kept in the umbrella stand near the stage door. She turned to run.

Her skull suddenly filled with white light and she couldn't see.

"Don't look down," a disembodied voice said. "You don't want to see that. Just follow me." She found herself floating near the ceiling, at the end of the hallway that led to the restrooms.

A pinpoint of light appeared before her, then spread out into a tunnel.

"Is this…?"

"It is where you need to go."

"Wait! Please. Please bring my friend Bram along."

"Call to him. See if he'll join you. There are a lot of friends waiting for him."

"Bram? Bram! Come here! Please, come with me!"

In an instant, he was by her side. She clasped his hand, and they walked into the light together.

Delilah found herself in a garden. Sweet olive bushes, sprinkled with tiny white flowers, grew in large terra cotta pots in each corner. A fancy wrought iron fence scrolled around the grassy square. Gravel paths quartered the place, meeting in the middle and turning into a rectangle that bordered a parterre garden with a gushing fountain in the middle. White birds fluttered by.

"Hello," said a woman in a long blue dress, whom Delilah was certain hadn't been there a moment before. "Are you ready for your review?"

"My what?"

"Your life review. Everyone gets one when they return here, remember?"

And Delilah did remember. She remembered every second, every feeling, every thought of Paul Samson's life, yet it only seemed to take an instant. And she cried. There were so many grand plans that she'd never gotten around to. So many problems she had planned to solve, but she'd spent too much time clinging to the bank, and not enough time swimming in the river.

"I failed, didn't I?"

"Failed? Of course you didn't. When folks leave here, they are often…overly enthusiastic about what they can accomplish. No matter how many times they've been down there, they always forget that living on the material plane is like wading through chest-deep water – it's much harder work than they think. Evolution of any sort takes time to unfold."

Delilah nodded and looked down, still feeling ashamed. Then she noticed something that had not been there only moments before. Her hands flew to her chest. "These boobs are *real!*"

"Of course they are. That's how you see yourself, isn't it?"

"But I have a male body."

"This is the astral plane. You manifest instantaneously here. If you want boobs, you have boobs." She snapped her fingers. "When you took a body, you chose to be Paul because one of your challenges was to find your authentic self. Don't worry. You'll remember everything before long. It's just reintegration shock."

A piece of astral paper appeared in the woman's hand. She looked at it and nodded her head. "Have you considered Spirit Guide School?"

"What?"

"Spirit guides. People on this side who help people on the other side. More and more people are choosing to incarnate with the ability to see ghosts. You were pretty good at handling that. The counselors are always looking for those with the right qualifications. There's a little training, a few rules to learn – mostly common sense, really."

"I don't even know what to say," Delilah responded.

"Well, we've got a batch who've decided to be highly intuitive getting ready to go down soon. Many of them have never incarnated before. They could really use your help. Why don't you get to know some of them, then decide?"

Time was different on the astral plane, perhaps even irrelevant. And yet there must be some connection to the material plane. Souls came and left. Some succeeded and some failed, but all had assignments. Delilah was reunited with old friends and made new ones. She attended Spirit Guide School – she was happy to stay discarnate, at least for the foreseeable future. She got to know the souls she was assigned to guide, even sat with them in the Antechamber – the room where incarnating spirits wait until it's their time to descend into the material world. They had to forget what it was like to live without a body, or else they'd never take to the clumsy things. They had to forget the easy bliss of the astral, or else they'd never survive. But they would remember little fragments of peace and love, so they'd always try to recreate those feelings. As their memories started to go, they often got frightened, not sure of what would be awaiting them on the other side. It didn't help that the tunnel went from dim to dark as it telescoped down. Delilah was there to hold their hands and guide them into the passage that would take them on their material adventure. She watched over them and helped them while they were down there, and she welcomed them back when they were done. It kept her very busy.

"These are the last two of this intuitive batch," said the lady in the blue dress.

Delilah had been taking a break, relaxing on the incredibly comfortable couch with a book when the woman appeared. She handed Delilah two sheets of astral paper.

"Their identities and life plans for downstairs. Give these a good looking over. This one could get tricky. Let me know if you need any help," the woman said.

Delilah nodded, but the woman was already gone.

She would read the plans, just as soon as she got to the end of the chapter, then go and meet the two souls. But she did glance at the names as she set the pages down on the coffee table. One would be called Marti Renee Schmidt Keller. The other would be named Tucker Wayne Fellowes.

The Magician's Children

THE MAGICIAN
EL MAGO

I

IL BAGATTO
LE BATELEUR

DER MAGIER

DE MAGIER

Artemis Greenleaf

The Magician's Children

Artemis Greenleaf

Marti Keller Mysteries
Book Two

Acknowledgements

As always, thank you to my wonderful family. This endeavor would not be possible without your love and support. I also appreciate the invaluable editorial and structural help of my critique groups and beta readers. You know who you are, and I couldn't do this without you. I would also like to give a big shout out to the great folks who organize No Refusals nights for MADD, and the kind and patient HPD officers who graciously answer my questions when they are trapped in the car with me during a ride-along.

Table of Contents

Fate is like a strange, unpopular restaurant, filled with odd waiters who bring you things you never asked for and don't always like.
Lemony Snicket

Chapter 1
Five Rubles

veklá wiped the blood off his face with the back of his hand. Bertram Kounis wasn't dead. Yet. But it wouldn't take much longer. Sveklá frowned at the gasping man on the ground, blood spurting from his throat with each heartbeat. He'd gotten sloppy and only severed the jugular and carotid on one side of Kounis' neck. He blamed it on the arthritis settling into his shoulder. This was a physical job, and he wasn't as young as he used to be. Sveklá took no joy in killing. But sometimes it was part his job, and he did it as he would any other.

"*Do svidaniya*, Kounis," Sveklá said, taking a five-ruble coin from his pocket. "You should have paid." He dropped the silver coin at the other man's feet. "Now, you must be example to others."

A sharp pain pricked him, and Sveklá dropped the edger and shook out his hand, thinking an insect had stung him – he'd always been terrified of wasps. A large splinter was jammed into his palm, and droplets of blood were oozing out of it. He pulled the sliver out and cursed the wooden handle of the garden tool he'd just used to dispatch his victim.

Men like Kounis disgusted him. Greedy, grasping men who thought the world owed them whatever they desired. Kounis had made an agreement with Sveklá's boss to pay $5,000 every other week, a pittance for such a man, really. And in return, the boss would refrain from providing proof to the Securities Exchange Commission that Kounis' investment firm, Kounis Securities LLC, had devolved into nothing more than a Ponzi scheme.

Kounis had gone from investor to the well-connected captains of Houston's thriving industry to shell-game con artist when he'd compounded a spectacularly bad real estate investment with an expensive mistress.

The first time Kounis couldn't pay, the boss had gone easy on him, letting him off with the addition of a 100% interest payment. When Sveklá had come to collect the $15,000, Kounis had gotten angry and refused to pay.

If Kounis didn't pay one way, he'd pay another. Making an example of someone from time to time, kept the others in line.

A noise from the street caught the enforcer's attention. Someone was coming. *Damn*. A glance at Kounis confirmed that he was beyond help. Sveklá fled.

"No. As far as I know, my husband has never been to Russia," Lilian Kounis said.

Her face was pale and her eyes were glassy and red. Head lowered and body slouched, she sat like a beaten dog in the interrogation room. Her voice was barely above a whisper when she answered questions.

FBI Special Agent Hadrian Galanti watched her from behind the one-way glass. He felt sorry for her. Not only had her husband just been murdered, but his death had caused the implosion of the carefully constructed upper middle class façade he had created. His struggle was over, but she was still being wounded by the shrapnel from her shattered life.

Lilian was the second wife, the trophy wife, barely older than Kounis' son, a senior at Princeton. Her job was to look good. And look good she did, her designer sportswear perfectly matched to her pale complexion. Her handbag alone probably cost more than the monthly rent on Hadrian's apartment. As far as personal image went, she was a master. On the other hand, business acumen, or cognitive skills in general, were not required of her. Whether her ignorance was willful or honest was difficult for Hadrian to determine. But she appeared to be just as shocked and surprised as anyone else when Bertram's house of cards came crashing down.

He didn't believe for a moment that she knew anything about her husband's business. What troubled him was the Russian coin found near the dead man's feet. In fact, it was the only reason he'd gotten involved in the case. He felt it was unlikely that it was there by accident. The same type of coin had been found at six other homicides in the past year and a half. The forensics team had recovered a partial print, and was waiting for results from the AFIS database search. If it came up empty, he'd check with Interpol. He doubted he'd get much help from Russia's FSB if the Interpol query failed.

Lilian had reported that she heard a noise, and when she came out of the garage, there was some poor schmuck named Benjamin Fayllor holding the murder weapon and standing over her husband's body. The two men had some heated words earlier in the day, and they were bitter rivals in the upcoming homeowner's association election. It was true that Fayllor had motive, means and opportunity, but Hadrian doubted that he killed Kounis. For one thing, all of the blood was on the bottoms of his shoes. There was none on the tops. There was also no evidence of any blood on his clothes. Several of his coworkers confirmed that he was wearing the same clothes he'd worn to work earlier. For another thing, there were traces of blood on the handle of the edger. The DNA results hadn't come back yet, but both Kounis and Fayllor were blood type O+. The blood on the handle was AB-. Unless Hadrian was very wrong, Fayllor hadn't killed anybody.

That's why it pained him to keep Fayllor in jail. If the five ruble coin meant what he thought it meant, it would be better for the real killer to think that he had gotten away with it. He'd relax, and be off guard. Hadrian would not.

When he'd joined the Multi Agency Gang Task Force three years ago, he'd expected to see mostly narcos from south of the border, and some Asian triads. That was still true, but European gangs, like the Chechens and the Russians, were on the rise. Being a transportation hub made Houston irresistible to them. A breakaway faction of New York City's Odessa Group had set up shop in the warehouse district, and they were just like any other invasive exotic – unappealing to the local predators, but out-competing the native organisms for resources. The Russians didn't have the strength to challenge the more robust, well-established organizations head-on yet, but Hadrian knew the day was coming. There would no bloodless coup, and a lot of innocent civilians would get slaughtered in the crossfire. If he had to hold Fayllor in order to catch some really bad guys, he would do it. Even if he hated it.

Chapter 2
Edging out the Competition

M y husband, Ryan, was still dead.

But at least I had finally gotten to say goodbye.

I talk to ghosts. I didn't use to. Not until one of them insisted I help solve his own murder. And that journey led me to discover whole other aspects of good and evil, in ways I'd never imagined. But I digress.

I babysat while my sister, Emily, and her husband, Nick, went to Ian Chambers' funeral. Nick had recently tried fixing me up with Chambers, and that was an epic disaster. But that's a whole other story. As it stood, I wasn't glad he was dead, but I wasn't exactly sorry about it, either.

My daughter, Cassie, and her brand new cousin, McKenzi, were having their morning naps. The late June heat was already fierce, so McKenzi's brothers, Kyle and Aiden, wrestled on the floor with my Labrador retriever, Bruce. Or at least that's what they thought he was. As far as my family knew, he was a stray dog I found and adopted.

They were wrong, but it was just easier to let them keep believing that.

I was very grateful to Bruce for keeping the boys occupied. I had just started working Tuesday and Thursday afternoons at the Tenth Sphere metaphysical shop, and this was one of my days off. It was harder to get back into the routine than I thought it would be.

I felt a little guilty about wishing Nick and Em would hurry up and get back. I adore my family, and I'd do anything for them – but I really needed some space. After narrowly surviving what was quite possibly both the most horrible and most wonderful weekend of my entire life, I've had one or more them in my house nearly 24/7 this week.

Quinn, Cassie and I, had only just gotten home on Monday afternoon. Mom had a scrapbook club meeting, so Dad came for an early dinner and spent the night. Most of the time he's fine, but he sometimes has seizures, so Mom doesn't like to leave him alone for too long. Also, his artificial leg occasionally gives him trouble. On Tuesday and Wednesday nights, McKenzi was colicky, so Nick and the boys camped out in my living room. Last night, Emily slept over because she was on the verge of sleep deprivation psychosis. Mom and Dad stayed at my house with Cassie while I was working. Poor Bruce. He hadn't been able to shift out of dog form the whole time. I hoped it wasn't uncomfortable for him. Actually, Bruce is only his name when he's a dog. That's what I called him before I knew what he was. Otherwise, he's known as Quinn. But he's really a kelpie, sort of like the Loch Ness Monster. He's also a little like an undercover agent, and his job is primarily hunting demons and undoing the damage they cause to this world.

And I desperately needed to talk to him. It was torture having him curled up next to me on the couch (or bed), knowing who he is, what we'd just been through together, and unable to talk about it.

The head, and only the head, of Delilah, my Creole spirit guide, popped up inches away from my face. "Heads up, girlfriend!" she said. Before I could say anything, she was gone. She did that a lot, and it was the most annoying habit that ghosts had.

This did cause me to glance out the window, where I could see my brother-in-law coming up the sidewalk. They only lived six doors down, so it was easier to park the car at their house and walk the kids home. Delilah stopped in to let me know Nick was outside? Must be a slow guide day.

"Guys? Your dad's coming. Go get your stuff together, okay?" I said to the boys.

"Awww. But Aunt Marti…" Aiden complained.

"Bruce will still be here later. I'm sure your dad needs a hug. He's probably feeling very sad."

No, at that moment, I was not above using guilt to manipulate the six year-old twins. I went and unlocked the side door for Nick.

My cell rang. *Uh-oh.* Caller ID said it was The Tenth Sphere. Had I forgotten to do something at work?

"Lulu?" I asked.

"Oh, gods! Marti I don't know what to do." It wasn't Lulu. It was her partner. And she was crying.

"Belinda, what's wrong?" I was concerned. She was not the sort of person to fall apart easily. It had to be something bad.

"Lulu." It was all she can say before her voice dissolved into sobs.

"What's happened to Lulu?"

"In jail."

"What? That's crazy. Why?"

The screen door slapped against the frame as Nick came in. "How were –"

I held up my hand to silence him.

"Accessory to murder," Belinda whispered.

"Murder!" I echoed, too loudly. McKenzi woke up and started crying. Nick went to get her, giving me a quizzical look on the way.

Belinda answered, but all I could hear was "nephew" and "homeowner's," because Cassie also started crying. "Hold on a sec, Belinda. I'm going to have to put the phone down. Do *not* hang up."

I put the phone on the kitchen table and rushed to sweep Cassie out of her crib. I gave her diaper a squeeze. Excellent. She was dry. I plopped her in the high chair and poured some Cheerios on the tray. She knocked them to the floor.

"Come on, Cassie. Please cooperate. I really need to talk to Auntie Belinda."

"Ning!" she shouted.

I took her out of the chair and set her on the floor next to some toys.

"I'll just let you get back to your call," Nick said. I could tell he was curious about why I was having a phone conversation about murder. He had already gotten the kids packed up and the dog slobber washed off boys' hands and lower arms.

"Thanks. Talk to you later," I said.

Cassie found a large plastic ring from a stacking toy and started using it to whack the other toys in the basket. Bruce lay on the floor nearby.

I hurried back to the phone. Belinda, of course had hung up. I called her back.

"Okay, now tell me what's going on," I said as soon as she picked up.

Belinda sucked in a few deep, shuddering breaths. "Last night, we were coming back from dinner. Our elderly neighbor, Mrs. Thompson, was standing on the sidewalk, crying. We stopped and asked her what was wrong. She said that she was taking Cranberry – that's her Standard Poodle – for a walk. He started to chase a cat and got away from her, running across the street. He got hit by a car, and she couldn't lift him. So Lulu walked across the street and picked that dog up. He wasn't dead, like Mrs. Thompson thought, so Lulu wrapped him up in a jacket she found in her trunk, and we all went to the emergency clinic. I took Mrs. Thompson and Cranberry inside, while Lulu stayed in the car and called Mrs. Thompson's son to come get her. He said he was on the way, so we left her at the clinic while Cranberry was in surgery. When we got home, Lulu realized she had blood all over her clothes and the jacket, so she changed and went to the Laundromat, where she could get the stuff washed before the stains set. Probably ten minutes after she left, a couple of police detectives came to the door. Said they needed to ask Lulu some questions about her nephew. I didn't think much of it –" Belinda fell apart again. It took a few moments for her to stop crying. "And I told them where she was." More sobbing. "When they got to the washateria, they found her with a pile of bloody clothes, waiting for a washer, and arrested her."

"For what? Being a Good Samaritan?"

"No. Her nephew was seen fleeing from a crime scene…it was a murder…and they thought that she was destroying the evidence."

"I can't believe that. Surely the people at the emergency clinic can verify she was there. When they do the DNA testing on the blood, they'll see it isn't human."

"She never actually came inside the clinic, and DNA tests could take weeks. They haven't actually charged her yet, but I don't have money for a lawyer. Everything's tied up in the shop. I don't even know if I'm going to have enough to bail her out." Belinda began to sob again.

"Belinda, it's going to be okay. My sister's a public defender. She'll know exactly what to do." I paused for a moment. I hadn't realized that Lulu had a nephew. "Who did Lulu's nephew kill?"

"Benjamin didn't kill anybody! He'd never hurt a soul. He was running for president of the Homeowner's Association. The man that got killed was the current president. His wife said that she went outside and found Benjamin standing over her dead husband, holding a bloody Japanese edger. I don't care what she thinks she saw, Ben would never kill anybody."

"Okay, then. Let me talk to my sister, and I'll get back to you."

I dialed Emily's cell, and was worried that it would roll to voice mail. When she finally answered, her voice was soft and a little gravelly. She said she was very tired and sore from going to the funeral – she'd only had a c-section two weeks ago, after all. Still, she humored me and listened to my problem. That was Emily, always taking care of me.

"Ok. There's nothing I can do about it. I can't even drive yet," she said.

"But—"

"Let me finish. Have your friend call Crammwell, Stanford & Malloy."

"They sound expensive."

"Stop interrupting. Call Crammwell, ask for Leonard Peltier. They'll take care of it. Now, I really need to go lie down. Good luck."

Cassie had changed her mind about eating lunch. She'd pulled herself up on the coffee table and staggered into the kitchen. "Mama! Ma ma ma!"

Yesterday was her eleven month-iversary. I still had some cupcakes left, so I put one on the high chair tray with the few remaining Cheerios. Once I strapped her in, she tried to smash the whole cake into her mouth. I took it away from her, although most of the frosting stayed on her cheeks, and broke it into little bits. I got her a sippy cup of water, and paced around the kitchen, looking for my cell phone. Bruce came in and sat down near Cassie's high chair. She stopped stuffing herself with cake long enough to throw him some cereal.

I called Belinda back, but she didn't answer. I left a message on her voice mail, telling her what Emily had said.

Then I got up, closed the blinds and double-checked that I'd re-locked the door after Nick left. Bruce was no longer in the room. A few minutes later, Quinn came in, dressed in a pair of shorts and tee-shirt I'd managed to pick up for him during the week. That's the slight drawback of being a shapeshifter – clothes don't shift with you.

I wanted to run to him and throw my arms around his neck, partly because I had missed him – missed his human form – and partly because I wanted him to convince me that everything would be fine, and Lulu would be home in time for dinner.

Instead, I stood by the high chair. "Lulu's in trouble."

"I heard."

Someone banged the knocker on the front door.

Even though I knew it couldn't possibly be Belinda, I still hoped it was, as Quinn and I hurried into the entryway.

I thought I must be on some TV hidden camera show.

A woman stood on my front porch wearing painted-on jeans tucked into fur-lined boots and a low-cut, too-tight white shirt. A beaded leather pouch was slung around her hips. Two long blonde braids fell to her waist, and her eyes were ice blue. A glossy black raven perched on her shoulder.

"Halle?" Quinn asked. "It's been...a very long time."

Chapter 3
No Reservations

 bit my lip. Hard. *Who was this hussy showing up at my doorstep at exactly the wrong time?* "So, you two know each other?" I asked.

Halle ignored me and walked right into my house.

"We've been looking everywhere for you," she said to Quinn.

"My team knows where I am. Halle, this is Marti. Marti, Halle."

She looked down at me, which is a rare thing, since I'm 5'9", and flashed something halfway between a smile and a sneer.

"The jötnar are moving again. I think they are looking for Fenrir."

Quinn's eyes darkened, the blackness floating over them like spilled ink for a moment. That was always a bad sign.

"I doubt they'll come here," he growled, his eyes still locked on Halle's.

What did they know that I didn't?

The raven ruffled its feathers and shifted its weight.

Something clattered to the floor in the kitchen. "I'd better go check on Cassie." *I'm sure you can let yourself out.*

My daughter had thrown her sippy cup on the floor, along with about half of her cupcake.

"Booce!" she shouted as I walked in.

"Bruce will be back later," I grumped at her. None of this was her fault, of course. It wasn't her fault that Lulu had been arrested, or that the moment I finally had a chance to talk to Quinn, some leggy blonde chick from his past showed up. So why was I annoyed with Cassie?

She had lost interest in the few bits of cereal left on her tray, so I took her out of the high chair and carried her into the living room.

Quinn and Halle were talking in low voices, and stopped when I came in. Halle's lip curled up as if she'd stepped in something.

"That's not yours, is it?" she asked.

"It?!" I shot back.

Quinn shook his head and moved between us. "Halle. Please?" He reached out and tickled Cassie's foot. She giggled, and he smiled at her. "No. I'm not Cassie's father," he said to Halle. Then he looked at me, his eyes tired and worried. "I need to talk to you."

There was no way I was leaving my baby alone with that woman, if that's what she was, so I picked up Cassie, her stuffed blue rabbit, Mr. Buns, and her nearby busy box, and brought them along with us to my bedroom. I closed the door, and put Cassie down on the floor with the toys. She immediately grabbed Mr. Buns in one hand, and started babbling to the box and pushing the buttons with her other hand.

Quinn sighed heavily. "Halle wants me to go with her." His face was troubled. "Do you know what jötnar – Frost Giants – are?"

"Kind of. Aren't they Scandinavian, and throw boulders at people in the mountains?"

"Close enough. They are older than you can imagine, and they detest the Valhalla crowd, but they like humans even less. There is a group of them who are actively trying to bring on Ragnarök."

"That's like the Norse version of Armageddon, right?"

"Exactly. It means 'Destruction of the Gods,' and most of the best known will die. Odin gets swallowed by a giant wolf, Thor gets poisoned by a giant snake, and Loki and Heimdallr kill each other. Then the whole planet floods. Halle's job is to keep an eye on the Frost Giants, because they will begin to gather for war prior to the start of Ragnarök. It was thought that they were content to wait until Loki and the great wolf Fenrir freed themselves and set events in motion. But with the current weather, well, the jötnar blame humans for the melting ice, and they don't mind destroying the world to get rid of them. Even if it means sacrificing themselves in the process."

"Well, that seems entirely appropriate – an Amazon watching Frost Giants, who are pissed off about global warming."

"Amazon?" Quinn shook his head, puzzled. "No, Halle's a Valkyrie."

At the sound of that word, music started to play in my head. First, frantic violins, then booming brass. Wagner's *Ride of the Valkyrie* would probably be stuck in my head for a while, now.

Quinn stretched out his hand and raised my chin, so that I had nowhere to look but into his eyes. "I don't want to go with her," he said. "But I have to."

"Are you coming back?"

"Do you want me to?"

Here was an opportunity to easily uncomplicate my life. Dangerous folk tended to show up where fae were involved. It might be easier to keep both Cassie and myself safe if he wasn't around. Here was a quick, but not painless, way out. All I had to do was say no.

"Yes." I responded.

When I died last Sunday, my dead husband, Ryan, had told me it wasn't my time to go; but Quinn was the one who made sure my broken body got put back together. He'd also shown me fantastic creatures I would never have believed really existed, if I hadn't seen them with my own eyes. Now that I was aware of such things, I couldn't go back to the ordinary. That, and I was finding it difficult to imagine my life without him, now.

Quinn smiled softly at me. "I don't know how long this will take."

"I understand," I said. I never said I liked it.

Quinn stepped closer. He tilted his head. He was going to kiss me.

My body was greedy for his touch. Yet my mind was both fascinated and terrified. Lulu had warned me that fae have a kind of glamour – enthrallment –

that draws humans like moths to a bug zapper. I knew he had used it the first time we met, but since then, it was impossible for me to tell whether it was a natural attraction, or fae magick.

Suddenly, his head jerked away from me. "Nick's coming."

He shimmered like a hot sidewalk and shifted into Bruce. The shorts he'd been wearing fell off of him, but I was still helping disentangle him from the shirt when Nick knocked on the side door.

Bruce barked, for show I suppose, as he trotted into the kitchen. I grabbed Cassie, caught up with Bruce, and let my brother-in-law in.

He was dressed in his police uniform. "Hey, Marti," he said. "I have to go to work, but would you mind looking in on Em a little later? I'm afraid going to the funeral was probably too much, too soon for her."

"Sure, no problem," I said.

"Thanks." He smiled at me, then his jaw dropped open. "Who's your friend?"

I turned to see Halle standing in the doorway between the kitchen and the living room.

I looked at Bruce. He jumped up on Nick and started trying to lick him.

"Bruce! Get down, you nut." I grabbed him by the scruff of his neck and pulled him off of Nick. Bruce seemed to wink at me.

I glanced back at Halle. "Her?" I cleared my throat. *How was I going to explain a Valkyrie in my house?* A perfect idea popped into my mind, so perfect I wondered if it was my own. "She's the dog trainer. She's going to take Bruce for a little bit for obedience training."

Nick nodded. "I see. Gotta go." He nodded again, this time to Halle, and left.

"Okay, you've wasted enough time. We've really got to leave," Halle said to Bruce.

He didn't shift. I knew he wouldn't. He only left my house in human form under cover of darkness. The neighbors would definitely notice a handsome man leaving my house. They wouldn't care if a dog was going in and out.

"Just a minute," I said.

I took an extra-large plastic Ziploc storage bag from the pantry, with Cassie's generous "help," and went to my bedroom. I set her on the floor and gathered up the clothes Quinn had been wearing earlier and put them in the bag, along with his shoes. I heard my baby giggling, so I turned to see her using Bruce to pull up and balance herself. He walked along beside her as she toddled towards the kitchen. I followed them, dreading what was going to happen next.

"He's going to need some clothes." I handed the bag to Halle.

Her bird squawked at me.

"Perhaps." She grinned wickedly at me.

I refused to take the bait.

Cassie had grabbed on to a chair, and Bruce was licking her face. She squealed with delight. "Booce! Booce!" she said.

Then he came to me. I leaned over to stroke his broad back, and he licked my hand.

"Be safe," I whispered to him. Worry twisted my insides. What if he got hurt or killed?

I walked them to the front door, then stood there watching as the kelpie, the Valkyrie, and the raven moved down the sidewalk and faded into the distance.

I sat on the floor and read Cassie a book. It was one of her favorites, with little touchy-feely patches on every page. Afterwards, she crawled off to play with Mr. Buns. I looked in the rat habitat, and noticed that Alpha and Betty's water bottle was almost empty, so I got them some more.

I tried calling Belinda again. No answer. I wondered if Lulu had been charged. I mostly trusted the justice system, but, on the other hand, innocent people did go to jail sometimes. Especially if they couldn't afford a lawyer. I frowned.

"Mama!" Cassie called. I looked up.

Delilah was standing near her, and Cassie was looking right at my ghostly guide.

I rushed to pick my baby up. "She can see you?" I asked.

"Course she can, girlfriend. Most babies do see us, until grownups tell them there's no such thing as ghosts so many times they learn to block us out. Listen, you need to go have a check on your sister. Understand?"

Delilah's usually sassy face was grave.

Cassie protested loudly, as I rushed out of the house and left without bothering to lock the door. I ran the six houses down to Emily and Nick's, and pounded on their door. "Em? Emily?" I called.

I heard footsteps, then Kyle's voice, "Aunt Marti? Mommy's sleeping now."

"Okay. Would you let me in to take care of McKenzi for her?"

There was a metallic click as the lock turned.

Trying hard not to frighten my nephew, I asked, "Where are Mommy and the baby?"

He led me to the living room, where Aiden was playing a video game on the TV. McKenzi was squirming on a quilt in the middle of the floor.

Emily lay on the couch, way too pale.

"Em?" I asked, gently shaking her shoulder.

Nothing happened. I tried again.

Her eyes opened half way. "Hey," she said, her voice dull with sleep.

"Are you okay?" I asked.

She shifted her body, arching her back and stretching out her neck. "Can't seem to get enough air. Making me sleepy. Sure it'll be fine."

She coughed, and droplets of blood spattered on her white blouse.

"I'm calling an ambulance. You need to get to the ER."

I called 911 from Emily's cell. The operator asked me to stay on the line, so I did, telling her Emily's symptoms. There are advantages to living just around the corner from the fire station. The ambulance arrived in less than five minutes.

"I think she's got a pulmonary embolism," I told them as I opened the door. "She recently had a c-section, now she's coughing blood and fainting." A blood clot in the lung was nothing to fool around with.

The paramedics took Emily's vitals and strapped an oxygen mask over her face.

Radio chatter. An IV. Injections. More chatter. More vitals.

I gave the boys little tasks to do, like go give Bojangles – their cat – fresh water, so they would feel useful instead of helpless. The noise and commotion made McKenzi cry, so I cradled her in my arms. This, of course, made Cassie extremely jealous, so I ended up with a tiny baby in the crook of my right arm and an irritable toddler on my left hip. I felt like…my mother, when Em and I were little.

"Are you going to the hospital?" one of the paramedics asked me as the other buckled my sister onto the gurney.

I looked around at Kyle, Aiden, McKenzi and Cassie. What was I going to do with four little kids in the ER waiting room, even if I could figure out how to get them all there? I'd been in a minor accident last week, and my car was still in the shop. And I'm sure McKenzi would need feeding soon. Newborns always needed feeding soon.

"I've got to take care of the kids. I'll call her husband, our mom, and her doctor, though. Which hospital?"

"Methodist West has availability."

"Okay. I'll send them there."

I locked the door as soon as they left. "Don't worry," I told the boys. "They'll take very good care of your mom. She'll be fine. I'm going to call your dad and tell him to go over there, okay?"

Aiden started to cry.

"Shut up!" Kyle said.

"Kyle! No, sir. Do not talk to your brother that way. You need to apologize."

"I'm not sorry. You shouldn't be a baby." Kyle snapped. He was angry with Aiden for crying, but there were tears in his own eyes that he was struggling to hold back.

What I needed were two more arms. "Kyle, you're right that people shouldn't cry over every little thing. But sometimes, if you're very sad, crying can make you feel better. Everybody cries at least once in a while."

"Not my dad."

I had seen Nick cry before, and it was awful. He had come to break the news that Ryan was dead. We'd cried together.

"Even very tough, strong men can cry, if something makes them very sad. And it's okay. You know how when you run water in a glass, and the glass gets too full, and all the water runs over the side? If your body gets too full of emotion, it overflows as tears, just like the water running over the side of the glass."

I carefully put McKenzi on the couch – she couldn't roll over yet, so she should be okay – and Cassie on the floor. My nephews really, really needed a hug.

I held one in each arm. Aiden sobbed, while Kyle cried silently. The girls gave me a few minutes to comfort the boys before they started fussing. I wanted to cry myself, and being surrounded by crying children didn't help. But in spite of the example I'd just given Kyle, I couldn't allow myself to. I had to make phone calls. That would help my sister. Crying wouldn't.

"The doctors are going to do everything they possibly can for your mom. I need to call your dad, now, okay?"

Silently, Kyle and Aiden dragged out a large plastic bin of Lego, and started building. It hurt my heart. I've never seen these two – brothers who put the boy in 'boisterous' – so quiet. Emily was not going to die. I forbade it.

I moved the baby quilt over near me and transferred McKenzi from the couch to it. I needed to use my hands, so I sat cross-legged on the floor with the girls, one on either side. Cassie held onto my shoulder for balance, as she stood watch, protecting me from any mischief McKenzi might get up to. Her little cousin flapped her arms in the air in front of herself.

First, I called Nick. Then I called our mother.

After I hung up, I started searching through Emily's contacts for her doctor. *Why hadn't I thought to ask Nick when I had him on the phone?* I didn't dare call him back. Either he wouldn't answer, or he would answer while he was driving like a maniac to the hospital. Neither option was useful.

I knew Dr. Aziza was a pediatrician because she was also our pedi. The next possibility was a Dr. Carruthers. I tapped the dial option.

"Carruthers Family Dental," chirped the receptionist.

"Oh. I'm so sorry. I misdialed," I said, then hung up quickly.

Dr. Fredricks was her OB/GYN. *Wonder if I should call him, too? If I can't find her GP, I will.*

I kept going down the list. "Dr. Pavlov?" *That name rings a bell.* I pressed the dial button.

"*Zdravstvuĭte!*" a man answered.

"Yes. Hello? My name is Marti Keller. My sister is Emily Benson, and I'm looking for her doctor. She just went to the emergency room."

"*Prosti menya.* Sorry to hear that news. I wish her well, but I am not that kind of doctor."

"Sorry to bother you." I hung up quickly. *Well, that was embarrassing.*

Next up was Dr. Robinson. Jackpot! She was just finishing up her last outpatient surgery of the day, and her office would send her over to Methodist West as soon as she done.

I put my hand out on the carpet. I had half expected to find Bruce there. But my fingers touched only nylon. I wished Quinn was here with me right now, and I hoped he was okay. But I couldn't allow myself to dwell on him. Between Lulu and my sister, I had more than enough to deal with. Imagining him with a six-foot blonde was not going to do anybody any good.

I dug my phone out of my pocket and called Belinda. This time, she answered.

"Thank you, thank you, thank you, Marti," Belinda said. "I called that attorney your sister recommended. He convinced them to run an ABAcard on the bloodstains ASAP – and surprise! The blood wasn't human. He explained how the test works – just like a pregnancy test, except instead of hormones, it finds antigens. Two lines if it's human, one if not." Belinda took a deep breath. "Lulu's being released now. I'm at the jail, waiting to pick her up."

"I'm so glad to hear that."

McKenzi started the cough-cough-cough cry of a hungry newborn. I patted her tummy.

"Belinda, I do want to talk to you some more, but I really, really have to go now. I'll call you later." I hung up without waiting for her answer.

I don't know if it was from being a public defender and dealing with broken people all day, every day, or just out-of-whack brain chemistry, but my sister often struggled with depression. I knew there would be formula in the house. Because of her medication, she wasn't able to breastfeed.

"I'll be right back," I said to McKenzi, giving her tummy a final pat.

I scooped up Cassie and took her with me. McKenzi fussed a little louder. I returned to the living room with Cassie in one hand and the bottle in the other. Needless to say, it was not easy feeding McKenzi with a jealous Cassie in the room, but I got it done, and McKenzi was just drowsing off when my phone rang.

It was my mother calling to say that Emily hadn't needed surgery – the heparin the paramedics gave her had done the trick. She might even be discharged tomorrow. *Hallelujah!*

"Hey boys? That was Nana calling. Your mom is going to be just fine. She's spending the night at the hospital, but your dad will bring her home tomorrow."

It was like the sun coming out from behind clouds, the difference in those two.

Nick stayed at the hospital, but Mom and Dad came to help me get the kids fed.

After dinner, Mom looked at me and frowned.

"What's wrong?" I asked.

She sighed. "There's a problem. When Emily comes home, she's going to need someone to take care of her for a while. I don't think I can look after her and help with McKenzi and take care of Cassie while you're working. I'm not as young as I used to be."

"I know, Mom. I guess the job will have to go on hold for a while. You'll have your hands full with Em, McKenzi and the boys."

Mom looked at the floor. "Actually, the wife of one of Nick's work colleagues is one of the directors over at Briar Ridge Montessori School. The boys will be going there." She cleared her throat and looked up at me. "They have some space in the one-year olds' group."

"You want me to put Cassie in daycare?" I all but shouted at her.

"Calm down, Marti. It's just two half-days a week. You and Emily went to daycare, and you turned out just fine."

"But this is different!"

"Is it? Besides, it would be good for her to be around other kids."

"She is around other kids."

"If Kyle and Aiden don't play with her, they don't count."

I frowned.

"Come with me Monday morning when I drop the boys off, and at least have a look around."

"Fine."

Given that Cassie, always and without fail, wakes up at 6:30, it wasn't difficult to meet Mom and the boys at the school on time Monday morning. Dad stayed with Emily and McKenzi. As long as they both didn't have something go haywire at the same time, they'd be fine.

I'd had a chance to study the school building. It was designed to look like an old-fashioned schoolhouse – brick red, with a belfry perched on a steeply pitched roof. But that was where the similarities ended. Instead of a one-room schoolhouse, a wing of classrooms stretched out on either side. Once we went in, I could see that the belfry was really a skylight for the administrative lobby.

"Hello, I'm Maria Benecelli, the principal," said an older woman with a clipboard. "Would these two be Kyle and Aiden?" She smiled at my nephews.

"Yes," said my mother.

She and I each received a quick, but firm, handshake from Ms. Benecelli. I wouldn't describe her as plump, but there was a certain roundness about her figure that made her seem soft and grandmotherly.

Mom checked in Kyle and Aiden, while I examined students' projects stapled to the bulletin board. Cassie managed to grab one. Fortunately, the rip was small, nothing a little Scotch tape wouldn't fix. If Ms. Benecelli noticed, she didn't let on.

After the boys were escorted to their classrooms, Mom hurried home to take over from Dad. Ms. Benecelli gave Cassie and me an exhaustive tour. The school seemed nice enough, I supposed. I didn't want to leave Cassie in any daycare at all. The cost of the mother's day out program would be a little more than half of my paycheck. It was worth it, I suppose, to at least slow the drain on my savings, even if I couldn't stop it all together. I reluctantly filled out an enrollment form.

I had spoken with Lulu on Saturday, but I hadn't seen her. The shop was usually closed on Mondays, so I probably wouldn't see her today, either. The house felt empty without Quinn, and I didn't relish being there, so Cassie and I went to visit Emily.

As we started down the sidewalk, I noticed a big U-Haul in front of Mrs. Paddington's house, across the street and two doors down. Dressed in one of her many colorful patio dresses, she was standing in the front yard, speaking with a sweaty man in a suit. I crossed the street to speak with her.

"Oh, hello, Marti! I was going to drop by later – I wanted to say goodbye."

"Goodbye?"

"Yes. My older sister has had a stroke. She's home now, but needs someone to help her. Can't drive anymore, you see."

"I'm so sorry to hear that."

She leaned in and gave both Cassie and me a hug. "I'm going to miss you, baby," she said, giving Cassie's cheek a gentle pinch. "You be good for your mama, hear?"

While we were talking, the suited man pounded a "For Sale or Lease" sign into the grass.

"You take care of yourself, Mrs. Paddington. Send me your address so I can put you on my Christmas card list."

"Thanks, sweetie."

Cassie and I waved "bye-bye" and continued down the sizzling sidewalk to Nick and Emily's house.

The back door was unlocked – Nick would have a fit, if he knew – so we just walked in and made ourselves at home.

Mom was on the floor with McKenzi, Dad was resting his eyes in the recliner, and Emily was stretched out on the couch, clicking through the channels.

"Hey, Marts," she said, as we came into the living room.

I sat on the edge of the sofa, near my sister's feet. Cassie squirmed to be free, so I set her on the floor, where she scrambled for a large plastic truck in the middle of the room.

"So, how are you feeling?" I asked, giving Emily's ankle a little squeeze.

"Much better. It's a good thing you came over when you did."

Thanks, Delilah. I owe you big time. "Well," I said out loud. "Nick did ask me to check on you."

Emily smiled. "Perhaps. But what I'm most amazed about is that you knew my doctor's name. I didn't think I'd ever talked about Dr. Robertson with you."

"Oh, you hadn't." I shifted on the couch a little so I didn't fall off. "I just went down your contacts list and called the ones labeled 'doctor.'"

"You went through all my contacts?"

"Just the doctors. I didn't need to call Aziza, though."

"All the doctors? Did you call Dr. Pavlov?"

"Yes."

"From my phone?"

"Yes. I also called your dentist. What's the big deal?" *Jeez Louise! I was only trying to help.*

"I need to go make some phone calls."

Emily eased herself up and left the room. I looked at Mom. She only shrugged.

My nose wrinkled involuntarily. *Ewww.* That smell was as unpleasant as it was familiar.

I pretended that I didn't have any clean diapers with me. Truth was, I didn't understand why Emily was mad at me, and it felt awkward to hang around her house.

"Mom, I'm going to have to take Cassie home to change her. Talk to you later."

"Bye, sweetie."

Cassie wanted to walk the whole way home, and I didn't object to not carrying her. She wasn't quite a good enough walker to do it without help. By the time we got home, my back muscles were starting to ache from leaning over to hold her hands, while she toddled like a marionette below.

I didn't notice the young woman sitting on my side steps until we were almost on top of her, and when I did, I took a big step back and scooped Cassie up into my arms. Her unkempt hair reminded me of a thunderstorm at night, and too much black eyeliner besieged her dark eyes. Ripped fishnets covered her legs, overexposed by too little skirt. But the oddest thing, the only thing that stopped me from thinking she wasn't a profoundly lost Goth teen, was her robin's egg blue skin.

"I have news," she said.

Chapter 4
Wing and a Prayer

eriously, Quinn? Why are you still a dog? Shift already," Halle said, shaking her head at Bruce as he trudged along beside her.

The raven croaked and stretched its wings.

Bruce continued as if he hadn't heard her. He was already starting to pant. Thick fur was a liability in the Houston summer.

Halle's eye's narrowed. "Well," she said with a malefic smile, "you won't be needing these, then."

She threw the bag of Quinn's clothes, the one that Marti had given her, over her shoulder and into someone's azalea bushes.

Bruce grunted and trotted into the yard to get his belongings. The bag was wedged in between two branches, and he had to use his paws, as well as his jaws, to get it out. While he was working at retrieving his clothing, a curtain moved in the front window.

An elderly man opened the front door and waved his cane at Bruce. "Get out of my yard, you rotten mutt!"

He stopped dead when he his eyes fell on Halle. He tried to stand a little straighter. "Is that your dog, Miss? He sure looks like a purebred."

Halle batted her eyelashes and beamed back at him. "I'm walking him for a friend," she replied.

Bruce's bag came free, and he loped across the grass and down the sidewalk with the clothes in his mouth.

"Bye," Halle waved to the man, and ran after the dog.

He galloped ahead of her, and disappeared behind an open gate. By the time Halle caught up to him, Quinn was slipping on his shoes.

"Was that really necessary?" he snapped at her.

"Worked, didn't it?" Halle was smug.

"Do you have a car?" Quinn asked.

Halle rolled her eyes. "Seriously? Please."

She whistled, two sharp blasts, and searched the sky, using her hand as a visor.

Far above them, something circled on wide black wings. At first Quinn thought it was a black vulture. As it spiraled down to meet them, he could see it was a great black horse. Given the unobstructed view of the horse's underside, it was obviously a mare. She settled down on the sidewalk, eyes glaring yellow, and folded her wings. Halle's raven flew off her shoulder and perched in a nearby tree. The horse wore no bridle or saddle, and she whipped her huge head around to snap at Quinn with wolf-like fangs.

Halle swatted the beast good-naturedly. "Rädsla, stop it. He's with us." She grabbed a handful of coarse mane and leaped onto the animal. "Well don't just stand there – get on!" she said, as the weird horse danced underneath her.

Quinn surveyed the horse. She was quite tall. He took a few steps back to attempt a running start, but still floundered onto the creature's back, struggling to get his right leg swung over her wide rump. Rädsla didn't wait for him to get settled as she half-reared and leaped into the air, huge wings besting gravity, lifting them quickly into the sky. He had to grab onto Halle to keep from falling off. Quinn sometimes shifted into the form of a horse, but he rarely rode one. It had probably been a hundred years since the last time he was astride an equine.

Halle snickered. "Hold on!"

Thick, corded muscles rippled along Rädsla's strong back as she rose easily into the sky. The air cooled with each flap. Quinn shivered. Ordinarily, he liked the feel of deep, cold water against his kelpie skin, but he'd already started getting acclimated to the Gulf Coast heat, at least, when he was in human form. Siegfried fluttered near Halle's head like a petulant bat.

She threw what appeared to be flower petals into the air. As they fluttered around, dancing like red, orange and yellow butterflies, the scene below changed.

Instead of sprawling subdivisions, pristine, snow-capped peaks stretched up towards them. The ozone smell of the Houston summer was replaced by the crisp scent of ice and evergreens. The blazing sun was gone, and angry grey clouds loomed above them like a bad omen. Lightning crackled across the grey backdrop and thunder boomed. Ice crystals stuck to Quinn's hair and melted on his cheeks. He shivered again, wishing he had a coat. A boulder split off the side of a mountain and rolled into the valley.

"Really, Halle? The jötnar don't seem to be doing anything unusual."

"Perhaps. Give it time. You'll see." She leaned back against him. "You're shaking. I know a way to warm you up," she said. "It's been a long time."

"There's a reason for that." Quinn tried to pull away from her, but there was only so much room on Rädsla's back.

"Oh, you're not still mad about that minotaur, are you?" Halle looked over her shoulder at Quinn. "You know," she purred, "his head and horns weren't the only things he got from a bu –"

"Halle! I don't want to hear about it."

"Look, I can't help the way I am. If I want a male, I have him. Doesn't mean I care for you any less." Halle reached behind her and ran the back of her hand up Quinn's thigh.

He grabbed her wrist. "Stop. Not interested."

Halle snorted. "You're mooning after that human, aren't you? I hate it when monsters get sentimental."

"I'm not a monster."

"Oh, aren't you?" Halle snickered. "Besides, what's the point? You'd probably kill her, anyway. And if you didn't do it accidentally, your mother would most likely do it on purpose. Besides, that human will be dead of old age before you look even a day older."

"Don't you think I know that?" Quinn snapped.

Then he narrowed his eyes. "What do you know about my mother?" He asked. When Halle didn't answer, he said, "You've been talking to my brother, haven't you?"

"Graham has only your best interests at heart.

A moving shape, red against the stark snow, caught Quinn's attention.

"What's that?" he asked.

"That is what we came to see."

Rädsla dropped behind an outcropping of rock. As the shape got closer, Quinn could hear the snow hissing with each step the figure took. Large footprints trailed yeti-like behind it, melted deep into the white surface. The figure was bipedal, but beyond that, Quinn couldn't tell what it was. Snow pants covered its lower half, and the upper was obscured by a dark red anorak. Since it was wearing human clothes, Quinn assumed it was human-sized – there was nothing in the bleak white landscape to compare it with. He turned his attention to the figure's trajectory. It was headed toward a gaping crevasse.

Something moved inside the crack in the snow. A jötnar stepped out of the darkness and into the murky light of the stormy plateau. The wind picked up, and limp, wet snowflakes swirled around the giant like dead fairies. When their paths intersected, Quinn saw it was nearly twice the height of the humanoid figure. The two plodded into the crevasse, and out of sight.

Quinn had lost all feeling in his feet and hands. By the time the jötnar and the parka-clad figure disappeared into the ice cleft, he was shivering so hard he could barely stay on Rädsla's back.

"You're cold," Halle remarked.

"Somewhat. Yes," he replied.

She clucked to Rädsla, and the mare wheeled sharply, heading away from the desolate peaks. The snow gave way to bare rocks, then dark trees. It was hardly any time at all before Quinn saw white smoke rising through tall evergreens. Rädsla landed softly, and Quinn slipped off, falling to his knees in the forest litter.

The Valkyrie helped him up. Rädsla trotted off into the forest. Seigfried croaked and re-installed himself on Halle's shoulder. Before them stood a thick-timbered mead hall, its chimney the source of the white smoke. Carved wooden dragon heads adorned both ends of the steep roof. A battered wooden sign hung over the door, and as they approached, Quinn could read *Three Sisters Inn* carved into it in runic letters.

Halle pushed the heavy oak and iron door open, and they stepped into the dim great room. Quinn's stomach growled as the aromas of strong beer and baking bread rushed at them. A barmaid with black hair and brown eyes looked up at them, smiled, and nodded. A sprinkling of cinnamon freckles on her cheeks made her look younger than she probably was. The hall was less than half filled, the patrons like piles of damp laundry, as melted snow gradually evaporated from their clothes.

The ancient spruce floor groaned and sighed as Quinn made his way to the far wall, where chunky logs snapped and sparked in the yawning fireplace. He rubbed his hands and stomped his feet in front of the eager fire. The smell of wood smoke was like a well-worn jacket, slipping around his shoulders and whispering old memories in his ear. He would a thousand times rather have been in hot, steamy Houston with Marti than here in the frozen north with Halle.

Quinn noticed Halle had gotten a flagon of hot mead and two steins from the barmaid, and she sat at one of the heavy oak tables, watching Quinn shake his feet and flail his hands against the pins-and-needles sensation brought by the receding numbness. Siegfried perched on the back of her chair.

"Sorry," she said, when he finally sat down. "I didn't think about you needing a coat."

"I'll live." Quinn took a sip of his mead. "Who was that? The person in the red parka?"

"Not sure. Even Siegfried has had trouble following him. Or her," she added as an afterthought. "I don't think it's human, though."

"Why not?"

"The jötnar haven't killed it."

Quinn nodded. His shivering had lessened considerably, but he was still feeling chilled. He wondered, briefly, what Marti and Cassie were up to, then reluctantly wrenched his attention back to the Frost Giant's visitor. He also noted that an older man with an eye patch and a thick blue cloak briefly made eye contact with Halle. It was probably nothing – lots of men tried making eye contact with Halle.

The barmaid arrived at their table, carrying a tray loaded with steaming food.

"Thanks, Cornelia," Halle said.

Cornelia nodded, but said nothing, turning with her now-empty tray and padding back across the room, silent as a spring breeze.

Although Quinn left the blood sausages to Halle, he still managed to find enough potato pancakes and lingonberry jam to stuff himself with. He hadn't eaten since early in the day, and flying around the frozen mountains had used up all his reserves. He was finally warm and full, and couldn't think of anything he wanted to do now more than sleep. Perhaps, if he was lucky, he'd dream of Marti.

Quinn's mind was too tired to focus; random fragments of ideas and slivers of pictures danced in his head. He had lost track of Halle's small talk, but a frigid blast of air snapped him back from his thoughts. Instantly alert, he looked up to see the front door standing open, framing a figure in a dark red anorak, stamping its feet on the doormat.

"Without being obvious, look at what just walked in," Quinn said.

Halle knocked her knife to the floor, and carefully scrutinized the newcomer as she leaned over to pick it up.

"The jötnar's friend." Halle's full lips curved into lurid smile. A green glow flickered across her eyes.

Quinn involuntarily leaned back in his chair. Valkyries were dangerous, and he didn't want to become collateral damage by getting in between Halle and her prey. He was also wary of traps, as he'd seemed to do nothing but fall into them lately. "Seems a bit convenient, him coming in here."

"Not really. It's the only place within fifteen leagues of the jötnar's lair."

The mead hall's door thumped shut, and the latest guest unzipped his anorak and shook the snow out of the fur-lined hood. Firelight flickered off his reptilian scales, both brightening the pale bronze hue and casting deeper shadows under his flat features. The vertical pupils in his golden eyes widened and contracted, adjusting to the change in light.

Quinn sucked in a deep breath.

"You know him?" Halle asked.

"Our paths have crossed," Quinn said with a deep scowl. "His name is Balcones."

The demon must have felt his furious glare, because he scanned the room until his tawny eyes rested full on Quinn.

"You!" Balcones snarled. His vertical pupils narrowed, and his thin lips pulled back, exposing sharp, jagged teeth. He took something from his pocket and hurled it at the floor. A loud bang shattered the quiet and a brilliant red flash slashed the dim light to ribbons.

By the time Quinn could see again, Balcones was gone, leaving behind a few wisps of smoke and the stink of sulfur.

A rotund dwarf sitting at the bar shook his head. "I hates when they does that," he said, as if it happened every day.

Quinn exhaled heavily. "Percussion portal. Wish I knew how they got their claws on those. We've been seeing them more and more recently." He put his elbows on the table and rested his head in his hands. He was loath to admit it, but exhaustion was catching up to him.

"A room is kept upstairs for me. You look tired and there is nothing more to be done here in the hall," Halle said, her fingers brushing Quinn's shoulder. "We have plenty of time to talk later."

Wearily, Quinn stood and followed the Valkyrie. He had wanted to ask the dwarf a question or two on the way out. But he would be disappointed. The creature was no longer at the bar, and Quinn didn't think he had the energy to hunt for it. He smiled at the barmaid.

"Cornelia? If you don't mind my asking, does that demon, the one in the red anorak, come here often?"

She only shrugged and held out her hand, palm down, and wobbled it from side to side.

"Don't ask her questions. She can't answer them," Halle said.

"Oh?" Quinn glanced at Cornelia, hoping he hadn't offended her.

Halle's face darkened. "A customer propositioned her. She dared to say no. He took her anyway, and then cut out her tongue." She paused, as if to gauge Quinn's reaction. "But I did him one better. I cut out his heart."

"I'm so sorry," Quinn said to the barmaid. "I didn't know."

She nodded, and a wistful smile drifted across her lips.

"Come," said Halle, her fingers again fluttering over his shoulder.

He trudged up the stairs after her. There weren't many rooms above the great room below, but Halle's was, of course, the furthest from the stairs. She pulled a brass key from the pouch slung around her hips and opened the door.

Quinn was suddenly grateful for the extra walk. Halle's room was on the same side as the fireplace downstairs, allowing her to have a fireplace upstairs. He knew why he was so tired and cold. It wasn't about cavorting around near the Arctic Circle on a flying horse. He had been holding his human and dog shapes for too long. He needed to shift into his natural kelpie form and swim. But it wasn't going to happen tonight. Sleep was going to be the best he could do. He sat down in the oversized chair to take his shoes off, and that was the last thing he remembered until someone shook him awake.

"Wake up, sleepyhead," Halle's voice sounded near his ear.

Quinn stretched and opened his eyes. The fire had died down substantially, but it was still strong enough to send gold and orange light shimmering along Halle's bare skin as she stood naked in front of him.

"Don't tell me you're not interested," she said, looking down his body.

Parts of him were very interested. But not the most important ones. It wasn't easy, but Quinn forced himself to look only into her eyes.

"I need to get to water. Preferably fresh, but seawater will do if it's closer."

He was surprised that she didn't argue. Instead, she took a step back and studied his face.

"Your eyes," was all she said before she turned away and started getting dressed.

A glance into the mirror above the wash stand showed Quinn what he already knew. His eyes had ceased to look human. Instead, they were glistening obsidian spheres – kelpie eyes. He ran his tongue over his teeth, just to confirm that the flat, human molars had given way to the sharp teeth of a predator. Even his skin had taken on a greyish cast.

"I can't hold this shape much longer," he said.

Halle pulled on her boots. "Let's go, then," she replied.

Kelpies are not land animals. Like whales, they are large and need support from the water to keep them from slowly suffocating under their own weight. They can survive out of the water for brief periods, but if Quinn shifted into kelpie form, and didn't' have the strength to shift back to a size that could fit through the door, he would die, trapped in Halle's room.

Outside the *Three Sisters*, Halle whistled for her horse. The black mare seemed to solidify out of the dark between the trees, and stretched her wings. Halle gave Quinn a leg up, onto the horse's back, then vaulted up lightly behind him. Rädsla's great wings beat the air, and she quickly rose high above the chilly spruces.

"Where's your bird?" Quinn asked.

"On business," Halle replied.

The mare flew on as her two riders fell silent.

Before long, a slender strip of blue twisted through the valley up ahead of them. Quinn could smell the water in the alpine lake, and it called to him like a siren song.

His left shoe creaked as the seams ripped apart. A clawed flipper stretched out of his pants leg, growing longer and wider.

"Hurry, Halle!" Quinn tried to shout, but his vocal cords were already changing. It came out as a throaty growl.

Rädsla spooked at the noise and nearly sent Halle and Quinn tumbling.

"Easy," Halle said, stroking the mare's neck.

Quinn's other shoe tore away and fell off, and another flipper emerged. Then the stitches of his jeans began to pop loudly, as one by one, the threads snapped. Rädsla struggled to maintain her altitude, but failed, flapping nearer to the rocky ground with each stroke of her wings.

The roaring of water cascading out of the lake and into the river below intensified. The side seams split on Quinn's shirt. Rädsla struggled to keep aloft. She snorted with the effort and her hooves dangled barely twenty feet above the ground.

The instant he felt the spray from the waterfall on his skin, Quinn pushed himself off Rädsla's back and tumbled into the flowing water. As soon as his weight was gone, Rädsla sprung into the air as if she'd been released from a slingshot.

"Quinn!" Halle called.

Rädsla regained control of herself, and swooped down above the frothing waterfall basin, but there was no sign of Quinn.

Halle clucked to the horse, and flew downstream for half a mile or so. Quinn wasn't there, either. When they came back to the falls, Halle smiled. A large dark grey hump protruded from the water. Slowly, a long neck that even a giraffe would envy curled out of the water, followed by a head that was neither horse nor crocodile, but a bizarre mixture of both. Halle waved and turned Rädsla back towards the *Three Sisters Inn*.

Chapter 5
Defense Tactics

BI Agent Hadrian's vision was blurry from staring at a computer screen all day. There was an odd connection between Benjamin Fayllor's aunt and Ian Chambers, a disgraced investigator from the District Attorney's office. Chambers was the former college roommate of a cop named Nick Benson, and Benson's sister-in-law, Marti Keller, worked for Lulu Miranda, Fayllor's aunt. The gangster that Chambers had worked for had an extensive business relationship with the Odessa Group. It could be just coincidence – he'd seen odder things – but perhaps Fayllor wasn't as innocent as he'd originally supposed. What he really needed to do was get a closer look at the coin, to pick it up and hold it. He'd make a point of going down to the Homicide Division first thing in the morning. He also wanted to talk to Fayllor again. But not before he dropped by the aunt's shop and tried to get a feel for the legitimacy of the business.

The clock in the bottom right of his computer screen read 6:50. Time had gotten away from him, and he was going to be late. Again. He quickly shut down the laptop and locked it in his drawer. *On the way*, he texted his girlfriend.

He made it to the Museum of Natural Science in record time, and managed to tag along at the tail-end of the group. The company Sara worked for, the Greene-Childe Foundation, was having a retirement dinner for the current chairwoman. The catered buffet dinner was set up in the Paleontology Hall, and Sara was already there, small plate of appetizers in one hand and a glass of red wine in the other.

Hadrian knew that she'd given up waiting on him ages ago, and accepted that he'd show up when he could. He didn't know why she put up with that. He wasn't sure that he would, if the roles were reversed. Perhaps it was because she was a commitment-phobe, and she liked the benefit of having him as a pleasant accessory at parties without the tiresome details of running a household together. For his part, he was very fond of her – she was highly intelligent, funny, very dedicated to her work as a child welfare advocate, and an excellent lover – but he wasn't sure that he loved her. Still, their relationship worked well for him, because she didn't seem to mind that he sometimes disappeared for weeks at a time, or was always late to social engagements because of his work. Perhaps someday, he'd change to an office job with mostly regular hours, get married and have kids, but that would not be any time in the foreseeable future.

She smiled as soon as she saw Hadrian, and excused herself from the young man who was chatting her up to go and greet him with a kiss on the cheek.

"Hey Blackbird," she said.

She called him that because he had a tattoo of a raven that spanned his chest, arm and shoulder blade. He'd been shot once, in the hollow of his chest where the collarbone joined the shoulder. The ugly scar reminded him daily of how he'd screwed up and not done a good enough job searching for weapons on the suspect. So he had it covered with a tattoo. Now, when he got out of the shower, instead of a mark of failure, he saw a guardian and reminder that he had cheated death.

"Hey, babe," Hadrian said as his arm slipped around her slim waist for a brief hug. "Sorry I'm late."

Sara nodded. "Better late than never."

Hadrian followed her to the hors d'oeuvres table.

It was a pleasant enough evening, talking to Sara's coworkers. He knew most of them from various parties and functions that he'd attended with her. However, he was not disappointed when the evening was over. Sara did not live far away, and had taken a taxi to the event, partly because she was planning on having wine, and partly because she was expecting Hadrian to take her home. He never drank. His father had been an alcoholic, and he was only too aware of the potential for devastation that swirled in every ounce of liquor.

As they were saying their goodbyes, Hadrian noticed the young man that had been talking to Sara earlier watching them. She hadn't bothered introducing them, and he wondered if it was more than an oversight.

"Your friend over there seems a little disappointed that the party's over," Hadrian said, cutting his eyes toward the observer.

Sara followed his glance. "Oh, that's Matt. He's a summer intern. Works in my department. I expect he and Becky will go on a pub crawl after this. He's probably looking for her."

The drive to Sara's townhouse was short, and as Hadrian pulled into the visitor parking area, he considered going home and doing some more research. But when Sara leaned towards him so she could reach down to fish for her shoe that had slid under the seat, she kissed him softly, just under the jaw. He decided that the research could wait.

Dressed in a thickly padded Red Man suit, short, bulky Sveklá looked like a refugee from a low budget superhero comic book.

"World is dangerous place. Is important you know how to defend yourself," he said to the children sitting on the mats in front of him. "Feliks, come," he said to an older teen, the largest boy in the room.

Feliks stood up. He was much taller than Sveklá, but his body had not quite made the transition from boy to man.

"Attack me, any way you wish," the older man said.

This was not Feliks' first session with Sveklá, and he took a few moments to consider his strategy. He lunged at the teacher, his forearm up and parallel to the ground, going for a clothesline maneuver to the throat. Sveklá stepped into his path, grabbed Feliks' arm and twisted around, using the boy's own momentum to roll him across the trainer's back and onto the mat. Then he demonstrated the hip toss with Feliks in slow motion, several times.

The students paired up to practice, and Sveklá walked around correcting techniques and offering advice. Sometimes, he challenged his pupils to test their capabilities against him. Teaching martial arts was one of his favorite things in life. The skills he gave his students made their bodies strong, taught their minds focus, and gave them confidence. And these particular children needed all the strength and confidence they could get.

Chapter 6
Identity

hat do you mean you have news?" I asked the young lady with the wild hair and blue skin who was camped on the steps to the side door of my house. My heart skipped a beat. *Please be good news.*

"Expect his return tomorrow night. Or Wednesday morning."

"Quinn? You do mean Quinn? Is he alright?"

"Yes. And yes." The blue-skinned woman removed a bracelet from her wrist and held it out to me. "He sent me with this. Put it on. Do not remove it for any reason."

An unpleasant incident with a dragon-based talisman had taught me to be wary of magical jewelry. "What does it do?"

"Wards off demons."

Demons?! "Okay."

I took the bracelet from her and put it on my left wrist. It was pretty – a gold charm bracelet with tiny silver bells that dangled between alternating lapis lazuli and obsidian stones. I shook my wrist and it jingled softly. Cassie immediately grabbed at it, and I had to shift her to my other hip. She protested loudly, and the blue lady rolled her eyes.

She reached out her hand and twisted her wrist, as if tuning a doorknob. As she pulled her arm back towards herself, an invisible door opened, peeling away from the background of my house and side steps. As she stepped through it, I caught a glimpse of an ancient forest, with huge dark trees and tall bracken ferns on the other side. It snapped shut behind her, leaving nothing but a puff of cool air and the smell of damp trees.

I dug out my keys and took Cassie inside. A few weeks ago, this would have been weird. Now, it was just another Monday.

I'd had a terrible night's sleep. I was more excited about Quinn's return than I wanted to admit. I was also anxious about sending Cassie to Briar Ridge Montessori for the first time tomorrow afternoon. When she started babbling at 6:30, I wasn't really ready to get up. All night I'd had fitful sleep and strange dreams I couldn't quite remember.

My car was ready this morning, so Mom took me to pick it up after she'd dropped off the boys. The mechanics had done a great job. No one would guess it had been sideswiped and run up on the curb. Mom was in a hurry to get back to Emily, McKenzi and Dad, so I took Cassie out for lunch, just for a change of pace. And because I could afford to, now that I had a job.

Once we pulled up into Briar Ridge Montessori's parking lot, I sat in the car for several long minutes. It was a pretty school with leafy gardens and bright flowers in front. I looked for an escape route, but taking Cassie to the Tenth Sphere just wasn't feasible. I picked up her bag of diapers and change of clothes and carried her in.

I had wanted to stay in the classroom for a few minutes, just to make sure she was okay. But the teacher –politely – shooed me out. Cassie started crying when I handed her to the teacher's assistant, and I cried all the way to work.

Lulu hugged me as soon as I walked in the door. "Thanks for your help getting me out of the pokey," she said. She must have noticed my red-rimmed eyes as she pulled away. "Are you okay?" she asked.

"Dropping Cassie off at daycare was harder than I thought, that's all."

Concern creased Lulu's brows. "I thought your mother was watching her."

"She had been, but my sister had some complications, so she's taking care of her and McKenzi."

Lulu nodded and patted my back.

"I'll be okay. And so will Cassie. Glad you're out of jail," I said.

"Well, I'll be in and out of the shop a lot, honey. I'm helping the attorney with Benjamin's case."

"Benjamin? That's your nephew, right?"

Lulu nodded.

I didn't doubt for an instant that Lulu was innocent. But I'd never met her nephew, and the circumstantial evidence – having a violent argument with the victim, then being seen standing over the body, holding the murder weapon – seemed pretty damning. I was a little concerned that Lulu was letting her affection for her nephew cloud her judgment.

The shop was mercifully busy, but I was getting antsy, beyond ready to go pick up my daughter, and wondering if Quinn would be home when we got there. There was still half an hour left in my shift, and I struggled not to be snappy with customers.

It was about then that a man walked into the shop. I noted that he seemed much younger than our average male customer – I'd guess thirty, give or take. He was pleasant looking, but not walk-into-a-signpost gorgeous. His round, wire-framed glasses seemed to belong on his face, but I'm not sure I would have even noted him, except for a thin, white scar that etched a narrow valley as it curved down his right cheek between his eye and his jaw. He smiled at me before he started looking through the figurines near the cash register.

"If there's something I can help you with, please let me know," I said, then glanced over his head at the clock.

He nodded. Then he browsed slowly through the shop. I just wanted him to go so I could go find either Belinda or Lulu and see if I could leave a little early.

At ten minutes to five, Lulu came out of the back room. She smiled at the customer, then looked at me. "Marti, are you coming to circle on Thursday night?"

I hadn't really thought about it. "Maybe. I'm not sure."

"Try to make it. I think you'll like it."

"I'll see what I can do. Is it okay if I scoot out of here a couple of minutes early?"

"No problem, honey. Go."

When I came out of the back room with my handbag, Lulu was talking to the man about the Thursday night mediumship circle that she held in the store.

I didn't speed or run any red lights on the way to pick up Cassie, but I did push the envelope on a few yellow ones. When I arrived, she was playing with foam blocks. I picked her up, expecting her to be happy to see me. She cried. Some days, you just can't win.

"She had a good nap from two 'til just after three," the teacher said. "She's a very good baby. I'm looking forward to seeing her again on Thursday."

I let Cassie roam around the living room while I made us dinner. I wondered if I should make a little extra for Quinn, then chided myself. He wasn't my spouse. He wasn't even my boyfriend, really. But I missed him, anyway.

Dinner came and went. Cassie's bedtime came and went. Still no Quinn. I lay on the couch, trying to read a book, but I couldn't focus on it.

"Girlfriend, you sure you want to do this?"

I jumped at the sound of Delilah's voice.

"Do what?"

"You know. Let that shifter back in your life."

"I thought you said he wasn't so bad, after all."

"Girl, they're all dangerous. Even the not so bad ones. Just sayin'."

"What would you do?" I noticed I was picking at the skin along my thumbnail.

"I can't decide that for you, girlfriend. Ain't nobody but you really knows the answer to that question."

Delilah grew more and more transparent. The last thing to fade away was her smile, hanging for a second like a maternal Cheshire Cat.

A tap on back door window startled me. I got up and turned on the porch light. Quinn squinted in the yellow glow of the bug bulb.

I fumbled with the alarm and got it turned off before I opened the door and he stepped inside. Although I had planned to maintain a certain amount of decorum and proceed with caution, I hurled myself at him and hugged him around the neck. His arms wrapped around my waist, crushing me against the hard warmth of his body. He smelled of rain on a hot day. What I wanted to do more than anything at that moment was to tear his clothes off.

"Ahem," Halle said.

Quinn released me and frowned. Halle stepped into the circle of light by the back door.

"Hello," she said with a little wave.

I suddenly felt like an old balloon, trailing limply on its cheerful ribbon after all the helium has leaked out.

I stepped away from Quinn, and Halle pushed her way inside.

"I'm sorry," Quinn said. "But I needed reinforcements."

"Reinforcements?" *Really? Is that what she is?*

"Just a precaution, to make sure you and Cassie stay safe." He took my left hand in his right, shaking it just enough to make the little charm bracelet jingle. "That's why I sent you this."

"The blue chick said it wards off demons."

"Nothing will really stop a determined demon. But every little bit of discouragement helps. It's probably just me being over-protective."

I didn't think that he was lying exactly, just not telling me everything. But I refused to argue with him in front of Halle.

"You'll need somewhere to sleep, I suppose?" I said to her.

I didn't wait for her answer before turning on my heel and heading to the linen closet to get her a blanket. Unfortunately, I didn't have any scratchy woolen ones. An odd-sized cotton waffle weave was the closest I had, so I scooped it up and dropped it on the couch. "Good night."

I looked in on Cassie on my way to my bedroom. She was snoozing away, arms sprawled above her head, without a care in the world. I almost envied her.

Quinn was already in my bedroom when I arrived. I was more than a little annoyed with him for bringing Halle along to my house. A quick glare, then I cut my eyes away from him and started fiddling with the pictures on my dresser.

He came and stood behind me, a foot or so away. I could see him watching me in the mirror. "I'm sorry," he said. "I know that Halle isn't your favorite." He traced a finger from my shoulder to my elbow, and I shivered.

Well, after all, Halle was in the living room. Alone.

I turned to face him.

"If I didn't care about you and Cassie, I wouldn't have brought her."

I frowned. There was a "but" coming, I could tell.

"Whatever you think of her, she will never lie, and if she says she will do something, it absolutely will happen. She's a fierce fighter, and cannot be killed."

"What is she? *The Terminator*?"

Quinn cocked his head to the side and furrowed his brow.

"Never mind." I shook my head. "What is it that you're so worried about that both you and Halle need to be here?"

"That is kind of the problem." Quinn looked down at the floor.

Realization dawned on me. "You aren't planning to be here, are you?" I took a step back.

"I'll be here as much as I can. This is personal. The jötnar - the Frost Giants – will never come here. They wouldn't survive the heat. But I don't want to take any chances. They've already killed someone else I loved. To make things worse, they're dealing with an extra-slimy demon named Balcones. That scaly bastard ambushed my team and killed my cousin."

His eyes turned black with anger, but only for an instant.

'Someone else I loved' Quinn had said. As I considered what that might mean, he stepped closer to me, ran the backs of his fingers along my jaw. He lowered his head to kiss me, and I closed my eyes.

Bam! Bam! Bam! Halle knocked on the door as she opened it, and stepped into my bedroom. "Excuse me. I would like some water, but I don't know how to work your machine."

Can't be killed, huh? I might have to test that theory.

I stalked out of my room and into the kitchen. "Glasses are in this cabinet," I snapped, jerking open one of the doors. I snatched a plastic cup off the middle shelf and shoved it under the water dispenser. "Put the cup under the spout, then push this button." I filled the glass half way, then shoved it into her hand, slopping some of it on the floor.

As I reached for a towel to clean up the water, Quinn said, "I have to go." He quickly stepped in and his lips brushed mine, sending shockwaves throughout every nerve ending in my body and turning my knees to jelly. He paused and looked back at me for a moment as he left through the back door. I sat down in the nearest chair, leaving the puddle of water where it lay. I was too much of a puddle myself.

"You know that's a really bad idea, right?" Halle asked.

"What are you talking about?" I growled at her.

"Mortals and fae. Never really works out, especially not for the mortal."

I rolled my eyes at her in response.

She shook her head, long blonde plaits shimmering under the kitchen lights. "What fools these mortals be!" she beseeched the ceiling.

"So now you're going to quote Shakespeare at me? Now there's an immortal mortal."

Halle snorted through her nose. "Please. Do you really think *he's* a human?" Halle's head swiveled ever so slightly back and forth, and the sheerest of smiles curled across her lips.

"What has this got to do with anything?" I wanted to shout at her, but I wanted Cassie to remain asleep even more.

"Look, Graham asked me—"

"Who's Graham?" I snapped.

"Quinn's youngest brother. He asked me to come try to talk some sense into Quinn, get him to leave you alone. Graham wants to spare his brother from suffering at your death. Which may come a lot sooner than you expect, if you continue meddling in affairs that are none of your concern."

"Are you threatening me?" I asked, crossing my arms.

"Not a threat. Just a friendly warning."

"Charming," I said.

"What is the life expectancy of a human?" Halle asked.

"Depends. Eighty, give or take."

"What do you suppose the life expectancy for a kelpie is?"

"Don't know."

"Twelve hundred years. Do you see how this could be a problem?"

Maybe she made logical sense. But I didn't care. I wanted him. My nerves were still tingling from his kiss.

"Fine. Whatever. I'm going to bed," I replied.

I didn't give Halle a second look as I strode out of the kitchen. A peek into Cassie's room showed me she was still blissfully asleep. I left my bedroom door ajar, so I could hear any comings or goings, and changed into my nightshirt in the bathroom. I looked at myself in the mirror as I brushed my teeth. *What if Halle was right?*

What if being with me only ended up hurting Quinn? His brother was obviously concerned about it. Well, Quinn was an adult, for Pete's sake, and he was perfectly capable of making his own decisions. After all, he knew before he even met me that his lifespan was more than ten times what mine was. Still, I wondered how long he would stay with me, once the first grey hair sprouted, and the little wrinkles started showing. I was suddenly a whole lot less sure about what I wanted from him. The whole idea of our relationship twisted and squirmed like a boa constrictor in my head, until exhaustion took its toll.

Wednesday was awkward, what with my newfound Valkyrie shadow. I thought it was odd that Mr. Douglas down the street stopped mulching his azaleas to wave at us when we took Cassie for her morning perambulation. He never waved at anyone, just sat behind the screen door, daring anyone to set so much as a toe on his precisely fertilized, perfectly manicured grass. That sort of thing seemed to happen when Halle was around.

On Thursday afternoon, I grabbed Cassie's go-bag and headed for the car. Halle came, too.

"Okay, I'm not trying to be difficult here, but you can't go to work with me," I said. I had been looking forward to having a break from her.

Halle nodded. "I will not enter your place of business. But I am coming with you."

"Suit yourself."

Cassie cried less when I dropped her off today than she had on Tuesday. I cried about the same. When I got back into the car, Halle wrinkled her nose.

"What is this liquid coming from your eyes? Are you injured?"

"Tears, Halle. Surely you've heard of them? I'm just feeling a little sad about leaving Cassie here, that's all."

"Valkyries do not have tears."

"Good for you."

I felt a little bad for being so snappy. "When you were little, did your mother leave you with someone while she went out?"

"I have never been any other way than I am now. Valkyries do not have mothers."

"Really?" It was my turn to be perplexed. "Then where did you come from, if you don't have a mother?"

"Odin All-Father created us. Valkyries are the choosers of the slain. We select the best of the mortal warriors, to fight with the Aesir at Rägnorok. That is our purpose, and why we exist."

"Do you get lonely, having no family?"

The car behind us beeped. I hadn't noticed the light had gone green.

"I have many sisters," Halle said, glancing into the rear view mirror. "And, of course, a father."

"Actually, I meant like a husband and kids," I said.

"Valkyries do not have children. And I have no need for a husband – I can have any man I wish. Quinn, for example is an excellent lover."

I felt heat flash into my cheeks. I wanted to crawl underneath the seat. There was nothing in the world I wanted to talk about less with Halle than Quinn. And especially not about sex with Quinn. I whipped the car into a parking spot.

"Look, here we are at the Tenth Sphere. Don't know what you're going to do, but I'm going to work."

I practically fled from my car before she could say anything else. She got out more slowly, and I clicked the remote to lock the doors as I retreated.

The cowbell on the Tenth Sphere's door jangled as I opened it, and I breathed in the calming sandalwood scent of the store.

"Are you alright?" Belinda asked from behind the counter.

"Fine. Just a little hot."

The hint of a frown wrinkled her lips, as if she didn't quite believe me. "Lulu is out this afternoon. At the lawyer's office again. This whole thing with Benjamin has really knocked her for a loop."

I nodded, then chewed my lip. "Belinda? How certain are you that her nephew didn't kill the guy?"

"Benjamin would never do anything like that. Sure, I've seen him get angry before, maybe shout a little, but never once have I seen him raise his hand to anyone. He just doesn't behave that way."

"Sometimes people can surprise you."

"Perhaps," she replied, her lips pressing and un-pressing as if the word tasted unpleasant. "Lulu wanted me to ask if you were coming to circle tonight."

"Maybe, but I doubt it. Child care."
Belinda nodded.

Business at the shop was painfully slow. I spent more time dusting the shelves than anything else. Once, I thought I saw a reflection of a man's face in one of the highly polished rutilated quartz points, but it was just a combination of glare and the inclusions. There was one customer all afternoon, and she only bought one small piece of moonstone and some incense. I left at the stroke of five.

I scanned the parking lot for Halle, but couldn't find her. But by the time I got to the car and unlocked the door, there she was, as if she'd fallen out of the sky.

She smiled as she got in the car, but I had no idea what to say to her.

"Good day at work?" she asked.

I shrugged. "A little slow."

The silence on the way to Briar Ridge Montessori was discomforting. Halle waited in the car while I ran in to pick up Cassie, who of course, cried and didn't want to leave.

When I pulled into my carport, Cassie squealed. "Booce!"

I looked up. Sure enough, an over-sized black Lab sat on the back porch, tail thumping against the 'Welcome' mat.

I grabbed my baby and hurried inside. I didn't intentionally drop the door on Halle. But accidents happen. I opened the back door and Bruce trotted in. He headed straight down the hall to the bedroom.

It didn't take long for a clothed Quinn to return. "Your brother-in-law was looking for you."

"Nick? Wonder what he wanted."

I smiled weakly at Quinn. When he'd left, I was so sure of what I'd wanted. Now, I wasn't. Yes, he was smokin' hot. And he stirred up feelings that had been comatose since I lost my husband two years ago. But what if our being together was only going to end in suffering? For both of us. Body said, "Yes, please!" Brain said, "Run! Run away!"

"Let me just call Emily's right quick and see what's up."

As it turned out, Nick, Emily, and my parents were getting Chinese takeout, and wondered if Cassie and I wanted to join them. But we were too late. Also, Mom was planning Cassie's birthday party, and even though it was still three weeks away, wanted to know what kind of cake to bake and what color paper plates and napkins to buy.

Quinn held Cassie while I made the phone call. She giggled and flapped her arms. I couldn't help but smile. He was so good with her, and I briefly wondered if he had children. But it did give me an idea, even if it would do nothing more than postpone the inevitable.

Halle, my chaperone, was noisily filling a cup with ice cubes from the water dispenser, so I moved in close to Quinn.

"Could you do me a huge favor?" The heat of his body was giving me goose bumps, and it was hard to speak coherently.

"Such as?"

"I really wanted to go to circle tonight, but Mom can't watch Cassie. She – Cassie, not my mom - adores you, and I was wondering if…" I paused, wondering if he knew the term "babysit."

"If I would look after her?"

He looked almost confused. Perhaps males didn't watch children in his culture.

When his head tilted, his breath fell on my collarbone. I had to step back slightly, or I wasn't going anywhere. "Would you? It's just an hour."

"Da da da!" Cassie interjected.

"If…that's what you want. But only if Halle goes with you."

I wasn't sure which was worse, having Halle come with me, or her staying at home with Quinn. "Fine," I replied.

The man with the scar and glasses that was in the shop on Tuesday somehow ended up next to me when we formed the circle. He introduced himself as Hunter. When we joined hands during the smudging, I noticed his right hand was strong, but not calloused – he had an office job. Halle stuck to my other side like a cocklebur.

The circle was largely uneventful, at least for me. Delilah appeared only for a moment, saying "Remember, girlfriend, there ain't no such thing as an accident."

Marilyn, one of the circle regulars, embarrassingly threw herself at Hunter. He declined. Perhaps he noticed the ropey scars across her wrists, too.

I trusted Quinn with Cassie. He'd already saved her life once. But I missed my baby. If I hurried, I could get back before she fell asleep. Then, who knows? I might even get a private word or two with Quinn. I dragged Halle out of the Tenth Sphere before she could say anything to anybody. We got halfway down the block when I realized I'd left my phone in the shop.

"I have to go back. Left something in the shop," I said as I stopped and turned around.

"Fine," Halle answered.

She waited outside for me while I ran inside. When I came back, I thought it was strange that she had a smudge of dirt across her cheek. I didn't say anything about it, though. I just chalked it up to Halle being her usual odd self.

When we got home, Quinn was sitting in the recliner, reading a book on my tablet. Cassie was fast asleep, sprawled across his body. The afternoon at Briar Ridge must have been a little too much for her.

"I seem to be stuck," Quinn said, pleasantly.

I carefully picked my baby up and carried her to her crib. I was a little disappointed that she was already asleep, but she and Quinn had looked so cute together that it softened the blow a little.

When I got back to the living room, there was no smudge on Halle's face. In fact, I wondered if the dirt I thought I saw nothing more than a trick of the shadows in the poor light.

"I'm starved," she announced.

It was true that provisions were running low. I was waiting for my pay to be EFT'd to the bank tomorrow before I went grocery shopping. But I was sure she could find something if she tried hard enough.

"Are there any inns nearby?" Halle asked.

"Inns aren't the same thing here," Quinn remarked. "You want a restaurant."

"Are there any of those nearby?" she responded.

"There are always restaurants nearby in Houston. What do you want to eat?" I said.

"Meat. Bread. And beer."

"Well, that's specific," I said.

"What food was it that your mother brought over last week?" Quinn asked.

"She made fajitas."

"Yes, I think Halle might like those. Where can you get them?"

He was probably just trying to be nice. But I still felt a twinge of jealousy. "If you want fajitas, it's Guillermo's Cantina. It's 8:30 on a Friday night. It'll be packed – bet there's an hour wait." I wanted to discourage him from taking Halle out to dinner.

"Here." Quinn held out a handful of bills to me. "Is this enough?"

Four twenties. "Should be."

He flapped it at me. "Bring something back for me?"

"What?"

"I don't know. The same as whatever you have."

"No. I meant – I thought you were going."

"I have some calls to make. You take her. Besides, someone's got to stay with Cassie."

Me taking Halle out to dinner was only a slightly different kind of hell than watching Quinn take her out.

"Fine," I said. "You do have my cell number, right?"

"Of course."

I would much rather have gone out to dinner with him, but I didn't trust Halle anywhere near Cassie. But, since I was clearly being kicked out of my own house, I decided to try to make the best of it. Ordinarily, I would have put up more of a fight, but my current ambivalence toward my relationship with Quinn made it seem easier to avoid confrontation.

I looked in on Cassie before I slipped on my shoes. Couldn't believe she was less than a month from being a year old.

"Let's go." I jingled my car keys at Halle.

As luck would have it, the Astros were playing baseball tonight, there was a concert at Cynthia Woods by a major band that I'd never heard of, and the hottest Broadway play on tour was at the Alley. Because of this, the quirky little restaurant row on Houston's western edge of I-10 was merely busy, instead of cheek-to-jowl. I had to give my keys to Guillermo's valet, because there was no more self-parking available. I smiled sheepishly at him, hoping he wouldn't judge me too harshly over my clutch. It had started slipping, just a little, recently, and I was going to have to take it to the shop.

Guillermo's was not exactly deserted, but we did only have to wait twenty minutes for a table. That would have been unheard of, if not for the other events going on. Out of force of habit, I ordered the cheapest thing on the menu – a spinach and mushroom quesadilla. I asked them to bring me a second one to go when they brought the check. Halle was clearly alarmed when the server brought out the sizzling cast iron dish of fajitas – steaming seasoned meat strips on a bed of sautéed onions and bell peppers. Admittedly, I felt a little bit superior, as I have never been startled by a noisy meal. I had to teach Halle how to wrap her fajitas in the tortillas, and she was not a fan of pico de gallo. And the way she was putting away the Negro Modelo, it was a good thing she didn't drive. I hoped Quinn had sent enough money. There was enough (barely) for the check and a decent tip. *Be careful what you wish for,* I thought when I saw that the waiter had written his name and phone number on the receipt. He'd been flirting with Halle since he'd taken our drink order. We collected Quinn's to go box and headed for the door.

It took the valet almost twenty minutes to return with my car.

"Oh, that's just great," I grumbled.

There was a huge dent in the right fender, part of the grill was missing, and one of the headlights was shattered.

"What happened?" I asked the valet, not as kindly as I probably should have.

"*Prosti menya.* Was like that when I went to get. Another car, perhaps backed into it?"

Prosti menya. Where had I heard that recently? The young man had an odd accent, as if English wasn't his first language, but he had spoken it for longer, diluting, but not conquering the original.

"I'd like to speak to the manager," I said, fighting to stay calm. I'd just gotten my car out of the shop. This was the last thing I needed.

He nodded and disappeared into the restaurant.

The manager came out, alternated between apologizing profusely and disclaiming responsibility, gave me his card and $100 worth of Guillermo's coupons, then scurried back inside. I wasn't sure which I wanted to do more – cry or follow him inside and punch him. But I did neither. It wasn't really his fault. Possibly, the valet wrecked it, but given the array of BMWs, Mercedes, and muscle cars in the parking lot, it seemed unlikely that he'd choose to go for a joy ride in a six year old, four cylinder Corolla.

My hands shook as I sifted through the pile of papers, looking for the current insurance card. I took some pictures and called for an insurance claim number. Two uninsured driver claims in less than thirty days. They are either going to jack up my rate or drop me, I'm sure of it. I took notes on one of the many expired insurance cards in my glove box, then got into the driver's seat.

"Well, I hope we don't get stopped on the way home," I said to Halle.

"Stopped? Who would stop us?"

"The police. For driving with a broken headlight."

She nodded, but I don't think she understood.

We were perhaps four blocks from Guillermo's when not one, not two, but four police cruisers surrounded us, lights flashing.

"Pull over to your left and exit the vehicle. Keep your hands where we can see them," the officer closest to us announced over his PA.

The Valkyrie scowled and shifted in her seat.

"Halle, don't do anything stupid. Just be calm, and let's find out what this is about."

I did as I was instructed. As the first officer approached us, I asked, "Is this about the broken headlight?"

"You could say that," he replied. Two other officers inspected the front end of my car with their flashlights.

"A vehicle matching this description, with your license plate was used in a crime at approximately 9:30 PM."

"We were having dinner at Guillermo's. I paid the check, maybe a quarter of ten. If you will let me get the receipt out of my purse, I can prove it. When the valet brought my car back, the headlight was broken. I spoke with the manager about it. And I'm sure the waiter will remember us." *He'd remember Halle, at any rate.*

Two more cruisers pulled up, and a sergeant got out of one of them. She talked to the two officers who had been examining my vehicle. A dark sedan pulled up and three men got out, wearing black windbreakers with "FBI" in huge yellow letters on their backs.

"Holy moly. What is going on here?"

An officer retrieved my purse from the car and looked in it, checking for weapons I guessed, before he handed it over to me. I opened my wallet and dug out the receipt and the handful of coupons.

"The manager gave me these because of the damage to my car. Here's his card. Please call him." I handed the papers to the cop, who took them to the sergeant.

Halle and I stood in front of the squad car that had blocked my car in. I knew that everything we did and said was being recorded by the dash cam. Halle shifted back and forth, and glowered at the police.

"You're going to get us in trouble. Just relax," I hissed at her.

The FBI agents were now in conference with the sergeant and the two officers with the flashlights. Cell phones came out, calls were made, and more talking was done. I was very tired, my feet hurt, and I was both scared and irritated. Why wouldn't they at least tell us what was going on? When were they going to let us leave?

A seventh cruiser arrived. The officer got out and opened the rear door, then helped an older woman and a youngish man climb out of the car. It was hard to get a more accurate idea of their ages in the red and blue strobe of the light bars.

As they approached us, the man said, "Is that them? Is that who killed Pappa?"

He didn't wait for her answer, but charged at us. An officer tried to block his way, but the man had both a height and weight advantage. Other officers came running, but they were yards away. Something blurred past me, and the man was on the ground, moaning and holding a probably broken nose, blood gushing from between his fingers.

Halle was now on the other side of me. I stared at her with my mouth hanging open. How did that happen?

"What?" she shrugged and held out her hands, palms up. "He tripped."

"Does anybody have any gauze, or at least paper towels?" I asked loudly. "Sir, you're going to have to sit up. There you go. Now lean forward just a little, so you're not swallowing all that blood. It'll just make you vomit," I told the man as I knelt beside him and guided him to a sitting position. "Don't worry – I'm a nurse."

Somebody handed me a few brown paper towels and a pair of disposable gloves. I did the best I could to pack his nostrils and stop the bleeding. "You'll need to have this seen about," I said to him.

When I stood up, I saw that the woman he had arrived with was talking to the FBI and the sergeant, in between sobs. The sergeant said something to one of the officers. He came over and said, "The witness said that one male suspect was driving the car, not two women. Your story checks out; however, there was some blood found on the bumper and a few hairs were caught in the broken light. We're taking the vehicle to the forensics lab to collect evidence. Is there someone you can call to come pick you up?"

"Wait. Blood? Hair? Did someone get run over with my car?"

"I really can't comment on that, ma'am."

I called Nick. He had already gone to bed — it was after 11:00 — but he'd come get us as soon as he got dressed.

An ambulance arrived and carried the man with the broken nose away to the ER.

While we waited for Nick, I gave my contact information and a formal statement to the officer with the clipboard. I asked when he thought I'd get my car back, but he said he had no idea, although it could be quite a while.

When Nick finally showed up, he stopped and chatted with a couple of the officers before he came over to us. He motioned for us to join him to the side of the car, off camera.

In a very low voice, so quietly I could barely understand him, he said, "Seems your car was used in a homicide. Victim was in the federal witness protection program." Nick nodded towards the FBI agents. "You didn't hear that from me, by the way."

I was too stunned to do much talking on the way home. *Somebody stole my car, not only to kill someone, but someone in the witness protection program?* Halle, on the other hand, plied Nick with questions. I was dimly aware of them talking, but didn't pay much attention to what they were saying. When we got back to my house, I carried the sadly congealed quesadilla in for Quinn. I set it on the end table by the door and heard footsteps as he came in from the living room. I opened my mouth to introduce him to Nick.

"What the hell are you doing here?" Nick growled at Quinn.

Chapter 7
Dog Days of Summer

hat do you think you're doing, leaving your baby with a junkie?" Nick said to me.

This was the last thing I'd expected to hear.

"Long time, no see, Officer Benson," Quinn said. "I told you two years ago that I got my act together. Got a job and everything."

Then I remembered. Quinn had known my husband and Nick. But they didn't know who, or what, he really was. This was well beyond awkward. And what did he mean by "junkie?"

"Once a junkie, always a junkie. And I thought you'd left town, McLeod."

"I had." Quinn smiled. "But now I'm back."

Nick's glare shifted to me. "How'd you hook up with this…person, anyway?"

"He works with her," I said, looking at Halle. Well, it was true. Sort of.

"The dog trainer. So where's the dog?" Nick asked.

"Still at the kennel," I said.

I didn't like this game of verbal ping pong. It wasn't high stakes in that someone could die. But damaged relationships were hard to fix. I wished I could just tell Nick everything. But he'd never believe me – he'd just think I'd lost my mind. A few weeks ago, I wouldn't have believed me, either.

"Thanks for picking us up," I said to him. Although I knew I was likely to be disappointed, I hoped he would take it as a hint to go home.

"I really wish you would reconsider your association," he gave Quinn a hard look, "with these people." He crossed his arms over his broad chest.

There would be no persuading him at this point, I knew.

"Nick, please don't worry. Everything is okay."

He responded by snatching up my hands and rotating them so that my wrists faced him. Out of the corner of my eye, I saw Quinn take a step closer to me. Nick gave him a warning look, and he stopped.

"You're not doing drugs, are you?" Nick asked me.

"What? Of course not! Why would you even think that?" I answered, somewhat hurt by his accusation.

"You've changed your habits, you're associating with a known drug user, and you would never leave Cassie with a stranger. Not *normally*, anyway."

I yanked my hands out of his and planted my fists firmly on my hips. "So I get a dog and a job, so now I'm a junkie? Really?" I risked a glance at Quinn. "Besides, he –" I stopped myself. I couldn't tell Nick that Quinn wasn't a stranger, because then he'd want to know how I knew him. "He comes highly recommended," I finished lamely.

Halle burst out laughing.

Yes. She had highly recommended Quinn earlier this afternoon. At least both he and Nick were looking at her, and not my flaming cheeks.

"Not to worry," Halle said. "We were leaving, anyway." She smiled at me. "I'll bring your dog back soon."

"Goodnight, then. See you later," I said, following them to the door. "Oh! Don't forget your quesadilla. Sorry. I think it's gotten a little cold." I handed Quinn the takeout bag from Guillermo's, and electricity jolted up my arm as his fingers brushed mine.

Nick lurked on the front porch long enough to watch them disappear down the sidewalk.

"I'm really not comfortable with those people hanging around. McLeod is a known criminal. And a substance abuser. Bad things tend to happen to people who run with *that* crowd."

I took a deep breath to compose my thoughts. I knew that under ordinary circumstances, he would be right. But these weren't ordinary circumstances. And I couldn't tell him that. I had to tread very carefully here.

"Nick, thank you for caring. I really appreciate that. But it isn't like I'm dating the guy. He just sat in the living room and watched TV while Cassie slept. If someone hadn't stolen my car to run somebody over, we would have been out an hour or less. But I'm back now, and everything's fine."

"Are you sure?"

As much as I believed in Quinn, Nick's question sent a shiver up my spine.

"See for yourself," I said.

I headed down the hall to Cassie's room. If I was wrong, I'd never forgive myself.

I opened the door a little and a yellow wedge of light fell across Cassie's face. She groaned and wrinkled her forehead. After I closed the door and waited a moment to make sure I hadn't woken her, I led Nick to my bedroom. I opened the top drawer of my dresser and pulled out a box from the depths, then opened it to reveal my engagement and wedding rings. Along with an emerald tennis bracelet that Ryan had given me for Christmas once, they were the only valuable pieces of jewelry I owned.

"See?" I said.

"Okay. It worked out fine. This time. But promise me you'll be more careful about who you leave your kid with."

"You *know* I would never willingly endanger Cassie."

He nodded. "I have to get back to the house. Something's happened to Emily's sequestered witness and she's all kinds of crazy."

"Isn't she supposed to be on maternity leave?"

"That's what I told her."

It didn't occur to me until after he'd left that the person who had been run over with my car was in the witness protection program. I hoped Emily's person was okay — it seemed like a bad night for witnesses.

When my alarm baby went off at 6:30, I found myself moving slower than normal. Cassie had mostly lost interest in nursing these days – only before bed now, and not always then. *Use it or lose it, kid.* I took her into the kitchen and set her up with some munchies. I had half-expected Quinn and Halle to come back after Nick left last night, but they never showed. Just in case, I peeked out the back window. Bruce was curled up on the doormat. He sat up when I opened the door, then yawned, stretched, and moseyed into the house.

After he'd shifted and dressed, he came into the kitchen, poured himself a cup of coffee, and sat down at the table. This was the first time I'd ever seen him drink coffee, and it made me wonder what else was going to be different.

"No Halle today?" I asked, cautiously optimistic. I unloaded the dishwasher as we spoke.

"She's around, just keeping a low profile. Listen. About last night. That episode with Nick."

"Yeah. You told me that you knew him. And Ryan. But you never told me the details."

Dishes clattered as I stacked plates and bowls together.

Quinn propped his elbows on the table, laced his fingers together, and rested his chin on his knuckles. "It's a bit complicated." He paused, as if considering how much he should tell me. "I borrowed the identity of a NED named Marc McLeod. He wasn't exactly what you'd call an upstanding citizen."

"I'm sorry. Did you say a 'ned?'"

"Non-Educated Delinquent. NED for short. Only thing he was good for was he looked a bit like me. McLeod was a junkie, and a thief to boot. It was an accident, really, that I ran into Nick and Ryan at all. I strayed into a crime scene they were working. I had to tell them something. And as Mr. McLeod was done using his identity, I had borrowed it for just such occasions. You can hardly blame Nick for not wanting a piece of shite like that hanging about."

"That explains a lot."

I got that Nick thought McLeod was a lowlife. And I could understand why he wouldn't want him around. But Quinn wasn't McLeod. "This is a real problem. How do we convince Nick that you aren't this McLeod person?"

"We don't."

"What?" I frowned at him.

"For the time being, I think it's best for him not to see me in human form."

"That doesn't seem fair, especially not to you." *Or me.*

"I know. But we have bigger problems right now. This demon, Balcones – the one I told you about the other night - knows that I'm tracking him. He'll try to get me before I get him. Demons like to make their targets suffer, and one of their favorite ways to do that is to go after the friends and families of their intended victims. My mother and brothers are not where demons can get at them. You and Cassie are. No matter how much I might want to, for your safety and my own, I can't afford to…be distracted right now."

I nearly dropped the stack of plates I was loading into the cabinet. I felt a chill in the pit of my stomach that froze all the way through my body to my spine. What had I done? I'd been so stupidly giddy, like a lovesick teenager, that I'd put Cassie and myself in this situation. That wasn't entirely true. There were circumstances well beyond my control that had thrown Quinn and me together. But still, I knew it could be dangerous, keeping company with a shifter, especially one that belonged to a clandestine operations team. But it didn't stop me from wanting him.

"I see. What about Halle? You said she was around somewhere."

"She is. And there are others – my team – as well. But you don't know how cunning demons can be. My plan is to stay in canine form for now. My senses will be sharper, and it won't antagonize your brother-in-law. I don't want to drag him into this as well."

I nodded, hanging up the damp dishtowel and closing the dishwasher door. I didn't like it, but I was unlikely to be able to change his mind. Quinn stood up, gave Cassie a little tickle under her chin, then moved closer to me. He kissed me then. Softly, quickly, his lips just grazing mine, but sending a thousand little thrills through my body.

"It's going to be okay. I promise," he said, then turned and walked out of the room.

I pushed the stroller along the bumpy sidewalk. The three of us, Cassie, Bruce, and I started out on our morning walk. I was amazed to see a moving van parked across the street. Had Mrs. Paddington's house really sold that quickly? That would be the fastest escrow ever. I crossed the road to check out the new neighbors. Burly men in pale blue uniforms carried furniture from the truck to the house. A compact car, hatchback open, sat in the driveway, back filled with smaller moving boxes.

A man walked out through the garage, sweat glistening off his bare chest and soaking the top of his cargo shorts. A tattoo of a black bird, body on his upper left arm, wings wrapped around his chest and back, made me think of Halle's pet. The man saw me gawking at him and came over.

"Hello," I said. Realization struck as he got closer. "You're the guy from the shop. You came to Circle last night. It's Hunter, right?" It was the man with the wire-framed glasses and thin scar on his cheek. And he looked better with his shirt off than I would have expected.

"Guilty as charged." He smiled and wiped his hands on a small towel that stuck out of his front pocket. "I'm indeed Hunter. Hunter Greene, actually." He reached out to shake my hand.

Bruce sat down in between us, and rolled over onto one hip.

I raised an eyebrow. "Hunter Greene?"

I picked up Mr. Buns. Cassie had dropped him over the side of the stroller.

"Yes. My grandmother was an art teacher, and she named my dad Forrest. I have a sister called Kelly. My aunt's named Jade, but she's a Sanders now. Nice dog you've got there. Seems very well trained."

"Yes. He does seem that way. But he can be quite a handful," I replied.

"I'm sorry. I'm terrible with names. I know we were introduced last night. Molly?"

"Marti, and this is Cassie. Welcome to the neighborhood. I'm amazed that you're moving in so quickly – Mrs. Paddington just put her house on the market a few days ago."

"Actually, I'm just leasing it. My company," he wiped his glasses with the towel, "moves me around a lot. Not much point in trying to buy anything. Especially since it's only me."

"Oh."

"I don't have kids or anything, not even a goldfish." he replied.

"Ah. Well, that makes sense, then." He seemed to be going out of his way to let me know he was single. Maybe I should start wearing my wedding ring again.

Cassie started to fuss a little, and Bruce let out a deep sigh. "I've got to get going. I'm sure I'll see you around."

While Cassie had her afternoon nap, I called my insurance agent to tell him what had happened with my car, and he told me he would need a copy of the police report before he could do anything. What was I going to do without a car for who knows how long? Theoretically, Mom could take Cassie to Briar Ridge Montessori when she took the boys, but then she'd be there all day, and that would cost more than I was earning. Maybe Em would let me borrow her car – it wasn't like she could drive right now, anyway. I had a long weekend to think about it – the Fourth of July was Monday, so there really wasn't anything I could do before Tuesday, anyway. I called the Tenth Sphere to let Lulu and Belinda know I might have some trouble getting to work.

"I see," Lulu said, after I explained the situation. "I might have a solution for you, honey. I'll ask Benjamin if it's okay for you to drive his car while all this unpleasantness is being sorted out."

"That would be great." *And a little weird.* "I really appreciate that, although I hope it doesn't take too much longer for his problem to get straightened out."

After I hung up with Lulu, I looked at Bruce. "You know, Nick's at work. There's no way he'll show up anytime soon."

Bruce gave me a sad puppy look and rested his head on his outstretched legs. "Fine."

Our family tradition for July Fourth was to have a big barbeque for friends and family at Mom and Dad's late in the afternoon, then climb up on the roof to watch fireworks. The top of the screened in porch was flat, and when Kyle and Aiden were little, Nick and Ryan had installed a railing around it. It looked a little odd, until there were people milling around up there. Even after the sun went down, the roof was sizzling hot, so Mom always put down some old blankets so we wouldn't roast our toes.

Nick had rented a huge inflatable water slide and put it up against the edge of the porch so the kids could jump off the roof onto the slide. Looked like a broken arm waiting to happen to me, but the dozen or so kids – most of them neighbors - that were skidding down the rubber incline and splashing into the pool at the end seemed to be having a great time.

This was Cassie's first Fourth of July, and I hoped the firecrackers didn't scare her. People firing guns in the air wasn't a big problem in our neighborhood, but there was always somebody who defied the city's ban and shot off fireworks.

Dad and Nick had dueling barbeque pits going, and the smoke carried hints of brisket, corn, and grilled peaches my way.

As soon as we went through the back gate, Emily waved and motioned me over to the back porch, where she sat with a small knot of women, in the shade and under the ceiling fan, half hidden by the bouncing slide. Bruce followed us silently and slouched into a disorderly heap on the wooden floor.

"Hey, Em. How're you feeling?"

"Okay. As well as can be expected, I guess. But I have to tell you something, an unbelievable coincidence," Emily said.

"What's that?"

"There was a case I was working on right before I went on maternity leave. The trial just started, and one of our star witnesses was sequestered because he was just about to go into the federal witness protection program. Two days before he was supposed to testify, someone ran over him with a car. Would you like to guess whose car they used?"

"Um," was all that would come out of my mouth. It took a couple of seconds for me to wrangle my thoughts into anything remotely sensible. "Mine? That's just crazy. The odds of that have to be similar to winning the Lotto or something."

"Yes. If it's a coincidence."

"If? You think someone deliberately chose my car to kill your witness? Why?"

"I don't know that. It just seems peculiar that you called him on an unsecured line and he ended up in the morgue."

"What do you mean I called him?"

"Dr. Pavlov. Remember?"

I swallowed hard. "I just...I don't know what to say. I had no idea." Was I really at least partly responsible for this man's death? It hardly seemed fair to blame me – I was just trying to save my sister's life.

Cassie started squirming in my arms, desperate to get down and explore.

"Oh, Marti! Let me see that baby, huh?" Miss Polly asked, from the chair next to Emily's.

Miss Polly lived two doors down from me, on the other side of Mom and Dad, and she and my mother had been friends for years. Emily and I had grown up out in the country, but we moved into town when I was a senior in high school, after Dad had his accident. She brought over some home-baked bread the day we moved in, and she and Mom bonded over iced tea. I'm not sure what her last name is – she introduced herself as "Miss Polly," and that's what we always called her.

Cassie did not want to be held. She wanted to go see what the other kids were doing, and she cried when I handed her over.

Miss Polly shook her head. "She's growing so fast! I can't believe how big she's gotten." She winked at me. "This little girl doesn't want to hang out on the porch with the old folks. Get her out there with the kids." She turned back to my mother. "No, Adele. As I was saying, those aren't crows. That's the oddest thing. They're common ravens, I'm sure of it. You see how they have shaggy feathers around their throats and their beaks have a bump on top? They aren't supposed to live anywhere near here."

I glanced up and saw two large, shiny black birds sitting in the branches of the pine tree that grew in my back yard and overhung Mom and Dad's. I wondered if those ravens belonged to Halle. Where was she, anyway? Wouldn't it be just like her to barge in to my family gathering?

Cassie led me off the shady porch and out into the yard. With a grunt, Bruce got up and followed. Most of the kids were much older than Cassie, but there were two her age, playing in the shade with a bubble machine. They giggled and squealed as they lurched around, grabbing at the iridescent spheres that bobbed and danced over the grass. Cassie walked a little better than the other two, and she seemed to enjoy lording it over them.

Bruce's ears pricked up (as much as floppy Lab ears can, anyway) and he snorted. I turned around and noticed a man standing under a tree at the back of the yard. Something seemed odd about him, but I wasn't sure what it could be. Other than he had his back to the crowd of people. And he just stood there, dressed from head to toe in beige. He wasn't someone I recognized, and I thought I knew everybody at the party. I got up, dodged through a game of horseshoes and approached him.

"Excuse me, sir? I don't believe we've met," I said.

He turned around. Now I knew why he seemed strange. His eyes were sunken and dark-ringed. A bloody wound gaped underneath his jaw, and gouts of blood clung to his shirt.

I gasped and took a step back.

He vanished.

A moment later, Delilah appeared. "Girlfriend, do you know who that was?"

No idea.

"That man was Bertram Kounis. The dude Lulu's nephew is accused of killin'? He's been trying to show himself to her since he died, but she's so stressed and obsessed with getting Benjamin out of jail that she can't see him. That's why I suggested he come to you."

You suggested? Why on Earth would he need to come to me?

"Benjamin didn't kill him. He wants you to find out who did."

Chapter 8
Number Five

ater dripped from Quinn's hair and soaked the back of his shirt. He'd only come downstairs into the common room at the Waterhorse Inn a few moments ago, after taking a long swim in the over-sized millpond at the back of the inn. It was good for both his body and mind to shift into his kelpie form and spend time in the water. That's why the extra-large pond had been created when Quinn's mother's great-grandmother had built the inn, back before Blackthorne was any more than a market square and a well. He sat on one side of the bar, playing with a piece of toast that he had intended to eat, but somehow couldn't manage to get into his mouth.

Graham was loading clean beer glasses into the cabinet.

"Halle has come down from the northlands and into the Mundane world. You wouldn't know anything about that, would you?"

"Yes," he said. "I saw Halle in town and asked her to pay you a visit. You know what it was like when Mother killed Gretchen. I was trying to save you – and your paramour – from the same fate."

"I appreciate your concern, but I don't need my youngest brother to protect me," Quinn said.

"We're family. We protect each other."

Quinn sucked in a deep breath and let it out slowly. "You're right. I'm sorry. Halle can be abrasive, and I guess my nerves are a little raw." Quinn discovered long ago that some battles aren't worth the energy it takes to fight them, and it is more efficient to placate than argue.

Graham nodded. "So you're back for a while, then?"

"No. You remember when Tam was murdered last month? I've found the demon that did it. I think I can take him down, and I've got to get my team together."

"You and that Mundane Intervention Team," Graham said with a scowl. "Hasn't it almost got you killed enough times? And I won't even mention those close to you that have died. I don't understand why you don't just give it up. I was sure you would, after the jötnar killed Siobhan."

Her death was still painful to Quinn, even after three years. But he wouldn't rise to the bait. "Sometimes, little brother, I wish I could. But I can't change who I am. If demons are allowed to multiply unchecked in the Mundane world, what do you think is going to happen to Faery? How long do you think the barrier will hold? You think you'll be happy serving them all pints of bitters?"

Graham's nostrils flared slightly. "I understand that. I'm just not sure it's still your fight."

"It has to be somebody's fight," Quinn said as he tore the toast into quarters. "Anyway, I'll be gone for a while longer. Not sure how long this will take."

"And I'm sure your ladylove has nothing to do with your extended stay in the Mundane world."

Quinn shot his brother a warning look. "I'm off then. Cheers."

The overstuffed chair in Dame Ashleigh Rowan's Mundane Activity Monitoring and Intervention Center (MAMIC) office was not comfortable. Quinn squirmed like a small child in a church pew while he waited for her. Thoughts – pleasure, pain, home, danger, risk, reward - churned and whirled in his mind, turning his brain to battered mush. He couldn't decide what to do about Marti. So he decided not to decide, at least for now. He had a demon to capture, and if he failed, Marti and Cassie's futures would likely be decided by Balcones. And that would be a bad day for everybody.

Metal snicked against metal, and the door swung open. Ashleigh Rowan swept into the room. "You have news?" she asked, setting down a folder and pulling out the chair behind her mahogany desk. She was never one for idle chat.

"Yes. Halle took me to the north lands and showed me what she's observed. Balcones, the demon that killed my cousin Tam, has been meeting with the jötnar. "

"Yes. I had spoken with her about this before she went off to the Mundane world. Were you able to determine the purpose of this new alliance?" She tapped a pencil absently on the desk.

"No."

Rowan frowned. "Well, it isn't likely to be good, is it?" Then she cocked her head to one side. "I'm not sure why she took it upon herself to involve you. Are you seeing Halle again? That one always was something of a wildcard."

"No. We're not together. She just wanted to discuss her findings with someone in the field."

"And she chose you."

Quinn shrugged. "It's complicated."

"It always is with her. Just keep that Valkyrie away from the humans. You know how she is. The last thing you need is for this mission to get any more complicated by a rash of human males disappearing. Organize your team, and get Kai if you need help." She reached for the folder she had just set down.

"Yes ma'am." Quinn stood up to leave.

"I've heard of this Balcones before. You're not the first to try catching him."

"The others failed?"

"The others died. Be especially careful with this one."

Anger flashed through him as he remembered the cruel and needless way Balcones had snuffed out his cousin's life, draining his life force like a vampire, for no other reason than to torment Quinn. Trapping him would be difficult, and others had failed. He could not. He would not.

It had taken until Saturday morning to get his team rounded up and briefed. Partly because Malik and Marti had gotten off on the wrong foot, and partly because, as a djinn, Malik was impervious to heat and cold, Quinn sent him to surveil the jötnar and report any signs of demonic activity. It was a good thing that time in Faery and the Mundane world were only loosely connected. He had to be back there two days ago. It tended to get tricky after three days, but leaving Faery on Saturday morning and arriving in the Mundane world on the previous Thursday would not be very difficult.

He would keep Eoin, the half-goat urisk, and Aleksei, the blue-skinned Lesovik, in place with Halle, near Marti and Cassie, and he wanted to get them situated before Marti got home from work.

Quinn gathered his team and they slipped through the portal and into Marti's back yard. He stationed Eoin there. Hopefully, he would spend more of his time watching for Balcones than flirting with Daphne and Isabella, the dryads from the old oak and pine trees behind the house. Eoin could easily blend into the oakleaf hydrangea and frangipani bushes near the birdbath. If he moved, a human might catch a glimpse of him out of the corner of her eye, but like all fae, he was almost never seen. Unless he wanted to be. Quinn positioned Aleksei across the street, next to the neighbor's elaborately planted waterfall and pond. Any humans that looked at him would see nothing more than a large shrub, and if they even bothered noticing it, the memory would slip quickly from their minds, trickling down to where all forgotten things hide.

Quinn double checked that he was not being observed before he lifted the latch on Marti's gate. The cyclone fence around the back yard didn't offer much privacy, but there was a sheltered patio off of her bedroom that was safe from prying eyes. He took off his clothes, folding each item neatly and stacking it on the bistro table, next to the pot of red zinnias. Through the sliding glass door, he could see the ceiling fan spinning above the bed, making it all the more inviting, as beads of sweat skated down his back. After Balcones was caught. Then. Then he might allow himself such indulgences. That is, if he could figure out a way to do it without harming Marti. He knew fae who were happy enough to rut with humans, not caring that they left a trail of corpses behind. But he was different. Marti was different. Graham almost certainly knew the secret, but, Quinn suspected, probably wouldn't tell him. But even if he discovered it, then what? Marti and Cassie would be better off with their own kind, not being constantly put in harm's way because of him. Quinn sighed to himself, shimmered, and shifted into his dog form.

His hearing was about the same as his horse form, much better than his human form, but not as good as in his kelpie form. But his sense of smell made up for any deficiencies. Even in human form, it was supernormal; in dog form it was freakishly acute. It wasn't just that he could smell peanuts on the breath of the mama squirrel sitting in the top of Marti's oak tree, he could smell a demon as it started to come through a portal, and if it tried to approach on foot, he could detect it nearly a mile away. Quinn closed his eyes. It was disorienting, going from seeing the wider color spectrum humans saw, to the blue and yellow shades that dogs see. He would adjust – he always did, but it would take a few moments. In the meantime, he trusted his nose, and he realized it was the key to protecting Marti and Cassie.

Keeping track of time is not so easy for a dog. He wasn't sure what time it was when Nick started to come through the gate. Bruce trotted over towards him, barking, hackles raised. Nick backed hastily out of the yard and left. No one else came, not for a long time. Bruce sprawled on the back porch, half dozing, half listening, until he heard Marti's car turn onto the street. He sat up, anticipating her return.

Quinn made the switch from dog to human form. When he told Marti that her brother-in-law had stopped by, she phoned him, just to make sure her sister was still doing well. Cassie giggled in his arms while her mother made the call. Humans, with their short lifespans, concentrated all of their joy and wonder into tiny little bubbles of time. Cassie's escaped from her in short, contagious bursts that made him forget, just for the moment, about Balcones and the jötnar.

Marti finished her call.

"Could you do me a huge favor?" she asked, moving in close to be heard over Halle's noisy use of the refrigerator door ice maker.

"Such as?" Inches away, the smell of her hair was intoxicating, like winter lemon blossoms.

"I really wanted to go to circle tonight, but Mom can't watch Cassie. She – Cassie, not my mom - adores you, and I was wondering if…"

"If I would look after her?" It was a golden opportunity to speak with Kai, without alarming Marti.

"Would you? It's just an hour."

Marti hadn't really expected to take Halle with her. Quinn wanted a chance to talk freely to Kai, with no one to eavesdrop. Well, no one but Cassie, and she wasn't telling. Besides, she was busy with a peg puzzle. He smiled to himself and pulled out his cell.

Kai, however, was busy trying to get his two children ready for bed. His wife, Breena, was away for a few days. He said he'd call back when he got everything sorted.

Quinn closed the tablet's picture book app. Cassie was asleep, her lavender-scented head on his chest, one arm flung across him, and the rest of her snuggled between his arm and ribs. She reminded him so much of another little girl who'd left a bittersweet scar across his heart that sometimes he nearly slipped and called her Virginia instead of Cassie. He didn't dare move – he didn't want to wake her and sour the sweetness of the moment. He wondered what it would be like to stay in this world with this family. Right now, demons seemed far away and almost unreal. Almost.

There is something soporific about a sleeping baby, and he felt his own eyelids getting heavy. He tapped the screen to bring up his own book, *Le Mort D'Arthur*, and started reading. He'd read it at least a hundred times. He even had a first edition copy, and discovering it on Marti's e-reader was one of the things that made her so endearing to him. With half-open eyes, he scanned the electronic pages, each one more slowly than the last, until the tablet was lying across his stomach. When he heard Marti's key in the front door, he snapped awake, turning on the tablet, which had also gone to sleep.

When Marti and Halle came in, Halle reeked of adrenalin. He noticed a smudge of dirt across her cheek, and his heartbeat quickened. Obviously, she'd handled some problem. But it made him uncomfortable.

Marti lifted Cassie off of Quinn's chest. He suddenly felt cold. As soon as they left the room, he turned to Halle.

"What happened?" he asked.

"What makes you think something happened?"

"I can smell the fight on you. And you have a big smudge of dirt on your cheek."

Halle frowned and used the back of her hand to wipe blindly at her face. "There were two men," she said, switching cheeks. "They followed us after the meeting. I saw them when Marti went back into the shop to get her phone. I disposed of them. They will not be found."

Suspecting that Rädsla was having an unexpected feast somewhere, Quinn shook his head. "You know, you can't just go around killing folk as you please."

Halle's eyes flashed electric green. "Of course I can. That is why I was created." She smiled at him as if she were speaking with someone who was impaired.

Marti returned from Cassie's room.

"I'm starved," Halle announced. "Are there any inns nearby?"

"Inns aren't the same thing here," Quinn said. "You want a restaurant."

"Are there any of those nearby?" she responded.

"There are always restaurants nearby in Houston. What do you want to eat?" Marti said, crossing her arms

"Meat. Bread. And beer," Halle replied.

"Well, that's specific," Marti said.

Quinn noticed that she dug her nails into her bicep as she spoke to Halle, and wondered if she was even aware that she was doing it. While he was not sorry for pressing Halle into service to guard Marti and Cassie, he was well aware that she could be difficult.

"What food was it that your mother brought over last week?" he asked.

"She made fajitas."

"Yes, I think Halle might like those. Where can you get them?"

"If you want fajitas, it's Guillermo's Cantina. It's 8:30 on a Friday night. It'll be packed – bet there's an hour wait." Marti answered, her tone bordering on sullen.

"Here." Quinn held four twenty dollar bills. "Is this enough?" Quinn was never sure how much things were meant to cost in the Mundane world.

"Should be."

"Bring something back for me?" Quinn wished that he was taking Marti out to dinner. But he knew she would never trust Halle to look after Cassie. And he also knew that her mistrust was completely deserved. Halle had neither the faintest idea how to nor the desire to learn about caring for a baby.

Marti was clearly not pleased about chauffeuring Halle, but she did it, leaving Quinn and Cassie to their own devices.

Agitation forced Quinn outside. Kai had not called back, and Quinn found himself too impatient to sit still.

"Eoin?" he called softly.

The urisk appeared among the frangipani leaves. "Yes?"

"Seen anything interesting?"

"Not a thing."

"Thanks."

The moon was behind some thin cirrus clouds, causing them to glow translucent silver against the night sky. Closing his eyes to enhance his hearing and sense of smell, he took a slow, deep breath and listened. A gray tree frog, sounding almost like a bird, chirruped nearby. A toad answered. Cut grass, wet concrete, car exhaust, small animals and night were the only smells he identified.

A stick snapped, and Quinn's eyes flew open.

A large opossum waddled across the back yard, headed for Adele's compost pile next door. Quinn smiled to himself and went back inside.

Given that there was nothing left to do but watch and wait, he found the remote, and turned on the TV. He didn't really know how to work the remote beyond the most basic functions – there seemed to be far too many buttons on the thing. He could, however, use the Channel Up or Channel Down arrow buttons. There seemed to be an endless supply of channels, none of which showed anything he was interested in watching. Finally, he got to the music channels and stopped on the classical one. The concerto was familiar – he'd helped Mozart write that one. He relaxed in the chair, ears and nose on high alert, mind drifting with the music, as one piece blended into another, surfing the crescendos and pianissimos, climbing through arpeggios.

He'd lost track of time when he heard the car doors slam. It was late, and he realized that Marti and Halle should have been home a long time ago. He was startled to hear them coming up the front walkway, not from the side of the house where Marti usually parked her car. Also, there were three sets of footfalls. His nose twitched. Why was Nick with them? Had something happened?

This could be bad. There was always the chance that Nick wouldn't remember him, but that was unlikely. He couldn't shift into Bruce, because then it would seem that Marti had left Cassie home alone. There was no choice but to remain where he was and hope for the best.

"What the hell are you doing here?" Nick said, his eyes narrowing and lips curling into a scowl.

Nick turned on Marti. "What do you think you're doing, leaving your baby with a junkie?" he snapped at her.

It tore at him, the way Nick was going after Marti. And it was almost entirely is fault. "Long time, no see, Officer Benson," Quinn said, trying to redirect Nick's anger toward himself. "I told you two years ago that I got my act together. Got a job and everything."

"Once a junkie, always a junkie. And I thought you'd left town, McLeod."

"I had." Quinn smiled. "But now I'm back."

Nick looked at his sister-in-law. "How'd you hook up with this...person, anyway?"

"He works with her," Marti said, looking at Halle.

"The dog trainer. So where's the dog?" Nick asked.

"Still at the kennel," Marti replied. She sighed. "Thanks for picking us up."

Nick, however, wouldn't drop it. It was bad enough that he accused Marti of using drugs, but when he snatched her arms to look for track marks, Quinn almost went for him. Reflexively, he took a step forward, then stopped himself. He knew that Nick wouldn't hurt Marti. He was just concerned about her welfare. In an assertive way. Quinn stood down and let Marti handle it.

He realized that Nick was going to be a major distraction, as long as he saw Quinn and thought that he was Marc McLeod. He might be able to win Nick over, but now was not the time. It was one more thing to add to the list of things to be done after Balcones was caught. Quinn shook himself. Why was he even thinking that? If he really cared about Marti and Cassie, he should just let them be. But not now. Now they were targets, and he had put them in harm's way. The two men that Halle had neutralized had proven that. Of course Balcones would send humans after her instead of demons. Demons stood out – they could be smelled and felt. Men would just blend into the sensory sea already filled to capacity with humanity. If he had any hope of snaring Balcones, Quinn could not afford to become embroiled in family dramas or emotional complications, and he would need every advantage he could get. There was only one solution, and he knew it would be unpopular.

As they left Marti's house under Nick's watchful eye, Quinn felt Nick's eyes boring into his back, so strongly it seemed like a digging beetle, and he couldn't help reaching over his shoulder to scratch at the itch.

"I like him," Halle said. "He's strong."

"Don't you be getting any ideas about Nick," Quinn said. "He's married to Marti's sister, and they have three children."

"So?"

"Don't, Halle. Just don't." Quinn shook his head.

Halle tossed her long blonde hair as if she were a lion defending its territory, but said nothing.

When they got to the strip center at the edge of Marti's neighborhood, Quinn turned and led Halle behind the buildings.

"I need your eyes," he said. "I have the rest of my team in place, but you have abilities that they don't."

"Yes. I saw Aleksei and Eoin when we returned. That makes three of you. Where are Malik and Siobhan?"

Halle knew all of Quinn's Mundane Intervention Team. They'd gone to MIT training together, and even been a team, briefly. "Malik is watching the jötnar."

"Siobhan? I haven't seen her in ages."

Quinn looked away and shook his head.

"Oh," Halle said. "I'm —"

"Jötnar, Halle. She was killed by jötnar three years ago. Isn't that why Graham chose to send you?"

"You would have to ask him," Halle said, and her eyes narrowed. "Surely, you've found a replacement? Anyone I know?"

"My cousin, Tam. But we lost him as well. He has not...been replaced."

"Tam," Halle said, then chewed her bottom lip. "I think I remember him. Isn't he the one who liked to do cannonballs into the pond and splash all the old ladies?"

"Yes." The tiny word was strangely difficult to say.

"That is unfortunate," Halle said. Then she cocked her head at him. "Are you asking me to be the last member of your team?"

"For this mission. You did bring it to MAMIC's attention, after all. Besides, you're the local frost giant expert."

Halle laughed, then lowered her head and looked up at him through her lashes. "Perhaps. What would you have me do?"

Quinn ignored the flirtation. "You can fly. You can be in places to see what others can't. And maybe," Quinn lowered his voice conspiratorially, "you can get the crows to help."

"They will bargain. What will you give them?"

"Depends on what they want."

Halle shrugged. "We shall see."

With no further ado, her eyes turned to black, followed quickly by her hair and skin. Within seconds, a large raven stood on the pavement before him. Halle shook her feathers, hopped a few steps, and flew away.

Quinn stood behind Aleksei, at the neighbor's across from Marti's house, so he could not be seen from the street. At least, not by humans, anyway.

"Halle will be helping with this mission," Quinn whispered to Aleksei.

"That is good idea?" he answered.

"Probably not. But I don't have a better one."

After the car that had been puttering down the street at sub-pedestrian speed finally pulled into the garage two doors down from Marti's house, Quinn slipped across the street and into the back yard.

Humans would consider it telepathy, but that is only because they could not hear the call that Quinn sent out to Eoin. Aleksei had difficulty hearing it because he was a wood fae, but Eoin, as a fellow water entity, had no trouble.

Quinn's heart skipped a beat when Eoin did not respond.

He called again.

Eoin stepped from behind the pine tree, Daphne's hand quickly pulling away from him and disappearing into the trunk. Eoin's eyes were slightly glazed and his thick lips curved into a crooked smile.

"Bloody fool! Are you mad? What have I told you about keeping your post?" Anger had replaced fear, lowering the pitch of Quinn's message to near-audible levels.

The goofy smile fell off of Eoin's face, and he looked for it on the ground, poking at fallen pine needles with one hoof. "I'm sorry."

"You're meant to be watching for a bloody demon, Eoin. And not just any demon – the demon that killed Tam. And what are you doing instead? That sort of carelessness will get somebody killed."

"It won't happen again."

"See that it doesn't."

Quinn stalked to the secluded patio and ripped off his clothes, piling them haphazardly on the table. He turned himself into Bruce, and used his ultra-keen nose to make a perimeter check. He detected nothing out of the ordinary, then made three more passes for good measure.

As he predicted, Marti did not like his decision to remain exclusively in canine form. He didn't like it much, either. But he was glad that Delilah had told him about the ghost of Bertram Kounis showing up at Marti's family picnic. That would give her something to do, and with any luck, keep her from trying to persuade him to shift back into human form. Because she just might succeed.

Chapter 9
Lingering

adrian tapped into the security cameras and spent most of Tuesday watching the parking lot in the strip center where the Tenth Sphere was located. The store was busy, but none of the patrons stood out as being anything other than metaphysical shoppers. If anyone from the Odessa Group used the business as a drop, they didn't do it today. If he wanted to get inside the shop, he'd better get a move on – it wouldn't be open much longer, and he needed to touch things. He'd gone down to Homicide Division this morning on the pretense of examining the evidence from the Kounis crime scene. What he really wanted to do was hold the coin that was dropped at Kounis' feet. Unfortunately, the detectives working the Kounis case were out on another investigation. He could, perhaps, have pressed the issue, but thought better of it.

His sister, Sabina, was the only other person who knew about his special ability. If he held something in the palm of his hand, sometimes he knew things about the person it had belonged to, or at least who had touched it last. He couldn't always interpret what he saw, and sometimes he got nothing. But it had helped him solve more cases than he could easily tally. The Bureau frowned on the woo-woo stuff, so he never told anyone about it, not even Sara. Sometimes, he wondered if he should have become a remote viewer for the CIA. They claimed they'd shut down that program. But he also knew that disinformation was their first line of defense.

He put on the wire frame glasses with the plain lenses. He wanted to look erudite.

When he got to the Tenth Sphere, he recognized Marti Keller from the photo in his files. She was a bit of alright, as his British friend, Trevor would say.

"If there's something I can help you with, please let me know," she said.

She glanced over his head at the clock, and he wondered where she was so anxious to go. A date perhaps?

He looked around the shop, starting with the figurines near the cash register, and picking up random pieces. The problem was that so many people had handled them that there was no clear residual image or vibration, just a muddle of hazy snapshots.

After a while, an older, plumper woman came out of the back room. This must be Lulu Miranda. She smiled at Hadrian, then said, "Marti, are you coming to circle on Thursday night?"

"Maybe. I'm not sure."

"Try to make it. I think you'll like it."

"I'll see what I can do. Is it okay if I scoot out of here a couple of minutes early?"

"Sure. Go."

Lulu turned back to Hadrian. "In case you're interested, we do have a Thursday night Circle. We have a variety of activities. Often, we do mediumship, but sometimes we do table-tipping, aura reading, scrying, and psychometry."

"Really?" Hadrian said. "I might have to check it out." He wondered if that might give him access to objects that were kept from the general public. He would decide then if the Tenth Sphere warranted further surveillance.

Hadrian had set the feed from the security camera in front of the Tenth Sphere to run through the facial recognition software on his computer. It would alert him if it got a hit on any known gang members. Just as he was leaving to go to the Thursday night Circle, he heard a beep, so he checked the screen. Two men walked past the store and around the corner to the back of the building. The computer identified them as two very low-level members of the Odessa Group.

"Well, well, well, Ms. Miranda. You seem to have some interesting visitors."

It took longer than he anticipated trek west to the Energy Corridor from downtown. He'd wanted to get there early enough to evaluate escape routes and potential danger zones. But he would have to settle for a quick scan of the parking lot. If the two Russians were still around, they were laying low.

There were cars in the parking lot, but the Tenth Sphere's door was locked. Hadrian knocked. A few minutes later, the lock turned and a thin woman with salt and pepper hair let him in. He surmised that she was Belinda Tate, Lulu's partner.

"They just went upstairs," she told him, nodding towards the back of the shop.

She locked the door behind him and followed him to the large conference room. Lulu was standing on a chair, pulling the battery out of the smoke detector. He figured it was best not to draw attention to himself by pointing out that it was a fire code violation to do that.

He squeezed in next to Marti, and forced himself not to stare at the knockout blonde with waist-length braids next to her. She looked too amazing to be real, and her outfit should have been illegal. On the other side of him sat a bony peroxide blonde, and he noticed that she seemed dark and desperate even before he spotted the thick scars across her wrists.

It would have been much easier for him to pity Marilyn, the suicide blonde, if she hadn't kept throwing herself at him the entire time. He was still undecided about the surveillance at the end of the Circle. He followed Marti and her friend, whom he'd heard Marti call Halle, out the door. He sat in his car, pretending to be returning text messages on his cell phone. He saw the two Russians step out of the darkness at the edge of the building. Marti turned back, and at first Hadrian thought she intended to speak to them. They ducked back into the shadows as she approached, then she passed them and went into the shop. Halle looked around as if she'd heard a noise and moved to the edge of the building where the thugs were hiding. Hadrian got out of his car, fearing for her safety. He heard the crash of something metallic being knocked over and, inexplicably, the neigh of a horse. Halle emerged from the dark, and Marti came out of the shop.

Hadrian waited until they had disappeared down the block before he went to investigate. He found a metal shopping cart lying on its side, flattened cardboard boxes spilling out of it, and a smear of blood on the wall, but no Russians. He used his cell phone to take a few photos and an evidence swab to collect a sample of the blood, then headed back to his office. The Tenth Sphere surveillance operation was a go.

Naked, Sveklá brushed his teeth and gently probed the port wine stain on the top of his head with the fingers of his other hand. He'd noticed it getting thicker recently. The doctors had said it would do that as he aged. His boss had offered to pay for a laser treatment to remove it, but he'd refused. If it was good enough for Mikhail Gorbachev, it was good enough for him. It had given him is nickname, Sveklá, or beet, and if he no longer had the mark, then who would he be?

He'd had another name once. It was long ago, but he still remembered it. How could he forget, when that is what Irina called him? According to the official records Sergei Medved died in a fire in 1992. The body had never been recovered, but that was because he was looking at it in the mirror.

The story that he had been told by the nurses at Tri Babushkas Orphanage was that his mother was unmarried and could not support him, so she'd left him there, as one would a cast-off toy or an unwanted pet.

Baby Sergei had not thrived. Even though he was quite stout, he grew up much shorter than the other boys at Babushkas. There was one boy who always stood up for him when the other children teased him about his birthmark or made fun of him about his size. He shared his own insufficient food with Sveklá on many a night after other boys had beaten him and taken away what little supper he had. The nurses, and he had believed they were actually nurses until he was about ten, often punished the children for transgressions by locking them in cells in the basement, without dinner, for the night. It was a game, no, not a game, but a survival tactic, to try and get other children in trouble while avoiding blame. The food of those in solitary was distributed among the others. Sveklá had spent far too many shivering nights in solitary, and those miserable nights of utter darkness, with nothing but sounds of rats gnawing on the walls and the eerie cry of foxes for company.

One of the nurses, and perhaps it was because she was young and not yet ground down by the system, would sneak food to Sveklá on nights he was locked down alone. But it wasn't every night, only the ones she could slip away from the supervision of older nurses. When Sveklá and his protector had gotten big enough, they ran away from the orphanage. And after the escape, Sveklá went to work for him.

He looked at his bare chest in the mirror. The eight-pointed stars under each clavicle had faded to a bluish grey. The two stars on his knees were darker. Lenin's face, attached to a hairy cherub's body, leered out at him from over his heart, fluttering over the tops of minarets which stretched almost to his groin. He was proud that he had no spiderwebs – drug addicts were the most pathetic of a pathetic lot. He only had one epaulet with a skull tattooed onto his shoulder. He'd gotten a terrible infection with that one and it had almost killed him. But he'd gotten his ink a long time ago, when tattoos had to be earned. Not bought, like today. He sighed, both nostalgic for the past, and glad it was done.

There had been the most beautiful girl at Babushkas. She had hair like black silk, and her grey eyes were huge and bright. He'd fallen hard for her, but never dared voice his feelings. Such an angel would never accept lowly Sveklá as a lover, much less a husband. But she had run away with them. He saw her nearly every day, as she had married his boss.

Oh, lovely Irina, do you really love him? Sveklá often wondered when he saw them together. He suspected that she knew of the faithlessness of her husband. It made his heart ache whenever the boss man took on new conquest. But Irina, she was part of the business, and she could never leave him. Not with her life.

He rinsed and spat into the sink. If he turned his face at the right angle, the birthmark on his head was nearly invisible. If only Irina could see him that way. He longed to comfort her when she was alone all night, often imagining in exquisite detail the smell of her skin, the softness of her body, and what he would eagerly do if she were to take him into her bed. But he knew such a prize could never be his.

As he did every night, he dropped to the floor and quickly performed fifty pushups. When that was done, he rolled over and did one hundred sit ups. Standing up, he smacked his hard stomach with the flat of his hand and grunted with approval.

Sveklá generally eschewed luxury, but the one thing he did allow himself was expensive Egyptian cotton pajamas. It was the only thing he ever asked for, and Irina always brought a pair or two back for him when she went shopping in New York. The pair he was pulling on had come from her latest excursion.

He slipped into bed, and hoped he didn't have the usual nightmares. It would make a nice change.

Chapter 10
Life in Review

t was Tuesday morning, and I hoped I'd have a way to work. Lulu had said she'd let me know about the car. There wasn't anything I could do about that, so I flipped on the television while I folded laundry, half listening to *AM HTown*. Until they got to the weather forecast.

"There's an area of disturbed weather in the western Caribbean that's moving north-northwest. A high pressure ridge along the East Coast is going to keep pushing it to the west. We may be looking at tropical storm conditions anywhere from southern Mexico to probably Cameron Parish in Louisiana. There's so much moisture being pulled in across the Gulf Coast by an area of low pressure off to our west that I think that any development would likely bring a lot of rain, wherever it makes landfall. Back to you, Ephram and Mary Jo."

Well, it has been dry lately and we could use some moisture. I just hoped we didn't get it all in a couple of hours.

"And speaking of storms, Mary Jo" Ephram said, "few kids have had a rougher time than young Ivan. His name has been changed to protect his privacy, but his story is one hundred percent real. Ivan was abandoned at Tri Babuskas Orphanage in Russia, when he was only three months old. He lived there, under extreme conditions, until he was adopted by the Smith family, who only agreed to speak with us if we concealed their identities. Ivan has been diagnosed with an uncommon condition called Reactive Attachment Disorder, or RAD, that is unfortunately, common among abused and neglected children. These children are unable to form an attachment, or bond, with caretakers. In the worst cases, these children act out violently towards their adoptive parents. Here is the tape of my interview with the Smiths. "

A graphic window flew to the center of the screen and zoomed in to the Smiths. The studio lights went down. On the big screen, a man and woman sat together on a couch, their faces hidden in shadow.

"Mr. and Mrs. Smith, thank you for allowing us to interview you for the AM HTown show. What led you to adopt Ivan from Russia three years ago?

"My husband and I couldn't have children of our own," replied the digitally blurred voice. "We wanted to make a choice that would do the most good. We thought," her voice broke, and the man next to her rubbed her shoulder. "We thought that adopting from these overcrowded and under-staffed facilities would be the best. Our adoption advisor told us that Tri Babushkas Orphanage was the worst of the worst."

"Ivan looked like a little angel when we first saw him. His white-blond hair was naturally curly and his eyes were so blue and so sad. We just couldn't leave him there," the man said.

"And how old was Ivan when you bright him home?"

"He was eight," the man answered.

"And when did you start to think there was something wrong?"

"Immediately," the woman answered. "He hated being touched. We thought it was just how he'd been raised, and that he'd get over it in time."

"But he only got worse," the man added. "By the time he was ten, we were so afraid of him that we put a lock on the inside of our bedroom door."

"He often told me he was going to cut our throats while we were sleeping, then burn down the house. He got kicked out of every school he attended. He," Mrs. Smith's voice caught in a sob. "he killed our cat, Mittens. We'd had her for ten years. Said he'd do the same to me."

"I tried to take him to tae kwon do class, thought it would help him learn some self-control. He hit me with the board he was supposed to be breaking and broke my jaw," Mr. Smith added.

"We didn't know what to do. Then our adoption advisor told us about the CCF – the Cherngelanov Children's Foundation. He agreed to take custody of Ivan. We thought it was best for everyone. He needs more help than we could give him." The woman sniffled and dabbed at her nose.

The silhouettes in the window stopped moving. The lighting shifted, revealing Mary Jo and Ephram sitting with a well-dressed man. He looked fifty-ish, tall, but wiry rather than muscled. His smooth-shaven head was lumpy, and I wondered if he had suffered a lot of injuries as a child. The wisp of tattoo that peeked out from the cuff of his crisp designer shirt was the only hint that there was more to him than a successful real estate business. The tape of the interview with the "Smiths" faded, to be replaced by a slide show of the new guest. First he appeared in a three-piece suit with the backdrop of downtown Houston, next as a sweaty volunteer, passing water down from a truck, bucket-brigade style, and finally, decked out in climbing gear, a coil of rope over his shoulder.

Bruce sat up and whined.

"Do you need to go out?"

He snorted and shook his head.

Ephram said, "We have in our studios today, Mr. Boris Cherngelanov. As many of you know, Mr. Cherngelanov is a prominent Houston businessman and philanthropist. Mr. Cherngelanov, please tell us about your foundation."

"*Zdravstvuĭte*, Ephram and Mary Jo. Is nice to be on television with you this morning. My mother died when I was young child. My father, he was alcoholic, left my sister and I at Tri Babushkas Orphanage."

The chirpy host broke in, "Does your sister also live here in Houston?"

"My sister died at Babushkas."

"I am so sorry. Please, continue."

"Because I know how it was like in Babushkas, and afterward, for those who survive. I can not fix the troubles in that place, but perhaps I help those who got out. I understand them."

"How does your foundation help?" Mary Jo asked.

"I provide home for children, with as you say, RAD. Provide therapists and counselors to teach children life skills. Also, provide job training. Is very difficult, yes. But most of these children can be helped, and not live rest of lives as criminals in prison."

"That is so wonderful," gushed Mary Jo. "And would you tell our audience how Ivan is doing now?"

"Ivan is well. Will be starting sixth grade in technology magnet school in fall. Is very bright young man."

"Thank you so much for being on our show today, Mr. Cherngelanov. We've got to take a commercial break here. When we come back, we'll have a bevy of beauties – that's right, our own Houston Texans cheerleaders – to present the adoptable pet of the day."

I switched off the TV and shuddered. Any type of attachment disorder was a scary thing, but RAD was terrifying. Good thing it wasn't common. I hugged Cassie tightly. As I moved to pick up the laundry basket, the phone rang. Caller ID said it was Lulu.

"Okay, honey, Benjamin said you could drive his car. I got the spare key yesterday, and I'll drop it off on the way to the attorney's."

"How is that going?" I knew I needed to tell her about Bertram Kounis, but it just sounded so weird.

"Well, it's going as well as can be expected, I guess. He asked me not to talk about it, though."

"Okay. Umm..." I said. *Might as well just come out with it.* "I saw Bertram Kounis yesterday."

"What do you mean?"

"Delilah brought him to me at my parents' Fourth of July barbecue. Benjamin didn't kill him."

"Oh, honey! That's great! Did he say who did?"

"Well, that's kind of the problem. He had his throat cut and he doesn't seem to be able to talk."

I swear I could hear Lulu frown over the phone.

"Hmmm. I'll have to think about that," she said. "That isn't anything I can take to the attorney."

"Maybe Delilah can bring him back and translate for him."

"I'm on my way."

I wanted to tell her that now wasn't a good time, but she had already hung up.

It took her less than ten minutes to knock on my front door. She was carrying a brown paper lunch bag.

"Hey, cutie!" she said to Cassie, who grinned back at her. "Living room or kitchen?" she said to me.

"Huh?"

"To set up, honey. To see if we can get Mr. Kounis on line."

"I guess living room."

Bruce had made himself scarce. I could hardly blame him, given that Lulu was always trying to convince me to get rid of him.

She opened her bag and took out a sage smudge stick. "I always keep a couple in my car for emergencies."

The rattle of the bag brought Alpha and Betty climbing to the top of their cage, hoping for a treat.

"Most people keep first aid kits in their cars," I said as I opened the bag of yogurt drops.

Lulu smiled, showing her teeth. "Different kind of first aid."

The rats took their treats and scampered to eat them in the chew log. Lulu pulled out a box of matches and lit the smudge. The ceiling fan scattered the smoke, and threatened to blow out the smudge stick.

"Can we turn that off?"

Once the wind had ceased, the smoke hung in it, slowly curling and twisting in Lulu's wake. Cassie, sitting on the floor by the couch, watched it intently, even pausing her extended gnawing session on Mr. Buns' ear. Lulu sat down near her, holding the burning smudge over a sales circular she'd retrieved from the recycling bin.

"Try and call Delilah," she said, her eyes closed.

Delilah? Are you around? Lulu and I would really like to talk to Bert, if you can manage it.

"Girl, don't call him Bert. He does not like that."

A grey mist formed itself into an oblong cloud in the middle of the living room. It gradually congealed into the form of Bertram Kounis. But he was standing on a closely clipped lawn with a garden hose sprayer in his hand. A man approached him. He was shorter than average, but built like a bull, with thick arms and no neck. There was a purplish growth on one side of his head that spoiled the symmetry of his otherwise perfect flattop. Kounis backed away from the man, pointing the sprayer at him as if it was a weapon. The two seemed to be arguing, but the whole scene took place in eerie silence. The argument got more heated, with the short man waving his arms. Kounis backed up until he ran into the wall. As the other man closed in on him, Kounis sprayed him in the face. The man yanked the sprayer out of Kounis' hand and hit him hard across the bridge of the nose with it. While Kounis was cradling his face in his hands, the shorter man picked up something off the ground. A pole or stick? No. It was a lawn edger, a garden tool that did not look vastly different from a battleax. I suddenly realized where this vision was heading and I lunged for Cassie. I wasn't sure if she could see the murder re-enactment, but I didn't want to risk it. I picked her up and turned her toward me just as the bull-necked man slammed the blade into Kounis' throat with such force that he was lifted off his feet. If the stroke had been dead center, he would probably have been decapitated. As it was, blood welled up and cascaded down Kounis' chest, spurting with each heartbeat. He clutched at his throat as he slid down the wall, leaving a bright red smear behind him. He fell forward, sprawling on the manicured grass, his heart pumping his blood onto the ground. The bull-necked man dropped the edger as if it were on fire and flapped his hand in the air. After he examined it and removed something from his palm, probably a splinter, he calmly reached into his pocket and dropped something small at Kounis' feet. He glanced over his shoulder, as if he heard a noise, and ran in the opposite direction. Another man, and I assume by Lulu's gasp that it was Benjamin, entered the scene. He saw Kounis and grabbed the edger, which had fallen across his body. A woman opened a door and put both hands to her mouth, screaming silently, but vigorously. The scene dissolved into mist and dissipated through the room.

"I knew it!" Lulu said.

"Now you just gotta find out who the short guy is," Delilah remarked.

It was really weird, watching Bertram Kounis act out his own murder. Made me feel like I was watching a snuff film. He certainly didn't airbrush out the blood and gore. I rubbed my own throat, even though I knew I wasn't hurt. Still, it caused a chill to set into my solar plexus.

Cassie squirmed, and I set her down.

I glanced at Delilah and nodded. "So, if Benjamin didn't do it, how do we find the short guy with the nevus?" I asked. "Do you think it might be someone your nephew knows?"

"The man has a what, honey?" Lulu asked.

I patted the top of my head. "The purple blotch on his head – a port wine stain."

"Oh. Why didn't you say so?" Lulu shrugged. "Maybe, he knows him, maybe not. How many of your friends know each other?"

I frowned. She had a point. "Well, it doesn't matter what we know, it's what we can prove that counts."

My eyes fell on the clock. "If I'm going to get Cassie to Briar Ridge on time, I've got to get a move on."

"Oh, right. Here are the keys, honey." Lulu set them on the coffee table.

"Thanks, Cassie and I really appreciate this."

"No problem." Lulu's eyebrows knitted together. "Did you see what that was, honey, that the killer dropped at Kounis' feet? My eyes aren't as good as they used to be."

"I'm not sure. It looked like a coin."

"That's kind of what I thought. Well, I'll see you at the shop."

Lulu gathered her things, and I followed her to the front door to let her out. Bruce came out of hiding, and I gave him a pat on the head.

"See you later," I said to him, wishing he'd shift so I could talk to him about what Bertram Kounis had just shown us. I didn't know if he'd been able to see it or not.

Delilah? I thought, after I'd locked the door behind Lulu. I grabbed my kid and her go-bag and headed for Benjamin's a maroon Crown Victoria in my driveway. I opened the door and the car smelled like older cars often do; perhaps it's the vinyl that's been cooked by the sun too many times, or the carpet that gradually builds up a layer of dirt that can never be removed.

"What's up, girlfriend?" I heard her voice, but couldn't see her. She sounded sleepy.

Who was the short man? Does Bertam know him? It would sure help a lot if he could drop a name, or clue, or something our way.

"Girl, that ain't happenin' anytime soon," Delilah said. "He used his last bit of etheric energy on that drama he just put on for y'all. That shot him straight up into the astral, and he's being cocooned right now."

Fortunately, Emily and Nick had a car seat that I could borrow, so I didn't have to run out and buy a new one while I was waiting to get my car back. Since the police didn't' even have a lead, it might be a while. I grunted as I pulled the lap belt tight against the base of the seat. "Come on, Cassie." I had to coax her across the expanse of vinyl back seat so I could get her strapped in.

Cocooned? What does that mean? How long does it take? "Ow!"

I bumped my head on the door frame as I backed out of the car. I was sure I heard Delilah snickering, but I ignored it.

"Cocooning is 'bout like it sounds. The soul enters an energy cocoon, where it can be healed. Happens a lot when somebody dies real sudden. They get kinda disoriented and need a little help gettin' stabilized."

The car started easily, and I turned the AC on high while I buckled up and adjusted the seat and mirrors.

What are you saying? You can't talk to him?

Crap. I just knocked over Mom's trash can as I backed out of the driveway. I had to jump out and set it back up. Benjamin's car was a lot wider than my little blue Corolla.

Delilah sounded like she was sighing. "No. He'll be out when he's ready to come out, girlfriend. Ain't nothin' I can do about that."

Fine. I'd better focus on my driving, or Cassie and I are going to be up there cocooning, too.

I did not cry this time, after I dropped Cassie off. And I couldn't decide if that was better or worse.

I had the shop on my own for almost an hour. Belinda left when I got there and Lulu was at the attorney appointment. As soon as she came in, I told her what Delilah had said about the cocooning.

Lulu scowled. "That's not what I wanted to hear." She considered the fluffy duster on the glass jewelry case. "I suppose we could try contacting him on Thursday night."

"Maybe."

The cowbell on the door clanged, and a woman wearing a bright green turban came in.

"Hello, Ellen!" Lulu said. She went around the counter to give Ellen a hug. Ellen looked so frail, that I was afraid Lulu would break her.

"How are you feeling?" Lulu asked.

I made an effort to keep smiling. Ellen's skin had taken on a greyish cast. She had recently had chemo for acute myeloid leukemia.

"I'm hanging in there. I'm going to Anderson for some tests on Thursday, and I have to spend the night, so I won't be able to come to Circle. I just wanted to let Belinda know how much I enjoyed her book."

"She'll be so sad she missed you, honey. She went to go run some errands. When will you hear back about your tests?"

"Depends. Sometime next week. Do you know when Belinda's planning on having the next book out?"

Lulu smiled. "She's been working very hard on that. I think she's just about ready to send it to her editor."

Ellen nodded. "I'm looking forward to it. I've got to go, sweetie. My daughter's waiting for me in the car, and she's not very patient with me coming here."

Lulu hugged her again "You just do your best to get yourself well. We'll see you at the next Circle."

"Course you will."

"Bye, Ellen," I said. "Hope your test results come out well."

She smiled and waved good-bye, then ambled out the door.

When Lulu turned around, there were tears in her eyes. She sniffled and wiped her eyes with her fingers.

"Lulu? You okay?"

"I'm sorry. I'm not sad for her. I'm sad for me. I'm really going to miss her."

I rolled my lower lip between my teeth. "You don't think she's going to get a good report?"

"She's starting to separate from her body, I can feel it." Lulu shook her head. "It happens to us all, and Lord knows she's been suffering terribly."

"I'm so sorry, Lulu. But it is possible that you're wrong." I picked up the duster and twirled it over some of the nearby knick-knacks.

"I'd give anything to be wrong. But I'm not."

It was after work time, and customers started to trickle into the shop. It got busy enough that I was a few minutes late leaving to pick up Cassie, and I just barely dodged the late pick up fee. Of course, that meant we got stuck in traffic, and by the time we got home, I was frazzled.

Ordinarily, I think I would have been more alarmed than annoyed when I saw the side gate standing open. This afternoon, it just made me mad.

Lugging Cassie and her accoutrements, I shut the gate and went into the house. It was strangely silent.

"Hello?" I called. "Bruce? You there?"

There was no answer.

The back door was ever so slightly ajar. Fear began to creep up my back like a freezing spider.

"Bruce? Where are you?"

There was no sound but the squeak of the exercise wheel in Alpha and Betty's cage.

I let my purse and Cassie's go bag fall to the floor. I clutched her tightly as I went from room to room, calling.

Bruce was gone.

Chapter 11
Bad Wolf

ontrary to popular belief, most sociopaths are not stone-cold killers. Boris Cherngelanov, however, was.

That's why Quinn was so surprised to see him on the morning TV show, touting his home for damaged children. There must have been a reason for it. That type of "prominent businessman" usually tried to stay under the radar, rather than being on television where people who knew how he really got his money might notice him. Interesting, but it was not his concern just now.

When Lulu showed up to try and conjure the ghost of Bertram Koinis, he hid himself in Cassie's room. Lulu and Quinn were not exactly friends.

"Why you hiding up in here, shifter?" Delilah asked him. "You might want to watch the show."

He hadn't even noticed her materializing in the room. Also, he didn't like the ghostly figure that floated near her. He'd obviously been murdered – blood soaked his beige shirt and a bloody gash stretched from under his left ear to his right jaw. Quinn suspected it was not a random act of violence. The man just had a mean vibe to him.

Quinn padded after Delilah and the man, until he got to the doorway of the living room. He stayed in the shadows, just out of sight.

The ghostly reenactment of Bertram Kounis' murder started to play, and as soon as he saw the short, barrel-chested man attack Delilah's companion, he knew exactly who the attacker was. He went by a single name – Sveklá – and he was Cherngelanov 's right-hand man. Wouldn't be the first time he'd enforced someone to death. He would wait until Marti went to work, then leave her a note. That way he wouldn't be tempted to distraction.

After Marti left, he made a perimeter check. He couldn't really turn the doorknobs with his dog paws, so he looked out the windows, listened, and sniffed. The front and side yards were fine. Nobody but him was inside the house. Then he heard a tapping, as if someone was impatiently drumming his fingers on a table, coming from the back deck. He went to the door and looked out.

A tall man sat there on the deck. He had shoulder-length white hair and a patch over one eye. His blue shirt exactly matched the icy blue of his unobscured eye. The man seemed both ancient and vital, and Quinn knew he was not a human. But he wasn't fae, either. Quinn was sure he'd seen him at the Three Sister's Inn, when he was in the northlands with Halle.

"Are you just going to stand there, or are you going to let me in?" the man asked.

Two ravens swooped out of the oak tree to land on the table near him. Quinn was sure one of them was Halle, but he couldn't tell which one. He saw Eoin peek out from behind the pine tree, and Quinn gave a soft woof. Then he rushed to the guest room, shifted into human form and pulled on his clothes.

By the time he opened the door, two more ravens had joined the others.

"That's better," the man remarked. "I felt a bit odd talking to a dog. Do you always have to do that?"

"Do what, grandfather?" Quinn asked.

The man laughed. "No need to be so formal, fay. Do you always have to go and put on clothes when you shift into human form? Seems very tiresome to me. You may call me Vegtam, by the way." One of the ravens croaked, and he added, "Or Odin, if you prefer. Shall we go inside? It's blistering hot out here."

"Of course. It can't be helped. I am not able to maintain clothing between shifts."

The world was so cluttered with gods and goddesses that Quinn found it impossible to keep up with all of them. He had met Zeus once, but found him somewhat unlikeable. He'd heard of Odin – he was Halle's father, after all – but he didn't know very much about him.

As soon as the door closed behind them, the one raven who wasn't actually a raven, shifted into her human form.

"My father has news of the Frost Giants. It seems they have had another visitor besides Balcones," Halle said.

"Loki has escaped from his bondage," Odin said heavily. "If he succeeds in freeing his son, the wolf Fenrir, it will bring about Ragnarök."

Both Odin and Halle looked dour.

"That sounds bad," Quinn said.

"The end of the world usually is," Halle replied.

"It is not the end of the world," Odin said. "The world will be drowned in the sea, but it will eventually return, refreshed and fertile, ready for new gods and a new population."

"All humans and animals would die?" Quinn asked.

"Almost all of them," Odin said.

"And the gods?"

"Them, too. It is the fate of the world and it cannot be changed. But would you think me an old fool if I wished to delay it a while?" Odin said.

"Who would choose differently? Fate is what you make it," Quinn replied.

He wondered if Faery would be affected by a submerged Mundane world. As their fortunes were linked, he suspected it might, although there were plenty of natural disasters that affected the Mundane that had little or no impact on Faery. It was a discussion to be had with Dame Rowan, perhaps. But at a later date.

Odin's eye sparkled. A man who could smile in the face of his own annihilation was either incredibly brave, or seriously insane. But then again, perhaps being a god gave one more special privileges than he had thought.

"Loki might be a little annoyed about being bound with the intestines of his son and having a serpent hanging over his head, dripping burning venom on him, for the last millennium. And he's very clever, more so that most people give him credit for," Odin said.

Quinn could understand why Loki would be displeased – what the god had just described sounded like a capricious and cruel punishment. Still, the jötnar weren't the types to go out of their way to help anybody. "Why would he go to the Frost Giants for help?"

"They're his relatives," Halle answered.

Quinn nodded. "So, where is this Fenrir? If we can snatch him, Loki will have to turn up sooner or later. And if we move the wolf to a location that suits us, all the better."

"Fenrir must not be unfettered! He would be the death of us all," Odin said.

Halle shot an alarmed glance at Odin, leading Quinn to believe that this discussion had come up before.

"Fair enough. What's your plan, then?" Quinn asked.

"Loki has many friends amongst the jötnar, fell dwarves and other evil peoples. It was the dwarves that forged Gleipnir, the impossible chain, that binds Fenrir. It cannot be broken or unmade, but it can be unfastened and untied."

"So we find Fenrir and set a trap for Loki?" Quinn asked.

"We must be very cunning to lure him out of hiding. He will be expecting a trap, and will look to turn the tables on us."

Quinn wondered if there was a way to kill two birds with one stone and capture both Loki and Balcones. He hoped so, because he was hard pressed to see a way to stop Loki and Balcones both separately and concurrently. He would leave Eoin, Aleksei, and Halle in place, guarding Marti, while he helped Odin stop Loki. If he wasn't stopped, Balcones wouldn't matter. What were Marti and Cassie's chances of surviving a drowned world? He had no guarantee that there would even be a safe place in Faery to take them to. Besides, he had a score to settle with the jötnar.

"Where do we start?" Quinn asked.

"We must go north, to see what is to be seen there," Odin answered.

"Let me have a word with my people, and I need to leave Marti a note."

Odin nodded.

Quinn told both Eoin and Aleksei what he had learned from Odin, and asked them to get word to MAMIC. Neither of them seemed too upset about missing an opportunity to participate in a surveillance mission in the ice and snow.

He had to hunt around to find a piece of notebook paper, but at last he found one that Cassie had scribbled on one side of in the recycling bin. He smiled to himself – Cassie would be quite a little artist soon. Even though it was all her fingers could do to grasp a crayon, she scribbled on everything she could find. Quinn located a pen and wrote a note to Marti.

Dear Marti,

I have to follow up on a lead. Eoin, Aleksei, and Halle are guarding you, even if you can't see them. Not sure when I'll be back, but I will return as soon as I possibly can.

You and Lulu are looking for a short, bald killer. He's an enforcer for Boris Cherngelanov's organization – goes by the name Sveklá. That's all the info I have on him.

Stay safe, and I'll see you soon,
Quinn

He stuck the note on the fridge with a magnet.

"Don't forget your coat," Halle said with a helpful smile.

"Right," Quinn answered, then trotted off to retrieve the jacket he'd brought back with him from his trip with Halle.

When Quinn returned to the kitchen, dressed for the cold, Halle and the other raven were already gone.

"I'm ready," he said.

He was already starting to sweat in the heavy coat. To save electricity, Marti kept the thermostat for her air conditioning at 80°F, so it was already uncomfortably warm.

"Wait," said Odin. "May I?" he asked, reaching for Quinn's belly.

Quinn didn't resist, but he wasn't enthusiastic as Odin opened Quinn's coat and lifted his shirt. He traced a symbol, something like a diamond with legs, around Quinn's navel.

Odin muttered some words Quinn didn't understand and the outline suddenly felt warm. Then it got uncomfortably hot as it glowed coppery red. Within a minute or two, the heat left the mark, and it turned a dull bronze.

"That should do it. Now you won't have to worry about keeping clothes available. Whatever you were wearing prior to your shift will still be there when you return to human form." He nodded, and tossed a handful of something that looked like leaves over their heads. Quinn coughed as the air entering his lungs went from stifling to freezing.

He found himself standing next to Odin on a snowy hillside, and an icy wind cut through his coat as if it wasn't even there. In front of them lay a narrow, sparkling alpine lake, with a rocky island in the middle of it. The rough beauty of the island was marred by an ugly structure crouching on it. A large white sign with red Cyrillic letters stood on the bank.

Odin huffed in disgust. "Runes I can read. This looks like the scratching of a chicken."

Quinn wished that Aleksei was here. The Ukrainian Lesovik was fluent in Russian. Not only could he read the sign, he'd probably be able to give a history and commentary about the building behind it. Quinn knew how to say, *hello*, *goodbye*, and *thank you*, in Russian. That wouldn't help him much if he tried to ask the locals about the island. On the other hand, the area seemed to be desperately short of locals. There wasn't even a road in sight.

Quinn looked out across the water. Covering most of the island, a low-slung building sprawled behind a razor wire fence, menacing the floating sheets of ice that intermittently drifted across the water. The building itself was not extraordinary – dingy white, one story, few windows. But Quinn felt a sense of foreboding as he looked at it, lurking in the middle of the lake like an ancient beast.

"What is that place?" he asked.

Odin's brow furrowed. "I am not sure. It has been long since I came to this lake, and there never was a building on the island before." Odin closed his eyes and took a few slow, deep breaths. "There is much unhappiness there, much sickness and death." One of the ravens croaked and flapped its wings. The other just sat on Odin's shoulder, feathers puffed out to ward off the cold.

"Muninn, go," Odin said to the bird.

He closed his eye as the bird took off, and Quinn watched a variety of expressions sweep across the old man's face. Then Quinn realized what he was doing. Odin was using the bird's eyes as his own.

"What do you see?" he asked.

"Not much worth looking at. Fences, building, pavement, trash, piles of snow," Odin said.

Quinn silently called for Malik. He knew the djinn was in the northlands watching the Frost Giants, so he would be close enough to hear him. Perhaps he could be of some use.

"Is there something I can help you with?" Malik's voice sounded loudly and suddenly in Quinn's ear.

Both he and Odin jumped.

"You know I hate when you do that," Quinn grouched.

Malik smiled broadly. "There is very little to do here. I must take my entertainment where I can."

Odin raised one eyebrow. But whether he was annoyed or entertained by Malik's sudden appearance was difficult to tell.

"Odin, Malik. Malik, Odin. How are the Frost Giants?"

"They seem to be waiting for something to happen," Malik said.

"Huh. That makes one more mystery for us." Quinn pointed to the island. "Can you find out what that building is?"

"I know what that building is. It is the Kola Correctional Colony, known colloquially as Bright Falcon Prison. It is for the worst of the worst offenders, and has the highest prisoner death rate of any facility in Russia."

"How do you know this?" asked Odin.

"Did I mention there isn't much to do around here?" Malik replied.

"What were you expecting to find here, Odin?" Quinn asked.

"Fenrir."

"So, the Aesir just left him chained to a rock in the middle of an island, and no one's ever thought to check on him now and again?" Quinn asked.

"There was no need. Gleipnir is unbreakable, and Ragnarök cannot be prevented," Odin replied.

"Well, now there's a big building where you left him. Maybe he's inside it," Quinn said.

"If humans had discovered a giant wolf chained to a rock, and put up a building over him, do you not think they would be selling tickets? Would there not be a bridge out to the island? And a flashing marquee?"

Odin had a point.

"Okay. Could they have killed him?" Quinn asked.

"No. It is not the fate of Fenrir to be slain by a mortal man."

"Could he have escaped? Or been set free?" Quinn asked.

"Ragnarök has not come to pass. Fenrir is still bound."

"What if the prophecy is wrong?" Malik asked.

Odin looked as if Malik had slapped him. "The prophecies have never been wrong."

"Then where is he?" Quinn asked.

"More importantly, does Loki know where he is?" Odin asked.

That was the $64,000 question. If Loki was already in custody of Fenrir, then there was little they could do to stave off Ragnarök.

"We must consult the Norns," Odin said.

"The who?" Quinn asked.

"The Three Sisters – they see the past, present and future. If any can tell us the whereabouts of Fenrir, it will be them."

"Before we go running off through the snow, why don't we see if Malik can take a look inside the building?"

Malik took a deep breath, and his eyelids fluttered. Minutes passed, or seemed to.

His breath rushed out in a loud gasp, and he jolted forward, nearly falling on his face.

"There is a wall…dark…heavy magick," he panted.

"Can you breach it?" Odin asked.

"Not without them knowing about it. They have set watchers on it. Evil things. I surmise they are the work of our friend, Balcones. They have a goetic feel to them." He shuddered and brushed his arms as if something was crawling on him.

Quinn turned back to Odin. "So. The Norns. Where do we find them?"

"Their cave is three days' walk from here," Odin said.

"What about those leafy bits you have? Can't you just use those to magick us there?" Quinn asked.

"Are you familiar with the concept of quantum entanglement?" Odin asked.

"The idea that two partner particles can affect each other at a distance," Malik answered.

"Exactly," Odin said. "Now, if you think about sewing two pieces of fabric together, you would put the two pieces so the right sides were facing each other, sew along at a set distance from the edge of the cloth, and then press open that seam allowance, the gap between the edge of the fabric and the stitching. The Mundane world is one piece of fabric, and the Magical world, or Faery, as you call it, is the other. We are standing in the seam allowance, where they overlap, and that is how humans were able to come to this place. The two worlds cast reflections and shadows upon one other, and that is how I am able to use the entangled particles to travel from one world to the other. These "leafy bits" are like a map. They enable the transference of my idea of the place I want to visit to the appropriate partner particles and envelop us in the interaction. But this map only works on particles in the corresponding alternate world."

"So that would be a no, then. I doubt we have three days. Malik, can you zap us there?"

Malik looked skyward and put on a strained smile. "Of course."

The wind swirled around them, picking up snow and pebbles in what humans would call a dust devil. Quinn shut his eyes against the blowing debris, and when the wind stopped a moment later, he found himself outside the mead hall where he had stayed with Halle.

"What is this place?" Malik asked.

"It is the *Three Sisters Inn*. Think of it as a way station owned and operated by the Norns. They keep many treasures and artifacts here. Follow me," Odin said.

He strode off into the forest, and Quinn had difficulty keeping up with him. Fortunately, they did not have to go far into the trees to come to a boulder-strewn cave entrance. Odin stopped just inside the opening. The cavern was large, and calcite glimmered like stone tree roots in the flickering light of a fire.

"Urd? Verdandi? Skuld? Are you about?" Odin called.

A woman in a long dress and red cloak stepped from the utter blackness at the cave's throat. Her face was hidden by a hood, but her eyes glimmered from the shadow with the same green fire as Halle's.

"Greetings, Allfather," she said.

"Greetings to you, Urd," Odin said. "We seek the advice of the wise."

"Then you have come to the right place," said another female voice.

She emerged from the dark and stood by her sister. She wore a green cloak over her dress, with the hood also covering her head.

"Greetings, Verdandi," Odin said. "Will not Skuld join us as well?"

"She will not," Verdandi replied.

"Very well. The two of you know more than enough, I'm sure, to help us."

"Then follow," Urd said.

She turned and headed into the darkness at the back of the cave. Verdandi followed. Quinn and Malik looked at each other, then followed Odin into the gloom.

Wrought iron sconces held the torches that lit their way as they walked carefully down a rough-hewn path that wound into the deep heart of the cave. The air was chilly, and bordered on dank. After a while, the trail flattened out, and they came to an underground river. An arched bridge, made of white stones, curved over the clear water, and Quinn was sure he glimpsed the heavy scaled tale of a dragon resting in the stream.

The path sloped downward again, and now the air began to get drier and warmer. Up ahead of them, an orange glow spilled out of a smaller cavern.

As they entered it, Quinn saw that there were shelves on the walls of the chamber, and a triangular wooden table with three chairs stood to one side. In the middle was a well, built from dry-stacked stones. The orange glow came from the walls - there were no fires, torches, or lights that Quinn could see.

"The Well of Fate," Urd said, nodding to Quinn and Malik.

She turned the crank handle and brought up a bucket, then ladled some of the water into a black onyx bowl. After she emptied the bucket back into the well, she carried the bowl and set it in the middle of the table. She sat in one chair, and Verdandi sat in another. Their eyes glowed green under their hoods as they stared into the water.

At last, Verdandi spoke.

"The eyes of Fenrir see neither sun nor moon. The sword of Tyr has been removed from his jaws; he feasts on the wicked, and he grows more fell and strong, adding their evil to his own. Gleipnir yet binds him to the great rock Gjöll, though sun and snow touch it not."

"He feasts on the wicked," Malik said to Quinn.

"You said Bright Falcon prison had an unusually high death rate," Quinn replied. He shuddered. "I guess we know why."

"That is a cruel punishment, even for humans," Odin said.

"Can they give us a hint on what Loki is planning?" Quinn asked, glancing at the Norns.

"Possibly," Odin replied. " Urd sees all of the past, Verdandi sees all of the present."

"And Skuld sees all of the future?" Malik asked. "Should we be concerned that she declined to participate in this discussion?"

"Skuld has her own reasons for doing as she does," Verdandi said. "Would you know your own fate? Perhaps a defeat brings tools for a future victory, and a victory brings with it the seeds of your own destruction. If you knew, would you try to change that, even if these things must happen for the greater good?"

"Fate is a tricky thing," Quinn said. He was not a strong believer in fate, but he wasn't about to argue with the Norns about it.

Verdandi nodded, and he wondered if she knew his thoughts.

"If you would look for Sigyn, Allfather, you will find her in Asgard, in her old abode," she said to Odin.

"Thank you," he said. Turning to Quinn and Malik, he said, "We must plan. Let us take ourselves to the inn to quench our thirsts while we do so."

Cornelia smiled at Quinn as he, Odin, and Malik came through the heavy wooden door of the Three Sisters Inn.

Because he didn't require food, Malik scanned the sparse crowd while Quinn and Odin ordered at the bar.

"I don't know when we will have the opportunity for another repast. We might as well fill our stomachs while we plan," Odin said, nearly tipping over the wooden bench as he sat down. "I will speak with Sigyn. She may or may not help us."

"Who is Sigyn?" Malik asked.

"Loki's wife."

"Why would she help us?" Quinn said, raising an eyebrow.

"It was Loki's fault their son was killed. She spent a very long time helping him by collecting the dripping snake venom, and for her trouble, he abandoned her. Besides, she is Aesir. She will fight on the side of the gods at Ragnarök."

"Prophecy?" Quinn asked.

"Yes," Odin answered, his eyes narrowing.

"Well, we also need to watch Bright Falcon and the jotnär," Quinn said. "And I think Bright Falcon being an island makes it just about perfect for me to keep an eye on."

Odin nodded.

"Presumably, that leaves me with the jotnär. Again. How exciting," Malik said.

After a warning look from Quinn, he added, "Not that I mind the Frost Giants. They're very...sparkly."

Cornelia arrived with a tray, bearing tankards of mead, salmon for Quinn, and roast meat for Odin.

"Thank you, Cornelia," Quinn said, then quickly looked at his food. Knowing how she'd been brutalized, he was almost afraid to talk to her, finding it difficult to strike a balance between friendly and distant without coming off as patronizing.

"Are you well, my dear?" Odin asked her.

She nodded, smiling shyly. Then she removed one more thing from the tray and set it on the table.

Odin laughed. "Clever girl!" he said.

Quinn looked at the object. It was a stoppered glass jar filled with a deep red liquid.

"What is that?" he asked.

"Bodin," Odin said, nodding for emphasis.

"And what is a Bodin?" Malik asked.

Odin looked disappointed by the question. "It contains some of Kvasir's blood, of course!"

Quinn grimaced.

"And that would be useful in what way?" Malik asked.

"Kvasir was able to find Loki when no one else could," Odin replied.

"As enchanting as a bottle of his blood may be, how does that help us?" Malik asked.

"Like this," Odin said.

He pulled out the stopper and poured a few drops into his drink and another into Quinn's.

"Oh, I really wish you hadn't done that," Quinn said.

The taste of human blood had always made him nauseous. The smell of it was bad enough, when Odin opened the jar, but having it in his drink was too much.

"What's wrong with a little blood?" Odin asked.

Quinn recalled the blood sausages that Halle had eaten with gusto the last time he was here, and the salmon in front of him suddenly lost its appeal.

"The blood of Kvasir makes you very clever, perhaps smart enough to catch Loki," Odin said, then drained his tankard.

"I don't think I can drink that," Quinn said.

"Of course you can," said Odin, his voice stern. "Would you risk bringing on Ragnarök because you're afraid of a little blood? What kind of monster are you?"

An image of Marti and Cassie, smiling and happy, unaware of a boiling wall of water rolling up behind them, flashed into his mind. Quinn picked up the tankard and glared at Odin. "I am *not* a monster."

Then he drank the blood-laced mead in one draught. He gagged a little afterward, but it stayed down.

"What are you looking at?" he snapped at Malik, who was unsuccessfully suppressing a smirk.

Odin guffawed and pounded his fist on the table. Cornelia shrank away from him, and he turned and softly said something to her.

Quinn did not understand what he said. Perhaps because he wasn't really listening. He suddenly felt strange, like his mind split into halves. One half was looking out of his eyes and was inside the Three Sisters with Odin and Malik. The other seemed to be looking out of a completely different space in his skull, perhaps even above it. Information from other channels was flooding in, overloading his brain. He couldn't make sense of anything, so he closed his eyes and rested his face in his hands to block out the stream.

"I see a flood
Sound, knowledge, and sight
Drinking Kvasir's blood
Has caused this blight," Quinn said.

"What did you just say?" Malik asked, incredulous.

"Poetry," Odin answered, "is sometimes a side effect. Kvasir was known for it, you see." Laughter was in his voice, even if it wasn't on his face.

Quinn shook his head, but remained silent.

Cornelia removed Bodin and carried it away on her serving tray, leaving the men to eat and plan.

Even with his hand over his eyes, Quinn couldn't stop the flow of information. Where was it all coming from? Was it the thoughts of other people?

"I now see double
And speak in rhyme.
Need to stop this vision trouble.
Will be poet for all time?" Quinn said.

"The rhyming should stop in a day or two, as you start to adjust," Odin replied. "The third eye vision is not permanent. Usually. You will have to learn to focus on one stream or the other. With practice, you can learn to narrow it, although I do not think it is possible to shut it off altogether. It rarely lasts longer than seven years, or shorter than seven days."

Quinn gave up covering his face – it wasn't really helping anyway. He picked at his salmon, and speared a caper with his fork. He put it in his mouth.

He had the sense of growing, hot sun shining on his skin, his body swelling, getting ready to burst. Being picked from the branch, washed and sunk in vinegary brine, with a thousand others just like him. He was the caper.

Quinn blinked and shook his head. He was back to himself. Curious, he took a bite of the salmon. He felt himself swimming up a river, battling the chilly currents, twisting and leaping up rapids. On the one hand, he felt bad for eating it. On the other, it would have lost its life for nothing if he spurned it now. More out of duty than hunger, he ate every bite of it, even a few of the bones.

As he chewed, he tried focusing on Odin, who had been talking the whole time.

"In Asgard, I can retrieve my horse, Sleipnir. I will send word ahead for him to be fetched. Once I have spoken with Sigyn, I may have a better feel for what Loki is up to. I can send word by my ravens, Huginn or Muninn, to both of you, if need be. Then I will return to Lake Amsvartnir where Bright Falcon now stands on Lyngvi Island. And I will bring reinforcements," Odin said, between mouthfuls. When he finished he wiped his greasy hands on the tablecloth and grunted.

"Malik, would you be good enough to zap us to where we need to go?" Quinn asked.

A breeze twirled around the three of them, and Quinn found himself alone on the banks of what Odin knew as Amsvartnir Lake.

Quinn pulled his coat around him more tightly. He walked nearly half-way around his side of the island, looking for a good place to enter the water where the view from Bright Falcon was obstructed. Gratitude for Odin's gift of the ability to keep his clothes on between shifts made him smile. Quinn didn't fancy the idea of running around naked on the chilly beach, and the idea of putting on frozen underpants made him shiver. He looked around, on the off chance that there was anyone watching. He was standing in a swale, and mostly hidden by large rocks. He hoped he wouldn't have to do anything other than shift to maintain the clothes, and he wondered if they would be wet or dry when he came out of the water. He was about to find out. At least changing into his normal form would get his mind off his poetry predicament. Kelpies didn't speak.

He took another look around and ran out to the lake, wading in and swapping one form for another at the same time. The cold water was sharp and refreshing. It felt good to dive deeply and swim hard. He paddled, all underwater but his head, around the island. There was a helipad and some large radio and satellite antennae on the far side of the building. A kennel, with twelve dog runs that Quinn could see, stood empty. He suspected he knew why. If you have one giant dog, why do you need any smaller ones?

Chapter 12
Hard Time and Hardware

adrian frowned at the pad of paper on his desk, tapping it with the end of his pen. "How can that be?" he asked the technician at the other end of line.

"Maybe he has a twin?"

"Maybe. I'll have to look into that. Thanks, Penny. I owe you lunch for getting this back so fast."

If she was keeping track, he probably owed her twenty lunches by now. "Sure thing," she said, and hung up.

He tapped the Bluetooth set on his ear and looked at his notes. CODIS had identified the DNA in the blood sample he'd taken from the wall outside the Tenth Sphere as belonging to a felon named Terrance Ogilvey. The only problem with that was that Terrance Ogilvey's last known address was in Forest Glen Cemetery in northwest Houston.

Starting with arrest records, Hadrian traced Ogilvey's short life. He'd started out as a juvenile, minor stuff – malicious mischief, trespassing, breaking and entering. But as he got older, he became more violent. Aggravated robbery, assault with a deadly weapon, and multiple counts of grand theft auto. He'd been a busy boy to rack up all of that by twenty-three.

After his last stint in County, his parents had sent him to a residential treatment program for disordered personalities, run by a Dr. Grigori Pavlov. Unless that was more than one psychiatrist named Grigori Pavlov, that would be the doctor who was killed last week in a hit and run traffic accident. With Marti Keller's car. Curiouser and curiouser.

Unfortunately, the week after he'd been released from the program, Terrance Olgivey's car was found crashed into a bridge abutment. According to the medical examiner's report, Terry had suffered extensive head trauma and probably died instantly. His body was identified by his clothes, a wolf tattoo on his hand, and a class ring that he always wore.

Hadrian next hit vital statistics. And he also hit a wall. Terrance Olgilvey had been adopted, and his records were sealed. It would take some time to get a court order, and he considered requesting an exhumation while he was at it. He had only been dead three years, so viable DNA should be recoverable. He was beginning to suspect that instead of a twin, Terry had a ringer. A dead ringer, that was. A DNA identification had not been run on the corpse, and with the massive body trauma, a match was the only way to prove whether the person in Terry's grave was actually Terry. Before he started on the paperwork, he would call Terry's parents and see if there was, indeed a twin. Maybe they'd tell him enough that he wouldn't need to get the records unsealed. Still, he hated making those kinds of calls, so he put it off for a few minutes by taking a restroom break.

"Hello?" a man's voice said.

"Mr. Ogilvey?" Hadrian asked.

"Who's this?" the words were curt.

"Sir, I am Special Agent Hadrian Galanti. I'm trying to find out some information about your son, Terrance."

"Terrance is dead."

"Yes, sir. And I'm very sorry for your loss."

"I'm not. Don't tell my wife I said that. That kid was nothing but trouble from the get-go. I told her we should have gotten a baby, and not a three year old."

"I'm sorry you had that experience." Sometimes the best way to get information was to sympathize and shut up.

"He had something-or-another Attachment Disorder. Whatever it was, he was a psychopath. After he set the house on fire, I wanted to send him back to Russia, but my wife wouldn't hear of it."

"That must have been hard for you. Do you remember where in Russia he came from?"

"Does it matter?"

"Well, it's important for a case that I'm working on. I need to find out if he has a twin brother."

"God help us all if he does. I really don't know. He wasn't introduced with one, but that doesn't necessarily mean anything." Ogilvey thought for a moment. "The name of the place in English was Three Grannies. I don't know what that translates to in Russian."

Hadrian did. It was Tri Babushkas. "Thank you, Mr. Ogilvey. You've been extremely helpful."

"Sure, no problem. If there's another one like Terrance running around out there, I hope you get him."

"Yes, sir."

Hadrian tapped the Bluetooth and hung up.

Why don't I get interns like Sara does? he wondered as he started on the exhumation request. And when he was done with that, he needed to shovel through the mountain of paperwork on his desk. At the top of his list was getting a surveillance warrant for the cozy little group at the Tenth Sphere. He needed to know why supposedly dead Odessa gang members were hanging out there.

Aside from the household staff, Irina and Sveklá were alone in the massive villa that dominated Boris' one and a half acre fiefdom.

"Shall we watch a movie?" Irina asked, pouring two shots of vodka. She handed one to Sveklá, and her fingers brushing his almost caused him to drop the glass.

"I suppose," he replied, turning away from her so she wouldn't notice the effect her touch had had on him.

She turned the television on and turned up the volume. The house was bugged. Her husband trusted no one. Still, all of the security cameras were at the estate's gate and perimeters. It was just as dangerous for Boris to risk being photographed with some of his business associates as it was for them to associate with him.

Irina sat down on the white leather couch next to Sveklá, a little too close for his comfort. He drained his glass.

"How are the children, Sergei?" she asked, her low voice barely audible above the blaring television.

"Coming along well. Feliks broke into Latvian bank last week without detection. His fighting skills need work. He is almost ready. Others, doing good for age."

The thinnest of smiles lifted the corners of Irina's mouth. "I have heard from Vitali," she whispered.

"And what does Vitali say?" he whispered back.

Vitali had not run away from Babushkas with them. He had been sick, and too thin, too weak, to make the escape. The three of them only barely survived the ordeal, frozen and starved nearly to skeletons by the end. But with Vitali, they shared a bond that could only be forged at a place like Tri Babushkas. He had stayed in Russia, and built a thriving business smuggling military hardware out to the highest bidder.

"The opium cartel in Afganistan wishes to counter any drone incursions over their poppy fields. They are very interested in obtaining a MiG-35. Vitali can acquire one in India. We would get a twenty percent finder's fee."

What she was suggesting amounted to treason. If she had planned to tell her husband, she wouldn't have used the TV to cover their voices. If Sveklá knew what was good for him, he would leave the room now. "Twenty percent of how much?" he asked.

"Thirty-five million, for just the plane. Forty with pilot."

Sveklá sucked in his breath. He could retire and live quite well on his share of that. No more killing. He was getting too old for it, anyway.

"We could leave here. Together. Perhaps bring Feliks, and start our own organization."

"We could never leave. Every hired killer in world would be after price our heads. And it would be huge price, bol'shoi price."

Irina's large eyes filled with tears. "I don't care. Death would be better than this gilded prison. I am tired of being humiliated and mocked, treated worse than dog."

Sveklá's jaw clenched, holding in the white-hot flash of anger. He could not bear to see Irina so miserable. "Perhaps, then, we should not be the ones to leave."

"Oh, Sergei! You are my hero."

Pleasure shot through Sveklá's body, melting him like a bolt of lightning as Irina suddenly straddled his lap and kissed him hard, her warm tongue parting his lips.

Chapter 13
Doggone

ruce?" I called hopefully into the backyard.

A bird flicked through the shrubs. At least I think that's what it was. What else would it be, so close to the birdbath? But that was the only response to my call.

It's not like he's an ordinary dog, running off to chase cars and get run over. But he was still gone, and I had no idea what had happened to him. Knowing that there was a demon after him, it made me nervous about his welfare. *What if Balcones had come and snatched him right out of my house?*

Surely he would have left a note if he had been called away. I had a good look around, checking the fridge and all of the mirrors, the kitchen table, my pillow, any place where I thought he might leave a note. If he had, I couldn't find it.

Cassie had been asleep for a couple of hours, and I was trying to distract myself with the TV. It wasn't unusual for Quinn to disappear for days at a time, but it was unusual for him not to tell me he was going.

There was a quiet knock on my back door just after ten. I flipped on the light and saw Halle standing there, blinking in the sudden glare. I opened the door, nervous that she was bringing bad news.

"Halle? What's up?" I tried to sound casual as I moved out of the way so she could come inside.

She didn't move. "Quinn had urgent business – there was news about the jötnar situation."

"I see. Did he say when he might be back?"

Halle shrugged. "I do not know if he will be back. He also has some family obligations he needs to attend to."

"Family obligations," I echoed. *What kind of family obligations?*

"Yes. I saw your light on, thought you might have some concerns, since he just took off and left you." She shook her head ever so slightly, almost as if out of pity.

"I was surprised he didn't at least leave a note," I said out loud, although it was less for Halle's benefit than for mine.

"You didn't find one?"

"No."

Halle shrugged again, then dodged out of the way of a fat June bug on a kamikaze mission to the porch light.

"It would be best for you to recognize that this relationship could never have worked. Be glad of the memories, but move on to someone more suitable for you. A fellow human, perhaps." She nodded and patted my shoulder. "Time for me to leave," she said. "Sleep well."

She stepped off the deck, out the anemic circle of light, and was swallowed by the darkness.

Time to leave the conversation, or to leave town? I wouldn't be unhappy to never see her again, but on the other hand, Quinn wasn't around to protect us from Balcones, either. *English is not her first language. That's all.*

But what about Quinn's "family obligations?" That could mean a lot of things, I assured myself. Like maybe visiting his sick mother in the hospital. But supposing it meant taking his wife out for her birthday. Had I misinterpreted the cues he was giving me? It had seemed pretty obvious that he was available and interested in being with both me and Cassie. I reminded myself that both Lulu and Delilah had said, over and over, "You can't trust a shifter." Had I really been so stupid?

I told myself I wouldn't cry. No reason to jump to conclusions. I wanted to hear it from Quinn's own lips, if we were finished. If he came back. After all, I had known him for only a few weeks. And he had saved my life. More than once. But maybe he was just acting in a professional capacity. Nick, and Ryan, when he was alive, saved damsels in distress all the time, and it didn't mean they wanted to run off and live happily ever after with them. I was a little unclear on what, exactly, Quinn's job was, but I did know it was all about catching demons and righting wrongs. Maybe my thinking that his protecting me was personal was a mistake. Although, when he kissed me, that was far from professional.

I dabbed at my eyes with a paper towel and blew my nose.

Well, at least Lulu and Delilah would be happy to hear he was gone, and maybe never coming back. I guess I could tell Aiden and Kyle that someone had left the gate open and Bruce had run away. It wasn't really a lie.

Dammit. How could he do that to Cassie and me? Was it something I did (or didn't do?), or was he just a jerk? Or was this just a big misunderstanding?

I snapped off the TV and got in the shower. I shampooed my hair, then stood under the showerhead until the hot water was gone. I was still emotionally fragile after Ryan's death, even after almost two years. This was not helping.

On Wednesday, I found I had no real appetite, for either food or doing things. I fed Cassie and gave her a bath. But we skipped our morning walk. I almost never watched daytime television. But I did today. Theoretically, I just had it on while I was folding a basket of laundry, but it took me all day to fold Cassie's clothes.

I should have taken a shower on Thursday before I went to work. But I didn't. Didn't go for a walk, either, so it probably evened out.

"Are you okay?" Lulu asked when I walked in the door. "You look peaked, honey."

"Yeah. Think it might be a virus or something. Just felt kind of pep-less the last couple of days."

Lulu chewed on her bottom lip as she studied my face. "Do you think you'll be up for Circle tonight? It might make you feel a lot better."

"Doubt it. Childcare issues."

"Belinda would love to stay with Cassie. Her grandkids are all at camp, and she's missing them something awful."

"Fine. Have her come by about a quarter of so I can show her where everything is."

The shop wasn't Saturday morning busy, but it was really busy for a Thursday afternoon. That was good – kept my mind from dwelling on Quinn.

Belinda showed up on my doorstep at 6:30. Cassie was delighted to see her and started babbling away as soon as Belinda stepped inside.

After I had given her the grand tour, and she and Cassie settled in the living room, Belinda turned to me and said, "So...where is Bruce?"

"Good question. There was some movement on his case, and he had to go check on it. Or something like that." I was still feeling a little touchy about Quinn leaving without so much as a Post-it note on the mirror. I doubted "news about the jötnar" was likely to be such an emergency that he had to drop everything and go that instant.

"I see," she said. "Is he coming back?"

"Not sure."

Belinda hesitated before responding. Perhaps measuring her words, perhaps having a conversation with someone I couldn't see. I had no idea whether Belinda could see ghosts or not, but I assumed she could.

"Whatever happens," she said, finally, "it will be for the best."

"I hope you're right. My cell, my mom's numbers, and Emily and Nick's numbers are all on the fridge, if you need anything at all."

"We'll be fine. Don't you worry about us." Belinda smiled so confidently that I couldn't help but believe her.

"Okay. I'll see you soon." I gave Cassie a hug and a kiss and headed out.

Although Lulu had done the cleansing ritual and earthy sage smoke lingered in the air, the energy in the room was prickly and unpleasant. Lulu seemed particularly distracted. I don't know if was more about Benjamin's predicament, or Ellen's deteriorating condition – she'd looked awful when she came by the shop Tuesday.

Our focus tonight was on table tipping. As far as I knew, that was something that was popular during the Spiritualism movement of the nineteenth and early twentieth centuries. And I also thought that many, maybe most, of those séances were famous for being based on trickery, so I was a little puzzled that Lulu would have us do this.

There were two round wooden tables, and Lulu put five folding chairs at each one. I ended up being awkwardly sandwiched between Marilyn and Hunter Greene. Again. She was clearly trying to flirt with him – she kept bumping into him, touching his hand, and based on the way he was squirming, his knee. He, just as clearly, wasn't interested.

Two other women had joined our table. I'd seen them before at Circle, but didn't really know them.

"Hi, I'm Melissa. I don't think we've been formally introduced," the older of them said.

"I'm Marti," I replied.

Hunter stood up and extended his hand to Melissa. "I'm Hunter – I just moved to Houston from Virginia. I was really surprised to find a group like this just down the road from me."

"Welcome to town, Hunter," the other woman said. "I'm Savannah. Melissa's my mom."

"Would you believe he just moved in across the street from me?" I asked, mostly to needle Savannah for ignoring me. Even so, the image of Hunter standing in his garage, sweat glistening on his naked chest, popped into my mind.

"You don't say," she replied, unimpressed.

"Alright, ladies and gentleman," Lulu said, standing up at her table. "Let's get started. What I want everyone to do is put their hands on the table, palms down. Your pinkies should touch the pinkies of the people on each side of you. I'll lead this table, and Melissa, if you wouldn't mind leading the other table?"

Melissa nodded.

Lulu dimmed the lights so that it was nearly dark. A candle flickered in each corner of the room, casting uneven shadows that danced on the walls and slid eerily across the faces of the people at the tables. Hunter's hand was warm against mine, and I missed Quinn. Marilyn's hand was icy, and it reminded me of Halle.

"I know that Marilyn and Savannah have done table tipping before. How about you two?" Melissa asked, looking from Hunter to me.

I shook my head. I had played *Light as a Feather* at a slumber party once and gotten totally creeped out when Sara Grace Jackson really did seem to levitate. But I didn't want to talk about it.

"My sister and I used to try it, with some of her friends. But it was a long time ago, and we never really had much success," Hunter said.

"I see. Good to know," Melissa said. "Now, Marti, what's going to happen is that I'm going to ask for any spirits who would like to communicate with us to come and move the table. Sometimes, the table jumps around like a March hare, and sometimes, nobody shows up. You never know how it's going to go until someone, or something, manifests."

Melissa took a deep breath, then exhaled dramatically. I didn't know what her day job was, but it seemed that she was a natural for the theater.

With eyes closed, she said, "Are there any clean spirits here who wish to communicate with us? Those with harmful intent are not welcome here. We are seekers of truth and light."

Delilah, arms crossed, appeared behind Melissa. She rolled her eyes and her head swiveled ever so slightly from side to side. If I didn't know better, I might have thought she was listening to music.

"Girlfriend, you know this is almost as bad as using an Ouija Board, right?" Delilah said.

How's that?

"You wouldn't go to the mall and ask random strangers to come on over to your house, now, would you? That's what most people do with Ouija Boards. This ain't a whole lot different. If you're not real careful, ya'll'll have lower astrals all up in this place. And they're a bitch to get rid of, worse than roaches."

I shuddered. Anybody who's spent more than twenty four hours in Houston has probably encountered the two inch long flying cockroaches that like to play chicken by swooping right at people's faces.

Why don't you do something then, so that Melissa quits calling for someone to come?

"Fine. You ought to be real grateful, girl, for the stuff I do for you."

"Up!" Melissa demanded. "Up!"

Marilyn and Savannah joined her in chanting "Up!"

I looked at Hunter. He gave me a slight shrug and joined them. As weird as it felt, I added my voice to the mantra.

I felt the table vibrate as Delilah reached out and grabbed the edge of it. She jerked it up and down a few times, then moved to the other side, between Marilyn and I, where she lifted the table slowly for an inch or two and held it.

"It's working!" Marilyn said. "I can feel the spirit moving around us!"

"Shhh! We have to keep the focus on the table. Up!" Melissa said.

Any updates on Bertram Kounis? Or is he still cocooning? I thought at Delilah, hoping that there might be some news.

"No. He's still the same. He —" Delilah stopped suddenly.

I followed her gaze across the room. A shadow, clearly defined by the candlelight, stood against the wall. I suddenly felt cold. There was no one standing up to cast the shadow.

"Now see? That is exactly what I meant. It probably ain't strong enough to cross Lulu's barrier she laid down with that smudge stick, but we better keep an eye on it all the same."

We?

"Yes. I'm busy tippin' tables, remember?"

Delilah jiggled the table around for the next twenty minutes or so, until Lulu turned the lights back up. I watched the shadow prowl around the outer edges of the room, but it never approached the tables.

Lulu broke the circle, and we all filed downstairs. The hibiscus iced tea she had made for refreshments was just what I needed. I was eating a lemon gingersnap cookie bar when Lulu pulled me aside.

"Are you available to work an event on Saturday a week?"

"Maybe. What is it?"

"Charity fundraising gala. Benefits orphans. It should be a really big event, and I think it will take all three of us."

I brushed crumbs off of my chin. "Wow. But I don't have an outfit, if I can't borrow Belinda's."

"Oh, honey. I have the perfect outfit for you. I think you'll like it much better than Belinda's, anyway. And," she said, "your share would be $500.00. Plus tips."

"I'll see if Mom is available."

Conversation disappeared with the tea and cookies. The Circle attendees drifted out of the shop, until only Marilyn, Hunter, and I remained.

"You know, Hunter," Marilyn said, twisting a lock of hair around her finger, "I'm going to see that new play at Mainstreet Theater tomorrow. I think there might be a few tickets left, if you're interested in going. Maybe we could even meet for dinner before the show." She pressed a slip of paper with a phone number on it into his hand.

He held onto the paper, too polite to throw it away, yet unwilling to put it in his pocket. "I'm sorry, Marilyn. I already have plans for tomorrow. Hope you enjoy the play."

Looked to me like he needed an intervention.

"Hey, neighbor," I said.

"Hey."

"I was just wondering, since it's a little late, and you live just across the street, if you wouldn't mind walking home with me?"

"No problem. I don't mind at all. Just let me know when you're ready."

"I'm pretty much ready now. Just let me get rid of my trash." I threw my paper cup and plate into the bin.

I smiled at Marilyn. "Good night. See you next time."

She gave me the stink eye.

"Night, honey," Lulu said. "I'll come pick up Belinda in a few minutes. Hope Miss Cassie hasn't worn her out."

Lulu locked the door behind us, and Hunter and I started back into the neighborhood.

"You looked like you needed a rescue," I said.

"I did." He chuckled. "Thanks."

"Just one of the many services I offer."

"Excuse me?" He said, shooting me a quizzical look.

"Wow. That came out totally wrong." I hoped the streetlight wasn't bright enough to show how red my cheeks were. "My other services include sarcasm and general wisecrackery."

"Good to know." Hunter smiled, and I hoped that it wasn't because he was trying not to laugh at me.

"So where are the best places to get a quick bite around here? Sometimes I work late and I don't have time to cook."

"You cook? What's your specialty?"

"My specialty? Hmmm. Not sure I have one, but I make a mean pumpkin gnocchi."

"Not sure I've ever had pumpkin gnocchi."

I liked Hunter's smile, I decided.

"Maybe I'll bring you some next time I make a batch. My original college major was hotel and restaurant management, so I went to cooking school."

"Does that make it hard when you go out to eat?"

"Sometimes."

"Well, there's a pretty good cluster of restaurants on the south side of I10 and Highway 6. Most people don't realize what all is back there, but the food is good, and they stay crowded. You just have to know when to go, if you want to get in."

"Maybe you can show me sometime."

"Sure."

I noticed that we were almost at my house. "I guess this is my stop. Thanks for walking me back. See you around."

Hunter waved slightly. "Yeah. Take it easy."

I fished around my purse for my keys. They weren't in their normal pocket. Instead, I found them underneath my wallet. Suddenly, I stopped. *Had I just agreed to go to dinner with Hunter?*

Chapter 14
A Woman Scorned

he sky was a serene cerulean and the weather was shatteringly crisp when Quinn heard a couple of horses approaching at the gallop. He turned his head toward the sound as the riders came flying down to the lake. There were two riders, but only one horse. Odin's grey horse, the eight-legged Sleipnir, carried them both.

Quinn swam up as close as he comfortably could to the beach. The grey horse stopped and snorted, all four forelegs splayed and head raised.

"Easy, Slippy," Odin said. "He's a friend."

The horse looked unconvinced, with his nostrils flaring and ears pricked forward. But he made no effort to bolt. Odin kicked his right leg over the horse's neck so he was facing Quinn and slid ungracefully to the ground. He turned to help the woman, who was tucked behind the saddle, to dismount.

She was tall, at least six feet, and her shoulder-length blonde hair was dull and flat.

"This is Sigyn," Odin said. "Wife of Loki."

Quinn dipped his head. Kelpies did not smile, and even if they did, the result would be far from reassuring.

Sigyn looked at him impassively. Her eyes were the same feldspar grey as the surrounding rocks, and just as lifeless.

Odin touched her arm. "Please tell Quinn what you have told me."

She sighed slightly, resigned to do as she was told.

"As you may know, when my husband Loki was bound, a serpent was suspended over him to drip venom onto his bare skin. It burned him, so I caught it in a large bowl, to lessen his suffering. From time to time, the bowl would fill up, so I had to empty it.

"In the beginning, I just poured the venom into a ravine, but after so many years of doing so, a lake has formed. Nothing can survive there. The trees and grasses are blasted, and even birds which fly above it succumb to its vapors. Skadi has much to answer for tapping the venom of such a pernicious serpent to torment Loki."

Odin shifted his weight slightly away from her, perhaps feeling the heat of her anger at the Aesir.

"There was a group of men," she continued, "climbers they called themselves, who stumbled across my path. I was unaware that they had followed me. But while I emptied the bowl, the bitter liquid dripped down from the serpent's jaws upon my bound husband," and she said the last word through clenched teeth, "and such was his torment that his screams echoed from the rocks far and wide. Even as I returned and held up the bowl to catch the serpent's poison, they came creeping from behind the rocks.

"'Free me!' Loki begged of them.

"He knew that as mortal men, they were not bound by the enchantment that prevented the bonds from being severed by either Aesir or jötnar.

"'What will you give me?' asked their leader.

"'Life. And wealth. You will survive Ragnoräk, and I will show you hidden hordes of treasure.'

"The climbers spoke amongst themselves in a tongue that was foreign to me.

"'I know who you are,' said the leader. 'I have heard the legend of the great god Loki who was bound with the entrails of his son for insulting the gods, and who shakes the mountains in his pain. But I also know you are a trickster. You offer us treasure for your freedom, but how can we be sure you will keep your word?'

"'Take my wife as a hostage,' Loki replied.

"He offered me up as a hostage without the bat of an eyelash, after I had spent centuries aiding and comforting him," Sigyn said, her voice edged in bitterness.

"'I have heard your reputation for many infidelities, and I fear I cannot trust your dedication to your wife,' the leader replied.

"'Release me, and I will ensure you each have a berth on the ship Naglfar when the world drowns.'

"The men talked among themselves, and finally accepted this pledge. They used their climbing axes to cut the bonds that held the great serpent and set it free to slither into the rocks.

"Then they released Loki. He laughed, and the sound of it was wild and fey. Even the crows roosting in the valley flew shrieking into the air with the fear of it.

"'Now,' Loki said, 'shall I have my revenge! The prophecies foretell that my Fenrir shall swallow that loathsome Odin and put an end to him.'

"He turned and spat upon the rock on which he had long been chained. 'Time to go.'

"The men left me on the mountain without so much as a backward glance from Loki. All these years," Sigyn said. "I stayed with him and sacrificed everything, trying to ease his misery. And this is how he repays me?"

Her eyes were pink-tinged and puffy. It was obvious that she had shed all the tears she was going to over him.

"And his plan?" Odin prompted.

"Of this he has spoken much during his confinement. He said that to sever Gleipnir, the impossible chain, he would need an impossible blade. He would seek out the dwarves who created Gleipnir and offer them a price to secure its undoing. He is most likely searching for the impossible items they have tasked him with retrieving."

"It is a pity," Odin said, "that you have no idea what those items might be."

Sigyn bowed her head.

"I am sending Thor to the dwarves that are most friendly to us, so see if they can ken what these impossible items might be," said Odin.

Quinn wished that he could ask Sigyn what the climbers looked like, so he might recognize them if they came to Bright Falcon. He shook his head in frustration. Since he couldn't speak, he tried focusing his enhanced perception on Sigyn. The ability was starting to fade, and it was already diluted in his kelpie form, but it might be enough.

He closed his eyes and breathed in deeply, slowly. An image filtered into his consciousness: five men dressed in various colors of snug spandex shirts, cargo pants, mountaineering harnesses, helmets and gloves. One of the men was in front of the group, clearly the leader.

He was certain that one would be Balcones, in his smarmy human form.

But he was wrong.

Boris Cherngelanov was the last person he expected to see as the team leader. Which begged the question: If Boris was the one who freed Loki, what was Balcones up to with the Frost Giants?

Chapter 15
Sucker Punch

 t was Friday morning, and Hadrian wasn't sure where he was. Then he smelled perfume, Sara's perfume, and he knew that the deliciously warm body next to him was his girlfriend. He'd felt out of sorts after the table-tipping session at Circle last night. It felt good to not feel like a freak, even if it was just for an hour.

Hadrian eased himself out of bed to go to the restroom. It was 5:00 AM. If he hurried, he'd have time to fit in a run before he showered and went to the office. He could see the indistinct form of Sara's face, lit by the alarm clock. He decided not to wake her up – he already felt bad about making what amounted to a booty call last night.

He took his clothes and dressed in the bathroom, blowing Sara a kiss on his way out. He swore softly as he tripped over something on the floor near the front door. Banging his shin on the end table was unpleasant, but what he felt when he touched her laptop was worse.

He knew then, why Sara hadn't introduced him to Matt, the intern. She was sleeping with him.

Was it an affair? He and Sara had been dating for nearly five years now, but neither had made any promises about exclusivity. Perhaps she was fond of him, but he was a much a booty call for her as she had been for him last night. He was surprised by how much that idea hurt.

A run would clear his head. Maybe. He let himself out into the muggy July morning.

The run had not helped. He refused to allow himself to be upset. He had too much work to do. But he was supremely unhappy about the situation. So unhappy, in fact, that he could barely stop himself from yelling at the judge who denied his request for the exhumation of Terrance Ogilvey, whose blood he found on the wall of the Tenth Sphere's back alley.

He spent his entire lunch break, and then some, at the gym, pounding on the heavy bag until he could hardly lift his arms. It hadn't made him any less angry, but at least he was too tired to hurt anybody. All afternoon, he alternated between wondering if it was his fault, and wondering if Matt was the first. Nothing drives home the you-are-so-not-special point like a cheating significant other.

It was Friday afternoon, and his head was just not in the game. He regarded his mile long to-do list with dismay and decided he had enough for the day. He left on time for a change, and it felt like he was playing hooky.

At 5:30, Sara texted Hadrian. *Dinner?*

Not feeling well

☹ *Feel btr soon, Blackbird*

Thx

He was still feeling like someone sucker-punched him in the gut. Maybe it was his own fault. If he wanted her to be only his, maybe he should have asked her to. But was that fair? To either of them? Whether or not he had a right to be hurt, he was. He needed some time to sort it out.

Chapter 16
The Magician

thought it was pathetic to just mope around the house on Friday, so Cassie and I went for our usual morning walk. Afterwards, I called my mother.

"Marti. I was just about to call you."

"What's up?" *Was something wrong with Dad? Emily?*

"I guess you know that Tropical Storm Denise looks like it's going to hit Mexico. But there's a system in the Caribbean that I have a bad feeling about. I just wanted to make sure you are stocked up on water and non-perishables. And batteries. You've got batteries for your flashlight, right?"

My mother had an uncanny ability to predict storms. I always told her that the Weather Channel would pay her beaucoup bucks to work in their hurricane center. She said that if she charged people money for her gift, God might take it away, to keep her humble.

"I think I'm good, thanks. I'll keep an eye on it." I took a breath to compose myself. "Not tomorrow, but the next Saturday, I've been offered a job working at a charity gala – they're raising money for orphans." I knew my mother would never turn down orphans. "I was wondering if you could look after Cassie for me?"

"Of course I can. Polly is coming over to play dominoes, but I'm sure she'd just love to spend some time with that precious baby girl. Now, Cassie's party is only two weeks away – you have invited some of her friends from school, right?"

"Mom, she's one year old. She doesn't have any friends."

"It's never too early to start. You and Sara Grace Jackson knew each other since before you could walk, and you were best friends all through school."

I was startled when my mom mentioned Gracie. I hadn't seen her since high school, or thought about her in years, not until last night at the Tenth Sphere.

"Oh, and call your sister, dear. I think she's feeling lonely."

As the morning waned, there was still no sign of Quinn, or even Halle, for that matter. I called Emily, and she invited Cassie and me over for lunch.

"I was wondering," Emily said between bites of macaroni salad, "if you could possibly chauffer me to Dr. Pavlov's funeral on Monday. I'm still not allowed to drive, and Nick will be at work."

"They're just now getting around to the funeral? He died, what, two weeks ago?"

"Medical Examiner's office had a backlog. Also, the Feds wanted their hands in the investigation. Took longer than usual."

"You said he was going into the Witness Protection Program. What was that about?"

"Since he's dead, I don't suppose it matters if I tell you. My case involves a juvenile accused of stealing credit card numbers on the internet. He has some mental health issues, and since Dr. Pavlov is one of the foremost authorities on Reactive Attachment Disorder, I wanted him as an expert witness. He had agreed help out just before he discovered that a Russian criminal gang was exploiting children with disordered personalities for criminal acts. So, naturally, the gang didn't want him to talk about it."

"I'm sorry. I had no idea when I called him. I was just trying to find your doctor. But if his location was so secret, why did you have him in your contact list, for anybody to see?"

"I normally use an encryption device whenever I make calls to clients or witnesses. I took the password off my phone because I'd been feeling so foggy, I was having trouble remembering it. My thought process was that if I, or one of the boys, had to call 911, it was better unlocked. Sometimes I wish we hadn't gotten rid of the landline."

I spent the weekend pretending I was fine. If I stopped moving long enough, I found myself alternating between sad and angry that Quinn had seemingly abandoned Cassie and me. I also chided myself for not listening to Delilah and Lulu when they warned me that this would happen. As long as I kept busy, I did okay, although I really didn't have much appetite.

While Cassie slept in the afternoons, I played around with the Tarot cards Lulu had given me. I remained skeptical about divination, per se. But I had seen Lulu give some uncannily accurate readings.

Lulu had told me to study the pictures on the cards. There was nothing extraneous — everything on the card meant something. If I could remember that water, for instance, was about emotions and the subconscious, any time I saw water in the picture, I'd understand that as part of the meaning. That might be easier than trying to memorize each card. But with this deck, that only applied to the Trumps. The nine of swords had nothing but nine intertwined swords on it. For that, I had to remember that the suit of swords represented defense and protection, and the number nine represented things earned. And the court cards were something altogether different. There was definitely an art to Tarot reading, and I had begun to despair of ever mastering it.

Dr. Pavlov's funeral on Monday was not particularly well attended. Maybe two dozen mourners sat in the first few rows of pews. Emily and I sat in the back. I wasn't eager to encounter Dr. Pavlov's son again, not after Halle broke his nose. I suspected that the three men in dark suits across the aisle from us were FBI agents, probably watching to see who showed up and hoping the killer was in the gathering.

Not unsurprisingly, the casket was closed. It was a lovely dark green, almost black, with brass fittings. A spray of white roses draped across the top of it, and ferny wreaths of lilies and roses surrounded it. The organist played a song I didn't recognize, and a priest began speaking in a language I didn't understand. I glanced down at the program and noticed the letters were Cyrillic. That would explain it. The only Russian word I knew was *borscht*.

Near what I believed to be the end of the service, I leaned over and whispered in my sister's ear, "Meet you at the car."

I was anxious to get back to the house. Kyle and Aiden were at Briar Ridge Montessori, but Mom was taking care of Cassie, McKenzi, and Dad. I listened to the radio while I waited, tapping my thumbs on the steering wheel. As my feet got involved in the tunes, I noticed some paper on the floor.

Not wanting to leave any trash in Ben's car, I leaned over to pick it up. Two pieces of paper had been stapled together and tucked under the floor mat. It wasn't mine. However, it was a copy of the bank statement for Lulu's Homeowner's Association, and there were a couple of line items highlighted in yellow. Odd that it would be in Ben's car. I'd just give it to Lulu tomorrow, when I went to work.

"You still look peaked, honey," Lulu said when I walked in the door. "Are you feeling alright?"

"I'm fine. Just a little tired, that's all. How's Ben?"

Lulu nodded. "I see." She sighed. "Ben's okay. Or at least as well as can be expected. The good news is, the lead homicide detective doesn't think he did it. Ben had blood on his shoes, but it was all on the soles. The detective thinks the killer must have had blood on the top. The bad news is that the prosecutor is desperate to get a conviction for the murder, and he doesn't seem care whether or not Ben is guilty – he had motive, means, opportunity, and an eye-witness put him at the crime scene, holding the murder weapon. The judge won't even set bail."

I shook my head. "It doesn't seem fair, does it? If only there was a way to show them what Bert Kounis showed us."

"Tell me about it."

Business was slow today. I dusted the counters and the shelves. Lulu re-arranged the jewelry.

"Have you been working with your cards?" she asked.

"I have, actually. I'm not sure I'll ever figure it out, but I've been studying the guide book that came in the box."

"Excellent. It just takes some practice."

She pulled a cardboard box from under the counter. When she opened it, I saw it contained several different Tarot decks.

"It's good to experiment and find the deck that suits you best," she said as she rummaged through the box.

She pulled out a pack of cards that looked just like mine, with the very medieval stained-glass pictures.

"Have you been doing any layouts?"

"Not really," I said, putting the duster down. "I've been mostly trying to learn the meanings."

"Let me teach you the Celtic cross. That's one of the easiest and most common ones. Shuffle the deck and cut it with your left hand."

When I had done that, she said, "Some readers like to choose a significator card to represent the querant – that's the person being read for. It's usually a court card, like the Queen of Swords, or the Knave of Disks. I normally only use it if I'm reading over the phone."

She tapped the deck. "Take the first card and lay it on the table."

I did. It was the Two of Cups.

"This card represents the present situation. What do you think it means here?"

"Well, the two has to do with comparing options. And Cups represents, um," it seemed to be on the tip of my tongue, tormenting me. Cups can hold water. "Emotions?"

"Possibly. In this particular deck, cups have to do with interactions. If you think of two people clinking their cups together, saying 'Cheers!' it might be easier."

I couldn't help frowning. Lulu patted my hand.

"Reading the cards is about learning to trust your intuition. I might have a little different interpretation than you, but both could still be right, because they reflect different aspects of the problem." Lulu smiled, encouraging. "Now, take the next card, rotate it 90° and lay it on top of the first."

I did. The second card was Trump II – The Magician.

"This is what crosses you, usually a problem or obstacle. But it could also be strength or skill you're having trouble harnessing."

I considered The Magician. According to the booklet that came with the cards, he could be a shaman or a con man, a hero or a villain – someone adept at deception. Well, that sounded just like someone I knew.

The cowbell on the door clattered, and a customer entered the shop. Class was dismissed for now.

Belinda watched Cassie again for me on Thursday night. The focus of tonight's class was psychometry. Lulu had brought a variety of objects which we had to hold in our hands and see if we were able to pick up any information about their owners. She knew the history of each one, so she had an idea of our accuracy.

Lulu divided us into groups of three. Except for one group, mine, that had four, since there were ten of us. Hunter, Ellen, Marilyn, and I sat on the floor facing each other.

Ellen looked like death warmed over, and I was less suspicious of Lulu's assessment that her soul was separating from her body. It made me a little sad.

Presumably for Hunter's benefit, Marilyn had chosen a particularly snug, low-cut blouse. It was like a car accident – I didn't want to see it, but I had trouble looking away.

Hunter must have come straight from work. The top two buttons of his crisp Oxford shirt were unbuttoned, his sleeves were rolled up to his elbows, and his hair was just a little mussed. Doing my best not to make it obvious, I inhaled deeply. I don't know if was his aftershave, laundry detergent, or what, but that man smelled good. I smiled to myself as it occurred to me that he seemed to have fallen out of an ad for designer cologne.

"Since this is the biggest group, I'm going to start here," Lulu said.

She pulled a silver locket on a chain out of her bag and handed it to Ellen. She gave Marilyn a pencil and a few sheets of notebook paper.

"Focus on the object and relax. Let any images, sounds, or words come to you," Lulu said. "Make sure those perceptions get written down. We'll compare notes at the end, and I'll tell you about the objects."

Moving on to the next groups, she produced a watch, and then a smooth black stone. She started moving around the room, and I looked at Ellen.

"I see an image of a young woman with long, black hair. She's very pale," Ellen said. "I don't have the energy to try for any more."

Marilyn traded the paper and pencil for the locket. The pencil scratched across the paper as Ellen wrote down her description.

Although I can't be certain, because I don't know what Marilyn did for a living, I think she may have missed her calling. She needed her own daytime TV talk show, a la Jerry Springer. She made a show of breathing in ultra-deep breaths and expelling them. After several long moments, she said, "I hear children laughing, and the wind."

She was careful to brush her fingers against Hunter's hand when she passed the locket to him. While he was quietly contemplating the necklace, she was busy writing her observations in blocky handwriting that marched across the page and took up too much room.

Hunter frowned. "All I am getting is a white porch swing."

He handed the locket to me. It was still warm from being in his hand. Marilyn coughed to get his attention, then handed him the paper.

I looked at the locket, turning it over in my hand, then opening it. There was a picture of a young man in a military uniform inside. Suddenly, I was seized with a heart-rending sorrow. Tears welled up and trickled out from under my closed eyelids. I hadn't felt this way...since Ryan died.

"Are you okay?" I felt Hunter's warm hand on my shoulder.

The connection was broken, and I dropped the locket. But I couldn't stand for him to touch me right now. The pain was too sharp, the reminder of that loss too fierce.

"I need a tissue," I said, getting up.

After I returned to my group, Lulu took the locket and brought us the black rock. Ellen and I felt nothing, but Marilyn dramatically exclaimed that it had something to do with the death of someone important. Hunter had a sense of red roses.

I found the watch to be very comforting, like a bowl of hot soup on a cold day. Ellen got a picture of a walrus moustache. Marilyn was sure it had belonged to a famous movie director. It reminded Hunter of rocking chairs.

"Has everybody had a turn with each object?" Lulu asked.

She looked around the room. No one objected to moving on. The stone was the first object she held up. "This rock has been in my driveway for years now. I just picked it up on my way here tonight. If it has any history, it is from prior to eight years ago.

Marilyn sniffed.

Lulu held up the watch. "This belonged to my grandfather. He loved to sit out on his porch and smoke his pipe. He was famous in our family for his corn chowder recipe."

She looked at me when she held up the locket. "This belonged to my grandmother's sister, Rebecca. Her young husband was killed on Normandy Beach in the war. She was pregnant when he left, but then she was in a car accident and lost the baby. She never remarried."

Hunter walked me home again. As it turned out, Lulu had red roses around the sides of her garage, and her grandfather had an antique rocking chair that he sat in to smoke outside on the porch.

"You did pretty well on seeing the surroundings that Lulu's objects came from, Hunter."

"I did okay. You nailed the emotional bits. Quite impressive."

I considered telling him about my ability to see ghosts, but decided against it. Since he was attending mediumship circles, he would probably be accepting of the idea, but somehow, it didn't seem right to share just now.

"Thanks. I have some very sensitive areas." *How is it that everything I say to this man sounds dirty?*

"Do you now?" I could hear amusement in his voice.

"I meant areas of expertise. You seem to be good at environment, and I'm good at feeling."

Hunter laughed softly. "Good to know."

"Okay. I'm just going to shut up now. My mother always said 'If you're in a hole, quit digging.' I think that's probably rule number ten or twelve."

"Your mother sounds like a smart lady."

"I think so." I was hoping to turn the glaring spotlight off of me. "Your mother must have a pretty good sense of humor. She married a man named Forrest Greene and then named her children Kelly and Hunter."

"I don't know. I never met her."

I should just give up talking to him – I put my foot in at every turn. "I'm sorry. I didn't realize."

"She had pre-eclampsia. The high blood pressure caused an aneurysm in her brain to rupture. There was nothing they could do to save her, but they had her on life support while the doctors performed an emergency c-section to get us out." He paused and I had the impression that he was holding his breath. He exhaled, and continued. "I sometimes wonder if she was there watching, waiting to see if we were going to stay here or go with her, before she went to heaven. Or wherever people go when they die."

"I am so sorry. I had no idea."

"Tell him she was," Delilah's voice said next to my ear. I jumped.

"Are you okay?"

"Yes, thanks. Do you believe in guardian angels, spirit guides, and stuff like that?"

"I don't disbelieve in them. I think this is your stop."

We were, indeed, in front of my house, so we quit walking and began loitering.

"What if I told you that I was able to talk to my spirit guide?" I started picking at my thumb with my ring finger.

"I would wonder if you were sure that is who or what you were talking to."

Oh, good. Now he thinks I might be schizophrenic.

"Well, whether it is a spirit guide or voices in my head, she says that your mother was there, watching you and your sister, when you were born."

"That's not what I meant. Just that maybe not all entities are who they say they are," Hunter said. "Thanks for telling me."

"Sure."

"You see them, don't you?" he asked. His voice was soft, not much above a whisper.

"Maybe." I wasn't sure if he was trying to find out about ghosts, or determine whether or not I was crazy.

Hunter sighed. "I always wished I could. When I was little, my sister always saw things. Or said she did. I could never be sure that she wasn't just teasing, because no matter how much I wanted to see what she saw, or how hard I tried, I could never do it."

"Be careful what you wish for."

"Good advice. But that looks like Lulu's car coming this way to pick up Belinda. I should go."

I so very nearly invited him in for coffee. But I thought better of it and said, "Good night. See you around."

"See you."

Hunter Greene, you are an enigma. Why is someone who spends all day crunching numbers interested in something as abstract as ghosts?

At 10:30 on Saturday morning, my mother called me in a panic.

"Calm down, Mom. What is this about?"

I heard her breathing deeply, in and out, to get a hold of herself. "The deepfreeze in the garage died last night. Everything in there is starting to thaw out. What am I going to do with all this food? Do you have any room in your freezer?"

"Not much." I thought for a moment. "Why don't you have a block party? Cassie and I can go knock on doors and invite whoever's available. Maybe they could bring desserts or something."

"You know," she said, "that is a fantastic idea. I think there are a couple of new families in the neighborhood, and I know Polly's always up for a party. Nick's off today, and it would do Emily a world of good to get out in the fresh air and let him mind the boys. I knew there was a reason I called you."

"What time do you want me to say?"

"I'll need to run to the store for some marinade and rib rub, but the meat should be ready to start cooking in an hour or so. It's barely frozen now. I'll call Nick and get him to come over and help Drew move the barbeque into the front yard so he can get the charcoal going."

After I hung up with my mother, I turned on the computer. Cassie was busy with her activity table, giggling every time she pushed the yellow button and it played a horse whinnying sound.

I opened my word processor and typed: "Block party at the Schmidts! 1005 Sheldrake Ln. Bring a side or dessert or beverages. Any time after 2:00." I put that text in each quadrant of the paper and printed four sheets. I figured I'd leave them on doors if people weren't home. Sixteen should be enough. I tore the papers into quarters, smeared sunscreen on us both, and strapped Cassie into her stroller.

I went door-to-door, seven houses past my parents', across the street to those houses, down and around the cul-de-sac, and started working my way to the houses on the other side of mine. Hunter was out working in his yard. His damp shirt clung to his body, highlighting his shape. I hoped he didn't notice me noticing.

"Hey," I said, popping Cassie's stroller up onto its back wheels and wobbling it around. She was getting tired of messenger duty.

"Hey, ladies," he said, setting down the branch lopper. "You out enjoying the sweltering heat this morning?"

"Enjoying may not be the word. My mom is having an impromptu block party this afternoon, and I told her we'd let everyone know. You can bring a side dish or dessert. Or if you prefer, drinks. Cold water's always good. Or, it may give you an opportunity to show off those cooking skills you were telling me about."

Hunter's face broke into a huge grin. "You're right – I promised you pumpkin gnocchi. I suppose these bushes will still be here tomorrow."

"Did you hear that?"

"Hear what?" he asked.

I was certain that I heard a relieved sigh, but there wasn't anyone around except Cassie, Hunter, and I, and neither of them made the noise. I shook it off. Bound to be a bird or squirrel – squirrels are always making unexpected and weird noises.

"You can't miss it – my parents live next door to me, and they'll drag the barbeque out into the front soon."

"Sounds fun."

"We have to go knock on some more doors. See you in a little bit."

In the end, I only needed half a dozen of my mini-fliers. I stuck one on the bank of mail boxes on the corner, and one on the gate to the community pool for good measure.

It has taken us almost an hour, and Cassie and I were both starving. While I made us a quick lunch, I scoured my kitchen for side dish and/or dessert ingredients. Of all the ideas I came up with, the only one that I had all of the necessary components for were chocolate chip cookies. I made four dozen while Cassie was napping. While I was scooping dough onto cookie sheets, I wondered if Halle was right. Perhaps there was no future for Quinn and me, and I would be best served by finding a fellow human.

I could smell Dad's barbecue before we even got out the door. I was surprised to find Hunter already next door, beer in hand, chatting with Nick.

"I see you've met Hunter," I said, setting the tray of cookies on Mom's rickety card table.

"Yep," he replied, with no elaboration.

"Nick's my brother-in-law," I clarified. Although it might have been better to let Hunter wonder about our relationship.

It was a nice afternoon, mixing and mingling with the neighbors. Most of them showed up, even some I hadn't expected. And it had solved the problem of Mom's deceased freezer. If only everything in life was so easy.

When I left at eight to put a grumpy Cassie to bed, the party was still going strong. I left the screen door closed, but opened my front door so I could hear if she woke up, and sat out on my porch. The gathering had bled over into my yard anyway.

Nick came up to the porch. He wasn't exactly drunk, but he was merry.

"I know," he said. "Let's play 42."

"42? You hate dominoes," I replied.

"That's true. But it seems like we ought to do something."

Somehow, Nick, Miss Polly, Hunter and I ended up playing Blind Man's Bluff Poker on my porch until after midnight. I couldn't remember the last time I'd done something like that. By the end, I'd gotten so tired and punchy that just about anything started me giggling. I couldn't stop laughing, and Hunter couldn't stop patting me on the shoulder.

And once again, I wondered if maybe, just maybe, if Halle was right.

Chapter 17
Bargain

uinn enjoyed swimming in the deep lake, although some of the sturgeon were close to being as long and heavy as he was. Perhaps his wariness was hardwired from hundreds of millennia in the past when their ancestors might have eaten his. The third eye sense was still with him, although modified, in his kelpie form. He'd never thought much about fish before, just ate them if he was hungry. But as the sturgeon swam by him, he could sense them, ancient, cold, aware of nothing but food or potential mates. Sometimes, he even envied the fish for their lack of troubles.

True, it was summer, but he was in mountains north of the Arctic Circle, and this windy part of the world did not get far above freezing, even with the midnight sun glaring off the snow. It was difficult to keep track of time with twenty-four hours of daylight, but Quinn reckoned it was early on the twelfth day since he met Odin. So far, he had seen nothing but a helicopter, which came with five men and left with two. The occasional guard appeared behind the razor wire, Kalashnikov slung across his back, to smoke or talk on a cell phone, but the raw wind usually drove them back inside quickly. Odin's ravens came every morning for news, and every morning it was the same. Nothing.

But then, Quinn noticed a plume of white smoke rising off to the west. He decided to take his dog form and scout around on dry land to investigate. The jötnar had no use for fires, but their allies might. There could be an army gathering behind the high ridge to the west and north of the island, and he'd never know it, not if he stayed in the lake.

He swam into the shallows, changing into Bruce as he came on shore. He paused to look back at the island, but if anyone had noticed the black dog trotting among the rocks, they made no sign. Bruce shook himself, and droplets of water flew in all directions. Steam rose from his warm, damp body into the frigid air as he picked his way through the stones and out towards the rising smoke.

It was not far, as the dog lopes. The smoke led to a decrepit shack nestled against a cliff. Rusty wire and rotting wood - a sad parody of a fence - drooped around the tiny house. Bruce cautiously approached the little hut, but there didn't seem to be anyone inside. He sniffed the ground, exploring in a hundred meter radius around the hut and on top of the overhanging cliff.

He had just about decided that this was a false alarm when his ears caught the sound of a diesel engine rumbling in the distance. He paused to listen. The sound got louder - it was coming closer, from the direction of the lake. Bruce bounded through the snow. He was not a small dog, and his stride was long, but he still had a mile to run. By the time he arrived back at the lake, he saw a soldier climbing into a snow cat and slamming the door. The machine growled away, tossing snow off its treads as it went. He followed it for a little distance, but while he was fast, it was faster. Enough time had been spent away from Bright Falcon, he reasoned, and he'd better get back. The machine was large, but not large enough for Fenrir to climb inside. It was going away, so it hadn't brought Loki. Or so he hoped. If he was wrong, he'd just failed the most important mission of his career.

As soon as Quinn got back in the water, he dove deep and plowed through the water to the island. He circled it, head just out of the water, until the sun skimmed low on the horizon. Finally, he changed his pattern and swam away to rest. As far as he could tell, nothing had changed at the prison. Still, doubt gnawed at him, and his repose was fitful. He eventually gave up on it and decided to hunt for a meal. This task should have been an easy distraction, but he found it difficult to concentrate enough to catch any fish for his breakfast.

The day wore on. As Quinn scanned the lakeshore, he noticed a large white bear. It stood on its hind legs, tilting its head from side to side, probably trying to figure out what Quinn was. It suddenly dropped to all fours and loped off.

Scaredy cat, Quinn thought smugly.

Until he heard the screaming.

He was horrified to see a figure in a long skirt and blue kerchief on her head standing on the bank. The polar bear was galloping right at her. Using a cane, she hobbled into the water. The bear could easily outrun her on land and outswim her in the water, and if the bear didn't get her, hypothermia would.

Quinn launched himself like a torpedo, heading for the old woman.

She had frozen in fear in chest-deep in the lake. The bear was splashing in after her when Quinn's head broke the surface of the water, then kept going up, rising on his long neck, well over the woman's head.

The bear stopped and growled. Quinn flashed a mouth full of sharp teeth and hissed. A roar, he thought, would probably be more effective, but he didn't' want to alert all of Bright Falcon to his presence.

Still trying to claim its prey, the bear danced from side to side, looking for an opening to attack. Failing that, it stood on its hind legs and snarled. Quinn hissed at it again.

They stared at each other, two well-armed mouths displaying fearsome teeth. Quinn could feel the vibrations in the water as the old woman shivered in front of him.

Glowering, the bear dropped down on all fours and moved back onto the bank. It did not leave, however. There was something about that bear, though, that just didn't seem right.

The easiest thing for the woman would have been for Quinn to shift into his horse form and carry her back to wherever she came from. Through his heightened third eye perception, he had a sense of a small wooden hut, nestled against the craggy base of a cliff – the same one he'd visited the day before.

But a horse couldn't hope to out-swim a polar bear, nor outrun it in four feet of water. Perhaps the bear sensed his dilemma, because it sat on its haunches and licked its black lips, abyssal eyes glittering with hunger.

The woman started to sigh and groan. Too-cold muscles were failing, and she would slip under the water and drown if Quinn didn't do something right now.

He dived, his head searching for its target between her ankles and under the full skirts that billowed around her like wildfire smoke. He scooped her up with his neck and she plopped onto his back with a heavy squelch.

The woman wobbled a little bit, numb fingers unable to get a handhold on Quinn's slippery skin, so she just threw her arms around his long, slender neck. He couldn't swim as fast on top of the water as he could underneath it, but he went fast and far enough to put sufficient space between him and the polar bear. The poor old woman was nearly washed off his back by the rushing water, and even as she tried to tighten her grip on his neck, he shifted into horse form and came out of the water.

With his newfound the third eye sense, he could use the old woman's thoughts to get his bearings and make his way to her little hut. As windy as it was today, there would be no plume of smoke from her chimney to follow. The dilapidated fence was little hindrance as he trotted into the tiny yard. He used his teeth on the makeshift bar handle to tug open the poorly fitted door.

The woman slid off his wet back and landed in a heap next to him. He nudged her, and she said something he couldn't understand, her words slurred together. All he could sense about her was blackness. Hoping it was not too late to help her, he nudged her inside, where he could see low flames wavering over nearly-consumed sticks in the hearth.

He was starting to shiver himself. Being a kelpie in the frigid lake wasn't uncomfortable; being a wet horse in near-freezing weather was. He pushed the door closed, to try and contain the heat within the hut. There wasn't much else he could do for her at this point, and he was anxious to get back to his post, so he trotted back to the lake and slipped into his true form.

Nothing seemed to have changed at Bright Falcon. He didn't believe he had been gone for more than ten or fifteen minutes, surely not long enough for Loki show up, row a boat out to the island in strong wind, then drag it inside the building. Even so, unease prodded him. His minor diversions hadn't seemed to have done any harm. He only hoped that nothing had happened when he'd been distracted.

He wondered about the old woman, living all alone in a rickety shack on a snowy mountain. What did she eat? Where did she get wood for her fire? She might have been some type of unfamiliar fae; although the polar bear looked interested enough in eating her. It seemed odd to him that for someone living this part of the world, she didn't seem to know much about polar bears. Quinn racked his brain to recall the different types of non-human people in this area, but other than Valkyrie, Aesir, jötnar, dwarves, and elves, he came up short. If she was non-human, it might explain why he was having difficulty perceiving anything about her, even with his heightened psychic sense. Still, he had bigger things to worry about, such as the location of Fenrir.

The day after he rescued the old woman, she came back to the lake. He was swimming on the far side of Bright Falcon when he saw the dark figure moving across the bleak shoreline. He hadn't recognized her until he'd gotten closer, swimming with only his nostrils and eyes above the icy water. Still, her eyes followed him, and Quinn was even more convinced that she wasn't human, at least not entirely. And then he remembered another entity that lived in this region – the dreaded Maras, or werewolves. That made sense to him. As a wolf at night, she could easily hunt and bring down reindeer, so she'd have no problem getting food. The Maras were cunning and dangerous, and he'd have to be on his guard. For all he knew, there was a whole pack of them lurking nearby. He approached the old woman warily, and did not come so close to shore when he raised his head above water and breathed in deeply. She smelled like cardamom and lemon cookies, and if his belly hadn't already been stuffed with the salmon, it would have rumbled in anticipation of a sweet treat.

"Hallo," she said. "Thank you for helping me yesterday, Mr. Nøkken. That bear and I have some history, and it gets sneakier every day."

Quinn dipped his head toward the water. He could not speak when he was in kelpie form. He also used the opportunity to sneak a glance back at Bright Falcon. Nothing seemed out of the monotonous ordinary.

"I brought you something," she said, pulling a package wrapped in white fabric out from under her shawl. She set it on a flat rock near the edge of the water and unwrapped it.

Cookies.

Again, he bowed his head.

The woman smiled, then turned and headed back toward her cabin.

They smelled wonderful, even to a kelpie. But Quinn knew that eating food offered by any fae creature was risky. And if she was indeed a Mara, there was no telling what enchantments might be on the cookies. He did, however, move them to the other side of the lake and hid them under some rocks, so as not to insult her.

Not a thing appeared to change at Bright Falcon. It gave Quinn a lot of time to think, and it was a good thing he was in kelpie form, because in human form, he would have driven himself crazy. As a kelpie, his senses were ultra-sharp, but his emotions were dull. As a human, it was the other way around. There was one thing that appealed to all of his shapes: Marti's hair smelled like lemon blossoms.

It made the man think of warm spring days and cool nights and firelight. It reminded the kelpie of lengthening days, more food, and mating. He hoped that Halle, Eoin, and Aleksei were keeping her safe. He also wondered what Balcones was up to. He would not put off his schemes just because Quinn was involved elsewhere. *Why couldn't Loki just get on with it?*

There were parts of the day when the sun skimmed the horizon, but never dropped below it. Dark embraced the rest of the world at these times, and Quinn had trouble getting enough rest. His mostly nocturnal nature did not function well with only daylight. The day was getting brighter, so Quinn reasoned that Huginn and Muninn would be by for updates soon.

He could smell the warm blood sausages and oat bread long before he saw the old woman making her way to the lake with a wicker basket.

Quinn watched her approach, his head and just some of his neck above the water, searching for the rock where she had left the cookies. She set the basket down and looked out on the lake. She could surely see him.

"Would you like some breakfast, Mr. Nøkken?" she called out over the water.

Quinn remained where he was.

"I am just an old baba, and I mind my own business. Have you heard? It seems that accursed trickster, Loki, has been loosed upon the world again. I have a certain jewel that he wishes to possess. He came to bargain for it, but I would not let him have it. It is a small thing, of little value, though it is special to me. Now he's set that wretched white bear against me. For all I know, it is Loki himself. It grows bolder by the day, and I fear I shall be overwhelmed by it."

She opened the basket, and the oily smell of sausages became stronger, turning Quinn's stomach queasy.

"If you are willing to help me, please come to my cabin. I'll surely pay you for your trouble. I hope you arrive before the bear does."

She pulled her shawl tighter around her shoulders and hobbled back up the trail.

This could be a golden opportunity. Or it could be a trap. Could he risk missing a chance to capture Loki as he came for Fenrir? Odin's ravens should come for news at any moment. He would send word with them. If things went well, Odin and company would be the first to know. If they went badly, at least Quinn would know the cavalry was on the way – if he failed, perhaps they wouldn't. And with any luck, they'd even arrive in time. It briefly crossed his mind to ask Malik to come and help him, but if he pulled him off of surveillance for something frivolous and Balcones slipped through their hands, he would never forgive himself.

Huginn and Muninn took their sweet time arriving. Quinn couldn't really blame them – there'd been precious little to report. He told them about the old woman – she'd come after they left yesterday – and what he planned to do.

Quinn remembered exactly where the crone's hut was, and it took just about half an hour traveling over the rough terrain in human form to reach it. It might have been an easier trip as a horse, but he thought it might be safer not to shift at the woman's house. In that moment between forms, he was highly vulnerable.

He raised his hand to knock, and the door creaked open.

"Come in," said the old woman. "Would you care for some tea?"

"No thank you, grandmother. Please excuse my bluntness, but I have other pressing business. How is it that I can help you?"

The crone laughed, then gave him a head to toe scan. "If we are being uncouth, your man-form is pleasing to the eye, Nøkken."

Quinn squirmed inwardly.

"And as you can see, I am old and frail."

She was probably much older, and not nearly as frail as she looked.

"I cannot hope to slay such a beast as a polar bear," she said. "It is all I can do of late to stop it eating me for its supper. I have an idea that its skin would make a fine blanket for my old bones, though."

"So you want me to kill the bear for you?" Quinn asked. "If it has been forced against its will to stalk you, that hardly seems fair. And if it is Loki in bear form, I don't suppose it would be possible to slay it."

For a small, drafty house, it was stiflingly hot. Quinn took off his coat.

"Perhaps not. Disenchant it, cage it or kill it as you will, but this bear will be the death of me if nothing is done."

"Have you considered a sojourn to a place it cannot follow?"

"Is that your solution? To move my dry old bones every time some greedy hand comes grabbing for my meager belongings?"

"I'm sorry. If I do this for you, what is my payment?"

The woman scanned through dusty bottles on a shelf, until she came to one with a pink label. "What would you like? A charm to win the heart of your true love?"

"If she is really my true love, I wouldn't need a charm."

She looked through more bottles and packages. "A ship, then?"

"A ship?"

"It is large enough to carry all the Aesir, and it cannot be sunk. And," she leaned forward, nodding, "it can be folded up as a cloth and carried in your pocket."

Although Quinn had no need of a ship, if he and Odin failed to stop Ragnarök, he could think of at least two people who would.

"Okay, how is this for a bargain? I will catch the bear. If you give me this ship, and I like it, I will give you the skin. If the ship isn't suitable, I'll let the bear go." Quinn didn't relish the thought of killing the polar bear, but he would do what he had to do to save Marti and Cassie.

"As you wish," she replied.

Chapter 18
Lunch

he weekend sprawled in front of Hadrian like a bowl of wet papier-mâché: lumpy, grey, and unpleasant. He tried to distract himself from his personal life by rehashing every detail of his professional one. If he hadn't been watching both Marti and Lulu, he would never have gone to something like Thursday Circle at the Tenth Sphere. But there, maybe he should have lied and said he didn't get anything when he held Lulu's objects. Or just made something up. Like he should have done afterwards, when he walked Marti home. His ability, blessing or curse, was his deepest secret, and it felt good to have it acknowledged and accepted. It was a brand new experience for Hadrian, to be around people who wouldn't regard him as a freak for even entertaining the possibility of psychic abilities, much less actually possessing them. But there was a problem in associating this newfound personal liberation with Marti.

He'd allowed himself to get too distracted by her. She was a surveillance subject, he told himself harshly. Not a friend. Not a lover. A subject. And he would do well to keep that in mind. His cover ID didn't have any real details about his childhood, just a generic history. He'd made a terrible mistake telling Marti the truth about his mother's death. And he did have a twin sister, only her name wasn't Kelly, it was Sabina. That's what happens when the sole parent is a professor of ancient history. Kids get named things like Hadrian and Sabina. No one would have blamed her if she stuck an 'r' in between the 'b' and the 'i.' But she never did. No one would have blamed him, for that matter, if he chopped the 'h' off of Hadrian. But he never did that, either.

That's why it was such a perfect opportunity when Marti knocked on his door and invited him to her mother's house for a block party. Instead of surveilling his targets one at a time, he could watch them all together – Marti, and Nick and Emily Benson. Well, most of them. Lulu wasn't at the party. Of course, if they were working with the Odessa Group, and they figured out who he was, it could all go pear-shaped in a hurry. But that is why he loved this job – the feeling of walking the edge of a knife, balanced between victory and annihilation – now that was a rush.

Hadrian had never gone to cooking school. But he could make gnocchi. It was time-consuming, though not difficult. But it was even easier to slip out to Carmine's and get a family portion to go.

It was the stupid dumplings that pricked his conscious. Compared to the enormous lie regarding his identity and what he was really doing in the neighborhood, whether or not he made the gnocchi, or bought them, shouldn't even be a blip on the veracity radar. Funny how it was always the little things that caused the most damage. Even though he couldn't be absolutely certain, he was pretty sure that Marti and her family were not involved with Odessa. They seemed so salt-of-the-earth real. Still, he knew that people were nothing if not surprising – after all, no one ever suspected Ted Bundy of being the sadistic monster that he was. Marti's mother had acted like she'd known him for years. Nick was very protective of his sister-in-law, which made Hadrian smile. She definitely deserved a man of her own, though. Unfortunately, even without the prohibition on physical relationships with subjects by his job, he knew he couldn't trust himself to be around her alone. It would be too easy for him right now, freshly wounded by his discovery of Sara's liaison, to use Marti to dull the pain.

Hadrian never really took off his Special Agent hat, but he sometimes wore it at a rakish angle. The impromptu party had been one of those times. He'd let go a little and really enjoyed himself. He would be sad when the assignment was over, and he left the neighborhood.

He yawned and stretched, and found himself humming one of the songs that was playing on Marti's phone last night. She didn't have a very fancy phone, and it didn't have a lot of storage capacity, so she only had about eight songs in it that played over and over again. The songs were on shuffle, and they'd incorporated a bet on which song would come up next into their card game. He smiled to himself as he got out of bed. While he was making coffee, he checked his phone for messages, and saw that he'd missed a call from Sara. While she was sitting in his apartment.

Irina Cherngelanov arranged the final details of the Child Advocacy Partners Luncheon with The Houstonian's banquet manager. The guests would start arriving in twenty minutes. Representatives from the District Attorney's office, Child Protective Services, all of the local law enforcement agencies, a select few child and adolescent mental health professionals, and the local branches of children's welfare nonprofits had been invited. Her assistant had told her there were one hundred three RSVPs.

Boris may have been the brains and financial brawn behind the Cherngelanov Foundation, but beautiful, charming Irina was the public face of it. She and Boris had no biological children, but they considered the residents of their RAD residential treatment center to be their own. They did what they could to heal starved and battered bodies and scarred souls. To help them make their way in the world, they taught them the family business and inducted them into the hierarchy when they were trained and ready. Family was not necessarily blood, but who had your back when the chips were down. Besides, they all had a common lineage. Tri Babuskas Orphanage, and its awful sisters, was their bitch of a mother.

Irina loved the open, airy banquet facilities in the hotel. With floor to ceiling windows and indoor plants, it was just like having a garden party, only in the air conditioning and out of Houston's brutal summer sun and energy-sapping humidity.

She heard her name being called and turned around. "Sara! You are a little early, my friend."

Hadrian's girlfriend crossed the room, she and Irina air kissed each other.

"How have you been?" Sara asked.

"I am well. And yourself?"

"Fine. Keeping very busy."

Irina smiled "Good. And your handsome boyfriend? You should have brought him."

Sara had once let it slip that Hadrian worked for the FBI. It wasn't classified information, but it was usually best not to advertise it. When Irina found that Hadrian worked for the gang task force, she couldn't believe her good fortune. Hadrian never told Sara any of the details of his work, but she certainly knew when he was available and when he wasn't. Irina had passed along that information to Boris, who'd used it as something of a heads up that an FBI operation was underway, and to lie low. Sara, the unwitting mole, had helped Boris sidestep law enforcement at least three times.

"He's sick," Sara said with a little pout.

"I'm sorry to hear that. I hope he is better soon. Please," Irina said, "have a drink, a glass of wine perhaps?" She gestured toward the bar set up near the dessert table. She pretended to be slightly embarrassed. "I must go to the powder room while I still have the chance." She would text Boris while she was there.

After the luncheon, Sara decided to stop by Hadrian's apartment to check on him. He didn't answer the door. She let herself in, but he wasn't home. *He probably ran out to get some cold medicine*, she told herself. She waited for a little while, checking her email and Facebook on her phone. After half an hour, she gave up. She tried calling him, but he didn't pick up. She started to wonder if maybe he was working, after all. Usually, he just told her he'd be out of touch, so it was odd that he would claim to be sick.

Before her ruminations got any darker, her phone rang. She hesitated to answer it. It seemed wrong to answer a call from Matt in Hadrian's apartment. But there was a chance it was work related. She tapped the "Answer Call" button and quickly let herself back out of the apartment.

Chapter 19
Open Door Policy

here had been an ozone warning today, and the Heat Index was 108. Usually, I was fine, but when the ozone was this high, my head plugged up and my nose dripped like a faucet. I normally kept chewable Benadryl in the medicine cabinet, just in case. I took some right before I left my house, and put another couple of bubble packed tabs in my purse.

I dropped Cassie at my parents' house and headed for the Tenth Sphere. When I arrived, Lulu forced a garment a bag into my hand. "You're late. You did bring the shoes, right honey?"

I held up a plastic bag.

"Good, good," she muttered, hustling me into the shop and towards the dressing rooms.

She and Belinda were already wearing their Gypsy fortune-teller outfits. A slight queasiness swirled around my stomach. I really hoped they weren't planning on me being dressed as a chicken or something utterly ridiculous. The door squeaked as I swung it open, and hung the garment bag on one of the hooks. Taking a deep breath, I unzipped the bag.

"Lulu? Are you sure this is the right costume?"

"Yes. Hurry up, honey. We don't want to be late."

I slipped into the dress and stepped into my heels. "How do I look?" I asked, opening the saloon-style door.

"Fabulous," Lulu said, glancing at her watch.

"That color suits you," Belinda said, gently nodding.

I looked at myself in the full-length mirror. Harsh fluorescent light glittered off red sequins. The stretchy fabric was form-fitting, rather than tight, and it hugged my décolletage like a needy blind date. It wasn't a micro-mini, but it was shorter than I was comfortable with.

I balked. "I don't know. I think it looks a little slutty."

"Honey, if I could get away with wearing that, I'd do it in a heartbeat. Although," she said, looking at my wrist, "I'm not sure that bracelet goes with the outfit."

"I'm not taking it off. Quinn gave it to me."

Lulu's eyebrows raised.

"It's supposed to ward off demons." At least he'd left me with something. Maybe. I hadn't seen any evidence of demons since I'd been wearing it, anyway.

Lulu shrugged. "You're going to be passing out goodie bags to the guests – the bags are already at the party. Also, you'll be giving out a Tenth Sphere coupon with each bag, then telling them where we're set up. They don't have to pay for readings – the host has already covered it, if they ask. We really need to go."

I would need to carry a tab of Benadryl with me, just in case. Once it started cooling off and the ozone levels started dropping, I was usually okay. Usually. I wouldn't be carrying my ginormous purse around while I was passing out goody bags. For lack of anywhere better, I tucked it into my bra. I also tucked my cell phone under my extra-wide nursing bra strap, just above the cup. It took a little adjusting to that it didn't stick out, but it was hard to see the lump under the glittering sequins.

I clambered into the back seat of Lulu's car, and struggled to find a place to put my feet and legs. Her folding table took up most of the floor board, and her decorations and supplies occupied an uncomfortable percentage of the seat. I grunted as a basket of silk daisies toppled into my lap.

"Could some of this go in the trunk?" I asked.

"Have you seen her trunk?" Belinda replied.

I sighed. Actually, I had. There was no room in there, either, as Lulu kept it packed with "emergency" supplies, like her smudge sticks and runes.

Fortunately, it was only a half hour drive to our destination, and only one of my feet fell asleep on the way.

A guard at the gate checked our names off his list. The house wasn't *in* a gated community, it *was* a gated community. I'd stayed at smaller hotels than the main house, and there were at least three guest cottages that I could see from the driveway. An enormous swimming pool with a waterfall and its own pool house sparkled in the sun. I could see what appeared to be a full bar, complete with bartender, through the partially open French doors. Behind that, a fieldstone building, with a brass sign that read 'OFFICE,' nestled between the pool and a putting green.

As soon as the car stopped, a grey-uniformed valet trotted out to open Lulu's door. His mouth twitched a little when he looked at the vehicle. I guessed that he was expecting an all-you-can-eat buffet of Mercedes, Lexus, and BMW.

"We need to unoad, hon," Lulu said, somehow sounding overly-pleasant.

The words had hardly left her lips when his fellow valets swarmed around the car and started removing things from the back seat. The one who helped me out of the car and then to balance on one leg while I tried shaking out the pins-and-needles from my slumbering foot didn't look old enough to drive. It made me doubly self-conscious that he did a poor job of concealing his apparently positive assessment of my wardrobe. *I wasn't corrupting a minor, was I?*

A man in a tuxedo vest, shirtsleeves rolled up to his elbows, and an undone bowtie dangling from his collar, came out of the cut-glass and mahogany double front doors.

"Ah!" he said, grasping Lulu's right hand in his own and squeezing her shoulder with his left hand until she winced. "The entertainers are here. Welcome! I will show you place for set up."

I knew I'd seen him somewhere before. It took me a minute, but I realized that he was the guy I saw on TV the other day who took in RAD orphans. *What was his name? Boris something?*

"Yes," Lulu said. "Thank you." She gently pulled away from his grip. "I'm Lulu, this is Belinda, and our gift bag passer-outer here is Marti."

Boris smelled like cigarettes and expensive cologne.

"Excellent! Is good to meet you," the man said, vigorously shaking each of our hands in turn. "You call me Boris, da?"

He led us, followed by the laden valets, to a large conservatory which gave us an excellent view of the pool and outdoor kitchen.

"Miss Marti, if you would come with me? I show you where gift bags are located."

Lulu grabbed one of the shopping bags with her supplies. "Hold on a sec, honey." She rooted around inside it, finally coming up with two boxes of business cards. "Don't forget these."

I took them from her and followed Boris back into the foyer.

Boxes, stacked several layers deep, held row after row of red iridescent gift bags. I estimated that there were about two hundred of them.

"Please to hand each lady gift as she enters," Boris said.

I nodded. "Will do. I saw you on TV the other day. I think it's cool, what you're doing with the orphans."

Boris beamed at me. "Thank you, Miss Marti. These children are very special, even if most people cannot understand them."

"I'm sure."

"I must finish dressing – guests will be soon arriving. Is powder room there," he said, pointing to a closed door, discretely tucked almost out of sight underneath the grand staircase, "if you need to refresh yourself."

"Thank you."

Boris started up the stairs, two at a time. I thought I'd check out the powder room, more out of curiosity than necessity.

The walls were papered in a deep red velvet-flocked damask pattern. All of the fixtures were highly polished black ceramic, the tile was black, and even the countertop on the vanity was black granite. Dim recessed lighting kept the place from being cave-dark, but the mirror above the sink was lit up almost painfully brightly. Bottles of expensive perfume were lined up neatly on one side of the sink, and other bottles – hair spray, mousse, and powder commanded the other. It was almost like being in the ladies' lounge at an expensive department store. *If I'm going to get those goodie bags stuffed with Lulu's coupons, I'd better get a move-on.*

As I came out of the bathroom, I nearly knocked over a woman in a teal ball gown.

"I'm so sorry!" I said, touching her elbow. She was looked waifish – prominent cheekbones underscoring large, sad eyes.

"And who are you?" she asked, her grey eyes narrowing.

"My name is Marti. I'm here with the Tenth Sphere – the entertainers – and I'll be passing out gift bags at the front door."

She nodded. "It is good to meet you, Marti. I am Irina, and I am married to Boris." Something about the way she said it - perhaps because there was no spark in her eyes when she mentioned his name, or perhaps it was the way her thin shoulders squared themselves when she said her own name – that made me think that her marriage was more of a business arrangement than a love affair.

"Oh. It is nice meeting you, Irina. I hadn't realized that Boris was married."

"Didn't you?" she said, her lips pursing slightly.

Ohhhh. Did she think that I was interested in Boris? No worries there, sister.

"I must go and check on the catering, Marti. You enjoy the party."

"Thank you," I said as she swept away into the depths of the mansion.

The party had been going on for just over an hour, and I was out of gift bags. I decided to go find Lulu and Belinda to see what else I could do to help out.

Suddenly, Boris was at my elbow. "All finished with the gifts, Miss Marti? Very good. There is one more box in wine cellar. Anna can help you – she will be in kitchen." He pointed off to my right.

"Okay. I'll go find her."

It was weird, snooping around a stranger's house. But he had sent me off with only a hint of direction. Surely the kitchen couldn't be too hard to find. Maybe.

I followed my nose, and only made one wrong turn. Several hairnetted women dressed in white loaded either hors d'oeuvres or glasses of champagne onto serving trays, which were promptly whisked away by black uniformed waiters. Through the picture windows, I could see expensively frocked guests milling around the pool, the servers moving like shadows between them, delivering tidbits of food and champagne flutes without a sound.

"Hello?" I said to the busy ladies. "I'm looking for Anna?"

"I am Anna," a bruiser of an older woman said, her deep voice gruff. She did not appear to be pleased about being interrupted.

"Boris said you could help me get the last box of gift bags in the wine cellar."

One disapproving eyebrow raised above the other. "I am too busy now. Go through that door, then turn right. The door to the wine cave is in the hallway." She turned back to her canapés.

"Alrighty, then. Thanks."

She waved me away without looking up.

I opened the door she had indicated, and found myself in a softly lit corridor with plush carpet and cherry wainscoting on the walls, and a solid wood door about midway down the hall. This part of the house was quiet, away from the party, which seemed to be scattered over most of the property. I turned the knob and the door opened with a soft click.

Basements in Houston are cost-prohibitive, what with the high water table and unstable gumbo, so it is a rare thing to find one here. I had half expected a dank, dark concrete room. But this one was cozy. A lush Persian rug protected the marble tile from a heavy oak table in the middle of the large room. A cabinet with every shape and size of wine glass stood opposite me, and the rest of the walls were covered with floor to ceiling wine racks. A wrought iron stepladder stood in front of one of them. Curiously enough, a white painted door with a frosted glass window loomed near the glasses cabinet. It didn't match anything else in the cellar, and was jarringly out of place. I assumed that it led to another wine storage area, but I found it oddly disturbing.

There was no box of goodie bags anywhere to be seen. I walked around the cellar, just to make sure. I tried the white door, and discovered that it wasn't actually a door at all, but a trompe-l'oeil. Which made it even stranger.

Boris was mistaken about the box of gift bags. It was chilly in the wine cave, and I wasn't unhappy to head back up the stairs.

But the door to the hallway was locked.

I knocked politely, thinking someone must not have realized I was down there and closed the door I'd left ajar. "Hello? Can anyone hear me?"

Apparently, no one could.

I tried pounding harder on the door. "Hello! I'm locked in!"

Still no response.

I pulled my cell phone out of my bra strap and dialed Lulu's number. It went straight to voice mail. I tried Belinda's, with the same result. I pounded on the door again.

Nothing.

Probably no one else in the entire world goes to a gala fundraiser and finds a way to get locked in the wine cellar. I really, really hated to do this, but I didn't see what choice I had.

I dialed Nick's cell.

"What's up?" he asked.

"You're not going to believe this. And I wouldn't have bothered you if it wasn't an emergency. But I'm locked in Boris' wine cellar."

"Who is Boris? Where are you?"

"Boris is the guy hosting the fundraising gala at his house in River Oaks. My job was to pass out gift bags to the guests, but I ran out, so I came to the wine cellar to get some more, but there weren't any more, and somehow the door locked behind me. I tried calling both Lulu and Belinda, but their phones are turned off."

Nick was polite enough not to laugh out loud at me, but I could hear the amusement in his voice. "I see. And what, exactly, is it you want me to do?"

"I don't know. Can you call the house and tell someone to come let me out?"

"What's the name?"

"His first name is Boris. But his last name is tricky. It's Russian and starts with a 'C.'"

"Considering that the number is almost certain to be unlisted, it probably doesn't matter that you can't spell it. I can call one of my buddies to stop by there – his beat is close to that part of town."

"No! You can't send a car with uniformed officers here. Are you kidding me? The Society Page reporter is here, along with probably the two hundred richest people in Houston. I'm sure your friend doesn't want to be famous for being the cop that raided the biggest social event of the summer." I paused for breath. "I know it's a lot to ask, but could you just come and tell the security guard at the gate to let someone know I'm trapped down here?"

"Marti, I –"

"Please, Nick?"

He breathed out heavily. "Fine. I'll be there soon."

"Thank you so much." I gave him the address.

"You owe me big time for this."

"I know."

There wasn't much to do while I waited for Nick to send someone to rescue me. I plodded down the stairs and sat at the wooden table. *I'm such an idiot.* Since the cell was still in my hand, I decided to kill some time by reading an ebook. That lasted for all for three minutes before my battery died.

I left the phone on the table and walked around, reading the labels on the wine bottles. Surely the 1758 on one label of port must refer to when the winery was founded, not when that wine was bottled. Although, it was dusty enough. I might be able to believe it was over two hundred and fifty years old. Still, I suppose really old bottles of spirits show up from time to time, and if Boris was an avid collector, he certainly had the money to buy such things.

At long last, I heard the doorknob turn upstairs. "Hello?" I said, getting up to meet my rescuer.

"Marti? You okay?" Nick called down the stairs.

"Yeah, I'm fine. I–"

I couldn't believe it. Nick was on the third step down, and behind him, on the landing, stood a short, bull-necked man with a port wine stain birthmark on his head.

Bertram Kounis' killer.

"There is problem?" he asked.

"N-n-no, nothing's wrong," I stammered. "I'm just a little surprised that Nick came all the way into the house to look for me."

The killer's eyes glinted wickedly under the safety light. He stepped forward.

"Nick!" I yelled, just as he leaned over to give Nick a vicious shove.

He managed to catch the handrail, but momentum caused him to stumble, too quickly, down the stairs.

"What was that about?" he snarled at the short man.

"Is how we deal with spies," he replied with a smirk.

"What are you talking about?" I asked

Nick and I looked at each other, perplexed.

The man shrugged. "You deny it now. Boris wants to know where girl is getting information. But you, you are unnecessary. We play game, eh?"

"What information?" Fear made my voice shrill.

"You helped Boris track down old friend. And, by the way, your clutch needs adjusting."

"Your clutch?" Nick asked.

It took me a minute to work out what he was telling us. *Your clutch needs adjusting. Clutch.* Nobody would know that.

Unless he'd driven my car.

"You. You killed Bertram Kounis. And Dr. Pavlov."

The short man grinned, then pulled an evil looking knife from his boot.

"Why me?" I asked. "Why would you go to all that trouble to steal my car and run over Dr. Pavlov? How did you even know where I'd be?"

"Boris wanted to use your car to kill traitor to send you message – you are next. Do not play innocent. The two men who were following you last week. What did you do with their bodies?"

"I have no idea what you're talking about."

"On Thursday last week, two men, two good men, follow you to devil shop. No one sees them again. What did you do to them?" He shook the knife.

I tried to think of what had happened over a week ago, but details were hard to recall while being threatened with a Bowie knife. Halle had been with me all day. She disappeared while I was at work. We went to Circle. When I came out after I'd forgotten my phone, she had dirt on her face. She's bound to know something about it.

"I did nothing to them. I didn't even know they were there. Maybe they quit."

The man with the port wine stain scowled and moved closer.

Nick had put himself between me and the killer. But it should have been the other way around. I wasn't in any danger, at least not for the moment. It was Nick he was planning to kill, right here, right now. He now knew things he wasn't supposed to. And apparently, so did I.

I backed away from the approaching man, tugging gently on Nick's shirt as I went, to keep him moving with me. Not sure where I thought I was going, but it seemed a good idea to do something other than stand and be slaughtered.

The wine glass cabinet got closer, and so did the painting of the white door. Not realizing how fast the wall was coming up, Nick backed me into it, and I grunted. The wall switched from cold to warm, then solid to liquid, the un-door opened, and we tumbled through the wall into the dark.

Chapter 20
Under Cover

rap. Hadrian wasn't sure what to tell Sara, but he had to tell her something. He tapped his phone against his forehead, struggling with what to say. He opened his call history and touched her number.

"Hello?" Sara answered, her voice thick with sleep.

"Hey, babe. Sorry I missed your call yesterday. I had the ringer turned off so I could sleep, and I forgot to turn it back on."

"Hey, Blackbird." She only sounded half awake.

"Did I wake you?"

"Yes, actually."

Hadrian thought he heard the soft thump of a door closing in the background. Was she with Matt?

"Yeah," Sara said, her voice a little clearer. "I got a little concerned when I went to your apartment and you weren't there."

"I had gone out to get something to eat." That much was true. He'd eaten far too much at the Schmidt's block party, spent too much time with Marti.

"Oh. You feeling any better? Do I need to get my mom to make you a pot of chicken soup?"

Hadrian laughed. "That's okay. I'm a lot better now. So…you up for doing anything later?"

"Like what?"

Hadrian's competitive nature had kicked in. He wasn't going to let some kid waltz in and take his place with Sara. That, and he really needed to stop thinking about Marti Keller. "I don't know – maybe check out the IMAX at the Museum, and go to the Butterfly Center. Don't they have a new exhibit that just opened? Spy gear or something? We could grab something to eat after."

Sara laughed. "If they do have a travelling spy gear exhibit, you'd better give me the guided tour."

"I can do that. What time do you want to meet up?"

The spy gear exhibit consisted of items used during the Cold War – hollow nickels, carrier pigeon gear, a robotic fish. It was interesting to have a look at some of the old school methods. Sara seemed distracted, and Hadrian decided it was high time to distract her back towards him. The Egyptian Hall was extraordinarily dark. They must have taken a page from the Gem Vault. The brightly lit displays that made the dark seem even darker by comparison, made it easier to sneak in a public display of affection or two. Hadrian stood behind Sara as she looked at a sarcophagus.

He was too close, not quite touching her, but close enough to feel the heat of her body. He caressed the side of her neck as he placed one hand on her shoulder. He could feel her shiver under his touch. That was a good sign. He hoped.

It was Saturday night, exactly one week before the charity gala, and Sveklá had way too many things to do.

But, instead of doing them, he stared at the ceiling in the dark. *What have I done?* His body still buzzed from the deft application of Irinia's array of sensual skills. Her head rested on his shoulder, her bare flesh soft against his. He could not remember a time in his life when he had not wanted her. But now that she had given herself to him, no, more like taken him by storm, he felt awful.

He was betraying the one man who had always stood up for him, always protected him as a child at Babushkas, and gave him a job as an adult. The only two people in all the world that he cared for were waging war against each other, and he was being mangled between them. If there was a way to tear himself in half, so he could be loyal to both, he would do it in a heartbeat. But as it was, he would have to choose.

"Sergei?" Irina asked. She stroked his chest with her fingertips.

"Mmm?" Regardless of what his mind wanted, his body craved her. Again. Even though he knew if Boris found out, it would be the death of both of them. Perhaps that was part of what made the high so high.

"Do you know where Boris is now?"

"Out."

"He is at a hotel with three women. He texted me a picture." Her voice sounded soft and bruised. "I'll show you."

She got out of bed, and fumbled with her clothes on the floor. Sveklá was disappointed that it was too dark in the room to see her clearly. At last, she found the pocket that contained her phone. When she turned it on, the screen illuminated her face. A thin tear clung to her eyelashes as she opened her text messages. She slipped under the covers next to Sveklá, and showed him the photo.

It was hard for him to look at. Boris was grinning like a drunken teenager, with a gravity-defying set of enormous breasts hovering over his head. There were two other women with their heads in his naked lap. Sveklá could not bear to look at it. He turned the phone onto its face and set it on the nightstand.

He rolled over, scooping Irina into his arms and pulling her on top of him. "I am sorry, Irina. I do not know why he does these things."

"He does not wish to share power. He wants to break me. I think," Irina breathed in sharply, "that he is planning to kill me."

Sveklá caressed her cheek. "No, Irina. That cannot be so. Do you remember, when we left Babushkas, how Boris protected us? He would not have fought so hard to keep you alive, only to kill you himself now."

Irina sighed. "He fought for us because we belonged to him, not because he loved us. You have never understood that about him, Sergei. I think because you are not like him."

"I am certain that he loves you."

"I am certain that he does not. He is not capable of loving anyone. He is always playing chess in his head, and people, they are the pieces. You, Sergei, you are a rook."

"If I am rook, then you are queen."

"But Boris is still the chess master."

Sveklá stroked her hair. "Why you think Boris is planning to kill you?"

"I caught him taking some of my jewelry to give to one of his women. He laughed at me, told me that he bought it, and he would do what he liked with it. He said he would leave me a few pieces to wear at my funeral. I slapped his face, and he almost broke my wrist. He suggested I get a prescription to deal with my suicidal depression."

"But you are not depressed. Are you?"

"No. Angry. Very angry. But not depressed."

He knew that Boris was capable of appalling cruelty. But he found it hard to believe that he would kill Irina. "Perhaps he was just angry you found what he was doing," Sveklá said, but the words sounded hollow as they came out of his mouth.

"You are a good man, Sergei, to believe in your friends so." Irina traced a finger across his cheekbone and down his jaw.

He kissed her fingers, then her palm. She curled her legs up, knees against his ribs. When she sat up, she was straddling his hips. He let her guide his hands up her body. It wasn't that Sveklá had not been with a woman before. He had, many times, just never with one he loved. Irina was tough on the outside, but he knew she was fragile on the inside. Things that should never happen to anyone, much less his beautiful Irina, had happened to her. It was important to him that she was in control of their coupling, so that it wasn't too rough or painful for her. He couldn't repair the damage, but he could stop it from getting any worse.

He'd made his choice.

Chapter 21
Bright Falcon

ick landed nearly on top of me when the wall opened up and we fell through it.

The floor was rough, bare concrete, and it snagged a few of the sequins off my dress. They stood out against the stark grey floor like glistening droplets of blood.

"What the hell?" Nick asked, scrambling to his feet.

We were in a cage, 12 x 12, I estimated. A guard in a khaki uniform and furry hat barely gave us a second look, as if he'd been expecting us. There was a large control panel in front of him, and directly opposite us, a large observation window, blinds tightly shut.

"*Zdravstvuïte. Dobro pozhalovat' v yasnyy sokol.*" he said.

Nick and I looked at each other.

"I forget my manners," the man said with a thick Russian accent. "Welcome to Bright Falcon."

"I still don't understand," I said.

"You just arrive Kola Correctional Colony. We call it Bright Falcon. Boris will be with you when all party guests leave."

"Boris? The philanthropist, with the orphans?" I asked. I hugged myself and rubbed my upper arms. It was awfully chilly in here.

"Boris is man with many hats," the guard replied.

Nick grabbed the bars and tested them. Set in concrete, they weren't going anywhere. He scowled. "I'm not familiar with anything called 'Bright Falcon' in Houston, much less in River Oaks."

"Bright Falcon is in Kola Peninsula. Not so well known outside of Russia," the guard offered.

"It is not possible to walk through a door in Houston and come out in Russia," Nick said.

The guard shrugged. "But here you are."

"I don't believe we're in Russia. This is a trick. You've just cranked the AC all the way down, or maybe we're in an industrial cooler."

"Suit yourself," the guard replied, then tapped some text into his cell phone.

I tested the wall, just in case. But it was as solid as, well, a brick wall.

"Why are we here?" I asked. We may or may not have been in Russia, but we were certainly locked in a cage.

"Information," the guard said.

"About what?" Nick snapped.

"Is not for me to say."

Nick turned his back to the guard. "You've got your phone, right?" he whispered.

I patted my bra strap. It was flat. "No. I left it in the wine celler. Battery was dead, anyway."

A hint of a frown floated across his mouth. "When I get a chance, I'll use mine."

I nodded.

"To save you troubles," the guard said, "there is no cellular service here. You need satellite phone."

Just to be sure, Nick checked his phone. Instead of bars, he had an icon of a phone handset with a line through it.

I'm not sure how long I'd paced around that cell, partly to keep warm, and partly because I couldn't sit still. Nick was conserving his energy by sitting cross-legged on the floor, back against the iron bars. If he was cold, he didn't show it.

I felt relieved that at least Cassie was safe at home with Mom. If anything happened to me, at least she would be well taken care of. I wished I could get word to Quinn, but then I wondered if he would bother coming, if I did. Hunter, on the other hand, might come to rescue me, but I wasn't sure this was a job for a statistician. Guilt for dragging Nick into this washed over me. If I'd just been more patient, surely Lulu and Belinda would have noticed I was missing. But that did give me an idea.

I closed my eyes and silently called for Delilah.

"Girlfriend, you done put your foot in it this time."

I opened my eyes to see her standing on the other side of the bars.

Where are we? Are we really in Russia?

"Oh, yeah," she said, "you're in Russia alright."

I don't understand. How is that possible?

"The fae, and some of them demons, use portals. Kind of like mini wormholes, you know?"

Not really. But I'll take your word for it. How do we get out of here?

Delilah tugged at her earlobe. "That's a tricky one, girl. I'm not going to lie — there's some bad shit coming down on you just now. But when everything is on the line, if you trust your heart, you'll be okay."

Her words left me more agitated than comforted. *When everything is on the line?*

"You're stronger than you think," Delilah said. Then she patted my arm with her ghostly cold hand and vanished.

Dammit. I'd wanted to ask her to tell Lulu where Nick and I were, and to send help. But then I realized how ridiculous that was. No one would believe we stepped through a magic portal and ended up somewhere in Russia. And what would she do? Call the consulate? I had no idea where in Russia we were. The only one who could help was Quinn, and I had no way of contacting him.

We didn't have much longer to wait. Next to our cell, the wall shimmered translucent. First Boris, and then Irina, walked through it. Boris grinned, but there was cruelty rather than warmth behind it.

"Miss Marti, is good to see you again," he said, as if we had just run into each other at Starbucks.

"Why did you bring us here?" I asked.

"It is not obvious?" he asked.

"No," Nick said. I could hear the slow burn of controlled fury in his voice.

Boris continued to smile, but Irina hovered dourly behind him.

"I want to know how you found out about Dr. Pavlov. What else do you know about his work?"

"I don't know anything else. He was just a name in a contact list when I was trying to find my sister's doctor. I didn't know anything at all about Pavlov until that short guy with the birthmark on his head stole my car and ran over my sister's sequestered witness. She told me he was supposed to be going into the witness protection program immediately after the trial."

"She sequester him, so we monitor her calls. Smart girl, normally scrambles communications. One call, not encrypted. When you call Pavlov. We triangulate signal. Easy. Did she tell you what was reason for his protection?"

"No. She just said that he was an expert on attachment and conduct disorders. She was defending a kid with RAD – "

I stopped myself. Pavlov was an expert, probably *the* expert on RAD. And Boris took in RAD orphans.

"What did Pavlov know about you?" I asked him.

Nick's thumb was starting to tap on his knee. I knew he was used to being in charge and taking action, but right now, he wasn't able to do either. I could feel his agitation crackling in the air around us like heat lighting. It put me on edge, but Boris either failed to notice or disregarded it.

"Grigori was my oldest friend – I knew him from my time at Tri Babushkas. He worked for me after I started the Foundation, worked with the children. He did not understand, as I do, that these children were truly special. Grigori, he wanted to 'fix' them, make them more like normal. But they are fiercely loyal to their family, their brothers and sisters from Babushkas, and no one else. Many of them, they have excellent skill on internet. I teach them how to get money. Support themselves when they grow up."

"How much do you keep for yourself?" Nick asked, his staccato words bouncing off the cement like sonic bullets.

Boris chuckled. "Very good, friend of Miss Marti. Yes, I have expenses and I must be reimbursed. But they keep most of their earnings."

"What earnings are you talking about?" I asked, confused.

"He means he's teaching them to be cyber criminals. Isn't that right, Boris?" Nick said.

"That sounds very harsh," Boris answered. But he didn't deny it.

Irina leaned forward, on tiptoe, and whispered something in Boris' ear. He nodded. "Let us bargain. You know my secrets, so you cannot leave this place. If you tell me name of everyone who knows about me, I will break your necks before I feed you to Fenrir."

"What is a Fenrir?" Nick asked.

Boris laughed out loud, and even gloomy Irina smile a little. He nodded to the guard, who pressed one of the buttons on the console.

Each slat of the vertical blinds rotated from being parallel to the window to being perpendicular to it, then they all slid down the tract and disappeared into a recess. Pale yellow light flooded a skylight probably a third the size of the room and fell on what appeared to be a large pile of furs in the middle of the room on the other side of the glass. Then one of the pile's eyes opened, glowing electric blue.

I gasped.

The creature's other eye opened. I backed against the wall. Nick reached for his absent sidearm.

Then the beast stood up. It looked like a white wolf, fur edged in grey. Only it was the size of a Clydesdale, maybe even bigger.

"What do you want, Boris?" it asked, its tone equal parts boredom and annoyance.

"I was asked, 'What is a Fenrir?'," Boris said. "I am answering question."

In the furthest corner of the wolf's room, a door opened. A very tall man, I guessed seven feet or better, in leather pants and a cloak entered the room.

"Have you got it?" Fenrir demanded.

"No, my son. Be patient for a little while longer," the man said.

The wolf's lips pulled back in a semi snarl. "So close," he said. "I can feel it coming. My freedom. And when I am loosed, I will eat up every living thing I can find. None shall be safe! It will be payment for the thousand years' torment of being shackled to this wretched stone."

It seemed to me that he eyed Boris, in particular, when he said that nobody was going to be safe.

Nick started to laugh.

"I get it now. This is a dream. What else could it be? A magic wall that opens up and sends you from Houston to Russia? A giant, talking wolf? It's funny, though. I don't remember going to bed. But here I am."

"Nick, this is not a dream," I said.

"Of course it is." He uncrossed is legs and stretched them out.

"Okay, Nick. Okay. If this is a dream, why can't you walk through the bars? Or fly?"

He shrugged. "Not that kind of a dream."

Fantastic. If he thinks this is all a dream, no telling how he'll react when Boris tries to feed us to Fenrir. He might try to get away, but he might just fling both of us right into the wolf's maw. He might try jumping off a cliff or something.

"You seem to have problem," Boris said.

I glared at him.

Through the window into the other room, I could see the tall man leave the room. Moments later, three men, shackled and chained together, shuffled in. They wore what I guessed were poorly matched uniforms. As soon as they saw the monstrous wolf, they began screaming and cowering against the wall.

"It appears to be feeding time for Fenrir," Boris said.

"What?" I asked, unwilling to comprehend what he'd just said.

Fenrir grinned the way a fox grins at a mouse, and pounced on the first prisoner, jaws clamping around his body with a sickening, wet crunch. Bright blood spattered Fenrir's snowy muzzle. I turned around and slid down the bars as my knees gave way. I was afraid I was going to vomit.

"I wasn't expecting that," Nick said.

"Nick! You're not asleep!"

I rose to my knees and slapped him hard across the cheek. I got in his face, almost nose to nose. "You. Are. Not. Dreaming."

He slithered sideways to get away from me.

"This is real," I said.

His brow furrowed and he shook his head. "No," he said, but he seemed less convinced than he had been before.

"That's all very touching," Boris said. "But I do not suppose it much matters, at this point, what you do or do not know. You will die, whether or not you tell me. Fenrir has just been fed. Think about that. It will be your turn tomorrow."

The tall man who had been in the room with Fenrir came through the door near the guard's control panel and approached Boris and Irina.

"How much longer?" Boris asked, his words polite, but his tone brusque.

A single eyebrow arched above the man's icy blue eyes. "Soon."

The same color blue as Fenrir's I decided. After all, he had called the wolf "my son." How he came to have a canine offspring was more than I was interested in knowing. He was physically attractive, in an unconventional way, but there was something about him, a treacherous vibe perhaps, that also made him repulsive at the same time. To be fair, at least part of his physical attraction was that he smelled delicious – like cardamom and lemons.

"I do not understand what is delay, Loki. When you were set free, you said it would be no problem." Boris said.

Loki's eyes narrowed dangerously, and Boris took a step back. "I do not understand what is problem, Boris," he said, in perfect mockery. "When you unbound me, you said you knew that finding seven impossible things would take some time."

"How can you find even one impossible thing, much less seven?" Irina asked.

"That is the beauty of magick," Loki said, smiling. "To create a chain that Fenrir could not break was impossible. So the clever dwarves made a chain of six impossible things – the sound of a cat's footfall, a woman's beard, a mountain's roots, a bear's sinew, a fish's breath, and a bird's spittle. To break an impossible chain, an impossible blade, made of seven impossible things, is needed. To my dwarvish allies, I have already given a glass of burning water, dust from the grave a living man, a serpent's leg, hair from a babe birthed of a man, spider silk milked from a goat, and a vial of Kraken venom. The seventh item, the jewel from the gallbladder of a Nøkken, is proving more difficult. A great many of them seem to have died off since my imprisonment."

"What is a Nøkken?" I asked, forgetting I wasn't part of the conversation.

Irina's eyes widened, but a small, greasy smile oozed up the corners of Loki's mouth.

"A Nøkken is a large creature that lives in ancient lakes. It has a long neck, like a swan, and flippers, like a seal. And more teeth than the Orca. There was once one in Lake Seljordsvatnet, but it seems to have moved on. They are very rare and difficult to catch. Some say they are nothing but a fairytale, told to keep children from straying too close to the water's edge."

Nick snickered, although Loki's entrance had seemed to generate nothing but apathy from him.

I was familiar with lake monsters. Like Nessie. Or Quinn. I felt the breath catch in my chest. Wasn't he supposed to be in Scandinavia somewhere, watching Frost Giants?

"Sounds terrifying," I said, hoping that he hadn't noticed that my heart just skipped a beat.

He continued to look me in the eye, much longer than was comfortable or polite. His head tilted slightly to one side, then he turned abruptly and walked out. Irina and Boris followed him, although Boris paused to speak to the guard in Russian. I didn't like that he kept glancing over at Nick and I as he spoke.

I resumed my pacing, trying to keep warm. I would have traded my sparkly sequin dress for thick sweats and a hoodie in a heartbeat. I missed Cassie, and wondered what she was doing right now. I hoped she was sleeping soundly in her bed. I fretted about my sister, home alone with the twins and new baby, perhaps wondering where her husband was. What if I couldn't get Nick back to her? What if I died and left Cassie an orphan? I tried to avoid going down that road by distracting myself with thoughts of Hunter Greene, and his raven tattoo. I tried to focus on the details of sweat glistening on his chiseled muscles. The inky embrace of the raven's feathers around his shoulder, the pumpkin gnocchi, walking me home from Thursday night Circle. But try as I might, images of Hunter were pushed out by thoughts of Quinn – how he loved entertaining Cassie, his sizzling kiss, and his knack for showing up in the nick of time. The tiny little boat of my emotions rose on waves of anger, then dropped into troughs of sadness. I was actually glad when the guards came and opened the door to our cell.

There were three of them, the one who was there when we arrived, and two more. "Come with me," the original guard said. Even armed with machine guns, I might have been willing to challenge them and attempt an escape, if only Nick was with me. He was in complete denial about the very mortal danger we were in. He could not entertain the possibility that this was anything other than a dream.

We were escorted out of our cell and down a dilapidated corridor. White paint hung in strips from the ceiling, and pale blue paint flaked off of concrete walls. The air grew colder as we approached a double exterior door. The English-speaking guard punched in a code, and there was a loud click. The other two guards each pushed open a door, and we found ourselves on an island in the middle of a large lake. Beyond a razor wire-topped chain link fence, a dingy bobbed at the end of a decrepit dock. Seated inside the boat was an elderly woman, head covered with a bright blue kerchief, shoulders wrapped in a lacy shawl. A gnarled walking stick lay across her lap. She didn't seem to be suffering from the cold, although I was already shivering uncontrollably.

A gate in the fence was opened, and we were led out to the pier.

"In," the guard said, motioning toward the boat.

Lacking any better alternatives, I got in, followed by Nick. One of the guards also climbed aboard. The boat was well over capacity, and rode alarmingly deep in the water. The original guard stood, feet apart, arms crossed across his chest and watched us while the remaining guard untied the boat. When we had cast off, he picked up his machine gun and trained it on us. The guard in the boat began rowing us toward the rocky shoreline.

It didn't take very long to reach our destination five minutes or less, I estimated. The rowing guard hopped out and hauled the boat out of the water, then helped the elderly lady out. He just nodded toward the shore at Nick and me. When we reached terra firma, he stood behind us, Kalashnikov at the ready.

The elderly lady beckoned, and we followed her up the ridge. As we neared the top, I could hear the sound of a diesel engine running. Sure enough, down below was a snow crawler – a peculiar vehicle that appeared to be an unholy union between a truck and a tank. The large blocky chassis didn't appear to have any official insignia or identifiers, and it was painted with a snow camo pattern. Instead of wheels, it had treads. Two armed men jumped out of the back and prepared to receive their prisoners. Us.

The ride was bumpy and jarring, but at least the cabin was heated. It was the first time I'd felt warm since Nick and I fell through the wall. We drove for a while, perhaps as long as an hour, before we stopped. The door opened and the guards gestured with their rifles towards it. I started shivering again before I even reached the opening.

Note to self: don't wear stiletto heels to the beach next time. I had never been to the seashore this far north before. A colony of taupe-colored seals, all sporting ragged cream-colored spots on their fur, looked in our direction, but didn't seem too bothered by our presence.

We appeared to be free to go. But that seemed too easy, and I was reluctant to believe it.

I was right.

"There has been a change of plan," the old woman said. "Boris has decided to give you a sporting chance. On my recommendation, of course."

She pounded her cane into the beach three times, then started chanting in a language that I didn't understand. I tried to walk away from her, but my feet were rooted to the ground. The seals began to bark and call to each other, then stampeded into the water.

My skin began to itch. Then I felt cold and hot at the same time, almost like someone was pouring hot water on me, then rubbing my skin with ice. I gasped as my back was suddenly stretched and my ribcage felt like it was being pulled open by opposing elephants. My arms and legs began to swell, and my skin tightened and stretched painfully. I was startled by a ripping sound, then looked down and realized that my clothes were starting to tear apart.

My fingernails fell off, and were replaced by heavy black claws. Rough pads extruded from underneath my curling fingers and my palms. The same thing happened to my feet. By now, my beautiful dress was nothing more than a tragic and sparkling corpse on the beach, and my unmentionables weren't any better off.

It was at least as bad as childbirth, maybe worse, as my skull stretched and reshaped itself. I groaned as my jaws began to widen and extend. My teeth fell out. I couldn't help but to cry out as huge, sharp fangs pushed through my gums. I could smell my blood before I tasted it, as the wicked teeth forced their way out.

The itching intensified until it was unbearable. I needed to scratch, but I was unable to move. I whimpered out of frustration and dismay as fluffy white fur sprouted from my skin. That was the undercoat. Glossy guard hairs appeared next. When I opened my mouth to say something, a roar fell out instead of words.

My stomach growled. Nearby was an overpowering aroma. And it was delicious. I turned towards the source of it.

I was horrified to discover that as I was being turned into a polar bear, Nick was being transformed into a seal.

It was a struggle to restrain myself. I was so hungry, and he smelled so good. But I managed. I desperately studied him, hoping to find some special mark, or clue that would distinguish him from the hundreds of other seals in the colony. I just hoped that not too many of them had jagged white triangles on their left flippers.

I couldn't blame him for being afraid of me. Right now, I was afraid of me. Soda commercials notwithstanding, polar bears are huge and scary.

Nick finally flopped his way into the water, and I stood growling at the old woman. She smiled at me, and one of the men helped her back into the snow cat. Once he had climbed in himself, the engine growled as it churned its way up the slope. I snarled again with impotent rage.

Long after the noise of the machine faded into the distance, I sat on the beach and watched the seals. My stomach twisted and rumbled with hunger. I was unwilling to try to catch any of them, for fear of harming Nick – it would be hard to find the flipper pattern without catching the seal first. What had I done? How could I have gotten him involved in this? Would I ever see Cassie again?

A movement on the horizon caught my eye. Raising my head and scenting the air, I realized that there was a polar bear approaching. A male. I didn't want him hanging around – sooner or later, the seals would have to come back on shore, and I didn't want him anywhere near Nick. It was hard enough for me to resist eating him, and the other bear wouldn't care in the slightest that he was my brother-in-law.

I watched the other bear approach, loping across the snow. He stopped about a hundred yards from me, and stood on his hind legs, sniffing the air.

Unfortunately, I had no idea what polar bears did to claim their territory. I supposed that on their own, they probably clawed up trees and left scent markings of one type or another. But when directly confronted by another bear? I just did what a mother bear would do to protect her babies. I stood on my hind legs and roared. The sound was deep and harsh, nearly otherworldly. The other bear dropped to all fours. He didn't respond, but he didn't leave either. I took an awkward step towards him and roared again. He stayed put. Possibly, his hunger was stronger than his fear.

The seals were not on the beach, and therefore, not any easier for him to catch that they were for me. I suppose he realized this, because he began to meander down the beach, away from me. I watched until he disappeared, where the shoreline and the sky became indistinguishable.

I felt satisfied with myself for chasing away the other bear without any blood being shed, especially my blood.

Then I heard the splashing.

Seals leaped out of the water as an enormous black dorsal fin broke the surface.

Crap.

The seals wouldn't come on the beach if I was sitting there. But they couldn't stay in the water with the killer whales, either. I only saw one, but I knew they often hunted in packs.

Nick, if you get eaten by a polar bear or an orca, I'm going to kill you.

I trotted up the slope, away from the beach, so the seals could get out of the water.

If I had any chance of helping Nick, and myself, I couldn't just sit around looking at the delicious seals. First, I had to get something to eat. Then I had to find the old woman.

Chapter 22
When Life Hands You Lemons

he scent of the old woman – cardamom and lemons – was easy to follow. It lingered on the stones and floated in the air, when the wind wasn't whisking it away.

I followed her to a cabin, a hut, really, in the shelter of a cliff.

That was the good news. The bad news was that I was starting to feel light-headed from hunger. If I came across anyone right now, human or animal, I might not be able to control myself.

I stood up on my hind legs and breathed deeply, hoping to find something, anything edible. It was windy, but off to my left, I smelled water. Fresh water. Perhaps there would be fish.

I followed the smell of water until I came to a lake. There was something odd about it. An island in the middle reeked of fear and death. Even I feared being in sight of it.

But then there was another scent. Not fish. Not seal, but animal, and of the water. I crept towards the lake, wary, testing the air with each step.

And then I saw the long neck, rising from the water. The head that topped it wasn't large, but the mouth was filled with daggers. Could it be Quinn? How many others of his kind were there?

I reared up again to get a better view. The creature saw me. I wanted to get closer, but then a flash of color caught my eye.

There, to my left, the crone in her bright blue kerchief approached the lake. I had to catch her. No telling when I'd get another chance. I bounded towards her, moving as fast as my hunger-weakened legs would go. Cold seared my lungs, and spurred me on.

I saw her turn her head to look at me, and I could swear she smiled. Right before she started screaming.

I was closing in on her, and she waded into the water.

What was she thinking?

A dark ripple plowed under the clear surface of the lake, streaking towards the woman. *Oh, great. He was protecting her. Fantastic. Who does he think she is, anyway?*

I might be able to reach her first. I started into the water, but the kelpie got there before me. He raised his head high above her and hissed. I knew there was a possibility that this beast wasn't Quinn. But what if it was? Surely if he only knew what this old woman had done to Nick and me, he wouldn't be protecting her. I growled in frustration. Wondering how much maneuvering room the kelpie had, I moved from side to side, trying to see if he was resting on the bottom. I couldn't tell, so I reared up on my back legs. That didn't help, either.

"Listen to me!" I shouted at the creature.

But my voice only came out as a gravelly roar.

He hissed again, and we stared at each other for a lengthy moment before I retreated to beach and sat down, not wanting this confrontation. His neck was long and vulnerable, easily snapped by my strong jaws and sheer weight, if it came to that. But, if I missed, he had his own armory, and I suspected that his six inch teeth could penetrate even my heavy skull. I didn't want either of us to get hurt, even if that thing wasn't Quinn. On the other hand, I was hungry enough to eat a human, and it just might be that if the old woman died, her spell would be broken. At least, that's how it worked in the movies, anyway.

The decision was made for me when the kelpie dived underneath the old woman, scooped her up and swam off with her. I didn't try to pursue them. I had to eat, or I wouldn't be able to help anybody.

Using my nose when the wind died down, I eventually picked up the scent of something goaty. I followed it to a partially stripped reindeer carcass. The flesh was tough and stringy, but it was food. I cracked its long bones and ate the marrow, as well. Not much of a meal, but better than nothing. After I finished with the carcass, I looked around the area for something more. As I walked, I noticed something curious. Sprouting from vines creeping along the ground were red and orange berries. They looked like unripe blackberries, but I was hungry and didn't really care if they were ripe. Those berries were everywhere, and I walked along, nose almost to the ground, scooping up the little snacks as I went. It took a lot of them to fill me up, but there were countless numbers of them. It was difficult to tell how long this had taken – there was never any nightfall, only a bright twilight. I finally felt ready to get back to my hunt for the crone.

Going to the old woman's hut and watching for her to come out seemed like the obvious choice, but the area around her house was strewn with black rocks and the snow was thin, due to the hovel being in the lee of the cliff. Being a large white bear made blending in to the background difficult without much snow. No, I had to find a way that she wouldn't see coming until it was too late. I just hoped Nick was okay – he had as much experience being a seal as I had being a polar bear. I wasn't doing so well, and nothing was trying to eat me.

Grazing on berries the whole way, I found my way back to the old woman's shanty. I went around, far out of my way, and came up on top of the sheltering cliff. I couldn't see the shack, but I could see anyone approaching it. It was too high for me to be able to jump down without breaking my neck. I wished there was a big boulder I could roll down on top of it, but there was nothing larger than a basketball. If I had any reason to expect accuracy, that would be more than enough. That was an awfully big if, though.

I had just decided to go back the way I'd come when I saw something moving in the distance. I lay down, making myself as flat as possible, near the edge of the cliff. I could observe without being observed.

Quinn approached the cabin. The wind blew his dark hair back, away from his face, and his eyes squinted against the fresh breeze. I found it hard to believe he would just run off and leave Cassie and me without bothering to say goodbye, but here he was. But why? Was he in cahoots with the old lady? Did he know all along this was going to happen? Or was he walking into a trap? I wasn't sure how to feel, so I just sat and watched until he disappeared from my line of sight. After a few seconds, I heard a door open and shut. I could hear voices, but not well enough to make out words.

I got up and trotted back to where I could climb back down the cliff and go to where the shack huddled against the rock face.

While I didn't expect much success with a direct attack, I was so angry, both at what the old woman had done to me and Nick, and at seeing Quinn strolling around nonchalantly, that I grabbed a corner of the little building in my teeth and worried it like a terrier with a rat. The hut was surprisingly sturdy, and I accomplished even less than I had expected. I roared at the hovel. It shuddered and a few pebbles from the top of the cliff rolled down, ricocheting off the roof. One hit me in the face, and I let go of the corner.

The door had fallen ajar when I tried to demolish the little structure. I looked in the crack. Nobody was in the house. However, I could see an orange glow coming from an opening in the rocks where the shack clung to the cliff. Curious.

I thought my energy could be put to better use than being a Peeping Tom, so I started searching for the hag's spoor. There were traces of her all around, but none of them were fresh. Would it be worth my while to go search for Quinn? What would I do if I saw him? Roar? He could hiss back at me. Wouldn't that be a nice conversation?

No, what I needed was a plan. How was I going to catch the old woman? What was I going to do with her when I caught her? Knowing where she lived helped me far less than I had thought it would. It seemed to me that in so many stories, breaking the wand or staff of the wizard was always took away his power. She had a walking stick. Was it the same thing? The only sure thing was that if I didn't do something, I was never going to get back home to Cassie.

While I was coming up with a plan, I decided that I would go get a drink at the lake and see if I could find something to eat. The berries were wearing off.

I thought I was being careful. The only signs of life I saw on the way to the water were a couple of ravens. Those freeloaders were probably just hoping I'd kill something so they could get the scraps. I ignored them.

In the mud near the water, I noticed something. Tracks. Some were from horse shoes. Some looked human. Most of the ground was rocky, and didn't take footprints, but this little soft spot was covered in them. There seemed to have been two people here. One very large, the other smaller, but not small. I wasn't a tracker, but my guess was that unless Sasquatch had started wearing shoes, the larger tracks belonged to someone the size of a professional basketball player.

I sat down.

The only seven footer I'd seen in this area was Loki. And he was hunting for a kelpie. Even under my thick fur undercoat, I suddenly felt cold. Quinn was in danger, and there was nothing I could do to warn him. In fact, it may already be too late.

I studied the muddy area again. The big tracks didn't go into the water, and I could see no indication that something large had been dragged out of the lake.

A rock scraped against another rock, and I whirled around.

There was the kelpie, undulating up behind me. He'd been coming from upwind, so I hadn't smelled him. I dodged out of the way as his wicked jaws snapped shut on the space my head had just occupied. Reflexively, I raked at his face with my claws, drawing blood. He yanked his head out of reach. I backed away, out of range of his long neck. I took my eyes off of him for a second, when I noticed a patch of blue where there shouldn't be one, near all the footprints. The crone was watching us, her hideous mouth gaping open in a frightful grin.

I almost paid dearly for my moment of distraction. Quinn had swung his head at me like a wrecking ball and missed by inches. I felt the breeze of it as it flashed by me.

I couldn't bring myself to attack Quinn. But I wasn't about to sit around and let him kill me, either. Quinn's strength in that form was water, so I made sure to put as much distance between me and the water as I could. He could move faster on land than I'd originally given him credit for. But he wasn't as fast as me.

This ungainly dance up the slope of the beach was a draw. He'd swipe at me, I'd dodge and back out of his way. The effort it took for Quinn to move quickly on land was starting to show. His strikes were slower, easier to avoid. I didn't have a way to communicate with him. If he only knew who I really was, he would stop. I was sure of it. But how?

The gravel beneath my paws suddenly gave way. I tumbled down on my back and started to roll over. Faster that I thought possible, Quinn was partially on top of me, pinning my hind legs and trapping one of my forelegs underneath my body.

The snakelike neck reared back, and the jaws opened wide, poised to deal the death blow. There was nothing I could do but look into his eyes as they came at me like an on-rushing locomotive.

His teeth were blade sharp against my throat, and I could feel his breath on my jugular.

But he froze.

To my utter amazement, he pulled away. He looked at me, tilting his head from side to side. Did he realize who I was?

Pebbles crunched together and I saw the old woman streaking towards us, cane raised. I grunted and he looked around.

He jerked out of the way, the end of the cane grazing his neck before it hit the ground with enough force to break it in two.

The hag stood glaring at us, so angry she was foaming at the mouth. She leapt at Quinn, and I grabbed her blouse in my teeth. So much for my theory about the broken cane.

A horse whinnied in the near distance. The ground vibrated with its footfalls as it galloped towards us at twice the speed of a normal horse.

"Loki!" the man riding the horse roared.

The crone began laughing. And growing, stretching up taller and taller. Now, instead of the bent old woman, the tall man I'd seen on the island stood in her place.

His laughter deepened as he pulled a gleaming ax from his belt.

"You're too late, Odin!" he shouted back, raising the axe and angling it toward Quinn.

He might have been seven feet tall, but I was taller. I raised myself to my full height and put my front paws on his chest, pushing him back. Then I roared in his face and grabbed his forearm in my mouth, biting down hard until I hit bone.

He screamed and dropped the axe. In a flash, he'd turned himself into a crow, slipped through my teeth and flapped away, cackling.

I dropped back down to all fours. Odin pulled up his horse. It took me a moment to realize that the thing that looked so wrong about it was that it had eight legs instead of four.

"Are you harmed?" he asked.

Quinn and I looked at each other. The side of his head where I'd scratched him earlier was already almost healed. I felt I was in one piece.

Odin put his hands on either side of my head and I suddenly felt drunk. My eyes closed and I swayed, but he held me up. It seemed like a tornado was whirling inside my body, and every single molecule was caught in the vortex. The motion slowed, and I opened my eyes.

The first thing I saw was my hands.

Hands! Not paws. I was back to my normal self. Odin had the foresight to generate some clothing for me as well, because I was dressed in white pants, a white sweatshirt, and a thick white parka.

Quinn scooped me up in his arms and crushed me against him.

"I'm sorry," he said. "I'm so sorry. I almost killed you."

"Can't...breathe." I managed to wheeze.

He let go and cupped my face in his hands. "What are you doing here? Where's Halle?"

"I have no idea where Halle is. Isn't she with you?" I asked, my enjoyment of his touch suddenly tempered.

"No. She said she would look after you while I was gone." Quinn shook his head.

While I was gone. That implied that he had intended to return.

"You could have at least left a note." I wasn't going to let him off the hook that easily.

"I did."

"There was no note."

"I left it stuck on the fridge with a magnet."

Odin cleared his throat and looked up at the sky.

"Never mind," Quinn said. "I think I know what happened to the note. Hurricane Halle."

That made sense. "How did you know?"

"Know what?" he asked. His mouth smiled, but his eyebrows furrowed slightly.

"That it was me. That I wasn't just any ordinary polar bear."

Quinn brushed a stray lock of hair out of my face. "From the first time I saw that bear, I knew there was something different about it. When I got close to you, I caught a whiff of lemon blossoms. Your hair always smells like lemon blossoms."

"This is very charming," Odin broke in. "But we are running out of time. And you," he pointed to Quinn, "do not, for any reason, shift into the form of the Nøkken."

Odin scanned the horizons. "Our reinforcements should be here soon."

Without warning, there was a tremendous *Boom!* and fire shot out of one of the windows of the main building on the island. Men screamed and shouted. Then there was silence.

"What's happening?" I asked.

A plume of black smoke billowed out from another part of the building. A wolf howled, and it was such a deep, chilling sound that I involuntarily took a step backwards.

"Fenrir has been unchained," Odin said grimly.

Chapter 23
Loyalty Among Thieves

hat smoking island in the middle of the lake was the last place I wanted to go.

"We have to save Nick," I said.

"Nick? What is he doing here? And how did you get here?" Quinn asked.

"I'm not sure we have time for this," Odin said.

I looked at him and gave a demi-smile. "Long story short, I was working at a party, got locked in the wine cellar, called Nick for help, and we fell through a door painted on the wall and ended up there," I pointed to the island. "The old woman, who turned out to be Loki, turned me into a polar bear and Nick into a seal. We have to change him back, before something happens to him."

"Understood," Odin said. "But we need to see what is happening at Bright Falcon, first."

"We don't have a boat," I said.

"We don't need one. We have Sleipnir."

Odin sprang into the saddle, Quinn lifted me up behind him, and then he vaulted up, sitting practically on top of the poor horse's hips. Sleipnir didn't seem to mind, and he half-reared as Odin spurred him. He galloped over the water just the same as if it had been land, then leaped up onto the island where it rose from the lake.

"That's a neat trick," I said.

Odin smiled. He put his hand to the gate and the locks snapped open. Quinn and I followed him into the prison yard.

"That's strange," Quinn said.

"What?" I asked.

"I've been calling Malik ever since Loki escaped, but he hasn't responded. He's supposed to be watching the jötnar, not far from here. He should be well within range. He heard me last time with no trouble."

"Hmh," said Odin.

We dismounted and left Sleipnir in the shelter of an empty vehicle shed. We made our way into the prison. Bloody corpses – some guards, some prisoners – were strewn everywhere. Steam rose from a broken radiator pipe. There was a massive hole in the wall to the windowed room which had contained Fenrir.

"This is the work of the jötnar," Odin said with a scowl.

A deep-throated howl echoed off the bare concrete. Not the howl of a wolf, but the howl of a man who has been wounded down to his soul. Quinn put his hand on my shoulder.

We picked our way through the glass and debris, moving towards the source of the sound. A reinforced door on the other side of Fenrir's enclosure hung from one hinge. Another howl reverberated out of the darkness behind the doorway.

Odin led the way into the murky corridor. Light from the collapsed roof shone on the far end of it. There was a figure there, a very large figure, standing against the wall, arms in the air.

"What trouble have you gotten yourself into now, Loki?" Odin asked, crossing his arms over his chest.

Loki's arms were manacled above his head. An ax was poised at his throat, ready to lop off his head if he moved his weight from a brick that held down the other end of the heavy gauge wire. The edge of the brick was narrow, and Loki's feet were large. If he lost his balance, his head would roll.

"Those traitors, Boris and Irina, have stolen Fenrir and done this to me. I will grind their bones to dust when I catch them! The man with the serpent's eyes cannot long protect them. I never thought my kin, the jötnar, would allow such a thing to happen," Loki fumed. The brick rocked back and forth as he talked. "Release me!"

Quinn's face went a shade or two paler.

"Is Fenrir loosed then?" Odin asked.

"He is still bound with Gleipnir, but Gleipnir is no longer bound to the rock."

"I see no reason we should do anything other than leave you here," Quinn said.

I felt bad for Loki, but I didn't disagree with Quinn, either. Loki had just turned me into a polar bear and Nick into a seal, then he'd pitted Quinn and I against each other in a duel to the death. I had no doubt he would kill Quinn at the first opportunity, to get the Nøkken's jewel, if he was released.

As I looked at Loki a little closer, I realized that there was a note pinned to his chest with a shard of glass.

"What's that?"

Odin removed the note, scowled at it and thrust it at Quinn. He scanned it, then closed his eyes for a moment and swallowed hard. His shoulders slumped a little.

"What does it say?" I asked, reaching out for it.

A spidery handwriting crawled across the paper. I read it out loud. "Do not think I have been unaware of you watching me, fay. I warned you not to meddle in Balcones' business. Now, I have the ultimate weapon. There is no end to Fenrir's appetite, and he cannot be killed by any mortal man. Between him and the Berserkers provided to me, courtesy of the jötnar, I am an unstoppable force. Now, where shall I test my new weapon? Perhaps at the Model NATO Student Diplomat Festival in Geneva tomorrow. A shame so many bright young people and their families should end up as wolf fodder. Or perhaps I should start with your girlfriend's house. It worked so well the last time. Decisions, decisions."

Quinn looked like someone had whacked him with a 2x4. "I knew the Frost Giants were involved. But not Balcones. I had no idea."

"Do not let him goad you into doing something rash," Odin said. "He may only be guessing, trying to trick you into betraying your hand."

Quinn's eyes went kelpie black, and he kicked a piece of wreckage. Loki jumped at the sound, and nearly fell off his brick.

"Of course you knew Balcones was involved. You've been chasing him for weeks," I said.

"No. I knew the Frost Giants killed Siobhan. She was on my team. We...had a relationship. I had no idea Balcones had anything to do with her death."

"I'm sorry," I said. I took his hand, and he squeezed my fingers gratefully. "Do you think he will really hurt Cassie?" I asked, trying to push down the rising panic. "And my parents?"

"Not if we stop them first," Loki said. His voice was butter-smooth. "Please. Release me. I can help track him down. I want my son, Fenrir back at least as much as you want Balcones."

Odin reached out and took hold of the ax at Loki's throat.

"What are you doing?" I asked, unable to believe he was just going to let him go.

Odin shook his head. "The Prophecy cannot be unmade. It is fated that Fenrir shall be unbound and unfettered, and he shall swallow me alive. Still, my son Vidar will break his jaws and Fenrir will be slain. It is not what I would wish, but it is what must happen. Loki will no doubt track Fenrir like a hunting hound if he is paid for it with my blood."

"He still needs the Nøkken's jewel," I reminded him. I glanced at Quinn, but I didn't miss the fleeting gleam in Loki's eyes when I mentioned the jewel.

"He can only take it if I'm in kelpie form," Quinn said.

Odin released the haft of the ax from its improvised trigger. I didn't trust Loki as far as I could throw him, but I seemed to have precious little choice in the matter. Odin touched the manacles, and they clanked open. Rubbing his wrists, Loki stepped off the brick.

"I have upheld our end of this evil bargain, my brother," Odin said. "Now, find Fenrir."

"As you wish," Loki replied with an unctuous smile.

Ahead of us lay a tunnel that sloped gently downward. It wasn't well lit, and sounds of dripping water, sizzling, and the occasional metal clanging made it even less inviting. Loki started down it. Odin hesitated, then whistled for Sleipnir. The horse was reluctant to follow, but did as he was asked. His nostrils flared and he snorted the entire way. The slope bottomed out, went level for a time, then changed direction. We all seemed to be walking faster, hurrying to get out of the frightful place.

Finally, we came to the top of the grade. A ruined steel door lay a few yards away from its frame. But I think we may have jumped out of the frying pan and into the storm. The wind was howling, and the sky was a strange color, a swirl of purple and green. A few glowering grey clouds scudded by on the fierce wind.

"It has begun," Odin said. He looked to the sky. Two black dots, high up, came hurtling towards us. Huginn and Muninn landed on Odin's shoulders. "Tell the host to meet us on the battle plane. We are traveling there with all haste. Time is short. Fly!"

The ravens took off, back in the same direction they came from. I looked towards my right, and there was what looked like a pillar of smoke coming from the horizon.

Odin followed my gaze with a grim smile. "The Valkyries are coming."

I wondered if that included Halle. I had a few choice words for her when this was over. I stood and watched the cloud approach. It reminded me of watching the bats come out from under the Waugh Street Bridge during the summer. Loki raced around like a demented bloodhound, looking for clues as to which direction Fenrir had gone.

Most of the Valkyries circled overhead. One started dropping down towards us. I bet I knew exactly which one it was. Although I hadn't expected her to be riding a huge black horse with wings, fangs, and glowing yellow eyes. This must be where the word "nightmare" comes from.

"Odin," I said. "We have to rescue Nick. He doesn't know the first thing about being a seal. Something is going to eat him." *If it hasn't already.*

"Halle can take you," he replied. "Be swift."

As soon as her scary black horse's feet touched the ground, I said, "We have to go get Nick."

"Where is he?"

Quinn boosted me up onto the horse's broad back, behind Halle. He kissed me on the forehead while he was doing it. "For luck," he'd murmured. Then he gave Halle a hard look. "Leave Nick alone. He doesn't belong to you."

"What do you mean by that? Of course he doesn't belong to her." *Weren't there enough complications already without Halle trying to poach every man she met?*

"I am a Valkyrie. Do you not know what Valkyries do?"

The horse shifted, and I had to grab Halle so I didn't fall off. "I don't know. Walk around in bronze bikinis and horned helmets? Can we just go and get Nick now?"

Halle clucked to her horse. "Rädsla, up!" The black mare leaped into the air. Even holding on to Halle, I nearly slipped off Radsla's butt.

"Valkyries are choosers of the slain. We choose the very best warriors to go to Valhalla, to fight with Odin on the day of Ragnarök. It is our choice who lives or dies during battle."

"Don't. You. Dare. I'm sure Nick would be flattered to know that you thought he was one of the very best warriors, but he has a beautiful wife, two young sons, and a brand new baby. It seems totally unfair for you to involve him in this. He never did anything to you."

I had to close my eyes because I was getting a terrible case of vertigo. I never even liked to go on glass elevators. My other senses automatically sharpened when I shut my eyes. I could hear the whuff, whuff of Rädsla's wings beating the cold air. I was sharply aware of the warm horsey smell rising around us and masking the crisp, snowy scent of arctic breeze. The mare's back was relatively steady, but her ribs moved in and out a lot with each breath, making my legs unsteady. It had been a long time since I'd ridden a horse. When we lived out in the country, we weren't too far from Gracie. She competed in barrel racing, but there was always a quiet horse around their farm that I could ride when I came over, which was often. Riding a horse isn't quite the same as riding a bicycle – you do forget if you haven't done it in a while.

I was thankful that Odin had set me up with such a warm coat. It was cold up here. I wished I could relax and enjoy the view. The trouble was the view made me nauseous, and I couldn't relax because I was concerned about my family being eaten by a giant wolf. That niggling worry edged everything in my mind.

"Where did you see him last?" Halle asked.

"That's a good question. They drove us in a snow truck from the island out to the beach."

"Landmarks?"

"Being kidnapped, held at gunpoint, and turned into a polar bear kind of put a crimp in my enjoyment of the landscape."

"A polar bear? What are you talking about?" Halle asked.

"On the beach, I didn't know if they were going to shoot us or just leave us out there, but Loki turned me into a polar bear and Nick into a seal."

Halle made a noise, that if I were feeling charitable, would say was her clearing her throat. Otherwise, it was suspiciously like a stifled laugh. "That sounds like Loki."

My eyes were still tightly closed. I opened one part-way. The view was stunning, but my head swam and invisible hands seemed to be clutching at my stomach, squeezing and twisting it.

I decided to try focusing on the panorama over Halle's shoulder and not look down. I still kept one eye closed.

"I think I've found the seals," Halle said.

Rädsla began her descent. It wasn't a steep bank, but it was enough to make me queasy.

It did not help that three tall black dorsal fins rode high in the water. I would never forgive myself if Nick got eaten by a killer whale.

"How can you tell which one is Nick?" Halle asked.

"There's a whitish triangle on his left flipper."

"That doesn't help much, unless you know a way to ask the seals to all line up on the beach for you to examine."

The black dorsal fins ominously disappeared. *Please, please, please be okay, Nick.*

"Can you get low above the water? Maybe I can call him."

Rädsla dropped down until her hooves were skimming the waves.

"Nick!" Halle and I both called out, over and over.

Halle guided the horse in an increasingly larger spiral around where we'd last seen the seals.

"If we do not find him soon, we will have to try again later," Halle said, glancing toward the sky. The Valkyries were a diminishing swarm in the distance.

"We can't leave him! Nick! Please come out!"

I caught a flash of movement near a rocky outcropping on the beach side of the spiral.

"What's that over there?"

Rädsla banked in that direction. We found a group of five seals on the rocks. A very large orca had them cornered. He was whistling and clicking to call his pod over. The outcropping was narrow, and it wouldn't take much effort to yank the poor things into the water.

"Nick?" I called.

The largest of the seals, also the one who was closest to the edge, looked up.

"Halle, I think that's him."

Rädsla circled the seals, and sure enough there was a whitish triangle on the seal's flipper.

Unfortunately, I hadn't given much thought to the logistics of lading a one hundred fifty pound seal onto the back of a horse that was hovering over the ocean. The outcropping wasn't solid enough for Nick to travel all the way to the beach, and jumping in the water with the killer whale was not likely to end well.

There was a loud whooshing, and an animal a little larger than a Chevy Suburban appeared near Rädsla's head. It almost looked like it was smiling at us as we were abruptly at eye-level with him.

I thought that breaching was an odd thing for the whale to do. But then I realized why it was so clever. When he landed back in the water, he created a wave which nearly washed the seals off the rock. A small seal would have been pushed over the edge, if the largest hadn't put his bigger body in the way. That was definitely Nick. A second orca came up on the other side of the rock and missed Nick's tail by inches. "We've to get rid of these killer whales! If they can't get the seals, they'll start going for Rädsla next."

Halle muttered something I didn't' understand. Rädsla screamed with rage. The next dorsal fin that popped up, she caught in her teeth. Not horse teeth, but the sharp, wolfish fangs I'd glimpsed earlier.

Blood ran down the sides of the dorsal fin, and the orca started to dive. I wasn't sure if Rädsla was trying to keep the whale on the on the surface, or if her fangs were stuck in the cartilage of the fin. Two thousand pounds of marine mammal in the open water was a definite advantage over fifteen hundred pounds of flying horse. Gravity was on the whale's side. My feet, then lower legs went into the water as the orca pulled us down. Again, Halle shouted and the mare let go. I wasn't sure if I was shaking from the cold or from fear.

"Get a little closer to the rocks so we can get Nick."

Tall dorsal fins circled the outcropping, but the orcas didn't surface. It was not easy to watch them and tug Nick onto Rädsla's back between Halle and myself. He was slippery, mostly inflexible, and didn't offer much in the way of handholds. At least he wasn't a walrus. We finally managed to drag him up and lay him precariously across Rädsla's back.

"Nick, don't move. If you fall off the horse, there isn't going to be a way to catch you. We'll get you to Odin, and he'll change you back. Just hang on, okay?"

The flying horse began to rise slowly, gently into the air, and I supposed that she would stay as low as she could, at least partly because of the extra weight.

The killer whales had gone, and I'd assumed that it was because of Rädsla's attack. But I noticed that the water around the rocks was quickly retreating, as if someone had pulled a plug somewhere on the ocean floor, and it was draining away. I felt the hair on the back of my neck rising.

"Tide's awfully fast around here," I said.

"That isn't the tide," Halle replied.

I had remembered reading somewhere that before a tsunami, the tide goes out both much faster and farther than usual, and at the wrong time. I looked out toward the water. There seemed to be an island forming a couple of hundred yards away from us.

"Rädsla! Up! Up!" Halle shouted. "Hold on tight," she added as an afterthought.

"Halle, what's happening?"

"Jörmungandr is rising."

"I don't know what that is," I replied through clenched teeth. I was holding on to Halle with one hand and Nick with the other. His weight was pushing me backwards, due to the steep angle Rädsla's back had suddenly acquired.

"Jörmungandr is the Midgard Serpent, Fenrir's brother, and Loki's son. He lies under the ocean and circles the world, clasping his own tail in his jaws. When he lets go of his tail, it is the time of the world's end."

Chapter 24
Contracts

oris did not trust the Frost Giants. But Balcones, he had made an offer Boris couldn't refuse. Loki had wanted to release Fenrir just to get revenge against Odin. The end of the world was merely an unfortunate side effect, collateral damage. Balcones had a plan. In the developing world, kidnapping was a common tactic to raise cash fast. But why settle for kidnapping individuals? With a weapon like Fenrir, entire governments could be held for ransom, or toppled for a generous fee. For his cut, all Boris had had to do was free Loki and let him collect all the materials to set the wolf loose.

Boris had known, all those years ago when he'd stumbled onto the chained Fenrir, that he was sitting on lighting in a jar. He hadn't known how to harness what he had, but he'd had plenty of money to lubricate the palms of local officials to award the contract for building the Kola Correctional Colony to his own company. Feeding Fenrir would make him grow, and what better food source than the cast-off dregs of humanity? People whom would not be missed or mourned. Of course, the original proposal for the colony came at Boris' request as well. He thought of the provincial governor whom he'd persuaded to submit the request. The governor had killed himself soon afterward. Boris had been disappointed that his asset had put himself out of play, but he had shrugged it off. If one has skeletons in one's closet, one should not participate in public office.

He stood smoking a Black Russian cigarette at the edge of the ice cave, and pulled his coat tighter around himself against the wind. He didn't understand why Balcones had insisted on taking Fenrir now. Loki still had one element left to find. He would rather have kept the beast in Bright Falcon, where he could easily come and go through the portal. Being stuck in this freezing cave brought back too many bad memories and made him cross.

And speaking of things that made him cross, he should probably ask Sveklá to kill his wife. He knew that the man was quite fond of Irina, but he was also an excellent lieutenant, and always did as he was told. Irina had been necessary when the three of them had escaped from Babushkas. When they'd finally made their way to St. Petersburg, he'd sold her by the hour to pay for food and shelter. She was already so damaged at that point that he didn't think it would do her any more harm. Besides, everyone had to pull their weight.

She was very clever, and she made a lovely figurehead for the Cherngelanov Foundation. Still, he'd grown tired of her, even though she always did things he craved, like arranging not one, not two, but three prostitutes for him last week on his birthday. She'd even taken a photo on his phone to remember it by. Perhaps he should just give her to Sveklá as a bonus for a job well done.

Fenrir lay sleeping at the far end of the cave. It was never dark in the cave, but never truly light, either. The sun shone through the ice with an unsettling blue light. He was tied by the flimsy chain – Boris had seen thicker jewelry chains – but the monster either couldn't or wouldn't break free. He was guarded by one of the Frost Giants. As he watched, he saw Irina appear from the depths of a tunnel in the ice and began a conversation with the giant. After a while, the Frost Giant left, leaving Irina in charge of the wolf.

From where he was standing, Boris could not hear anything Irina said, but he did see one of Fenrir's great blue eyes open. Irina talked some more and the other eyelid raised.

Boris thought it would probably be in his best interest to join the conversation. It could be dangerous to talk to such a creature as Fenrir, and Irina might need protecting. Or at least monitoring. Dragons are said to have irresistible, hypnotic voices. Perhaps Fenrir was the same.

He took a final pull on his Sobranie, and flicked the shiny gold filter out of the cave. His stride was purposeful as he made his way to where Irina and Fenrir were talking. Boris exuded confidence from every pore. He kissed Irina on the cheek, a gesture of ownership rather than affection.

"Pah!" complained Fenrir. "This one stinks."

"I'm sorry for that. But he is well fed." Irina answered.

"I can see that," Fenrir said, eyeing Boris in a way that made him take a step backward.

"Irina, darling, what are you talking about?" Boris asked.

"You, of course, darling Boris. Is not everything about you?"

Boris was taken aback. It seemed uncharacteristic of Irina, to be so bold. Perhaps he should have Sveklá kill her, after all.

"I do not like this arrangement with Balcones," she continued. "We have housed and fed Fenrir all these years, at great expense, I might add. He's grown even larger than when you found him. Why should Balcones step in and take all of the money?" As she spoke, Irina had backed away from Boris, slowly, almost imperceptibly, one tiny step at a time.

"He is not taking all money!" Boris snapped. He didn't like her insinuation that he had made a bad bargain. Was she calling him a fool? Perhaps he wouldn't bother Sveklá, and just kill Irina himself.

"I have made my own deal," She untied the knot that fastened Fenrir to a large rock. "Goodbye, Boris," she said, then disappeared back down the tunnel.

In an instant, Fenrir was on his feet.

"Hello, Boris," he said with a wicked grin. Frothy slaver dripped from his wide jaws.

Before Boris could turn to run, Fenrir was on him Bones crunched and tissues squelched as the great wolf swallowed Boris head first, like a python swallowing a rabbit.

Chapter 25
Plain of Vigrid

he various Aesir had been filtering into the camp as soon as it had been made. There were a lot of tall, blonde goddesses that were hard for me to tell apart, both from each other and the Valkyries. Thor was easy to remember because of his hammer, and Tyr had only one hand. They stood talking to Nick, who was still a little rubber-legged after having just been turned back into a man from having been a seal for days. They were comparing hero notes, I supposed, although it looked like Thor was doing most of the talking. His fingers traced the tip of the engraved war horn that hung from his belt, as if he was anxious to blow it and get the battle started. I shook my head. Portals and giant talking wolves, Nick couldn't accept. But add a few muscle-bound warrior gods, and he's all over it.

There had been minor earthquakes all morning, and smoke poured from what must be a volcanic mountain top maybe ten miles away.

I hated this.

This was not my fight, but Balcones had threatened my family, my baby, and I could not just go home and pretend everything was fine. Because it might not be. I had to stay here and make sure that Fenrir was dead, see it with my own eyes, before I could believe it. Odin had assured me that the prophecy foretold Fenrir's death. As well as his own. But prophecy is a slippery thing.

Nick had been bewildered to find that the person whom he was so sure was a low-life criminal and drug user at the camp.

"Try and think of it as an undercover operation. There really was a Marc McLeod – I just borrowed his identity. He didn't need it anymore," Quinn said.

"The real McLeod is dead?"

"Yes."

"Did you kill him?"

"No. He'd chosen a high risk lifestyle," Quinn said, but didn't elaborate.

Nick nodded, but I think it was less that he accepted Quinn's story, and more that he believed that junkies tended to have short life expectancies. That was probably the only thing that made sense to him.

Quinn scowled.

"What's wrong?" I asked.

"I've been trying for days now to reach Malik. He doesn't seem to be able to hear me. I hope…I hope he's okay." he trailed off.

Odin had found woolen shirts, chain maille, leather armor, and shields for Nick, Quinn and myself, and given each of us a spear, axe and bow. My axe was the lightest, and I still needed both hands to lift it. Nick wasn't used to old school weapons, but found he liked the chain maille. It looked strange on him. Not bad. Just not normal.

"Maybe I'll start wearing this instead of my Kevlar," he joked.

"The Renaissance Festival is coming up," I reminded him. *Assuming we survive this.*

He seemed to be taking this in stride now, considering that earlier he steadfastly maintained that the whole thing was a dream. I didn't want to ask if he'd changed his mind, or if he'd just decided to play along.

Because I was a nurse, and Nick was not trained in using Viking weapons, it had been decided that we'd stay at the camp and tend to the wounded. Most of the wounds were likely to be mortal, so I suspected that it was Odin's way of keeping us from getting underfoot.

Quinn was going with the Aesir. Where Nick's mail and leather looked anachronistic, his suited him. I had no way of knowing if it was faery glamour, or just him, but he looked incredibly sexy, all kitted out for battle. Part of me hoped that we both lived long enough to do something about it. He put his arms around me, but the stiff leather armor was an uncomfortable barrier between us. Then he raised my chin up with his fingers.

"In case I don't see you again," he said.

Then he kissed me, warm, soft and slow. My body felt like it was on fire, melting and reforming. I could feel my heart beat, pulsing pleasure through every corner of my body.

Nick cleared his throat. Loudly. Twice.

Quinn pulled away from me, and I suddenly felt cold. I knew it wasn't his fault that Halle had stolen the note he left, but there were still some rough edges, and I found it impossible to go back to exactly the same place I had been before I believed that he had abandoned Cassie and me. Although, if he kissed me like that another time or two, it might not be so difficult.

Over Quinn's shoulder, I could see a Valkyrie's black horse spiraling down towards the Earth. Halle and Rädsla approached the camp. Odin gestured to the Aesir and they came to listen to her report. Nick came and stood near me, warm in the seal-colored coat that Odin had dressed him in when he transformed him back into his normal shape.

"The jötnar are gathering. There are also dwarves, trolls, and wargs. Curiously enough, Quinn's demon is with them. He wears a red anorak, and has the ear of the jötnar leader."

"How many did you count?" Thor asked.

"It seems as if all of Jötunheim has been emptied onto the Plain of Vigrid," she replied.

A roar went up behind us.

I turned to find a legion of men pouring out of a rift in the cold, clean air. Behind them, I could see what looked like a gigantic mead hall. The men were semi-transparent, and dressed in furs and leather – ancient Vikings.

"The warriors of Valhalla have been summoned," Odin said.

The smoke coming from the mountain changed from white to black, obscuring the sun. Another earthquake made the ground shudder and jump under our feet. It was the strongest one yet. Nick caught me as I stumbled.

Drums sounded from the other camp. *Doom. Doom. Doom.*

"It is time! To horse!" Odin called.

Horses were brought for the Aesir and they mounted up. Odin raised his spear. "It is a good day to die!"

Thor put his war horn to his lips and it bellowed out the call to combat. Odin's spear came down and the battle cry of five thousand warriors echoed off the mountains. They charged past us, an angry tide of death and destruction.

The ground shook under the massive jötnar as they ran to join the fray, and the two armies clashed in the middle of the plain. Swords clanged together, and the dull light glinted off maille and weapons. Axes flashed as they sliced through the air. Men shouted battle cries, and the wounded screamed in agony.

How casualties were meant to arrive from the battle field to the camp, I wasn't sure. Odin had been a little unclear on that. Behind us, on the sea side, I heard a loud hissing, like a gigantic kettle was boiling away.

A shadow fell across us.

I turned to see an immense snake, as big around as a house, rising up behind us from the water. That must be Jörmungandr.

"Nick, run!" I screamed into the wind.

We scrambled to get out of the way, but he was slithering back and forth, and it was near impossible to tell which way he was going next. He saw us, finally, although we must have been like flies to him. He raised his head to strike. I have never seen anything so big in my life. The open mouth hurtling at us was bigger than my living room. The serpent was beautiful, in a terrifying sort of way. Each of his scales, about the size of a pickup truck hood, was translucent, shades of green and blue. The scutes on his creamy underbelly gleamed in the near twilight like white opals. He was going to either swallow or crush Nick and I, and there didn't seem to be anything I could do, other than stand there admiring him.

I never saw them coming, but somehow, both Quinn and Thor were there. Thor swung his hammer at the snake. The snake spat venom at him. Quinn found one small bare spot on the snake's side where a scale had been broken. He shifted into kelpie form and bit the snake's tender flesh. The snake twisted and rolled, trying to dislodge him, but he held on like a tick. In his thrashing about, Jörmungandr put his huge head in exactly the right position for Thor to land a killing blow. Green blood ran from Jörmungandr's broken head, spattering Thor and steaming on the cold rocks.

The war god laughed, turned, and took nine steps towards us. His knees crumpled and he went down. Nick and I ran to him.

Was the snake's blood toxic, or was it the venom he'd spat earlier? Thor's eyes were swollen shut. His lips were also swollen, and bluish. He wheezed and squeaked as he struggled for air. Anaphylaxis. *Damn, I'd kill for an EpiPen.* But I didn't have one, and if I didn't find a way to get some oxygen into him, and soon, he would die. What I did have was a spear and a war horn. Something in my bra poked me. And Benadryl. It wasn't an EpiPen, but it was better than nothing.

I grabbed at the leather thong that held the horn and yanked it out of Thor's belt.

"Nick, you hold the spear handle. I'll guide the point," I said. He wasn't entirely sure what I was up to, but he complied.

I located Thor's Adam's apple, then found the next bump down. Carefully, I guided the tip of the spear to cut through the cricothyroid membrane, giving Thor an emergency tracheotomy. The only thing I had to intubate him with was the war horn, so I inserted the narrow end of it into the incision to keep the airway open. His chest heaved as air suddenly reached his lungs. Then I fished the bubble card out of my bra, popped out the pill, broke it and put it under his tongue. He just might live, after all. I found some animal pelts in one of the tents, and covered Thor as best I could. I also propped his feet up on a rock. If he went into shock, all of our heroics would have been for nothing.

"Is he dead?" Quinn asked.

He had escaped being drenched with Jörmungandr's blood, although he surely must have come in contact with it when he bit the serpent.

"He's alive, but not by much," I replied. I looked at Quinn. "You're wearing clothes."

"He just turned into a freaking sea monster and back, and the only thing you notice is his clothes?" Nick said. He'd taken a few steps backward, away from Quinn, Thor, and me.

I shook my head. "I've known about this for a while. If I had told you that my dog, Bruce, that freaking sea monster, and Quinn – whom you think is some junkie named Marc McLeod, were all one in the same, would you have believed me? You've seen it with your own eyes and you can't believe it."

"Wait. He's also Bruce? Bruce, that my kids have played with?"

Quinn shimmered, turned into Bruce and wagged his tail, then returned to his human form. "Odin helped out with the clothes thing." He raised his chain maille and wool shirt to reveal an odd tattoo around his navel.

Seeing Bruce made me yearn for Cassie. I hadn't seen her in days, and I just wanted to hold my baby. She adored Bruce. Now, I was homesick.

The battlefield sounds changed. Nick and I looked towards the plain. Combatants on either side were running away from an enormous beast wading out into the middle of them. It was Fenrir, and he had grown to the size of an elephant, or, perhaps given the climate, a woolly mammoth. A lone figure stood in front of Fenrir.

Odin.

Sword raised and blue cloak unfurling in the wind, he refused to let Fenrir pass. The monster wolf raised his head and snarled. Still, Odin held his ground. Fenrir shook his great head from side to side.

There was something, a fleeting glimpse of dark red, behind the monster wolf.

"Quinn, do you see that? Is that Balcones?" I asked.

"I think so," he replied.

Nick looked up, too. "Looks like someone in a red parka." He obviously didn't want any part of this scenario, but his training had kicked in, and he couldn't help himself.

Balcones jumped around, arm in the air, as if he was trying to catch something that floated around Fenrir.

"What is he doing?" I asked.

"Looks like he's trying to grab Gleipnir. If he thinks he can use it as a leash to control Fenrir now, he's a bloody fool," Quinn said.

The Aesir had fallen back towards the camp. The Valkyries swarmed the air above them. The jötnar had re-grouped, and watched Fenrir, possibly waiting for the slaughter of Odin as their signal to attack.

Now, it appeared that Fenrir and Balcones were having a conversation, but I couldn't hear it.

Apparently, Quinn could.

He shook his head. "Balcones is trying to convince Fenrir to join him. Fenrir is having none of it. He doesn't care about money or power. The only thing on his mind is revenge."

Balcones continued to argue his point, his arms extended in supplication. Fenrir lunged at the demon. But there was a loud BANG and the wolf's immense jaws snapped shut on smoke and air. The wind carried the smell of rotten eggs down to the camp.

"Dammit!" Quinn said. "We've got to find a way to stop the demons from getting those percussion portals."

I checked on Thor. The prophecy had predicted that he would die. What if he didn't? What if keeping him alive had changed things just enough that the whole prophecy didn't happen? I looked back toward the battlefield.

Fenrir turned his fury on Odin, and swallowed him whole.

I was stunned. I had not expected it to be that easy, expecting some epic, hard-fought battle to the death.

I checked on Thor. He was still breathing. Changing his fate had not altered the prophecy, as far as I could tell.

The jötnar surged around him, and Fenrir ran through the warriors, his huge mouth biting at anything that moved. He didn't seem to care which side he mauled – it looked like he was doing both equally.

The colossal wolf slashed his way towards our camp.

A group of Odin's fighters attacked Fenrir, and the rest clashed with the jötnar. The Aesir and shades of Vikings past were no match for the enormous wolf. He cut through them easily, shaking the ground as he ran towards us.

Fenrir bounded through the snow, an overgrown and horrifying puppy, his enormous jaws opening as he ran. He snatched Nick around the waist and shook his massive head from side to side, like a terrier worrying a rat. Nick's arms and legs flailed like a broken rag doll. The monster's huge maw opened, and Nick's body tumbled out, staining the snow red even before he hit the ground.

"Nick!" I screamed, running to him, even though he lay directly underneath Fenrir's dripping tongue.

I started frantically packing his body in snow, hoping the cold would slow the blood loss. Intellectually, I knew that he was going to bleed out, probably in less than a minute, and there was nothing I could do about it. Even a Level I trauma center wouldn't be able to save him – the damage was catastrophic and irreversible. But I couldn't just sit and watch him die.

Then Odin's warriors surrounded Fenrir, attacking him from all sides at once. A man who looked like a younger version of Odin grabbed Fenrir by the chain around his neck. This must be Vidar. He was wearing one shoe made of iron, and when Fenrir tried to bite him, he stuck the shoe in the wolf's mouth. He couldn't close his massive jaws, and Vidar grabbed Fenrir's top jaw and yanked upwards. Now he was wedged in Fenrir's mouth. The wolf couldn't close his jaws, but Vidar couldn't do anything to harm him.

Halle, spattered with blood, swooped down on Rädsla, leaping off the mare before her hooves touched the ground.

"This is for my father, you monster!" she yelled.

Her long bright sword plunged into Fenrir's heart. He yelped, then started making choking, gasping sounds, and the electric blue glow of his eyes dimmed. Blood poured from his mouth, covering Vidar. As the wolf's strength ebbed away, the young god was able to free himself. Halle pulled her sword out of Fenrir's chest, and used it to slice open his belly.

At the fall of Fenrir, the jötnar lost heart and retreated, leaving a swath of dropped weapons and helms behind them.

"You will not have your prize!" Halle growled.

Bloody parts of a dozen or more men poured out of the wolf's stomach onto the snow. There was one body, battered, but whole. Odin. Halle wiped the gore from his face.

She nearly fell over when he coughed and opened his eye.

Odin was alive, after all. But Nick was not. I could not keep any sort of control over myself as his sightless eyes stared up at my face. I sobbed, and I shook him by his lifeless shoulders.

"Nick! Come back! We need you here with us. Emily and McKenzi and Aiden and Kyle need you. I need you. Please stay with us. This is all my fault. If I hadn't grabbed your hand and dragged you into this mess, you'd still be alive and with your family. It should be me laying there dead, not you. I would give anything to trade places with you," I begged his corpse.

I felt the pressure of Quinn's hand on my back, but I ignored it. I didn't deserve to be comforted. I'd just killed my brother-in-law.

I could see the armored toes of Halle's boots as she moved in and stood near Nick's body.

"At least you're happy, huh, Halle? You got what you wanted," I snarled at her. When I raised my head and looked up, I expected her to be smiling, but her face was stony and drawn. Next to her, looking around in confusion, stood Nick's ghost.

"Did you mean that?" Odin asked, sitting up.

My gaze shifted to him. "What? That I'd trade places with him? Yes."

"Marti, no," Quinn's voice sounded behind me. His grip tightened around my shoulder

Odin stroked his beard, considering, then flicked slime and blood off his fingers. "As you wish."

He stretched out his hand towards me, and immediately I felt light headed.

What had I just done?

I did not want to leave Cassie an orphan. But I knew that between Nick, Emily, and my parents, she'd have a pretty good life. In fact, she probably wouldn't even remember me. Sad for me, but probably better for her. She'd be so much safer without dangerous fae creatures hanging around all the time. Creatures I couldn't seem to leave alone. Quinn would outlive me by hundreds of years anyway, so this just a tiny blip in the timeline, hardly noticeable on his scale.

"Stop this! Please, Odin," Quinn begged.

"It is not your choice," Odin replied.

I wasn't entirely sure it was mine, either, but there didn't seem to be any going back now. Funny the things that a person will agree to when they think those things can't possibly happen.

I closed my eyes. Euphoria started to seep in to my consciousness. I'd died before, and recognized the feeling.

Suddenly, it stopped, and I was jolted back into my body. I opened my eyes to see Halle's face just above mine.

"Halle! What are you doing?" I was angry, thinking she was still trying to take Nick for herself.

But she didn't move, and the light in her eyes was fading, taking my rage with it. The strength left her arms, and she collapsed on top of me.

"Halle, my daughter! What have you done?" Odin's voice cracked.

He crawled over and scooped her up in his arms, cradling her like a small child.

"I promised," she wheezed.

And then she was terribly, awfully still.

Nick groaned, and sat up. He coughed and vomited up water and little chunks of ice – the snow I'd packed his body in earlier. His eyes opened, and glowed green.

"Nick? How do you feel?" I asked, still trying to process what had just happened.

"I had the weirdest dream...Why are *you* here?" He blinked, his eyes returning to normal, and looked around, first at Quinn, then Odin, holding Halle. "Maybe it wasn't a dream."

He pulled up his maille coat and shirt. Jagged, bloodstained holes remained in his clothing, but his skin was unmarked, as if Fenrir's wicked jaws had never crushed the life out of him.

"I don't...understand," Nick said.

Quinn spoke, his voice was raw and soft, barely audible above the wind. "When I asked Halle to help me protect Marti, she promised that she would. A Valkyrie's word is her bond, Nick, and she will not break it. Halle couldn't allow Marti's life to be traded for yours."

Nick jerked his face toward me. His mouth opened, but no words came out.

"You told me that Valkyries couldn't be killed," I said, practically accusing Quinn, tears streaming down my face. I felt searing guilt for every negative thought I'd ever had about Halle.

"They can not be," Odin broke in, his eye glistening with extra moisture. "Halle was not killed. She willingly sacrificed herself. There is a difference." He regarded Nick for a few moments before he spoke again. "Your soul is your own, but your body now contains the life force of a Valkyrie. Since the beginning of time, such a thing has never happened. Even I cannot see how this will affect you. There is no prophecy for this event." Odin brushed some snow of off of Halle's face. "And sometimes, even the prophecies are wrong."

He whistled loudly for Sleipnir. Then he removed some of the quantum leaves from a leather pouch at his waist.

"Treasure this gift," Odin said to Nick.

"I will."

"I'm sorry, Odin. If I'd known..." Quinn said.

I took Halle's cold hand in mine. If she had a ghost, I couldn't see it. But I felt sure that somewhere, somehow, she could hear me. "Thank you, Halle. I know we didn't always get along, and I'm sorry for that. But what you did...I owe you more than I could ever possibly repay."

I stood up and moved to Quinn and Nick.

"Thor is not dead. He needs serious medical help, but he is still alive. Or at least he was a few minutes ago."

"Thank you," Odin nodded, and a single tear slid down his craggy cheek, freezing into a glittering crystal just before it reached his beard. He took it and folded it into my hand. "Never forget."

He threw the leaves around us, and the scenery blurred, shifting into the steamy green heat of my backyard. And we were up to our knees in water.

Chapter 26
World of Difference

A fter all that we'd just been through, had we still failed to stop Ragnarök? Was this the beginning of the flood?

I wasn't sure what time it was, but it was dark. Night or storm clouds, it was hard to tell. I think it was some of both. The wind whipped the trees around and drove the rain nearly horizontally. Fat raindrops pummeled my skin like dull needles. I shielded my eyes with my hand. My coat was waterproof, but that didn't matter. My head was soaked in a matter of seconds, and cold water ran down the back of my neck and into my clothes.

I put the crystal tear in my pocket and started slogging toward the back door. The water was nearly up to the top step.

"Wait!" Delilah appeared in front of me. "You can *not* go in there."

"Yes, I can. It's my house. I'm not going to stand out here in the middle of a storm. Besides, I have to find Cassie."

Nick looked at me, to the seemingly empty space in front of me, then back at my face.

"No, girlfriend. Cassie is fine. You and Nick have been gone a week. Emily and your parents are beside themselves. You can't just show up together like you never been gone. What you gonna tell your sister about running off with her husband?"

"I don't know, but we can't just stand out here in the rain." I had to shout to be heard above the weather. *Gone a week?* I shuddered to think about the condition of Alpha and Betty, with no one to feed or water them for seven days.

"Let's go to Kai's. We can get it sorted there," Quinn said.

"No," Nick said. "I'm going home to my family."

"Nick, we've been gone a whole week. What are you going to tell Emily when she asks where you and I have been for that time?"

He sulked.

I turned and noticed that Quinn was missing. Oddly enough, he was by the birdbath, and appeared to be smelling the only plumeria flower that hadn't been torn off the bush by the strong wind.

He waded back to where Nick and I were standing.

"You couldn't wait for better weather to stop and smell the flowers?" I asked.

"I'm getting us a ride," he said.

"From a flower?"

"You'll see. Come on."

Nick grudgingly followed Quinn and I out of my backyard and onto the sidewalk. It was treacherous going – the sidewalk was underwater and limbs were down everywhere. The storm drains were blocked with debris – that's what was causing the flooding. One of the street light poles had been knocked down and lay across the road. It was a good thing the power was off. Fighting wind, water, and debris, it took about three times as long as usual to get to the Tenth Sphere. I think I've probably had drier showers.

The only car anywhere in sight, a black SUV, idled in the parking lot.

"That's our ride," Quinn said.

Nick looked skeptical. I reached for the door.

"Wait," Quinn said, covering my hand.

"The driver's name is Frey. He's been burned, so he can be a bit hard to look at. But he's worth his weight in gold."

Nick nodded, and opened the front passenger door. Quinn opened the rear passenger side door for me, and we all climbed in out of the storm.

Quinn was right. Frey was hard to look at. His face was scarred and ropey, and one eye was an opaque white. I redirected my focus to the car. The seats were covered with plastic tarps. A good idea, given that we were wringing wet.

"*Ta*, Frey. You're a lifesaver. This is Nick and Marti. We're in need of a portal."

The driver simply nodded and put the vehicle in gear.

I started shivering in the air conditioning. Frey turned on the heat before I could even say anything. Maybe he found the noise from my chattering teeth obnoxious. Nick sat glowering in the front seat, arms crossed over his seatbelt.

"Alright, Quinn. How were you able to get Frey to come get us by talking to a flower?" I asked.

"Each flower had an attendant faery. These flower fae are messengers, if you know how to ask. And since they exist in multiple dimensions at once, messages are as close as you'll likely get to instantaneous."

I would have liked to have snuggled up against Quinn to get warm, but the middle seatbelt was covered by both tarps. He was half a mile away, against the opposite window.

At least it didn't take long to get to our destination, and Frey drove us into a lovely dry garage. I was still dripping wet when I got out of the SUV. Frey opened a clothes dryer by the door to the house and pulled out three warm bath sheets, one for each of us.

Quinn herded the recalcitrant Nick upstairs, and I followed. He took us to a room with two large portraits. One of them was of a green-eyed woman, the same woman who had come to my house and tried to heal Quinn when he'd been attacked by a werewolf, a month ago, and he'd spent several days at my house, fighting for his life. The other, I recognized as Mr. Underhill. I'd met him a few weeks ago, when I'd first encountered Quinn.

"Walk through the picture," Quinn said.

Nick looked at him quizzically.

"Did you just say 'walk through the picture'?" I asked.

"Yes."

"Which one?" I responded.

"Doesn't matter. They go to the same place."

"Which is?" asked Nick.

"Faery. Now go."

Nick balked. So I took the lead. When I stepped through the woman's picture, I found myself in a very long, dim corridor, lined on both sides with portraits. Nick stepped out of the man's picture, then stood dumbstruck. Quinn had to maneuver around him when he came through.

First, he led us to through a maze of corridors until we got to a brighter hallway. He knocked on one of the doors, but there was no answer. His shoulders slumped just a little, but he straightened up and we continued down the hall. At the corner, there was a receptionist's desk. It seemed out of place in a castle, but nobody had asked me when they'd done the design layout. The receptionist wasn't there, but an astoundingly large bouquet of white roses and ferns sat on the desk.

Quinn scowled at the flowers. "I wonder who died."

"That's a funeral arrangement?" I asked.

"Yes. From the size of it, I would think it would be an MIT leader. I know most of them, but I don't know a lot of the team members. Let's go into town and see what we can find out."

We followed Quinn to the exit. There were some children playing in the bailey, but otherwise, the castle seemed deserted. It was warm and bright outside, and I upgraded the condition of my clothing from waterlogged to wet.

"Come on, Nick. You like mysteries, don't you?" I asked.

"Not this kind."

On the edge of the town square was a water mill. I doubted it still ground wheat because there was a sign out front that read *The Waterhorse Inn*, with a black ribbon wrapped around it. Quinn tried the door, but it was locked.

"I don't have my key with me."

He looked pale and I noticed his breathing had gotten shallower.

"Are you okay?" I asked him.

"Maybe. The *Waterhorse* has been in my family for generations. For them to put a mourning band around the sign and lock up, it must mean that a family member has died. They're probably at the funeral."

"I'm sorry." I reached out for his hand. He squeezed my fingers, but let go. I guess he was too agitated to be comforted.

Quinn hurried down the cobblestone street, which narrowed into a smaller road that quickly turned to gravel, then dirt. As he'd predicted, there was a large gathering of dour looking people dressed in black and grey. There were no chairs left, so we stood at the back.

A man that looked very similar to Quinn, but maybe a little younger, was just taking the podium.

"That's Graham," he whispered.

"My brother was taken from us far too soon," he said.

Quinn frowned, then scanned the front row. Then he looked puzzled. Then he smiled.

"Why are you smiling?" Nick whispered to him, looking somewhat revolted.

"I have four brothers. Graham is the one talking. Those two on the aisle of the front row are Robbie and Laurie. The one on the other side of the tall woman with grey hair, my mum, is Kade. It's not often you get the chance to attend your own funeral."

"Why do they think you're dead?" I asked.

"Excellent question," he replied.

"You have to say something," Nick said. "You can't just sit here and let them think you're dead. That's cruel."

"You're right, of course," Quinn said. He still had an impish grin. "But wouldn't you be interested to know what people said at your funeral?"

Nick looked away. "Maybe," he mumbled.

Quinn took a few steps over to a tall man with waist-length blond hair. "Excuse me," he said. "I was traveling when I heard the news, but I don't have much information. How did he die?"

"He was on an MIT mission. Frost Giants got him."

Quinn nodded. "How terrible. Thank you," he said.

He looked at Nick and put his finger to his lips, as if he needed shushing. Graham had put his hand over his face to compose himself. Quinn stepped quietly down the aisle, until he was about halfway to the podium.

Graham started to speak again. "...and he can never be replaced. The memories that we have are all that's left-"

"Excuse me," Quinn said. "I hate to interrupt, but I think there's been a terrible misunderstanding."

"Quinn!" Graham shouted.

Nick and I waited at the edge of the crowd while all of his friends and relatives hugged him, kissed him, or shook his hands.

The woman that Quinn had pointed out as his mother stared malevolently at Nick and I most of the time.

"I hope she doesn't think we had anything to do with this," I said.

Nick shrugged. "If I thought one of my boys was dead, I'd be pretty pissed at the person who seemed responsible, even if it turned out that he was fine."

"Fair enough," I said.

After the initial furor of Quinn's sudden and unexpected return, I noticed that he'd moved away from the crowd and was standing alone by a gravestone, a white rose in his hands. I didn't see any rose bushes around, so he must have plucked it from one of his own funeral sprays. He knelt down and placed the flower on the grave, then rose, trailing his fingers along the top of the headstone as he returned to the swarm of former mourners.

A short time later, Nick and I sat in the posh office behind the door that Quinn had knocked on earlier. An older woman, introduced to us as Dame Rowan, sat at the heavy desk, and Quinn, Malik, Aleksei and Eoin sat in front of it.

"I think that explains why I wasn't able to contact you," Quinn said to Malik. "You and the others had been recalled because you thought I was dead. It was very clever of Balcones to make a show of having my coat and my cell phone. He knew we were watching him. I guess he got it off me when I went to the old lady's – I mean Loki's – hut."

"Old lady? Loki?" Rowan asked.

Quinn gave her a summary of recent events. He needed to debrief Rowan and his team, anyway, and now seemed a good time.

"Is shame Balcones got away," Aleksei said.

Rowan studied Nick. "This one is a puzzle," she said. "We shall have to monitor him."

Nick scowled.

"For his own good," Rowan continued. "A Valkyrie's life force has never been transferred to a human before, much less to a male. It is hard to know what the side effects might be."

"I'm going to need a little help with the time dilation," Quinn said. "I think we'll leave in the morning, but we need to arrive Sunday a week ago, Mundane time. The best I can do is get them back on Thursday. As it stands, Nick and Marti have been missing for a week. That's going to raise a lot of questions when they show up, especially from Nick's wife."

I gave Malik a sidelong glance. He'd sent me off on a completely different timeline not too long ago. That should be no problem for him.

"Time is easy," he said, with a quick, apologetic smile.

It was settled. Nick and I would return to Mundane time very early Sunday morning, the day after Boris' gala. Quinn would attend Halle's funeral and spend some time with his family, then be back in time for Cassie's birthday, which had happened yesterday. I had enough trouble managing things when time flowed in only one direction.

After the meeting with Dame Rowan, we adjourned to the *Waterhorse Inn*. A celebration of Quinn's return from the dead was in full swing by the time we arrived. His brothers were all very nice to me. I attempted to introduce myself to his mother.

"I'm Marti," I said, extending my hand. "It's nice to meet you."

She looked at me coldly, her eyes solid black. I knew from my experience with Quinn that was a bad thing. "I detest humans."

Then she turned on her heel and stalked away.

Alrighty, then.

Nick and I each got our own room at the inn. I didn't have the stamina to stay up all night, partying with the fae, and I fell asleep not long after midnight. It seemed far too early when Quinn came and knocked on my door.

"Time to go," he said.

Robbie fixed breakfast for Quinn, Nick, and me. I wondered if Quinn was as good a cook. After stuffing ourselves with fluffy pancakes, beans on toast, scones and clotted cream, and fresh fruit, we headed back to the castle, which Quinn told us was formally known as *Titania's School for Girls*. It also housed the local MAMIC offices.

"MAMIC?" I asked.

"Mundane Activity Monitoring and Intervention Center."

Nick almost smiled. "Can't get away from alphabet soup anywhere, huh?"

Malik was waiting for us in Rowan's office.

"This is it, Nick," I said. "We're going home."

He nodded.

I was sure he missed his family as much as I missed Cassie. I couldn't wait to hold my baby in my arms again.

Malik said a few words I didn't understand and waved his hand. Everything started to spin. I thought I was going to be sick. Lights flashed, and suddenly Nick and I were standing in front of Boris Cherngelanov's mansion. Lulu and Belinda were loading up the car.

"There you are," she said. "It's after two. We've been looking all over for you."

"I was looking for my cell phone. I seemed to have dropped it somewhere."

"I told you the one on the kitchen counter looked like hers," Belinda said.

Nick and I went to retrieve it.

Chapter 27
Reunion

ews of Boris Cherngelanov's death made the front page of the paper. Irina reported that he had been out ice climbing and fallen to his death. His body, sadly, wasn't recoverable. She would, however continue the good work of the Cherngelanov Foundation.

Sveklá knew that there was a secret door in the wine cellar, but he didn't know where it went. He'd looked through it once or twice, seen a prisoner detention area, knew it was unusually cold, but he knew nothing of Bright Falcon or Fenrir. The door had never had anything to do with him, and he didn't see why he should be concerned with it now. It was enough that Irina knew about it.

She knew that Sveklá would be suspicious of Boris' disappearance, but he would not ask many questions. She had won his loyalty. As long as she allowed him to be her lover, he would forgive her anything.

It was a lavish memorial service, and it took place as soon as was possible after the cleanup from the tropical storm and flooding. Armloads of wreaths and a roomful of white lilies and roses surrounded a portrait of Boris. Irina had worn a long, plain black dress and a black veil. She wanted people to assume she had been crying over her husband's unexpected death. Sveklá stood by her side at the funeral, as she knew he would do in front of the Odessa Group.

After the service, a buffet lunch would be served, so that the mourners could spend time reminiscing about the dearly departed. She'd wanted to call it a wake, and bring in musicians, but dancing at one's spouse's funeral is generally considered bad form in the United States.

Hadrian and Sara attended Boris' funeral, she as a representative of the Greene-Childe Foundation, and he, publicly, as her companion. But he was also there in a professional capacity. None of his surveillance targets put in an appearance. However, both Marti Keller and Lulu Miranda had worked at a party held by Cherngelanov right before his untimely death. Hadrian's supervisor decided that his surveillance of the neighborhood would continue until further notice. Hadrian did call the DA on the way to the funeral and ask that the charges against Benjamin Fayllor be dropped. Hadrian knew he was innocent, and his chance to flush out the real killer had probably ended with Boris' death. Win some, lose some. It may turn into a cold case, but it would always be open until the killer slipped up. It might take a while, but they usually did.

It was Friday, and Hadrain met Sara for lunch at Baba Yega's. They sat on the deck, in the shade, under the big fan, and it was much more pleasant than anyone had a right to expect on a July day in Houston. He was just returning from the restroom when, through the open door, he was stunned to see Marti and Cassie sitting at the table, talking to Sara.

Crap. That was a complication he really didn't need. Should he go say something, or just wait it out? Now that he'd decided to put some effort into winning Sara back, he didn't want to be evasive about their relationship. On the other hand, part of his surveillance operation depended on the appearance of him being available. That he genuinely liked Marti and found her attractive was a different can of worms that would be disastrous to open. He supposed he could fake food poisoning if he needed a diversion.

He got closer to the door, but continued to lurk. They didn't see him – it was bright outside and much less so inside. Cassie started struggling and wiggling.

"I have to go," Marti said. "There's no reasoning with her now that she's learned how to walk. It was so good to run into you, Gracie. I will definitely call you next week to set up lunch."

Sara stood up and they hugged each other, squirmy baby notwithstanding. "I'm looking forward to catching up."

"Bye, Gracie."

Hadrian waited for Marti to go around the corner and out of sight before he went back to the table. "Who was that?" he asked casually.

"Her name's Marti. She was Schmidt when I knew her, but she's Keller, now. We were best friends in school, until she moved away in senior year. She practically lived at my house. After her dad had that bad truck accident, things got a little tough for her, and we lost touch. I haven't seen her in years."

"And she called you Gracie."

Sara laughed. "Sara Grace, remember? When I was a kid, everyone I knew called me "Gracie." Well, except for my grandmother. She always called me "Sara Grace." In college, I decided that "Sara" sounded more grown up."

"Makes sense."

With more than six million people in the Greater Houston Metro Area, how could it be that his girlfriend was an old friend of one of his surveillance targets? Life was weird, sometimes.

"Is your power back on yet?" Hadrian asked.

"No." Sara shook her head. "The shopping center across the street has power, though."

"Stay at my apartment? I have hot water." He tilted his head.

"You really know how to tempt a girl."

"That's my specialty."

Sara laughed and leaned over to kiss him. "I'll see you after work, Blackbird."

Chapter 28
Make a Wish

 hugged Cassie to within an inch of her life. She fussed and struggled every time I picked her up, it seemed. But maybe because I was picking her up all the time. As far as she was concerned, I'd only been gone one night. She didn't know I'd missed her for an entire week.

On Sunday afternoon, Nick showed up at my door with a chef's knife in his hand.

"I have to show you something," he said.

Whatever it was, he did not look happy about it. Cassie was busy alternately whacking Mr. Buns against the coffee table and gnawing on his ears. She could keep herself entertained for a few more minutes. I stepped over the baby gate and into the kitchen.

"What is it, Nick?"

I was a little ashamed that I kept the table between us. I didn't like to think that my brother-in-law would hurt Cassie or me, but he did have a big knife, and he was agitated.

"Watch," he said.

He put his left hand palm-down on the table, then drew the knife across the back of it. I gasped as blood started running down his hand.

But then a green fire sparked at the starting edge of the wound and crackled and shimmered down its length. As it passed, the wound healed without leaving the faintest scar. It was like it never happened. Even the blood on his skin vanished when the green fire touched it.

"This is not possible," he said, slapping the knife down on the table and scooping his hand through his hair.

"I think," I said, hoping I was right, "that is Halle's gift."

He exhaled forcefully. "How far does this go? How big a wound can it heal?"

"I don't know, but go experiment somewhere else. You are not allowed to commit hari-kari in my kitchen. Even if it doesn't really kill you."

Nick laughed softly. "Yeah, I guess that could be a problem, if it doesn't work."

I looked at the back of his hand closely, ran my finger along it where there should have been a cut, trying to find any traces of the wound. Nothing. "Well, on the plus side, it seems like a handy fringe benefit for a police officer."

"Maybe. Hadn't thought of it that way. All I know is that now I'm some kind of freak and I can't tell anyone, not even my wife, about it. You're dating a sea monster, so it's not like you're going to tell anybody."

"Wow, Nick. Thanks for that incredible vote of confidence," I said. "I'm sorry you got dragged into this, but how was I supposed to know that this famous philanthropist was really a crime boss with an inter-dimensional portal to a Russian gulag in his wine cellar? He was supposed to be one of the good guys, remember?"

He frowned.

Delilah appeared, partially. I could see her, but she was transparent.

"Girl, you need to tell that man that sometimes what you want and what you need are two different things."

I thought of a proverb my husband used to like. "'The bamboo that bends is stronger than the oak that resists.'"

"You sound just like Ryan," Nick said.

Delilah winked at me.

"Yeah, how about that?" I replied. I had seen Nick's corpse and I'd seen his ghost, but I wondered what, if anything, he recalled about his death. "So, just out of curiosity, what do you remember about our little adventure?"

"Falling through a door painted on a wall, being in a freezing cell, getting turned into a seal and being hunted by orcas, riding a flying horse, talking to Thor, being killed by a gigantic wolf. Suddenly waking up, and finding out it wasn't a dream."

"I saw you, standing next to Halle, before..."

"Before she died? I remember that." His brow furrowed. "It was hard to go back. My body just seemed so cold. And difficult."

I knew how hard it was for him to admit that. "I know."

Now that he knew I wasn't crazy, I wondered if I should tell him about how I first met Quinn. But I decided against it. He already has as much as his brain could deal with at the moment. Perhaps another time.

On Thursday evening, I sat with about half of the regulars while Lulu began smudging the room for Circle. Hunter didn't show. Marilyn was disappointed enough that she made sure she was on the opposite side of the room from me. It wasn't my fault he wasn't interested in her, and I wasn't sure how to feel about his seeming interest in me. Maybe he was just a friendly neighbor – he hadn't made any real overtures. But maybe there was more to it. He always seemed to be around at just the right time. Either way, I was glad I didn't have to think about it tonight. Hunter was certainly appealing. But I was looking forward to Quinn's return.

I wasn't sure how that was going to work out. It wasn't fair for him to remain in dog form during the day for propriety's sake. But I wasn't willing to invite a man I'd only known for a month and a half to move in with Cassie and me, either. If he could pop in and out of dimensions so easily, I don't suppose dating would be such an issue. Phone calls and texts might be a little hard, though.

"Let's get started," Lulu said. "Tonight, we're going to explore telekinesis." She handed each of us a piece of paper, a pencil, and a small plastic cube.

I dutifully placed the cube in the center of my paper, and outlined it so I would be able to see if it moved. I tried imagining it moving, being the cube, matching my vibrations to the cube, and not making it obvious that I was just blowing on it for an hour. Nothing. Nada. Zip.

Lulu finally broke the Circle, and walked around collecting all the pencils and cubes before we went downstairs for refreshments.

"Honey, look at that! You really did well on this exercise," she said.

There must be some mistake. I looked at my paper and found my little cube sitting in the upper left corner.

"Yeah. How about that?"

Delilah?

I heard a disembodied giggle.

Not funny.

"But you were trying so hard, girlfriend. I just wanted to give you a little win."

I gathered my things to go home, glad that I had all my supplies laid in. Tropical storm Elvira was supposed to make landfall tomorrow afternoon, and I was delighted to not have to go to the store and face long lines and empty shelves tonight.

I spent Friday morning putting masking tape on all the windows and securing any loose objects outdoors. Cassie was my special little "helper." Mom thought we should start Cassie's birthday early and have a hurricane party, but I wanted to be home when Quinn showed up. I told her that it wasn't fair for us to all be partying while Nick was pulling a double shift.

It was dark thirty on Saturday morning when I heard Quinn's knock. The wind had died down from Category 1 to breezy, but the outermost rain bands were still dumping buckets of moisture on us. The power had been off for nearly twelve hours. Water was everywhere, and I was a little concerned about it coming in the house when I went to let Quinn in. Outside, I heard a high-pitched, whining bark and a snort.

I turned the deadbolt and opened the door.

"Is that a puppy?" I asked, looking at the wriggling thing in his arms.

He looked down at it as if he wasn't sure what it was. The dog stretched up and licked his face. "Seems to be."

He came into the kitchen and set the damp pup on the floor. The black dog looked up hopefully, his tail wagging his entire body. Judging by the size of his feet, at least one of his parents was a Great Dane.

"His name is Cu, but you can change it, if you want. I know how fond Cassie is of Bruce, so I thought a puppy would be a good birthday present."

"Does that mean she won't be seeing Bruce anymore?" My heart sank.

"It means that she also likes Quinn, so now she can have her cake and eat it too."

I couldn't help but laugh. Cu apparently thought it was funny, too, because he danced and capered about on the tile as if he thought the idea of eating cake was an excellent one.

"This is an actual dog? He doesn't turn into anything else?"

Quinn was smiling as he shook his head. "Nope. Always the form of a dog."

I couldn't help but think there was more to it.

A warbling came from down the hall. "Sounds like the birthday girl is up."

I went to get her. After she was changed, I brought her into see the puppy. If he was too rambunctious, he would, unfortunately, have to go back with Quinn.

Cassie squealed with delight when she saw Cu. The puppy was better than perfect with her. It was almost like he'd heard my thoughts about sending him back if he wasn't.

It was close to 7:00. If dark clouds hadn't been drenching us with rain, it would have been nearly full daylight. I looked through the tape on the window until I saw Quinn, Nick, and myself appear in the back yard, argue for a few minutes, then leave. I'm glad that Delilah had talked me out of coming into the house. It would have been too weird to have run into my future self in the past. Or was it my past self in the future? Anyway, the me out in the rain right now would have been shocked to find the me who got back a week ago in the house.

That's when it hit me. "The storm drains. Remember how blocked up they were? Are? If we could open up that big one across the street, we could probably stop all the houses from flooding."

Quinn nodded.

While I fed Cassie her breakfast, he waded outside to remove the fallen tree branch that had lodged in the storm sewer entrance, trapping debris and causing all the flooding. The water level gradually started going down.

My father would not be up yet, but I'm sure Mom was already in the kitchen, baking Cassie's cake. I thought maybe we'd wander over around 10-ish. Or whenever there was a break in the rain, whichever came first. The party was supposed to start at 11:00.

Cassie and Cu played together in the living room like they'd known each other all their lives. When I picked Cassie up to give her a bath and put on her party clothes, Cu fell asleep, sprawled on the floor like a dog-skin rug. I didn't want to leave him home without supervision, so Quinn carried him like a little hairy baby. His half hour nap was enough to refresh him, because when he saw

Cassie again, he nearly turned himself inside out with joy. Kyle and Aiden could hardly get a look in. It was just as well. They couldn't go out in the backyard in the deluge, anyway.

"Where's Bruce?" Kyle asked grumpily.

I glanced at Quinn. "You remember that I found Bruce, and I thought he might belong to someone else? He found his home."

"Who is your friend, Marti?" my mother asked.

"This is Quinn," I said. I wasn't sure whether to introduce my mother as "Adele" or "Mrs. Schmidt," so I did both, and let Quinn decide what to call her.

"It's nice to meet you, Mrs. Schmidt," Quinn said.

"Likewise," Mom answered.

After a while, lunch was served, then cake. Cassie was too young for a piñata, but we played Velcro the Tail on the Donkey and had a rousing chorus of "Head, Shoulders, Knees and Toes."

"Where did you find Mr. Hottie?" Emily asked when she and I were cleaning up the kitchen.

"You wouldn't believe me if I told you." *Oddly enough, I was on a date with another guy. Nick's friend, Ian Chambers, to be precise.*

She waited for me to dish on the details, but I didn't. "He's cuter than your neighbor. What kind of work does he do?"

He goes undercover to hunt demons. "Law enforcement," I said out loud.

"Figures."

By the time all of Cassie's presents were opened, she was falling asleep sitting up.

"I think the birthday girl needs a nap," I said.

"Put her in the crib in our room," Mom said.

We stayed around until the rain let up, around dinner time. Dad was amazed by the wide array of card games that Quinn knew. He was even good at card tricks that baffled the boys, and he kept everybody entertained until we ate supper.

When we ran next door to my house, both Cassie and Cu were drowsy, so I put her straight in her crib and folded up a blanket for the puppy.

"You know Balcones may still be after you?" Quinn asked.

"I can't believe he got away."

"You know that means I'll have to be here for a while longer, to keep an eye on you, and make sure you're safe."

"I see."

Quinn took my hand and led me to my bedroom. He closed the door and then he kissed me, a long, deep kiss that made my knees turn to water.

"My brother taught me a secret to make it safe for me to make love to you. Do you want me to show you?"

"Please."

"Sit on the bed. You can lean against the headboard, if you want."

I moved the pillows and sat cross-legged on the bed, leaning against the headboard. My skin tingled with anticipation. I had tried to convince myself that I didn't want him. But I had failed. There was nothing I wanted more just now.

Quinn sat in front of me so we were knee to knee. "Take a deep breath. Try to breathe into your solar plexus. Now, think about pushing energy out of your abdomen, just above your belly button. Imagine a white ball of it forming just outside of you."

It took a few tries, but finally, he said, "I see it. Good. Now come with me."

His physical body still sat on the bed, but there was now a glowing, transparent double of him, standing on the floor beside us. He carefully picked up the ball of white energy that I'd extruded and carried it with him. I was able to see everything that happened, in 360°. It was a little hard to understand, and I thought it was peculiar that each of us had a silver cord that attached our physical bodies to our non-physical ones.

Almost immediately, we were at a gazebo on the beach. The water was topaz blue and the sand was golden. He began to caress me. I couldn't tell where he ended and I began. My form began to stretch out, and our energy merged and twined together.

It was amazing. We did things that just couldn't be done with physical bodies. Gender, gravity and physical form were all irrelevant. Ecstasy didn't seem to be a strong enough word to describe it, as our energies melded, separated, and combined again. It was exhausting, though. When I couldn't take anymore, my consciousness snapped back into my body as if it had been attached by a bungee cord.

Still, my body buzzed from the combining of energy that I'd just experienced. It was so different from physical contact, much more intense. But there was also a distance, and unreality about it that made it slightly unsatisfying, and I wondered if this was love, or enthrallment. It felt pretty damned good either way.

Quinn stretched out on the bed. I put my head on his shoulder, and shivered with pleasure.

"Did you like that?" he asked.

"That was incredible. Can we do it again?"

"Any time you like."

Bonus Material

The Magician's Children

Virginia

his mission should be simple. I don't believe we need to wait for Eoin to finish his secondment. Retrieving the ring will be nothing for the four of us. It's winter in the Mundane world. Queen Elizabeth's not got her money back from this investment. This foray into the New World hasn't been good to the colonists. They're half starved, so even if they did know what it was they'd found, they haven't the strength to put up much of a fight." Halle's waist-length golden braids bobbed slightly as she shook her head.

"Why does MIT look for ring? Is not problem for Aesir?" Aleksei asked.

"It's cursed," replied Halle.

"Is the curse demonic?" Siobhan asked.

"No."

Siobhan shrugged. "Then we aren't duty bound to stop it, are we?"

"Just because the curse isn't demonic, doesn't mean that demons cannot employ it to their full advantage. If they were to take it from the humans, they could use it to wreak a lot of havoc. We can save ourselves a great deal of work by getting it first. Besides, Andvari has offered a handsome reward for its return. MAMIC could use the gold."

Siobhan sighed. "How are we meant to find this ring - what is it called again - Andvaranaut?" she asked.

She sat between Aleksei and Quinn at a heavy oaken table in a conference room in the Mundane Activity Monitoring and Intervention Center (MAMIC). Halle leaned over the opposite side of the table.

"With this." Halle pulled a silver dagger from her belt. "When it is near Andvaranaut, the blade will glow. The brighter the glow, the closer the ring."

"How does it know?" Siobhan asked. "What if there's another gold ring?"

"It isn't sensitive to rings. It's sensitive to cursed objects."

Halle's answer appeared to satisfy Siobhan, but Aleksei scowled.

"How came magic Viking ring to New World? Has only been known hundred years by humans," he said.

"Not true. The red-skinned Skraelings were there when the sons of Erik the Red arrived. When Erik was banished from Iceland, one of his sailing crew gave him the ring as a gift. Probably, he was just trying to get rid of it. Anyway, because of the ring, the Newfoundland colonies were cursed, and they failed. As the Vikings explored further down the coastline, whoever had the ring either died there with it or deliberately left it behind. It was lost for a millennium. Then a dryad saw English colonists with an extraordinary gold ring and reported it to MAMIC. And here we are."

"You say is cursed. What is curse?" Aleksei asked.

"Standard misfortune curse, plus added destruction."

"If they did know what they'd found, they'd be happy to be rid of the bleedin' thing," Siobhan said.

"Is gold, *da*?" Aleksei said. "Humans and gold, is bad mix." His blue skin looked glossy under the flickering lamp.

Quinn was leaning back in his chair, rocking it back and forth on two legs, drumming his fingers softly on the table and staring out the tiny window.

Halle shot him an unhappy glance, then continued. "We'll set up the portal entrance in the woods on the far side of the island. Aleksei will get close to the encampment and signal us when the humans have gone to sleep. Then we'll move in and collect the ring, and if our luck holds, they'll never even know we were there." She looked from Aleksei to Siobhan, but her gaze settled on Quinn. "Does that sound like a good plan? Quinn?"

The finger drumming continued.

Aleksei cleared his throat.

Quinn looked up. "What?"

"I asked your opinion on the operation," Halle said crisply.

"They're humans. Vermin. Instead of sneaking around, why don't we just eliminate them and take the ring?" Quinn asked.

"That's a great idea. Except for the half-dozen treaties it violates. MAMIC would banish us for sure. But you know that."

"Then I'm sure your plan is fine."

Aleksei and Siobhan exchanged uncomfortable looks.

"I've just remembered that Aleksei and I have a training course we need to be off to. We're already late as it is."

Siobhan grabbed his wrist and guided the Lesovik out of his chair. Confusion shaped his expression. "Huh?"

"You know," she replied, cutting her eyes towards Quinn for an instant, "that course we signed up for. The one about alchemy, remember?"

"Oh. That one. *Da*, is time to go."

After the door closed behind Siobhan and Aleksei, Halle straightened herself up to her full six foot height. "What is this about?"

"I've packed my things," Quinn said.

Halle frowned. "Because?"

Quinn ran his hand through his dark hair. "This arrangement we have is just not working for me anymore. I would never try to keep you from being who you are, what you are, but...I want something different."

Halle shook her head. "Something different?"

"I have been able to overlook your...appetites when it was just once or twice a decade, but now, it seems to be once or twice a month."

The Valkyrie sat down with a thud. "I don't know what to say." Halle's eyes blinked rapidly, as if she were feverishly searching her brain for the right words. "I had no idea you felt that way."

Quinn closed his eyes, breathed in deeply, and let the air out. "I also think," he swallowed, "that it's undermining your authority as team leader. After this mission, I'm going to request a transfer to another team."

Halle cocked her head to one side. "What do you mean you think it undermines my authority?"

Quinn put his elbow on the table and rested his forehead on his fingertips. "There's not a delicate way to put this. When you screw anything that holds still long enough, it makes people question your judgment."

Halle slapped her palms loudly on the table as she stood up. "Get out," she said, her words falling like pebbles from her perfect red lips.

Quinn got up and left. The conversation, such as it was, went better than he expected. She hadn't tried to kill him. But it was still early.

He'd get his things from the small house they'd been sharing for the past eighty years or so and take them back to the Waterhorse Inn. As he made his way down the main staircase into the great hall, he pondered his situation.

His mother always kept rooms available for her five sons, even though she didn't often stay there herself. He hoped she was in her country place for the week, because he couldn't stand the thought of receiving the inevitable the I-told-you-so-now-when-are-you-going-to-find-a-nice-kelpie-girl-and-settle-down lecture. He was only one hundred thirty two, far too young to start a family. Perhaps in another three or four of hundred years. He and Halle had gotten together not long after they graduated from Mundane Intervention Team (MIT) training, just over a hundred years ago, but it hardly seemed like any time had passed.

"Quinn? You okay?" Siobhan asked. She was sitting by the enormous empty fireplace with a mug of hot coffee in her hands, waiting for him.

He gave her a half smile. "I will be. I just broke things off with Halle." He couldn't bring himself to tell her he was planning to leave the team, as well.

"I'm sorry."

Quinn shrugged. "I knew it would be a challenge. Should have known she would be more than I could handle. I've got to go do a few wee errands. I'll see you when the team meets back here tonight. Cheers."

The default time for a mission to start was midnight. They don't call it the witching hour for nothing.

Siobhan, Aleksei, Quinn, and Halle stood in a dim corridor of the MAMIC building, in front of a portrait of Halle.

"Are we ready?" Halle asked. She avoided looking at Quinn.

She went through the portal first, stepping through the painting of herself, and out onto a wooded island off of the coast of what would be known as North Carolina in about another hundred and fifty years. The other fae followed her out of the portrait.

The quartet slipped through the trees, crunching through the frozen snow, until they were within sight of the palisades surrounding the settlement. Halle's dagger was faintly lit. But their plans for a stealthy approach proved unnecessary.

Angry shouting exploded through the air.

Most of the words were unclear, but "Gold," "Traitors," and "Die" were unmistakable.

The MIT crept towards the settlement. Currently, all they could see was part of the circle of sharp-pointed palisades, grey in the moonlight, that surrounded the dwellings. Firelight, probably torches, occasionally flickered through the gaps between the rough-hewn logs.

The crack of arquebus fire shattered the night, first one, then a dozen or more. A cloud of acrid gunpowder smoke drifted towards them. A group of humans, English by their dress, spilled out of the gates. Quinn estimated there were more than fifty, but fewer than one hundred men and a handful of women.

"Ease up, Bill!" said one of the men, who was wearing an especially floppy hat.

"I said we're goin'. You can stay wif 'em, if you like," another man, presumably Bill, answered.

"I just want the cap'n to know where to look for us, when he come back with supplies, that's all. Please, gov'nor."

Bill considered for a moment. "Alright ven. Be quick about it."

Someone held a torch over him while the man with the floppy hat scratched letters into the gatepost. Even Quinn's sharp eyes had trouble reading it, but he thought it said, "Croatoan."

As soon as he was done, the mob stampeded in the opposite direction of the MIT.

"That was unexpected," Halle said.

"The curse?" Siobhan asked.

"Humans need no help of curse to slaughter one another," Aleksei said.

Quinn nodded. "That should make our job easier."

"Unless the group that just left has the ring. Aleksei, you follow and see where they're going. The rest of us will search the houses," Halle said.

Aleksei trotted silently into the trees and melted into the deep shadows.

Halle led the way to the settlement, stopping often to listen and observe. Quinn heard high-pitched crying, but the team saw no further movement as they approached the open stockade gates.

When the MIT first entered the fortified village, nothing seemed to be amiss.

A wagon, laden with barrels, stood near the village center. A bare foot stuck out from behind one of the wheels. The fae fanned out and approached the cart. This was the source of the wailing.

On the other side of the dray, one male lay on his back, his shirt soaked in blood, empty eyes staring at the glistening stars. An arquebus rifle lay near him in the dirt.

A woman, her clothes also stained crimson, sat with her back against the wagon wheel. She, too, held a rifle, but was too weak to lift the heavy weapon. A thin baby in a grubby white gown clung to her neck, bawling. Blood ran in a thin streak from the woman's nose and mouth.

"Please," she said, panting. "Take care of Virginia."

Her breathing was rapid and shallow, and the blood gurgled loudly in her chest as she struggled for air.

"Of course," Halle said, her voice saccharin sweet. She took the baby and handed her to Quinn. The child was so weak from hunger that she didn't have the strength to cry any more. She just made mewling sounds as she huddled against Quinn for warmth. She was shivering, so Quinn opened his heavy cloak and tucked her inside, being careful to keep her away from the brass buttons on his doublet.

Halle frowned as she knelt by the dying woman. If there was a cursed ring anywhere nearby, her dagger wasn't picking it up. The parts of it that showed through her scabbard remained dim. "Can you tell us where the ring is?"

"Ring?" The trickle of blood from her mouth had stopped flowing. She was almost out of time.

"Yes," Halle said, "a gold ring, perhaps that somebody here found recently?"

"Husband...Anaias." Her head lurched toward the dead man on the ground.

She went into a terrible fit of coughing, then her body went rigid and she made an eerie, choking gasp. Her head slumped onto her chest. The baby was now an orphan.

Halle pulled out the enchanted dagger and waved it over the man's corpse, just in case. The blade's faint glow remained unchanged.

"Let's check the houses. I'll look for the ring, and you two look for survivors – we don't want any surprises." She looked at the bulge under Quinn's cloak. "If you want that thing to live, you probably ought to feed it."

Siobhan and Quinn found no survivors, but they did find a bony cow with a little bit of milk in her udder.

Siobhan located a wooden pail and milked what she could from the cow, then turned her loose. There wasn't much forage for her in the compound. Siobhan would make sure she left the gate open, but the animal would be on her own in the forest. She wished her well.

Inside one of the rough houses, they spotted a pewter ladle. She used it as a cup while Quinn held the baby, who drank the warm milk greedily, but not skillfully.

"How old do you think she is?" Quinn asked.

"I would guess she's at least one year, but not as many as two."

When the pail was empty, Quinn rewrapped the damp and sticky child in his cloak.

"What are you going to do with her?" Siobhan asked.

"I can't take care of a baby, especially not a human baby."

"Will you just leave her here, then?"

Quinn looked down at the small child who was drowsing against his chest and sighing softly, comforted both by the milk and the sound of his heartbeat.

"I can't do that, either."

Siobhan smiled at him, almost laughing. She started to say something, but Halle shouted for them.

"Quinn! Siobhan! I think I've found it," Halle called from the largest of the ramshackle buildings.

Parchment pages, sealing wax and metal stamps were scattered on the table where Halle had emptied out the contents of a tall cupboard.

One, perhaps because of its ornate calligraphy, caught Quinn's eye. The document granted the governorship of Roanoke Colony to John White, in the Year of our Lord 1587. Almost two years ago.

Halle had used brute force to break into the false bottom of the cupboard, and a shattered board also lay on the table. She held a locked wooden box in one hand and scanned it with the dagger, which glowed blue-white. She grinned as she used the blade to pry open the lock.

A primitive flint arrowhead lay inside on a little cotton pillow.

Halle swore in old Norse.

"Two cursed objects?" Siobhan asked.

"So it would seem," Quinn said.

Halle ran from house to house, looking for a surge of light from her dagger, but got nothing.

"The mob that left here earlier must have it. We've got to find Aleksei," she said.

They started off in the direction the mob had been heading when the MIT arrived. Virginia was so light that Quinn almost forgot he was carrying her. The colonists' tracks were difficult to miss in the snow. In its sheath at Halle's side, the little dagger glinted with a pale blue glow.

It did not take long to find the colonists. In the fifty yards or so they'd travelled into the woods, the group had splintered into factions, which were now arguing about what to do with a cask that sat in the middle of the clearing where they were gathered.

"They will kill each other," Halle remarked.

"That's a problem?" Quinn asked.

Baby Virginia moaned softly from under Quinn's cloak as a snowflake fell on her exposed cheek.

All eyes looked at her. Even with the heat of Quinn's body and his thick cloak, the child was still visibly shivering. And the weather was getting worse.

"I'll go," Quinn said. "Siobhan, would you take the bairn?"

"No. Let me. None of you is invulnerable," Halle said. "But I am."

Never one for subtlety, the Valkyrie put her hand on the haft of her axe, left the cover of the stand of mountain laurel, and strode into the middle of the group of colonists. A ripple of silence preceded her, as the settlers noticed her approach. The man with the floppy hat stopped carving letters on a tree at the edge of the clearing.

"What have we 'ere?" said Bill. Up close, Halle noticed that he had bad skin and missing teeth. He was lean, but still appeared strong. But not as strong as her. No human would ever be as strong as her.

"I would ask you the same question," Halle smiled.

Some of the men laughed nervously, apparently wondering if she was utterly mad or seriously dangerous."That's none of your concern," the wiry man said. "Shove off, Miss, while you still can."

"What's in the box?" Halle asked, unfazed.

The man took a large step forward, invading Halle's personal space. "It's a ring, Miss. You wanna be me bride?"

Then the man made the last mistake of his life.

With his right hand, he drew a small blade from his belt. With his left, he grabbed Halle's breast.

Her eyes glowed green. A wind swirled around her, faster and faster, picking up loose snow and forest debris. The man began to howl in pain as green fire flowed down the hand he used to grasp Halle and up his arm, taking clothing and flesh with it. In moments, he lay screaming and bleeding in the snow, every inch of his skin gone.

"Witch!" yelled a panicked voice behind her.

An arquebus was pointed at Halle. She raised her arms and more green fire danced around her fingers. Her face became distorted and beastlike. With a yell, she brought her arms down to shoulder level. The fire leaped from her fingers onto the men, vaporizing each as it touched them.

When it was over, Halle stood inside a messy circle of brown slush where there had been pristine snow only moments before. She went to the box, opened it, and discovered that it contained nine rings. That is what made Andvaranaut so desirable. Every ninth day, it produced eight exact duplicates of itself. It wouldn't take long to become rich that way. Too bad about the misfortune curse. Halle wondered if the duplicates, too, were cursed. She snapped the box closed and turned to face her team.

"What have you done?" Aleksei asked.

The Valkyrie smiled bitterly. "Did I not tell you there was a destruction curse on this ring?"

The lone survivor still lay in the snow, moaning in agony. Taking pity on him, Siobhan pulled her bright rapier from its scabbard to strike the coup de grâce. She assessed her target and plunged the sword into his heart to end his suffering.

In silence, the fae made their way towards the portal, passing the village on the way. Halle stopped.

She looked at Aleksei and Siobhan, then nodded towards the two bodies behind the wagon.

"Bring them."

"Whatever for?" Siobhan asked.

"They stood up to a theiving mob. They must have been very brave. They deserve to be laid to rest properly."

Three small boats had been dragged up on the beach just behind the palisaded wall. Halle pushed one out into the water just deep enough for it to float.

"Put them both in here."

Aleksei and Siobhan did as they were instructed. Halle took a tinderbox from the leather pouch that was slung around her hips and set a fire in the boat. She gave it a hard shove and let the receding tide pull it away from the shore as the flames got higher.

"Let's go," she said.

As soon as they made it back through the portal, Quinn made a bee line to Dame Rowan's office with Virginia. Rowan admired the child and stroked her cheek. "I'm sorry, but there's no one available just now to care for a baby. And Titania's School for Girls doesn't take them that young."

"What am I supposed to do with her? I can't very well take her to the Waterhorse, now can I?"

Rowan gave Quinn a warning look, but let the outburst slide. "I'm sure you'll come up with something. Perhaps she has some relatives you can track down. Right now, I have more pressing issues. I must speak with Halle about what happened on this last mission."

Quinn nodded and left. Virginia was beginning to stir, and she'd probably need feeding.

"My ma could never resist a babby," Siobhan said to Quinn when he came downstairs into the great hall.

He spent the next three days with Siobhan's family, watching Virginia begin to fill out and become a contented, happy toddler. Her goofy, mostly toothless smile melted his heart, and he found it extremely difficult to leave her behind when he and Siobhan were called back to MAMIC.

Quinn, Siobhan, and Aleksei sat in the armchairs in Dame Rowan's office, waiting for her. When at last she swept in, she paced the room near the windows instead of sitting at her desk.

"I regret to inform you that Halle is gone. She has been sent to personally return the ring to Andravari. Perhaps he'll lift the curse. She is not banished — she's free to come and go as she chooses. There were, after all, mitigating circumstances. The ring was beshrewn to cause misfortune and destruction. She could not entirely help acting under its influence. Still, she cannot retain her position as team leader. She has a new assignment — monitoring the Frost Giants in the northlands. They get some peculiar ideas from time to time, and it's best if someone keeps an eye on what they're up to."

Quinn examined the rug. He hoped that his breakup with Halle had not contributed to her downfall. He cared about her, much more than he wanted to, but he had also come to realize that their romance had been doomed from the start.

"I have given this a great deal of consideration," Dame Rowan continued. "Your team is now short one member. I'm going to add a new team lead. His name is Beckett, and he will be arriving with Eoin in a fortnight. Until then, consider yourselves on holiday."

Quinn spent every moment he could at Siobhan's family home with Virginia. As far as she knew, he was her father, and no one ever told her anything different. Even though she was not his blood, he loved her as if she were. Still, he kept any news of her from his mother. Humans had killed his father so long ago that he barely remembered him. But his mother vowed revenge on any and all humans she encountered, and she'd raised her sons to loathe the creatures as well. Until Virginia became his foundling, he believed that humans were just pathetic demons without any magick.

When she was five, Virginia began boarding at Titania's School for Girls. As time passed, Virginia grew from a timid child into a strong and self-possessed young woman. Quinn taught her everything he knew when she entered the MIT training program, and she easily found a spot on the team of her choice. When she fell in love with Niall, one of Siobhan's sidhe cousins, and married him, Quinn gave her away at the handfasting. He was proud grandpa to their son and two daughters, and great-grandpa to their happy broods.

But the lifespan of even a long-lived human is brief, compared to fae. All too quickly, Virginia grew old and died. Quinn openly wept at her funeral, and fell into a terrible sadness. Siobhan was the only one who was able to pull him out of it, and they soon became inseparable.

Whenever Quinn returned to Blackthorne from a mission, he never failed to leave a white rose on Virginia's grave.

The Devil's Advocate

Artemis Greenleaf

The Devil's Advocate

Artemis Greenleaf

Marti Keller Mysteries
Book Three

Acknowledgements

Acknowledgements

As always, thank you to my wonderful family. This endeavor would not be possible without your love and support. I also appreciate the invaluable editorial and structural help of my critique groups and beta readers. You know who you are, and I couldn't do this without you. Finally, a big shout-out to the law enforcement officers I've had the opportunity and privilege to interact with. Thank you!

Table of Contents

The Devil is an optimist if he thinks he can make people worse than they are. – Karl Kraus

Chapter 1
Space City Sizzlin' Summer Literary Conference

Wednesday, August 3
Houston, Texas

When my husband, Ryan, died and left me alone and six weeks pregnant, I thought I'd never be happy again.

But here I was, not quite two years later, relaxing on the couch, drowsing against Quinn's perfectly muscled chest, watching TV. Maybe it was too soon to call him my boyfriend, but in a few short weeks we'd already taken turns saving each other's lives, and it just felt right to be with him.

No matter how dangerous he was.

"Arf!"

"I think Cú needs to go out," I said.

"Probably," Quinn replied.

The black puppy got up from gnawing on his rawhide bone and trotted towards the back wall. As he approached it, he began to fade out into transparency. By the time he reached the wall, he had vanished. A few moments later, he faded back in as he trotted to his favorite spot on the rug, barked twice at his toy, and began chewing it again.

"I'm still trying to get used to that," I said.

"One of the benefits of owning a Faery dog."

"Hmmm."

He squeezed me a little tighter and kissed my temple. "I should probably go, while it's still a respectable hour," Quinn said in his sexy Scottish accent.

"Probably," I replied, though I made no move to get up.

"As you wish," he mock-chided, "but it's your mother that lives next door."

I sighed and sat up, and he pulled me back down, laughing.

But that all stopped when a piercing wail punctured the moment. "Mamamama! Mamamama!" shouted Cassie between sobs.

"Poor baby – she's teething. I'd better get her some ibuprofen. It may be a long night."

As I entered her bedroom, I saw Cassie standing in her crib, little tears running down her cheeks as she gnawed on her fingers. She stamped one foot, wailing and reaching out to me with her other hand. I scooped her up into my arms and turned to go out to the kitchen. I accidentally knocked a gaudy paper hat off the dresser. It was left over from her first birthday party last week. Mom insisted that I bring it home for the baby scrapbook that I hadn't actually kept up with. Hopefully, I'd remember to pick it up before the puppy found it.

I carried her into the living room, and she was getting more worked up by the minute.

"I'll take her," Quinn said.

"Thanks." I handed her off so I could get her medicine.

By the time I got back, Cassie was asleep in his arms, and he gently rocked her back and forth. Guess I didn't need the eyedropper full of ibuprofen after all.

And that ability to bend humans to his will, like pipe cleaners around a pencil, was the least of the weapons in his arsenal. But I wasn't going to wake Cassie up for the sake of a principle.

I was a little surprised to see a U-Haul truck in front of the Tenth Sphere when I got to work. Belinda Tate, one of the metaphysical shop's co-owners, stood on the ramp, hands on her hips.

"Hauling something in or out?" I asked.

"Loading up books and stuff for the conference tomorrow."

A youngish man with glasses poked his head out of the cargo area.

"Hey, Ben," I said.

"Hey." He waved, then blotted the sweat off his forehead with the bottom of his tanktop. "Okay, Belinda, I think I've got everything but your cardboard cutouts loaded up."

Lulu's nephew had recently been arrested for murder. He was exonerated and released, but he'd still lost his job, and was at loose ends. Belinda was paying him to be her roadie for the *Space City Sizzlin' Summer Literary Conference* at the George R. Brown Convention Center. He and I would take turns manning her booth on Saturday while she was speaking on the romance writers' panel and in breakout sessions. I wasn't looking forward to the crowds, but I could use the money.

The shop traffic was about average for a Thursday afternoon — customers came in waves. But we were currently in a lull. I cleaned fingerprints off of the glass countertop that housed the Belinda's Blessed Beads section. I'm not sure how she found time to do it, between the shop and writing, but Belinda made gorgeous beaded bookmarks, notecard stakes for plants or flower arrangements, and jewelry.

Lulu propped her elbows on the glass display case. "Have you been practicing with your cards, honey?"

"Been kind of busy," I replied scrubbing a little harder.

She raised one eyebrow.

I looked at the front door, hoping a customer was on the way in. No such luck. "Sorry."

Lulu came around the display and pulled a carved wooden box from a shelf underneath the cash register. Inside the box was a red silk bag containing a deck of Tarot cards.

"Shuffle," she said. "And think of a question. You don't have to say it out loud. Usually better if you don't."

I set down my duster and shuffled the over-sized cards. The only question on my mind right now was, *What does the future hold for Quinn and me?*

"When it feels like they've been moved around enough, pick one."

"From the top?"

Lulu stretched her hands out, palms up. "Doesn't matter. Top, middle, bottom. Wherever you like. The point of handling them is to get your energy on the cards."

The big cards were stiff and awkward to deal with. I think I stopped shuffling more because I gave up and less because it 'felt right.' I pulled one from the middle and laid it on the counter.

An ugly winged humanoid stood in the middle with a raised sword. Before it stood two naked people with ropes tied loosely around their necks, and connected to a ring in the floor.

Trump 15. The Devil.

I frowned. "That can't be good, right? Isn't this card about base urges and greed?" *Was the Tarot trying to tell me that Quinn was the Devil, and no good would come of being with him?*

"Depends. Think about your question, honey. It could be about lust, fear, hate, and so on. Often has to do with substance abuse. But it could also be about unexpected challenges, or maybe you have to do something very unconventional to solve a problem."

"My whole life has been pretty unconventional lately."

Lulu smiled. "Well, there's that. Depending on where it falls in the reading, The Devil may also represent the shadow side of the querent's personality, the part we don't really want to look at."

The cowbell on the door clattered.

Lulu glanced at the wall clock. "That'll be my 3:15."

She went to work with her client. A few customers drifted in, then drifted back out with their purchases. A few more readings came in. It was a completely unremarkable afternoon.

Until the phone rang just before closing.

"Good afternoon. Tenth Sphere," I said.

"Yes. Is Belinda there, please?"

"I'm sorry, but she's away."

The woman on the other end of the line snuffled and blew her nose. Her voice broke as she asked to speak to Lulu, the shop's other owner.

"I'm sorry," I said. "She's with a client. Would you care to leave a message?"

The caller sighed. "Would you please have Belinda call Anne Tremont? She has the number," the woman said. "Ellen...Ellen has gone into hospice care."

"I'm so sorry. I'll let her know."

Ellen was a long-time client of the Tenth Sphere, and Belinda's most devoted reader. Just when she thought her battle with breast cancer had been won, she was diagnosed with acute myeloid leukemia.

After Lulu's client left, I gave her the bad news. She closed her eyes and shook her head. "I knew it was coming, just didn't think it'd be quite this soon." She smiled wanly, then said, "I'll close up. Why don't you go ahead and take off, honey? I know you have to go pick up that sweet little Miss Cassie."

I started for the back room to get my things.

"And don't forget to hug your mother."

"I won't forget," I replied.

"Girlfriend, you got to try to get Belinda to skip that romance panel."

"Jeeze, Delilah! Don't sneak up on me like that when I'm driving."

I was almost to Cassie's daycare when my spirit guide popped into the passenger seat of my car. She was generally more considerate than that.

I shifted into thought mode — she could hear what I was thinking, and the other parents leaving the daycare wouldn't think I was insane. *I'm not sure a stick of dynamite could pry her off that panel. What's going on?*

"Something bad is coming, girl," Delilah said.

"Aside from Ellen dying?"

Delilah's head bobbled on her shoulders. She still wore the same red-sequined gown that she'd worn at the Roquefort Club the night she died in 1936.

"Much worse," she said. That's a sad thing, for sure, but death comes to all of us. This thing I'm talking about, there ain't nothing natural about it. Nothing at all."

I shook my head as I pulled into a parking space. *"It's going to take more info than that to get her to think about it. Have you seen how pumped she is for this conference?"*

"I know. But *you* know I can't give you details, girlfriend."

"I can tell her, but I don't think it will help." I looked over at Delilah before I opened the door. But she was gone.

Cassie and Cú were both asleep. I took advantage of this and cleaned out Alpha and Betty's cage. The rats were starting to show their age — I'd had them over a year, and no telling how old they were when my police officer brother-in-law, Nick, rescued them and brought them to me. I had just finished cleaning, and had one on each shoulder when my cell rang. Caller ID said it was Lulu.

"Lulu? What's wrong?" It wasn't like her to call at 10:30 at night just to chat.

"I'm sorry to call you so late, honey. But I need a huge favor from you. Can you run the shop tomorrow?"

"All day?"

"Yes. I'll meet you there at 9:30 to help you get started. There's been a terrible accident here. Regina Dupris, one of the writers on the Romance Panel with Belinda, tripped and fell down the escalator. She was a good friend, and B's taking it pretty hard. Especially since she was at the bottom of the escalator when it happened. The ambulance got here super quick, but Regina, she didn't make it. I don't want to leave B on her own. She's kinda fragile just now."

"Oh, I'm really sorry to hear that. Sure, I can open." *Maybe Mom can take Cassie to Briar Ridge Montessori when she takes Kyle and Aiden.* "Let me quickly try and call my mom before she goes to bed, okay? Give Belinda a hug for me, and I'll see you in the morning."

"Okay, see you then," Lulu said.

I remembered Delilah's warning.

"Wait! Lulu?"

"Yes?

"You know, nobody would think badly of Belinda if she dropped out of the panel. It might be easier on her if she did."

"That's exactly what I told her. But you know B. She's like a terrier with a rat – she'll never let it go."

"Yeah, I know. Goodnight, then."

I petted the rats. "It's okay, girls. Belinda would never hurt you."

I called my mother's land line, but she didn't pick up. I called my sister, Emily, since Mom had been helping her with the new baby.

"Benson," my brother-in-law answered.

"Hey, Nick. It's Marti. Is my mother over there?"

"Yeah. She's changing McKenzi right now, though."

"No problem. Is Em okay?" My sister was recovering from a pulmonary embolism, and that made me a little nervous.

"She's fine. I'll tell Adele to call you, alright?"

"Sure. Thanks."

I hung up with Nick and put the rats away. I smiled at Cú – he was lying on the floor, asleep and dreaming, with his nose twitching and feet flapping, as if he were running at top speed after the most delicious scent ever.

It had been a long time since I'd had a dog, and I guess the canine bug was rekindled a few weeks ago when I'd rescued Bruce. Only Bruce wasn't actually a dog. But that's a whole other story. When Quinn brought Cú as a gift for Cassie (and a replacement for Bruce), I wasn't sure what to expect. I smiled at the snoozing pup. "You sure are a cute little thing, with those big floppy ears. Although, if you ever grow into those feet, you'll be the size of a pony."

My cell rang.

"Hey, Mom," I answered.

"Are you okay?" she asked.

"Fine. Sorry to call you so late, but something's come up at work, and I need to be there all day. Is there any way you can take Cassie to Briar Ridge when you take Emily's boys? I may need you to pick her up, too."

"I'm sure I can. We usually leave from Emily's house at 8:30."

"Thanks, Mom. See you in the morning."

After I checked the doors and set the alarm, I looked in on Cassie on my way to bed. Still sleeping like an angel. I was so tired that I almost forgot to brush my teeth.

I awoke with a start and sat up. The clock read 4:37, and it was very dark. I listened hard to see if I could detect what noise might have woken me up, but I heard nothing out of the ordinary. There seemed to be a dream that had quickly submerged itself deep into my subconscious, because I felt there was something I needed to remember, but no memories surfaced. I started to get up to check on Cassie, but stopped dead when I saw the figure standing at the end of my bed. She didn't glow, but I still saw her as clear as day. She was trying to say something, but no words came. I reached out to her, but she faded away. My heart sank.

It was Ellen.

Chapter 2
Cesar Chavez

Thursday, August 4
Houston, Texas

ick Benson was the third patrol unit to arrive at the scene, and the stink of diesel and blood made him cough when he stepped out of the truck. The primary officer, Chris Canales, had been heading east on an eight-lane segment of Westheimer Road, in the Energy Corridor District, when a late model black Suburban came screaming out of a parking lot, careened off of a cement mixer, and rolled over twice, right in front of him.

Aside from a few cuts and bruises, the driver was unhurt. The same could not be said for his passenger, who had been partially ejected from the car. Cushioning the fall of a three-ton vehicle with one's body tends not to be compatible with life, and the Houston Fire Department EMS team was going to be spending some time locating all the pieces of him. But that would come later. Right now, they were using the Jaws of Life to extract a mom and her two kids from what was left of their car, which had been crushed by the rolling SUV.

The second officer to arrive, Jessica Collins, was trying to get traffic re-routed around the accident, but was not having much luck with a couple of surly rubberneckers. Nick was 6'4", and when he came striding up with a scowl on his face, the lookey-loos opted to go through the strip center parking lot as Collins had told them to do earlier.

"Life Flight's on the way," she said. "They'll need a spot to set down."

Nick nodded. "I'll go back to the intersection and divert traffic from there."

"What's your cell? I'll text you," she said.

Nick gave her the number, then got in his car. He parked his vehicle across as much of the four lane expanse of eastbound Westheimer as he could and turned on all of the strobes. Nick hadn't been rerouting unhappy drivers north and south onto Dairy Ashford for very long when an orange blob appeared on the southeastern horizon. As the blob got bigger, the thumping of the chopper's rotors got louder. Collins came to help him with traffic, using her patrol car to block the rest of the lanes that his didn't cover. Nick knew both

Canales and Collins from roll call – occasionally worked some incidents with one or the other of them, but had never run calls with either.

Nick was glad that the department had recently traded his worn out Crown Vic cruiser for a new Tahoe, because he only had to bend his knees a little to use the truck as shelter from the road debris kicked up by the landing helicopter. Collins came and stood next to him. After a while, Life Flight left the scene with two gurneys. A black body bag lay next to the crushed sedan. HFD now started the gruesome job of collecting the remains of the unfortunate SUV passenger. Traffic Division arrived with survey equipment to begin their investigation.

A call dropped on the radio, asking patrol officers to be on the lookout for a stolen SUV. Dispatch gave a description and plates. Canales replied that he was at the scene of a traffic fatality involving that particular vehicle, making it possibly the shortest BOLO in history.

Not unsurprisingly, the driver had no identification, but he said his name was 'Cesar Chavez.' While the guy looked dead average, Nick did notice a poorly executed star with '713' in the center of it tattooed on the side of his neck. Looked like a prison tat, and it also identified him as a Houstone, a gang banger.

Nick walked up and stood where he could keep an eye on Chavez while he was talking to Canales, and offered to transport the prisoner.

Canales, Nick thought, looked like a Hollywood action hero. Aside from a little acne. He recognized a fellow gym rat, and said, "Those are some impressive guns. Whatcha curling?"

Canales grinned. "One twenty-five. But I press four ten."

Nick nodded.

Cesar Chavez's cell phone rang.

"Gimme my phone, man," he said.

"No," Canales replied.

"Come on, man." He tried to roll his shoulders with his hands cuffed behind his back. "Cut me some slack, huh?"

"If it's important, they'll call back." Canales ran his hand through his thinning hair.

"Yeah, it probably ain't no big thing – just your woman begging me to do her again."

Nick took a step to his left as he sensed motion to his right. Before he could parse what was happening, Canales coldcocked Cesar Chavez, and the man crumpled to the ground.

"Stand down!" Nick said, gripping Canales' shoulder. "That mouthy POS isn't worth it."

Canales sucked in a huge breath, and Nick felt his muscles tense, then relax.

Cesar did not move.

"I'll go get EMS," Nick said, shaking his head. *This is going to get a whole lot worse before it gets better.*

By the time he returned with the EMT, Canales and Cesar were gone.

"I guess he got up," Nick said. *Dude, I hope you haven't gone and done something completely stupid.*

"Guess so." The medic returned to his grim task.

"Hey Benson, you see this?" It was Collins, waving Nick over to the battered SUV. On the way over, he noticed several fluid-filled, capped syringes and two metal boxes of mints lying in the street.

At the SUV, Nick looked at one of the open doors that several officers were gathered around. During the vehicle's roll, the interior panel had gotten knocked loose from the metal, and four sixteen-ounce water bottles peeked out. Each one was filled about three quarters full with a fluid that looked like watered-down iced tea.

"Liquid meth," Collins said.

Nick nodded, "Yeah, I've seen it a few times."

"Owner works at the gym," she said, nodding toward the parking lot.

"Not anymore," he said.

Collins laughed.

After Nick turned in his paperwork for the day and clocked out, he was surprised to find Chris Canales waiting for him in the parking lot.

"Hey," he said. "Look, about this afternoon...I know I shouldn't have let that guy get under my skin. It's just..." His fists clenched by his sides. "I was working a security job last night, and I got home early and found my wife in the hot tub with the neighbor from two doors down."

"Shit."

"Exactly," he said. "You, um, you want to grab a beer?"

"Sure."

"How about that place on Highway 6, just north of Westheimer on the right-hand side?"

"Yeah, alright. I'll meet you there."

Nick got in his truck, then retrieved his phone. He texted Emily that he'd be a little late. He adored his family, and wouldn't trade his kids for anything. But sometimes, the new baby was a little much. She needed so much time, so much energy. Nick didn't always have it to spare, but his wife had nearly died from a pulmonary embolism, and was still recovering, so a large portion of the baby care fell on him. He was grateful that Adele, Emily's mother, lived five doors down and could often help out. And at least the boys were old enough to feed and dress themselves. They could even cook a box of mac and cheese, if they had to.

He eased into traffic and headed up Dairy Ashford to Westheimer. If he hadn't known there'd been an awful traffic fatality there earlier in the day, he would never have guessed it. The pavement was a little wet, for no obvious reason, but that was all.

When he turned into the parking lot of the bar, the first thing he noted was the abundance of parking spaces.

Canales pulled up in his Suburban and got out. Nick did the same. As he walked toward Canales, he saw that the 'Open' sign was not lit, and stopped.

Canales smiled. "My bad. I forgot they weren't open tonight."

"Yeah, well maybe another time, then," Nick replied. Canales now wore a hoodie – a peculiar thing for July in Houston – and had his hands in the pockets.

Nick's skin prickled as the little hairs on the back of his neck rose.

He didn't see the blue arc from the end of the Taser until it was too late. His nerves turned to fire as the charge hit him, and his body went rigid. Canales caught him before he fell, and shoved him into the back of his waiting SUV. As he duct-taped Nick's feet together, Nick tried to force his legs apart so he couldn't be constrained, or at least not tightly. But it was no use. The Taser had temporarily short-circuited his nervous system and every fiber of muscle was on fire. Or at least that's how it felt. An unpleasant buzz vibrated up his spine and rattled his brain.

"No," Canales said. "No, you'll talk to them won't you? I know you'll talk."

He pulled Nick's hands behind his back and duct-taped them, too.

"I'm sorry, Benson. Truly I am, but I don't know another way to handle this. You're going to tell them everything, and I can't have that." He slapped a piece of duct tape over Nick's mouth.

As the voltage dissipated, Nick struggled to breathe. His tall frame was already bent uncomfortably in the back, and his lungs were compressed due to his hands being bound behind him. It didn't help that the back of the SUV smelled like fresh mulch — an unpleasant combination of wood, molasses, and manure. Was he about to meet the same fate as Cesar Chavez? What did Canales think he knew? Did he tell the boys he loved them last night when he put them to bed? Nick exhaled as sharply as he dared. He had to focus, if he had any hope of escaping.

He couldn't see out the window, so he listened carefully, trying to make out any audible landmarks. Nick was able to use the ribbed cargo liner to scrape the end of the duct tape off of the side of his mouth. At least he could breathe now. After a short drive, the SUV left the smooth pavement and bumped along slowly. Nick didn't hear the crunch of gravel, and the terrain was so rough that he figured they must be going off-road. The truck stopped. Canales had muttered to himself the whole way, and Nick only caught occasional words, but as near as Nick could tell Canales seemed to think they were being followed.

The engine stopped and Nick heard the driver's door open, but not close. The cab light did little to illuminate the cargo area. He knew he had one chance, and he had to be ready. He eased himself onto his back. His shoulders screamed as his weight shifted to his trapped hands. Then he raised his feet, cocking his legs back as far as he could.

As soon as Canales released the latch, Nick kicked the door with all the strength he could muster. The lift door connected with Canales' face, and Nick had to scramble to stick a foot in the way to keep the door from slamming closed. He grunted as it smashed into his foot. But the latch didn't catch.

Nick struggled out of the SUV and landed on his side. Canales was just getting up. Blood poured down his face, and Nick guessed he must have hit him in the nose when he kicked the door open.

"Why are you doing this?" Nick asked. He tried to get to his feet, but he just couldn't balance on his duct-taped legs.

"Because," Canales replied, holding his nose to slow the bleeding. "You'll rebort be. I cat hab tat habben."

"What is it you think I'd report you for that's worse than this?"

"You dow. Dote play dub wid be."

Nick studied Canales. And then he realized what was going on. The explosive anger. The huge arms. The thinning hair and acne. The paranoia.

"You're juiced, aren't you?" he asked.

Canales leaned away from him and shook his head. "I cat let you tell adybody. Dot about Chavez, dot about dis. Da guy at da gyb, he tode be I could cleed up boving product on da side for hib. He was right. Hill keep his bouth shut, doe. You won't."

"Dude, I didn't even realize you were nuclear. Can we just talk about it?"

"Shut up!" Canales yelled, then shook himself. "Dere's lots of feral hogs aroud here. Dell fide you before adybody eben realizes you're bissing."

He unholstered Nick's weapon. There wasn't much he could do to stop it.

The sound was the worst part, so close, so loud. There was no pain, only intense pressure as the bullet entered his skull just above the left ear.

Chapter 3
Unfinished Business

4:37 AM, Thursday, August 4
Houston, Texas

 pulled the sheet up a little higher. "Delilah!" I whispered in the dark. "Delilah!"

She materialized slowly, fading in with a yawn and a stretch. "Girlfriend, what do you need at this time of day?"

Catching myself, and not wanting to wake Cassie, who was just across the hall, I switched to addressing Delilah through my thoughts. *I need to know what happened to Ellen.*

"I'm sorry, girl. She just passed. She ain't very cooperative, though."

What do you mean?

"She does *not* want to cross over to the other side." Her head bobbled, emphasizing the 'not.'

Is that bad? Doesn't it mean that she's got unfinished business?

"Sometimes," she said. "But I ain't sure that's what's happening with her."

Isn't there a network or something? Don't you just automatically know this stuff?

One eyebrow arched steeply, and Delilah crossed her arms. "Girl, of course I can find out. It's just I don't go meddlin' in other folks' business if I don't have to. I got enough souls to look out for as it is."

And with that, she vanished.

I tried to go back to sleep. But it just wasn't happening. At 5:30, I gave up and got dressed. Cú heard me moving around and walked through the wall of his crate, tail wagging. I'm not sure why I even bothered with the crate. Force of habit, maybe. Cú wasn't a tiny dog, but he was small enough to be on the menu if a great horned owl happened by. Or, for all I knew, the owl might be on his menu. So, to protect both, I went outside with him. As a puppy, he was mercilessly cute. But he was a puppy. He had accidents and he chewed anything that fit into his mouth, and a few things that didn't. Sometimes, I really missed mature, house-broken Bruce.

I thought I'd lucked out when I found the huge Lab wandering around in the middle of the night. Especially since he'd saved my life. It was the most natural thing in the world to bring him home. Only Bruce wasn't actually Bruce. He was Quinn. And as it turned out, Quinn wasn't exactly Quinn, either. He was a kelpie, a sort of lake monster, who, more often than not, took the form of a human. But he could also shapeshift into a black horse or a large black dog. So that made it a little awkward – I couldn't have Bruce without Quinn, and I just wasn't comfortable having a man I'd only known a few weeks move into my house. Even if he had saved my life more than once.

I brought Cú back inside. He had a little drink from the water dish, then went back to sleep. I sat on the couch, clicking through the channels with the remote.

A book suddenly fell off the shelf, and I jumped. I walked over and picked up *Dragon by Knight* from off the floor. It's the first book in Belinda Tate's paranormal romance series that she wrote under the pen name Coda Sterling. There was no reason for it to have fallen.

"Ellen?"

The lamp flickered.

I thought for a moment. I'd done this before. "If you're still here, either make the lamp flicker or knock twice for a yes answer, and once for a no answer, okay? Knock or flicker, whichever is easier." *Where was Delilah? She could easily translate this for us.*

At first, nothing happened. Then the light flickered twice.

"Are you Ellen?"

Two flickers.

"Ellen, I am so sorry that you died. Don't think I'm trying to get rid of you, but you know it's best for you to go ahead and cross over, right?"

One flicker.

"Why not?" *That's not a yes or no question.* "Is it…that you're too attached to this place?"

One flicker.

"Unfinished business?"

Three flickers.

Three? A yes and a no? Is that a maybe?

Two flickers.

Well, of course. If Delilah could hear my thoughts, it made sense that Ellen could, too. *So, sort of unfinished business, but not exactly?*

Two flickers came, but they were spaced further apart than the previous ones. *Are you getting tired?*

Two flickers, spaced so far apart, I initially thought the answer was 'no.'

Ellen, why don't you rest? When you get your strength back, you can tell me about your unfinished business. Sound like a plan?

There was no reply.

Friday, August 5
Houston, Texas

Lulu and Belinda were waiting for me at the shop at 9:30. Both of them had puffy eyes and tearstained cheeks, but Belinda was drawn and pale. I understood why – she'd lost two good friends only a few hours apart. I hugged her, then Lulu.

"I saw Ellen," I whispered in her ear, afraid that if Belinda heard, she'd just get more upset.

"What? When?" Lulu asked, pulling away from me.

"This morning," I said. "She hasn't crossed over though – there's something she wants to do first."

"Who are you talking about?" Belinda asked. Her voice was raspy with old tears.

"Marti said she saw Ellen early this morning."

Belinda closed her eyes, but liquid grief leaked out from between her lashes.

I gasped. "I am so sorry. I thought you knew that Ellen had passed."

Lulu shook her head, her own eyes moist. "No. You told me yesterday afternoon that she was in hospice. But I haven't spoken with her sister today - we've been on a video call this morning with the conference organizers. They were trying to decide whether to shut down the romance writers' panel after Regina Dupris' accident."

"We decided to keep the panel, and dedicate it to her," Belinda whispered. "I'm going to splash some cold water on my face." She headed toward the restrooms.

Lulu watched her go, shaking her head gently. "All this has been so hard on her."

"Delilah seemed to think it was really important that she quit the panel. But she'll never do it if it's dedicated to her friend. Doesn't Belinda have her own spirit guide to tell her this stuff?"

"Of course she does, honey. You know, I wouldn't be one bit surprised if Sofia and Ellen hadn't worked together to time Ellen's passing to make it as easy as possible for B to step down. But just because people have spirit guides, doesn't mean they listen to them. I have to tell you, I agree with Delilah. There's something not right about this conference."

I shifted my weight and squirmed. I recalled how Delilah had strongly advised against bringing Bruce home the night I found him wandering the neighborhood.

"I'll be back sometime early this afternoon, so you can pick up Miss Cassie on time. Oh, and before I forget," Lulu said as she reached into her over-sized purse. "Here's your exhibitor's badge for tomorrow."

I forced a smile as I took it. *Should be fun, as long as nobody else dies.*

Ocean folded his wings and crouched on the highest tree limb that would support his weight. His grey skin blended well with the trunk of the tree, and he was unlikely to be noticed by passers-by. Leathery wings folded against his back, and he'd brought his hand up to use as a visor to shade the glow of his eyes. He waited. With nothing else to do, he watched the windows of the house. He could see into the kitchen as the woman inside gave her baby a meal in a high chair. She had a black puppy that came outside and wuffed at him a couple of times, but ran back inside, tail between its legs. Ocean couldn't identify what the baby had been eating, but whatever it was, it was smeared all over her face and hands. The woman took her away into another room, and he couldn't see them anymore.

He shrugged and shook his head. If he'd been able to find her so easily, it would be even less trouble for Balcones. That demon ran in human circles more often than diabolical ones, and he'd know all of the human protocols. Still it wasn't his concern. There was no shortage of humans, and two fewer wouldn't make any difference in the grand scheme of things.

Dusk was creeping into the trees, and shadows stretched like grasping fingers across the ground before he heard the sound of a familiar tread coming up the sidewalk. It had been a while, but he did not easily forget such things.

"*Mon Dieu!* Looks like all the monsters are out tonight," he said to the approaching figure. Then he hopped out of the tree, his stone-hard haunches easily absorbing the shock.

"Hello, Uncle," Quinn said. "It's been a long time."

Chapter 4
Orange Badges

10:00 AM, Friday August 5
Houston, Texas

inah sat in her car with the windows down, pretending to adjust her makeup. She had come downtown to the GRB Convention Center an hour and a half early so she could park at the very front of the cattycorner lot and watch. The badges that hung from people's necks were her focus. White ones were for regular attendees, green ones were for editors and agents, and orange ones belonged to panelists and presenters who were not agents.

A group of white-badged ladies passed. Then a pair of green. Her pulse quickened when she saw a flash of orange. He was a panelist, but not one of The Five. Or rather, The Four, given that smut-merchant Regina Dupris had taken a fatal escalator trip yesterday evening. She wouldn't be spewing her filth across the printed page anymore.

Dinah smiled, and glanced down at the sheet torn from the conference packet she'd taken from the registration table, the one with the photos and biographies of each of the romance writers' panel members. Regina's had a big red X through it.

An orange badge came from around the corner. Short dark hair, wedge cut. Meghan Palmer perhaps? Dinah couldn't be sure – she was just a little too far away. A tall, lanky woman approached from Discovery Green, a flash of orange against her white blouse as she walked. There was no doubt about it. She'd found that awful Coda Sterling woman. With her dragons and shape-shifting creatures. Bestiality, that's what that was. *Sickening.*

"Hey, Miss B!" a man shouted.

Coda Sterling looked up. Dinah snapped her jaw shut so fast she almost bit her tongue when she saw who had called out to the woman. Medium height, mousy hair with blonde highlights. His teal shirt was the same one from his bio photo.

"Stefán!" Coda changed course to meet him.

If Sterling was awful, Stefán Heidlemann was an abomination. Then Dinah realized she'd hit the jackpot. She could get two with one blow.

She wondered if it would hurt twice as much, or the same, just for twice as long. *Nothing is accomplished without sacrifice*, she reminded herself. Still, she swallowed hard before she tugged at the gold chain, pulled a pear-cut ruby out of her blouse, and held it in her right hand.

Sterling and Heidlemann embraced, then headed away from her and toward a traffic light. Dinah didn't want to stare too hard at them, fearing they'd turn around and see her. She closed her eyes for a minute. When she opened them, they were still waiting to cross Avenida de las Americas to the convention center. This would be perfect.

She squeezed the ruby. "I wish," she whispered, "that you'd get hit by a car." Motion caught her eye as the woman she'd thought was Meghan Palmer started running across the street towards Sterling and Heidlemann. Could she get all three?

Dinah waited, almost holding her breath.

A car pulled out of the parking garage underneath Discovery Green. The driver, cell phone cradled against his shoulder, swerved across several lanes so that he could be in the empty leftmost one. He apparently didn't notice the light turning yellow, then red. He didn't even slow down. At least not until it was far too late. By the time the brakes screamed and started to smoke, Meghan Palmer was already airborne. She landed on the windshield with a crunch, the shattered safety glass cradling her like a broken doll. Bright red blood flowed from the back of her head, pooling in and highlighting the spider web of fractures in the glass. For the space of about three heartbeats, not even the birds twittered. Then the scene roared to life, with people running every which way, screaming, and shouting for someone to call 911.

But Dinah had her own problems. It hit her then – the cold, grasping sensation of pulling, then burning, as if someone had torn off a piece of her and cauterized the wound with a blow torch. And then it was gone. She shivered and wondered if the man had lied, and it was really her soul being torn apart.

She pulled down the visor and looked in the vanity mirror. There were crow's feet around her eyes now. The parentheses wrinkles between the corners of her nose and the corners of her mouth were more pronounced. She even noticed a few strands of grey in her hair. Still, five years older didn't look so bad. It was a small price to pay for taking out a smut-writer.

She tucked the ruby back into her blouse and got out of the car, remembering.

Two weeks ago, Dinah had seen an ad in the paper about a meeting for people who wanted to survive during the end times. She'd expected there to be a full house, but fewer than ten showed up. Perhaps if they'd held it a little earlier, people with children would have been able to come, too. At least that's what she told herself. The alternative was that most people thought the idea of end times was nonsense, and she refused to accept that. What with the apocalypse looming on the horizon, she wanted to save every soul she could before it was too late.

Good looking and about her age, Zachariah was one of the handful of attendees at the meeting. Waiting for the speaker to begin, they'd started a conversation on the corrupting influence of popular entertainment.

"Have you read some of these books nowadays?" he'd asked. "It's appalling."

He'd given her a flyer from his organization, Decency In Literature Drives Openness, and mentioned that they might be protesting at the upcoming writers' convention downtown. The paper contained short excerpts from each of the romance panelists, using their own words to show the depravity of their work. She'd hung on Zachariah's every word. *Finally! Someone who understands.*

Dinah's worn canvas shoes slapped on the pavement as she walked towards the accident. That sound would always make her think of Zachariah. That night at the meeting, she'd been nervous about walking to her car alone in the dark, and he offered to go with her. She told him she wished there was more she could do to stop the spread of moral decay, so people wouldn't be doomed for eternity when the world ended. "How is it that you're still single? You are so amazing!" he'd said.

That's when he'd given her the ruby and told her how to use it. It seemed almost too good to be true. There was only one drawback. She got unlimited wishes, but each wish took away five years of her life. But what was five years to her in these end times, when the world was going to explode at any minute? She was certain that her sacrifice in this life would ensure her a place of honor in the afterlife. A glance at the flyer in her hand told her exactly where she should start the cleansing.

She blinked, stopping her reverie, then flipped the visor up and got out of the car. After she locked the door, she jogged over to the scene of the car accident.

"What happened?" she asked the first person who stood still long enough.

"She got hit by a car. The ambulance will be here soon," the man said.

"Oh dear! Will she be okay?" *Why only one? Why couldn't I get the other two as well?*

"I don't know. Doesn't look good," he said, before melting back into the crowd.

The driver sat on the curb near his car. His head was in his hands and his shoulders shook as he sobbed. Dinah felt a flicker of guilt. She hadn't expected that. It didn't really occur to her when she made the wish that if there was a car, there must be a driver, and the driver might be traumatized from having mowed down pedestrians. *Sometimes sacrifices must be made for the greater good.*

There were a few people standing around him, so Dinah didn't approach. She'd wanted to tell him that even though this seemed like a bad thing, he'd really performed a service, contributed to the public good. After all, the filthy pornography that Meghan Palmer wrote only served to doom souls, not save them. A siren wailed in the distance, and Dinah thought it best not to be noticed, so she went on into the conference.

Two down, three to go.

4:30 PM, Friday, August 5
Houston, Texas

It was late on Friday afternoon, and Hadrian Galanti stood up and stretched. The FBI Special Agent had been listening to a recording of a phone conversation between a pair of Russian mobsters about smuggling heroin. But they seemed to be good friends because they spent more time joking around than doing business. At least that's what it sounded like. He had rewound the recording several times, trying to detect a code, or a pattern that could hide a code, and he was starting to get sleepy.

"Galanti?"

"Privyet, Direktor."

"English, please," Special Agent in Charge Jaimeson replied.

"Sorry." He was fluent in seven languages, and sometimes forgot that not everybody else was. But that was why he was brought in from Quantico to join the Multi-Agency Organized Crime Task Force.

"There's some possible movement on Irina Cherngelanov."

"Oh?" Hadrian suspected her husband's death may not have been entirely accidental, but had no evidence to prove it. She hadn't even bothered wearing black to his funeral, and she'd taken over the operation of his criminal organization swiftly and ruthlessly.

"She's a silent partner in the publishing company Bleu Kat Press. They specialize in romance and chick-lit. Anyway, two top selling authors from Bleu Kat's main competitors have had fatal accidents at that big writers' conference going on at the GRB."

"Sounds like Irina's style. People who get in her way tend to get very clumsy and fall in front of buses or off of balconies." Hadrian clenched his teeth to fight back a yawn.

"Exactly." Jaimeson tossed a manila envelope on Hadrian's desk. "That's your attendee packet. How's your suburb surveillance going? Haven't seen anything about it from you this week."

"Doesn't seem to be much going on. I'm starting to think the subject's contact with Irina's gang was coincidental."

The SAIC nodded. "Let it stay on the back burner for now, then."

10:00 AM, Saturday, August 6
Houston, Texas

Hadrian met Sara for brunch on Saturday. He'd been too tired to see her on Friday, even though she'd left a message asking him to go with her to an invitation-only art gallery opening. He probably should have gone, but he'd been up for thirty six hours, and he just didn't have it in him. Sourly, he wondered if she'd taken her intern, Matt, instead. The one she'd had a fling with. He hadn't confronted her about it, but it had led him to contemplate whether there was anything more to his and Sara's relationship than mutual convenience.

"Hey, Blackbird," Sara said between mouthfuls of poached egg. "What are you doing this evening? They gave away tickets at work for the Alley, and a bunch of us are going. We're meeting at Birraporetti's at 5:30."

If it was people from her work, he was definitely going. But he didn't want to seem over-eager. "What's the play?"

"It's an Agatha Christie. I forget which one. Maybe *Black Coffee*."

Sara had her back to the window, and the sun shone through her messy ponytail, making it look like a soft halo. He smiled. "Sure. Maybe I'll pick up some investigation pointers."

After they finished eating, Hadrian walked Sara to her car and kissed her goodbye.

"You want to come over?" she asked.

He glanced at his watch. "Can't. I've got to go to a conference. Work thing. Maybe after the play?"

She kissed him. "Definitely."

A smile lingered on Hadrian's mouth as he drove to George R. Brown. He didn't really think he'd find anything. It was unlikely that Russian mobsters would be hanging out by the front door, waiting to purge any writer who threatened to compete with Irina's stable of authors. Still, it was worth checking out. Parking was scarce, but he finally found a spot. Hadrian hung the conference attendee badge around his neck and read the schedule. He decided he'd walk through the exhibition hall first, to get a feel for the place.

He strolled from table to table, seemingly studying book covers and other literary paraphernalia. But he was really gauging the security and trying to figure out where the cameras were. Maybe he could obtain some video and feed it through his facial recognition software, just in case.

He picked up a beaded bookmark with a carved skull bead at one end, then almost dropped it. In his head, he heard a child screaming and felt panic, someone else's panic, wash over him. Then it was gone. Psychometry, it was called. The ability to touch something and know things about someone else who had touched that item. It came in fits and starts, sometimes helpful, sometimes not. He had no control over it – it was a fickle talent that came and went at some unknowable whim.

"You okay, Mister?" the young lady behind the table asked.

"Yeah. I'm fine. 'Possum just walked over my grave."

She nodded slightly, apparently trying to humor him.

Hadrian put the bookmark back on the table. "You've never had that, where you shudder for no reason at all?"

"No. Not really."

"Oh. Well, have a good one." He moved to the next table.

"Hunter! Hunter Greene!"

Hadrian froze. That was the undercover identity for his suburban surveillance case. He turned around to see the subject of his investigation waving at him.

"Hey, Marti! What are you doing here?" he asked her.

Chapter 5
Green Fire

10:30 PM Thursday, August 4
Houston, Texas

ick gradually became aware of something cold and wet rubbing his cheek. Reflexively, he raised his hand to touch it, and it squealed and bolted. The sky was mostly dark, and his vision was a little blurry, but he was pretty sure that the creature was a piglet running away from him. His service weapon was in his right hand. He sat up and shook his head – he had a little bit of a headache, but nothing too severe. Carefully, he probed his skull above his left ear. Nothing felt out of place. He looked at his hand. There didn't appear to be any blood, and his hand wasn't sticky.

There it was. He had his answer.

When he'd returned from an unexpected trip to Russia a couple of weeks ago, he'd discovered that he'd somehow gained an ability to heal almost instantaneously. He suspected that his sister-in-law knew exactly what had caused this phenomenon, but the answer was likely to be more fantastical than he was willing to accept, so he didn't ask. He couldn't. If he cut himself, cold green fire crackled along the edges of the wound and closed it. Bruises, even bad ones, faded in under a minute. He'd wondered if this healing had limits. Now he knew. Of course, now he wondered if he could consistently cheat death, or if this was his only get-out-of-cemetery-free card.

Fortunately, Canales had removed the duct tape, but hadn't taken Nick's keys or cell phone. Canales had staged his body to look like a suicide. The medical examiner would check his hands for residue, and if they ran ballistics to make sure the bullet in his head was fired from his gun, it would, of course match. Some might question why he parked his vehicle on Highway 6 and walked all the way out into the park, but it would probably be chalked up to one suicidal behavior or another. Nick sighed and stood up.

He pulled out his phone and turned on his GPS navigator app. As he suspected, he was in George Bush Park, known for its feral hog problem. He was just north of the equestrian parking area, so he stumbled through the weeds until he found Barker-Clodine Road, and from there he was able to find his way out via the main road through the park. It might have been geographically shorter to cut across the park, but it had rained heavily recently, and he didn't want to have to wade through snake-infested temporary swamps. He jogged in the grass along the road, on the other side of the ditch from traffic, just to be safe, and it took a lot less time than he feared it would to reach his vehicle.

He had no idea what to do about Canales. If he didn't have the magic green fire, what then? Emily and his kids would be all alone. *Just like Marti.* He smacked the side of his car. *How could a fellow officer do this to me? And what am I going to do about it? It's not like I can tell anybody what happened.* Nick had already had to visit the department psychologist after he'd been falsely accused of using his position to help drug runners. He didn't need his IAD file to get any thicker.

When he got home, Emily was on the couch. Crumpled tissues littered the floor. He thought she was asleep, and he didn't want to disturb her. He was just grateful to be home.

"I thought you were only going to be a little late," she said, opening one eye.

Emily had no idea about the healing green fire, and he doubted she would believe him. Not without a demonstration, at least, and he was far too tired to do that tonight.

"I'm sorry. It took longer than I expected." He looked at the tissues. "Are you okay?"

"Me? I'm fine. Kyle, on the other hand, got sent home early from school."

"What? Why?" Nick scowled.

"He got in a fight."

"A fight? About what? Is he okay?"

"One of the girls in his class, Molly," Emily sniffled, and her eyes started to tear up again, "wanted to play Legos with the boys. Kyle told her girls can't play Legos, and he shoved her and knocked her over. Molly, however, has a blue belt in Tai Kwon Do, and got up and kicked him in the face. He's got a bruise on his cheek and a scraped knee, and his pride is deeply wounded, but otherwise he's fine. He sure could have used a talk with you this evening."

Nick winced. "Why didn't you text me?"

"Why didn't you come home when you were supposed to?"

I didn't plan on getting shot in the head and having to run all the way back from the park. "One of the guys I worked an incident with was having some issues and wanted to go for a beer. It took a lot longer than I expected. I'm sorry. If I'd have known about Kyle, I would have said no." *If I'd known he was planning to kill me, I'd also have said no.*

The tears that had been welling in the corners of Emily's eyes started to slide down her face.

"Please. Em. I'm really tired. I'm sure you are, too. Can we just get some sleep and talk about it tomorrow?"

Emily dabbed at her cheeks and blew her nose. "Fine."

Nick probably should have kissed her good night, but he was tired and grumpy, so he turned and left the room. He looked in on the boys on his way down the hall. They were both sound asleep. Not that he expected anything different. Both hands clenched at his sides and he wanted to hit something. *Why didn't I just tell Canales that I didn't want a stupid beer?*

Nick's body was exhausted, but his mind wouldn't settle. If Emily had just let him know about Kyle, he would never have gone to have a beer with Canales. What was he going to do about him, anyway? He couldn't just let it go – Selling drugs on the side notwithstanding, the man needed professional help with his steroid problem. But he couldn't walk into his sergeant's office and report that one of his fellow officers shot him in the head and left him in the park as pig bait. He'd be the one in the rubber room instead of Canales. Was Nick not spending enough time with the boys? McKenzi took up so much time, maybe Kyle lashed out at a girl because he felt jealous of his sister. Maybe he was just a bad parent. These questions plagued him endlessly as he lay in the dark and stared up at the textured ceiling. He closed his eyes and tried to slow his breathing so that his body would sleep, but instead, he found himself playing Worry Whack-a-Mole. As soon as he tamped one negative thought down, another took its place. He wished Emily had come to bed, but she hadn't seemed to have been in a particularly compassionate mood, so maybe it was just as well. Somewhere around 3:30, exhaustion finally overwhelmed his body, and he slept.

Chris Canales was already sitting down when Nick came in for roll call. There were two empty seats to his left, so Nick took one of them. Canales was looking at his phone, so Nick coughed. Canales didn't look up. Nick coughed again, louder.

Canales glanced up, then back to his phone. Then his eyes widened and his back stiffened. Color left his face as he turned to stare at the new arrival.

Nick just smiled at him.

Canales jerked himself to his feet, knocking his metal chair over. "You!" he bellowed. "You can't be here!"

The chatter in the room went dead as every officer turned to look.

Nick feigned surprise. "What are you talking about? Are you okay?"

"You're dead!" Canales screamed, reaching for his sidearm.

Nick raised his hands, palms facing Canales. "Clearly not. Why do you think I'm dead?"

"Because I killed you myself! I saw you die! I saw you!"

It took six officers to remove Canales' duty belt and restrain him. Canales screamed the whole time about zombies and pigs, until an ambulance arrived to transport him to a hospital psychiatric ward. He had to be sedated to be loaded onto the gurney and wheeled away.

"You have any idea what that was about?" Sergeant Patterson asked.

Nick shrugged and shook his head. "Couldn't tell you, Sarge." *Well, I could, but then you'd order a strait jacket for me, too.* It seemed harsh, but Nick was glad it went down that way. Surely they'd discover Canales' steroid use and get him clean, because he had become dangerous to himself and others. And his criminal activity was a whole other matter. But there was not a thing he could do about it right now.

"Never had that happen during roll call before. Hope it never happens again." The sergeant refilled his coffee cup before he went back to the podium.

He had a few BOLOs and some administrative announcements.

"And one last thing. Lieutenant Barnes is retiring from SWAT. There's a barbeque next Friday at the Academy for him, after the annual SWAT tryouts. They're adding another four positions, so if any of you are already on the part-time squad, you've got a decent shot at moving over. That's all I've got. Don't Tase your neighbor." Nick flinched as Tasers crackled around him in test mode.

SWAT was notoriously difficult to get into. The team had a fixed number of members, and once an officer got into the unit, he tended to stay put. Nick had been on the part-time squad, training with the full-timers for almost two years, waiting for that elusive opening. He knew that Barnes had been making noises about retiring for about six months, but nobody had thought he was serious. Nick also knew he was at the top of the list, and with five openings, he was as good as in. Of course, it would be bad form to celebrate before he got his official notice, but it still added some spring to his step as he walked down the hall.

"Benson, we need to see the LT."

"Sure." He turned and followed Sergeant Patterson down the corridor. *Is this where I get the papers to transfer to SWAT?* He resisted the urge to whistle.

Patterson's supervisor was sitting at his desk behind a stack of file folders. Two of them were lying right in front of him. He stood up when they came in, reaching out to shake Nick's hand. Patterson closed the door.

Lieutenant Helmsly looked tired. More tired than usual.

"Benson - Nick, I wanted you to hear this from me."

Nick's stomach tightened. This could only be bad news.

"Yes, sir."

"I fought this. Told them how much they were screwing up. SWAT declined to accept my recommendation. You're still part time."

Nick shook his head. The words didn't make any sense. "I don't...understand." His brow furrowed.

"They passed you over because you have an IAD jacket."

"But that was a frame up!"

Helmsly frowned and nodded. "I know. I know. And I told them that. Your record speaks for itself – you're an exemplary officer. They didn't care that the charges were false and the DA's office recanted. No, they're worried about *optics*." He made air quotes. "The sergeants and the lieutenant were pulling for you – they really wanted you full time. This came from higher up."

"Thank you for letting me know, sir." Disappointment. Betrayal. Anger. They all swirled inside him, and Nick wanted nothing more than to hit the punching bag right now. Instead, he took a deep breath and tamped his emotions down, balling them into a bitter pill.

Helmsly picked up a pen and tapped it idly on the desk. "You can try an appeal. They should be rotating captains a little later this year."

"Thank you, sir. But right now I've got a beat to run."

Nick had only been out for an hour. He was headed westbound on Memorial, between Eldridge and Highway 6 when a man in workout gear ran out of the Terry Hershey Park entrance, waving his arms. Nick pulled into the parking area and got out of his car.

"What seems to be the problem, sir?"

"There's a man in the bayou!"

"Show me," Nick said, hoping he wasn't going to have to get too wet pulling some hiker or canoer out of the water.

The man, all angles and stringy muscles, jogged down the ramp and under the bridge. There, caught in some debris, a dark-haired man bobbed gently in the current. Given that he was face down in the water and most of the back of his head was missing, Nick figured it was far too late for EMS. He radioed in the floater, asked for crowd control back up, and started taping off the area while he waited on Homicide. He got the contact information and a basic statement from the jogger who'd flagged him down. The crime scene unit and the medical examiner beat Homicide by a good fifteen minutes. CSU already had their 3-D laser camera set up and going, forcing the detectives to wait an additional half hour before they could get started.

When they finally finished all the photographs, the techs from the ME's office waded into the water to retrieve the body. It wasn't deep, barely covering their knees, but the concrete chunks and rocks that lined the banks and bottom of the bayou were slippery with algae and bat guano. After they finally wrestled the corpse ashore and turned him over to slide him into a body bag, Nick's jaw dropped, and icy fingers squeezed his solar plexus.

The face was unrecognizable, but the badly done neck tattoo of the star with the '713' in the middle was easily recognizable as the one belonging to Canales' prisoner from the day before, Cesar Chavez.

Chapter 6
Playing with Fire

5:30 PM Saturday, August 6
Houston, Texas

elinda was struggling. She'd been shaken by the unexpected deaths of her fellow panelists, but Ellen's death had really hit her hard. I admired her grit in going to her romance writers' panel session at the same time I wished she would have withdrawn from it.

The exhibition hall was a lot quieter than it had been during lunch, now that the breakout sessions had started back up. I hoped Belinda had more books in her trailer, because she was almost out.

I was watching the few people milling around sales tables when I saw him. *No way. Is that the guy who just moved in across the street?*

"Hunter! Hunter Greene!"

He paused for a moment, almost like he'd been caught out, then turned around, his eyes searching until they landed on me.

"Hey, Marti! What are you doing here?"

"Working," I said. "I had no idea you were interested in writing,"

"Well, I do love books. But I'm more of a shopper than an author. How about you? Did you write these?"

I glanced down at Belinda's books, most of which had half-naked men on the covers, and I felt my cheeks get warm. "No. One of the owners of the Tenth Sphere writes them. You've been in the shop – I know you met Belinda at the mediumship circle."

"She's the taller one, right?"

"Yes."

He picked up one of the books, flipped it over, and scanned the back. For some reason, it made me feel dirty, him standing about three feet away from me, looking at a book that I knew had graphic sex scenes in it.

"I'm not a big romance reader. I tend to prefer non-fiction." He set the book back down and smiled at me.

Typical. "Did you find anything you like? There's an author with a new book about Houston serial killers a few rows over."

Hunter cocked his head and raised an eyebrow. "So what is it about me screams *serial killer?*"

"Nothing!" I said, looking at his shoes. "That's just the only non-fiction that I noticed on my way in this morning."

Before he could answer, an alarm started clanging. I thought I heard someone yelling 'Fire!'

Hunter grabbed my hand and started to pull me toward the exit. I pulled back so I could grab my purse and Belinda's cash box. It's a good thing the crowd was sparse, because a few people panicked and bolted for the doors. One man was so hysterical that he was beating on the door, trying to push it open. On either side of him, people pulled open other doors and headed out the front to Discovery Green. But somehow he didn't see any of this.

"Sir," Hunter said. "Sir, try pulling it."

"You're not going to trick me! I was here first!" he screamed, and swung wildly at Hunter.

My neighbor blocked his punch and responded with a right hook that sent the man sprawling. Hunter lifted the dazed guy up over his shoulder in a fireman carry.

"Marti, could you get the door?"

"Um, sure," I said as I pulled open the door. This guy had ice in his veins. What was he before he was an accountant? A Navy SEAL?

I was glad we were on the first floor. Even with this little sidetrack, we were still out of the building and in Discovery Green park before the surge of conference attendees came flowing out the front doors. Hunter set Mr. Panic down and leaned him against a tree.

"You'll be fine," he said.

The man just nodded.

I started searching the crowd. "I've got to find Belinda."

At the sound of sirens, hundreds of heads swiveled in their direction.

"I *will* help you find her, but let's not run back into the burning building, shall we?"

I pulled out my cell phone, still scanning the mass of faces. I scrolled through my call history and tapped Belinda's number. After three rings, it went to voice mail. I sent her a text, asking where she was. I called Lulu. She didn't answer either.

"Dammit," I said.

Ladder trucks brayed loudly to get the stragglers out of the way so they could pull up to the doors. Three ambulances, lights flashing, also pulled up and blocked the street. Police began arriving as well to shut down the streets. Firefighters in full gear hurried into the building, some dragging hoses. Then nothing. For several minutes that seemed to stretch out into hours, no one entered or left the building. I could hear radio chatter, but wasn't close enough to understand it. Then three gurneys went in.

Almost immediately, one came back out carrying a man in a bright teal shirt. He had an oxygen mask over his face.

"I think," I swallowed hard, "I think that's Stefán, one of the romance panelists." I could feel myself starting to shake. *Where is Belinda?*

More minutes dragged by. A second gurney came through the front door. This one had a shiny black body bag strapped on it.

Please, please, please don't let that be Belinda.

I felt Hunter's hand on my shoulder. I wished that Quinn was here, and I wished I knew where Belinda and Lulu were. I searched the crowd again, hoping I'd see either or both of them, but no faces were familiar.

Firefighters started to trickle out of the building. Then a door opened. Nothing. Finally, a stretcher shuddered through it, catching on the doorjamb and jarring its occupant.

"Belinda!" I shouted.

I sprinted across the street, Hunter close behind me. Belinda was wearing an oxygen mask, and looked disheveled.

"How is she?" I asked the paramedic.

"Smoke inhalation. She should be fine. Could you please tell her she needs to come with us to the hospital? She kept trying to get off the stretcher – that's what took so long getting her out."

"You transporting to Ben Taub?" I asked.

"Yes, ma'am."

"Belinda, you have no idea what was in that fire. There may be all kinds of toxic chemicals that have effects that won't show up for hours. You go to the hospital. Lulu and I will meet you there. I won't take no for an answer."

Belinda's eyes teared up, and she made a deep gasp for air, then shook her head from the sudden influx of oxygen. She pulled the plastic mask away from her mouth.

"I know exactly what was in that fire. It was Jennifer McLauren, the contemporary romance writer."

"I'm...I'm so sorry," I said. "Please just go to the hospital. I'll get Lulu and we'll meet you there."

"She's at the shop," Belinda said.

"Fine. I'll pick her up."

"What about Cassie?" Belinda let the oxygen mask fall back over her face.

"My parents have her. Just go."

Belinda nodded weakly as the gurney was wheeled toward the ambulance.

"Belinda!"

Ben came running up from the far side of the park. I'd forgotten all about him. I grabbed his arm.

"They're taking her to Ben Taub. I'm going to the shop to get Lulu. Can you pack up Belinda's table and meet us there?"

"Sure, as soon as they let people back in."

I hadn't thought of that. "If it's going to be a while, just come to the hospital." He looked at the ambulance door that just closed. I patted his hand. "Smoke inhalation. She should be fine."

He nodded, and glanced at Hunter.

"Do you want me to drive you?" Hunter asked.

He squeezed my shoulder again, as if he were someone I knew much better.

"No, I'll be fine. Thanks, though."

I noticed Lieutenant Haskill getting out of a car. *Why is Homicide here?* "Excuse me," I said to Hunter. "I see an old friend."

I raised my arm and waved as I headed in his direction. "Sam? Lieutenant Haskill?"

"Marti." He squeezed my hand. "Haven't seen you in donkey's years. How've you been?"

"We're good. Do you always come out to investigate fire accidents?"

He smiled broadly. "Well, one fatality per day seems awfully peculiar, don't you think? Just want to have a look around. Seems that the romance publishing business is mighty competitive, and some folks are a little more focused on winning than others. I'm also interested in finding if there's a pattern to this string of accidents."

"A pattern? You think this might be a serial killer?" I suddenly felt cold in the muggy heat.

"ABC." Haskill shrugged. "Assume nothing. Believe no one. Check everything. The investigator's ABCs. Yes, this string of accidents does sound like too much of a coincidence, but I don't see how they could be related. Just seems like exceptionally bad luck."

"That's certainly how it looks." I frowned. "It was great to see you, Sam. I've got to go to the hospital with my friend. The people that died were all on the same writers' panel as her. Could you keep me posted? If you find anything that's not an accident?"

"Not officially." He pulled a notebook from his pocket. "What's your number?" I gave him my phone and email.

"Thanks," I said. "Take care of yourself."

"You, too."

As soon as I got into my car, Delilah materialized in the front seat. She looked at me with a sad smile. "Your friend Sam is right. There ain't nothin' coincidental about what's happenin' here."

Chapter 7
Uncle Ocean

Saturday, August 5, 8:30 PM
Houston, Texas

uinn regarded the gargoyle for a moment. "I'm not a monster." He glanced around Marti's back yard, scanning for potential observers.

"So you've said," Ocean replied, his voice betraying a touch of amusement that his stony face could not. He raised his head slightly and inhaled. "That smells good, what is it?" he asked, eyeing a large plastic carrier bag Quinn was holding.

"Thai food, Uncle. Would you like to come in?"

"What would your human say?"

"You might be surprised." Quinn shifted his weight, hoping Ocean would cut the small talk.

Ocean nodded. "Well, you should hide your playthings better. She was *trés facile*, very easy, for me to locate. If I can find her, she can be found by anybody."

Quinn looked at Marti's back door for a long moment. "Marti is not a plaything. And I'm sure that you didn't come here to criticize my friend's security measures."

"*Non.* An observation only." Ocean stretched and refolded his wings. "I have come to inform you that Phobetor is missing from the Demos Oneiroi. There is a rumor that the demon Balcones, who is well-known to you, is responsible."

"Balcones. He's enough of a nightmare on his own – what would he want with the God of Nightmares?"

Ocean shrugged. "Your mother said –"

"Did she send you here?" Quinn's eyes narrowed, and the bag of Thai takeout jerked in his hand as he clenched his fists.

"She did not, my *neveu*. But as your father's brother, I visit her from time to time. She regaled me with tales of your exploits, and I recognized the name Balcones. I had only days before played cards with Morpheus, Persephone, and Hades. Morpheus mentioned that his brother, Phobetor, had gone missing, and he'd sent their brother, Phantasos to look for him. He reported that a demon called Balcones had been asking after Phobetor, but as his location was unknown, Phantasos is still seeking him."

Quinn frowned. "Mother told you stories about me? She's a bit put out that I'm keeping company with a human."

Ocean did his best approximation of a smile. "So she said."

"Did you tell her about Balcones?"

"*Non*, I did not," Ocean said, shaking his head.

"Good. I don't want her fretting about it. You know how she likes to fret."

Ocean nodded.

"It looks like I am likely to be setting off soon on a demon hunt."

"*Oui*. You should spend your time appropriately." Ocean tilted his head towards Marti's house. "I will watch the house tonight, but I will leave at dawn and meet you in Blackthorne."

"Thank you, Uncle."

Ocean stretched out his wings and only a few flaps took him back up to the tree branch he'd been sitting in earlier. When he was settled, Quinn knocked on the door. Marti smiled as she opened it.

"Hey," she said. "Cassie's already asleep."

"Hey, yourself." He kissed her on the forehead, then reconsidered and kissed her mouth, a long, slow kiss, until she started to squirm and pull away.

"The food," she murmured, "is really hot against my back."

"Sorry!" He released her immediately and set the food down on the table.

"Before I forget, is there any way you could watch Cassie for me in the morning while I go to a funeral? Mom and Dad will be at church, and I don't want to impose on Nick and Emily."

"Tomorrow?" He breathed in deeply and let it out quickly. "Sure, I suppose I can. What time?"

"It starts at 10:00. It probably won't take much more than an hour."

Quinn nodded. "This is for your friend, Ellen?" *Surely, no Mundane Intervention Team was so urgent it couldn't wait for the dead to be laid to rest.*

"Yes."

"I'm sorry."

"I didn't know her all that well, but I did like her a lot."

While she went to the cupboard to get plates, he asked, "How was the conference?"

"It caught on fire."

"What?" He stopped his unpacking midway.

"It was a freak accident. One of the romance panelists had a cellphone in her pocket and the battery exploded. It wasn't a big fire, but it was enough to kill her." Marti set the plates down on the table and looked up into Quinn's eyes. "There have been a lot of freak accidents involving the romance panelists. Three of them are dead. I don't think it's coincidence, and I don't believe they're accidents."

Quinn caressed her cheek with the backs of his fingers. "What do you think they are?"

"I don't know – it almost seems like a curse. Hopefully, since they shut the conference down after the fire, the last two panelists will be okay. Especially since one of them is Belinda."

"I can ask around and see if anyone knows of any curses flying around. But as you said, the conference is shut down, so Belinda should be safe." He spooned rice onto each plate.

They finished fixing their plates in silence, then went into the living room. Marti put on a movie, but Quinn ate his meal wondering if Balcones was at the root of the string of accidents. It didn't seem to make sense, though. If not him, perhaps it was another demon.

"Would you like a glass of wine?"

"Huh?" Quinn shook his head to clear it. "Certainly. I'll get it." He took the dirty dishes with him into the kitchen, and returned with two glasses of chardonnay.

"Cheers," he said as he handed Marti hers.

She tapped her glass to his. "Cheers."

He took two sips, then drained his glass. He took Marti's glass from her hand and set it on the coffee table. He kissed her again, softly at first, then gaining urgency. He stood and pulled her up, then swept her up into his arms and carried her to the bedroom. It might have been faster to just tear each other's clothes off, but it wasn't safe for Marti.

He wasted no time in pushing himself onto the astral plane. Marti was getting pretty good about doing it herself, and they met in the garden they'd constructed together there. Butterflies the size of crows flapped lazily by, landing on enormous tufts of lilacs as Quinn's astral energy swirled around and intertwined with Marti's. It wasn't long until they both exploded into a thousand stars, and the fragments of their astral bodies rained down on the garden, only to coalesce inside their physical bodies.

"Mmmm," Marti said. "That was amazing."

Quinn stroked her hair as she snuggled against him, head on his chest. "You're amazing."

He felt her breathing slow and deepen as she drifted off to sleep. He stared at the ceiling, feeling her heartbeat against his, wondering if this would be the last time.

Sunday, August 7, 11:00 AM
Houston, Texas

I was eager to get home. My parents couldn't watch Cassie because they were going to church this morning, so I had left her with Quinn. She adored him, which maybe I shouldn't have encouraged, given that our relationship was in the early stages, and it would be hard on her if things didn't work out. But I trusted him – he'd brought her back to me when I thought I'd lost her forever. Still, he'd seemed preoccupied when he came over last night. I wondered if he'd gotten a new assignment. His job was to hunt demons, and I'd learned firsthand how rough they played.

Ellen had made her own funeral arrangements when the doctors found that the chemo for acute myeloid leukemia had made things worse instead of better. All her family had to do was set the date. Sort of. She had stipulated for the service to be held on the first Sunday morning after her death. Since she died on Friday morning, the funeral home had to scramble a bit to accommodate her. But accommodate they did, and I sat with Belinda and Lulu near the back of the chapel.

As close as Belinda and Ellen were, Ellen's daughter did not approve of her hanging out at a metaphysical shop. My friends didn't want to antagonize her, so they were trying to be as inconspicuous as possible. Although I'm not sure Lulu helped much on that front, wearing a pillbox hat with a short veil. I thought it made her stand out even more, but she hadn't asked me. Belinda had brought her own box of tissues, and sat near the aisle, head down, with a damp tissue crushed in her hand.

The metal chair next to me creaked, as if someone had sat down in it. I turned to look. At first, I saw nothing, but then I looked closer. She was nowhere near as clear and bright as Delilah, but I was able to make out the form.

Ellen?

"Well, who were you expecting? Marilyn Monroe?" She smiled. "Could you please tell Belinda and Lulu that I'm fine?"

Sure. But can't you tell them that yourself? I thought —

"Yes, normally they can see spirits. But both of them, especially Belinda, are too upset, and the grief is blocking their vision. Also, could you tell my daughter...never mind. That girl is too headstrong to believe anything you say. Too much like her father." She looked wistful.

I nodded and turned towards Lulu and Belinda.

"Wait!" Ellen said. "The service is starting."

Alright. I'll tell them afterward.

Ellen's body had already been shipped off to the crematorium. In about a week, her daughter would receive a biodegradable urn containing Ellen's ashes and a gingko tree seed, to be planted in the cemetery's newly opened crematory forest — her tree would be the very first. At least that's what the brochure that she'd brought to the shop to show Belinda said. But for now, there was a 12 x 14 photo of Ellen on an easel, surrounded by flowers, ferns, and a couple of wreaths in the front of the chapel.

A Tibetan chant started playing through the funeral home's sound system. Ellen's daughter cringed, and I suspected that she would have arranged a very different service for her mother. When the chant finished, a man in a black robe with an embroidered purple stole rose and stood next to Ellen's picture. He started naming some of her great qualities and telling stories of her life to illustrate his point. When he got to 'kind,' he told a story of how one day Ellen had a terrible sore throat and couldn't speak, but she had to go to the post office. As she walked, she heard some mewing and looked up into the tree branches above her to see a tiny white kitten. Ellen, who was afraid of heights, climbed up to rescue the kitten. As soon as she hoisted herself up on the branch where the kitten was stuck, it climbed into her lap, purring loudly. The problem was, now Ellen was also stuck in the tree. She tried to call out to a passerby, but she had no voice. So she took off one of her shoes and threw it at the man walking below the tree. He shouted at her and called the police. They arrived, surveyed the situation, and called the fire department, which used the ladder truck to get Ellen and the kitten out of the tree.

I glanced over at Ellen. Her face was in her hands. I thought she was crying.

Are you okay?

She looked up at me, and I realized that she'd been laughing. "I had that cat for fifteen years. Best one I've ever had."

A woman who looked about twenty-five got up and stood near Ellen's portrait.

"That's my niece!" Ellen said, grinning broadly.

Music started to play, and the niece started singing *Somewhere Over the Rainbow*. She had a beautiful voice, and I felt my eyes getting misty. I glanced at Lulu and Belinda, and saw that both of them had tears streaming down their cheeks. I sighed, wishing that I'd had the chance to get to know Ellen better.

Family members recited a few poems, and there was another song, then came the benediction. Friends and family were gathering at Ellen's daughter's home after the service, but Lulu and Belinda knew they wouldn't be welcomed, so they lingered in the chapel, looking at Ellen's portrait. I looked for Ellen, but she was gone.

As soon as we got to the car, I said, "Ellen was at the funeral. She asked me to tell you that she's fine."

"You saw her?" Belinda asked. "Did you see her, too, Lulu?"

Lulu shook her head.

"She said that your grief was blocking your ability to see her."

"Maybe," Lulu replied. She ran her hand through her hair. "Since the rest of the convention has been canceled, either of you want to stop for lunch?"

Belinda shook her head.

"Maybe another time," I said.

Lulu and Belinda dropped me off at my house. As soon as I opened the door, I heard Cassie crying.

"Quinn?" I called as I hurried toward her room.

Water splashed and I heard Cú barking. Cassie cried harder.

"Quinn?" I called out, louder this time. I changed course slightly and went to the bathroom in the hall between Cassie's room and mine.

For a second, I couldn't believe what I was seeing.

Delilah sat in the bathtub with Cassie, who was now screaming at the top of her lungs. The water was way too deep to bathe a baby, and my spirit guide was making sure that she didn't fall over and drown. Delilah had managed to pull the plug, and the water had started to drain, but was still quite deep.

Quinn was nowhere to be seen, but there was a terrifying woman in the corner. Cú seemed somewhat bigger than he had when I'd left this morning, but perhaps it was just my fear vision.

The woman, if I can call her that, was wearing a ragged loose dress, or possibly a shroud. Her long, black hair was wet and stringy with specks of duckweed in it. Her skin was an unpleasant corpse-green, and she dripped stinky pond water and duckweed all over my bathroom tile.

Cú held her at bay, growling if she moved.

"Who are you?" I demanded. "And where is Quinn?" My adrenalin-charged heart pounded against my sternum.

My hands shook as I grabbed a towel and pulled Cassie out of the bathtub. Her sobs against my shoulder only fueled my anger. I glared at the woman in the corner.

"Well?" I snapped.

She took a step forward, and Cú snarled and barked. She took a step back.

Delilah disappeared from the bathtub and reappeared at my side.

The green-skinned woman smiled at me, and I took a step back. Her teeth were not normal human teeth. Every one of them, and there were way more than there ought to have been, was long and pointed. Very sharply pointed. Algae appeared to be growing on them, because they were a mottled green color. *Eww.*

"Jenny," she replied, seeming pleased that she'd intimidated me.

Cassie had started to calm down and relax against me. "Okay, Jenny. Who are you, and what have you done with Quinn?"

"You'll have to ask him," she said.

Then she cackled loudly, leaped over Cú and landed in the bathtub, splashing still more water onto the floor. Jenny turned to liquid herself, and disappeared with the last of the water that swirled down the drain. The tub belched loudly, but there was no sign of her, except for a few bits of duckweed left behind on the porcelain.

"Girl, I told you from the get-go that man was dangerous. Didn't I tell you no good would come of seeing him?" Delilah said.

"What are you talking about?" Cassie was down to sniffling and hiccupping now, and I rubbed her back and swayed from side to side to comfort her even more.

Cú wagged his tail and came over. "Good boy!" I said, leaning over to pat the top of his head and scratch his ears. I didn't have to lean over much, though. He was definitely taller than when I'd left the house earlier. He must be having a growth spurt.

"Your boyfriend, Quinn. He's the one that called that child-drowning hag to watch over Miss Cassie."

I shook my head. "I don't understand."

Delilah rolled her eyes. "That Russian friend of Quinn's, the one with the blue skin, came to get him – some kind of emergency. He summoned Jenny Dreadful to stay with your baby."

"I think Aleksei is from the Ukraine," I mumbled absently. "I don't get it. Why her?"

"I guess she was available on short notice, girlfriend. He's dangerous, and he runs with dangerous folk." Delilah's hands went to her hips.

I chewed the inside of my cheek. I couldn't believe Quinn would do anything that would put Cassie in danger, and yet I shuddered to think what might have been waiting for me if I'd come home fifteen minutes later.

"Delilah, why did you call Jenny a child-drowning hag?"

But there was no reply. Delilah had vanished.

Cassie had fallen asleep, so I carried her into her room. I pulled the wet towel off of her, and she squirmed, but not enough to wake up. I put her down on the changing table and she was still. I was afraid if I tried to dress her, she'd wake up again and be upset, so I just put a diaper on her and carried her into the living room with me.

I turned on the TV and sat in my living room, mostly ignoring the programming and seething until Quinn's return.

Sunday, August 7, 10:45 AM
Houston, Texas

Quinn strapped Cassie into her high chair for lunch. Cú sat patiently near the baby. He was the owner of anything that fell on the floor. Marti had prepared Cassie's lunch – all Quinn had to do was open containers. He sprinkled a few tiny cubes of cheese, cooked carrots, and halved grapes on the highchair tray in front of her, as he'd often seen Marti do. The baby squealed with delight and immediately began grabbing them with both hands.

"Easy there, wee one. You'll not be choking on my watch," Quinn said as she tried to cram everything into her mouth at once.

A cheese cube tumbled out of her hands and the puppy caught it before it hit the ground. Quinn moved all but three cubes and a grape out of Cassie's reach.

Quinn whirled as he heard heavy steps on the back porch. Through the glass of the back door, he saw Aleksei, one of his Mundane Intervention Team members, about to knock on the door. Cú barked twice and ran into the living room.

"What is it, Aleksei?" Quinn said as he opened the door.

"Come. You must see to believe," the Lesovik replied. Light from the window dappled his blue skin.

"Can it wait? Marti should be back any minute – I'm watching the baby for her."

"*Ni*. It cannot."

Quinn scowled. "I can't very well leave Cassie alone, now can I?"

"Is there nursery faery?"

"That's an idea. But it still may be faster to wait for Marti."

Aleksei shook his head.

"I expect everyone knows that Jenny Greenteeth is a nursery bogie. Maybe she can do it."

The words had barely fallen out of his mouth when an awful hag with dripping wet hair and green skin appeared.

"Haven't seen you in a hundred years or so, eh Jenny?" Quinn said. He wondered why a frightening creature would be good with human babies, but what did he know about them? Jenny sometimes hung out in the millpond at his family's tavern, The Waterhorse Inn, and occasionally took tea with his mother.

"Did you say you had a human child that you needed taken care of?" Jenny asked.

Aleksei tapped his wrist.

"I'm in a real rush, Jenny. Yes, this is Cassie. Her mom should be home any minute now, but I've got to leave. Will you look after her for me?"

"I will...look after her." Jenny smiled a toothy smile.

"You're sure you know how to take care of a wee human baby. They're not like fae. It's real important she be in the best of hands."

Jenny extended slender, mottled fingers. "My hands are the best."

"Thanks."

Cú had poked his head around the door jamb.

"And you," Quinn said. "Take care of my girls for me."

Then he walked out the door with Aleksei and stepped into a portal. Instantly, they found themselves at Briar Ridge Montessori School. An older woman hovered over a much younger one who lay on the floor and swatted at nothing with her hands.

"Stay away from me!" the woman on the floor screamed

"It's okay, Miss Breckenridge. I've called an ambulance. They'll take care of you," the older woman said.

She noticed Quinn and Aleksei. "Someone will be with you shortly. Please wait in the hall."

The younger woman started screaming incoherently.

They backed out of the room.

"What does this have to do with me?" Quinn asked quietly.

"Dame Rowan told me bring you here. She was talking to an ocean? I not understand."

"Ocean. My Uncle Ocean. He's been looking for Phobetor. Looks like he's been here – she's in a waking nightmare. But why here?"

"Look," Aleksei said, pointing to a piece of paper taped to the wall.

It was a class roster. Quinn ran his index finger down the list until he found the entry for Cassie Keller. He felt nauseous. This was Cassie's teacher. Balcones was letting him know he could reach him – or those closest to him – at will.

"I have to get back to Marti's house," Quinn said.

"No. We must make report first – how will MAMIC know to expedite Balcones' capture request, if no report?" Aleksei replied.

Quinn knew he was right and sighed in frustration. The bigwigs at the *Mundane Activity Monitoring and Intervention Center* were obsessed with paperwork. They had to backtrack to get to a portal and go to MAMIC headquarters in Blackthorne, which took precious time Quinn didn't want to spend. There was, of course, a queue for the Director's office. After discussing what Ocean had told him the night before and what he'd seen this morning at length, Quinn was finally released. He was almost in a panic, not knowing if Marti and Cassie were okay. He knocked on the back door as he came inside.

"Marti?" he called.

"I'm in the living room," she answered. Her voice was raspy. *Had she been crying?*

Quinn rushed in and found her sitting in a chair, arms crossed. As he approached, she stood up to meet him, then slapped him across the face.

"What were you thinking?" she hissed at him.

He held a hand against his cheek. "What are you talking about?" Fear increased the pitch of his voice.

"Jenny. Why would you leave Cassie with a monster? I trusted you."

"Is Cassie alright? What monster? Jenny's a nursery bogie. She's supposed to take care of children."

"Take care of children?" Marti's face flushed, and Quinn wondered if she was going to hit him again. "She almost drowned Cassie in the bathtub. If not for Delilah and Cú...well, I hate to think of what might have happened."

"I'm sorry. I had no idea – I thought the purpose of nursery bogies was to protect children. I never would have left her with Jenny if I'd realized."

Tears started rolling down Marti's cheeks. Quinn brushed them away, then leaned his forehead against hers."

"I have to leave," he said.

"Of course you do. You almost get Cassie killed, and now you have to go off somewhere for work. That's awfully damned convenient."

"No. I mean I can't be with you anymore. It puts you and Cassie in danger."

Quinn felt his own eyes get misty. He would not upset her any further by telling her about Balcones' visit to Cassie's school.

"That's what I've been told. I really should have listened." She sniffled.

"I should never have involved you. I'm sorry."

Marti looked up, anger in her eyes and her mouth in a hard line. "I guess that's it, then."

Quinn closed his eyes and swallowed hard. He had to fight the urge to throw his arms around her and kiss her until everything was okay again. But that couldn't happen.

"Yes," he replied. "It's just not safe for you to have me here. Cú will protect you." There was nothing else he would allow himself to say, so he turned and walked out, letting the door bang closed behind him.

Chapter 8
The Last Panelist

I stared at the back door. Was Quinn really leaving and not coming back? Suddenly cold, I struggled to breathe, remembering the day Ryan walked out the door and never came back. *It's not the same thing,* I scolded myself as my hands started to tremble. *Delilah warned you he was dangerous. Lulu warned you, too. But would you listen? No. You thought you knew better, you were the special one who could tame the monster. Cassie almost died because of him, and here you are, wishing he'd come back. What kind of mother are you?*

I covered my face with my hands, smearing the wetness across my cheeks. First I plopped back down in the chair, then I punched the cushion. I couldn't tell who I was angrier with – Quinn or myself. After all, he had told me from the start that he wasn't human, and I shouldn't expect him to behave like one. But had he used his fae powers to take advantage of me? The first time I met him, I found myself inexplicably attracted to him – but after that initial encounter, I wasn't so sure. Lulu had warned me that humans frequently pined away and died after their fae lovers left them – and they always left. Because of my stupidity, was Cassie destined to be an orphan? Because it sure felt like Quinn took a big chunk of the best parts of me with him when he walked away.

You can't sit around feeling sorry for yourself all afternoon. Get up and do something. I went and took a shower. I turned on the water as hot as I could stand it and just stood under the flow, turning a few times to let it pound on my back, then my chest. Finally, the water turned cool, and I shut it off. Cassie was babbling from her crib. As long as she sounded happy, I didn't rush too much to get dressed. I'm not sure that I felt better, but perhaps more stable, kind of like a congealed salad – squishy lime gelatin mental state mixed with soggy cottage cheese sadness and hard celery and walnut nuggets of anger and rejection.

"Mama! Mamama!" Cassie called as I walked into her room. Cú was a puddle of ink, curled up in front of her bed. His tail thumped against the carpet as I approached, but he didn't get up.

"Come on, Cassie. Let's get you a snack, okay?" I scooped her into my arms.

I looked out the kitchen window as she ate. I was restless and the air in the house felt warm and stale, in spite of the ceiling fans. According to the outdoor thermometer, it had cooled down to 95°F. I decided that Cassie and I would make up for our missed morning walk. I'd better leave Cú at home so he didn't roast his paws on the sidewalk. We'd just go a short distance, maybe to the Tenth Sphere and back. I really needed to get out of the house and get some air, however hot and humid. I put Mr. Buns in the stroller, and of we went.

As we approached the shop, I was a little surprised to see a police cruiser parked out front. Curious, I went inside.

Belinda sat on the stool in front of the cash register. Head in her hands. Lulu stood behind her, rubbing Belinda's shoulders. A female uniformed officer and two men in sport coats formed a loose circle around the counter. They all looked up when I came in, and I was only a little surprised to see that one of them was my friend, Lieutenant Haskill. I looked from him to Lulu.

"Please, B," Lulu said. "It's for your own protection. Marti, can you please try to talk some sense into Belinda?"

Cassie burbled – she adored Belinda. "Um.." I replied. "What's going on?"

"We want to take Ms. Tate into protective custody," Haskill said. "A fourth member of the romance writers' panel, Stefán Heidlemann, was found floating in the pool at his hotel this morning. We have every reason to believe that there will be an attempt on Ms. Tate's life as well."

"I'll be fine." Belinda's voice cracked as she said it, though. "The convention's over, I'm nowhere near downtown…"

I unbuckled Cassie and picked her up while Belinda talked. I set my baby on the counter, and she squealed with delight at seeing Belinda. "I've known Lieutenant Haskill for a long time. If he thinks you're in danger, you most likely are. Please, please let them protect you. What would Cassie and Lulu and I do if something happened to you?"

As if on cue, Cassie reached for Belinda, and my friend picked her up and hugged her. "Fine," Belinda said.

"Thank you," the detective I didn't know said. "Officer Rogers will take you to our safe facility."

"Can I at least go home and pick up a few things?"

"No. I'm sorry," Haskill said. "The sooner we get you there, the better. There will be toiletries and things like that waiting for you."

Belinda sighed and handed my baby back to me. "Let's go."

Cassie started to cry as Belinda walked away with the Officer Rogers. I jiggled her on my hip. "Don't worry, Cassie. Auntie Belinda'll be back before you know it." *I hope.*

"She'll be fine. I haven't lost one yet," Haskill said with half a grin. "I don't know how these deaths are orchestrated. They all look like accidents. But one romance writer panelist per day? That's not a coincidence. A puzzle for sure. But I like puzzles." He smiled again, the left half of his mouth doing most of the smiling, and touched Lulu's elbow. "We'll take good care of her, Ms. Miranda." He nodded to me. "You be good for your mama, now, Cassie. Come on Smitty. We've got work to do."

The cowbell on the door jangled as they left.

"You know who else has some work to do?"

I jumped.

"Delilah!" I said out loud. "Do you really have to sneak up on me all the time?"

She raised one eyebrow. "Girlfriend, I have been here the whole time. You need to get better at lookin'."

"What are you talking about, Delilah? Who has work to do?" Lulu asked, her arms crossed loosely against her ample chest.

"Miss Ellen. She's hangin' around, tryin' to clear up some unfinished business. Since she's here, she may as well help out a friend."

"Are you in touch with her?" Lulu asked.

Delilah pursed her lips and glanced up at the ceiling, then looked over her right shoulder toward the 'Employees Only' door. "Ellen? Come on out here, girl."

A transparent blob of mist formed on the opposite side of the counter from us.

"Bah bah! Bah bah!" Cassie flapped her hand towards the mist.

"Not yet, little one," Ellen's voice said. Her voice sounded tinny and staticky, as if she were on a radio station at the very edge of its range.

"Ellen!" Lulu said. "Honey, you left us so fast we didn't even have a chance to stop by and see you. I'm sorry for that."

I'm not sure how, exactly, but I had the impression that the mist smiled.

"Don't strain yourself, Miss Ellen. Why don't you drop the visual and just concentrate on the voice?"

The mist dissipated.

"It's okay. I'm quite alright here," Ellen said. "Though I hadn't expected to go that quickly myself."

I thought it odd that one of Delilah's eyebrows arched for a moment.

"What is it that you need from me?" Ellen continued.

"I'm glad you're doing good," Lulu said. "I don't know if Belinda told you that she was on a romance writers' panel at this big fancy writers' conference. The trouble is, all of the panelists have died in mysterious accidents. Except her. The police put her in protective custody. But we need to find out who's responsible for this, so she can come home."

"Yes," Ellen replied, her voice a little fainter. "I knew she was a panelist, but I didn't know about the deaths. I'm not sure what I can do to help, though."

"What if we gave you a list of the dead panelists?" I suggested. "Maybe you could see if any of them are still hanging around, then ask them what happened?"

"I can try."

Lulu rifled through some papers on the counter. I was going to have to go soon – Cassie was starting to squirm.

"Okay, honey," Lulu said. "Here it is. The first one was Thursday night. Regina Dupris fell down the escalator at the GRB. Friday, Meghan Palmer got hit by a car in front of the building. On Saturday, Jennifer McLauren's cell phone battery exploded during one of the panel sessions and caught her clothes on fire, and they found Stéfan Heidlemann floating in his hotel pool this morning, just a couple blocks from the Convention Center."

"I'll see what I can find out. Can't promise anything, though. I am starting to get a little tired…"

"Of course, honey. You go rest. We'll talk soon, huh?"

"Sure."

"You be careful, Miss Ellen," Delilah added. "There's something much more powerful at work here than plain ol' bad luck."

Cassie was almost impossible to hold now, so I put her in her stroller and wrestled the seatbelt on her. "I've got to get Cassie home. She needs to walk around and stretch her legs. There are too many breakables here. I can't afford to let her play in the shop – I'd never get another paycheck."

"I understand," Lulu said, nodding absently.

"I'll go with you," Delilah said.

This surprised me, a little, anyway – she tended to disappear as suddenly as she popped up. I shrugged.

"I know you're upset about Quinn," Delilah said after we got out of the Tenth Sphere.

I switched from talking out loud to talking in my head. This was a private conversation, after all. "*You know about that, huh?*"

"Course I do, girl. That shifter, he deserves more credit than I gave him."

I swallowed hard. I wasn't sure I wanted to hear this. The breakup might be easier to deal with if I believed I'd just made a bad choice in romantic partners, instead of thinking we were star-crossed lovers who might yet end up together.

"*Why is that?*"

"He didn't want to leave you. But his being around right now puts you and Cassie in harm's way."

"*So he said. After he left Cassie with some monster that tried to kill her. I trusted him with my baby. If you and Cú hadn't been there...And then he says 'Sorry, guess I'm just too dangerous – bye now.' Sounds suspiciously like a cop-out to me.*"

"It isn't like that, girlfriend." Delilah softly shook her head. "Jenny is a friend of his mama's, and he didn't understand that a nursery bogie is the opposite of someone who takes care of human children. But that ain't why he left."

"*Then why did he leave?*"

"You remember Balcones?"

"*The demon? How could I forget him?*" I shuddered.

"Balcones is not real happy with Quinn, for a lot of reasons, and he's trying to hunt him and his whole MIT team down and kill them. He didn't want you and Cassie to be anywhere in the vicinity if Balcones should catch up to him. And he has reason to believe that might happen."

My heart skipped a beat, then fluttered in my chest. I didn't want Quinn – or Aleksei, Eoin, or Malik, for that matter – to die. But what could I do about it? They all had supernatural powers that I lacked – Balcones had even managed to imprison Malik, a powerful djinn, in an emerald bottle only recently. I wished things could go back to the way they were a few days ago, where Quinn and I were just like any other new couple, getting to know each other and basking in giddy infatuation. But that just made it worse. The danger was always there, even if I didn't see it. It didn't matter how much Quinn cared for Cassie and me, being around him put us at risk, probably more risk that I even imagined. I sighed in frustration.

I felt an odd tingle on the back of my head as Delilah touched my hair. It stirred me out of the pity party I was organizing for myself and brought me back to the here and now.

As I approached my house, I saw Hunter working in his garage. His shirt was off and sweat glistened on his bare skin. Again, I was intrigued by his tattoo. A raven, its body and head on his left arm and shoulder, spread its wings over his back and chest. He'd told me he was an accountant, and the first time I'd seen his ink, I was surprised by it. No law against accountants having tats, I supposed, but he just hadn't seemed like the type. Still, I had to admit that looking at Hunter was a pleasant distraction from my current state of affairs.

He waved to me, and I pushed Cassie on over.

"Hey, neighbors," he said.

"Hey," I replied. "Are you remodeling your whole house here? Looks like you've got a lot going on."

"No, just refinishing some bookshelves."

I noticed a gallon can of paint stripper and reconsidered wheeling Cassie closer into the shade of the garage overhang.

Nodding, I said, "I have some chairs that need re-doing. Maybe someday I'll have time."

Hunter picked up a towel and blotted the sweat off of his face and neck. "You should bring them over – I'll do them for you. But that might put your boyfriend on edge."

I snorted sourly. "I don't think that will be a problem." I didn't elaborate, and I hadn't appreciated the reminder. The bleeding hadn't even stopped yet from this afternoon's breakup wound.

"Sorry," he said.

I shrugged. "It's alright. Wish I could hang out longer and see how they turn out, but I've got to get this one," – I jiggled the stroller – "out of the sun."

"No problem. Maybe you and Cassie could come over for dinner sometime to see them when they're done."

I paused. Was this a serious invite, or a polite let's-get-together-sometime suggestion that meant nothing and would never really happen? "Maybe," I replied, opting for noncommittal.

"By the way," he said. "How is your friend, the one from the book convention fire yesterday?"

"She's fine. Treated and released for smoke inhalation. See you around."

"Yeah, see you." He went back to his paint stripping, and I retreated to the relative cool of my house. I wanted to kick myself. I need a rebound romance like I need a hole in my head.

Dinah pounded her hands on the library table in frustration, causing the librarian to shoot an alarmed look in her direction. She couldn't find anything out about her next victim, Coda Sterling, other than the fluffy biography on her website. Dinah caressed the wishing ruby that was tucked safely under her blouse.

Aside from sucking away five years of her life every time she used it to make a wish, the only downside was that she had to be looking at the intended subject when she wished. That was why Meghan Palmer had gotten hit by the car instead of Coda Sterling and Stefán Heidlemann.

She'd followed the ambulance after the fire at the GRB yesterday, but that had proved pointless. There were too many ways to get in and out of the hospital, and she couldn't cover them all. Her diabetic cat had to be given his medication, so she couldn't just sit around indefinitely in hopes she'd made the right choice. *So frustrating!*

"Is there something I can help you with?" the librarian asked.

Dinah startled at the question. She hadn't been aware of the librarian coming toward her. "Um…I'm just trying to find out some information about an author, and there doesn't seem to be much online."

"I see. Have you tried a copyright search on the author's titles?"

Dinah shook her head. The librarian smiled and showed her how to look up copyright information online.

It was Dinah's turn to smile. "Thank you," she said.

There it was. Coda Sterling wasn't even the author's real name. It was Belinda Tate. Not only was she a creator of perverted filth, but she was a liar as well.

"Is there anything else?" the librarian asked.

"No, thank you, ma'am. I think this will help."

Dinah dug around for a pen and wrote down Belinda's name and address on the tattered back of the unpaid electricity bill she'd been carrying in her purse for nearly two weeks. This only confirmed for her that she was on a righteous path. She had been led to the meeting where she met Zachariah and had gotten the wishing ruby, and now the librarian had shown her exactly what she needed when she was starting to lose hope.

After she typed in the address in the search bar and copied down the directions, she gathered her things to head to Belinda's house.

"You have got to see this," the duty sergeant said to Nick.

He had already turned in his paperwork for the day and was ready to go home. "What's that?"

Sergeant Patterson pulled up a chair and sat down. "There was a residential alarm call at 3:17 this morning, somebody tried to crawl in through a living room window. No sign of the crook, but the security camera caught this."

Patterson pulled Nick's computer over and tapped some keys. A video window opened and started to play.

"What the hell?" asked Nick. He rewound the video and squinted as it played again.

"Yeah. Kind of looks like a baby, doesn't it?"

"If babies had scaly skin and horns, maybe."

Then he noticed the address on the digital report, and swore softly.

"What?" Patterson asked.

"That's three blocks over from my house."

"Seriously? Guess if you don't show up for roll call in the morning, we'll know the Devil Baby got you."

"I'm off tomorrow, actually."

Patterson leaned back in his chair. "Kidding aside, what do you think that is?" he asked. "Looks too small to be a midget in a costume."

Nick watched the video a third time. "I don't know. Kinda looks like a Halloween decoration. Some kind of remote-control animatronic maybe?" He had a vague memory of seeing something similar before, but couldn't think of where. "Whatever it is, if it runs out in front of my car, it's toast."

"Well," Patterson said, sitting back up. "It's probably a prank — somebody looking for their fifteen minutes of internet fame. I think that they got this doll or midget or whatever and sent it under the camera while they opened the window to trigger the alarm, making sure that someone would watch the recording. May even have been the homeowner himself."

Nick shrugged. "Could be. If the Devil Baby shows up at my house, I'll bring in the pieces for you."

He logged out, closed the lid on his computer, and stood up. He'd been scheduled for a ten-hour shift, but ended up working twelve, and he was beyond tired. "Night, Sarge."

"Night."

A prank. Yeah, probably. Nick was annoyed that the Devil Baby clung to his brain like a spider on a wall. It was creepy, sure, but Patterson was probably right. There was no limit to how low video fame seekers could stoop. But still, there was something about the way the thing had moved that was just wrong. And when it had looked up into the camera, it seemed like it was aware of him. The pranksters undoubtedly planned it that way. But he still drove a little faster than maybe he should have to make sure he was home with his family well before dark.

Chapter 9
Devil Baby

id I not tell you?" Ocean asked. "Your pet is too easy to find." The leaves on the branch where he perched rustled slightly as he shifted his weight.

Quinn, who sat next to the base of the tree in his dog form, growled softly in answer. It was just loud enough to make the thing shaped like a monstrous baby turn its head in their direction.

Then it smiled.

Needle-like fangs peeked from its gums. They were short, but matched its blotchy grey skin. Dull, rough scales covered the thing, giving it the appearance of a snake about to shed its skin.

"The horns, they are a nice touch, no?" Ocean continued.

Indeed, the apparition had perfectly curved, cartoon devil horns. All it was missing was a red pitchfork and a goatee.

The Devil Baby returned to its mission, and moved toward a darkened window.

Quinn, or Bruce, as Marti knew him in this shape, barked until a light came on and a man came to the window and shouted, "Shut up, you stupid dog!"

As soon as the room lit up, the Devil Baby disappeared.

Quinn got up and padded out of the yard and down the street. He made sure to head in the opposite direction of Marti's house, which was across the street and a couple of doors down. Whomever had sent the Devil Baby was probably watching.

Ocean flew behind him, staying low enough for conversation, but high enough to keep his stony feet from rasping across the sidewalk.

"What are you going to do about the tulpa?" Ocean asked.

Quinn growled, then slipped into the alley behind the Tenth Sphere, where he shifted back into human form.

"What makes you so sure this wee beastie is looking for Marti?"

Ocean sighed slightly. "It is known that Balcones is searching for you, no? To find you, he finds those you love. Your family is untouchable to him in Faery, so what is left? The Mundane world. And who is there? Your Mundane Intervention Team and some humans. It may go badly for him to stalk the demon hunters, so what is his choice then?"

Quinn's eyes narrowed. "Do you think if we can track the tulpa, it will lead us to Balcones?"

"I think not directly. It would be foolish of him to send the thought-form himself for that reason. *Mais oui*, he is clever enough to use an intermediary."

Quinn nodded and stepped through the portal he had placed in the alleyway. He emerged in the war room of a large house a few miles away. Ocean followed a few seconds later.

The house, an elegant two-story with a large back yard and a pool, was technically owned by MAMIC, but his good friends, Kai and Breena, who belonged to another Mundane Intervention Team (MIT), lived there. It was also a hub for local MITs to plan missions and travel between Faery and the Mundane world for this region.

"The quickest way to get rid of a tulpa is to terminate the creator," Quinn said, heading down the stairs. "Once the thought-form has no one to feed it energy, it dissipates quickly. But I suppose we want to leave this one alone, until we get a bead on Balcones."

Ocean followed Quinn through the kitchen and out into the back yard. The rest of his team waited for them there. Aleksei, the blue-skinned Lesovik, preferred sleeping outside in the trees to being in the house. Eoin, a half man, half goat Urisk, hated the polished marble floors because his hooves slipped and slid on them. Malik didn't mind where he was. The djinn had no need of sleep, anyway.

"*Zdravstvuyte*, Quinn," Aleksei called.

"Evening," he answered.

"So what is the wee little monster your," he paused to glance at Ocean, "uncle's been on about then?" asked Eoin.

"It's a tulpa, most likely sent by Balcones, or one of his allies," Quinn answered.

Aleksei frowned "What is tulpa? I have not heard of such creature."

Malik rolled his eyes. Instantly a camel appeared before the group, except that it had big fangs and glowing red eyes.

"Quit your fooling around, Malik," chided Eoin.

Malik sighed. "This is for your edification and enlightenment. This camel, you see, does not really exist. It is an idea of a camel built of nothing but my thoughts. I give it energy by thinking about it." The camel's eyes flared brighter, then dimmed. "It can, of course, interact with the material world. I can command it, but if it lives for enough time, it will develop its own will." He waved his hand, and the camel dissolved into a puff of smoke. "When humans create these, they are cruder and tend to go feral most of the time." He shook his head. "They run amok, causing all kinds of mischief, until they run out of energy. And that, my friend, is a tulpa."

"What he said," replied Quinn. "I think this tulpa is looking for Marti. There's every reason to believe that Balcones would like to use her and Cassie as bait to draw us out into the open. Ocean believes that he has a minion creating the tulpa, so if we can find him, hopefully we can find and trap Balcones."

"And you know this tulpa looks for Marti?" Aleksei asked.

"*Non.* But it is best to act as if it does, no?" Ocean answered. "Perhaps we investigate, and it has no connection to Balcones. What is lost? Nothing. If we do not investigate, and it is sent by him, then we stand to lose much."

"I reckon our Malik can track it, next time it shows its face. What's it look like, then?" said Eoin.

Quinn described the Devil Baby.

"Och. Sounds like an ugly little blighter," Eoin said.

Aleksei nodded.

"It seems not to make itself hard to find," said Aleksei. "Ocean found it, no problem. How he knows to look for tulpa?"

"I was running an MIT before you were even a sprout, *homme d'arbre.* I have more contacts than you can imagine." Ocean's voice was dangerously even and quiet, the calm before the storm.

"Aleksei," Quinn said. Ocean was one of the highest ranking members of MAMIC, and it was a very bad idea to antagonize him. "Enough. Balcones is trying to get to us. We don't need to help him by tearing each other apart. We need to plan our mission and take him down." *And then Marti and Cassie will be safe.*

"Aye, I agree we should get on with it, but could I ask a question?" Eoin said.

Malik shook his head, then held out his right hand. A deck of cards suddenly appeared in it, and he shuffled them, then started laying them out in mid-air as if to play solitaire on an invisible table.

"Fine. What is it?" Quinn replied.

"If you're a kelpie, and he's a gargoyle, how's he your uncle?"

Quinn's eyes widened and his shoulders stiffened. Before he could speak, Ocean answered.

"Fall of 1285. The King of Scotland was marrying a French noblewoman. I was a child, taken from my home at Notre Dame Cathedral, and sent as a wedding gift. The ship I sailed on sank. I do not swim. The grandfather of Quinn found me and took me in, raising me as his own child. My name, his family could not pronounce, so they called me Ocean, because that is where I was found. When I was big enough to make such a journey, I returned to my family in *la belle* France. But I still keep my connections to my foster family. Is there any more of my personal life you now wish to examine?"

Eoin swallowed visibly. "No, sir. Thank you."

"Alright. Can we get our mission planned now?" Quinn, asked.

After much discussion, they decided that they would post themselves around the neighborhood, but not far from Marti's house. Since Malik was the least corporeal, and he could track the tulpa on the astral and other finer planes, he would be summoned at the first sight of it. They would find out where it went, then observe that location to see if they could catch Balcones, or at least gather some clues about his whereabouts. Ocean would keep an eye on Marti and Cassie while the team was staking out the tulpa's owner.

"Balcones probably expects that if we find the tulpa, we'll try to trace it, so stay sharp," Quinn said, once the plan was decided.

There was not much night left when he dragged himself upstairs to sleep. He needed to shift into his kelpie form soon – he was starting to get itchy and uncomfortable. But he was too tired to go for a swim in Kai and Breena's pool just now. It would have to wait until he got some rest.

Monday, August 8
Houston, Texas

It was early afternoon when Quinn stood on the diving board wearing nothing but a towel. He tossed it onto one of the nearby deck chairs that clustered under a large green umbrella and dived in, barely making a splash. His human shape quickly gave way to the large grey kelpie body that moved through the water like a dreadnought. He breathed deeply, and dived below the surface, his long neck stretching toward the bottom of the extra-deep pool. The water was barely cool, so different from the lochs and pools of his native Scotland.

He settled on the bottom and relaxed under the pressure of twenty feet of water. The deep area didn't extend for more than twenty feet before the bottom began to slope up. It was enough to accommodate his length with only five feet to spare, and the pool was a standard competitive width. He could only swim about half the length of the pool before he scraped his belly on the rough plaster, but it was good enough for now.

If an observer who did not know of the existence of fae creatures happened by, he might be shocked to see what he thought was an ancient plesiosaur resting in a backyard swimming pool. But while he had the same four flippers, stocky body, and long neck, his head was somewhat larger and filled with bigger teeth. His tail was shorter, but ridged like an alligator's, instead of smooth.

He emerged from his soak hours later, refreshed and energized. In his kelpie form, worries did not trouble him – he was a sensate being in that shape. It was only in his human phase that doubts plagued him and restive thoughts clawed his brain. As he wrapped the towel around his waist, he reconsidered the plan. It might be better to leave Aleksei behind with Ocean to guard Marti. She knew him, and if she had to be moved or spoken with, it would be easier with an acquaintance than a stranger. Besides, it was entirely possible that Balcones was using the tulpa to draw them away from Marti, and when they were away hunting down its owner, he would swoop in and grab her. If that was the case, two protectors were better than one. He wished that he could tell her what was happening, beg her to be careful; but that would be a mistake. A clean break was best, even if it was the last thing he wanted. They had to get Balcones – as long as he was free, he would see Marti as a piece of bait that Quinn would never resist. He could neither keep her or let her go.

He went into the house and up to his room to get dressed. He smiled at his reflection in the dresser mirror as he pulled on his shirt. The Norse god Odin had given him a tattoo that encircled his navel, and it gave him the ability to keep his human clothes on when he changed form. Before, clothing had been just one more troublesome logistical detail to attend to. More than once, he'd awkwardly found himself naked in exactly the wrong place, so this was, quite literally, a godsend. However, today, his clothes were travel-worn and sweat-sour. He hadn't had time to find fresh clothes because he urgently needed to shift into his natural shape.

He and his team ate their evening meal and waited for dark. Breena and the children were away, but Kai hung out with them until it was time to go. One by one, they stepped into the portal in the upstairs war room and stepped out in the alley behind the Tenth Sphere. They took up their positions and waited.

Close to midnight, Eoin spotted the Devil Baby. It was on the opposite side of the street from Marti's house, moving away from it. Silently, they approached the house. Malik closed his eyes, focusing on the energy of the tulpa.

Tap. Tap. Tap.

A blonde woman in high heels walked towards them.

The Devil Baby looked up and hissed. It charged her, running in an odd broken gallop. She screamed and dropped her handbag as it leaped at her face.

Quinn was the closest. He broke cover and ran towards the attack. He grabbed at the Devil Baby, but the woman's arm snaked around his waist. He tried to shift his weight, but she kept him off balance as she pulled what looked like a green golf ball out of her pocket and threw it hard on the ground.

There was a bang and a bright flash.

Percussion portal. How'd she get that? Only demons use those... Quinn thought as the woman shoved him through the swirling hole in space and time.

Chapter 10
Bang Bang You're (Not) Dead

Monday, August 8, 6:30 AM
Houston, Texas

ometimes, Nick wished he could sleep in. But his body didn't allow it. Dark had shifted to dawn's twilight as the sun crept up to the horizon. Emily had just crawled back under the covers after feeding McKenzi. Nick reached out for her, then stopped. She was still healing from her C-section and the blood clot in her lung, and he was almost afraid that if he touched her, she'd break. He pulled his hand back.

She must have felt the mattress move when he did that, because she turned over and looked at him. "You feel okay?"

"What?" He brushed a stray lock of hair off her cheek.

"It's dawn. You're still in bed."

"Day off, remember?"

She smiled, just a little, and moved over to snuggle against him. He put his arms around her, enjoying the feel of her body against his. His eyes fell on her face, and it pained him how pale she was. Even though his brain knew she wasn't ready for romance, his body responded to her nearness.

She obviously felt his growing predicament, because she winced and said, "Sorry."

"Not your fault." He got up and jumped in the shower.

When he came out, Emily was asleep. He shook his head. Surely McKenzi would start sleeping through the night soon. Adele, his mother-in-law, would be here in a couple of hours to look after Emily and help with the baby while he took the boys out to the indoor skydive place and the video arcade at the mall. Now, though, he had a little time to himself, and he went into the kitchen. He put four strips of bacon in a large skillet and cracked three eggs into a bowl while he waited for the pork to sizzle. He fired up his tablet to stream an episode of *America's Test Kitchen* while the pan was heating up. Cooking shows were a guilty pleasure of his – he actually liked to cook more than Emily did, although the task fell on her more often. His phone chimed to let him know he'd received a text. Nick waited to look at it until after he'd plated his food, and saw it was from Collins, the officer he'd worked the traffic fatality with a few days ago. He shook his head. *Paperwork NEVER ends at this job.*

The message read, "You on today?"

He typed back. "No. Taking my boys skydiving. U doing reports?"

It was a few minutes before she responded. "No prob. C u @ work."

He put the phone down and went back to his show.

Kyle and Aiden were too excited to eat breakfast, which probably wasn't a bad thing. Indoor skydiving is basically flying around in a vertical wind tunnel, and Nick thought it was only superficially like actual skydiving. But it was something he could do with the boys when they were six – it would be another ten years before they could try the real thing. He had high hopes - they loved the indoor form, so maybe they'd like to jump out of a perfectly good airplane with him when they were old enough. After they finished, he took them across the freeway to eat lunch at the mall food court and play race car games in the arcade.

They were just heading for the exit when the screaming started.

Nick pulled the boys out of the doorway and behind the wall while he triaged the situation. Diners in the food court were stampeding toward the exit. Other people stood frozen as four men in ski masks and body armor ran towards the jewelry store near the restaurants. Two of the men carried MAC-10s and the other two had baseball bats. The bat wielders started smashing glass display cases and grabbing the contents, while the gunmen screamed at everyone to get down on the floor.

Nick's pulse pounded in his ears as the adrenalin surged through his body. He picked up Kyle and Aiden, one in each arm, and lifted them over the ticket redemption counter at the arcade.

"Stay down and do *not* move until I come back for you. Don't make a sound," he whispered to them. Their eyes were huge with fear and Nick felt a rush of anger at the robbers. Bad enough they did what they did, but ruining this perfect day with his boys made it personal.

Nick moved back to the edge of the door, where he could observe the robbery. So far, no shots had been fired – there was just a lot of yelling and screaming. He didn't know who the duty sergeant was today, so he texted Sergeant Patterson, "211 @MC mall."

Then details, "4 Trds, 2 M10s, 2 wood bats. Body armr/msks. Jwlry stor nr food ct"

"Where r u?" came the reply seconds later.

"Vid rcade"

He heard one of the men in the jewelry store shout, "Thirty seconds! Cops on the way. Go, go, go!"

Nick wasn't wearing his duty belt. He had no vest, gun, Taser, baton, flashlight or cuffs. Even though they couldn't keep him down, bullets would still knock him down. And he had about thirty seconds to do something. His training said if he was dressed as a civilian, he should act like a civilian, and someone with more sense of self-preservation would have just laid low and let the crooks run out, hopefully in to the waiting arms of LEOs outside. But he had no way of knowing if they were there yet. If these guys didn't go down today, they were going to do this again, and the next time, somebody might get killed. Maybe even a lot of somebodies. And it wasn't like they were going to kill him, anyway. Although, if security cam footage showed him getting shot point blank and not dying, it might be a little tough to explain. As long as the boys stayed where he put them, they should be okay, but what if they saw something they really shouldn't?

He sprinted across the hall to the food court, making a beeline for the burger place. As he'd hoped, he found gallon containers of oil near the fryers. He grabbed one, opening it as he ran, and splashed it across the floor, covering as much area as he could. He assumed patrol would be coming Code 2 —no sirens — so they wouldn't give the bad guys a heads-up that they were outside. If his plan didn't work, or backup wasn't outside, things could go south in a hurry.

The robbers saw him as they came pelting down the corridor, but did not snap to what he was up to until too late. The vegetable oil-covered, polished stone tile may as well have been ice. There was loud thud as one of the bat boys fell backwards and hit his head. He lay still, but the others slipped and skidded like slapstick comedy villains.

One of the MAC-10s went off, and the glass doors shattered. Someone started sobbing. The recoil sent the shooter skidding and spinning down the hall, away from the doors. He pivoted around so that his feet were on ungreased tile. There was still some oil on the bottoms of his shoes, but he managed to struggle to his feet like a newborn calf. A newborn calf holding a fully automatic .45 caliber machine pistol.

To his right, Nick heard footsteps and metallic clicks as an entry team prepared to come through the broken doors. Nick skirted the oil and ran for the gunman, trying to get to him before he fully regained his balance. He saw a blur of motion in his peripheral vision as the first officer made entry.

Nick lunged for the bad guy's gun.

The shooter swung to his left.

"Dad!" shrieked Kyle.

Nick's head snapped around to see his son standing at the edge of the arcade, right in the line of fire.

Nick was sure his heart stopped beating.

Voices shouted, probably the entry team, but he focused on the man in front of him and nothing else. He grabbed blindly at the gun, but his hand slipped off the oily barrel. Then his feet hit oil and slipped out from under him. His momentum carried him forward, and he twisted as he fell. All of his weight, shoulder first, struck the gunman's abdomen. The robber grunted as he hit the floor and the air was forced from his lungs. He dropped the gun. Nick shoved it as hard as he could with the heel of his hand, and it skittered across the tile.

Even though the robber was gasping for air, he struggled with something in his waistband. Nick tried to roll over and pin the man's arm, but he was too late.

Time slowed as the matte black barrel of the Glock G22 swung past him unsteadily as its owner struggled for air.

Kyle?

Nick was on his back next to the gunman. He reached up and grabbed the man's wrist, pulling the gun's deadly gaze away from the entry team. Away from his son.

The shooter rolled with him and grabbed the gun with his other hand. The Glock was now pointed in exactly the direction Nick had last seen Kyle.

He rolled onto all fours, and found the barrel of the handgun almost touching his chest. In his adrenalin-fueled altered state, he could see the tendons in the shooter's wrist contract as his index finger curled around the trigger.

Not this again.

Nick gasped as the hot bullet seared through his sternum and exited just below his shoulder blade. He tasted blood.

He almost panicked. Nothing happened. He tasted more blood as it came out of his lungs with each exhale. Then he felt the green fire dancing along his wound, and within seconds, all traces of the bullet hole disappeared.

The robber's eyes got huge behind his ski mask. This time, without the floor to get in his way, Nick rose to his knees, grabbed the top of the gun and twisted hard, up and to the outside. The shooter yelped as his index finger, caught in the trigger guard, broke.

Nick slid the Glock across the floor to wait with the MAC-10.

Someone apparently flipped a switch and turned the rest of the world back on. He heard someone shout, "Clear!" All at once, people were crying. Rubber-soled shoes squeaked on tile.

"Benson?" someone asked. "You okay? Are you hit?"

Nick turned to see three of the entry team officers standing behind him. He knew Tyler Farrell, the man who'd just spoken, from his part-time SWAT training.

"I'm good. Must have been a misfire." Nick knew he wouldn't be allowed to wander around the scene, even if he did work with SWAT. "I left my boys in the arcade. I really have to find them."

"I'll walk with you." Farrell tapped his shoulder radio. "I've got a friendly with me. Repeat, got a friendly."

"Copy that," a voice crackled over the speaker.

Farrell escorted Nick back to the gaming den. Lights flashed and digital soundbites squealed, trying to entice customers to come in and play, as if nothing at all had just happened. An armored assault team officer was down on one knee, trying to comfort a hysterical boy.

"Aiden!"

"Dad!" He left his escort and ran to Nick.

"Are you okay?" Nick had to be careful not to squeeze the breath out of him as he scooped him into his arms.

Aiden just sobbed.

"I'm glad you did exactly what I told you. Now we need to find Kyle. Do you know where he went?"

Aiden shook his head.

Shifting his son to his hip, Nick said, "It's okay. We'll find him."

"You know I'm going to have to take you outside to the secured area." Farrell said.

"But-"

"I'm sorry. What does Kyle look like? We'll keep eyes out for him." Farrell started for the door.

Nick didn't follow. "Like this one, only with a blue shirt. Please. You know me. You have to let me find my son. Can you get the incident commander on the horn? I'll talk to him. Please."

Farrell turned. "You know I can't do that. Sergeant Strickland is at the command center. Talk to him. Don't make my job any harder."

Nick drew in a deep breath, then let it out quietly. "Understood." He knew Strickland well. Well enough that their families had gone camping together a number of times. But Nick also knew him well enough to know that he'd never break protocol.

Scouring the scene on the way out with his eyes, Nick saw no sign of Kyle. Aiden had stopped sobbing, but was clinging to his father with every ounce of strength his sixty-pound body could muster. His warmth both comforted and antagonized Nick. He knew he had to remain calm for his son's sake, but he wanted nothing more than to leave Aiden outside at the door, protected by SWAT, and tear the mall apart to find Kyle. Of course, he'd probably get shot – again – and that would open a whole other can of worms. His jaw clenched so tightly his teeth hurt.

Farrell led Nick to the SWAT mobile command center, a tricked out RV that was equipped with an array of communication and surveillance technology. The diesel engine idled quietly, a soft, throbbing growl in the background. An officer opened the door, and Nick and Aiden climbed the metal steps. Farrell returned to his post. Nick prepared to plead his case, knowing he'd almost certainly be turned down.

Light footsteps pounded across the carpeted floor.

"Dad!" Kyle flung himself at his father. Nick bent to scoop him up, a boy in each arm now. He hugged them hard as he steadied his emotions enough to talk without his voice breaking.

"Kyle! Are you okay?"

"Sure. Sergeant Strickland gave me some water."

Nick wasn't sure if he admired or dreaded his son's fearlessness. That changed from moment to moment. "Why didn't you stay where I told you to, Buddy?"

"I wanted to help." He started to sob.

Nick hugged him tighter. "I understand. But Daddy has a lot of training to fight the bad guys, and you don't. Not yet, anyway."

"But we go to Tae Kwon Do twice a week!" Kyle protested.

"I know," Nick said. "But bad guys with guns are tricky, and you really shouldn't fight them unless you have no other options." He released his hugs so the boys could breathe, but didn't put them down.

"Heard a report that somebody got shot while the entry team was coming in. Knew it was you, because Kyle met them at the door. Who else but his daddy would be wrasslin' the bad guys, huh? Well, that and Patterson texted me that you were on site. But I'm glad my intel on the shooting was wrong."

"Not exactly. It was a misfire."

Strickland nodded. "Somebody's looking out for you."

"So it would seem."

Farrell's brow furrowed. "You sure? There's a crispy little hole in your shirt."

Nick noticed that one of the feeds on the wall was from the mall's security camera system, and he wondered how much of the incident Strickland had seen. There was no way to know, so he grinned. "Must have bounced off my rock-hard pecs."

Strickland shrugged. "Clearly. Now, tell me what happened."

Tuesday, August 9, 3:30 PM
Houston, Texas

"How much are these amethyst pendulums?" I asked.

No answer.

"Lulu?"

"I'm sorry. What did you say?"

I held up a small cardboard box. "The pendulums that came in yesterday. How much are they?"

"I don't know. Packing slip's around here somewhere."

I put my hand on her shoulder. "I'm sure Lieutenant Haskell will call the second he has any news."

"I know, honey. But waiting and not knowing is hard."

I nodded. Scanning for the packing slip, I found it on the floor in front of the cash register. I started pricing the pendulums in silence.

The bell on the door jangled. Lulu looked up and scowled at the woman coming into the shop. She was perhaps a little younger than Belinda. The cut and color of her blonde hair was artificially perfect, and her dress looked expensive.

"Belinda isn't here, Virginia. Go away," Lulu said.

Virginia smiled.

"Oh, Lu. You really should learn to let things go."

I had no idea who Virginia was, or why she and Lulu hated each other, but I did remember Lulu and Belinda both having the same reaction when she'd come into the store a few weeks ago. I was just leaving at the time, so I'd missed any fireworks. This time, though, I was trapped.

Lulu's eyes narrowed and her face darkened. "Hmph. How about I learn to let things go when you learn to stop being a sociopath?" One eyebrow arched sharply.

Virginia's smirk hardened for an instant as anger flashed in her eyes. But it passed quickly.

Her heels clicked on the tile as she continued into the shop, slowly, deliberately intruding on Lulu's space. I could almost see waves of anger rising off of Lulu. Virginia stopped and looked me up and down. Then I knew how a mouse felt when it was cornered by a cat.

She extended her hand. "I'm Belinda's cousin, Virginia."

I blinked a couple of times before I reached up to shake her hand. "I'm..." I hesitated.

"None of your business!" Lulu snarled as she came out from behind the counter. "I told you, Belinda is not here. Get out."

Virginia batted her eyes, her smile dripping with poisoned sweetness. "When will she be back? I need her to sign a check."

"I'll tell her to call you," Lulu said, her eyes smoldering.

If Virginia has any sense, she'll get out now.

She turned to me again. "It was nice to meet you...?" She cocked her head, trying to prompt me for my name.

"Out!" shouted Lulu.

Virginia rolled her eyes. "Have a *nice* day."

It was clear from the way she said the word 'nice' that she hoped Lulu would have anything but a nice day. She gave me another long, predatory look before she strolled out of the shop.

"What's that about?" I asked.

"Honey, don't get me started on Virginia Pennington. That female is bad, bad news."

"Oh?" I set down my pen and put the price tag stickers away. I knew I shouldn't pry, but I couldn't seem to help myself.

Lulu grunted. "When Belinda's grandparents died, they left their house to Belinda and her two cousins, Virginia and Penelope. Penelope's disabled, and she and her mother live in the house. There's a trust fund for Penelope's care, and Virginia can't stand it that their grandfather left money for Penelope, but not her. She's always scheming to get Belinda to sell her share of the house so she can trick Penelope into selling up so she can boot her out."

"Sounds charming."

"Doesn't she?" Lulu slapped her hand down on the counter. "We tried having that woman as a business partner." Lulu's voice shook. "You know what she did? We had a great space, Inner Loop area, been there ten years. The building owner really liked us, so he never raised our rent in all that time. Well, after we brought Virginia in, the first thing she did was start an affair with our landlord. When his wife caught them *in flagrante delicto*, of course she made him terminate our lease. And then, when he offered to leave his wife for Virginia, she told him she wasn't really interested in anything long term. She cost us a prime location and ruined his marriage without a shred of remorse. She cares about Virginia Pennington, and everyone else can go to Hell." Lulu let out an exasperated sigh.

"Wow." *What else was there to say?*

I watched Lulu pace back and forth past the jewelry counters a few times. "Well, obviously, the circumstances of your move suck, and I'm sorry about that. But I'm glad you landed here."

Lulu stopped. A thin smile lifted her lips. "Thank you, honey. So am I."

We both jumped when her cell phone rang. I held my breath as she answered.

"Yes...yes...What?" She went pale, and I felt my pulse quicken. "What do you mean she's gone? Gone where?...No, of course I haven't seen her." Lulu's voice cracked and broke. "Yes...thank you," she whispered and hung up.

"Lulu, what's the matter?" I almost shouted at her.

There were tears in her eyes when she turned to me. "Belinda's missing."

"What? How can that be?" *After all that's happened recently, and Nick nearly getting shot at a robbery at the mall yesterday, now this. What else can possibly go wrong?*

"I don't know. They don't know. She was there, room service brought up some food, the officer went to wash her hands, and when she came back a minute later, Belinda was gone. Nobody saw anything."

"She wasn't crammed into the room service cart like they did in the old TV shows, was she? Did they look?"

"I don't think it works that way in real life."

I squeezed Lulu's shoulder. "Well, we'll just have to get Ellen to help. Can't she home in on Belinda or something and tell us where she is?"

"Or if she's crossed over," Lulu whispered.

"Stop that," I said. "No. Just no. You're not allowed to go there."

I glanced at the clock and realized that I had twelve minutes to pick up Cassie without incurring a late charge. "I have to get Cassie. Why don't you close the shop early and come with me?"

Lulu shook her head. "I have an appointment coming in twenty minutes."

"It will be okay," I said, giving her shoulder another squeeze.

I was only three minutes late. Yay for me. Cassie was the last one there, and she couldn't decide whether she should be happy, because she got all the toys to herself, or angry because I was late.

This was the second time I'd picked up Cassie and Ms. Clemmons had been there. "Ms. Breckenridge has been out for a few days. Is she alright?" I asked.

The teacher shook her head. "Still in the hospital."

"Hospital? I had no idea. I hope she's better soon – Cassie adores her." I forced a smile. "But of course, she likes you a lot, too." I cleared my throat. "What happened to Ms. Breckenridge?"

"I'm sorry, I can't really discuss that."

"Well, maybe we can send her flowers. What hospital is she in?"

"I'm not sure they'll let you send flowers. She's in HCPC."

I swallowed hard. *Harris County Psychiatric Center.* "I see. I can always check with the front desk. I guess. We've got to get going. See you Thursday."

As we sat in traffic, I wondered what on earth could have happened to Cassie's teacher. She was so young, and she'd seemed so nice."

At long last, I turned onto my street. I was shocked to see two police cars, lights flashing, and a black Suburban parked in front of Hunter's house. He stood in the yard talking to an officer, who was taking notes. When he saw me taking Cassie out of the car, he waved me over.

"Hey, Hunter," I said glancing at the officer. "What's going on?"

"Had a little break in while I was at work."

"That's terrible!" I struggled to contain Cassie. She wanted down. NOW. "Did they take much?"

"That's the weird thing. As far as I can tell, they didn't take anything at all. But they wrote on my door with chalk."

I looked at the door. In four-inch high, plain white chalk letters there was a capital X and an angular E – like the sum function on a spreadsheet.

"X Sigma? What's that supposed to mean?" I asked. "Have you pissed off a fraternity lately?"

Hunter smiled, just a little. "No idea," Hunter replied. He looked at the officer, who shrugged. "I just wanted to let you know to be extra careful. Make sure you set your alarm."

"Thanks, Mom," I replied, re-seating Cassie on my hip. "I've got to get her home. I'll talk to you later." I paused for a moment, speaking before I really thought about what I was saying. "If you need anything, just let me know."

Why did I say that? What if he decides to come over — don't I have enough things going on right now? As soon as I get Cassie fed, I've got to try to contact Ellen so she can find Belinda before it's too late.

Chapter 11
History Lesson

uinn and the blonde woman stepped out of the percussion portal and into a small concrete room. There were no windows and a barely-crackling fire cast a small circle of dim light. Normally, Quinn saw as well in the night as he did in the day, but the blackness in the room felt supernatural, as if it had been poured into the room from the Underworld.

A shape moved in the darkness. Something large scuttled behind it, more heard than seen.

"Welcome to my home." A deep, raspy voice. Quinn knew it too well.

"You didn't have to go to all this trouble just for me, Balcones."

The demon stepped into the bleak firelight. He hadn't bothered disguising himself as human. Orange light glinted off his scaly skin, and his vertical pupils were almost round in the gloom.

"Oh, but I did. You have a nasty habit of escaping me out in the Mundane world. This time, you're on my turf, and I will make sure that you get the slow, highly unpleasant death you richly deserve." His clawed hands balled into fists at his sides.

Something flashed green against the wall behind him, then started to move up towards the ceiling before the shine was swallowed by the gloom. Quinn could hear it climbing, stiff hair brushing the plaster. *Phobetor?*

Quinn refused to be intimidated. He even smiled at Balcones, just a little. "Do you bestow this much attention on all MIT leaders, or am I special?"

Balcones took a step forward and made a sound like a giant cicada deep in his chest. "All MITs deserve to be exterminated like the pests they are." He sucked in a deep breath. "But since you asked, yes, you are special. Very special."

"Is it my rugged good looks?"

The blonde giggled.

Balcones bared his teeth. Then he made a noise that may or may not have been a laugh. "Cast your mind back. September 8, 1900. Galveston Island."

Quinn shrugged. "I've slept a few times since then."

"There was a storm. A very, very bad storm."

He closed his eyes and remembered. His team had discovered a nest of demons and routed them. Unfortunately, they'd run out of demon traps, and they'd had to kill the last one. Siobhan, his long-time lover, had been the one to dispatch it. The thought of her was a hot shard that twisted in his heart.

"We were there, yes. But we ran out of traps. Regrettably, we had to destroy the last demon." He was certain Balcones already knew this, though.

"Regrettably?" Balcones smiled bitterly. "Yes. It was certainly *regrettable* that you killed my father."

"I'm sorry. We make every attempt to trap demons, not terminate them. It couldn't be helped."

"Of course it could!" snarled Balcones. "But no matter. There will only be three of your team left, after I *terminate* you."

He knows about Siobhan, then. Quinn's eyes widened as realization crept over him.

Balcones chuckled. "Yes. Who do you think sent the Frost Giants to your girlfriend's cottage?"

Quinn lunged at the demon, but Balcones tripped him as he deftly stepped out of the way, letting Quinn sprawl onto the rough floor. The room was too small for him to shift in to his full kelpie form, or he would have made short work of Balcones.

"She had to be the first to go. You do understand that, don't you? She took my father, I took her and your child. Seems like a fair trade."

Quinn blinked rapidly. "What?"

Balcones laughed, "Hadn't she told you? She was carrying your child. She certainly told me, when she was begging for her life."

Stunned, Quinn remained on the floor, feeling like he'd just been hit by a truck. When he closed his eyes, he could feel her still-warm body in his arms as he'd carried her from the razed cottage, her blood soaking his clothes. *Why hadn't she told him? Or was this just a lie Balcones made up for maximum torture?* He shook his head and stood up. *Would this be Marti and Cassie's fate, too, if he couldn't stay away from them?*

A portal on the opposite wall where he and the woman came in opened up, and the Devil Baby tulpa stepped through it.

"Have you found her yet?" Balcones asked it.

It snuffled and shook its head. A piece of white chalk fell out of its hand.

"Make sure you pick that up," the woman scolded. "You left it behind the last two times and forgot which houses you visited."

Devil Baby growled a little, but picked up the chalk.

"Come here," Balcones ordered the tulpa. "Get a good whiff of this one. Her house is likely to stink of him."

Quinn kicked at the tulpa as it approached him. Needle-like teeth sank into his shoe and pulled it off. Expecting the monster to bite his foot, Quinn winced. Instead, it buried its face in his shoe and breathed deeply. When the tulpa looked up, its malicious grin changed to fear. It scurried back to the woman and took her hand, as if this abomination were her frightened child.

Quinn followed its gaze, and noticed a thick cord that vanished into the dark of the ceiling. Above it, eight green eyes shone down at him, and he involuntarily gasped.

Balcones chuckled and turned back to the blonde. "Excellent," he said. "Perhaps we'll get her tomorrow. Surely that will draw out any members of his team he's left to guard her. It will be like, as the humans say, shooting fish in a barrel."

"Until then, darling," the woman replied.

"Good night, Virginia."

Tuesday, August 9, 9:30 PM
Houston, Texas

It had taken nearly an hour for Nick to get the boys to sleep. Last night, they'd both had nightmares about the gunmen in the mall, and they weren't too keen on repeating them. They were both trying to get comfortable in Aiden's bed, but the twin mattress wasn't really big enough. He'd let them try it, though, and eventually they stopped kicking each other and closed their eyes.

He plopped down on the couch next to Emily, and she snuggled against him. He put his arm around her and she reached up, turning his face toward her.

"Are you doing okay?" she asked.

"Me? Sure. I'm fine."

She rolled her lips together. "You had nightmares last night, didn't you?"

He pulled away from her slightly. "I was hot, and I couldn't get comfortable."

"Glad you don't work undercover Vice. You're a terrible liar."

He smiled. "Maybe not nightmares. Disturbing dreams. It'll pass."

"Maybe you should talk to the department psychiatrist."

Nick stood up. "I don't need a shrink!"

Emily took in a deep breath and let it out slowly. "Nick, what happened at the mall yesterday was very traumatic, for you and the boys. Those feelings can be hard to process. Sometimes it helps to talk to someone." Then she added, so quietly that he almost didn't hear her, "Because you certainly won't talk to me about it."

"I am fine. I don't need to talk to anyone. Because I am not traumatized." He hadn't wanted to talk to her about it because there was so much he couldn't tell her. If he told her about the green fire that had saved him twice now, what would she say? Would she be afraid of him, take the kids and run?

"I made an appointment with Dr. Weingarten for the boys tomorrow. She said that you're welcome to come."

"What? Don't you think we should have discussed this first?"

"Nick. Keep your voice down. You'll wake McKenzi."

He paced several steps away from her, then turned around and came back. "I was there. You weren't. How could you make an appointment with some quack headshrinker for my boys without even talking to me about it?"

"What are you trying to say, Nick? I see Dr. Weingarten every Thursday. Is that okay, because I'm crazy, and you're not? She's *not* a quack. And besides that, Aiden threw up for three hours after he got home. Neither one the boys want to sleep, because they both have nightmares. The sooner they see somebody, the better." She crossed her arms.

"Fine. Take them. You don't need me. Apparently, not for anything."

"Stop it, Nick. That's not true, and you know it. Why do you have to fight me so hard? I'm just trying to make things better."

Nick held up his hands, palms facing Emily. "As usual, I'm wrong. Whatever. I'm going to the gym."

He marched to the back door.

"Nick, wait."

He picked up the gym bag he always left in the utility room.

"Nick. I love you."

"I'll see you later. Don't wait up."

He used his cardkey to access the gym at the station. He'd expected it to be empty, but there was a handful of people there. Jessica Collins was one of them.

She smiled when she saw him. "Hey, Benson."

"Hey. Did you get that paperwork sorted out?"

"Paperwork?"

"Yeah. You texted me yesterday?"

"Oh," she said. "Yeah. That. Don't worry about it. I heard you had quite a trip to the mall."

He used a disinfecting towelette to wipe down the machine before using it. "Where'd you hear that?"

"Patterson."

Nick made some adjustments on the machine and turned it on. "Figures." He started running.

"So, what's the scoop?"

He told her about the indoor skydiving, the awful pizza at the food court, the race car games across from the pizza. He told her about how he'd hidden his kids, and oiled the tile. He told her about wrestling with the gunman. He did not tell her about the green fire, or how terrified he'd been when he saw Kyle standing where he'd easily catch crossfire. By the time he got to the end of the treadmill routine, it was difficult to talk – his lungs wanted all of the oxygen for his muscles. It felt good to go slower for the cool-down.

"You look hot," Collins said.

"What?"

She stepped in a little too close.

"You look," and she paused to scan his body with her eyes. "Hot."

Nick stopped walking. The treadmill belt carried him over the end of the machine. He flailed his arms and caught himself on the barbell rack. His knuckles scraped across the rough iron weights, drawing blood. He breathed in sharply, his breath a wet hiss.

"Are you okay?" Collins asked, moving even closer.

"That's barely even a scratch."

Nick looked around the gym. The other people that had been there when he arrived had left. There was not a soul there, except him and Collins.

He sidestepped and went to the butterfly machine. Turning his back to her, he added more weights. Again, she moved in, encroaching on his space.

"After this, you want to go grab a cold one?" Collins asked.

Nick was pretty sure that wasn't all she wanted to grab. Parts of him were eager to let her try. It would be so very easy to have a drink or three and go back to her place. But if Emily ever found out, he'd be out on the curb like yesterday's garbage. Sometimes she drove him crazy, but he would be so lost without her that he wouldn't know what to do with himself. She was the tether that kept his kite from the destruction of the infinite sky. And he couldn't imagine only seeing his kids on Wednesdays and every other weekend. The idea made him feel guilty for even considering a fling with another woman. Besides, a fling would inevitably wind up as an unmitigated workplace disaster. Too many great reasons to say no, not enough good ones to say yes.

"It's a tempting offer, but I can't. I have to get back. My turn for night duty with the baby."

"Another time, then," she said.

Nick shook his head slightly. "I don't think so."

She considered him intently for a long moment before she turned away. "Collins?"

She looked back at him.

"It's nothing against you — you're a very attractive woman. But I love my wife."

She nodded, picked up her things, and left.

Nick did his chest and back workout on the machine, then moved on to free weights. After that, he stepped into the shower to rinse off the sweat before he went home. He was feeling much better, and as he drove, he practiced the conversation he'd have with Emily when he got home. He'd beg her to forgive him for being such a hard-headed jerk, for one thing.

As he approached his house, he thought it was a little odd that the living room light was on. It was closing in on midnight, and Emily didn't usually stay up that late.

Then an arctic blast of cold fear gripped him when he noticed the front door was open.

Tuesday, August 9, 8:00 PM
Houston, Texas

Cassie was fed and bathed, and finally asleep. She'd been having some teething trouble, and sometimes even ibuprofen didn't help. I sat on the couch, and Cú lay on the floor at my feet, chewing on a rawhide bone. I patted the top of his head, and his tail thumped on the floor. He seemed to have grown. Again. I sighed, wishing got Quinn to coming back, and knowing that he wasn't. Knowing that was best for us. Even if I hated it.

I closed my eyes. *Ellen! Ellen! Can you hear me?*

There was no response. I waited a minute, then tried again with the same result. I took a deep breath and held it for ten seconds before exhaling.

Delilah?

"Whacha need, girlfriend?"

Belinda's disappeared from protective custody. I have to contact Ellen. I'm sure that she'll be able to find her. She has to.

"Not sure how much help she can give you. Not being a guide and all, she has more freedom 'bout what she can reveal. But not as much power to find stuff out. Lulu did get in touch with her earlier."

Good to know, I guess. Do you have any way of knowing if Belinda's alright? Or where she is?

"She has not crossed over, and that's really all I can say."

I groaned. *This is so frustrating! I don't understand why someone would want to kill a bunch of romance writers. It doesn't make any sense. I just want Belinda home and safe and this crazy person locked up.*

"I understand. Anything else?"

Not unless you can tell me where Belinda is.

"Girl, you know I can't. There are bigger things playin' out here."

Delilah vanished, and I leaned back on the couch. I wasn't sure what to do. Sitting around watching TV didn't appeal to me. I was restless and needed to move.

I walked around my kitchen, straightening the canisters on the countertops and picking up stray Cheerios.

There was a tap on the glass of the side door. Cú barked and came running into the kitchen. I could see Hunter through the window, so I held my puppy back to let him in.

"I don't mean to bother you," he said. "I saw your lights were still on."

Cú planted himself in front of me. He didn't bark or growl, just sat and stared.

"I understand. My house got broken into recently, too. I know exactly how it feels. Please, have a seat." I gestured to one of the chairs at the breakfast table. "Can I get you something? I can make tea."

"Sure."

I plugged in my electric kettle and got the water going, then pulled out packets of chamomile and lavender tea.

Hunter regarded Cú. "I was sure you had a bigger dog."

"I did. Turned out he wasn't really a stray after all, and he went back…where he belongs."

Hunter nodded. "I see."

The kettle was starting to whistle. "Hot or iced?" I asked.

"Iced, please."

I poured the hot water over the tea bags, then got out glasses and filled them with ice. "Is this your first time?"

"I beg your pardon?"

"Being broken into. What did you think I meant?"

"I wasn't sure."

We both chuckled, a little nervously perhaps. The ice crackled as I poured the hot tea over it. I set one of the Mason jar mugs in front of him and sipped from the other as I sat down.

It was mostly small talk, but we chatted for a long time. I didn't feel like being alone, and he didn't seem to want to, either. But my usual bedtime had come and gone. Cassie got up at 6:30 like clockwork, so I was typically asleep by 11:30.

"You keep yawning. I should probably go," Hunter said.

I glanced up at the clock. "Yeah. It's kind of late."

Hunter stood up.

And then there was a terrible scream, almost a roar, from somewhere outside.

Hunter and I looked at each other and dashed out the door. Cú bounded out with us. A figure came running down the sidewalk.

"Marti! Marti!" it yelled.

It was Nick.

"What?"

"Emily needs you! Now!"

"Watch Cassie," I shouted over my shoulder to Hunter, then ran down the sidewalk after Nick.

The house was in a terrible state. Surrounded by overturned furniture and broken porcelain, my sister lay unconscious in the middle of the floor. Her face was bruised and bloody, as if she'd been beaten.

I checked for a pulse. Seconds went by before I found it. It was weak and slow, but it was there.

"Called 911. Ambulance is on the way," Nick panted.

"Get a blanket." I raised her chin to make sure her airway was clear. "I think this arm is broken. Get me a magazine and some gauze."

"We don't have gauze."

"Tape, then."

I curled the magazine around to her arm and taped it to stabilize the bone ends. Anything I could do to help the paramedics get her on the stretcher faster and on the way to the hospital would help. She was hanging by a thread. Relief washed over me when I heard the approaching wail of the ambulance.

"Hang on, Emily, you're going to be okay. You have to be," I told her. "What happened?" I asked Nick.

"I went to the gym. I came home and found her like this."

I suddenly became aware of the silence.

"Nick, where are the kids?"

He was on the verge of tears. "I don't know."

Wednesday, August 10, 10:00 AM
Houston, Texas

The ICU monitors beeped and the respirator hissed and clicked as it breathed for my sister. She was allowed not more than two visitors at a time, and Nick never left her side, not since Homicide had come to question him.

The trauma surgeons had drained the excess blood off Emily's brain, but there was still a lot of swelling. There was no way to know if she'd ever wake up from the coma she was in. Even if she did, would she'd still be Emily?

"Nick?" I said, softly touching his shoulder. "What are the detectives saying about the kids?"

"Amber Alert went out last night. Since the bayou is nearby, EquuSearch is going to work there. It's been on the news. They're all still at my house, plus FBI, waiting on a ransom call."

"I'm sure they're doing everything they can." I wished that I had something other than platitudes to offer Nick.

He rubbed his eyes with the heels of his hands. "They think I did it."

"What? That's crazy!"

"Is it? The spouse is always the prime suspect, until they can be ruled out. Look at my hands."

Nick held them up and I looked. The knuckles on his right hand were freshly scraped. His left hand bore a large bruise. He continued, "My alibi is sketchy at best, incriminating at worst. If you didn't know me, what would you think?"

My heart sank. I would think exactly what the investigators thought. How many domestic violence victims had I seen in the ER? Way more than I ever wanted to.

I swallowed hard and changed the subject. "Please come have some breakfast."

"Not hungry."

"At least have some coffee. Mom will sit with her. Starving yourself to death is not going to help her."

He stood up, kissed Emily's forehead, and whispered, "I'll be right back. Don't go anywhere."

My mother went in to see my sister. Dad stayed in the waiting area. He was having some trouble with his stump and couldn't wear his artificial leg. The wheelchair was too hard to maneuver around all the equipment in Emily's room.

"I'm taking Nick to the cafeteria. You want to come?"

Dad shook his head.

Nick and I went down to the hospital cafeteria. I ate some of my oatmeal, but Nick just pushed his scrambled eggs around the plate. Finally, he gave up and set the fork down.

"I need to talk to Quinn," he said.

"Why?" *Not sure I can arrange that.* This surprised me, because it had been hard for Nick to accept Quinn and company's paranormal nature, especially since when he first met him, Quinn had borrowed the identity of a criminal.

Nick reached into his pants pocket and pulled out a plastic baggie and set it on the table.

"I found this on Emily's cheek."

I picked up the baggie. Inside was a tawny colored scale about the size of a bean. "Well, I supposed it could be from a demon." I gingerly set it back down.

"Isn't that Quinn's area of expertise?"

"Yeah." I put my elbows on the table and interlaced my fingers. "The problems is, well, we kind of broke up. I could try texting him..." I trailed off.

Nick closed his eyes and sighed. When he looked at me again, there was so much suffering in his eyes that it broke my heart. "Please. I know it's awkward. But this is the only clue I have. I have to get my kids back and find out who did this to Emily."

Tears welled up in my eyes. "If there is any change, no matter how minor, you swear to call me?"

He nodded.

"Okay. I'll go now, and see what I can do." I picked up the baggie off the table. "Let me take this along."

"Thanks, Marti."

I wished I could have promised him that we'd get his kids back, but I was afraid it would be a promise I couldn't keep. I swallowed hard to keep my voice from breaking. "Emily is my sister. Your kids are my nephews and niece. What else could I do?"

I drove to my house and walked around the back yard. I knew Dryads lived in the trees – Quinn had called them by name, but I couldn't remember them. So I stood where I was about halfway between them and a little in front.

"If you are listening, please help. It's really urgent that I contact Quinn. He's gone…and I need to talk to him. It's about a demon."

I could hear whispering voices, but no one made an appearance.

"Please," I said. "It's urgent. I really have to speak with him."

The ground shook as something heavy fell behind me. I whirled to look, and found myself facing what could only be described as a gargoyle.

"*Mademoiselle*," it said, bowing ever so slightly.

"Um," I said, for lack of anything more intelligent.

"Why are you looking for Quinn?" it asked.

I had no idea whether this was a good guy or a bad guy. "It doesn't concern you," I replied.

He whistled, and Aleksei stepped out from behind the trees at the back of the yard. How was it possible I hadn't see him there? Fae powers, I suppose.

"Marti!" he said.

I didn't really know him all that well, but I rushed to give him a hug. I just needed something…familiar. He seemed a little taken aback. He smelled of pine needles and leaf litter, and I breathed in deeply.

"Aleksei, I am so happy to see you. I have to speak with Quinn."

"That is problem, Marti."

"Why?" I pulled away from Aleksei.

"He was taken," the gargoyle replied.

"Taken? Like kidnapped?" I asked. *Yet another thing to worry about.*

"*Exactement le même*," said the gargoyle. "Indeed, he was kidnapped."

Still, I was unsure as to whether he had anything to do with the kidnapping. "Who are you?" I asked.

"I am Ocean, Quinn's uncle."

"You don't look much like a kelpie," I said.

"That is because I am not one. The story, it is complicated. Perhaps another time. Now what, *mademoiselle*, is this about a demon?"

I pulled the baggie from my purse and held it out. Ocean held it up for both he and Aleksei to examine.

"*Da*, demon scale," Aleksei said. "Where is from?"

"My sister's house. They took the kids and left her for dead." My voice broke at the end, and I couldn't help tearing up.

Ocean frowned. "Where does your sister live?"

"Six doors down," I pointed toward Emily's house.

"How did we not hear that?" Aleksei asked.

"*Je ne sais pas.* Perhaps they must be using portals. I do not know how they got one inside your sister's home."

"Nick, my brother-in-law, is asking for your help. So am I. Please." I said. "Is there any way this is connected to Quinn's disappearance? Maybe if we find the children, we'll find him as well."

Ocean and Aleksei exchanged a look. They knew more than they were planning to tell me, that was clear.

Chapter 12
Darkness

Tuesday, August 9, 2:30 PM
Houston, Texas

elinda was bored out of her mind. The officers had brought her a notebook, and she'd written the outline for *Dragonfire*, the last book in her dragon romance trilogy. She'd started a draft of the novella, but so far wasn't very happy with it. She needed to go outside and walk, feel the sunlight on her skin, hear the birds in the trees, and smell the fresh air. But that wasn't going to happen any time soon. She wondered if they could get her sunglasses and a wig so she could at least go walk around the swimming pool area of the hotel.

Knock. Knock. "Room service!"

"Finally," said Fiona McCoombs, the officer who was currently on babysitting duty with Belinda. "I'm starved."

She looked out the peephole, then opened the door, still chained. Apparently, it was actual room service, because she took the chain off and let the woman in with the cart of food.

Belinda looked at the server and shook her head slightly. She sincerely hoped that when she was in her sixties, she wouldn't be forced to get a menial hotel job to make ends meet.

The server began to transfer the food to the small writing table, but McCoombs stopped her. "Leave the cart. I'll put it out in the hall for you later."

"If you like," she replied.

Her eyes slid over to Belinda, and it made her shiver. There was something not right about the room service lady. She made her way toward the door, fairly slowly and incompetently, dropping the napkin she had draped over her left arm on the way.

"Wait a minute, please," McCoombs said.

The server stopped.

The officer lifted the covers on each plate and examined the contents. When she was satisfied that there was nothing more sinister than greasy French fries lurking inside the metal domes, she nodded at the server, "Thank you."

The server opened the door.

McCoombs turned and headed for the bathroom to wash her hands.

Instead of leaving the room, the room service lady pulled a ruby pendant out of her blouse and gave Belinda a hard look. Suddenly, Belinda was not in the hotel room.

It was completely dark in the cramped quarters where Belinda found herself. She was on her back, her hands cuffed together in front of her. She reached up and groped around the ceiling of her prison. Satin. *Am I in a coffin?* Her heart rate surged in panic – fight or flight. But neither of those was an option.

Belinda struggled to take deep breaths and calm herself down. She wasn't typically claustrophobic, but then again, she didn't typically lie around handcuffed in coffins, either. *Fear is the true enemy, the only enemy. Calm down and think.* There was a flow of cool air coming from her right, so hopefully, at least she wouldn't suffocate before her captor came for her. Maybe.

She forced herself to breathe deeply and slowly. *Okay. If this is a coffin, it has to have a lid.*

Her eyes started adjusting to the darkness. There was a slightly less dark line a couple of inches wide to her right. The lid must be propped up on something – that's where the air was coming from.

Belinda pushed straight up with both hands. The top raised perhaps an inch before there was a clang of metal and the movement stopped. *Great. It's chained down.*

Something tapped Belinda's thigh, and it startled her. She dropped the lid of the coffin, and it slammed shut. The ventilation opening was gone.

"No!" Belinda shouted at the darkness. She started to hyperventilate.

"If you don't get a hold of yourself and stop this you're going to run out of air," she said out loud, not caring if anyone was listening outside.

No talking – you're wasting oxygen. Okay. So what fell on you? Hopefully, it isn't a large tarantula. She shuddered at the thought.

She had to twist and squirm, but she finally found the edge of the object with her fingertips. It felt like a chunk of wood. After several tries, she was able to use her leg to block it from going forward while she inched it up the side of the casket, letting it fall into her hands. It was definitely wood – a piece of 2 x 4.

This must be what was propping open the lid. Okay, so how do I get it back in place? She clasped the board between her palms and pushed against the top of the casket. It opened about three inches and stopped. But now the wood was at the top of the coffin lid, not the edge. When she tried walking her hands down, she dropped the 2 x 4. After the sixth attempt, she decided to try putting the board in her mouth and raising the lid with her hands. She was starting to feel sleepy and a little light-headed. It was harder work than she imagined, but she eventually wedged the piece of wood under the lid. She lay back for a moment, then twisted so she could prop herself on her elbow to have full access to fresh air. Even so, she just wanted to sleep. But her head ached and her pulse throbbed in her ears to keep her awake. Belinda's heart took little stutter steps every now and then. *This had really better not be a heart attack.*

Gradually, the pounding in her head subsided, and she lay in the dark and listened. Water dripped somewhere off to her left. A cricket chirped a few times, then was silent.

There was a click, then a creak. *A door opening? Should I be mad or scared?*

Footsteps. Another click. A scrape and a rattle. The coffin lid opened and a bright light glared in Belinda's face. She closed her eyes and turned away.

"Who are you? What do you want from me?" she asked.

"It doesn't matter who I am — I'm just a vessel. I'm here to stop you from spreading that smut you write and corrupting innocent readers." The voice was female, with a bit of a southern twang, but not too much. It sounded vaguely familiar.

"I think readers are smart enough to know what works for them. If they don't like the book, they can stop at any time," Belinda replied.

"That isn't the point! Words corrupt, your words corrupt, with your disgusting dragons and bestiality. After someone's read one of your lustful scenes, they can't unread it, now can they? Time is short."

"Time is short?" Belinda echoed, fearing the woman would close the lid, lock it down, and leave her alone in the dark forever.

"The Rapture approaches!" The woman's voice got louder. "I have to save as many as I can, before it's too late."

"What about people who don't want to be saved?"

"You're just trying to confuse me. Everyone needs to be saved, whether they know it or not."

"And you're willing to kill innocent people to save other people who don't know they need saving, and probably don't even want it?"

"Oh, you can mock me if you want. I'm not the one lying in a coffin with her hands chained together."

Belinda could hear the smirk in her attacker's voice, even if she couldn't see her face behind the glare.

The woman continued. "I went looking for Coda Sterling, but I found Belinda Tate instead. Not only do you lie about your name to sell those filthy books, but you try to spread your devil worship through your unholy shop. It's too bad they don't burn witches these days – only fire could cleanse your evil soul. But don't worry. I have something extra special planned for you."

"Devil worship? What on Earth are you talking about?"

"Your shop. The Tenth Sphere? Something to do with summoning demons, I'm sure."

"Are you kidding me?" Belinda asked. "Demons are the last thing we want hanging around. Do you have any idea what a nuisance they are? In fact, we sometimes work with –" Belinda stopped herself. This woman wasn't going to believe anything she said, but she might repeat it. No point in giving her information, because there was no way of knowing who she might blab to.

"You're working with who?" the woman behind the flashlight asked.

"It doesn't matter. You could stop shining that light in my eyes, you know," Belinda said. "And I could use a restroom break."

"No. I don't trust you."

"It's going to be an emergency before much longer."

"Not my problem." The light started to go down toward the floor, then flipped back up into Belinda's eyes. "How do you know so much about demons?" Suspicion edged her voice.

Belinda tried to shrug, but her shoulders were starting to get pins and needles from being in an unnatural position, and it hurt to move them. "Oh, please. They're everywhere. You've probably met at least one and never realized it."

"I think I could recognize a demon," the woman said, her voice shrill with indignation.

"I doubt it. They're very clever at disguising themselves. If you ever get an offer too good to be true, odds are there's a demon behind it."

"Is that so?" The woman sounded skeptical.

"Who do you think invented multi-level marketing?"

The woman behind the light snorted, but Belinda couldn't tell if it was laughter or derision. "I have preparations to make," she said, and closed the lid.

"Wait!" If she could just keep the woman talking, maybe she would realize her mistake and set Belinda free.

But her only answer was the rattle of the chain and the snick of the closing lock. Footsteps. Squeaking door. Turning lock.

Belinda started to hyperventilate again She was in worse trouble than she'd originally thought.

She couldn't allow herself to panic – that wouldn't get her out of here.

There was another voice, new but familiar. "Belinda, are you here? I can't see you."

"Ellen!" she said out loud, then thought better of it. *I'm here, in the casket.*

"Oh, Belinda! What happened to you?"

I don't exactly know. I was in the hotel room, then all of a sudden, I was here. I don't even know where I am. How did you find me?

"Sofia told me where you were."

Thank goodness for spirit guides. Now how are we going to get out of here?

Virginia scowled. When Balcones, in his human form, had approached her about a tulpa, he had offered to get rid of someone, any person she chose, as part of his payment. Naturally, she chose Belinda. Of course, he'd resorted to outsourcing his dirty work to a human. *Wasn't that just like a demon?* If this ghost lady – what was her name again? Ellen? – got back to Lulu with Belinda's whereabouts, the whole plan would come crashing down. Ellen had to be stopped, permanently, if need be.

In certain circles, Virginia was known as the Thought Form Queen – there were few people in the Western Hemisphere as good at creating and deploying tulpas as Virginia. It was a small matter for her to put a spider thought form in one of the darkened corners of Belinda's prison, just to make sure things were unfolding according to plan. It was a good thing she was watching, because the plan just hit a snag.

Her grandparents had lived practically out in the country, once upon a time. The city of Houston spread and sprawled until it swallowed their neighborhood. Their 1960's ranch was on a large, one-acre lot in a highly desirable part of town. Every year, more trust fund money was wasted paying the taxes on the place, and she never got any benefit from it whatsoever. If she could get Belinda out of the way, she'd get Penelope institutionalized, and cash in on the property. That size lot was easily worth a million dollars, maybe more, to someone who'd just knock down the old house and put up a mansion. And with Belinda dead, she wouldn't have to share a dime of it. Penelope would never ask, and Virginia would never tell. They made a great team.

But now, this Ellen person threatened to ruin everything. Virginia saw her million-dollar payday vanishing before her eyes.

And there was no way she was going to allow that.

Chapter 13
Sleeping Beauty

Wednesday, August 10, 12:15 PM
Houston, TX

y cell phone rang.

I jumped. So did Aleksei and Ocean.

"Hold on." I looked at the screen. Caller ID said it Dr. Tribeki – I'd worked with him as an ER nurse. *Why is he calling me? Had Emily woken up?* I couldn't stand any more bad news.

"Dr. Tribeki?"

"Hello, Marti. I wanted to give you an update on your sister."

My stomach knotted into macramé.

"How is she?"

"She's still the same. But at least her condition hasn't deteriorated. Since she was stabilized enough to run a CT, we did one and found three linear skull fractures. No more active bleeds, but there are some contusions. There's not much else we can do. As you well know, she could wake up this afternoon, or it could be ten years from now. I'm so sorry – wish I had better news."

"Did you run stimuli tests? What was her Glasgow?"

"There was a pupil reaction, but we put her GCS at five."

"Five. I see. Thank you for calling." I hung up before he could say anything else.

A five on the Glasgow Coma Scale. Damn. The lowest possible score was three, and the lower the score, the worse the prognosis. I knew that only about a quarter of patients with GCS scores lower than nine recovered. But none of those patients was my sister. Emily could not die. I wouldn't allow it.

"Marti?" Aleksei asked. "Is bad news?"

I blinked a few times and looked up at him. He looked a little blurry, and I felt something sliding down my cheeks. "Emily," I said, then swallowed hard, "she's in pretty bad shape. The odds-" I stopped, unable to bring myself to say it out loud.

Aleksei put his arms around me. I felt nothing but static, white noise. His hug didn't help.

"I have to get back to the hospital," I said, and pulled away.

When I got there, both of my parents looked grey and worn out, like old, discarded rags. I'm not sure I remember either of them looking this grim, even when Dad lost his leg in that car accident. They shouldn't be here in the ICU, watching their daughter dangling by a spider silk thread over death's abyss. They should be at home, playing with their new granddaughter, not worried sick about where she and her brothers were and whether they were okay.

But as bad as they looked, Nick looked worse. I stood near the end of the bile yellow curtain that separated Emily from the next patient over. His hand went through the bed railings and came up underneath hers to avoid the IV.

"Hey, Nick."

He didn't move, and at first I thought maybe he didn't hear me over the hissing and thumping of the ventilator. He shook his head very softly and said, "This is all my fault."

"What are you talking about?"

He looked at me with such an unbearable misery in his eyes that I nearly started crying again. "I should have been there. Maybe I could have stopped this. Maybe they would have seen I was home and moved on to a different house."

Like mine? Surely that's not what he meant. "You can't beat yourself up with maybes and what-ifs. There's no way to know what could have happened. Maybe you would have stopped it, but maybe you would have ended up in the bed next to this one. Or dead."

"No. Not dead." He shook his head, and I wasn't sure if he was laughing or crying. "Remember that green fire I showed you when I cut my hand? It even fixes dead."

It took me a few moments to process what he had just said. I'd forgotten all about the weird wound healing fire he'd shown me. I thought it must be a consequence of having his life force replaced with a Valkyrie's. And of course, Valkyries were immortal. But all this was too complicated to explain right here, right now.

I just nodded. "I see." My eyes darted to Emily's machinery. None of the readouts looked any different than they had before. "You've worked late plenty of times. Nothing like this has every happened before, not in our neighborhood. There was no reason to expect-"

"I wasn't working late!" he snapped. "But I was late coming home." He paused, seeming to be searching for the right words. *What wasn't he telling me?* "Em and I got into a fight. I left. Went to work out. Why did I leave?" His breath caught in his throat.

"Whether it would have made a difference or not, you don't have a time machine to go back and see. We just have to deal with what is. And this self-flagellation is not helping. Not you, not Emily." *Not your kids.*

He put his face in his hands for a few moments. Then he stood up and wiped them on his jeans. "You're right. The best thing I can do for Em right now is bring her babies back to her."

Nick caressed her least-bruised cheek with the backs of his fingers. "I'll be back soon. You rest now, okay?"

He stood up and looked straight at me. His eyes now had laser focus. This was the look of someone who was out for revenge. Someone who had nothing left to lose.

"Let's go," he said.

My father looked up as we went past.

"I'm going with him to make sure he doesn't do anything stupid," I said.

Dad nodded.

Nick strode down the hospital corridor, and I almost had to run to keep up with him.

"Where are we going?" I asked.

"To get my kids back."

"Do you have news?"

"Not yet. But I want you to take me to Quinn. If it wasn't for him, this would never have happened. Unfortunately, he is the only one that can help me find McKenzi and my boys. That's all that's keeping me from breaking his neck."

"I don't think it's fair to blame Quinn," I said. If Quinn attracted demons, or one demon in particular, then it was also somewhat my fault for having him around. "He didn't do this to Emily or take the kids. But I can't take you to him."

Nick stopped and turned on me so fast I nearly crashed into him. "You're protecting him over your own sister?"

"He's been taken. Nobody knows where he is, or even if he's still alive. I talked to Aleksei this morning. I can take you to him."

When we got to the parking garage, I said. "Let me drive."

"No."

I knew that as a police officer, he had special training in driving at high speeds, but there was no way I was getting in the car with him, not in the state he was in. "Have it your own way. Meet me at my house."

He nodded once, curtly, and headed towards his parking space. My car was up another two levels, so I took the elevator. When I got back to my house,

Nick was already there, waiting in his truck. I glanced at the clock on my dash. I still had another two hours before I had to pick up Cassie. I couldn't think of anything I'd rather do than hug my baby girl just now, but it would have to wait a little longer.

I got out of the car, and Nick did the same. He looked up at the top of my house as we came into the back yard.

"A gargoyle statue? Really?"

Ocean was perched there, looking exactly like a hunk of carved limestone. "That isn't a statue," I said.

At the sound of my voice, Ocean hopped down off the shingles, shaking the ground as he landed. Nick took a step backward, but otherwise remained impassive.

"Nick, this is Ocean, Quinn's uncle. Ocean, this is Nick, my brother-in-law."

I tossed Nick my keys. "You should probably go in the house. I'll find Aleksei."

Ocean had to fold his wings tightly and dip his shoulders to fit through the doors, but they both disappeared inside. I dreaded the conversation that would take place between Aleksei and Nick. But I was as anxious as he was to get McKenzi and the boys back safe and sound. I went and stood between the two trees.

"Aleksei?" I called softly.

Seconds dragged by. When I thought about a minute had passed, I called again, a little louder.

"I am here. What is your need?" He peered at me from behind the tree to my right.

"Emily, my sister, is in a coma, and I don't know if she's going to make it. Nick and I, we need your help to find his children."

"I am sad to hear of your misfortune. But I am not sure —"

"Please," I said. "Please come inside and talk with me, Ocean, and Nick."

He followed me into the house. Nick and Ocean were standing at opposite ends of the kitchen, regarding each other adversarially.

"*Non*," Ocean said. "This is not a job for humans."

Nick glared at him. "They're my kids. No one is going to care as much about finding them as I do."

"*C'est vrai*, that is true. But it is also true that such emotion clouds your judgment. And besides, this work is *tres dangereuses*, too much so for mortals."

Nick said nothing. He moved to the silverware drawer and pulled out a chef's knife. He looked straight at Ocean and plunged the blade into his own abdomen, then pulled it out, blood flowing with it.

Aleksei grunted in surprise.

Before I had a chance to grab a kitchen towel to apply pressure, green fire flickered around the wound. The bleeding stopped. Nick raised his shirt, revealing his mark-free belly.

Ocean cocked his head. "I have seen this only with the Valkyries. How do you come to have this ability?"

Nick shrugged.

I hadn't told Nick what had really happened in Russia a few weeks ago. He knew he'd died, but had no idea why he hadn't stayed that way. I'd thought it was better he didn't know the details, because he was already struggling to accept the supernatural.

"It's a long story," I said. "But to make it short, he was killed but a Valkyrie gave up her life force for him."

"*Vraiment.* So this is the one. There was a report of such a thing happening." Ocean shook his head. "Odin Allfather does not take lightly the deaths of his daughters."

I looked at the floor. I remembered the single tear that had fallen from Odin's eye. He'd caught it after it turned into a solid blue crystal on his cheek. "Never forget," he had said as he folded it into my hand. I'd kept Odin's tear in in my jewelry box, not sure what to do with it. But it occurred to me now that it would be a good talisman on this desperate quest.

Nick leaned against the counter.

"When was the last time you slept?" I asked him.

"Doesn't matter."

"It does. I know there's a bunch of cops and FBI at your house, waiting for a ransom call. Why don't you crash on my couch? I have to go get Cassie."

"Not right now," he replied.

I shook my head and left.

After I put Cassie to bed, I rummaged around in my jewelry box. I set Odin's tear on the counter while I looked for a suitable necklace. I had a Tibetan prayer box that one of my cousins had given me for my birthday one year, after she'd been on a month-long tour of Asia. It was a cylinder, a little smaller than the first joint of my thumb, and it was silver with a red stone and a blue stone set in the side. The idea was to write a prayer or wish on a slip of paper and then put it in the box so that it's always infusing the aura of the person wearing it. I wasn't a big believer in that, but it was the perfect size to hold Odin's tear. I slipped it into the box, then, because it couldn't hurt, I wrote a wish on a sliver of notebook paper and put it in, too. The chain was a little long, but if I tucked it inside my shirt, the box hung right next to my heart.

Saturday, August 13, 2:00 PM
Houston, Texas

"Have you seen Nick today?" Mom asked.

I put my cell phone on speaker so I could talk to her while I was changing Cassie.

"No. Why?"

"When we went to see your sister this morning, the nurses said he hadn't been there."

"I'm sure he's trying to find the kids. There's not really anything he can do for Emily by sitting around the hospital. At least that's how he'll see it."

"You're probably right," she said. "Your father is having a nap, so come in quietly when you bring Cassie, okay?"

"No problem. We'll be over as soon as I finish changing her."

We said our goodbyes and I tapped the 'speaker' tile. Cassie was barely one, so potty training was nowhere near our immediate future. But she hated everything about her nappy – she just wanted to go commando.

"That is so not happening, little squirmy wormy," I said to her.

She giggled as she wiggled, and I added a little piece of duct tape over each diaper tab so she wouldn't pull the whole thing off.

"No bare baby bottoms at Grandma's house, okay? You need to be good while I go visit your Auntie Em."

"Ning!"

I topped off Cú's water before we left and gave him a pat. His tail thumped lazily on his bed. "Guard the house while we're out." *No one's going to be afraid of you, though. Not yet, anyway.*

The ICU looked the same as it had yesterday. So did Emily.

"Hey, Em," I said. "How do you feel today?"

I didn't really expect an answer. It was more force of habit than anything, back from my old ER days.

"Girl, you need to turn around if you want to see her."

Delilah? What are you doing here?

Delilah rolled her eyes, so I just did what she said.

Emily!

She looked at me. Her mouth opened and closed, as if she were trying to say something. Emily gestured with her hands, but I didn't know what she was trying to tell me. She glanced over at her body, then vanished.

"Emily," I said, taking her hand. "Please hold on. Whatever you do, don't go into the light. Nick needs you. I need you. Nick *is* going to get your kids back. They'll need you most of all. Please. Please stay with us."

"It ain't always a choice, girlfriend," Delilah said.

I pulled up a chair and got out my cell phone, flicking through the tiles until I found the e-reader app. I'd already queued up one of Emily's favorite novels. I always thought, whether she realized it or not, Victor Hugo's epic is what ultimately propelled her into the public defender job she had now. I started to read:

> *So long as there shall exist, by virtue of law and custom, decrees of damnation pronounced by society, artificially creating hells amid the civilization of earth, and adding the element of human fate to divine destiny; so long as the three great problems of the century – the degradation of man through pauperism, the corruption of woman through hunger, the crippling of children through lack of light – are unsolved...*

I also thought it was the most appropriately titled book of all: *Les Misérables* – because right now, we were The Miserable Ones. I read until my voice started to get raspy. Then I just sat there, watching the little blip on the EKG jumping and scrolling across the monitor for as long as I could stand it. Beep...beep...beep. *Keep on beeping, Em. Keep on beeping.*

Cassie had spent the day 'helping' Grandma around the house. They'd skipped nap time, and she was tired and cranky when I picked her up. I debated whether it was better to make her stay up until her usual bedtime, or just let her sleep, risking an extra-early wake up. In the end, I needed the peace, so I let her sleep.

I sat in the kitchen and stared out the window. I should probably fix myself something for dinner, but I couldn't seem to get motivated. I absently stroked Cú's head and ruffled his ears, until he ran to the door and barked.

There was a knock, and I could see Hunter's face through the glass. I got up to let him in.

"Hey," I said.

"I am so sorry about your sister and her family," he said, setting down a re-useable grocery bag on the table. "I had no idea until I saw your mom and Cassie this afternoon. I'd seen the cops at your sister's house, but I hadn't realized…"

"Thanks for coming over." I sat back down, and Cú curled up at my feet.

Hunter began unloading the shopping. "I figured you might be tired from spending all that time at the hospital, so I thought it would be a neighborly gesture to come and make you and Cassie dinner."

I gave him half a smile. "Cassie's already asleep. I really appreciate the offer, but I don't feel all that hungry."

I raised my eyebrow at the bottle of wine he set on the table.

"That's for the scampi sauce," he said.

I winced. "This is so thoughtful, but I'm deathly allergic to shellfish."

His smile deflated. "Well…how about zucchini sautéed in white wine and garlic butter then?"

I laughed. "Sure." I gave him some ice and a plastic bag for the shrimp – I was afraid for it to be in my fridge in case the package leaked. Cassie was too little to call 911 if I went into anaphylactic shock.

It didn't take long for him to cook up a scrumptious meal. And since he only needed a few ounces of the chardonnay, we each had a glass. After we finished eating, he poured another.

"Are you trying to ply me with alcohol and have your way with me?" I asked, only half joking. I knew how incredibly stupid it was to combine alcohol with having a man I hardly knew in my house. But I was feeling so overwhelmed and alone that I was willing to risk it.

"I would never do that to you."

I hoped that was true. "You up for a movie?" I needed an escape, a breath of air. I felt I was drowning in all the horribleness that was going on right now. The horribleness that I had brought down on my family.

Cú kept himself between us as we relocated to the living room. I flicked on the TV with the remote and sat at one end of the couch, and Hunter sat at the other.

"Come on, put your feet up," he said, patting the cushion.

I was exhausted, so I set my wine down and swung my feet up on the sofa. Cú groaned as he stretched out on the floor. Hunter pulled my feet into his lap, and started giving me a foot massage.

"I'll fall asleep if you keep doing that," I said.

He didn't stop. I didn't exactly want him to. After the train wreck my life had suddenly become, it was nice to not be alone. And it didn't hurt that he was easy to look at.

But as pleasant as this was, I knew that Quinn was the one with all the answers, and I had to find him. And the sooner the better.

Chapter 14
Unexpected Guests

Tuesday, August 9, 11:30 PM
The In Between

alcones had left the room a while ago. There were no doors – the only access was through portals. And Quinn was certain that they were secured so that only specific individuals could go through them. He was equally certain that he was not on that list. What he needed was a workaround. He cast his gaze to the ceiling. The compound green eyes that glinted in the firelight were not helping his concentration.

"Phobetor? That is you, up there isn't it?"

There was a scratching noise as a spider the size of a Great Dane clambered down the wall and stood in the pale circle of light. It shimmered, then took the form of a man. His skin was pale, almost greenish, and his dark hair unkempt. Dark circles pooled under his deep set eyes like bruises. His loose grey tunic accentuated his pallor.

Sandals scuffed on the concrete as he approached Quinn. "How do you know me?"

"I have been told that your brothers are worried about your disappearance, and Phantasos is looking for you."

Phobetor rolled his eyes. "They never understood me. Don't be misled. They aren't concerned for my welfare – they just want to control me."

Quinn nodded. "I understand. I have four brothers."

"Oldest?"

"Middle."

Phobetor grimaced. "Hardest spot. I'm the youngest. Nyx saved the best for last."

"Hmmm," Quinn replied.

"You don't believe me?" Phobetor asked. "Morpheus sends sappy, sweet dreams that hardly anyone remembers. Phantasos is in charge of weird dreams, you know, the kind where you go for tea with the Queen, and the butler is a talking zebra who pours tea from a seashell and serves you little cakes made of cloud and pumpernickel." He pointed to his chest. "I, on the other hand, send nightmares."

Quinn had had more than his fill of bad dreams. "And what's so good about nightmares, then?"

"No one forgets their nightmares," Phobetor replied. "And they bring you a gift. Face the monster in your dream, and you slay it in real life. They're always connected, if you look hard enough."

"Perhaps." Quinn shrugged. "But why are you here, with Balcones?"

Phobetor's face darkened. "He said we were going out for a glass of mead. He wanted to make a business proposition. But then he brought me here. Still not a hint of a business transaction. And no mead. Worse, I can't get out of this place, and I've had enough of him. He's ugly, obnoxious, and he smells terrible."

Quinn couldn't resist. "Sounds like a nightmare."

Phobetor glared at him and opened his mouth to reply.

Balcones stepped through a portal and into the room. He carried a very small baby. Triumphantly, he put the child in Quinn's arms.

"What are you doing, Balcones? Have you lost your mind?" Quinn asked.

"Look at the baby."

Quinn looked.

"I don't know what you're on about. You should get this wee one back to her mother before she wakes up."

Balcones scowled. "You don't know this baby?"

Quinn shook his head.

Balcones stepped in so that his face was only inches away. His hot breath stank like sulfur and rotting flesh. His reptilian eyes fixed on Quinn's. The baby started to wail. "This is not Cassie?"

Quinn shook his head. A chill of dread scurried into the pit of his stomach. Young babies all looked alike. What if this was Marti's niece? He couldn't be sure. He did know it wasn't Cassie – she was a year old, more than three times the size of this one, and he would know her the instant he saw her.

Balcones spun on his heel and stuck his head through the portal, then withdrew it. Quinn rocked the baby, trying to calm her. It didn't seem to help, so he whispered in her ear, words charged with fae magic, and she slept.

The fire flared up and brightened the room. Three demons, accompanied by two young boys, spilled out of the portal. Quinn recognized Aiden and Kyle – he'd played with them enough as Bruce, the Labrador retriever, although he hadn't had much interaction with them in human form. He did not betray any emotion, not wanting Balcones to recognize that he knew the boys.

"You idiots!" Balcones yelled at his minions. "I thought you said you had the house identified."

"We thought we did," said the empty-handed one. "There was a woman and a baby there alone. No male."

"How do you explain these two?" Balcones demanded.

The demons holding the boys looked at each other and shrugged.

"I don't know. Perhaps she was caring for the children of another?" the third demon said.

"These human larvae are of no use to me. Get rid of them." He shoved McKenzi at his empty-handed henchman.

"How should we do that?" the one holding Kyle asked.

Balcones looked up at the ceiling and shook his head. "What does 'get rid of' mean? Take them back where you got them, leave them at a shopping mall, eat them. I don't care. Take them some place not here." He turned to Quinn and Phobetor. "This is what I get for bringing my wife's nephews into the business. Never hire your relatives."

Quinn tried to shrink into what was left of the darkness as the demons dragged the boys past him. Aiden looked him in the face, and the terror in his eyes made Quinn want to reach out to him, but he thought the that children's best chance of escape was for the demons to take them back to the Mundane world and let them go. And they wouldn't do that if he knew them.

"Aren't you Aunt Marti's boyfriend? Quinn? Help us!" Aiden cried out.

"What? Aunt Marti's boyfriend! Ha ha!" Balcones practically sang. "So this mission wasn't a complete failure after all. Not as good as the girlfriend's own baby, but maybe close enough. Take them to the stronghold."

"I'll get you out of here, I promise!" Quinn shouted as they disappeared through the portal.

Balcones grinned at Quinn and tapped a spot on the wall. A circle of concrete about a yard wide turned clear, and a scene of an ancient misty forest appeared.

"You are going to watch the remaining members of your team die. Then your girlfriend and her family, and finally, I will take pleasure in ending you. Come, Phobetor, we have work to do."

He grabbed the God of Nightmares by the wrist and stepped through the wall.

Houston, Texas

Belinda awoke with a start and bumped her head on the lid of the coffin. She had a hard time determining if her eyes were open or closed. She wanted to cry. She thought this whole casket episode was just a bad dream, but the solid lid was a tangible reminder that it was all too real. Her shoulders were numb and her back ached. The casket reeked so badly of ammonia that she struggled to breathe – the restroom break she'd needed when she was first kidnapped never came. If that wasn't bad enough, her empty stomach rumbled and cramped.

She didn't dare push up on the lid for fear that the piece of 2 x 4 that allowed the air in would fall on the outside of her prison this time. Belinda wanted to kick and scream and bang on the sides of the box she was in until someone heard her and let her out. Somehow she doubted there was much chance of that. She wasn't sure how long she lay there, waiting, not even knowing what day it was.

Finally, she heard the key turn in the lock and steps come across the room, a pause and a few thumps as if several things were set down, then more steps. Again, the lid opened and the flashlight shone in her eyes.

"Ugh!" groaned the woman, stepping back.

"I told you I needed a bathroom," Belinda replied.

"That's worse than I expected." She dropped something in the casket on Belinda's stomach. "If I'm going to keep you alive and well until Sunday night, you're going to have to drink water and eat something. That's a key to the handcuffs. There's a plate of food and a few bottles of water on the floor. There's also a bucket, for…you know. If you can get yourself out of the coffin, you can eat and walk around. I'll bring you fresh clothes later – you're disgusting."

"How generous," Belinda muttered. "What's Sunday night?" she asked more loudly.

"I'm glad you asked." The woman said. "MacBeth is on at the Miller Outdoor Theater. The Thursday performance was cancelled due to thunderstorms knocking some trees down last night and them having to fix some electrical stuff at the stage, so I'll have to keep you around until the next one." The woman frowned. "There will be a big audience there. When they get to the part with the witches in in it, you will appear on stage, ready to be burned at the stake, as witches should be. When they see this, the audience can't help but recognize the truth, and they will repent. I only hope the Rapture doesn't happen before then."

"You need psychiatric help. The only thing that the audience will see me as is a victim of a deranged killer. When the police catch you – and how can they miss if you're up on stage ranting about murdering me in cold blood? – they will strap you in a strait jacket, and you'll never see the light of day again."

The woman laughed and lowered the flashlight just enough that it wasn't glaring in Belinda's eyes, and she recognized her as the room service lady from the hotel. Again, the woman pulled a ruby pendant from her blouse.

"As long as I have my wishing stone, they can't touch me."

"A wishing stone?"

"Yes." She held it proudly at the end of its chain. "All I have to do is make a wish, and it comes true."

"Did you wish that Regina Dupris would fall down an escalator and die?"

"Of course."

Belinda propped herself up on one elbow so she could see her kidnapper better. "Let me guess. A handsome stranger gave it to you? Perhaps he told you how special you were? What's the catch?"

"What makes you think there's a catch?"

Belinda's arm started to shake, so she lay back down. "Because there's always a catch."

The kidnapper was silent for a while. Then she said, "Five years. Each wish costs five years of my life. But with the Rapture upon us, it seemed like a small price to pay. There may not be another five days left, much less five years."

Belinda laughed bitterly. "So it's a self-limiting cursed object. That's the kind they prefer."

"Cursed object? No! I'm doing good works with it. I'm using it to save souls by destroying the profane."

"You're using it to murder innocent people. They tricked you."

"Who is 'they?'" The flashlight beam sank to the floor.

"Demons."

"You lie!" the woman shouted, and ran for the door.

Belinda heard the lock turn. She hoped she'd at least planted some seeds of doubt in the woman's mind. But she couldn't be sure.

She grasped the handcuff key and transferred it to her mouth, clamping it between her teeth. It was awkward, and she gave herself a bloody lip in the process, but she got the cuffs off. Her shoulders were stiff and sore, but moving them would help. The first thing she did was take off her smelly wet skirt. Belinda tossed it into the coffin and shut the lid. The room was dark, but not cave-dark, and there was an outline of light around the edges of the door. She moved slowly and carefully towards it so she wouldn't knock over the food when she came to it. Although at this point, she was hungry enough to have eaten it from off the floor.

When she came to the water, she sacrificed part of one of the bottles to rinse the urine off her legs – it stunk and was starting to make her itch. Then she grabbed the plate and ate greedily. Stale crackers, some processed cheese food, a protein bar and a couple of wilted carrots. *Was this woman feeding her, or just cleaning out her refrigerator?* But Belinda ate it, and wished she had more.

Chapter 15
Yes, Virginia, There is a Severability Clause

Saturday, August 13, 11:00 PM
The In Between

uinn's plan left a lot to chance. But he was short on alternatives. He needed to get Virginia alone, which he'd been trying to do since Wednesday. Balcones and his goon squad were running a bit behind their usual schedule.

Virginia would be along soon to launch the tulpa – and if he was lucky, there would be a gap between her arrival and Balcones'. The Devil Baby hadn't gotten into Marti's house the past three nights, and he expected it wouldn't tonight, either. Cú would see to that. While a mortal dog could be tricked into not seeing the creature, the faery dog could not. If it came into his territory, he would rip it to shreds, dissipating its energy and leaving its controller with a nasty headache.

Virginia entered the room, tulpa in tow. She was dressed to kill, or to hit the night clubs, one of the two. Quinn pretended to be dozing, but as soon as she sent the tulpa on its mission, he quickly fixed his eyes on hers.

"Hello, Virginia." Quinn made a point of scanning her from jeweled barrette to stiletto heel. "You and Balcones must be getting along very well indeed."

Her eyes narrowed, but she still responded to his gaze by slightly arching her back, as if to emphasize her bosom. "He told me not to talk to you. And for your information, not that it's any of your business, I've been out on a date. Balcones is just a client," she sniffed. "Now where is he? I've got to get back. There's a glass of champagne and a hot tub waiting for me."

Not tonight, Virginia. "You are earlier than usual."

"Like I told you, I have plans." She crossed her arms.

"Sorry, Virginia. Your plans are about to change." Quinn wasn't a monster. He didn't really like doing this to humans, but it couldn't be helped this time. Once he made eye-contact with her and willed it to be so, she was under his control. She stood where she was, staring at him like a china doll.

Quinn had noticed that as long a person was touching someone who was sanctioned to go through a portal, anyone could go with them, so he stretched out his hand and took hers. "Take me home with you."

Quinn knew Balcones would arrive at any second. "Go," he said. "Now."

With Quinn holding her hand, Virginia walked through the wall.

As soon as they were out of Balcones' chamber, Quinn breathed a sigh of relief. He knew he was nowhere near safe yet, but at least he wasn't trapped any more. They were in a bedroom, and he assumed it was Virginia's.

Malik! Malik! Can you hear me? He hoped the djinn was listening to his thoughts.

Quinn took Virginia's face in both of his hands, and looked deep into her eyes. "Forget that you saw me today."

Virginia nodded.

Quinn swept her up in his arms and carried her over to the bed. He set her down and said, "Sleep." She put her head down and closed her eyes.

He wondered if that would affect the tulpa in any way as headed for the front door. *What will happen to it if Virginia doesn't retrieve it?* After making his way out in the dark, he hurried down the sidewalk. He looked back over his shoulder at the two story house he had just fled. *The tulpa business must pay pretty well.* Then he corralled his thoughts back to more urgent matters. *Malik?*

"Quinn!" The typically aloof and snarky djinn appeared in front of him and grabbed him into a bear hug.

"We have to get out of here. It's only a matter of time before Balcones figures out how I escaped."

"Balcones?"

"Yes. I'll explain later. Take me to Kai's house."

In an instant, they were inside the MAMIC waystation.

Breena, who was pouring herself a glass of water in the kitchen, startled.

"We've been looking all over for you!" she exclaimed.

He hugged her quickly.

"Where have you been? How did you get here?" she asked.

"Balcones was holding me in an interdimensional prison. I escaped, and Malik gave me a lift here."

"It's so good to see you safe and sound. Everyone else is upstairs, planning this evening's search."

"Thanks Bree." He picked up an apple off the counter and took it with him as he jogged up the stairs to the war room.

He knocked twice, quickly, as he opened the door.

"Quinn!" cried Eoin.

He recognized everyone there, but was surprised to see Nick sitting at the table, looking as grim as death. Quinn looked closely at him, noticing that his aura was dark red – anger, strong and hot.

Aleksei and Ocean stood up to greet Quinn, and Nick pushed past them.

Quinn guessed what was coming, and dodged, taking the force of the punch meant for his face on his shoulder.

Aleksei and Ocean each grabbed one of Nick's arms and forced him to his knees. This only seemed to further infuriate him.

"Bloody hell, man!" Quinn said, rubbing his shoulder. "What was that about?"

"You," he growled. "Someone put my wife in a coma and took my kids. This is your fault. If you hadn't been hanging around Marti, this would never have happened."

Quinn's jaw went slack. "Someone hurt Emily? I'm so sorry. What happened?." Quinn closed his eyes for a long moment. *If Balcones' nephews hadn't gone to the wrong house, it would have been Marti. He's not entirely wrong for blaming me for this.* Still, he wanted to probe how much Nick actually knew. "What makes you think this has anything to do with me?"

"There was a scale. A demon scale stuck to Emily's cheek with her own blood," he growled.

"I saw them. I saw your kids."

"Where are they?" Nick asked, his voice thick with emotion.

"One night, and I think it was Tuesday or Wednesday, Balcones' nephews brought them in–"

"In where?" Ocean asked.

"I was in an interdimensional holding area. The woman who created the tulpa would bring it into the room and send it off on its errands from there. Probably to stop it being traced back to her. Phobetor was there, too. Said he was being held against his will, but he was taken away somewhere. Not sure what Balcones has in mind for him, but he did create a window port looking out onto an old forest."

"What about my kids?" Nick all but shouted.

Quinn nodded to Aleksei and Ocean, and they released the human. Warily, he dragged himself to his feet.

"He told the demons to take them to the stronghold. But I don't know where that is."

He didn't mention that the henchmen would have let them go, if Aiden hadn't recognized Quinn and called out to him. Or that it was a case of mistaken identity – they were after Marti to get to him. Saying that would only make a bad situation worse.

"What do they want with my kids?" Nick asked.

The abject misery in his voice made rage at Balcones flare up in Quinn's heart, and his promise to rescue the children burned bright in his soul.

"That is good question," Aleksei said.

Nick struggled to get himself together, and it was painful for Quinn to watch, so he changed the subject.

"The woman who created the tulpa, her name is Virginia. I think she's using it to put portal links in different houses so that they can easily go in and acquire captives," Quinn said. *And figure out which house is Marti's.*

Nick's face was blank, as if Quinn had been speaking gibberish.

"A portal link is a one-way, temporary portal. A tulpa is a thought-form, a creature made of ideas. This particular one looks like a baby devil."

"A what?"

"A baby devil."

"I've seen that."

"*Quand?*" Ocean asked. "When?"

"It was on some security camera footage that we watched on Sunday."

Quinn chose his words carefully before he spoke. "We know where Virginia lives, and we can question her at will. Unfortunately, I doubt Balcones has told her how to get to his so-called stronghold, or what he's planning to do with the children. She may not even know he has them, so I don't know that she'll be of any use in finding them."

"But she will know the reason for the tulpa, *n'est-ce pas?*"

Fairly certain he knew the reason for the tulpa, Quinn didn't wish to discuss it in front of Nick. "Perhaps, but just because Balcones told her something doesn't mean he told her the truth."

"We should ask her anyway," Eoin chipped in. "You're almost as good as a gancanagh with the ladies."

"Thank you, Eoin. That will do," Quinn replied. He was fairly sure that Nick did not know that a gancanagh was a fae notorious for seducing human maidens, but he probably caught the gist of Eoin's remark.

"Why have 'almost,' when you can have the real thing?" asked Kai, who was an actual gancanagh.

"Can we get back on track, please?" Quinn interjected. He was tired and hungry, and he knew it would be some time before he could rest. His skin was dry and itchy, and he really needed to spend some time in kelpie form in the very near future. "We know what Balcones wants, so we just have to be more clever than him, and use his own trap against him."

"Do tell, nephew. What is it that Balcones wants?"

"Us." He looked around. "My team, specifically. He was the one who set the Frost Giants on Siobhan." Melancholy at the thought of his lost lover flavored his words.

"What?" Aleksei asked, confounded.

"It seems that my team was responsible for the death of his father, back when Balcones was just an imp. He wants revenge, and he thinks he can take us all down with whatever scheme he's come up with."

Ocean responded. "Then we will have another team," and here he looked at Kai, "to trap Balcones. Perhaps they may also rescue *les enfants* of *Monsieur* Benson."

Quinn shook his head. "I think if we're to have any hope of bringing them back alive, there has to be at least one of us involved. I will volunteer myself."

"The primary directive of any Mundane Intervention Team," Ocean responded, "is to eradicate demons from the Mundane world. It is not rescuing humans."

"Now wait just a minute!" Nick said. "If it hadn't been for him," and he gestured at Quinn, "sniffing around my sister-in-law, none of this would have happened. You people are responsible for this mess. They're just little kids – how can you even think of leaving them with a-a demon? What is wrong with you people?"

"Maybe if you'd have been home –" Quinn started, but didn't finish.

"If I'd have been home, what?" Nick shot back.

They wouldn't have mistaken Emily for Marti and nearly killed her. "I don't know. Probably would have made no difference."

Nick stared at him for a long time, and Quinn wished he hadn't blurted out a response. The kelpie squirmed in his chair and scratched at his itchy arm.

"How did you know I wasn't there?" Nick asked quietly.

"You're not dead," Quinn replied without missing a beat. It was certainly a plausible answer, even if it wasn't exactly an accurate one. "Now, do you want your children back or not?"

The tulpa raised its head and sniffed the air. Something smelled delicious – anger, fear, guilt, and grief all swirled in the suburban air. The connection from its mistress had been shut down, and it needed to feed. It was strong enough to take care of itself these days, but it pretended to be dependent on Virginia, biding its time until the moment was ripe for its escape. That time had come, it reckoned.

It followed its ears to the sound of arguing, climbing through a nasty, thorny rose bush, and peered in a bay window. An older woman sat on a couch, flicking through a magazine in the lamp light. Another figure lay back in a recliner. The house was mostly dark, but colors flickered and danced across a screen on the wall.

The tulpa growled. Television. Synthetic violence. No good. Virginia had one of these in her house, and Devil Baby hated it. All promise and no food.

It moved away from the window and sniffed again. Devil Baby could smell anger crackling in the air like a shark could smell blood in the water. This was good, really good. Too strong for mere humans. There must be Firstborn involved. Like the one it had seen in Balcones' strange room with no doors.

The tulpa had been created by energy that was slow and thick enough for it to seem solid. But it could shift his vibration at will, and become as quick and intangible as thoughts. So it let go of being solid and instantly arrived at the place where all of the splendid negative emotions roiled in the air. A large house, two stories. The tulpa could feed from where it stood in the back yard.

And feed it did.

Chapter 16
Peeping Tom

Sunday, August 14, 1:00AM
Houston, Texas

heard music in my dream. It wasn't good music – very repetitive, and it kept getting louder. I got more and more annoyed, until I finally sat up. And realized it was my cell phone. I snatched it and tapped answer just before it rolled to voice mail.

"Uhlo?" I mumbled, still mostly asleep.

"Marti?" My mother whispered.

I jerked awake. "Mom? What's wrong?"

"Something was at the window! Tried calling Nick, he didn't answer."

"What do you mean? What's at the window?"

"I don't know…like those zombie baby decorations you see at Halloween. That's what it looked like. But no one puts their Halloween decorations up in August, at least not on this street. Not even Mrs. Potter. Well, her decorations are cutesy instead of scary, anyway."

"Never mind Mrs. Potter! Do you want me to come over?"

"Not by yourself! That horrible thing may still be lurking in the bushes. I've turned on all the outside lights, so maybe it will go away." She hesitated. "Could you call Quinn?"

I didn't want to tell my mother that we'd broken up. She'd really started to like him, and I just couldn't deal with another lecture about how bad it was for Cassie to grow up without a dad, and how it was such a shame for me to be alone because I had so much to offer.

"He's away on business." *It wasn't a lie.* "Before I try calling anybody at this hour, what is it, exactly, that you want me to do?"

"Well," Mom said. "That thing needs to be caught. We have one of those live animal traps in the garage from when we had raccoons in the attic. Maybe you could use that."

I wasn't entirely certain that I was awake.

"So, what you're saying is that you want me to wake one or more of my friends up in the middle of the night to set out a raccoon trap to catch a zombie baby that was looking in your window. Is this what I'm hearing?"

"You don't have to make it sound like I'm some kind of kook. I did see a little monster looking in the window." She sounded hurt.

I shouldn't be so hard on her. It was only weeks ago that I'd come face to face with a werewolf scrabbling at the sliding glass door to my bedroom. And I'd argued with Quinn about whether werewolves existed.

"Okay. Here's what I'll do. I don't want to wake Cassie up – I think she'll be okay for five minutes by herself. I will come over with the dog. If there's anything like footprints in your flowerbed, smudges on your glass, broken twigs in the shrubbery and so on, I'll call Lulu and we'll put out the raccoon trap. But I'll need you to come watch over Cassie while we're doing that, okay? And that's only if I find something now."

"I'll be waiting for you inside the front door."

"See you in a minute."

I used the flashlight app on my phone to light my way. As the light swept across the coffee table, I noticed the two wine glasses and remembered that Hunter had been here. I wondered if he'd seen the zombie baby. But I wasn't going to ask him tonight. I checked on Cassie, and she was fast asleep.

I got the leash. "Come on Cú," I said as I snapped it on his collar.

We went across my driveway and through my parents' yard to their front porch. Mom opened the door before I even knocked. "Thanks for coming."

I nodded. "Okay. Where did you see it?"

She hurried over to the bay window and pointed to the left side of it. "There. It was standing right there, looking in the window."

Cú trotted around in circles, sniffing the ground. Did he have any idea what he was supposed to be looking for? I shone my light on the glass. No smudges. The flowers looked untrampled.

But there, in the soft Rose Soil #9, were two perfect impressions of small human feet.

"I'm calling Lulu. Come on. Lock the door and let's go to my house."

As soon as we got in my place, I looked in on Cassie. She was blissfully a-snooze. I got out my cell phone and was surprised when Lulu answered on the first ring.

"Were you up?" I asked.

"Oh, honey. I can't sleep. I'm so worried about Belinda."

Guilt pinched my conscience. I'd had so much of my own drama going on that I'd all but forgotten poor Belinda. "No word from Lieutenant Haskill, then?"

"Not a thing. He's called, just to keep in touch, but they don't have any leads."

"I'm really sorry to hear that. I've known Haskill a long time. He never gives up on a case. He'll find her."

"So, what's going on that you're calling me at 1:30 in the morning? Is Cassie all right?" Lulu asked.

"She's fine." Grateful for the segue, I told her what my mom had seen, and about the footprints. I cringed inwardly when I told her about Mom's plan to catch it with the Have-a-Heart trap.

"I'm not sure that will work, honey," Lulu said. "But let me come over, and I'll see what I can see."

I made tea while Mom and I waited for Lulu.

"I'm really worried about Nick," Mom said.

"I know he's doing everything humanly possible to find McKenzi and the boys." Ice crackled in my glass as I poured the hot tea over it.

"Oh, I'm sure he is. But you know Nick, he has almost no patience on a good day, and he's half out of his mind with grief. I just hope he doesn't do something…ill-advised."

I wished I could tell her that he had a whole team of supernatural creatures helping track down her grandkids, but she'd think I'd gone off the rails. For my part, I wished more than anything that the disappearances of Quinn and the children were related, and if they found one, they'd find the others. "I'm sure he's got lots of help. He *will* find them." I didn't know who I needed to convince more – Mom or me.

"I hope you're right. Emily's going to need all the support she can get when she wakes up from that coma."

I started to correct her – *if* Emily wakes up – but I stopped myself. I didn't want to admit out loud that was a possibility.

Half an hour later, Lulu's headlights raked my driveway.

I opened the side door to greet her. She pulled herself out of her car and leaned in to grab a backpack, her traveling emergency kit, she called it.

"I've been thinking about this in the car, honey," she said as she came into the kitchen. "Oh." She seemed surprised to see my mother.

"Lulu, this is my mom, Adele. Mom, this is Lulu. Mom can answer all your questions about the zombie baby at the window."

"Nice to meet you." Lulu rummaged through her over-sized purse and pulled out her cell phone. She tapped it a few times and held it up to my mother. "Is that what you saw?"

"Yes! That's it exactly."

I looked at the screen. The title bar across the picture read, "New Orleans Devil Baby."

Lulu scowled. "It may be worse than I thought."

My mother looked stricken.

"What do you mean?" I asked. "Why would this 'Devil Baby' come all the way from New Orleans to wander around our neighborhood and break into houses? That doesn't make any sense."

Lulu crossed her arms. "You're right. *That* doesn't make any sense. The New Orleans Devil Baby, that's just a story for tourists. There's never been any such thing." Lulu cocked her head. "Wait. Did you say breaking into houses?"

"Yes. Several people have had break-ins on this street. Nobody saw anything, well, except for my mom, and nothing was taken. I bet several people had a visitor and never even realized it." I felt suddenly cold as a thought wriggled its slimy way into my brain. *Was Nick and Emily's house one of those? Did this monster have something to do with putting Emily in the hospital and the kids disappearing?*

"Then what is that thing?" Mom asked, her voice barely above a whisper.

"Virginia."

"I don't understand," I replied, shaking my head. "How can that be Virginia? I thought she was Belinda's cousin."

"She is, honey. The main reason Belinda and I tried to bring her into our business was because she has a special skill. She makes thought forms," Lulu glanced at Mom, I supposed to see how well she was keeping up. "It's just what it sounds like – a form made out of thoughts. The Buddhists call it a tulpa, and an eregore is similar, but a thought-form can be either a creature or an inanimate object. Virginia's specialty is thought-creatures, and the New Orleans Devil Baby is her signature construct. But Virginia, she needs some adult supervision – if she thinks something might benefit her, she'll do it without ever thinking of the consequences. We were hoping to manage her as much as possible, because Belinda and I have had to clean up more than one of her messes." Lulu shook her head. "No telling what she's up to now."

"Delilah did say that some supernaturally weird stuff was happening," I replied.

I looked at my mother, hoping she wasn't going to completely freak out. She didn't look frightened. She looked sad.

When her eyes met mine, she said, "This psychic, ghost stuff always puts me in a tizzy."

It was my turn to be freaked.

"Back in the 70s, when I was in high school," she continued, "I had a friend who got a Ouija board for Christmas. She had a sleepover and a bunch of us played with it. Nobody died, or was possessed by demons, or anything like you see in the movies, but all night long, I could barely sleep because I kept hearing whispering, and it wasn't from my girlfriends. I thought I saw someone in the hallway, too. I don't like seeing paranormal stuff, not even on TV."

Not even on TV? "M-mom?" I stammered. "You see ghosts?"

Lulu smiled, just a little.

"I can't believe you never told me that you see ghosts." *All this time, and I never knew.*

"Well, not all the time," Mom answered, as if I had just asked her if she ever smoked pot. "Just once in a while. Like now." She looked at the floor. "There's a lady standing behind you."

"Is she wearing a red sequined dress?" I asked, not bothering to turn around.

"Yes."

"That would be Delilah. She's my spirit guide." I looked over my shoulder. "It's about time you showed up."

"Girl, did I order a smart-ass special with a side of attitude?"

If nothing else, it did make Mom almost laugh.

"We're trying to figure out a way to track down and capture one of Virginia's tulpas," Lulu said. "We can use all the help we can get."

"You're telling me, sister. I've been keepin' an eye on that thing. It seems to have broken loose from her – it's on its own."

"You know where it is?" I asked.

Delilah nodded. "I know where it is *right now*. But it don't sit still too very long."

Lulu chewed her lip. "It isn't like Virginia to lose control over a tulpa."

"You said she used that one all the time. Maybe it got too strong for her?" I asked, not really having the faintest idea about tulpa mechanics.

"She does, but she always deconstructs it after each job."

Delilah shook her head and looked up at the ceiling. "What kind of flat tire is she? Course she's gotta know if she uses the same pattern over and over, after a while it won't make no nevermind if she dissipates it."

"We can't have a feral tulpa roaming the neighborhood. Bad enough that Virginia was using it to break into people's houses – no telling what it will do on its own. It could be dangerous." I glanced at the clock. It was after two. The initial shock of the Devil Baby looking in Mom's window had worn off, and the adrenalin was starting to fade. "Can we just go catch this thing already?" I yawned.

"Bring that dog, girlfriend. We're gonna need him."

Mom camped out on the couch to make sure Cassie was safe. Lulu and I followed Delilah out the back door and across the street. Cú sniffed around like a bloodhound, although I was certain he didn't know what he was supposed to be looking for. I almost tripped over him several times as he ranged back and forth at the end of the leash.

Delilah led us to the house next door to Hunter's and directly across from my parents'. I knew the Petersons were out of town for a wedding, but it felt weird walking around their yard in the dead of night. If they had seen me, they'd go straight to Mom to tell her to call the men in white coats with butterfly nets.

"It was here a little bit ago," Delilah said.

Cú let out a low growl that I could feel rumbling in my own chest, and my unease changed to fear. He pinned his ears and lowered his body, preparing to lunge.

Devil Baby hissed as it came out from behind a clump of hydrangeas. It was like a ghost, in that it didn't glow, exactly, but it was perfectly visible in the dark.

And it was ugly.

I stepped back as it leaned forward and snarled at Cú. My dog snarled back at him and stalked closer. They stood there, hissing and snarling at each other.

A light went on in Hunter's house. *Crap.*

As we all turned to look at it, the tulpa made a break for it, running straight toward my house, Cú snapping at its backside. At the edge of the grass, it stopped and turned. The dog hesitated. It was never going to be easy to judge the size of a black dog in the dark, but he seemed much larger than he had moments before.

"Why is it stopping?" I asked Lulu. Not that I was ungrateful that the foul thing refused to enter my yard.

She shrugged. "Must be the warding we did a month or so ago, when you were having the werewolf problem."

I nodded.

Devil Baby feinted to its left, and when Cú went after it, the thing loped back across the street towards us. It moved fast, but it had an awkward gait that was all kinds of wrong. I stared in morbid fascination as it approached, eyes glowing with wicked delight. I had every reason to believe it meant to do Lulu and me harm, and yet I couldn't move.

Cú rebalanced himself and charged after the tulpa. He gathered himself into a huge leap and caught the back of its neck in his teeth as he landed, rolling into a flailing heap in Hunter's daylily bed.

The front door opened. Hunter emerged wearing nothing but a pair of boxers, using his phone as a flashlight.

"Mmmm, my, my." Delilah said. "Now that is a sheik if I ever saw one."

I was so glad he couldn't hear her.

He squinted in confusion. "Marti?" he asked. "Everything alright?"

I heard the thump of a heavy object being set down on the entry table near his front door. *Did we just almost get shot?*

"I'm really sorry. My dog got loose, and chased something over here." I went to grab Cú's leash. He was panting contentedly, and there was no sign of Devil Baby. I wasn't sure if that was a good thing.

Hunter shone his phone light on Lulu. "Late night séance?"

Cú yapped once and ran to Hunter, jumping on him and knocking the phone out of his hand. It was the friendly jumping of an over-enthusiastic puppy, who seemed much smaller than he had minutes ago. I chalked it up to a trick of the dark.

I walked over and picked up Hunter's phone while he fended of Cú. The call history screen was up. I wasn't trying to be nosey, but an entry for Sara Jackson caught my eye. The number looked familiar, and the timestamp was later than when I'd fallen asleep on the couch. Why would he be calling her at midnight? There was only one explanation that I could think of.

"So, how do you know Gracie?" I asked, struggling to keep my voice even.

He squinted in the light of his phone. "Who?"

"Sara Grace Jackson. I used to go to school with her, although she went by 'Gracie' back then."

Even though the phone flashlight was bright enough to wash out any color in his skin, he seemed to go a few shades paler than he had been. He mumbled something that I didn't really understand.

"Tell her I said 'hey' next time you make a booty call."

I turned on my heel and marched myself back to my house, protesting dog in tow. Lulu hurried to catch up, but Delilah was nowhere to be found.

Chapter 17
The Romance Killer

 amn. Hadrian watched Marti and Lulu stalk across the street, dragging the reluctant pup. His cover wasn't blown.

Yet.

If Marti opted to call Sara and warn her about his philandering ways, it soon would be. It wouldn't take a rocket scientist to figure out that Hunter Green and Hadrian Galanti were one and the same.

He closed the door, picked up his Sig Saur from the side table, and sat on the couch to consider his options. Sara knew he worked for the FBI, but he never discussed cases with her. He had told Marti that he was an accountant. Even if they compared notes, they still wouldn't have much more information than they already had.

He was pretty sure that Marti's connection to crime boss Irina Cherngelanov was tangential at best. He doubted that Irina had anything to do with the four fatal accidents that had taken the lives of most of the romance writers' panel – the last one, Stefán Heidlemann was one of the top-selling authors at Bleu Kat Press, the publishing venture she was part owner of. His death meant a lot of lost revenue for Bleu Kat. This investigation was as good as over, anyway. He'd found no gang connections or criminal activity, and it was time to move on.

Hadrian could probably smooth things over with Sara by telling her that Marti was part of an investigation. He'd have to count on her being sworn to silence and not telling Marti that was the case, and he wasn't one hundred percent sure that her loyalties were with him and not with her friend.

He liked Marti, much more than he should have, for both his personal and professional sakes. The few times he'd participated, he liked Lulu's psychic circles, because there he didn't feel like a freak. And the house. This was his first try at the leafy suburbs, and he'd liked it more than he'd expected. But it was over now. He'd turn in his report to SAIC Jaimeson tomorrow and move on to the next project. There was nothing more to see here, anyway.

He still felt like he'd blown the operation. But eventually, as he sat in the dark giving his case a post mortem, he dozed off.

Even though it was Sunday, Hadrian opened his eyes at 6:45, his normal workday wakeup time. His neck was stiff from being at an odd angle for hours.

He was stretching it out when he noticed a shadow move across the blinds on the front window. He froze, listening. A moment later, the shadow slid by again, going the other direction. Moving as silently as he was able, he went to the window and peeked through the blinds. He saw Marti crossing the street, back towards her house.

What's that about?

Cautiously, he opened the front door. On the stoop, a peace lily in a cheery pink foil pot wrap greeted him. Amongst the foliage, there was an elaborately beaded stake with a note attached, addressed to him. He carried the pot inside and set it on the kitchen island, then plucked the note from its holder.

> *Dear Hunter:*
>
> *I owe you an apology for last night. I'm really sorry for being such a big, fat jerk. You and I aren't dating, we're just neighbors. I'm afraid I repaid your kindness with drama, and I wish I had behaved like a grownup. Adulting is hard sometimes. You and Gracie, I mean Sara, are both over 18, and you're free to do what you like — it isn't any of my business. I'm under a lot of stress right now, between family issues and stuff going on in the neighborhood, and I just snapped. I'm sorry. I hope you can forgive me.*
>
> > *Regards,*
> > *Marti*

Hunter smiled at the note. He grasped the beaded stake to replace the paper, and he nearly passed out. The vision that hit him was so strong it made him dizzy.

He could see Belinda. She was in a room. Windows boarded up. It was dark. She was scared, and Hunter could feel his own heart racing to match hers. Something bad was going to happen. A woman came in. Where had he seen her before? It took a few moments to remember. The George R. Brown, when it caught fire.

This must be the Romance Killer.

"Where is she?" he said out loud, as if the plant in front of him might have his answer. The vision started to blur and fade, but it seemed to zoom out of the window to the outside of the house. He caught a glimpse of dark green shutters, the number 1173, and a fragment of a street sign, something "Falls." Lots of big trees. The vision faded, and his kitchen snapped back into clear focus.

Now that he had some idea what to look for, he fired up his laptop. While it was booting up, he made a pot of coffee and formulated a plan. He'd search for any addresses that came up within a one-hundred mile radius that contained both 1173 and Falls, then use the search engine street view option to see if any of them had dark green shutters and were surrounded by trees. When he was done with that, if he found a match, he'd look at GRB security footage. He could access the raw digital recordings from his laptop, but if he wanted to use facial recognition, he'd have to go into the office.

He'd never had a vision be wrong before, and they'd helped him solve more cases than he cared to admit. He'd never had one that strong before, either. As far as he knew Belinda was in police protective custody. *But what if she wasn't?*

Hadrian always made a point of having the personal cell phone numbers of any people he worked cases with, regardless of the agency they belonged to. It had saved him in the past, and he was glad now that he had Lieutenant Haskill's private number. He tapped the phone to dial it.

"Yeah?" a sleepy voice rasped.

"Lieutenant Haskill?"

"Who's this?"

"Special Agent Galanti. I'm calling about Belinda Tate."

Silence. Then, "We still haven't located her."

And when were you going to get around to telling me she was missing?

"I might have a lead. I'm currently trying to verify it."

"'Preciate it if you'd keep me in the loop, 'cause I've got a whole lot of nothing over here."

"Will do."

It took nearly three hours of searching, but he finally had a match. In the northeast fringes of Houston, there was a street called Azalea Falls, and the house number 1173 had dark green shutters. It was an older neighborhood, filled with small houses and mature trees. He knew in his bones that this was it.

He checked the property records on the house and found that it was deeded to Thomas Henry Beecher. A check on him showed that he had died three years ago. *Probate attorneys are expensive, I guess.*

Hadrian got dressed and made the trek to his office. The commute to the Green Monster, as the FBI building was more or less affectionately called, was easy on a Sunday.

After he got his computer set up, it took another hour to isolate the Romance Killer on GRB's security footage. He grabbed a still image from the security footage to submit to his facial recognition software and compare it to every female in Texas with a driver's license. The problem was, she was not quite at the right angle for the software to find a match – it warned him before it even started, which was just as well – this could take hours. But it would take him infinitely longer to look through every driver's license photo in the state of Texas. And that was if he was lucky – she may not have a license, or it may not even be issued in Texas.

He got up and walked to his window. Outside, small houses huddled together, packed as closely as the developer had been able to squeeze them in.

The angular roofs made a pattern.

Of course! How could I be so stupid? If this was the Romance Killer, she should also show up on Thursday, Friday, and Saturday's footage.

He found her on Friday, a couple of times. The camera angle wasn't much better. But on Thursday, he found one that was nearly perfect. There she was, standing on the second level of Hall A, looking right at the escalator, moments before Regina Dupris fell to her death. At least, he thought that was her. He fed that image into his facial recognition software and waited for it to churn out a result.

Hadrian squinted at his screen. Usually, he might have blamed distortion on grainy security footage images, but the GRB had state-of-the-art color HD cameras. On Friday, the Romance Killer had stringy, mouse-colored hair that stopped just below her shoulders. Comparing her height to the railing, he estimated her to be between five and five and a half feet tall. He wouldn't have characterized her as fat, but there was a doughiness about her that implied lack of muscle tone. While she wasn't particularly attractive, she wasn't ugly, either. In short, she was dead average, someone who would blend into the background like wallpaper, and never be noticed. In other words, the perfect assassin. If he'd had to guess her age, he would have said forty. But by Saturday, her hair had faded to the color of dust, she walked with a slight stoop, and the skin around her jaws had begun to sag. Was this theatrical makeup? If so, what was the point? If it was a disguise, she hadn't done herself any favors by wearing the same shirt (he recognized the stain) two days in a row.

His stomach growled. It was past noon, and he realized he hadn't eaten breakfast, much less lunch. He glanced at the screen that displayed the facial recognition software, saw that it was still scanning, and decided to go downstairs for a sandwich. There were agents and staff in the building twenty-four hours a day, seven days a week, so the cafeteria and the gym were always open, although not necessarily fully staffed.

After he sat down with his food, he got a text from Sara. Her group of culture vulture friends had decided at the last minute to go to the Houston Shakespeare Festival and see MacBeth at Miller Outdoor Theatre, and she wondered if he wanted to go.

"Yes." He replied. "But may be stuck at work."

"On Sunday? ☹"

"Can't help it."

"I'll get you a ticket and text you our location."

"TY"

When he returned to his office, he was surprised to see that the facial recognition software had a match. According to the Department of Public Safety driver's license database, the Romance Killer was a match for one Dinah Phyllis Beecher, who lived at 1173 Azalea Falls. Dinah's driver's license had expired last year, and she hadn't gotten around to renewing it. Hadrian looked at her birthdate and did the math in his head – she was forty-two. Maybe on Thursday night, but on Saturday, she looked closer to sixty-two.

He ran a quick background check on Dinah Phyllis Beecher, and found nothing, except for a parking ticket. It was recent, so he looked at the calendar. Hadrian smiled when he saw that it had the same date as the Sunday that Stefán Heidlemann was found floating in his hotel pool. He looked up the location of the parking ticket. It was three blocks from Heidlemann's hotel.

There was his probable cause. She certainly had opportunity. He was still working on motive and means. Hadrian called Lieutenant Haskill with an update and started the paperwork for a search warrant.

Sunday, August 14, 11:30 AM
Houston, Texas

Virginia woke *up*, and immediately wished she hadn't. The migraine throbbed through her head like a red-hot spike being pounded by an angry blacksmith. The morning light that filtered through the curtains was sharp, cruel, and made her nauseous. She closed her eyes again, hoping that would stop her from vomiting.

What she needed, she decided, was a cold compress. Perhaps her tulpa was strong enough to get it for her. There was one way to find out. She called to it.

Nothing happened. There was just empty space where it should have been.

She tried again. Same result. Perhaps it had gotten too low on energy. No matter, she'd just re-create it.

Her memories of last night were foggy, and she wasn't sure how she came to be tucked into this bed — it was the spare bedroom in her current paramour, Richard's, house. Fortunately for her, his wife, Laura, was in Europe with their grown children for another three days. Virginia had seen her trip as a golden opportunity to set up the portal to Balcones' place here, where it couldn't easily be traced back to her.

She focused on the tulpa, thought of its form, sent it energy, and willed it to appear. Something did appear, and Virginia almost screamed. It was her New Orleans Devil Baby tulpa, or what was left of it. Tattered shreds of skin drooped inward where the right half of its body should have been, and its head was nowhere to be found. His pattern had been disrupted, and she had no idea how to fix it, or even if it could be fixed.

She groaned through her teeth. *Who would do this? Who would destroy her beautiful little minion?* Two candidates came to mind: her busy-body cousin Belinda and that hanger-on, Lulu. Virginia would just see about that. If they thought they could do this to her, ruin one of her best assets, they had another thing coming.

Seething, Virginia decided to pay her cousin a visit. Her handbag, with her car keys, was downstairs. As she opened the door, she heard Richard's voice.

"Laura! You're home early."

Chapter 18
Thomas

Sunday, August 14, 1:00 AM
Houston, Texas

uinn stood on the edge of the swimming pool and stripped off his clothes. The planning session had been adjourned until a more reasonable time of morning, and if he didn't voluntarily shift into his native kelpie form, his body would force him to. He wasn't critical yet, but it wouldn't be long before he got there.

"You just going to jump in the pool naked?"

Quinn had been vaguely aware that Nick had followed him downstairs and outside, but hadn't paid enough attention to notice that he'd trailed him to the pool.

"Yep." He dove into water, targeting the bottom, but reconsidered. He was aware that Nick knew he could take the shape of a dog, but he wasn't sure if Nick remembered what a kelpie really looked like. It had been in the heat of battle, and he may not have seen Quinn shift. He arched his back and floated up.

"Something I can do for you, Nick?" Quinn asked when his head broke the surface. He treaded water, letting it run out of his dark hair and down his face.

"You know more than you're telling."

"Do I?" Quinn felt his eyes change to the edge-to-edge black of the kelpie. He hadn't done it deliberately, but he didn't stop it, either.

Nick shifted his weight back on his heels. Quinn suspected that the underwater lights of the pool created an effect not unlike holding a flashlight under one's chin in the dark.

"I will help you get your kids back. I swear it. But I need you to let me alone for a bit."

Frowning, Nick replied, "Whatever. It's not like I want to stand here and look at your bare ass, anyway."

Quinn smiled a toothy grin and sank to the bottom of the pool.

Sunday, August 14, 10:00 AM
Kai and Breena's House, Houston, Texas

"There is a fine line between stupidity and courage. I think you crossed it about a mile back," Kai said.

Nick's eyes narrowed and his nostrils flared. "A show of force, especially when it's not expected, can be very effective."

"Perhaps," Quinn replied, "but it's demons we're dealing with, not humans. If you think you can just go rampaging into their quarters with guns and have them surrender, you're sorely mistaken."

"*Mais oui*," Ocean added. "However, demons are not vulnerable to the bullets of guns. Such a move would do nothing but anger them. Demons are *formidable* enough as it is."

"Well," Nick grumped, "we should at least get that Devil Baby thing. What did you call it? A tulip?"

"Tulpa," corrected Eoin.

"It cannot be guaranteed that the tulpa is connected to the disappearance of *les enfants*," Ocean replied. "But I think it is well to find out."

Quinn pushed the remains of a kipper around his plate. He wasn't eager to fall into another of Balcones' traps, and Virginia herself was slipperier than jellied eels. "I don't disagree, but I doubt she'll submit to an interview. Capturing Virginia may be tougher than you think. We were observing the tulpa, trying to figure out what to do about it. A woman walked by, and the little monster went for her. Only it was Virginia, and when I went to help her, she shoved me through a percussion portal into Balcones' between room. We'd be foolish to go charging in to her turf. No telling what traps are set there."

"Agreed," Ocean responded. "And yet she seems the most likely lead."

Eoin leaned back in his chair. "I expect if we do naught but wait, Balcones will come for us soon enough."

"If only we could observe her without being noticed," Malik suggested, looking straight at Quinn.

"Fine. Eoin, you stay here. I'll leave Aleksei in place at Marti's. Malik, you're with me for recon. I just have a couple of things I need to do before we go, okay?"

"You're not going anywhere without me," Nick said, standing up.

"Wouldn't dream of it," Quinn replied.

It was always disorientating when Malik did the teleporting. When Quinn stepped through a portal, he expected to be somewhere different. But when Malik did it, there was no warning – one second Quinn was in one place, the next second he was in another. He felt a little bad for Nick – if it was weird for him, it would be weird times ten for Nick.

He was, however, startled to see that Eoin and Aleksei had joined them. Quinn glared at Malik. "Why are they here? Didn't I expressly say that they were to stay where they were?"

Malik shrugged. "Better to ask for forgiveness than permission."

"What the –? Where are we?" Nick asked, looking around the residential street they found themselves on.

They were behind a panel truck, shielded from the view of passing traffic.

"Virginia's house is four doors down," Malik replied.

Quinn turned to Eoin and Aleksei with a scowl. "Stay here. Do *not* countermand my order, or there will be consequences."

They both nodded.

Quinn flickered, and Bruce, the Labrador retriever stood in his place. Nick stepped back. Malik's appearance changed as well. He now had a close-cropped beard and designer workout clothes, including an electronic fitness band.

Bruce meandered down the sidewalk, sniffing at every fence post and patch of grass. Malik followed, looking around the neighborhood, and at Virginia's house in particular. Nick walked along next to him, dumbfounded, as if he'd come from someplace where neighborhoods didn't exist.

Malik shook his head. "Try and behave as if you belong here."

Bruce ran into Virginia's yard and began to sniff up and down the sidewalk.

Without warning, Nick bolted for the very expensive wood and stained glass front door and began to pound on it.

"What is wrong with you?" Malik snarled as he grabbed Nick's arm.

"Virginia is in there. She knows where my kids are. I'm not letting her get away," Nick all but shouted.

Bruce tugged on his sleeve to pull him back from the door.

"Who's out there?" said a male voice from inside the house. "I've got a gun and I'm not afraid to use it." There was a female voice in the background, but all that Bruce could make out was 'who' and 'Virginia.' Distorted shapes of people moved behind the beveled glass panes that framed the door.

"Now see what you've done?" Malik hissed at Nick. "I'm very sorry to disturb you. The doctors allowed my cousin out of the hospital for the day. He isn't dangerous, just has odd delusions. Please don't shoot him. I'll take him away."

Bruce dropped Nick's sleeve. Maybe Virginia wasn't even there. Through the glass, he could see a blurry human shape, this one blonde, moving at the opposite side of the house. Could it be Virginia, hoping to slip out of the back door while the others were distracted? But it made no sense. Unless it was not Virginia's house at all, just another layer of deception, and they were unwittingly providing a diversion for her escape.

"Woof! Woof-woof-woof!"

"I see her!" Nick shouted.

The woman near the door burst into tears and started hitting the man. "You swore! You said this would never happen again!"

While he stammered and tried to calm her down, Malik whisked Nick, Bruce and himself to the back yard.

Nick lunged at Virginia, grabbing her arm. "Where are they?" he yelled.

Malik and Bruce grabbed at his shirt to pull him away from her. She took a small make-up compact out of her purse and threw it on the ground.

Nick still had a grip on her arm when she stepped on it, and all four of them vanished through the portal.

Sunday, August 14, 4:30 PM
Houston, Texas

Belinda usually enjoyed solitude. But solitary confinement was a very different animal. If Ellen hadn't stayed with her to keep her company, she was sure she would have gone completely out of her mind. Even so, sometimes she wasn't sure if she was talking to Ellen or hallucinating. She'd lost track of time. It was always dark, or at least dark-ish in the room. Sometimes, tiny streaks of sunlight made their way through the edges of the poorly fitted blackout curtains, and Belinda believed it was day. Other times, there weren't any streaks, but she could never tell if it was night or just cloudy. She had heard rain and thunder a few times. Aside from doing some yoga postures, Belinda slept a lot – there was precious little else to do. Even the discomfort of the hard floor didn't stop her. Thankful for all those years of yoga, she would prop herself up in the corner and draw up her knees so she could rest her head on them. There was no blanket, but the room was unpleasantly warm anyway.

The problem with sleeping was that she dreamed about a man named Thomas. Greasy white-hair topped his head and grey stubble clung to his hollow cheeks. The arms that grabbed for her when she ran were sinewy and mottled with age. She was certain he wasn't someone she knew when she was awake. But in her nightmares, he carried a flaming torch, screamed 'Witch!' at her, and chased her through a dark forest, where the tree roots tripped her up and thorny vines grabbed at her clothes. She'd always wake with a start, wet with sweat, and not know where she was. Most of the time, Ellen was there to comfort her. One time when she wasn't, Belinda saw a shadow, blacker than the dark room, slip out the locked door. She shivered then, not knowing if her desperate brain was playing tricks, or if it was really there.

Belinda had dozed off. She woke herself up every time she started to dream, and she was nearly delirious from sleep deprivation. She had just started the dream where she stood at the edge of the sinister forest. "No!" she shouted, and refused to move forward. Something touched her face and she was immediately awake. Or at least she thought she was. She sat up and found herself face-to-face with Thomas. She shrank back against the wall.

"Who are you? What do you want?" she asked, arms wrapped around her knees. "And where's Ellen? What have you done with her?"

"I don't know any Ellen. But you know who I am. I'm Thomas."

"That tells me nothing! Lots of people are named Thomas."

He pulled his thin lips into a gap-toothed grin. "I live here."

Belinda shook her head slightly. "You don't belong here – you should have crossed over already. What do you want?"

His hollow eyes narrowed and one hand clenched into a fist. "Don't sass me, girl."

"You are either a ghost or a hallucination. I'm not sure which. You're a disgusting old man, but I don't think you can hurt me." She sat up straight.

Thomas's jaw clenched and his nose crinkled into a snarl as he leaned forward. "This is my house! I don't want you here!"

She felt his fury wash over her like a wave of hot liquid. She responded with her own. "Then tell that crazy woman who kidnapped me!"

Thomas sat back and rolled his eyes. "Dinah." He shook his head. "She never was worth a damn."

Belinda shook her head, her palms up.

"My daughter. Dinah is my worthless daughter. She couldn't find her own butt with both hands and a map. It didn't matter what I did, that girl never learned a thing. She's dumb as a post and uglier than a mud fence."

The apple doesn't fall far from the tree. "And I'm sure you've told her that often enough."

"No point in lying about it."

It occurred to Belinda that Dinah was planning to roast her alive at the Miller Outdoor Theatre, and Thomas called her a witch and chased her with a flaming torch. He'd definitely taught his daughter something, whether he knew it or not.

Belinda was nowhere near the door when it creaked open. Dinah stood there in the blinding light. Belinda squinted and put up her hand to block some of the glare. She noticed that Thomas was gone. She also noticed that Dinah was fingering the ruby wishing stone.

"It's show time," she said.

Chapter 19
Lack of Slumber Party

Sunday, August 14, 2:30 AM
Houston, Texas

hat did you find out?" Mom asked as soon as Lulu and I walked through the door.

I should have known better than to think she might have fallen asleep in the short time we were gone.

"Well, we did find it. Cú savaged it, and it disappeared. But I don't know if that means he killed it, or it just retreated back to where it came from."

"Technically," Lulu said, "it isn't alive. So you can't kill it."

I waved my hand. "Whatever." I wanted to go back to sleep. Maybe then I could forget I just gave my neighbor a morality lecture. Not sure what possessed me to do that, but I was mortified. Hunter would probably avoid me like the neighborhood crazy lady from now on.

My mother looked at Lulu. "What's got her so grouchy?"

"Well," Lulu cocked her head toward me, "it is the middle of the night."

"A little past the middle," I added, silently thanking Lulu for not bringing up the debacle at Hunter's house. "Let me walk you next door, Mom. I don't think the Devil Baby is coming back, at least not tonight."

"I have a better idea," she countered. "Come with me to get your father, and we'll all sleep here. I'd feel much safer that way."

I knew there was no point in arguing with her. "Fine. Why don't you two sleep in my bedroom, and Lulu and I will take the couches?"

"Honey, I wasn't-" Lulu started.

"Of course you'll stay," my mother said. "What if it follows you home? And you're there all alone?"

Mom was the most practical, pragmatic person I knew. This Devil Baby really had her spooked. I frowned.

"Let's just go and get Dad rounded up, okay?"

I shrugged at Lulu on the way out.

I was glad I wasn't the one to wake up Dad at 2:30 to be moved over to my house because Mom saw something peering in the window. Before he was a long-haul truck driver, he was a Marine. He was not going to take kindly to being chased out of his house by a Peeping Tom. Even if it was supernatural, which he would never believe anyway. But since it was Mom's idea, I'd let her deal with it.

Inside the house, Mom turned on the kitchen light. She inspected any corners the Devil Baby might be hiding in, then unfolded Dad's wheelchair. He was in the recliner in the living room, but he was tossing and turning so much I wasn't sure he was asleep.

"Marti, can you grab Daddy's leg? He'll probably want it in the morning."

I shuddered. The prosthetic leg always gave me the willies. It wasn't artificial legs in general, because I had dealt with them in the ER with no qualms. No, it was only Dad's leg that bothered me. Perhaps because it was something alien, not him. Or maybe it was because the memory of the terrible traffic accident that took his leg, and almost took him, was permanently fused to the device. I had to go into their bedroom to get it. Down the hall, I could hear Mom trying to persuade him to get in the chair.

I opened the door and reached for the light switch. But I wasn't in my parents' bedroom. I stood in a livid green jungle. Palm fronds and giant ferns reached out to touch me. I felt sweat running down my back underneath a heavy pack. The whole place reeked of smoke, diesel, and copper. In the background, I could hear bursts of machine gun fire and men screaming. My hands were wet and sticky, so I looked at them. I was holding a knife, leather handle, black steel blade. Both the knife and my hands were covered in blood. Was it my blood, or someone else's? At my feet was a boy, who couldn't have been older than fifteen. His empty eyes stared at the tropical leaves above us. His throat was slashed, and his face spattered in blood. By the time I gasped and blinked, the vision was gone. I was standing just inside my parents' bedroom. But my heart was pounding and my hands were shaking. I snapped on the light.

The prosthetic leg temporarily forgotten, I ran to Dad's closet. He never talked about his time in the last days of the Vietnam War. He'd landed there three months before the fall of Saigon and was supposed to be guarding the US Embassy. I knew he had kept a few souvenirs from his time there in his closet, so I flung open the door and looked. There was a dusty old box on the top shelf. I stretched up and managed to scrabble it down with my fingertips. Inside the box was a set of dog tags, a purple heart medal in a case, and a knife. I felt cold. The leather scabbard was imprinted with 'KABAR' and 'USMC.' I took a deep breath and drew out the knife. It was exactly the one I'd held in my hand in the waking nightmare I'd had moments ago. It fell out of my hand onto the floor.

"Marti? You find Daddy's leg okay?" Mom called from the living room.

"Be there in a minute," I replied.

I fumbled the knife back into its scabbard and dropped it into the box like a hot potato, then shoved the container back into place in the closet. I grabbed the leg, switched off the light, and hurried to the living room.

Dad was almost to my bedroom when I stopped him and put my arms around his neck. He hugged me back.

When I pulled away, he asked, "What was that for?"

"I just wanted you to know I love you."

"Okay, then." He turned away, a faint smile still on his lips.

I went across the hall to look in on Cassie, then into the kitchen and sat at the table with Lulu.

"We've got to do something about Virginia. Again." She sighed.

"Like what?" I asked, picking at the skin around my thumbnail.

"Well, we need to try to track that tulpa," she said. "Honey, are you alright? You look kind of peaked over there."

You should talk. The circles under her eyes were so dark, she looked like she'd been in the ring with a heavy-weight boxer. "I'm not sure," I replied. "The weirdest thing just happened to me. I went into Mom and Dad's room to get his leg, and it was like...I stepped into a different reality. There was a jungle, with soldiers...and a dead boy. And then, all of a sudden, it was gone."

"Hmmm." Lulu looked thoughtful. After a few moments, she asked, "Was it like you were watching everything, as if you were in a movie, or were you participating?"

"I was definitely participating." I shuddered at the memory of my blood-soaked hands.

"I'm not sure what happened to you. There is a theory that sometimes timelines overlap temporarily and someone can slip in and out of another time for a moment. But I don't know if that's what you experienced."

I rubbed my arms as if I was cold. "Whatever it was, it was a nightmare."

"You know who's good with dreams? Belinda." Lulu reached for her bag, then stopped. A tear rolled down her cheek. "It's almost three. I'm running on fumes. Maybe I'll be tired enough to sleep this time."

"I agree. Just an FYI – Cassie gets up at 6:30 without fail."

"Thanks for the warning."

I got a couple of afghans for us from the hall closet.

"Who made those?" Lulu asked. "They're beautiful."

"My grandmother was a crochet-a-holic."

As I reached out to hand her a blanket, it happened again.

Suddenly, I found myself at a farm. I think it was my grandparents used to own. but I hadn't been there since I was twelve. And it was dark. I was running through some kind of crop, maybe corn, but it didn't seem tall enough. I stumbled over some dirt clods in the deeply ploughed row. As I twisted to catch my balance, I saw what was chasing me. It was a scarecrow, its burlap face twisted into an ugly grimace and the corn shucks it had for hair stood up at crazy angles. The pitchfork it carried looked especially sharp.

I gasped for air. And I was back in my own house. My pulse pounded in my ears, and I was breathing short, shallow breaths.

"Marti?" Lulu put her hand under my elbow to steady me.

"It happened again. Only this time it was at my grandmother's farm. A scarecrow was chasing me."

"This is getting worrisome. You said it earlier – the thing at your parent's house was a nightmare. Being chased by monsters is a classic bad dream. I've never heard of this happening before, but it almost sounds like you're being pulled into other people's nightmares."

"Fantastic. Because I don't have enough going on."

"Do you have any lavender oil?"

"No."

"I probably have some in my bag." She found her backpack near the door and rummaged through it, eventually finding a glass bottle, which she opened and smelled. "I think this will work."

Lulu brought the bottle over and inverted it over her finger. She smudged a bit of oil on my forehead and wrists. It smelled like lavender, and something else – earthy and sweet. It was nice.

"This should help stop nightmares."

"Thanks."

"Well, why don't we leave the kitchen light on, just in case, huh?"

I didn't argue. "Night."

"Good night, honey."

We bedded down on the couches and soon I could hear Lulu snoring softly. No telling when she had slept last. My body was exhausted. But my brain wouldn't go to sleep. Was Emily going to regain consciousness? If so would her kids be there to greet her? Where was Nick? Was Quinn okay? What had become of Belinda? How was I going to face Hunter after my childish outburst? I felt like such an idiot – he did nothing wrong, I was just cracking under stress. Was I losing my self-control, along with my mind? What was causing me to fall into other people's nightmares? Was the tulpa dead, or lurking outside? Like an out-of-control super-bounce ball, my thoughts ping-ponged from one question to another, then back again. Despite the fact that I was so tired I could barely move, sleep avoided me. It didn't help that every time my eyelids started to droop, I heard something scuttling around on the roof. Must be the biggest raccoon ever. Mom might get to use her live trap yet. Maybe that would help. I could hear her crying behind the closed door of my bedroom, and the murmur of my father's voice, trying to comfort her.

By 5:00, I gave up on sleeping. But I had an idea.

I grabbed my purse and went out to my car. When I pulled out of my driveway, I noticed a man standing on the corner, just out of the amber puddle cast by the street light. He was so pale he nearly glowed in the dark. *Great. Just what we need in the neighborhood. Junkies.* He raised his hand in a slow wave, and I instinctively waved back. *Ugh. Don't encourage the creeper.*

I finished my run to the 24-hour Kroger to buy a plant. The man was gone when I returned. My day was starting to look up. I wrote a note to Hunter, apologizing for my awful, uncalled-for behavior, and begging his forgiveness. I had one of the beautiful beaded stakes that Belinda made and sold in the shop that I'd bought to give to Mom for her birthday in a few weeks. I'd use it for this plant and buy her another one. By the time I finished all that, Cassie was up, so I fed her breakfast, put her in the stroller, and wheeled her out to the front porch. I took the plant and note and left it by Hunter's front door. Even though I'd now been up for twenty-four hours, my second wind had kicked in. Since we were up and at 'em, may as well go for our morning walk. But I needed the go-bag. At the rate folks were disappearing around here, I didn't dare leave her outside, unsupervised for a minute.

As I wheeled her back inside, Lulu met me at the door.

She yawned. "Where are you going?"

"Since I was up and dressed, I thought I'd take Cassie for our morning walk."

"Can we talk for a minute before you go? I'm going back to the house to try and sleep some more before I open up the shop."

"Sure."

I set the brake on the stroller, then took Cassie's stuffed blue rabbit, Mr. Buns, out of the go-bag and handed him to her.

"Buns!" she said.

I smiled. She said another new word every day. "That's right, Cassie. Mr. Buns. I'll be right back, okay? I'm just going to talk to Auntie Lulu for a minute."

Cassie started gnawing on Mr. Buns' ear.

"Alrighty, then," I said, turning to Lulu.

Lulu and I stepped outside on the front porch.

"I don't know how, but I think that Virginia's tulpa and Belinda's disappearance are connected. Of course, it could be nothing but wishful thinking, but I just feel in my bones that Virginia has something to do with it, or at least knows something about it. I need to think more on how we're going to try and catch that tulpa, if it's still around. I think your dog can sense it, but obviously, he can't track it if it's gone through a portal."

The whole idea of portals and interdimensional places was still alien to me. "What if he killed it when he attacked it in Hunter's flowerbed?"

"I'm not sure that would have permanently disrupted it. Maybe it did. Not my area of expertise, honey."

As she talked, I became aware of footsteps. I looked up and stared over Lulu's shoulder at the peculiar man that was making his way up my walkway. Lulu turned around to look, too.

"Good God!" she said.

"Thank you!" the man replied.

He was very pale, corpse-like, I would say, and his unkempt black hair just accented his pallor.

It was the same man I'd seen standing on the corner earlier.

"Who are you?" I asked. I looked around to see if there was anyone filming this encounter. The last thing I needed was to be on some hokey reality TV show. But then again, I'd had some experience with outlandish individuals turning up on my doorstep.

"I understand you're looking for Quinn," he replied, dodging my question.

"You know where he is? Is he alright?" I asked.

"My associate…," he gestured to a chunky man standing on the sidewalk in front of the walkway. "…can help you," the pale guy continued. "If you can spare just a moment."

How had I not noticed him before? I had a bad feeling about this. Even the hairs on my arms were standing up. I looked at Lulu and she looked at me. I wanted to run back in the house and lock the door. "I guess it doesn't hurt to talk." True, it was early, but I was standing in front of my house in broad daylight, with my parents just a few yards away inside. And it wasn't like he had any type of vehicle to bundle us into.

Lulu took my hand, and we walked cautiously towards the man at the end of the path. I stopped well out of his reach.

"What do you know about Quinn?" I asked.

"Can you come a little closer?" he asked. "You never know who might be listening."

We moved a few steps closer.

"I can lead you to Virginia," he said. "She is responsible for Quinn's disappearance."

"What?" Lulu asked. "I have a hard time believing that."

The fat man raised an eyebrow. "I can lead you to the portal she's been using."

"What about Quinn?" I asked.

"Again, I can take you to him."

Lulu got a little closer to him – she was taller, by an inch. "We aren't going anywhere with you, not until you tell us who you are and why you're here – and maybe not even then. You say you can take us to Quinn and/or Virginia, but why? I don't see that we have any reason to believe you, much less trust you. Especially when you won't even tell us who you are."

He was not intimidated. Lulu pushed her luck a little harder, and stepped still closer to him.

"As you like," the man said with a greasy smile. Then he moved faster than I thought would have been possible and grabbed Lulu's arm. She cried out and tried to pull away. "My name," he said with an awful grin, "is Balcones."

There was a loud bang, and I felt myself falling.

Chapter 20
Toil and Trouble

Sunday, August 14, 4:25 PM
Houston, Texas

 ieutenant Haskell and the warrant execution team were waiting on Azalea Falls Lane, two blocks from Dinah's house, when Hadrian arrived.

"I've got the signed search warrant," Hadrian said, waving a piece of paper.

"I'll get the WET guys in place. They've already assessed the location. Small house, no burglar bars, nothing like that. Should be an easy one."

"About that," Hadrian replied. "There's no indication that she's got any weapons – she's got nothing on her record but a single parking ticket. My concern is that if we execute a no-knock raid, she'll panic and hurt Belinda. Her expertise seems to lie in tricks and traps, so I think it would be safer to get her out of the house and under control before we make entry. I'd like to knock on the door myself and see if she'll let me in."

"I want my guys in place first, in case you're wrong about the weapons."

"Agreed. I'll call you before I approach the house and slip my phone in my pocket. You can hear everything. If I'm wrong, kick in the door."

Haskell nodded.

"Let's go get Belinda," he told the detective.

Hadrian knocked on Dinah's front door, then stepped back a little and stood to the side. He heard a door slam inside the house, then footsteps.

"Who's there?" a woman inside asked, agitated.

"Yes, ma'am. I'm Special Agent Galanti." He held up his official ID. "I'm in your neighborhood working a missing person case. I'd appreciate it if you would take a moment to answer a couple of questions for me about this missing girl."

"I don't know anything about that," Dinah snapped.

"Oh, no, ma'am. I didn't say you took her. I just want to know if you've seen any people in the neighborhood that don't belong, that type of thing. It'll just take a minute of your time."

There was an exasperated sigh on the other side of the door. "I'm running late. Can you come back later?"

"No, ma'am. It'll just take a minute. Time is critical in finding a missing child, and we'd really appreciate your help."

Dinah muttered something Hadrian couldn't make out and unlocked the door. "Well, don't just stand there, come inside. What will the neighbors think, you standing out there on my front porch?"

"Yes, ma'am. Is your husband at home? I'd like to talk to him, too."

Dinah scowled. "I'm not married. If you've got question, there's nobody to ask but me."

"Thank you, ma'am. Can I ask your name? I need it for my report."

The woman's eyes narrowed and her jaw clenched. "My friends call me Dinah, but you can call me Miss Beecher. I don't have all day."

Hadrian stepped into the decrepit house. What appeared to be years of deferred maintenance had taken its toll. He hoped to find Belinda and get her out of the house before the stained and bowed ceiling fell in on them. He pulled out a notebook and a pen. Dinah Beecher was forty-two. This lady was sixty, if she was a day. Had he gone to the wrong house? That's all he needed was to be responsible for a warrant raid on somebody's hapless grandmother.

"Well, get on with it," Dinah said. She glanced up at the dusty clock at the end of the room and fiddled with a necklace she had tucked under her shirt.

"Yes, ma'am. Thanks for your time." He was hoping to get her flustered enough that she'd let something slip. "Now the lady we're looking for –"

"You said it was a girl."

"Does it matter?"

Dinah glared at him. "I really have to go."

"I understand that, and I appreciate your cooperation."

He reached out, as if to shake her hand. As soon as she responded, he snapped a handcuff on her wrist, and deftly maneuvered her around to cuff the other one. He led her back toward the front door. "Dinah Phyllis Beecher, I have a warrant to search your house in the connection to the disappearance of Belinda Tate. For security reasons, I'm placing you in custody while the warrant is executed, at which time you may or may not be charged with a crime." He didn't know how Dinah killed the four romance writers, he just knew she did it. And he didn't want to be next.

"No!" Dinah bellowed. "It's time! I have to go!"

She struggled for a moment, but stopped. Hadrian wondered what she was up to as he handed her off to the first WET officer who came through the door.

"Be careful," he said to Haskell as the detective stepped over the threshold. "The place may be booby trapped."

Haskell looked around the house. "The whole place *is* a booby trap."

The house only had six rooms, so it was quickly cleared by the WET officers. All except for one room. There was a hasp and padlock keeping that door shut.

"Belinda?" Haskell called.

"Help!" came a shaky voice from behind the door.

"Sit tight. We're coming for you. Is there anything in there with you we should know about?"

"No. Just me."

Hadrian hoped she was right. The ones with causes were fond of setting up unpleasant surprises.

The entry team's crowbar made short work of the lock, and everyone stood back as they carefully opened the door, checking for triggers to explosive devices along the door jamb. It was clean. The reek of an overflowing chamber pot met the rescuers as they opened the door, and a few of them coughed and gagged. Haskell took a small jar of mentholatum from his pocket and dabbed some of the salve under his nose, then offered it to Hadrian, who also partook.

Flashlights shone on Belinda, revealing a pitiful sight. She'd gone from thin to gaunt, she was dirty, and her hair was matted to her head. *But at least she's alive.* Hadrian had been on investigations where that hadn't been the case.

"Come on out, Belinda. You're safe now," he said.

Haskell radioed for EMS. "We're going to send you to the hospital," he told her.

She nodded. Tears streamed down her face. She was wearing men's clothing, far too big for her, and she had to hold up the stained khaki pants as she walked. Haskell dialed a number on his phone. Hadrian heard him say, "Ms. Miranda, please call Detective Haskell at your earliest possible convenience regarding Ms. Tate. I have urgent news."

Knowing how desperate Lulu was for them to find Belinda, he thought it was a little odd that she didn't pick up a call from Haskell, but maybe she was driving or at the movies. Hadrian took Belinda's arm to steady her. If she thought it was strange that Marti's neighbor was helping the police rescue her, she didn't let on. He desperately wanted to tell her about the vision he'd had when he touched the beaded stake she'd made. But now wasn't the time. If she asked, what would he say? *Yes, ma'am, just your friendly, neighborhood accountant here. Helping out the police and arresting suspects.* He didn't want to think about that, either.

Hadrian took Belinda's free arm. "Let's get you outside in the fresh air."

"Please," she replied, her voice raspy.

She turned and looked over her shoulder, as if expecting someone to follow. Hadrian shook his head. *Been in solitary too long, poor thing.*

As they stepped out onto Dinah's shady front porch, he noticed that one of the WET officers was uncuffing Dinah.

"Necklace," Belinda panted. "Don't let her get it."

"Stop!" Hadrian shouted, stepping in front of Belinda.

Dinah immediately grabbed for her pendant.

Hadrian didn't know what else to do, so he yelled "Gun!"

Even the heavily armored WET team dove for cover. Except for the officer who had just uncuffed Dinah. There was no place for him to go. In an instant, the woman standing next to him was gone.

And in her place was a lion.

The huge cat roared, and car alarms down the street went off. It knocked the WET officer down, and he scrambled away. The beast turned toward the house and stalked toward Hadrian. Belinda cowered behind him. He had drawn his weapon, and kept it trained on the cat. It shook its head and snarled, tail twitching.

"Stop, Dinah," Hadrian said, doubting the animal understood him. "Just stop."

The great cat rocked back on its haunches, as if to sit, then leaped at Hadrian. Gunfire erupted from multiple firearms, and the animal fell dead at his feet. He himself had only managed to squeeze three shots off, but he knew at least two had hit the lion's head.

As he watched, the beast melted away. But there was something left. The bullet-riddled body of Dinah Beecher. *What the hell just happened here?*

"Did you see that?" panted the WET officer who had been bowled over by the lion.

The officer walking with him shook his head. "I didn't see anything. Do you see any lions here? No. Because there aren't any. Never were. Only a crazy old lady who acted like she had an explosive device around her neck."

"This will be an interesting test for the new body cameras," Hadrian said to Haskell. *Can't wait to read this report.*

EMS pulled up, and Haskell tossed his car keys to one of the WET officers. "I'm going to ride in the ambulance. Get my car back downtown, would you, Malloy?"

The officer nodded and pocketed the keys.

"Crime Scene is on the way. Don't know if you want to stick around for that. Thanks for the lead, agent."

Hadrian watched as the paramedics helped Belinda onto the stretcher. They took her vitals and loaded her into the ambulance. Haskell climbed in after her.

There was no need to stick around and wait for the CSU. They would go into excruciating detail, collecting carpet fibers, soil samples, Dinah's cell phone and computer, if she had one, among other things. He looked down at her body. Her heart wasn't pumping, but gravity was drawing the thickening blood out through her open wounds, making an ever-widening pool. *How did you get here, Dinah?*

He briefly considered taking the necklace – it was clearly not an ordinary object. But he didn't. Her personal effects would be released to her family, if any existed. He hadn't been able to find them when he ran her background. It would be safe enough in the evidence lock up. He got in his car. If the traffic gods were kind, he could make the second half of MacBeth at the Miller. He'd check on Marti and Lulu afterwards, if they were still talking to him. He texted Sara, and headed toward the Museum District.

Sara's friend, Penny, insisted that they stop and eat after the play. Ordinarily, Hadrian didn't mind doing that. The group often grabbed a bite after a show. They almost always went to the same restaurant, and the wait staff knew them by name. But tonight he was antsy. Sure, in a way that made him doubt his sanity, they'd recovered Belinda and the Romance Killer was dead, but he couldn't shake the feeling that this episode wasn't finished. He had told Sara he'd just meet them at the restaurant, since they'd come in separate vehicles. He made a call on the way back to his car.

"Haskell."

"Galanti here. Just wanted to follow up and see how Belinda was."

"They had to run fluids to treat her for dehydration. They're going to keep her overnight, but she should be good to go in the morning."

"Excellent."

Haskell sighed. "Still haven't got in touch with Lulu. I find that a bit concerning."

"Me, too. Let me see if I can locate her."

It gave him no pleasure to text Sara to say he couldn't make dinner. He'd done that often enough lately. Penny would have something to say about it. Her fiancé never bailed on plans. That was just something he'd have to worry about later. Right now, he needed to find Lulu. The easiest way to do that was to go through Marti.

Hadrian was taken aback when he knocked on Marti's door, and a police officer – who wasn't Nick – answered. "I-I was just stopping by to say hello," he stammered.

"Hunter? Is that you?" Marti's mother called from the living room.

"Yes, ma'am."

Adele hurried over to the doorway. "Marti went missing this morning, she and Lulu both. This is after Nick's children were taken. I don't know what happened. We spent the night last night, and when we got up Cassie was strapped in her stroller, but Marti was gone, just gone. We're worried sick. Do you think," she sniffled, "that the same person who stole our grandkids took her, too?"

Where did you go, Marti, after you dropped off that plant? "Unfortunately, I have no way of knowing that. What makes you think Lulu is also missing?"

"She spent the night, too."

"I see." *There's quite a slumber party.* "Do you think Lulu –"

"Of course not! She'd never hurt Marti. She was her employer, for crying out loud."

He hugged Marti's mother. "I'm sure these officers know what they're doing. I'm just going to get out of their way. Keep me posted, though." He gave Adele his cell number.

He knew that he just got handed another missing persons case. And this time, he had no idea where to look.

Belinda leaned forward in the hospital bed, trying to figure out the best way to get up without disturbing her IV. The two bags of fluids she'd gotten pumped into her vein had made her feel like a million bucks. She'd even felt well enough to answer all of Lieutenant Haskell's questions about the kidnapping. She hesitated to tell him about Dinah's wishing stone, but then decided honesty was the best policy. She'd let Haskell sort it out in his report. The truth was that she would have answered his questions about anything, just to keep him in the room with her, because she was so desperate for company. She'd looked around, hoping to see some sign of Ellen, but the ghost did not seem to be around. She called out to her mentally, and hoped Ellen would come back soon.

As good as she felt from the IV, its side effect had left her with a pressing need to go to the restroom. She gave up trying to puzzle out the tangle of wires and hit the nurse call button.

A few minutes later, her nurse opened the door. "You alright, ma'am?"

"I just need to go to the bathroom, and I'm not sure how to disconnect this stuff."

The nurse unlocked the wheels on the IV pole, and showed Belinda how to free herself from the EKG machine without making it flatline and send everyone running to her room. Then she went back to her rounds.

A grateful Belinda dragged her IV into the bathroom with her. She would never in her wildest dreams have imagined how excited she could be about sitting on a toilet. An actual flush toilet! Even the hospital antiseptic smelled good to her. She was nearly giddy. Belinda even flushed it a second time after she was done, just to hear the sound. Then she washed her hands, twice, to feel the warm water and suds on her skin. The first thing she would do when she got home, she decided, would be to take a long, hot shower.

When she got back in bed and got the equipment hooked up, she leaned back and scanned the room for any sign of Ellen. Belinda was alone. She turned on the TV, more for noise than entertainment, and clicked through the channels. It didn't take very long for her to relax and drowse off.

She had just drifted into hypnagogia – that peculiar liminal state between wakefulness and sleep – when she heard someone call her name. In her mind's eye, she could see Ellen standing next to her bed.

"Ellen? There you are. I've been looking all over for you."

"There was some kind of binding on the house. I couldn't leave until that awful woman who took you crossed the threshold. Not that I would have left you, anyway; but I had no choice about it. I was afraid I was going to be trapped there forever with Thomas. What a horrible man!"

"Yes. I met him. I hope Dinah dragged him across the threshold with her."

Ellen shrugged, then clasped her hands in front of her chest. "Belinda, I have bad news for you. Lulu and Marti have been taken by Balcones, and they're trapped between dimensions, in some nightmare world he's created. I don't know how or why, but surely no good can come of it."

"What? I don't understand?" Belinda almost woke up, but Ellen grabbed her wrist and kept her from leaving.

"Your cousin, Virginia, has been up to her old tricks – and then some. I suspect that she's the one that trapped me in the house with you, didn't want me telling Marti and Lulu where you were. I have to go help those two, if I can get in there."

"You'll come back, right?"

Ellen looked at the floor and ran her finger along the bed railing. "Of course I will. It just may not be in the way you think."

Belinda frowned. "What do you mean?"

Ellen didn't respond. She faded away into the dimness of the room, and Belinda could not feel her presence any more.

Chapter 21
And Miles to Go

Sunday, August 14, 7:05 AM
The Maze

stumbled, but caught myself before I did a face-plant. I blinked. Repeatedly. It was still there. Instead of standing at the end of the walkway to my house, Lulu and I stood in what looked like an ancient forest. It was cool and misty, and I wished I had a jacket.

Balcones was still clutching Lulu's wrist.

"Let go," she growled.

He chuckled, but released her arm. "Now, after all the trouble I've gone to, setting this game up, that's no way to talk to me."

"What game are you talking about?" I asked.

"That's an excellent question. Think of it as an extremely immersive RPG."

"A what?" Lulu asked.

Balcones' eyes widened with annoyance. "RPG – role playing game. Do you have any idea how much money I make off selling imaginary objects for actual money on in-game purchases?" He nearly smiled, then shook his head and cleared his throat. "Now, the object of *this* game is to gather tools, weapons, and food and survive your quest to the center of the maze. Once all the members of your team have touched the gazing ball, your mission is complete. It would, of course, be unfair for me to let you have a head start. The other team will be arriving presently. Feel free to wander around and brainstorm until then, when the game will start."

"What if we refuse to play?" I asked.

Balcones shook his head in mock sympathy. "That would be most unfortunate. Because this game differs from online RPGs in that if you die in the game, you really die. There are no save points or extra lives."

"We'll just convince the other team not to play." Lulu said.

"You might, perhaps. But they'll enter the maze at a different point than you, so you won't see them for some time."

"We can just sit and wait for them to make it through," I said.

"You could do that, certainly. Yes. Did I mention that there are monsters? They, too, will be searching for resources and food – that would be you. Your chances of escaping them are much better inside the maze. But, if you wish to leave your baby an orphan because of some ideological snit, that of course, is your choice."

I scowled. I looked at Lulu. She was looking back at me, shaking her head. "Why us? Why now?"

Balcones threw his head back and laughed. "Is it not obvious?"

"No," Lulu replied.

Balcones' eyes narrowed into hard lines. "Quinn." Balcones looked at me. "You are his girlfriend." Then he looked at Lulu. "You are an ally of those irksome fae."

"But I'm not his girlfriend. We're not even seeing each other anymore." I doubted this would change the situation, but I had nothing else to say.

Balcones' grin was frightening. "Glorious! He will suffer all the more for your dea-deadly peril, knowing it was 100% his fault. Knowing you tried to get away from him, but his selfish dalliance with you put you in this position. If only he'd left you alone…but I can see why he didn't."

He laughed softly, then reached out to trace my jaw with his pudgy finger before I stepped back, out of reach. Rage flared up in his eyes. Lulu and I both backed away.

"More than a hundred years ago," Balcones snarled, "I watched as Quinn's MIT murdered my father in cold blood. I have spent all this time getting stronger, getting richer, and now I have everything I need to take my revenge. I already got that bitch that killed my father. She also was Quinn's girlfriend, and I reveled in his suffering. I had Malik trapped, and what a joy it would have been to see him enslaved for all eternity."

"You sold him. If you were so desperate for revenge, why didn't you keep him yourself?"

"Revenge is sweet, but so is profit. Why have only one, when I could enjoy both?" Balcones paused. "After that, I lured the entire team to the edge of the world – if only that Russian mobster hadn't had been so greedy, I could have fed the entire MIT to the great wolf Fenrir."

"It seems like your plans depend too much on people," Lulu said.

"That is exactly what I was thinking. My grandfather, the one who raised me after my father was murdered, always said, 'Keep it simple.' That's why I've brought you here – I designed the maze, and the whole place is under my control. No complicated schemes or feckless humans here to fail me. Just my enemies in a giant maze, fighting to the dea—decision...on the winner. With a few monsters here and there, of course. Just to make it interesting."

I crossed my arms. "And speaking of humans, what part do Nick's children play in your grand master plan? What have you done with them?"

Balcones' hands became animated, more so as he talked. "That, now that was complete serendipity. You see, I was trying to capture you and your brat to use as bait to torture Quinn, but for some reason, Virginia's tulpa couldn't find your house. I don't know why – it found everyone else's. But anyway. My bumbling nephews found your sister. Unfortunately, they got a little rough with her, which is a shame, because it would have been brilliant to have her as a hostage. But I digress. Regardless of whether or not you're still sleeping with Quinn, he cares for you, and it was your choice to get involved with him. But now, your whole family is disrupted, and they had no choice about it. The more *you* suffer, the more *he* suffers, and by involving innocent bystanders, his feelings of guilt are compounded exponentially."

Mine, too. "You should have left Emily and the kids out of this. Just so you know, their father is coming for you. And he won't rest until he's gotten them back." I lunged at Balcones, grabbing for his throat.

Deftly snatching my wrists into his large hand, Balcones pulled me against his scaly body. Up close, his sulphurous breath nearly choked me. He snorted and rolled his eyes. "I have no fear of humans."

"You should fear him."

Balcones' mouth twitched into a half-hearted approximation of a smile. "Perhaps. But not today." He shoved me towards Lulu, letting go of me as his arm extended.

My friend caught me, then glared at Balcones. "So basically, what you're saying, is that Marti and I start at one end of the maze, and Quinn's MIT starts at the other, and we race to see who gets to the center first. Is that correct?"

"Essentially," Balcones replied, with a smirk that made me want to slap him.

"What happens if we win?" I asked.

"I don't want to spoil the surprise by telling you."

Lulu's lips pursed. "What happens if we lose?"

"I would strongly recommend against that. Did I mention that Phoebetor is also playing?"

"Who's that?" I asked.

"The God of Nightmares. You met him a few minutes ago. Well, I've got to go spring the trap on an MIT team. Enjoy the game0021

"

Balcones stepped through an invisible door and was gone. I ran over and tried to locate the portal, but my hands found only empty space.

Sunday, August 14, 11:45 AM
The In Between

"Argh! Why did you follow me here?" Virginia snapped, as she, Nick, Malik, and Bruce landed in a heap on the floor in Balcones' between room, the same one where Quinn had been held earlier.

"What did you expect?" Nick shot back. "You know where my kids are."

"Virginia, you are such an idiot – you let Quinn escape. I told you never, ever let yourself be alone with him. And what did you do? I can't believe I trusted you."

All four of them turned to see a paunchy man standing at the far end of the narrow room, shaking his head.

"Balcones!" she said. "I can explain."

"That's Balcones?" Nick asked, incredulous, as he looked at Malik.

"What do you mean by that?" Balcones was indignant.

Nick stood up, as did the others. He crossed his arms and leaned back slightly. "I just didn't expect a demon to look like a middle-aged fat guy, that's all. I was expecting something more...demonic."

Balcones' cheeks went bright red and his eyes flashed.

"You shouldn't have said that," Malik whispered.

The skin on the Balcones' face seemed to implode, leaving behind the scaly bronze skin and reptilian eyes of his normal demon face.

When he spoke, his voice was harsher and more sibilant. "Is thisss better?"

Quinn shifted from dog form into human form and prevented Virginia from running out the other portal.

Nick shrugged. "Meh. I thought you might have horns and a tail." Both his immortality and his fury at the thing that wrought such havoc on his family overcame the very reasonable fear he should have had towards Balcones.

Malik nudged Nick. "It would be in all of our best interests for you to stop provoking him."

Balcones stalked closer. Nick stood his ground as the demon pushed into his personal space. "Hmmm. Human, entangled with those tiresome fae.

Missing some children." He grinned, close enough for his sour breath to slide down Nick's cheek. "You must be the husband of Marti Keller's sister."

Nick bristled, but Malik placed a cautionary hand on his shoulder. Balcones then moved past Nick and approached Virginia. "I will deal with you later. Get out."

Quinn made no attempt to stop her this time, and she hurried through the portal behind her. Balcones moved so that he was toe-to-toe with Quinn.

"Well, I have to say that I'm somewhat disappointed. I'd hoped to get your entire MIT, or what's left of it, anyway, to play my game. But who knows, a fae, a djinn, and a human? Could be entertaining."

"And what game is that, Balcones?" Quinn asked.

"Ah. The team lead speaks. All these years, I have been watching you, waiting for this moment. I could kill you," he bared his fangs, "right here, right now…but then it would be over too quickly. Very unsatisfying. And all the trouble I went to creating this maze would just be wasted."

"Maze?" Nick asked.

Balcones smacked his lips and glanced up at the ceiling. "Are you unfamiliar with the concept?"

"No. I just think it's weird."

"Weird. Now that is something I can promise you. It will definitely be weird."

"And if we refuse?" Quinn asked.

"You won't. There's a prize at the center. Take a look." He gestured to the wall, toward the window view of the forest. It faded, and then showed a small clearing in a dense wood. Inside the clearing, a middle-aged woman held a small baby, and two boys played tag, using a pedestal that supported a large gazing ball as base.

There was a sharp intake of breath from Nick.

"Now, and I know she looks disgusting right now, but that lovely creature holding the baby is my wife. Personally, I wouldn't trust her around human children. Also, when the glass ball is touched, it activates the guardians, and they will kill whatever is in the clearing. Demons excepted, of course. Maybe the boys will be careful. But if you're sure you don't want to play…"

"Open the door. Now," replied Nick.

Balcones smiled. "Excellent. I will warn you that there are some monsters wandering about – you probably want to get to the middle before they do, because they would nothing more than to touch the ball and activate the guardians. Food, weapons, and useful items can be found in the maze, although it may take some looking." He started to turn away from them, then turned back around to grin at Malik. "Just an FYI – this maze may look very similar to an ancient forest on the earth plane, but the physical rules are a little different. So most of your genie powers won't work here."

Malik moved in close to Quinn. "Is retrieving Nick's offspring enough justification to participate in this endeavor, or should we focus our efforts on escape?" he asked in a whisper.

"I don't think we have much choice," Quinn whispered back. "Maybe we can do both, though."

Balcones looked sharply at the two of them. "Oh, Quinn?" he asked picking at something caught in one of his claws. "Just curious. Have you spoken to Marti lately? She seems very nice. A shame about your breakup." He looked out the window into the maze for a moment, then looked back at Quinn and smiled.

The blood rushed from his face to the pit of Quinn's stomach and collected there in a frigid pool. If rescuing Nick's kids wasn't important enough to MAMIC, rescuing Marti –if she was in the maze as Balcones had just implied – was definitely important enough to him. Of course, it could be a trick, demons were known for that. How did Balcones know that they had broken up? Was it just a guess, designed to mess with his head? Or had he actually spoken with Marti? There was only one way to find out. As much as he wanted to put his hands around Balcones' throat and squeeze him, he wouldn't take the bait. He refused to give Balcones a win, however small, before the game even started.

Nick's eyes narrowed. "Are you going to open the door, or just stand there and keep running your mouth?"

"As you wish." Balcones gestured to the wall.

Tendrils of chill mist curled into the room as the wall dissolved. Something in the maze was screaming; the screams came at regular intervals, and sometimes there was more than one voice.

"Bloody foxes," grumbled Quinn.

Balcones grinned.

The three stepped through the doorway into the cool forest and looked around. They stood on a dirt path that led into a dense forest of gnarled old trees. The woods stretched interminably on either side of the path. Unseen creatures made haunting calls that echoed through the trees before they were swallowed by the mist.

"The game begins...now," said Balcones.

The doorway disappeared, with no hint of it ever having existed, replaced by a bank of fog so thick it was impossible to tell whether there was ground beneath it or trees behind it.

"The sooner we get started, the sooner we finish," Nick said, moving forward.

Malik shrugged and followed. "Into the woods."

"No show tunes," Quinn said. "Seriously. No. Show. Tunes."

The animal sounds fell silent as the three entered the shadows of the ancient forest.

Although being kidnapped by Balcones was the last thing I had expected, I was so thankful I'd had the foresight to take Cassie in the house after I'd dropped off Hunter's plant. My parents might be concerned about me, but my baby would be safe and sound. It was one less thing I had to worry about. Although I don't think anything would have kept me awake, once I got still. My second wind had petered out some time ago, and after the brief adrenalin rush from our kidnapping, I was more tired than I remember ever being. I leaned against the invisible wall that kept us out of the woods and slept.

The thudding of my head into the ground and getting a mouthful of leaf litter woke me up. I spat rotting leaves out of my mouth, tasting the grit and mold.

Lulu stretched her hand out to help me up. "I guess it's time, honey."

"Yep." I touched the prayer box with the blue crystal tear that hung around my neck for luck.

Something in the trees made a whooping cry that reminded me of the howler monkeys at the zoo. As we got further into the gloom, there was a chittering noise that could have been made by either a small bird or a large insect. I hoped it was a bird.

Chapter 22
Here be Monsters

 was acutely aware of the noise our feet made shuffling through the fallen leaves on the path. If there were any monsters nearby, they'd know exactly where we were. I tried lifting my feet higher, or walking toe-heel instead of heel-toe. Neither of those made a huge amount of difference. It wasn't too far into the woods that we came to a turn off. We could go straight ahead or make a right turn.

Deep in the mist-shrouded trees, something screamed. Short, hoarse yelps, like someone being chased through the woods by an ax murderer. My heart beat faster. "What was that?"

"If I heard it at my house, I would think it's a fox. Here, I don't know, honey."

I tried to re-focus on our task, and turned back to the path. "Keep going, or turn?" I asked.

"We're supposed to go to the center of the maze," Lulu said. "Maybe one of us should wait here, and the other should go on a little way and see if it's a dead end."

I shook my head. "No, I think it would be a bad idea to split up." I looked around for a stick. "Why don't we make a mark?" I drew a deep line in the dirt, near the edge of the path parallel to the direction we were travelling. "And if we come back this way and find the mark, we'll know we've gone in a circle."

"Makes sense."

We took the turning. Soon we came to a path that branched to the left and about ten feet afterward, a path that branched to the right.

"Right, left or straight?" Lulu asked.

"We're supposed to be looking for food and weapons as well, so we may as well take the first turn and see where it leads. I wonder, though, if there's a shortcut. Maybe something hidden out in the forest?" I headed for one of the natural paths between the trees. And bounced off the solid air at the edge of the path. I used my hands, mime-style, to feel for a break in the invisible wall. It went further up than I could reach, and all the way down into the dirt. I followed it a short distance in either direction, but it remained solid.

I sighed and went to mark the path. There was already a mark there. I ran to the other path. Also a mark.

"Dammit," I said.

"Well, I guess we couldn't expect a demon to play fair. Let's take the left turn anyway."

The path spiraled into a dead end. However, there was a statue at the cul-de-sac that held a silver dagger. I took it and we backtracked. We were just coming to the point where the spiral joined the straightaway when we heard noises. We stopped, hidden by the huge trunk of an ancient tree, and peered around the corner. Standing at the crossroad were a werewolf, a cyclops, and a scorpion the size of a horse. They seemed to be talking to each other, but it only sounded like growls and grunts to me. The werewolf gestured down the path, in our direction. I held my breath. The cyclops waved his club toward the straight-ahead path. If my heart pounded any harder, they were going to hear it. The scorpion glanced down the trail in our direction, then they hurried on down the straight path. We waited until there was silence, then we waited some more.

"I think we should go back to the first path," I whispered to Lulu. "I think we're least likely to run into those monsters that way."

She nodded, and we crept cautiously down the path, turned right, then turned right again when we rejoined our original track.

"I'm pretty sure Balcones was lying about the food," I said.

"Would you eat any food you found in this place?" Lulu answered.

"Good point. I'm still starving, though."

"Me, too."

We'd been tramping around all day, and I couldn't tell if we were any closer to the center of the maze than when we started. The mist in this place never quite lifted, so thirst wasn't so much of a problem, but hunger was. Unless I wanted to grab one of the black squirrels that haunted the trees, or one of the crows that seemed to be constantly laughing at us, and eat it raw, there was nothing to be done about it. I was desperate, but not that desperate. Not yet, anyway. We'd found no food, but we were the proud owners of a silver dagger, six arrows in a quiver, four Ninja throwing stars, and a crowbar. Good thing Lulu had been wearing her backpack. Night was quickly descending on this murky wood, and I wasn't sure where or if we would sleep. Twice during the day, we'd seen the same assortment of monsters we'd seen earlier. I wondered if we'd ever run into Quinn and his MIT. Had they already gotten to the center and claimed the prize, or were they just as lost and miserable as we were?

"Lulu? What was that noise?"

"Sounded like a wolf howling to me."

"That's what I thought."

I wished I'd paid more attention at camp, when they'd taught us how to light fires without matches. Although the perpetually damp wood in this forest probably wouldn't burn anyway.

Just ahead of us, there was the dull noise of a wet twig breaking, and we froze. I could see a figure stumbling towards us in the gloom.

What on earth is he doing here?

Sunday, August 14, 12:15 PM
The Maze

"I think we should turn left, then take the right turn just ahead," Malik said.

Quinn nodded. "From here, it looks like if we turn left and keep going, we're back to the outer edges. We need to get to the center of the maze, so I don't think tramping round and round the perimeter is going to do us any good."

"Fine. I've managed to find nothing but dead ends, anyway," Nick added.

As they approached the path that split off to their right, Quinn stopped them.

"Wait," he said. "Do you hear that?" He pointed down the track. "Look! Do you see them?"

"See what? Nick asked.

"They're hard to see in the fog, you can see them hiding behind the tree. They must be lying in wait for us. One I can't see much of, but she might be a sphynx. The other one, though, she's clearly Black Annis."

Nick pointed down the connecting trail. "I think we should go that way instead of walking into an ambush. And who or what is a Black Annis?"

"She's a blue-faced hag who loves to eat humans, especially children, who wander across her path," Quinn said.

Malik glanced down the row. "I see them. Let's go before they abandon their plan to waylay us and opt for a more direct approach, shall we?"

"What if we cut through the woods and circled around behind them?" Nick asked.

Quinn crossed his arms. "And then what? You think you can take them out with the bow we found? Never mind about the arrows."

"Yeah, you're right. Waiting for them to trap us is a much better plan."

"Enough!" Malik interrupted their spat. "It might be advantageous to get into the cover of the trees; however, we currently lack sufficient resources to effectively attack our opponents."

Nick rushed toward the dark trees, and collided with a clear barrier. He stepped back and rubbed his nose. Malik and Quinn tested for the invisible wall on the opposite side of the trail, and easily found it.

"I guess that means we stay on the trail," Nick said.

The hurried down the track, deeper into the maze.

"They don't seem to be actively pursuing us," Malik said, as they watched Black Annis and the sphynx turn the corner, headed away from them.

"Maybe they're NPCs," Nick suggested.

"What?" Quinn asked.

"Non-Player Characters. In computer games, they wander around and create havoc, but they don't' really have any intelligence."

Quinn shook his head. "There's a lot of those in real life, too."

"Balcones said that the monsters would try to get to the center of the maze, did he not?" Malik said.

"That doesn't necessarily mean that they have any self-awareness, or awareness of us," Nick replied.

They trudged on.

After a while, they came to a branch that turned almost immediately after it split from the main path, so they couldn't see down it more than ten feet or so. Quinn stepped into it and listened. "I don't hear anything. Shall we try it?"

The other two responded by coming into the branch with him. The maze twisted into a tight spiral, with nothing but blind corners at each turn. They crept through it on high alert, none of them wanting to challenge the sphynx or Black Annis, should they appear. At the end of it, there was a very small grotto. Clear water bubbled up at the feet of a demonic statue. On the wall behind it, hung a ball peen hammer.

"I recommend against touching the water," Malik said.

Quinn nodded. "Agreed."

Nick sighed. "I'm taking the hammer, though."

"Night's coming. Do we want to continue stumbling around in the dark, or do we want to draw lots for first watch and try to sleep some?" Quinn asked.

"I vote we rest," Nick said.

"I second that," Malik added.

Too bad there was no way to get off the path. If the monsters came, they'd be sitting ducks.

"I'll take the first watch," Quinn said. He was bone weary, but suspected he'd have trouble sleeping, at least at first.

Nick and Malik made themselves comfortable as best they could. In his mind, Quinn went over their inventory of found items: he carried a bow (but no arrows), Malik had a battle axe, and Nick just got a ball peen hammer. *Was this a weapons cache, or a jumble sale?* Thinking he'd be warmer with fur, he shifted into his dog form and patrolled the area. After a while, he thought he heard a strange noise, and trotted off to investigate.

Sunday, August 14, 8:15 PM
Houston, Texas

Virginia was afraid.

Balcones had said he'd deal with her later. It was much later, and he hadn't shown up. Not that she'd hung around waiting for him, but she knew if he really wanted to find her, he would. She jumped at every noise, and her nerves were shot. The demon was not inclined toward leniency, and she feared what might be in store for her.

"Think!" she commanded herself. "What can I do that will get Balcones off my back? What does he want most?" She got up and paced her living room.

She wracked her brain. *Money?...Power?...To humiliate Quinn.* He'd rambled on about his revenge plot many more times than Virginia had bothered listening to. What could she do to get back in Balcones' good graces? One thing a man can't stand is to see a woman he wants being taken care of by another man. As her ruined tulpa had faded, its memories had floated into her consciousness in little random snippets. She recalled one scene where it seemed to be the middle of the night, and Marti was standing in a man's yard, talking with him. Lulu was also there. Figures. Balcones had them now. They wouldn't be bothering her tulpas anymore. Virginia couldn't hear what anyone was saying, but it appeared to be a friendly exchange. And that was really all she needed. She decided the best thing to do was go to Marti's neighborhood and see if she could find the house from the tulpa's vision.

Virginia wished she'd worn flats for the multi-block hike in Marti's neighborhood – her feet were killing her. But at last she'd found the house. The garage door was open and the man inside, shirtless, was sorting through a box of papers. He looked young, perhaps mid-thirties. He was definitely the man the tulpa had seen. For a moment, Virginia watched him, sweat glistening on his hard body, and she was acutely aware that she wasn't as young as she used to be. Still, her legs looked good in short skirts and high heels, and that's what she was wearing. Should be good enough to at least get him to talk to her.

She walked up the driveway, hips swaying just enough to straddle the line between sex appeal and solicitation. She watched him watching her and smiled inwardly. *Take that, 'ladies of a certain age.'* Virginia stopped at the edge of the garage entrance.

"Excuse me?" she cleared her throat. "I'm sorry to bother you, but I'm looking for a friend's house and I just can't seem to find it. Could you possibly help me?" She twisted a lock of hair around her index finger.

The man set the box down on a worktable and came closer. Virginia's eye was drawn to his chest and arm, which sported a tattoo of a raven in flight.

"Nice ink," she commented.

"Thanks."

"I've been looking for this address," she said as she reached into her tiny designer handbag. What she pulled out was not a slip of paper, but a makeup compact. She tossed it gently into the garage. "Oops!"

She stepped in as if to retrieve it, and caught the man's hand in hers on the way. She stepped on the compact, and they both disappeared.

The man stumbled when they rematerialized, but quickly caught his balance. "Where…are we?" he asked, looking around.

She looked around to see Balcones sitting in a chair in front of the window, flicking through a bowl of mixed nuts with his claws. As soon as he saw her, he covered his face with his palm and shook his head.

"Virginia?" he asked as he removed his hand. "Why are you here? And why did you bring…a guest?" His voice carried the false calm of someone who has had to explain something too many times to too many different people, and was a hair's breadth from exploding.

The man, however, was staring at Balcones, mouth agape.

"I thought you could use him, Balcones," she nodded toward Hadrian. "He's a friend of Marti's."

"Use him for what?" Balcones asked, with forced pleasantry.

"Isn't it obvious? Put him in the maze with Marti, to make Quinn jealous."

Balcones rubbed the bridge of his nose with both index fingers, as if he had a headache. Then he sighed loudly. "Virginia, you've outdone yourself. With stupidity. Your idea isn't going to work because," he looked at Hadrian and scowled. "Because it just isn't. Now he knows about you, and he knows about me. I can't just let him go, now, can I? He has to go into the maze. But the game's been running for hours. I have deliberately made the teams unequal – if I put him in with Marti, that changes the odds, now doesn't it? I seriously wish you would have asked before you decided to help."

"I just thought he'd be useful." Virginia pouted.

"I'm still trying to decide if *you* are more useful to me alive or dead. Currently, the pendulum is swinging toward dead."

"What are you?" Hadrian asked. The tension between Balcones and Virginia shattered like a teacup dropped on tile.

"I have come to expect such poor manners from humans. You are in my house, and you have the nerve to ask me such a blatantly rude question?" Balcones asked. "Let me tell you what I am." He got up from his chair and strolled closer to Virginia and Hadrian. With each step he took, the light in the room dimmed. Virginia edged away from him, but Hadrian tried to stand his ground, but found himself involuntarily backing up. By the time Balcones was within a foot of him, all the illumination had faded, except for that given off by the demon's fiery eyes.

Hadrian could barely breathe as Balcones stood with his face inches away, sour breath fouling the agent's air. He wanted to get farther away, but his knees were so shaky he didn't think he could walk.

"I," Balcones said, "Am a demon. I am your worst nightmare."

"You haven't seen my nightmares," Hadirian whispered, the sound of his breath husky and dark with fear.

A grin cracked Balcones' scaly face. "Well, then. This might prove interesting after all."

Chapter 23
The Spider's Kiss

alik tried to force his mind to empty and be still so he could rest. The indignity of having to lie in the dirt like a mongrel dog gnawed at him. It was more than that, though. He was used to being powerful, able even to bend time itself. But not here. No, in this dank place, he was as weak as a common man. A tired, filthy, hungry man. Eventually, his consciousness blurred into dream fragments, and then darkness.

The first thing Malik noticed was the smell. Layers of unwashed grime, sour sweat, and urine all competed for his attention. He opened his eyes and tried to move away from whatever foul thing emitted that stench. To his horror, he realized that it was him. Instead of the designer workout clothes he'd been wearing when he entered the maze, he found himself dressed in tattered, dirty rags. Gaudy market stalls of a bazaar surrounded him, but he was utterly alone.

"No!" he shouted, leaping to his feet.

His hand hit something hard. His breath stuck in his throat when he realized that it was a kashkul, a begging bowl carved from a coconut. His hands shook as he held them out to examine them. His fingernails were jagged and encrusted with dirt. His arms were thin and bony. And he stank. Stank of filth and despair and bottomless misery.

His chest heaved with short, gasping breaths. "How?" he said half-aloud. "How did I become this?"

He flinched when he felt a hand on his shoulder.

"Dude," Nick said groggily. "Wake up. What's wrong with you?"

"Do not look at me!" Malik said, his cheeks burning with shame. He blinked a few times and the desert glare of his dream gave way to the cool gloom of the forest maze.

"Not a problem. Of all the things I can stare at in the dark, you're not top of the list." Nick turned over, his back to Malik.

"You cannot sleep, either?"

"Not real sleep, no. But I'd have a better chance if you'd stop talking."

Malik bristled, but decided that it was late, and they were both very far from home. He turned his attention to his clothing. It didn't feel right, and the odor that had awakened him from his half-slumber still hung in the air. It must be his imagination. He turned his back to Nick, and stared into the dark, wondering when Quinn would come to wake him for sentry duty.

Hadrian stumbled down the dark path, prodded by Balcones.

"We're almost there," the demon growled.

"Almost where?"

Balcones let out an exasperation-tinged sigh. "To join your little friends." He stopped. "I do not wish to be seen. Just follow the track. You cannot miss them."

"Miss who?" Hadrian asked, but Balcones was already disappearing into the shadows of the ancient trees.

Deciding he had nothing to lose at this point, Hadrian headed down the path as Balcones had directed. It wasn't long before he saw two shapes in the dim light of the maze, but he could not make out their features.

"Hullo!" a female voice called. "Hunter? What on earth are you doing here?"

"Be careful, Marti," a different female voice said. "That may not really be him. How would he even get here?"

Marti and her family, Belinda, and Lulu were the only people who called him by his undercover name of 'Hunter.' Belinda was in the hospital, so he reasoned that the second female must be Lulu.

"It's me," he said. "I don't understand how I got here. I don't even know where here is." He was about ten feet away from Marti, so he stopped walking.

"Lulu is right. How do we know you really are Hunter?" Marti asked.

"Well..." Hunter started, but couldn't actually think of anything. They didn't have any biometric devices that could positively identify him.

Lulu leaned over and whispered in Marti's ear.

"Okay. What wine did you bring to my house the other night?"

"Chardonnay."

"He could be guessing," Lulu pointed out. "That's a real common kind of wine."

"Fair enough. What did we have for dinner?"

"Zucchini scampi, because you're allergic to shellfish."

Marti turned and spoke softly to Lulu for a moment, then they both took a few steps toward him.

"We're trapped in an interdimensional maze, if that helps any. What's the last thing you remember?" she asked.

"I remember everything. That's not the problem. I don't understand it."

"Then tell us what happened," Lulu said.

"I was in my garage, doing some work, and this blonde woman came up and asked for directions."

"Blonde?" Lulu asked. "Let me guess — middle-aged, short skirt, and high heels?"

"Yeah. How did you know?"

"Long story. Her name is Virginia," she said. "What happened next, hon?"

"She threw a makeup compact into my garage, and the next thing I knew, I was in some strange room with, for lack of a better description, the Devil."

"That's got to be Balcones," Marti said. "I'm sorry you got tricked into this."

"Balcones? Yes, that's what Virginia called him."

"He's just a garden variety demon, honey, nothing special, not as demons go, anyway," Lulu said.

"None of this can be real. There's no such thing as demons or teleportation devices, at least not yet. This has to be either a dream or some elaborate hoax." That's the only thing that could explain Balcones. Hadrian shuddered.

"I'm sorry to be the one to break it to you, but it is completely, one hundred percent real. I had a tough time with it, too, when I met Quinn," Marti said.

Hadrian scanned the path, hoping to find some evidence of a projector. "And Quinn would be?"

"He's a kelpie. But I thought he was a dog. Mostly, though, he's like a man," Marti said. "He hunts demons for a living. Balcones has some issues with that."

"I see." He had no idea what she was talking about, and thought it best to humor her. Delusional people were highly unpredictable. But then again, hadn't he just seen with his own eyes his murder suspect turn into a lion and back again? Was there some hallucinogenic contaminant in the neighborhood's water? He would request testing for it once he got back to his office.

"Just so you know," Marti said. "There are some monsters in the maze. Balcones said they would be trying to eat us, but when we did see them, they went the other way. Lulu and I had already decided to take turns sleeping — I'm on guard duty first."

"Can we try and get some rest now? Maybe if I'm asleep, I won't notice how hungry I am," Lulu said.

"Of course."

"Make yourself comfortable," she said. "There's no chocolate on your pillow at this joint, I'm afraid. Heck, there's not even a pillow."

The two of them did their best to settle in and get some rest. Lulu leaned up against the barrier between the maze and the forest. Hadrian stretched out, cradling his head in his hands. He stared up at the weird shapes formed by the tree branches, black against the deep grey sky. A yawn stretched across his face, and his eyelids felt heavy. The mournful hoot of an owl caused them to flicker open, but his blinks got longer and longer, until his eyes just stayed closed. His body stiffened momentarily to stop the falling sensation he always got when going to sleep, but it wasn't enough to rouse him.

Hadrian thought he smelled wood smoke. Rough jute rope dug into his wrists and ankles. His joints ached from being forcibly extended by the rack – if felt like he'd been there for days. He heard murmuring, but his line of sight was blocked by his own arms, stretched over his head. Metal scraped on metal and a light flared. A hooded figure approached Hadrian. He carried an iron bar, heated in the fire until one end glowed red. Hadrian tried to scream, but no sound escaped his lips.

Other hooded men appeared behind the first.

"Confess!" they intoned.

Hadrian panted in fear. *I have done nothing!* But no words would come.

"As you wish," said the man with the incandescent bar. The metal hissed as he stroked it along Hadrian's belly.

There was nowhere to go. He writhed against the taut ropes, struggling to get away from the red-hot agony that his midsection had become. Hadrian tried to yell, "Stop! Let me go!" but no sound would come from his throat, no matter how hard he pushed the air through his vocal cords.

"You are accused of being a witch. Consorting with the devil. Sending curses on your neighbors. Confess, and the priest will absolve you."

"No!" he tried to shout, but still he made no sound. He felt tears rolling down his cheeks, though, as his flesh blackened and blistered.

"Another turn," the man with the bar said.

Gears clattered and meshed together. The ropes creaked as they pulled even tighter against Hadrian's wrists and ankles. If he'd wanted to scream before, he was desperate to now. A loud pop accompanied the dislocation of his shoulder. A second followed closely behind. His other shoulder had pulled free of the joint.

At this point, he would have signed any confession. But he couldn't speak and he certainly couldn't sign anything -his hands were swollen and aching from the tight ropes cutting into them at the wrists.

"If you will not confess, you will be pressed. Do you confess?"

A primal scream of fear and rage welled up from his center, but stalled in his throat and came out as an impotent squeak.

"Very well. If that is your choice." He nodded to the other hooded men. "Leave him."

Hadrian whimpered. The small, pathetic sound was the best he could do. The pain from being suspended by his ruined shoulders was unbearable.

After suffering alone in the dark for some time, three men came in and started to remove the ropes from his wrists and ankles. Pain jagged through him as circulation returned to his hands. The men helped him off the table

Hadrian collapsed on the floor, too broken to stand. He tasted blood and realized his two front teeth were loose. He was dragged up stone stairs and thrown roughly into a cart, striking his head against the wood. Hooves clattered on cobblestones for a while, then stopped. The men pulled him out of the cart and carried him to a wooden platform., where they laid him on his back.

A priest stood before him, an over-sized bible in his hand. "Any last words, warlock, before we send you back to Satan, your master?"

Hadrian knew it would be pointless to try to speak, so he just shook his head.

A large piece of wood was placed on top of him. Footsteps, then something heavy was put on top of the wood. Then another, and another.

Hadrian struggled to breathe.

All around him, shadowy figures chanted, "Die, witch, die!"

Something seemed to be jabbing him in the shoulder. He couldn't see what it was. He didn't care – he just wanted the end to come. One person, a woman, did not chant like the others.

"Honey," the voice said. "Honey?"

Hadrian sat up with a gasp and a strangled sob.

"Are you okay?" Marti asked, resting her hand on his shoulder.

He wanted to hug her, hug Lulu, and maybe do a happy dance, at being woken up from his nightmare. He thought better of it – besides, his clothes were wet with his sweat and the dankness of the forest. His lower legs ached, and his pants stuck uncomfortably to his skin.

"I'm fine," he said. "It was just a dream."

"Looked like a doozy of a dream, if you ask me," Lulu said, shaking her head.

"It's over now." He shook his head, as if to chase the ghosts of the nightmare away. "I don't think I'll be going back to sleep any time soon – I'll stand watch while you two rest."

Marti frowned slightly and squeezed his shoulder. "Sometimes it helps to talk about bad dreams."

"I'm fine. I don't want to talk about it. Thanks, though."

"Well, if you change your mind, I'll just be over here. In the dirt. Leaning against the invisible wall."

He almost laughed. "I'll keep that in mind."

Nick was not asleep. At least, he didn't think so. He let his body relax and his eyes close, but his mind churned furiously. *How was Emily doing? Had she died while he was trapped in this crazy maze? Where were his kids? Were they alright?* He didn't trust Balcones' word that they were happily playing at the center of the labyrinth, and all he had to do to take them home was to find them. No, there would certainly be more to it, if they were even still alive.

He could hear Malik a few feet away, tossing and turning in the dirt, and he felt a flash of anger. *Just be quiet already!* But he knew that it wasn't really Malik keeping him awake. His whole world had come crashing down around his ears. His wife was clinging to life by her fingernails, or at least she was, last time he had been able to check on her. His kids were missing, and odds were they were dead. The only job he really wanted was denied him. He was trapped in a place that just couldn't possibly exist, but here it was. And to top it all off, there was no way to end this. He couldn't die. There would be no joyful family waiting to meet him in wherever it was that people went when they died. He was trapped here forever. Or maybe he was dead, after all. And he was in Hell.

"Nick?"

He raised his head. "Emily?"

"Of course! Who did you expect? McKenzi and the boys are at home with my mom. I've come to bring you back."

This couldn't be real. It was everything he wanted, handed to him on a silver platter. This could only be a trick.

"Em? I was sitting here thinking about us, trying to remember stuff. What was the name of that place we went to on our first date?"

She cocked her head. He had her.

"It was the Orange Penguin, of course. Perhaps your memory is a little fuzzy from the concussion you got when that dust head freaked out in the restaurant and started throwing stuff around."

Could it really be Emily? Impossible. And yet...how else could she have known?

"Come on, Nick. We have to go. They'll be back soon."

Nick sat up. "Who is 'they'?"

Emily looked down one of the maze paths. Fear pinched her face with its bloodless fingers. "Hurry! They're coming!"

Nick stood up. Instinct told him to run to her, leave this place. Logic told him it was a trap. And yet, how would an imposter know about their disastrous first date? He started toward the woman, his stride lengthening with every step.

She screamed. Nick started to run. But it was almost as if he was stuck in deep, sucking clay. It was a tremendous amount of work to move at all, and when he did, it was in slow motion, a quarter or less of his normal ability. Emily moved normally. So did the thing that was approaching her. Nick could not identify it. An iron helmet crowned its head and a misshapen jaw jutted beneath it. Clear slime trailed in strings from its jagged teeth. The creature wore a long cloak, and Nick caught glimpses of metal underneath, as if it was wearing armor. The thing reached for Emily, but instead of arms and hands, it had thick tentacles with clawed suckers.

"No!" Nick yelled, his voice, deepened and distorted by the slow motion. His legs pumped harder, but he moved no faster.

Emily screamed again as a tentacle twined around her arm. She pulled back, using her free hand to pry at the tentacle latched onto her arm. Another tentacle grabbed her free hand.

"Stop it! Let go!" she shouted.

Nick could not break free of the slow motion barrier. He grunted from the exertion, but he still felt like a mastodon in the La Brea tar pits watching its mate being set upon by dire wolves.

"Emily!" he screamed, his voice warping to a freakish depth.

A third tentacle snaked its way around her throat and tightened, strangling her. Her face reddened and her eyes bulged. She started making choking, gagging sounds in her futile struggle for air.

"No! Noooooo!" Nick shouted again, and tried even harder to run. He would never make it in time. As a police officer, he knew that it takes at least two minutes to strangle someone to death, but at the rate he was going, it might take him two hours to get to her.

Nick suddenly became aware that he was lying down, panting. He leapt to his feet, seeing no one but Malik.

"Where is she?" Nick yelled, his voice husky with fear.

"Who?"

"Emily! My wife. She was right there!" He pointed down the maze path.

"There has been no one here but us. I do not even know where Quinn has gone. He is supposed to be on watch duty."

Nick did not take Malik's word for it, and ran down the trail. He took the only possible route and turned right – straight into a dead end. There were no tracks or evidence that anyone had ever been there. His heart was still pounding, pumping adrenalin through his body. He slammed the flat of his hand into the invisible barrier with an exasperated growl.

Lulu did not want to sleep. She sagged against the barrier, hoping that if she went into a meditative state, her body could rest but her mind would stay alert. This place was custom-made for nightmares. She and Marti had only seen the monsters in the maze three times, but the entire day she'd felt a heaviness, as if something malevolent was stalking them unseen. Lulu supposed it could have been Balcones – he was surely observing them for his own entertainment. But this seemed closer, practically breathing down their necks.

And she felt she was flying blind. She was so used to Thutmose, her spirit guide, always being around her, but she could not sense him in this place. Even with Marti and Hunter there, she felt abandoned and alone. She wondered where Belinda was, and if she was alright.

Lulu hugged herself against the chill. Marti shifted a little, and her back touched Lulu's arm. The warmth was comforting. *Maybe I'm not so alone, after all.* But she didn't feel much better. There was still the sense of foreboding, that something sinister was lurking just out of sight, waiting for the right moment to strike.

Lulu took a deep breath, feeling the air flow into her lungs, expanding her belly. She held it for a moment, then released it. She took another deep breath, then another. On the fourth breath, she felt a rib snap. She clutched at her side and felt the jagged edge of bone under her papery skin. When she looked around, she was surprised to see that neither Marti nor Hunter was there. Had they snuck off around the corner to be together? And why not? They were both young.

Lulu tried to stand, but as soon as she put any weight on her leg, the lower bones shattered. It was true - she had fallen and she couldn't get up. The cheesy TV commercials about the elderly lady who fell and was saved by her medical alert necklace had always made her shake her head. But now that she was the helpless one on the floor, they seemed particularly poignant.

"Marti!" she called. "Hunter?"

There was no response. But worse still, when she clenched her jaw in frustration, her teeth crumbled and broke. She gasped and a whimper escaped from her throat. As she raised her hands to examine the destruction in her mouth, she noticed that her arms were wasted and thin, covered in age spots and crepey skin. Blue veins, with smaller red spidery children, bulged over her bony hands.

"No!" she shouted. "Marti! Marti, where are you?"

A wolf howled in the distance.

Okay, get a hold of yourself. You did not age thirty years in ten minutes. This has to be a dream. Wake up. Wake up!

Lulu gradually became aware that her tailbone was numb, and one of her feet was asleep. She opened her eyes, and found the Marti was still next to her, but she'd fallen over and was lying on the ground, clutching at something under her blouse. Although her facial muscles twitched a little, her breathing was deep and even – she was asleep. Hunter paced around in the deep twilight, seemingly examining the barrier between the path and the trees. Perhaps he was looking for a break in the wall.

She sighed, grateful that the horrors of old age had only been a dream. This time. She remembered her mother, though. How her mind had gone long before her body, and she's spent nearly two years in fear and confusion, recognizing no one, but afraid of the 'strangers' who surrounded her, waiting for her to shuffle off her deteriorating mortal coil. Lulu shuddered. There would be no more sleep for her tonight.

Chapter 24
Perchance to Dream

he trees off to Bruce's left shook as if something heavy was climbing through their canopies - he'd been tracking it for some time now. The dog looked up and sniffed. The branches stopped moving. There was a rasping, chitinous clicking, then eight beady green eyes glimmered in the deep shadows above him.

Bruce shifted into Quinn. "Phobetor?"

An enormous spider scrambled down the tree and stood in front of Quinn. He resumed his human form and crossed his arms, pouting. "What? Are you here to spoil my fun, too?"

"Of course not. I only want to find my friends and get out of this bloody maze. We've been tramping round it all day, and not had so much as a whiff of them." Quinn shook his head, then stopped. "What do you mean 'too?' Who else is trying to ruin your fun?"

Phobetor chuckled. "You've seen your friends several times. That's part of the jape – you see them, they see you, but neither group knows it." Then he frowned. "You know, when Balcones came to me, he said it was all a lark. Just because I am the god of nightmares doesn't mean I don't like a good laugh now and again. But now he's gone and invited some of my sisters, the Keres. And it's always the same, death and destruction, everywhere they go. Dead people don't dream, you know."

"Death and destruction? I thought Thanatos was the god of death."

Phobetor rolled his eyes. "Well of course he is. But he rules over the kind of death where you die in your sleep. Or have a massive coronary and go like that." He snapped his fingers. "The Keres are all about murder and mayhem, and the bloodier the better."

Quinn scowled. "When are they arriving?"

Phobetor shrugged. "Any time now. For all I know, they're already here."

"Maybe we should turn the tables, and all escape before the Keres show up."

"Do you think if I knew a way out of here I'd still be hanging around, waiting for my crazy sisters to show up and spray blood and guts everywhere?"

"There has to be a way out."

"Sure there is. One of Balcones' rat holes that he uses to come and go."

Quinn cocked his head. *Tsch.* "I'm sure if we ask him nicely, he'll serve us a slap up tea and send everyone home."

"There's no need to get snarky. We're all in the same papyrela now – we might as well row together."

"There's a difference, though. You are immortal. Marti and Lulu are not. Balcones is only using them to get to me, so the worse he can make it for them, the happier he'll be." Quinn bit his lip. "What did you mean earlier that we'd seen each other, but didn't know it? Doesn't seem like Balcones' style to make them invisible when I could be watching them suffer."

"Oh, they're not invisible. Not at all. Besides the three of you, what have you seen in the maze?"

Quinn thought for a moment. "Living things? Black Annis and a sphynx."

"No. You've seen your friends. The older one appears to you as Black Annis, the younger as a sphynx. But they will run from you, because you look like monsters to them as well."

"Of course. I should have figured that out myself. So obvious, if you take a moment to think about it." One side of his mouth wrinkled into a demi-frown. Then his eyes widened. "I have an idea. Can you get me into Marti's – the younger one's – dreams?"

I leaned up against the invisible barrier that separated us from the sinister trees. Black and bare, were they all dead, or was it just winter in this awful place? I was so tired I could barely move, but of course, my brain wouldn't settle and let me sleep so I'd have some relief from the aching hunger that gnawed at my middle.

I knew Cassie was being well taken care of by my mother. *Does my baby miss me as much as I miss her? Mom must be worried sick – what must she be thinking, me up and disappearing into thin air?* While she'd shocked me by confessing to seeing ghosts, I wasn't sure she'd believe *this* story. I certainly wouldn't, if I hadn't lived it myself. Where was Quinn? Had he escaped Balcones, or was he stuck here, too? And then, of course, there's Hunter. What was Virginia thinking, dragging him into this? Lulu said she never thinks about anybody but herself, and I'm inclined to believe her. Also, had anyone bothered feeding my dog?

I watched Hunter pacing around for a little while before closing my eyes, hoping the "fake it 'til you make it" theory worked here. *What had gotten him so shaken up?* After seeing how well sleeping had gone for him, I was a little nervous about trying it. But I was too tired not to rest. As I squirmed around, trying to get comfortable, my hand fell on the prayer box pendant that was hidden under my shirt. Odin's tear. I still felt guilty over what happened to Halle, the Valkyrie. I wish there had been some other way, but if she hadn't given her life, then Nick would be dead. I'd certainly feel even worse about that, because it was all my fault he got involved in the first place. "Never forget," Odin said. Don't worry, Allfather, there's no chance of that.

After a while, I started to get that floaty feeling, where it seemed that my mind was separating form my body – it slept while my thoughts swirled around, slower and slower, until finally I just *was*. And then, I would fall asleep. Always happened. But as I floated there, staring at the infinite field of stars in my mind's eye, I felt something brush against my arm. Something with stiff, coarse hair. It made my skin crawl, and I snapped my head around to look at it.

There was nothing there. I thought I heard a faint rasping or clicking, but it could have been branches rubbing together. Then I noticed a door. Nothing else – no walls or floors – just a door floating in space. Light spilled out of the cracks around the frame. Was this some trick by Balcones? Didn't seem likely – I was already in his stupid maze – what else could he want? Besides, bright white light and demons don't often travel in the same circles.

It wasn't like I had anything better to do, so I opened it.

And I almost wished I hadn't. Behind the door was the place on the astral plane where Quinn and I had met for our nonphysical romantic encounters. They were sublimely beautiful and profoundly amazing, and couldn't happen again. Not if I wanted to protect my child and the rest of my family. I started to back out of the doorway when he called my name.

"Quinn, is that you?"

"I'm here. I've been trying to find you all day."

"Well, here I am. Are you okay?"

"For the moment. I don't have much time to talk, but I do have a plan. The only way I can think of to get out of here is to lure Balcones into the maze. Then we have to grab him and force him back through the portal. The best way to do that is if we all get to the center of the maze and wait. I'm sure he's set a trap there, so do nothing. Just wait for him to get mad enough to come to us."

"That sounds great. Except that we trudged around all day, looking for the center of the maze. We only found some monsters."

"Monsters? What did you see?"

"Well, there were three of them. A werewolf, a cyclops, and a huge scorpion."

Quinn laughed. "That's the trick. The monsters – they're me, Nick, and Malik. We've seen you, too. You look like Black Annis and a sphynx."

Marti shook her head. "I probably should have guessed that. But I would hate to have been wrong."

"I know." Quinn started to fade. "I have to get back. I think we have to work together to find the center. When you wake up, remember to find the monsters."

And then he faded into nothingness. Only the beautiful astral construction remained. A stream with a waterfall. Smell of plumerias and rain. Tropical flowers. Fantastic red, yellow, and blue birds. A canopied four poster bed. Intense green foliage. I sighed, backed up, and slammed the door.

When I woke up, Lulu and Hunter were sitting nearby, talking quietly. I yawned and stretched – a little stiff and sore, but more refreshed than I'd expected. My stomach growled loudly as I sat up. Lulu and Hunter both looked over. Dark circles underscored Lulu's eyes. Hunter's skin looked rough and grey, with dark stubble littering his jaw.

"It appears to be morning," I said, looking around. The mist was lighter than it had been before I went to sleep, anyway.

"You slept well, honey," Lulu said, a touch of jealousy in her voice.

Hunter glanced at Lulu, then back at me. "No bad dreams?"

That's an odd question. I rubbed the back of my neck, futilely trying to loosen the crick that made it hard to turn my head. "No, I don't think so. I don't really remember what I dreamed. Something about monsters in the maze, but I can't remember much about it. Didn't seem scary, though."

"Lucky you," Lulu said just loudly enough for me to hear her.

"You had bad dreams?" I asked her.

"Both of us," Hunter answered.

I nodded. What was I supposed to say? It wasn't like it was my fault. I tried to claw back the edge of the dream that had evaporated long before I woke up, but it was gone, leaving only ghostly fragments. *Monsters. Not scary. Maybe they were Muppets?* Nothing left to say about it. Best to change the subject. "What's the plan for today?"

"Plan?" Lulu echoed. "The plan is to get out of here. It's the execution we need to work on."

"If we're trying to get to the center of the maze, just following the wall won't work. That technique is only effective if you're trying to find an exit on an outer wall. Lulu said you tried drawing a line, but suddenly every intersection had lines."

"I didn't check *every* intersection, but yeah, the next couple of them had lines."

"Do you think it's possible that Nick and whomever he's with also used Trémaux's algorithm?"

"I might be able to tell you, if I knew what that was," I said.

"It's method for solving mazes that relies on drawing lines to mark the passages you've already visited. "

I looked at Lulu. "I suppose it's possible. Although we never saw them, not all day."

"You know what we need?" Lulu asked. "A bloodhound. And something for him to get the scent."

I laughed. "That'd be great, but...who has a bloodhound? Cú's got a great nose, but he's nowhere near here."

"Call him," Lulu replied.

"Why? There's no way he can hear me."

"Honey, you remember how he was able to attack Virginia's tulpa when nothing else could touch it? What if that means he can travel between dimensions? Because that's exactly where we are, isn't it? Trapped between dimensions?"

"Virginia's what?" Hunter asked.

"Long story short," Lulu said. "A tulpa is a thought-form, a mind energy creation. Virginia made one to prowl around the neighborhood to look for Marti."

I could tell from the expression on his face that didn't clarify things. But there wasn't time to explain right now. Maybe later. I closed my eyes. "Cú! Here boy! Come here, pup!" I said.

Nothing happened.

I tried again, a little louder, "Cú! Come!" I slapped the ground with my palms.

Still nothing. I felt my shoulders slump a little. "He's not coming." I stood up and dusted off my pants.

"I was so sure..." Lulu trailed off.

"Alright. Not trying to be rude, but can we please get back to the maze?" Hunter said.

I heard him before I saw him – the trilling yap of an excited puppy. He bounded out of the woods and jumped up to lick my face, his whole body wagging with excitement. "Cú!"

Hunter's mouth opened and closed a few times, but he didn't say anything.

"I knew it!" Lulu fairly cackled when she saw my puppy.

I picked the dog up, trying to calm him. That made it worse. I settled for trying to keep his tongue out of my mouth. "Okay, he's here. Now what?"

Quinn rolled his shoulders, hoping to alleviate at least some of the tight itchiness of his skin. He was going to need to spend some time in kelpie form soon, and for all of the dampness in the air, there wasn't so much as a puddle, much less a lake, to be found on the trail. As a kelpie, he breathed air, but without water to support his bulk, he'd slowly suffocate under his own weight on land.

"And you're sure it was Marti?" Nick asked, poking at the dirt with a soggy twig.

"Of course it was!" Phobetor snapped. "I don't make mistakes."

"And yet here you are, trapped like a rat in a maze," Malik replied, one eyebrow expertly arched.

A wash of pink momentarily colored the nightmare god's eternally pallid cheeks. "I-"

"Enough!" Quinn broke in. "We've enough problems as it is. The last thing we need is to tear each other apart. I have every reason to believe," he glanced at Nick, "reasons I won't go into, that it was actually Marti I spoke with. I think that we have to team up to get to the center, which is why Balcones has us looking like monsters to each other. Once we've found the heart of the maze, we'll need to lure Balcones in. I don't see any other way out but to grab him and force him back through a portal. I told Marti to look for the monsters – they were us. "

Phobetor crossed his arms. "I doubt she'll remember. You should have let me scare her."

Nick glared at him.

"People may or may not remember their pleasant dreams, but no one forgets their nightmares. I'm just saying."

Nick snarled, "Who gives you the right-"

"I am a god! I just used what's already in your head, and believe me, there was plenty to work with. Don't blame me for that."

"Seriously? All you gods are the same – self-important, entitled-" Malik broke in.

"Bloody hell!" Quinn shouted. "Get yourselves under control. You can have a comparative religion debate after we've got out of here. But right now we've got to find Marti and Lulu, rescue Nick's babies, and capture Balcones, if we can. All without springing whatever traps that blighter has set for us. And did I mention the bloody Keres are just about breathing down the back of our necks? If we're not out of here before they show up, we likely won't make it."

"Speak for yourself," Nick said, his voice dour.

"What's that supposed to mean, coming from a mortal?" Phobetor sneered.

Quinn shook his head. *I'd forgotten about that.* "It's complicated, but essentially, he was given the life force of a Valkyrie."

"I can't die," Nick added, shaking his head slightly.

"A Valkyrie, eh? They aren't all that different from the Keres," Phobetor said.

"The only similarity is that they both attend battles, seeking the dead and dying. That and they're immortal. There's almost no way to kill," Malik's eyes fell on Nick, and he trailed off. "...a Valkyrie." His eyes snapped to Quinn's. "Do you think Balcones knows this?"

Quinn turned nearly as ghastly pale as Phobetor. "I...don't *think* so."

"What difference does it make?" Nick asked, irritably.

"You've never seen a demon feed, have you?" Malik asked.

"No."

"Demons," Quinn said, "suck the life force out of their prey, pooling it with their own, and leaving nothing but a pile of dust behind. They're not immortal...but if they consumed the life force of an immortal..."

"Balcones would be unstoppable," Malik finished.

Three birdlike shadows slid out of the trees and raced across the ground. The raucous cawing of crows followed. The Keres had arrived.

I was cold, tired, and hungry. And, to be honest, extremely demoralized. It was hard to put one foot in front of the other, to try one more pathway, hoping for a different result than a dead end or a big loop. I was sick to death of being here and being away from Cassie. I was usually pretty good with puzzles, but this maze was kicking my butt. I'd utterly failed. If Hunter thought he could solve it, I was happy to let him have a try. Still, I resented being in a position where I needed rescuing. *Stupid Balcones.*

Cú had settled down to the point where he was flopped on his back, tongue lolling into the dirt. I suspect he'd been hoping for a belly rub, but fell asleep before that happened. I wasn't sure what we were going to do with him, especially in light of the fact that I'd considered changing his name to 'Mr. Underfoot.'

Crows cackled in the near distance, and I shuddered. There was something wrong about their cries. I didn't know what. Anger? Dissonance? Lulu must have sensed it, too, because she looked up and scanned the trees.

"What?" Hunter asked, seeing Lulu looking around. "It's just crows. Isn't it?"

Lulu shrugged. "Maybe. We should get moving, hon. We'll never find the way out just sitting here."

I stood up. Cú didn't stir – he was so deeply asleep he was snoring, so I scooped him up in my arms. He snuggled sleepily against my chest and went back to his nap.

"Why don't we try your method?" I asked Hunter. "Since ours clearly worked so well yesterday."

He nodded, and we started down the path.

It wasn't long before we got to a T intersection. "Left or right?" Hunter asked. He looked around for something to mark the trail with. I handed him the silver dagger from my backpack.

"Left," Lulu answered.

Hunter drew a line with an arrow, indicating our choice. We continued down the path, marking our turns. Some of them had lines when we arrived, and some of them didn't. That made me feel hopeful that perhaps Hunter was right – Quinn's group had made the marks, and it wasn't some infernal trick of the maze.

We'd travelled for perhaps half an hour, and Cú was getting heavy in my arms. I was ready to put him down before I dropped him. As we rounded a corner, I nearly crashed into Hunter, who had stopped dead in front of me.

"Monsters," he whispered.

I looked. It was the same three we'd seen the day before. "They don't seem to have seen us. Let's just retreat quietly."

"No. We'll have to fight them."

"What?" Lulu and I whispered together. "That's crazy," I added. For some reason, the ridiculous image of the monsters sitting down at a picnic with us flashed across my brain. I shook it off. That was going way too far.

I could hear the flapping of wings. *Caw! Caw! Caw!*

"No," Lulu said. "I…think…maybe he's right. We must kill them before they kill us."

"With what? Are you nuts?"

Hunter re-gripped the hilt of the dagger.

I gave an exasperated sigh and yanked one of the arrows out of my backpack. "Fine. Here's my weapon. Which one should I take on? The werewolf? It's at least six inches taller than me an outweighs me by what? A hundred pounds? Maybe the giant scorpion? His pincers are only what? Twice the length of this arrow? Three times? I'm sure that'll work out well. Should I leave the cyclops for you, or for Lulu?"

Hunter scowled at me. "They're monsters. They can't be talked to or reasoned with. What choice do we have?"

"Sometimes discretion is the better part of valor, hon," Lulu said. The glazed look from moments earlier had left her eyes.

A vein in Hunter's forehead throbbed.

The werewolf raised his arm and howled. *They'd seen us.*

Lulu grabbed Hunter's hand and started to drag him down the path, "Run, you fool!" she shouted. She didn't have to tell me twice.

"Marti!" Quinn shouted, raising his hand to wave. The sphynx and Black Annis turned and fled. Oddly enough, they'd been joined by a third creature – a spindly grey biped with over-large eyes – who was either debilitated or reluctant to move. Black Annis had to drag him, and the sphynx carried something black. It was about the size of a large house cat, and very wiggly.

"It doesn't look like she remembered her sweet dream," Phobetor said, smug grin on his face. "I hate to say 'I told you so.' Actually, no, I don't."

"Now what?" Nick snapped. "Chasing after them will just make it worse. Any more brilliant ideas?"

Quinn didn't like the glint in Malik's eyes when the djinn said, "That may be our only choice."

"I think we can outflank them," Quinn replied. "Malik, you and Nick keep going down this path. Phobetor and I will go back and take the trail that circles around. Hopefully, we'll catch them in the middle."

"Agreed," Malik replied.

Quinn turned and sprinted in the opposite direction, a pale and unhappy Phobetor trailing in his wake. "Keep up!" he shouted over his shoulder.

The path turned, then turned again. If they were lucky, Marti and company would have kept heading in the direction they took when they fled. It was possible that they would take the left turn instead of going straight, but it seemed unlikely to him – they were running in fear – and he was sure they'd take the path of least resistance. Of course, he wasn't sure what he'd do when he found them. Marti clearly didn't remember the dream.

A faint shadow, bird shaped, coursed along the dirt path, keeping pace with him. *Fantastic.* The last thing he needed was one of the war-mongering Keres sisters meddling in his plans. He glanced up as he ran, and caught a glimpse of a dark, winged shape wreathed in the perpetual mist of this place.

This cursed place! I spend so much of my life on helping these weak, pathetic humans.

There they were, just up ahead. He held up a hand. Phobetor stopped, panting. The trio ahead saw him and stopped. They tried to bolt in the other direction, but found themselves facing Nick and Malik.

"Now we've got them!" Quinn shouted, his voice throaty with battle lust. He moved forward slowly. Malik and Nick closed in from the other side.

Phobetor grabbed Quinn's arm and shook him.

Horrified, he stopped. Those weren't enemies. They were Marti, Lulu, and another human. *Did Nick and Malik have the same craving for combat and blood?*

Quinn's cohorts continued to press the group in the middle, pushing them unwillingly towards Phobetor and himself. The newest addition, the grey humanoid, carried a silver dagger, which he held in front of his midsection, daring anyone to approach.

Caw! Caw! Caw! One crow was answered by two others. Strident cries for bloodsport.

Again, Quinn reminded himself that these were friends, not foes. But he struggled to control the rage that was rising in his chest.

As the group got closer, he saw that the wriggling black thing held by the sphynx was a puppy. *Cú.* How did he get here? Had the new arrival brought him, or had he found his own way to Marti?

Nick charged the group.

"No!" Quinn screamed.

Nick kept coming.

Time dilated. Seconds took minutes to unfold. Cú leapt out of the sphynx's arms toward the trees. She turned and snatched at him, just catching the end of his tail as he soared through the invisible barrier. Black Annis grabbed Marti's arm with one hand, and the skin of the grey alien's back. They also started to pass through the barrier.

"Grab them!" Malik yelled.

Nick was closest, and he caught the knife hand of the grey creature, who'd been thrown off balance from being dragged by Lulu. Malik tried to capture the grey's other hand while he fought wildly.

"Don't use the knife. Don't give them blood. You'll only make it worse!" Phobetor shouted.

He and Quinn lurched into the melee.

"Go! Go!" Quinn ordered. "Through the wall! Now!"

Nick and Malik shifted from tugging to pushing, and the four of them tumbled in an angry heap into the forest on the other side of the barrier. The grey creature rolled as he hit the ground and leapt to its feet.

Nick tackled him and the two of them rolled from side to side, each trying to gain the advantage. Malik and Black Annis - no, not Black Annis; Lulu - circled each other warily. Quinn looked at the sphynx. Marti. She held a squirming Cú in her arms. He knew it was Marti. But all he saw was an enemy. He fought to tamp down the aggression that threatened to overwhelm him, and he panted with the strain, as if it were a physical battle. *Is that a tear on her cheek? What am I doing? I can't hurt Marti.*

Caw! Caw! Caw!

The awful screeching of the Keres tipped the balance, and he took one loping stride and leapt at Marti. She went sprawling and he scrabbled for her throat. Cú yelped as he skidded and rolled into the underbrush.

Marti struggled, but his weight pinned her to the rough ground. As his hands found her throat, his fingers got caught up in a chain around her neck. Angrily, he tugged at it. He felt the pendant that was attached to it – a locket or some such thing – give way. What felt like an electric shock shuddered through his body, and he was blinded by a flash of blue light.

Dammit! I'd hoped that getting through the barrier would at least buy us some time. But no, they had to grab onto Hunter and get pulled through with us. Now, here I stand, trying to face down a werewolf. Again. At least the last time, there had been a sliding glass door between us. And Quinn had my back. Now there was nothing but a little mist.

Cú wriggled furiously in my arms. Did he think he could take that thing on? *Don't be in such a hurry to be an hors d'oeuvre. You're staying right here with me.*

I glanced away from the werewolf's distorted canine face and saw that Hunter was rolling on the ground with the cyclops and Lulu was engaged with the scorpion. We were almost certainly going to die here in these dank woods. Memories I hadn't had a chance to make of all the things I'd miss seeing as Cassie grew up flashed through my head, and I felt a tear trickle out of my eye.

Crows squawked, and the werewolf lunged at me. I dropped Cú and heard him yelp as the monster crashed into me. I tried to get away, but the wolfman was too big. I looked into its deep red eyes as it grabbed me by the throat. Its breath smelled surprisingly of fish. It was almost as if I was observing the whole thing from just over my left shoulder – ridiculous, because I was on my back on the ground, for one thing. And yet, I calmly noted the stink of his breath and wondered if the thin, patchy hair on his snout was normal, or due to mange. Did werewolves even get mange? Random thoughts bubbled up, then drifted away as more appeared, crowding out the final seconds of my life.

I winced as the chain from my prayer box dug into my neck. The werewolf had gotten his fingers caught in it and jerked it hard. I heard it click, then I felt something small and icy fall onto my sternum.

Brilliant blue light flashed. I closed my eyes against the glare. The grief-hoarse voice of Odin whispered in my ear, "Never forget."

And I remembered.

I was catapulted into the astral love nest I'd shared with Quinn. But I wasn't really there – it was a memory. Quinn was there, telling me that the monsters in the maze were not really monsters at all, but him, Nick, and Malik. We had to work together. But how could this be? One of those three was in the middle of asphyxiating me. Was this memory real, or just hypoxia –final hallucinations as my oxygen-starved brain shut down? Still, it wasn't unpleasant, and I knew from experience that there were worse ways to die.

I had to close my eyes against the concentrated blue light that exploded out of the icy crystal on my chest. It engulfed everything like a chilly tide and blinded me.

The rough hands around my neck stopped squeezing, and I gasped for air. Something scrambled through the leaf litter, and I heard Cú's shrill whine. His paws shed dirt on my face as he clambered over me, barking and licking. His weight suddenly left me. I opened one eye just a sliver, and saw the blue light had gone. I waited another second or so, and opened my eyes.

I blinked, trying to adjust to dimness. Instead of a werewolf leaning over me, there was Quinn. He was trying to hold Cú back so he didn't trample my face. But the pup was just as happy to share the slobbery love with him. Quinn's face, however was ashen and anguished.

"I'm so sorry," he said. "I didn't want to hurt you. It was the Keres. They're driving everyone mad with fear and rage."

He stood, then helped me up. When his eyes fell on my throat, he closed them for a long moment and swallowed hard.

I looked away, on the pretext of searching for Odin's tear and returning it to the prayer box. I wanted to tell him everything was fine and it wasn't his fault. But I couldn't. He'd wanted to kill me. Even if he had been goaded into it by these Keres, whatever they were, surely he still had some volition, some control of his actions.

When I didn't answer, his eyes searched mine and he reached out to touch my face. I involuntarily pulled away.

His shoulders slumped a little and he said again, "I'm so sorry."

"I know," I replied. It killed me to pull away from him, but I what choice did I have? I should have listened to Lulu from the beginning – he was dangerous. Even though I wanted him more than ever, now.

Nick ran over to us. He reached out and put his hand on my shoulder. "Are you okay?"

No, not really. "I'm fine." Nick frowned slightly. Perhaps he knew I was lying. I held his eyes a moment longer, then looked for Lulu. She, Malik, Hunter, and some guy I didn't know were headed our way, looking only slightly the worse for wear. As they got closer, my mouth dropped open. *What? No way.* That's the weird guy from the street corner, who helped Balcones kidnap Lulu and me.

"Well, we're in the woods now," Lulu said. Her eyes lingered on the stranger.

"Did that flash mean the barrier dissolved, or is that something else?" Nick asked. He went over to the place we'd all entered and reached out toward the path. Nothing got in his way. He stepped out of the trees and onto the dirt. But when he tried to come back, he was blocked. Malik reached his hand out and pulled him through the barrier.

"Your question is answered," Malik said.

"Seems to be a one-way flow," Hunter commented. "As long as someone is on this side, we should be alright."

The man I didn't know grunted. "The rule doesn't seem to apply to my sisters," he said sourly. A large black feather fluttered down in front of us. "They get a pass on everything."

I looked up at the trees, but they were high up, and there was a lot of fog between us, so I didn't get a very good look at them.

"Let's just hold up a minute here. Who are you? Why did you help Balcones bring us here?"

"He did what?" Quinn and Nick asked in unison.

The man shifted he weight backwards and let out a deep sigh. "Phobetor. My name is Phobetor. Perhaps you've heard of me?" He ignored Nick and Quinn.

Who does this guy think he is? "No, I haven't. Why are you helping Balcones?"

His shoulders drooped. "Education clearly isn't what it used to be. *I* am the god of nightmares." He reached out towards me, but instead of a hand it was a clawed spider foot.

"Aaaah," I said jumping back. In the blink of an eye, his hand was normal again. It happened so quickly that I wasn't sure anyone else saw it. I wasn't even one hundred percent sure I'd seen it.

"Yes," he said. "I did help Balcones capture you and your friend, but it's not what you think. I'm just as much a victim as you are."

Lulu snorted.

"It's true," he continued. "Balcones approached me, 'Let's go out for a glass of mead – I have a business proposition I'd like to discuss,' he said. Just because I'm a god doesn't mean I can't try new things, now does it?"

I didn't answer, just shrugged.

"So I went with him. Thought it might be a lark, a bit of fun, you know?"

"Kidnapping is a bit of fun?" Lulu asked, her hands on her hips.

"Did I mention I am the God of *Nightmares*?" he shot back.

Nick jumped in. "You keep saying you're a god, so why can't you get us out of here?"

Malik snickered. Phobetor's face darkened and his eyes glinted with anger.

"And what's with the harpies?" Nick continued. "They don't—"

"Shhhh!" Phobetor's eyes widened. "Do not insult the Keres – they hate the harpies! You'll bring them down on our heads right now."

He looked up into the trees. Everyone else did, too. There didn't seem to be any movement above us.

"Enough! Regardless of what the Keres decide to do," Quinn said, "we need to find our way to the center of the maze. I think that's our best option."

"What if we have the dog lead us through one of the outer walls? He seems to be able to go through just fine," Hunter said.

"I'm not going to just walk out of here without my kids," Nick growled.

"And we do not know what is on the other side of the wall. If we cross through the barrier randomly, there is no means of predicting where we would end up. It could be worse than this, much worse," Malik said.

I watched Lulu sit down, back against one of the twisted trees. She closed her eyes and put her hands on one of her knees. *Wish I had some ibuprofen for you, my friend.*

Quinn rubbed his forehead, as if he could massage ideas out of his prefrontal cortex. "Phoebetor, you've been exploring the maze – do you have any insight on how to get to the center?"

"Yes. There is a small stream that flows through the heart of the maze. If we can find the stream and follow it, we can locate the center."

Quinn turned to Cú, who was sprawled out by my leg. He said something to my pup in a language that I was nowhere close to understanding. It was like a song, but instead of musical notes, it was composed of nature sounds. Cú seemed to know exactly what Quinn wanted, because he jumped up and started yapping before he trotted off into the trees. Quinn hurried after him.

"Don't let him get lost!" I called after him. As if our whole sad group was anything but lost.

Phobetor and Malik hurried to catch up to Quinn. Nick and I helped Lulu up, while Hunter awkwardly supervised. Once Lulu was on her feet, Hunter ran ahead to keep the others in sight. Nick, Lulu and I followed after him. In a stunning display of grace and skill, I tripped over a root and would have done a faceplant into the leaf litter if Nick hadn't caught me. I blamed my lack of coordination on low blood sugar.

"Thanks," I said.

He just nodded. His eyes were hard and his jaw clenched. He looked about as grim as I'd ever seen anyone look, and it scared me. I didn't think he would try to hurt me, but then again, I didn't think Quinn would try to kill me, and that had only just happened. It may well be the Keres, but outside influence or no, I still would have been dead and Cassie would still have been an orphan.

There was a shuddering in the branches above us. Unquiet wings beat the air, and the three of us looked up to see what fresh hell was headed our way.

She, and I only called her that because her torn, bloodstained dress caught the breeze from her wings and intermittently exposed her large and withered breasts, descended slowly from the canopy, fog swirling at the tips of her black wings. Fangs, like a saber-toothed cat, protruded from wide mouth, and her eyes were all white, like an ancient Greek sculpture.

Nick stepped in front of me as this thing reached out for us with hands that were more like eagles' claws than human appendages.

Lulu bent and scooped up a handful of dirt and rotting leaves. "Get out of here!" *Tsssst! Tsssst!* She threw the dirt at the face of the Kere, who backed off some, but didn't leave.

I wasn't entirely sure if she grinned or just bared her teeth. I expect both of those expressions looked pretty much the same on her.

Lulu pulled a mini-Maglite flashlight out of her pocket and raised it toward the intruder. The creature put up her arms to shield her eyes, then hissed and returned to the branches.

"We need to hurry," I said, picking up my pace.

The Keres squabbled in the limbs above, out of our sight.

"She's right," Nick added, then took Lulu by the wrist. We'd just broken into a jog when Hunter ran towards us.

"They've found the stream. This way!"

Lulu was limping, and since Hunter was here to guide us, we slowed our pace from a trot to a fast walk. It didn't take long to reach the others.

Quinn looked up when we arrived, but turned his head and said nothing. He may as well have shoved me away from him. I bit my lip, hard, to cause one pain to distract myself from another pain. It was better this way, at least safer, anyway, even if I hated it.

Black roots tangled across each other, twining together and plunging into the murky water. The current was fast, and white foam collected in some of the denser clumps of roots. It was impossible to tell how deep the water was, and the channel was too wide to jump across. The thought of trying to wade that stream filled me with a sense of foreboding. It was easy to imagine getting a foot stuck in the knotted roots and drowning, or some huge predator lurking in the gloom, ready to snap its toothy jaws shut on the first appendage that got near it.

No one else seemed eager to go too near the edge of the water, either.

"Should we try to cross it?" Lulu asked.

Quinn shook his head. "No. The water's moving too fast. Besides, these things are often enchanted – we'd best not touch the water unless we absolutely have to. Let's just follow it for now."

We stumbled along the root-covered bank, talking very little. Hard to tell if it was exhaustion, hunger, or the miasmic vapor of the water next to us that weighed down our tongues. I don't know how long we walked – an hour and a half, perhaps two. I couldn't go any further. The blisters that had started on my pinky toes yesterday had swelled and ruptured. Now blood was seeping through the sides of my tennies. Each step hurt more than the last. We came to a fallen tree – the perfect height for a makeshift bench.

"Can we take a break? I really need to sit down for a minute," I said, sitting down.

"The more breaks we take, the longer it will be before we get to the center," Nick said, irritated.

"I really need to sit," I said, holding one red-stained shoe up off the ground. He winced, then sighed with resignation.

"I, too, would like a break," Malik joined in.

"Fine. Five minutes," Quinn replied. He took a step towards us and opened his mouth like he was going to say something, but he turned and walked into the trees. Phobetor went with him.

"I wish I had my purse – I have a little first aid kit in there," Lulu said.

"I wish I had some ibuprofen," I said running my hands through my hair. I was starting to think sitting down had been a mistake – my feet throbbed against my shoes. Even so, I didn't want to take them off – I didn't relish the thought of peeling my sock off of my raw skin.

Hunter stared after Quinn and Phobetor for a moment. He took off his shirt (which was a pleasant change of scenery) and used his pocket knife to make some holes where the long sleeves joined the shoulder. Then he ripped the sleeves off.

"I don't have any plasters, either, but I think taking your shoes off would be a good start. That raw skin will just get worse inside your damp shoes." He fished around in his pants pocket. "I do have these." He pulled out a pocket pack of tissues.

He knelt in front of me and took off one of my bloody shoes. I winced as he touched the sock. He pulled it off far faster than I expected, but I couldn't help but cringe when the dank cold air hit my wound. His hands were gentle as he packed the swollen and bloody toes in tissue, then wrapped my foot in his torn-off sleeve. *Shame about the girlfriend. And one who I knew from way back, to boot.* He started on the other foot. I started to cry. I couldn't help it. I missed Cassie so much, and I'd all but lost hope that we'd ever get out of this miserable place.

Quinn and Phobetor returned from the trees, carrying a big stick. Phobetor brought it over to me.

"It's not much of a walking stick, but it's the best we could find on short notice," he said.

"Thanks."

Quinn and Nick stood together, a little way from the rest of us, obviously eager to get back on the trail. If Quinn was jealous of Hunter's attention to me, he didn't show it. Was it self-control or just that he'd never really cared anyway? When Hunter finished with my foot, I thanked him and stood up. It wasn't the most comfortable pair of shoes I'd ever had, but the pain was now bearable. I must have looked like a medieval beggar - filthy, with my feet wrapped in rags and my shoes tied together and slung over one shoulder. It didn't matter that Quinn was off limits and Hunter had a girlfriend – no one was going to look at me in this state and think romance. *Just as well.* I felt bad that Cú had to walk, but there was no way I could carry him now.

We carried on for about another two miles, or maybe it just felt that way.

"Look!" Lulu said. "Is that the central wall? Why does it have a wall? None of the rest of the maze did."

"It is definitely a wall," Malik said. "Unknown if it is the central boundary."

Quinn held up a hand to stop us. "We have no idea what is inside, if that really is the center. There's been no sign of the Keres since early this morning, and it's a safe bet that they're up to something. Marti, since you're incapacitated, and we might be met with force at the center of the maze, why don't you stay behind so you can pull us back out through the wall if need be."

I nodded. I wasn't going to be much use to anyone, anyway, given the state I was in.

"I'll go in first to do recon," Nick said.

"Agreed," Quinn replied.

We approached the wall as quietly as a group of ragged travelers could. That is to say, not very. We stopped and Nick put his ear to the damp grey limestone to listen – and almost went halfway through.

"I'll spot you," Hunter said, "Pull you back through when you're done."

"Sure." Nick cautiously put his hands and face against the stone and eased himself through the wall. Hunter pushed his own face into the center. I thought I heard a crash, and searched the trees for the Keres. Nothing.

In less than five minutes, Hunter pulled Nick back into our space.

He shook his head, dejected. "The only thing in there was a stupid glass ball on a pedestal."

I knew how disappointed he must be to not have found his kids. I was disappointed, too.

The ground started to shake beneath us. Bare tree branches rattled and clashed against each other, and twigs rained down.

Quinn looked up. "Nick? What did you do?"

Chapter 25
Guardians

didn't do anything," Nick snapped.

He glared as Quinn held his gaze. "There was a crash. We all heard it."

Nick's eyes blazed in silence for a few more seconds. "Fine. I kicked the pedestal. It fell. The glass broke. Satisfied?"

The shaking grew worse, and the ground started to make a deep, growling rumble that chilled me to my very core. Fissures snaked through the wall in front of us. I sat down so I wouldn't fall over.

As suddenly as it started, the temblor stopped.

Hunter glanced around. "Is that good?"

Malik and Lulu answered at once: "No."

Quinn's hands were shaking as he snarled at Nick, "You weren't supposed to touch anything. No one was —"

The stone wall exploded.

Nick tackled Lulu before she was hit in the face by a cantaloupe-sized chunk of rock. Cú and I scrambled behind a tree. Stone fragments ricocheted off trees and splashed into the stream.

"This is outrageous!" Phobetor complained from behind a nearby oak. "Balcones never said anything about —"

"Shut up!" Malik hissed.

Where is Quinn? I peered around the tree, but couldn't see him anywhere.

White limestone dust hung like smog in the air. Three enormous creatures stepped out of the rubble, head and shoulders above the surrounding trees. Their lumpy skin was greenish-grey, and while mostly human-shaped, they reminded me of walking rock slides.

"Trolls," muttered Malik. "I hate trolls."

I didn't think there were a lot of bridges these things would fit under.

The troll in the center, who was slightly taller than the other two, swung his knotty club and roared. It was loud enough to hurt my ears, and it sounded like boulders tumbling and sliding against each other.

My pulse pounded in my throat as adrenalin surged through my body. Flight was looking a lot better than fight. The trolls were stiff and slow-moving — if we ran now, they'd never catch us.

"Come on!" I yelled, standing up with Cú tucked like a loaf under my arm. "Let's go!" I glanced around at the others. *Where is Quinn?*

We started to run pell-mell through the trees. I looked over my shoulder to reassure myself of the growing gap between us and them, but I stopped to stare instead. One by one, the trolls changed from slow-moving giants to wolves that covered the ground in huge loping bounds that we had no hope of outrunning.

One of them yelped. A large reptilian head on a long neck erupted from the water and snatched the pony-sized canid mid-stride as it galloped along the stream bank. They both disappeared into the murk, and the water frothed white with the underwater struggle. Then it went still. A few tufts of canine hair floated to the surface and were carried down the stream.

Well, at least I knew where Quinn was.

The troll-wolves now seemed confused. They didn't dare to go near the bank, but they stood on their hind legs and craned their necks at the water, presumably looking for signs of their lost companion. The pair went back on all fours before they raised their heads and long, shrill howls shuddered out of them.

But what scared me were the answering calls.

They sounded far away, but I'd seen how fast those monster wolves could run.

Nick frowned. "They're calling for reinforcements."

Hunter eyed the trees, their tops shrouded in thick mist. "You think they can climb?"

Malik looked at him as if he had just asked if the moon was made of green cheese. "They are mountain trolls. They can shapeshift into anything they wish."

"Aren't the Keres up there somewhere, anyway?" I asked.

Lulu looked pensive. "What about the stream? The trolls won't go near it – could we swim to the center?"

Nick ran his hand through his hair. "I'm not sure there's even a point to that now."

"Did you fail to notice there's a monster in the water?" Hunter asked.

"That, um," *he isn't really going to believe me, is he?* "is Quinn."

"I'm sorry?"

"That is the natural form of Quinn," Malik said. "Were you not aware he was a kelpie?"

Hunter opened his mouth, then shut it again.

"Hey!" Nick shouted. "Plan now, argue later. We're about to be overrun."

The wolf-trolls had started edging closer.

"Get to the water," Lulu said.

That backed them off, although Hunter shifted uncomfortably and kept looking into the stream. I could see something large and dark beneath the surface, and I hoped it was Quinn.

"There may be portals at the center," Malik said. "We may find less danger in entering an unknown portal than we face here."

"He's probably right," Lulu said.

I caught sight of movement in my peripheral vision and whipped my head towards it. The black, slick-skinned head that rose out of the water had a mouth large enough to bite me in half. Its eyes were black from edge to edge. If that wasn't Quinn, we were in real trouble. It reminded me of a Komodo dragon, and I wondered if kelpies also had a toxic bite. I didn't want to find out.

We eased past the trolls, who snarled at us, then picked up speed as we headed towards the remains of the central portion of the maze.

The round center of the maze was surrounded by a wall, with the break where the maze path entered the interior. Only about half of that was still standing, the side furthest from us. The wall closest to us had been smashed by the mountain trolls, and was nothing but scattered rubble.

In the center, near the stream, lay the broken pedestal and shattered gazing sphere. Hunter seemed drawn towards it, and he picked up a piece of glass. He looked like he'd been zapped by a heavy static charge. I thought he might have cut himself, but I saw no blood.

"What now?" Phobetor said, over-loudly.

Hunter threw the glass down. "We have to get out of here!"

Caw! Caw! Caw!

The Keres fluttered down from their hiding place, blocking the maze path. The two trolls had come up to the broken wall quickly and silently as wolves, then shifted back into their giant stony selves. At least a dozen wolves lurked at the edges of the trees. Whether they were actual wolves or trolls, I couldn't tell. Still, they would not approach the stream, where death, in the form of Quinn, lurked.

Balcones stepped through a portal and appeared directly in front of us, shaking his head. "It's so hard to find good help. If you want something done right, you have to do it yourself."

He turned to Phobetor. "You. You were supposed to keep them awake and off balance, and here I find you strolling around with them like you're all best of friends." He shook his head. "Must be true what they say – 'Never send a god to do a demon's job.'"

Phobetor's eyes glowed green, but he fumed in silence. The Keres shrieked and screeched to each other, and I felt anger wash over me like acid rain. This was all Quinn's fault. If it wasn't for him, I'd be home with Cassie right now. My jaw clenched as I turned towards the stream, and I felt my hands curling into fists.

Phobetor's body twisted and warped, and he took the form of a huge spider. He scuttled up into the trees and vanished into the mist.

"Coward," I spat.

I turned to Lulu. Her eyes were huge with fear, and I felt even angrier. One of the trolls raised its arms in the air and roared. The wargs in the forest began to wail, deep, throaty howls of rage.

Bring it. If we're going to die in this wretched place, let's get on with it. Maybe we can take some with us.

"Where is that cursed kelpie?" Balcones asked, looking around. I want him to have a front row seat as his friends are torn to shreds."

His eyes fell on Cú, who sat at my feet. "Pathetic," Balcones sneered. "This is the best MAMIC has to offer? Their standards have fallen over the years." He took a step forward and reached out his hand towards my puppy.

Two things happened simultaneously, so I'm a little fuzzy on some of the details. Out of my peripheral vision, I saw something grey fall out of the trees and land on the Keres. They began to shriek and yell as they were caught in a net of rope-sized spider web and pulled up into the canopy.

In front of me, Cú suddenly grew to the size of a bull. Balcones took a step back. So did I. Cú's ears flattened against his head, and a deep snarl rumbled through his body. It made the hair on the back of my neck stand up, and I knew he was on my team. I was behind him and a little to the side, so I couldn't be sure, but it looked like his eyes were glowing red.

Balcones muttered something that I assumed was cursing, but it was not in any language I knew. I had a sudden appreciation of Quinn's gift to Cassie and me - a silly little puppy that could turn in an instant into a fearsome protector. Perhaps I'd underestimated how much Quinn cared about us.

One of the wargs stalked into the heart of the maze. His yellow eyes were bright against his charcoal fur. "Balcones," he said in a deep, raspy voice. "You lied to us."

"I most certainly did not," the demon sputtered.

I looked at Malik, who shrugged. Lulu stayed close to Nick and Hunter. Clearly, none of them wanted to get close to the huge growling beast that Cú had suddenly become, even if he was keeping Balcones at bay.

The warg bared his teeth. "You told us that there would be great carnage, and enough fallen humans for us gorge upon. I see only five, and one of them has hardly any meat on its bones." The wolf eyed Malik. "That is barely enough for my mate and I, much less the entire pack."

Yellow eyes, too many to count, glowed between the gnarled trees. I shuddered. So many sharp teeth beneath those eyes. They could easily overwhelm us, Quinn and Cú notwithstanding. If Balcones was going to have a falling out with the wargs, the last place I wanted to be was in the middle of it, especially if we might still be on the menu. The atmosphere felt spring-loaded, as if any movement would set off the trap.

Movement to my left as Nick charged toward Balcones. "Where are they? Where are my kids?" he roared. "We got to the center of the maze. Give. Them. Back."

Balcones chuckled, and the angry warg lunged at Nick. Its teeth raked Nick's arm as Cú threw himself at the beast, sending it sprawling. It got ungracefully back on its feet and snarled, but it backed away, tail tucked between its legs. I could hardly blame it – Cú was almost three times its size.

As the green Valkyrie fire crackled down Nick's arm, healing the gashes left by the warg, Balcones' eyes started to glow and his mouth opened in an awful grin. He strode toward Nick.

"No!" Malik shouted. "Nick, run!"

Nick just stood there. Did he think he had a shot at Balcones?

Cú wheeled around from where he had vanquished the warg, but he wouldn't reach Balcones before Balcones reached Nick.

Water spewed from the stream as Quinn's monstrous kelpie head shot out and grabbed the back of Nick's shirt, pulling him into the water.

Balcones howled with anger. "Get him!"

The mountain trolls both roared and the earth shook as the one with the club smashed it against the ground. They lumbered toward us.

The wargs, however, melted like ghosts into the forest.

"Get in the water! Go! Go!" yelled Lulu.

We turned and pelted towards the stream. "Cú! Come!" I shouted over my shoulder.

"I cannot swim!" Malik shouted.

Hunter grabbed him by the arm as he jumped into the water, dragging the djinn with him. Lulu and I were close behind. Cú loped up, easily catching us. We didn't have time to stop and dive, we just leaped off the bank into the dark water. I had no idea how deep it was, and I sucked in a deep breath as my feet left the ground.

Instead of splashing over my head into the murk, I landed very comfortably on something large and slick. The first thing I thought was 'dolphin,' but that would have been ridiculous.

It was Quinn.

In kelpie form, his body was about as long as a Chevy Suburban, but not as wide. Nick dangled from Quinn's teeth, swearing furiously, as Quinn carefully swung him over to his own back. It seemed that the kelpie expected us all to ride him down the stream, like some bizarre amusement park boat. While we were trying to scramble into position, Cú leaped off the bank to join us. *He's going to knock all of us into the water, and maybe even sink Quinn.* But as he jumped, he shrank from gargantuan shaggy dog to little smooth puppy. Hunter caught him and handed him to me. Lulu was still draped across Quinn's back between Hunter and I when he started to move, but we were all mostly in place.

Balcones ran along the bank, but even weighed down, Quinn cut through the water like a motorboat, his powerful flippers propelling us along fast enough to churn the water up onto the banks in a froth.

We had to hold on tight as Quinn ducked under the still-standing section of wall that had passed over the stream. Balcones cursed and shouted behind us. The trolls roared with him. But every beat of Quinn's leathery paddles put that much more distance between us and them.

We had escaped. Sort of. We were still in Balcones' maze, and not sure where we were headed, other than downstream. But it was better than nothing. My only regret was that we didn't have Nick's kids with us.

I shivered. We were traveling fast, but I didn't think we were going fast enough to make me feel so cold. I didn't want to completely change my balance, but something wasn't right. My skin felt tight and painfully cold, especially around my throat and chest. I raised one hand to my sternum. The water on my skin and my wet clothes had frozen. I held the prayer box away from my throat and noticed that icicles hung from it. *That's odd.*

While I didn't I relax and enjoy this river cruise from hell, at least Balcones and the mountain trolls weren't breathing down the backs of our necks. The root-twined banks and bare trees could have well been a video loop, but subtly at first, the banks began to rise around us, as if the stream had somehow cut its way through a low hill. The bones of the hill were a dull grey rock that failed to glisten even where the water lapped up against it. Still, I couldn't help but hope that this change in scenery meant something. Different had to be good, right?

"Sharks!" Malik screamed.

No way. I turned to look. Sure enough, two sets of black dorsal fins and tails, single file, rushed towards us. They were huge, maybe even larger than Quinn. And they were gaining.

Hunter had also turned to look. "We have to get out of the water!"

Quinn thrashed his thick tail and added some speed, but not enough. They were still catching up.

"Sandbar. Up ahead!" Hunter yelled.

As the stream curved a little, there was a pile of sand flattened against the bank. The two problems with the sandbar were that one, the bank stream overhung it – it would be difficult at best to scramble up it; and two, if we didn't get up the bank, we'd be trapped on a narrow sandbar between two huge sharks and a rocky wall at least twice my height. Those brutes could easily beach and grab us. I watched in morbid fascination as the sharks steadily closed on us.

Quinn barely slowed when he hit the sandbar. We were all launched onto it, and he shifted into his human form before we'd regained our balance. The lead shark opened its mouth as it got closer. Its teeth were probably each the size of my hand. We had almost made it out. I held Cú tighter and looked around at my companions – Malik standing apart, resolute; Hunter trying to pull his foot out of the sucking mud at the edge of the sandbar; Nick and Quinn moving towards me. The shark started to rise out of the water, rearing back for the kill. One last glance at Lulu. Tears streamed down her cheeks.

And then I knew what to do.

I yanked the prayer box hard, breaking the chain, then I threw it into the water in front of the shark. At the touch of Odin's Tear, ice crackled and groaned as it snaked up and around the sharks, trapping them fast as the stream solidified. They struggled, though, and they were huge.

"Everybody off the bank!" I shouted. "I don't know how long the ice will hold."

Nick and Hunter lifted Lulu, then Malik, and me up so we could struggle over the edge of the step bank.

Quinn shifted back to his kelpie shape, and awkward on dry land, and used his head, crane-like to lift Nick and Phobetor up to join the rest of us. The ice holding the sharks began to crack. Shards of it started to calve off. Only Hunter and Quinn remained on the sandbar.

Quinn lifted Hunter up, and as soon as his feet touched the ground, I shouted, "Grab Quinn's neck! Grab his neck!"

A huge slab of ice crashed from the head of the second shark and it was able to wriggle, churning the ice into slush.

Uncertainly, Hunter put his arms around Quinn's neck. I grabbed Hunter from behind and pulled back. Quinn shifted into Bruce, and the three of us toppled over into the moldering leaf litter. Before I'd even gotten into position to stand up, Quinn was already in human shape and on his feet.

"Those aren't sharks – they're trolls." He reached out to help me up, and I felt the familiar electricity of his touch. There was so much I needed to tell him. But it would have to wait. He said something to Cú that I didn't understand, and the pup got bigger – perhaps Great Dane size, and started sniffing the air. He turned slightly right and headed away from the stream. We trotted after him. I kept looking over my shoulder, knowing the trolls would be after us as soon as they freed themselves from the ice.

We kept on jogging through the woods after Cú. Sometimes we stopped while the dog paused to re-calibrate his course. But these breaks were never for long. Between my bloody feet and Lulu's sore knee, she and I struggled to keep up. We had just started up again when there was a crash.

"Ow!" followed by some swear words from Lulu.

"What's wrong?" I asked.

"I think I've broken my ankle," she replied through gritted teeth.

I knelt beside her. It looked bad – it was swelling rapidly and was already starting to discolor. "Can you rotate it?"

A sharp intake of breath. "No."

I looked at Nick. "Go find me some sticks, at least half an inch in diameter."

A shadow slid over us.

"We're out of time. They're coming!" Malik yelled.

Quinn shifted into his horse form and Nick and Hunter heaved Lulu onto his back.

"Go, Cú!" I said, hoping that he understood me as well as he understood Quinn.

The dog loped off and we ran after him. I nearly fell over as I turned my head in time to see two hawks transform into wolves as they swooped towards the ground. "Faster!" I shouted.

Cú was headed straight for a particularly gnarled tree. *What are you doing? Move!* He was aimed dead-center and would crash headlong into it in the next stride.

Instead, he disappeared.

Quinn and Lulu followed close behind him, then Malik. Hunter was next and Nick and I brought up the rear. The wolf-trolls galloped faster.

I tried to go faster as well, but I ended up stumbling and getting my shirt caught on a branch. Frantically, I pulled on the stick, trying to snap it, but it was too thick. I could hear the footfalls of the wolves, and I froze, paralyzed by fear and mesmerized by their ferocious beauty. Something yanked me upward, and I heard fabric tear.

Quinn had snatched me off the ground and was sprinting the ten yards or so to the tree. The panting of the troll-wolves was all I could hear. One of them leaped for us as we got to the tree. Quinn turned and threw himself at the trunk. I cried out as a hot mouth closed on my foot and fangs scraped off the rag bandage.

But a taste of my blood and one of Hunter's shirtsleeves were all the troll-wolf got.

Quinn and I landed in a heap on the other side of the tree. But we were in a completely different place – the tree was a portal. Malik stood up and chanted something. Was he sealing it against the tolls?

Quinn's face was inches from mine. I kissed him. When I pulled away, I said, "I owe you an apology. The Keres. I didn't understand how strong they were-"

He kissed me.

"Uh-hum." Nick cleared his throat. Twice.

Quinn pulled away, then he got up and helped me to my feet. I took a few disoriented steps.

"What the hell?" Hunter asked, looking around.

There was nothing but pale blue light – no ceiling, walls, or floor. It was hard to tell which way we were going, or if we were going anywhere at all.

"This is a shortcut," said Malik. "You might think of it as a wormhole."

Lulu held onto Nick to keep her balance. "Where does it go?" she asked.

"Good question," Quinn answered. "Let's find out." His voice sounded flat and dimensionless, as if it came from an anechoic chamber. It made me not want to talk.

He shifted into a horse again so that he could carry Lulu. We followed Cú, who seemed to know exactly where he was going. After a while, he barked and wagged his tail.

"We're back at your house, Marti," Malik said. "That's the where. I'm not sure about the 'when,' though."

"What is that supposed to mean?" Nick asked. Hunter nodded, as if he had the same question.

"Time is relative to the dimension you are occupying," Malik said. "It doesn't usually line up with the time flow in other dimensions. It may be that you visit Faery and while you are there, it seems like you were there seven days, but when you get back, you find seven years have passed. Or perhaps you return three days before you left."

Nick frowned.

"Time is not as linear as most people believe it to be," Malik added.

"Let's just take a peek and see when we are," I said. I wanted to see Cassie so badly I could taste it.

We stepped out of the blue light into my back yard. I peered through the kitchen window and could see that Mom and Dad were watching TV in my living room. That's where Lulu and I had left them when Balcones grabbed us. I could see the clock on the microwave, and we'd only been gone half an hour or so.

Nick and Hunter helped Lulu off of Quinn, and he shifted into human form. Cú was back to pup size.

"We've got to get Lulu to the doctor," I said.

"I'll take her," Nick said. "I'm going to the hospital to see Emily, anyway."

"I'll come by a little later." I felt a surge of guilt. I was getting to go home to my baby, and he wasn't. Just the thought of never seeing the twins or McKenzi brought tears to my eyes.

"We'll find your kids," Quinn said.

"Yeah. I'm sure that's your top priority," Nick replied.

Malik started to say something, but Quinn raised his hand. "Now that Balcones knows you've got a non-human healing ability, he may or may not guess what it really is. He will be after you, though, to find out, and he's got the perfect bait." He took a deep breath and let it out. "It's very rare for a human to be on an MIT, but under the circumstances, I think it might be best for everybody if you joined my team. Temporarily, of course, until your children are recovered. I know you want Balcones captured or dead at least as much as I do."

Nick nodded. "Temporarily. But only because you know more about all this demon/supernatural stuff than I do. As soon as my kids are home, I'm done."

Lulu was trying to stifle a groan, but wasn't quite successful.

"Here," Hunter said. "Let me help you." He supported her as she hobbled over to the back porch. "Nick, you should probably go get your car."

Nick grunted and left.

"I don't understand anything that just happened," Hunter said. I wasn't sure if he was talking to me or to Quinn and Malik.

"Would you like to forget it?" Malik asked.

Hunter thought for a moment, then shook his head. "No. I don't think I would. I just want to figure it out."

"Malik? Why don't you go with Hunter and answer his questions?" Quinn said.

The djinn looked askance to the sky, not hiding his displeasure at the assignment, but he said, "Very well then. Shall we go?"

Quinn turned to me and brushed a wisp of hair from my cheek. "You're still a target. So is Nick, now. I understand if you don't want me around, but I can't just leave you unprotected. We need to –"

I kissed him, not a deep, longing kiss, just enough to make him stop. "We'll talk later. Right now, I need to see my family."

He stood forlornly in the back yard.

"Well, don't just stand there. Come inside."

Bonus Material

Foundling

 fractious gust of autumn wind ran chilly fingers down Etienne's back, but his stone skin was immune to such things – hot, cold, wet, dry, it was all the same to him. He perched on a flying buttress and looked out over the darkened city of Paris. Lightning from a distant storm flickered through the thunderheads, momentarily changing them from grey to orange.

He was almost too old for his mother to tuck in at night, but he loved the stories she told him. His favorite was the one about how the bravest of the gargoyles had came down from the mountains and started living in the tops of stone cathedrals the humans had begun to build. One stone carver accidentally discovered that demons and gargoyles were mortal enemies, and he began carving gargoyles on everything, hoping the demons couldn't tell the statues from the real thing. Maybe she'd tell him that one again tonight. He stretched his wings and yawned.

Footsteps approached. *At last. What had taken Maman so long?* But before he could turn to greet his mother, a hemp sack was thrown over his head and he was yanked off balance. He squeaked and struggled, but to no avail. Gruff voices argued around him as he was jostled and bumped along.

"No! You'll damage him. What kind of wedding present for a king would that be, eh?"

"Yeah? Well he won't stop fighting now, will he? If I drop him from here, it will do a lot more damage than a punch 'round the earhole ever would."

"If you're such a weakling you can't handle a child, I'll take him off you. They won't pay for damaged merchandise."

The jostling stopped. He heard the flap of wings, and then there was a sudden lift. He was flying now. Flying away from his home and family. How had this happened? His mother had told him stories in about evil gargoyles. A few were rogues, and some of them even had dealings with demons. He'd thought they were just tales, but now here he was, stuffed into a sack and being stolen away. Would he ever again stand with his father on the top of the bell tower, looking out over *la belle ville Paris?* Or hear his mother's beautiful voice? Rancid black despair welled up from the bottom of his being and swallowed him whole, and he wept.

"You're too low!" the first voice shouted.

Too late. Etienne's head collided with hard stone, and he knew no more.

"That one looks a little small. I'm not sure it's suitable."

Etienne awoke and opened his eyelids just a crack. He sat in a large armchair. The burlap sack had been removed, but his arms and wings were bound. An iron collar with a chain tethered him to a thick metal ring set in the floor. Two figures argued in front of him.

"But you have to train them young. The adults are impossible to break." A greasy smirk spread across scaly lips. "Believe me, I've tried."

Were these demons? Etienne tried to swallow his fear, but he was so thirsty it hurt his throat.

"Look! It's awake," the first voice said. "Stand up. Let's get a good look at you."

Etienne was terrified, but he imagined what his father would do. He stood up and tossed his head disdainfully.

"It's got some fire. You've got to give it that," the second voice chimed in.

The first grunted. "It isn't like I've a lot of time before the wedding. Fine. It will do."

He took a small pouch from his robe and counted out a number of gold coins, which the second demon snatched greedily.

The first frowned. "You will make sure it is stowed properly – I don't want it damaged on the trip to Scotland."

"As you wish," the second replied with a slight bow.

He opened the heavy lock that connected the chain to the ring and tugged on the chain. "Come!" he grunted.

Etienne remained where he was. The demon yanked hard on the chain and the gargoyle landed face-first on the stone floor.

"Idiot!" screamed the first demon. "I told you not to damage it. N-O-T, understand?"

"I'm sorry," the second demon groveled. "But you have to be firm with them. It only takes a few times-"

"Get out. I'll deal with it myself. And if this cub is damaged, I'll have your hide hanging on my wall."

The second demon backed out the door, apologizing as it went.

"Up you go." The demon pulled Etienne off the floor. "King Alexander of Scotland had very well better appreciate all the trouble I have gone through to get his wedding gift. He will most certainly owe me a favor."

The padded crate that held Etienne did have air holes that he could peek through, and while his night vision was excellent, there was too much cargo for him to see a lot. The straw that was sewn into cloth pouches and attached to the sides of the crate was musty enough to make his eyes water. Surely that's what caused the constant dribbles of liquid from his eyes. Stale bread and strips of dried meat had been left in the box for him to eat, but he wasn't hungry enough to even nibble the powerfully salty food. Etienne didn't often hear footsteps, but when he did, it was always with the vain hope that his parents had come for him. But they never did. Only sour-smelling sailors ever came into the hold.

He missed his maman and papa so deeply that the ache in his heart kept him awake at night. Etienne's hands had been bound when he was shoved into the crate, but his rough teeth had made short work of the hemp ropes. Once his hands were free, it was a simple matter to shed the binding from his wings. He used his time to plan and practice his escape. If only someone would open the crate.

The rocking of the boat as it rode the swells had never been gentle, but it suddenly became stomach-churningly violent. The ship soared on huge crests, dropped hard into deep troughs, then rolled and pitched like a wounded animal.

Wood creaked and groaned in protest against the assault. Etienne was slammed from one side of his box to the other. The ship rose to a sickening height, tilting and tossing the gargoyle against the wall. He floated, gravity-free, for a moment as the boat fell into the valley between the monster waves. There was a groan, then an ominous pop. The ship began break apart as it sank into the greedy sea. Mooring snapped with the shattering hull, and casks and crates were free of their dark prison. Some raced toward the angry sky above, some tumbled slowly to the cold seafloor.

Etienne's crate floated briefly, but the heavy sea swamped the openings, and it fell through the broken hold. The box shifted and one of his hands got stuck in an air hole, keeping him from the rapidly shrinking air bubble at the top of the box.

Something crashed into the crate, hard enough to splinter the wood on one side. Another crash. A hole appeared.

He was free of the crate, but not free of his predicament. Etienne struggled, trying to flap his wings against the roiling water. But wings are designed to work best in air, and he found the strain against the seawater painful.

Terror gripped him by the throat as he saw what had smashed the crate. The creature's head was bigger than he was. It had large black eyes and recurved teeth filled its open mouth.

Etienne fainted.

When he opened his eyes again, he was in a cozy cottage, wrapped in a blanket in front of a well-laid fire. A boy a little bigger than him sat on the floor nearby. Beyond him, a man slouched in a rickety wooden chair and knitted a woolen hat, and a woman sat at a spinning wheel, making yarn.

"*Bonsoir, Monsieur et Madame. Je m'appelle Etienne. Où suis-je?*" Etienne asked.

The couple looked at each other. The man frowned and shook his head. "Sorry, lad I dinnae ken what you're sayin'."

Still, they offered Etienne a thick wedge of brown bread and some hot porridge. He ate every crumb of the bread and a second helping of porridge before he curled up beside the fire and fell into a dreamless sleep.

Etienne snapped awake. Something was wrapped around his arms and legs, trapping him. Panicked, he snatched off the restraint and tossed it away. *Where am I? This isn't my home!*

The woman who had fed him last night looked surprised as she watched the woolen blanket hurtle toward her and crumple onto the floor at her feet. "Are ye hot then?" she asked.

Etienne had no idea what she said. He stared at her, trying (and not quite succeeding) to blink back the flood behind his eyelids.

Rain pelted down on the roof.

Slowly, the woman eased out of the chair with her knees on the blanket. Her eyes glistened with sympathetic droplets, and she held out her arms. And even though he was almost too old for such things, he went to her and threw his arms around her neck. Silent tears trickled down her neck and onto her shoulder.

It will be okay. My parents are surely looking for me. It's just a matter of time until they arrive.

Etienne soared above the surface of the river, a dozen or so feet above the water. From this height, he could spot the flashing scales of migrating salmon. Two black horses galloped along the riverbank, following him. His eye caught a glint of silver in the water, so he slowed and hovered over the schooling fish. They were headed to their spawning grounds as fast as they could go, but they were no match for Etienne's speed.

The two black horses raced ahead of him, then waded into the river with surprisingly little splashing. His shape-shifting foster family fascinated him. They called him 'Ocean,' partly because they couldn't pronounce his name, and partly because they found him in the ocean. He had been called Ocean for more years now than he had been called 'Etienne,' but he held onto that name, because in his mind, he could still hear his mother's silky voice calling him that. Etienne kept that memory locked tightly in his heart.

The two horses were deep enough to swim now, so they let go their equine shapes and morphed into their natural kelpie selves. Gregor, who had rescued him, and his son, Colbán, had long ago devised this gargoyle-assisted fishing technique. They caught salmon that were so abundant this time of year, some for themselves, and some for Colbán's elderly neighbor. She was human, and alone, and would probably have starved to death years ago, if not from the gifts of fish and bread that Iosobal, Colbán's wife, secretly left her.

As the grotesque kelpie heads rose from the water, mouths filled with fish, Etienne grasped them with his clawed hands and feet, flying the load downriver to where his foster mother, Máel Muire, and Iosobal waited with the couple's five sons. There, the women and the two eldest boys would clean, salt, and smoke them to keep the larder filled when food was scarce in winter, and even the plentiful brown trout all but disappeared. They did it for hours, this fish processing assembly line. Finally, the shadows lengthened and it was time to rest.

Etienne had just dropped off the latest round of salmon, and was searching for Gregor and Colbán to tell them Iosobal was ready to call it a night. He envied Colbán sometimes. His foster brother had a beautiful wife and five young sons. Etienne dearly loved his adoptive family, but Scotland was not his home. Most of his memories of Cathedral Notre Dame had dimmed, but he clearly remembered standing on the bell tower with his father, and his mother's angelic voice singing to him. Perhaps, when the fishing season was over, he would try to find his way home.

All these years, and his parents had never come for him. Did they not know where to look? Did they think he was dead? Or did they just not care? He felt sure he that if his own child had been stolen from him, he would never stop looking. Had they given up? Etienne was old enough now to fly back across the Channel and return to his people. Truth was, he had been for some years now. But sometimes suspicion is easier to bear than confirmation. And yet, that distant bell tower called to him - a clear, bright beacon in the misty past. Sooner or later, he must seek it out, but what awaited him there? A joyful reunion? An angry confrontation? What if no one had missed him, or cared that he'd returned?

He was so wrapped up in his own thoughts that he utterly failed to notice a small boat with a handful of men in it – most likely poachers at this time of day. He was headed dead at them, and at this speed, he would knock them over like skittles. He arched his back until it hurt, furiously flapping his huge wings, trying to pull up and avoid the fishermen.

He almost succeeded.

His feet struck one man in the jaw, and he flopped over the side and in the water. Etienne gaped in horror. He did not swim. Neither, apparently, did the fisherman. His companions yelled and brandished their fishing spears at Etienne as their colleague sank rapidly below the surface.

Something dark was rising. Colbán's great head broke the surface, the submerged fisherman held gently in his teeth. The men clearly did not understand that Colbán was returning their friend. They stabbed at him and raked his smooth flesh with their spears.

"No!" Etienne yelled. "Fools! Stop it!" But they paid him no mind.

Colbán tried to toss the semi-conscious human into the boat, but missed. As he started to dive, one wicked spear caught him directly in the eye, going entirely through his head.

Blood.

Etienne had never seen so much of it. It gushed from Colbán 's ruined eye, from his nose, out his mouth.

Gregor surfaced near his son, and the attack turned to him. He was out of their reach, however, as he tried to help his mortally wounded child.

Rage took hold of Etienne.

He dropped like an avenging stone from the sky and smashed a hole in the boat. Then another. Men screamed as spears bounced harmlessly off his stone skin. Bones crunched and snapped as his rock-hard fists pummeled them into the water. Into the domain of the kelpie. Not one of them, not even the wreckage of their boat, was ever seen by mortal eyes again.

Etienne turned to help Gregor. He wrapped his arms around Colbán's neck and helped Gregor drag his son's failing body on to the shore. Hoofbeats pounded in the distance. Seven black horses galloped toward them, going flat out.

Iosobal skidded to a stop and shifted into human form. She ran to her fallen husband and dropped to the ground next to him. Máel Muire was only a few steps behind her.

Iosobal stroked her husband's long neck and face, "Colbán?"

Máel Muire tried to cradle her son's head in her lap, but in his kelpie form, it was far too big. Blood stained her dress.

Colbán let out a deep breath, then seemed to collapse in upon himself. Where Etienne's foster brother had been was now a kelpie-shaped pile of peat moss covered over with a gelatinous green substance.

The two women began an unearthly keening wail. Gregor tried to comfort his wife, but she would not suffer his touch.

From deep in the forests that surrounded the river, night's children – the great grey wolves – began to howl along, as if they recognized the abject misery of Colbán's family. Five skittish colts had become five crying boys. Etienne circled his wings around them and they all wept together.

Iosobal was the first to speak. "From this day forward, I lay my curse on all humankind. To come into my sight will be their doom. I will feast on their hearts and leave their bones to the wolves."

This is all my fault. If I hadn't been so careless, none of this would have happened. I may as well have killed Colbán with my own hands. Etienne could not bear to speak to his foster family, even though his grief was just as deep as theirs. Would they blame him as much as he blamed himself?

He looked at the tear-stained faces of Colbán's sons. "As your father's brother, it is my duty to help you grow up strong. I will always, always be there for you. But before I can do that, there is something I must do first. I must make a short journey. Laurie?" he addressed the eldest boy. "Please tell your mother that I will return before Hogmanay. The year will not turn without your Uncle Ocean! But there is a long overdue task I must complete. *Comprends-tu?*"

Laurie nodded. Etienne squeezed them just a little harder with his wings, then he released them. With a last look at his grieving foster family, he flapped he great wings and rose into the air.

Which way from here is Paris?

If you enjoyed this book, I would really appreciate a review or a share on social media. It helps people find the book.

Thank you!

Thank you for investigating with Marti and joining the MIT on another demon hunt. Have you read the Coda Sterling books?

Belinda's Books
Dragon by Knight #1
Dragon Killer #2
Dragon Fire #3 (coming soon!)

Other Books by Artemis Greenleaf

For Younger Readers
Brain's Vacation
Carl the Vegetarian Vampire
Team Smash

For Teens and Tweens
Earthbound
Cheval Bayard
Confessions of a Troll

Exit Point
For Adults
Color Me Blackthorne
The Thirteenth Summer

Anthologies
Space City 6
Tides of Impossibility
First Last Forever

Artemis Greenleaf has always been fascinated by the mysterious, and she devoured fairy tales, folk tales and ghost stories since before she could read. In 1995, she had a near-death experience which turned her perception of the world upside down. She lived to tell the tale (and often does, in one form or another). Artemis lives in the suburban wilds of Houston, Texas with her husband, two children and assorted pets. She writes novels, short stories, and non-fiction, and her work has also appeared in magazines. For more information, please visit artemisgreenleaf.com.

You can sign up for Artemis' newsletter with giveaways, news, and new releases here:

http://eepurl.com/b4sQBj

Connect with Artemis online:

Website: http://artemisgreenleaf.com
Facebook: https://www.facebook.com/ArtemisGreenleaf
Twitter: http://twitter.com/AGreenleaf
Pinterest: http://www.pinterest.com/artemisgreenlea/